PENGUIN BOOKS

RABBIT REDUX

John Updike was born in 1932 in Shillington, Pennsylvania. He attended Shillington High School, Harvard College and the Ruskin School of Drawing and Fine Art at Oxford, where he spent a year on a Knox Fellowship. From 1955 to 1957 he was a member of the staff of the *New Yorker*, to which he has over the years contributed poems, short stories, essays and book reviews. Since 1957 he has lived in Massachusetts as a freelance writer.

John Updike's first novel, *The Poorhouse Fair*, was published in 1959, followed by *Rabbit, Run*, the first volume in what has now become known as the *Rabbit* books, described by John Banville as 'one of the finest literary achievements to have come out of the US since the war'. Two of the volumes, *Rabbit is Rich* (1981) and *Rabbit at Rest* (1990), have been awarded the Pulitzer Prize for fiction. Other novels by John Updike include *Couples*, *Marry Me*, *The Coup*, *The Witches of Eastwick*, which was made into a major feature film, and more recently *Memories of the Ford Administration* and *Brazil*. He is also the author of many volumes of short stories: a selection from the volumes *The Same Door*, *Pigeon Feathers*, *The Music School* and *Museums and Women* is published in Penguin as *Forty Stories*. Many of his essays and criticism, which first appeared in magazines such as the *New Yorker* and *The New York Times Review of Books*, have been collected in four volumes. His *Collected Poems 1953–1993* brings together almost all the poems from five previous volumes including *Hoping for a Hoopoe*, *Telephone Poles* and *Tossing and Turning*, as well as seventy poems previously unpublished in book form.

ALSO BY JOHN UPDIKE IN PENGUIN

Novels

The Poorhouse Fair
Rabbit, Run
The Centaur
On the Farm
Couples
A Month of Sundays
Marry Me
The Coup
Rabbit is Rich
The Witches of Eastwick
Roger's Version
S.
Rabbit at Rest
Memories of the Ford Administration
Brazil
The Afterlife and Other Stories

and

A Rabbit Omnibus
(*containing the first three* 'Rabbit' *books*)

Short Stories

The Complete Henry Bech
(*containing* Bech A Book *and* Bech is Back)
Your Lover Just Called
Trust Me
Forty Stories

Poems

Collected Poems 1953–1993

Essays and Criticism

Hugging the Shore
Odd Jobs

Memoirs

Self-Consciousness

John Updike

Rabbit Redux

PENGUIN BOOKS

PENGUIN BOOKS

Published by the Penguin Group
Penguin Books Ltd, 27 Wrights Lane, London W8 5TZ, England
Penguin Books USA Inc., 375 Hudson Street, New York, New York 10014, USA
Penguin Books Australia Ltd, Ringwood, Victoria, Australia
Penguin Books Canada Ltd, 10 Alcorn Avenue, Toronto, Ontario, Canada M4V 3B2
Penguin Books (NZ) Ltd, 182–190 Wairau Road, Auckland 10, New Zealand

Penguin Books Ltd, Registered Offices: Harmondsworth, Middlesex, England

First published in the USA by Alfred A. Knopf 1971
First published in Great Britain by André Deutsch 1972
Published in Penguin Books 1972
Reprinted in Penguin Books in this setting 1995
10 9 8 7 6 5 4 3 2 1

Printed in England by Clays Ltd, St Ives plc
Set in Monotype Plantin

Contents

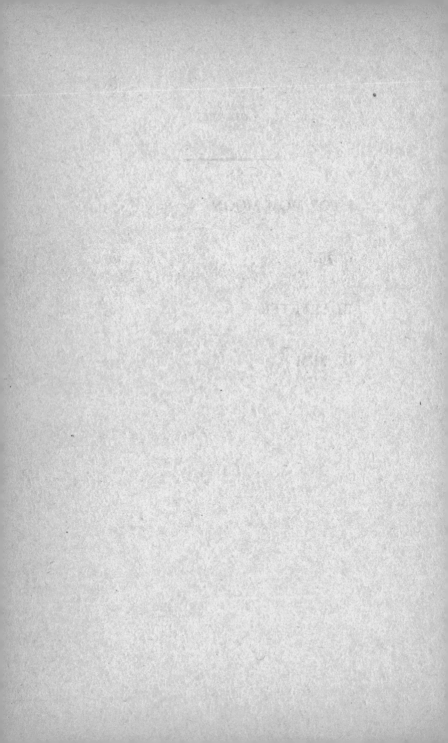

RABBIT REDUX

LIEUT. COL. VLADIMIR A. SHATALOV: *I am heading straight for the socket.*

LIEUT. COL. BORIS V. VOLYNOV, SOYUZ 5 COMMANDER: *Easy, not so rough.*

COLONEL SHATALOV: *It took me quite a while to find you, but now I've got you.*

I. POP/MOM/MOON

MEN emerge pale from the little printing plant at four sharp, ghosts for an instant, blinking, until the outdoor light overcomes the look of constant indoor light clinging to them. In winter, Pine Street at this hour is dark, darkness presses down early from the mountain that hangs above the stagnant city of Brewer; but now in summer the granite curbs starred with mica and the row houses differentiated by speckled bastard sidings and the hopeful small porches with their jigsaw brackets and gray milk-bottle boxes and the sooty ginkgo trees and the baking curbside cars wince beneath a brilliance like a frozen explosion. The city, attempting to revive its dying downtown, has torn away blocks of buildings to create parking lots, so that a desolate openness, weedy and rubbled, spills through the once-packed streets, exposing church façades never seen from a distance and generating new perspectives of rear entryways and half-alleys and intensifying the cruel breadth of the light. The sky is cloudless yet colorless, hovering blanched humidity, in the way of these Pennsylvania summers, good for nothing but to make green things grow. Men don't even tan; filmed by sweat, they turn yellow.

A man and his son, Earl Angstrom and Harry, are among the printers released from work. The father is near retirement, a thin man with no excess left to him, his face washed empty by grievances and caved in above the protruding slippage of bad false teeth. The son is five inches taller and fatter; his prime is soft, somehow pale and sour. The small nose and slightly lifted upper lip that once made the nickname Rabbit fit now seem, along with the thick waist and cautious stoop bred into him by a decade of the linotyper's trade, clues to weakness, a weakness verging on anonymity. Though his height, his bulk, and a remnant alertness in the way he moves his head continue to distinguish him on the street, years have passed since anyone has called him Rabbit.

"Harry, how about a quick one?" his father asks. At the corner where their side street meets Weiser there is a bus stop and a bar, the Phoenix, with a girl nude but for cowboy boots in neon outside and cactuses painted on the dim walls inside. Their buses when they take them go in opposite directions: the old man takes number 16A around the mountain to the town of Mt. Judge, where he has lived his life, and Harry takes number 12 in the opposite direction to Penn Villas, a new development south of the city, ranch houses and quarter-acre lawns contoured as the bulldozer left them and maple saplings tethered to the earth as if otherwise they might fly away. He moved there with Janice and Nelson three years ago. His father still feels the move out of Mt. Judge as a rejection, and so most afternoons they have a drink together to soften the day's parting. Working together ten years, they have grown into the love they would have had in Harry's childhood, had not his mother loomed so large between them.

"Make it a Schlitz," Earl tells the bartender.

"Daiquiri," Harry says. The air-conditioning is turned so far up he unrolls his shirt cuffs and buttons them for warmth. He always wears a white shirt to work and after, as a way of cancelling the ink. Ritually, he asks his father how his mother is.

But his father declines to make a ritual answer. Usually he says, "As good as can be hoped." Today he sidles a conspiratorial inch closer at the bar and says, "Not as good as could be hoped, Harry."

She has had Parkinson's Disease for years now. Harry's mind slides away from picturing her, the way she has become, the loosely fluttering knobbed hands, the shuffling sheepish walk, the eyes that study him with vacant amazement though the doctor says her mind is as good as ever in there, and the mouth that wanders open and forgets to close until saliva reminds it. "At nights, you mean?" The very question offers to hide her in darkness.

Again the old man blocks Rabbit's desire to slide by. "No, the nights are better now. They have her on a new pill and she says she sleeps better now. It's in her mind, more."

"What is, Pop?"

"We don't talk about it, Harry, it isn't in her nature, it isn't the type of thing she and I have ever talked about. Your mother and I have just let a certain type of thing go unsaid, it was the way we were brought up, maybe it would have been better if we hadn't, I don't know. I mean things now they've *put* into her mind."

"Who's this they?" Harry sighs into the daiquiri foam and thinks, He's going too, they're both going. Neither makes enough sense. As his father pushes closer against him to explain, he becomes one of the hundreds of skinny whining codgers in and around this city, men who have sucked this same brick tit for sixty years and have dried up with it.

"Why, the ones who come to visit her now she spends half the day in bed. Mamie Kellog, for one. Julia Arndt's another.

I hate like the Jesus to bother you with it, Harry, but her talk is getting wild and with Mim on the West Coast you're the only one to help me straighten out my own mind. I hate to bother you but her talk is getting so wild she even talks of telephoning Janice."

"Janice! Why would she call Janice?"

"Well." A pull on the Schlitz. A wiping of the wet upper lip with the bony back of the hand, fingers half-clenched in an old man's clutching way. A loose-toothed grimacing getting set to dive in. "Well the talk is *about* Janice."

"*My* Janice?"

"Now Harry, don't blow your lid. Don't blame the bearer of bad tidings. I'm trying to tell you what they say, not what I believe."

"I'm just surprised there's anything to say. I hardly see her any more, now that she's over at Springer's lot all the time."

"Well, that's it. That may be your mistake, Harry. You've taken Janice for granted ever since—the time." The time he left her. The time the baby died. The time she took him back. "Ten years ago," his father needlessly adds. Harry is beginning, here in this cold bar with cactuses in plastic pots on the shelves beneath the mirrors and the little Schlitz spinner doing its polychrome parabola over and over, to feel the world turn. A hopeful coldness inside him grows, grips his wrists inside his cuffs. The news isn't all in, a new combination might break it open, this stale peace.

"Harry, the malice of people surpasses human understanding in my book, and the poor soul has no defenses against it, there she lies and has to listen. Ten years ago, wouldn't she have laid them out? Wouldn't her tongue have cut them down? They've told her that Janice is running around. With one certain man, Harry. Nobody claims she's playing the field."

The coldness spreads up Rabbit's arms to his shoulders, and

down the tree of veins toward his stomach. "Do they name the man?"

"Not to my knowledge, Harry. How could they now, when in all likelihood there is no man?"

"Well, if they can make up the idea, they can make up a name."

The bar television is running, with the sound turned off. For the twentieth time that day the rocket blasts off, the numbers pouring backwards in tenths of seconds faster than the eye until zero is reached: then the white boiling beneath the tall kettle, the lifting so slow it seems certain to tip, the swift diminishment into a retreating speck, a jiggling star. The men dark along the bar murmur among themselves. They have not been lifted, they are left here. Harry's father mutters at him, prying. "Has she seemed any different to you lately, Harry? Listen, I know in all probability it's what they call a crock of shit, but—has she seemed any, you know, different lately?"

It offends Rabbit to hear his father swear; he lifts his head fastidiously, as if to watch the television, which has returned to a program where people are trying to guess what sort of prize is hidden behind a curtain and jump and squeal and kiss each other when it turns out to be an eight-foot frozen-food locker. He might be wrong but for a second he could swear this young housewife opens her mouth in mid-kiss and gives the m.c. a taste of her tongue. Anyway, she won't stop kissing. The m.c.'s eyes roll out to the camera for mercy and they cut to a commercial. In silence images of spaghetti and some opera singer riffle past. "I don't know," Rabbit says. "She hits the bottle pretty well sometimes but then so do I."

"Not you," the old man tells him, "you're no drinker, Harry. I've seen drinkers all my life, somebody like Boonie over in engraving, there's a drinker, killing himself with it, and he knows it, he couldn't stop if they told him he'd die tomorrow. You may have a whisky or two in the evening, you're no spring chicken any more, but you're no drinker." He hides his loose mouth in his beer and Harry taps the bar for another daiquiri. The old man nuzzles closer. "Now Harry, forgive me for asking if you don't want to talk about it, but how about in bed? That goes along pretty well, does it?"

"No," he answers slowly, disdainful of this prying, "I wouldn't exactly say well. Tell me about Mom. Has she had any of those breathing fits lately?"

"Not a one that I've been woken up for. She sleeps like a baby with those new green pills. This new medicine is a miracle, I must admit, ten more years the only way to kill us'll be to gas us to death, Hitler had the right idea. Already, you know, there aren't any more crazy people: just give 'em a pill morning and evening and they're sensible as Einstein. You wouldn't exactly say it does, go along O.K., is that what I understood you said?"

"Well we've never been that great, Pop, frankly. Does she fall down ever? Mom."

"She may take a tumble or two in the day and not tell me about it. I tell her, I *tell* her, stay in bed and watch the box. She has this theory the longer she can do things the longer she'll stay out of bed for good. I figure she should take care of herself, put herself in deep freeze, and in a year or two in all likelihood they'll develop a pill that'll clear this up simple as a common cold. Already, you know, some of these cortisones; but the doctor tells us they don't know but what the side effects may be worse. You know: the big C. My figuring is, take the chance, they're just about ready to lick cancer anyway and with these transplants pretty soon they can replace your whole insides." The old man hears himself talking too much and slumps to stare into his empty beer, the suds sliding down, but can't help adding, to give it all point, "It's a terrible thing." And when Harry fails to respond: "God she hates not being active."

The rum is beginning to work. Rabbit has ceased to feel cold, his heart is beginning to lift off. The air in here seems thinner, his eyes adjusting to the dark. He asks, "How's her mind? You aren't saying they should start giving her crazy pills."

"In honest truth, I won't lie to you Harry, it's as clear as a bell, when her tongue can find the words. And as I say she's gotten hipped lately on this Janice idea. It would help a lot, Jesus I hate to bother you but it's the truth, it would help a lot if you and Janice could spare the time to come over tonight. Not seeing you too often her imagination's free to wander. Now I know you've promised Sunday for her birthday, but think of it this way: if you're stuck in bed with nobody but the idiot box and a lot of malicious biddies for company a week can seem a year. If you could make it up there some evening before the weekend, bring Janice along so Mary could look at her—"

"I'd like to, Pop. You know I would."

"I know, Jesus I know. I know more than you think. You're at just the age to realize your old man's not the dope you always thought he was."

"The trouble is, Janice works in the lot office until ten, eleven all the time and I don't like to leave the kid alone in the house. In fact I better be getting back there now just in case." In case it's burned down. In case a madman has moved in. These things happen all the time in the papers. He can read in his father's face—a fishy pinching-in at the corners of the mouth, a tightened veiling of the washed-out eyes—the old man's suspicions confirmed. Rabbit sees red. Meddling old crock. Janice: who'd have that mutt? In love with her father and there she stuck. Happy as a Girl Scout since she began to fill in at the lot, half these summer nights out way past supper, TV dinners, tuck Nelson in alone and wait up for her to breeze in blooming and talkative; he's never known her to be so full of herself, in a way it does his heart good. He resents his father trying to get at him with Janice and hits back with the handiest weapon, Mom. "This doctor you have, does he ever mention a nursing home?"

The old man's mind is slow making the switch back to his own wife. Harry has a thought, a spark like where train wheels run over a track switch. Did Mom ever do it to Pop? Play him false. All this poking around about life in bed hints at some experience. Hard to imagine, not only who with but when, she was always in the house as long as he could remember, nobody ever came to visit but the brush man and the Jehovah's Witness, yet the thought excites him, like Pop's rumor chills him, opens up possibilities. Pop is saying, ". . . at the beginning. We want to hold off at least until she's bed-ridden. If we reach the point where she can't take care of herself before I'm on retirement and there all day, it's an option we might be forced into. I'd hate to see it, though. Jesus I'd hate to see it."

"Hey Pop—?"

"Here's my forty cents. Plus a dime for the tip." The way the old man's hand clings curlingly to the quarters in offering them betrays that they are real silver to him instead of just cut-copper sandwich-coins that ring flat on the bar top. Old values. The Depression when money was money. Never be sacred again, not even dimes are silver now. Kennedy's face killed half-dollars, took them out of circulation and they've never come back. Put the metal on the moon. The niggling business of settling their bill delays his question about Mom until they are outdoors and then he sees he can't ask it, he doesn't know his father that well. Out here in the hot light his father has lost all sidling intimacy and looks merely old—liverish scoops below his eyes, broken veins along the sides of his nose, his hair the no-color of cardboard. "What'd you want to ask me?"

"I forget," Harry says, and sneezes. Coming into this heat from that air-conditioning sets off an explosion between his eyes that turns heads around halfway down the block and leaves his nostrils weeping. "No, I remember. The nursing home. How can we afford it? Fifty bucks a day or whatever. It'll suck us right down the drain."

His father laughs, with a sudden snap to retrieve his slipping teeth, and does a little shuffling dance-step, right here on the baking sidewalk, beneath the white-on-red BUS STOP sign that people have scratched and lipsticked to read PUS DROP. "Harry, God in His way hasn't been all bad to your mother and me. Believe it or not there's some advantages to living so long in this day and age. This Sunday she's going to be sixty-five and come under Medicare. I've been paying in since '66, it's like a ton of anxiety rolled off my chest. There's no medical expense can break us now. They called LBJ every name in the book but believe me he did a lot of good for the little man. Wherever he went wrong, it was his big heart betrayed him. These pretty boys in the sky right now, Nixon'll hog the credit but it was the Democrats put 'em there, it's been the same story ever since I can remember, ever since Wilson—the Republicans don't do a thing for the little man."

"Right," Harry says blankly. His bus is coming. "Tell her we'll be over Sunday." He pushes to a clear space at the back where, looking out while hanging onto the bar, he sees his father as one of the "little men." Pop stands whittled by the great American glare, squinting in the manna of blessings that come down from the government, shuffling from side to side in nervous happiness that his day's work is done, that a beer is inside him, that Armstrong is above him, that the U.S. is the crown and stupefaction of human history. Like a piece of grit in the launching pad, he has done his part. Still, he has been the one to keep his health; who would have thought Mom would fail first? Rabbit's mind, as the bus dips into its bag of gears and surges and shudders, noses closer into the image of her he keeps like a dreaded relic: the black hair gone gray, the mannish mouth too clever for her life, the lozenge-shaped nostrils that to him as a child suggested a kind of soreness within, the eyes whose color he had never dared to learn closed bulge-lidded in her failing, the whole long face, slightly shining as if with sweat, lying numbed on the pillow. He can't bear to see her like this is the secret of his seldom visiting, not Janice. The source of his life staring wasted there while she gropes for the words to greet him. And that gentle tawny smell of sickness that doesn't even stay in her room but comes downstairs to meet them in the front hall among the umbrellas and follows them into the kitchen where poor Pop warms their meals. A smell like gas escaping, that used to worry her so when he and Mim were little. He bows his head and curtly prays, *Forgive me, forgive us, make it easy for her. Amen.* He only ever prays on buses. Now this bus has that smell.

The bus has too many Negroes. Rabbit notices them more and more. They've been here all along, as a tiny kid he remembers streets in Brewer you held your breath walking through, though they never hurt you, just looked; but now they're noisier. Instead of bald-looking heads they're bushy. That's O.K., it's more Nature, Nature is what we're running out of. Two of the men in the shop are Negroes, Farnsworth and Buchanan, and after a while you didn't even notice; at least they remember how to laugh. Sad business, being a Negro man, always underpaid, their eyes don't look like our eyes, bloodshot, brown, liquid in them about to quiver out. Read somewhere some anthropologist thinks Negroes instead of being more primitive are the latest thing to evolve, the newest men. In some ways tougher, in some ways more delicate. Certainly dumber but then being smart hasn't amounted to so much, the atom bomb and the one-piece aluminum beer can. And you can't say Bill Cosby's stupid.

But against these educated tolerant thoughts rests a certain fear; he doesn't see why they have to be so noisy. The four seated right under him, jabbing and letting their noise come out in big silvery hoops; they know damn well they're bugging the fat Dutchy wives pulling their shopping bags home. Well, that's kids of any color: but strange. They are a strange race. Not only their skins but the way they're put together, loose-jointed like lions, strange about the head, as if their thoughts are a different shape and come out twisted even when they mean no menace. It's as if, all these Afro hair bushes and gold earrings and hoopy noise on buses, seeds of some tropical plant sneaked in by the birds were taking over the garden. His garden. Rabbit knows it's his garden and that's why he's put a flag decal on the back window of the Falcon even though Janice says it's corny and fascist. In the papers you read about these houses in Connecticut where the parents are away in the Bahamas and the kids come in and smash it up for a party. More and more this country is getting like that. As if it just grew here instead of people laying down their lives to build it.

The bus works its way down Weiser and crosses the Running Horse River and begins to drop people instead of taking them on. The city with its tired five and dimes (that used to be a wonderland, the counters as high as his nose and the Big Little Books smelling like Christmas) and its Kroll's Department Store (where he once worked knocking apart crates behind the furniture department) and its flowerpotted traffic circle where the trolley tracks used to make a clanging star of intersection and then the empty dusty windows where stores have been starved by the suburban shopping malls and the sad narrow places that come and go called Go-Go or Boutique and the funeral parlors with imitation granite faces and the surplus outlets and a shoe parlor that sells hot roasted peanuts and Afro newspapers printed in Philly crying MBOYA MARTYRED and a flower shop where they sell numbers and protection and a variety store next to a pipe-rack clothing retailer next to a corner dive called JIMBO'S *Friendly* LOUNGE, cigarette ends of the city snuffed by the bridge—the city gives way, after the flash of open water that in his youth was choked with coal silt (a man once tried to commit suicide from this bridge but stuck there up to his hips until the police pulled him out) but that now has been dredged and supports a flecking of moored pleasure boats, to West Brewer, a gappy imitation of the city, the same domino-thin houses of brick painted red, but spaced here and there by the twirlers of a car lot, the pumps and blazoned overhang of a gas station, the lakelike depth of a supermarket parking lot crammed with shimmering fins. Surging and spitting, the bus, growing lighter, the Negroes vanishing, moves toward a dream of spaciousness, past residential fortresses with sprinkled lawn around all four sides and clipped hydrangeas above newly pointed retaining walls, past a glimpse of the museum whose gardens were always in blossom and where the swans ate the breadcrusts schoolchildren threw them, then a glimpse of the sunstruck windows, pumpkin orange blazing in reflection, of the tall new wing of the County Hospital for the Insane. Closer at hand, the West Brewer Dry Cleaners, a toy store calling itself Hobby Heaven, a Rialto movie house with a stubby marquee: 2001 SPACE OD'SEY. Weiser Street curves, becomes a highway, dips into green suburbs where in the Twenties little knights of industry built half-timbered dream-houses, pebbled mortar and clinker brick, stucco flaky as pie crust, witch's houses of candy and hardened cookie dough with two-car garages and curved driveways. In Brewer County, but for a few baronial estates ringed by iron fences and moated by miles of lawn, there is nowhere higher to go than these houses; the most successful dentists may get to buy one, the pushiest insurance salesmen, the suavest opthalmologists. This section even has another name, distinguishing itself from West Brewer: Penn Park. Penn Villas echoes the name hopefully, though it is not incorporated into this borough but sits on the border of Furnace Township, looking in. The township, where once charcoal-fed furnaces had smelted the iron for Revolutionary muskets, is now still mostly farmland, and its few snowplows and single sheriff can hardly cope with this ranch-house village of muddy lawns and potholed macadam and sub-code sewers the developers suddenly left in its care.

Rabbit gets off at a stop in Penn Park and walks down a street of mock Tudor, Emberly Avenue, to where the road surface changes at the township line, and becomes Emberly Drive in Penn Villas. He lives on Vista Crescent, third house from the end. Once there may have been here a vista, a softly sloped valley of red barns and fieldstone farmhouses, but more Penn Villas had been added and now the view from any window is as into a fragmented mirror, of houses like this, telephone wires and television aerials showing where the glass cracked. His house is faced with apple-green aluminum clapboards and is numbered 26. Rabbit steps onto his flagstone porchlet and opens his door with its three baby windows arranged like three steps, echoing the door-chime of three stepped tones.

"Hey Dad," his son calls from the living room, a room on his right the size of what used to be called a parlor, with a fire place they never use. "They've left earth's orbit! They're forty-three thousand miles away."

"Good for them," he says. "Your mother here?"

"No. At school they let us all into assembly to see the launch."

"She call at all?"

"Not since I've been here. I just got in a while ago." Nelson, at thirteen, is under average height, with his mother's dark complexion, and something finely cut and wary about his face that may come from the Angstroms. His long eyelashes come from nowhere, and his shoulder-length hair is his own idea. Somehow, Rabbit feels, if he were taller it would be all right, to have hair so long. As is, the resemblance to a girl is frighteningly strong.

"Whadja do all day?"

The same television program, of people guessing and getting and squealing and kissing the m.c., is still going on.

"Nothing much."

"Go to the playground?"

"For a while."

"Then where?"

"Oh, over to West Brewer, just to hang around Billy's apartment. Hey?"

"Yeah?"

"His father got him a mini-bike for his birthday. It's real cool. With that real long front part so you have to reach up for the handles."

"You rode it?"

"He only let me once. It's all shiny, there isn't a speck of paint on it, it's just metal, with a white banana seat."

"He's older than you, isn't he?"

"By two months. That's all. Just two months, Dad."

"Where does he ride it? It's not legal on the street, is it?"

"Their building has a big parking lot he rides it all around. Nobody says anything. It only cost a hundred-eighty dollars, Dad."

"Keep talking, I'm getting a beer."

The house is small enough so that the boy can be heard by his father in the kitchen, his voice mixed with gleeful greedy spurts from the television and the chunky suck of the refrigerator door opening and shutting. "Hey Dad, something I don't understand."

"Shoot."

"I thought the Fosnachts were divorced."

"Separated."

"Then how come his father keeps getting him all this neat junk? You ought to see the hi-fi set he has, that's all his, for his room, not even to share. Four speakers, Dad, and earphones. The earphones are fantastic. It's like you're way in*side* Tiny Tim."

"That's the place to be," Rabbit says, coming into the living room. "Want a sip?"

The boy takes a sip from the can, putting a keyhole width of foam on the fuzz of his upper lip, and makes a bitter face.

Harry explains, "When people get divorced the father doesn't stop liking the kids, he just can't live with them any more. The reason Fosnacht keeps getting Billy all this expensive crap is probably he feels guilty for leaving him."

"Why did they get separated, Dad, do you know?"

"Beats me. The bigger riddle is, why did they ever get married?" Rabbit knew Peggy Fosnacht when she was Peggy Gring, a big-assed walleyed girl in the middle row always waving her hand in the air because she thought she had the answer. Fosnacht he knows less well: a weedy little guy always shrugging his shoulders, used to play the saxophone in prom bands, now a partner in a music store on the upper end of Weiser Street, used to be called Chords 'n' Records, now Fidelity Audio. At the discount Fosnacht got, Billy's hi-fi set must have cost next to nothing. Like these prizes they keep socking into these young shriekers. The one that French-kissed the m.c. is off now and a colored couple is guessing. Pale, but definitely colored. That's O.K., let 'em guess, win, and shriek with the rest of us. Better that than sniping from rooftops. Still, he wonders how that black bride would be.

Big lips, suck you right off, the men are slow as Jesus, long as whips, takes everything to get them up, in there forever, that's why white women need them, white men too quick about it, have to get on with the job, making America great. Rabbit loves, on *Laugh-In*, when Teresa does the go-go bit, the way they paint the words in white on her skin. When they watch Janice and Nelson are always asking him what the words are; since he took up the printer's trade he can read like a flash, upside down, mirror-wise too: he always had good quick eyes, Tothero used to tell him he could see the ball through the holes of his ears, to praise him. A great secret sly praiser, Tothero. Dead now. The game different now, everything the jump shot, big looping hungry blacks lifting and floating there a second while a pink palm long as your forearm launched the ball. He asks Nelson, "Why don't you stay at the playground any more? When I was your age I'd be playing Horse and Twenty-one all day long."

"Yeah, but you were good. You were tall." Nelson used to be crazy for sports. Little League, intramural. But lately he isn't. Rabbit blames it on a scrapbook his mother kept, of his basketball days in the late Forties, when he set some county records: last winter every time they would go visit Mt. Judge Nelson would ask to get it out and lie on the floor with it, those old dry-yellow games, the glue dried so the pages crackle being turned, MT. JUDGE TOPPLES ORIOLE, ANGSTROM HITS FOR 37, just happening for the kid, that happened twenty years ago, light from a star.

"I *got* tall," Rabbit tells him. "At your age I wasn't much taller than you are." A lie, but not really. A few inches. In a world where inches matter. Putts. Fucks. Orbits. Squaring up a form. He feels bad about Nelson's height. His own never did him much good, if he could take five inches off himself and give them to Nelson he might. If it didn't hurt.

"Anyway, Dad, sports are square now. Nobody does it."

"Well, what isn't square now? Besides pill-popping and

draft-dodging. And letting your hair grow down into your eyes. Where the hell is your mother? I'm going to call her. Turn the frigging TV down for once in your life."

David Frost has replaced *The Match Game* so Nelson turns it off entirely. Harry regrets the scared look that glimmered across the kid's face: like the look on his father's face when he sneezed on the street. Christ they're even scared to let him sneeze. His son and father seem alike fragile and sad to him. That's the trouble with caring about anybody, you begin to feel overprotective. Then you begin to feel crowded.

The telephone is on the lower of a set of see-through shelves that in theory divides the living room from a kind of alcove they call a breakfast nook. A few cookbooks sit on them but Janice has never to his knowledge looked into them, just dishes up the same fried chicken and tasteless steak and peas and French fries she's always dished up. Harry dials the familiar number and a familiar voice answers. "Springer Motors. Mr. Stavros speaking."

"Charlie, hi. Hey, is Janice around?"

"Sure is, Harry. How's tricks?" Stavros is a salesman and always has to say something.

"Tricky," Rabbit answers.

"Hold on, friend. The good woman's right here." Off-phone, his voice calls, "Pick it up. It's your old man."

Another receiver is lifted. Through the knothole of momentary silence Rabbit sees the office: the gleaming display cars on the showroom floor, old man Springer's frosted-glass door shut, the green-topped counter with the three steel desks behind: Stavros at one, Janice at another, and Mildred Kroust the bookkeeper Springer has had for thirty years at the one in between, except she's usually out sick with some sort of female problem she's developed late in life, so her desk top is empty and bare but for wire baskets and a spindle and a blotter. Rabbit can also see last year's puppy-dog calendar on the wall and the cardboard cut-out of the Toyota station wagon on the old coffee-colored safe, behind the Christmas tree. The last time he was at Springer's lot was for their Christmas party. Also Springer is so tickled to get the Toyota franchise after years of dealing in second-hand he has told Harry he feels "like a kid at Christmas all year round." "Harry sweet," Janice says, and he does hear something new in her voice, a breathy lilt of faint hurry, of a song he has interrupted her singing. "You're going to scold me, aren't you?"

"No, the kid and I were just wondering if and if so when the hell we're going to get a home-cooked meal around here."

"Oh I know," she sings, "I hate it too, it's just that with Mildred out so much we've had to go into her books, and her system is really zilch." Zilch: he hears another voice in hers. "Honestly," she sings on, "if it turns out she's been swindling Daddy of millions none of us will be surprised."

"Yeah. Look, Janice. It sounds like you're having a lot of fun over there—"

"*Fun?* I'm *work*ing, sweetie."

"Sure. Now what the fuck is really going on?"

"What do you mean, *going on?* Nothing is going on except your wife is trying to bring home a little extra bread." Bread? " 'Going on'—really. You may think your seven or whatever dollars an hour you get for sitting in the dark diddling that machine is wonderful money, Harry, but the fact is a hundred dollars doesn't buy anything any more, it just *goes*."

"Jesus, why am I getting this lecture on inflation? All I want to know is why my wife is never home to cook the fucking supper for me and the fucking kid."

"Harry, has somebody been bugging you about me?"

"Bugging? How would they do that? Janice. Just tell me, shall I put two TV dinners in the oven or what?"

A pause, during which he has a vision: sees her wings hover, her song suspended: imagines himself soaring, rootless, free. An old premonition, dim. Janice says, with measured words, so he feels as when a child watching his mother levelling tablespoons of sugar into a bowl of batter, "Could you, sweet? Just for tonight? We're in the middle of a little crisis here, frankly. It's too complicated to explain, but we have to get some figures firm or we can't do the paychecks tomorrow."

"Who's this we? Your father there?"

"Oh sure."

"Could I talk to him a second?"

"Why? He's out on the lot."

"I want to know if he got those tickets for the Blasts game. The kid's dying to go."

"Well, actually, I don't see him, I guess he's gone home for supper."

"So it's just you and Charlie there."

"Other people are in and out. We're *des*perately trying to untangle this mess Mildred made. This is the last night, Harry, I promise. I'll be home between eight and nine, and then tomorrow night let's all go to a movie together. That space thing is still in West Brewer, I noticed this morning driving in."

Rabbit is suddenly tired, of this conversation, of everything. Confusing energy surrounds him. A man's appetites diminish, but the world's never. "O.K. Be home when you can. But we got to talk."

"I'd love to talk, Harry." From her tone she assumes "talk" means fuck, when he did mean talk. She hangs up: a satisfied impatient sound.

He opens another beer. The pull-tab breaks, so he has to find the rusty old church key underneath everything in the knife drawer. He heats up two Salisbury steak dinners; while waiting for the oven to preheat to 400°, he reads the ingredients listed on the package: water, beef, peas, dehydrated potato flakes, bread crumbs, mushrooms, flour, butter, margarine, salt, malto-dextrin, tomato paste, corn starch, Worcestershire sauce, hydrolyzed vegetable protein, monosodium glutamate, nonfat dry milk, dehydrated onions, flavoring, sugar, caramel color, spice, cysteine and thiamine hydrochloride, gum arabic. There is no clue from the picture on the tinfoil where all this stuff fits in. He always thought gum arabic was something you erased with. Thirty-six years old and he knows less than when he started. With the difference that now he knows how little he'll always know. He'll never know how to talk Chinese or how screwing an African princess feels. The six o'clock news is all about space, all about emptiness: some bald man plays with little toys to show the docking and undocking maneuvers, and then a panel talks about the significance of this for the next five hundred years. They keep mentioning Columbus but as far as Rabbit can see it's the exact opposite: Columbus flew blind and hit something, these guys see exactly where they're aiming and it's a big round nothing. The Salisbury steak tastes of preservative and Nelson eats only a few bites. Rabbit tries to joke him into it: "Can't eat a TV dinner without TV." They channel-hop, trying to find something to hold them, but there is nothing, it all slides past until, after nine, on Carol Burnett, she and Gomer Pyle do an actually pretty funny skit about the Lone Ranger. It takes Rabbit back to when he used to sit in the radio-listening armchair back on Jackson Road, its arms darkened with greasespots from the peanut butter cracker-sandwiches he used to stack there to listen with. Mom used to have a fit. Every Monday, Wednesday, and Friday night it came on at seven-thirty, and if it was summer you'd come in from kick-the-can or three-stops-or-a-catch and the neighborhood would grow quiet all across the backyards and then at eight the doors would slam and the games begin again, those generous summer days, just enough dark to fit sleep into, a war being fought across oceans just so he could spin out his days in such happiness, in such quiet growing. Eating Wheaties.

In this skit the Lone Ranger has a wife. She stamps around a cabin saying how she hates housework, hates her lonely life. "You're never home," she says, "you keep disappearing in a cloud of dust with a hearty 'Heigh-ho, Silver.'" The unseen audience laughs, Rabbit laughs. Nelson doesn't see what's so funny. Rabbit tells him, "That's how they always used to introduce the program."

The kid says crossly, "I *know,* Dad," and Rabbit loses the thread of the skit a little, there has been a joke he didn't hear, whose laughter is dying.

Now the Lone Ranger's wife is complaining that Daniel Boone brings his wife beautiful furs, but "What do I ever get from you? A silver bullet." She opens a door and a bushel of silver bullets comes crashing out and floods the floor. For the rest of the skit Carol Burnett and Gomer Pyle and the man who plays Tonto (not Sammy Davis Jr. but another TV Negro) keep slipping and crunching on these bullets, by accident. Rabbit thinks of the millions who are watching, the millions the sponsors are paying, and still nobody took time to realize that this would happen, a mess of silver bullets on the floor.

Tonto tells the Lone Ranger, "Better next time, put-um bullet in gun first."

The wife turns to complaining about Tonto. "*Him.* Why must we always keep having him to dinner? He *never* has *us* back."

Tonto tells her that if she comes to his teepee, she would be kidnapped by seven or eight braves. Instead of being frightened, she is interested. She rolls those big Burnett eyes and says, "Let's go, *que más sabe.*"

Nelson asks, "Dad, what's *que más sabe?*"

Rabbit is surprised to have to say, "I don't know. Something like 'good friend' or 'boss,' I suppose." Indeed come to think of it he understands nothing about Tonto. The Lone Ranger is a white man, so law and order on the range will work to his benefit, but what about Tonto? A Judas to his race, the more disinterested and lonely and heroic figure of virtue. When did he get his pay-off? Why was he faithful to the masked stranger? In the days of the war one never asked. Tonto was simply on "the side of right." It seemed a correct dream then, red and white together, red loving white as naturally as stripes in the flag. Where has "the side of right" gone? He has missed several jokes while trying to answer Nelson. The skit is approaching its climax. The wife is telling the Lone Ranger, "You must choose between him or me." Arms folded, she stands fierce.

The Lone Ranger's pause for decision is not long. "Saddle up, Tonto," he says. He puts on the phonograph a record of the *William Tell* Overture and both men leave. The wife tiptoes over, a bullet crunching underfoot, and changes the record to "Indian Love Call." Tonto enters from the other side of the screen. He and she kiss and hug. "I've always been interested," Carol Burnett confides out to the audience, her face getting huge, "in Indian affairs."

There is a laugh from the invisible audience there, and even Rabbit sitting at home in his easy chair laughs, but underneath the laugh this final gag falls flat, maybe because everybody still thinks of Tonto as incorruptible, as above it all, like Jesus and Armstrong. "Bedtime, huh?" Rabbit says. He turns off the show as it unravels into a string of credits. The sudden little star flares, then fades.

Nelson says, "The kids at school say Mr. Fosnacht was having an affair, that's why they got divorced."

"Or maybe he just got tired of not knowing which of his wife's eyes was looking at him."

"Dad, what is an affair exactly?"

"Oh, it's two people going out together when they're married to somebody else."

"Did that ever happen to you and Mom?"

"I wouldn't say so. I took a vacation once, that didn't last very long. When you were about three. You wouldn't remember."

"I do, though. I remember Mom crying a lot, and everybody chasing you at the baby's funeral, and I remember standing in the place on Wilbur Street, with just you in the room beside me, and looking down at the town through the window screen, and knowing Mom was in the hospital."

"Yeah. Those were poor days. This Saturday, if Grandpa Springer has got the tickets he said he would, we'll go to the Blasts game."

"I know," the boy says, unenthusiastic, and drifts toward the stairs. It unsettles Harry, how in the corner of his eye, once or twice a day, he seems to see another woman in the house, a woman who is not Janice; when it is only his long-haired son.

One more beer. He scrapes Nelson's uneaten dinner into the Disposall, which sometimes sweetly stinks because the Penn Villas sewers flow sluggishly, carelessly engineered. He moves through the downstairs collecting glasses for the dishwasher; one of Janice's stunts is to wander around leaving dreggy cups with saucers used as ashtrays and wineglasses coated with vermouth around on whatever ledges occurred to her—the TV top, a windowsill. How can she be helping untangle Mildred's mess? Maybe out of the house she's a whirlwind of efficiency. And a heigh-ho Silver. Indian affairs. Poor Pop and his rumor. Poor Mom lying there prey to poison tongues and nightmares. The two of them, their minds gone dry as haystacks rats slither through. His mind shies away. He looks out the window and sees in dusk the black lines of a TV aerial, an aluminum clothes tree, a basketball hoop on a far garage. How can he get the kid interested in sports? If he's too short for basketball, then baseball. Anything, just to put something there, some bliss, to live on later for a while. If he goes empty now he won't last at all, because we get emptier. Rabbit turns from the window and everywhere in his own house sees a slippery disposable gloss. It glints back at him from the synthetic fabric of the living room sofa and a chair, the synthetic artiness of a lamp Janice bought that has a piece of driftwood weighted and wired as its base, the unnatural-looking natural wood of the shelves empty but for a few ashtrays with the sheen of fairgrounds souvenirs; it glints back at him from the steel sink, the kitchen linoleum with its whorls as of madness, oil in water, things don't mix. The window above the sink is black and opaque as the orange that paints the asylum windows. He sees mirrored in it his own wet hands. Underwater. He crumples the aluminum beer can he has absentmindedly drained. Its contents feel metallic inside him: corrosive, fattening. Things don't mix. His inability to fasten onto any thought and make something of it must be fatigue. Rabbit lifts himself up the stairs, pushes himself through the underwater motions of undressing and dental care, sinks into bed without bothering to turn out the lights downstairs and in the bathroom. He hears from a mournful smothered radio noise that Nelson is still awake. He thinks he should get up and say good night, give the kid a blessing, but a weight crushes him while light persists into his bedroom, along with the boy's soft knocking noises, opening and shutting doors, looking for something to do. Since infancy Rabbit sleeps best when others are up, upright like nails holding down the world, like lamp-posts, street-signs, dandelion stems, cobwebs . . .

Something big slithers into the bed. Janice. The fluorescent dial on the bureau is saying five of eleven, its two hands merged into one finger. She is warm in her nightie. Skin is warmer than cotton. He was dreaming about a parabolic curve, trying to steer on it, though the thing he was trying to steer was fighting him, like a broken sled.

"Get it untangled?" he asks her.

"Just about. I'm so sorry, Harry. Daddy came back and he just wouldn't let us go."

"Catch a nigger by the toe," he mumbles.

"What sort of evening did you and Nelson have?"

"A kind of nothing sort of evening."

"Anybody call?"

"Nobody."

He senses she is, late as it is, alive, jazzed up, and wants to talk, apologetic, wanting to make it up. Her being in the bed changes its quality, from a resisting raft he is seeking to hold to a curving course to a nest, a laden hollow, itself curved. Her hand seeks him out and he brushes her away with an athlete's old instinct to protect that spot. She turns then her back on him. He accepts this rejection. He nestles against her. Her waist where no bones are nips like a bird dipping. He had been afraid marrying her she would get fat like her mother but as she ages more and more her skinny little stringy go-getter of a father comes out in her. His hand leaves the dip to stray around in front to her belly, faintly lovingly loose from having had two babies. Puppy's neck. Should he have let her have had another to replace the one that died? Maybe that was the mistake. It had all seemed like a pit to him then, her womb and the grave, sex and death, he had fled her cunt as a tiger's mouth. His fingers search lower, touch tendrils, go lower, discover a moistness already there. He thinks of feathering the linotype keys, of work tomorrow, and is already there.

The Verity Press lives on order forms, tickets to fund-raising dances, political posters in the fall, high-school yearbooks in the spring, throwaway fliers for the supermarkets, junk mail sales announcements. On its rotary press it prints a weekly, *The Brewer Vat*, which specializes in city scandal since the two dailies handle all the hard local and syndicated national news. Once it also published a German-language journal, *Der Schockelschtuhl*, founded 1830. In Rabbit's time here they had let it die, its circulation thinned down to a few thousand farmers in odd corners of the county and counties around. Rabbit remembers it because it meant the departure from the shop of old Kurt Schrack, one of those dark scowling Germans with whiskers that look tattooed into the skin rather than growing out of it to be shaved. His hair was iron but his jaw was lead as he sat scowling in the corner that belonged only to him; he was paid just to proofread the Pennsylvania Dutch copy and hand-set it in the black-letter fonts no one else was allowed to touch. The borders, and the big ornamental letters used on the inside pages, had been carved of wood, blackened by a century of inky handling. Schrack would concentrate down into his work so hard he would look up at lunchtime and talk in German to Pajasek the Polish foreman, or to one of the two shop Negroes, or to one of the Angstroms. Schrack had been likable in that he had done something scrupulously that others could not do at all. Then one Monday he was let go and his corner was soon walled in for the engravers.

Der Schockelschtuhl has gone and the *Vat* itself keeps threatening to take its custom to one of the big offset plants in Philadelphia. You simply paste it up, ads and photos and type, and send it off. Over Verity hangs a future that belongs to cool processes, to photo-offset and beyond that to photocomposition, computerized television that throws thousands of letters a second onto film with never the kiss of metal, beamed by computers programmed even for hyphenation and runarounds; but just an offset press is upwards of thirty thousand dollars and flatbed letterpress remains the easiest way to do tickets and posters. And the *Vat* might fold up any week. It is certainly a superfluous newspaper.

BREWER FACTORY TOOLS COMPONENT HEADED TOWARD MOON, is this week's front page story. Rabbit sets, two-column measure, his white fingers feathering, the used matrices dropping back into their channels above his head like rain onto tin.

When Brewerites this Sunday gaze up at the moon, it may look a little bit different to them.

Why?

Because there's going to be a little bit of Brewer on

No. Widow. He tries to take it back but the line is too tight to close so he settles for the widow.

it.

Zigzag Electronic Products Inc., of Seventh and Locust Streets, City,

Oops.

Locust Streets, city, revealed to VAT reporters this week that a crucial electronic switching sequence in the on-board guidance and nabifiation computer was the on-board guidance and navigation computer was manufactured by them here, in the plain brick building, once the cite if Gossamer Ho¢irey Co, that thouing, once the site of Gossamer Hosiery Co., that thousands of Brewer citizens walk unknowingly by each day.

If the printed circuits of their switches—half the size of a postage stamp and weighing less than a sunflower seed—fail to function, astronauts Armstrong, Aldrin and Collin will drift past the moon and perish in the infinite vacuum of so-called ''deep space.''

But there is no danger of that, Zigzag Electronics general manager Leroy ''Spin'' Lengel assured the

Jump after twenty lines. Switch to single-column lines.

VAT reporter in his highly modern, light-green office.

''It was just another job to us,'' he said. ''We do a hundred like it every week.

''Naturally all of us at Zigzag are proud as punch,'' Lengel added. ''We're sailinggeatoin added. ''We're sailing on a new sea.''

The machine stands tall and warm above him, mothering, muttering, a temperamental thousand-parted survival from the golden age of machinery. The sorts tray is on his right hand; the Star Quadder and the mold disc and slug tray on his left; a green-shaded light bulb at the level of his eyes. Above this sun the machine shoulders into shadow like a thunderhead, its matrix return rod spiralling idly, all these rustling sighing tons of intricately keyed mass waiting for the feather-touch of his intelligence. Behind the mold disc the molten lead waits; sometimes when there is a jam the lead squirts hot out: Harry has been burned. But the machine is a baby; its demands, though inflexible, are few, and once these demands are met obedience automatically follows. There is no problem of fidelity. Do for it, it does for you. And Harry loves the light here. It is cream to his eyes, this even bluish light that nowhere casts a shadow, light so calm and fine you can read glinting letters backwards at a glance. It contrasts to the light in his home, where standing at the kitchen sink he casts a shadow that looks like dirt over the dishes, and sitting in the living room he must squint against the bridge lamp Janice uses to read magazines by, and bulbs keep burning out on the stair landing, and the kid complains except when it's totally dark about the reflections on the television screen. In the big room of Verity Press, ceilinged with fluorescent tubes, men move around as spirits, without shadows.

At the ten-thirty coffee break Pop comes over and asks, "Think you can make it over this evening?"

"I don't know. Janice said something last night about taking the kid to a movie. How's Mom?"

"As good as can be hoped."

"She mention Janice again?"

"Not last night, Harry. Not more than in passing at least."

The old man sidles closer, clutching his paper cup of coffee tightly as if it held jewels. "Did you say anything to Janice?" he asks. "Did you search her out any?"

"Search her out, what is she, on trial? I hardly saw her. She was over at Springer's until late." Rabbit winces, in the perfect light seeing his father's lips pinch in, his eyes slide fishily. Harry elaborates: "Old man Springer kept her trying to untangle his books until eleven, ever since he started selling Jap cars he's a slavedriver."

Pop's pupils widen a hairline; his eyebrows lift a pica's width. "I thought he and his missus were in the Poconos."

"The Springers? Who told you that?"

"I guess your mother, I forget who told her, Julia Arndt maybe. Maybe it was last week. Mrs. Springer's legs they say can't take the heat, they swell up. I don't know what to tell you about growing old, Harry; it isn't all it's cracked up to be."

"The Poconos."

"It must have been last week they said. Your mother will be disappointed if you can't come over tonight, what shall I tell her?"

The bell rings, ending the break; Buchanan slouches by, wiping his morning shot of whisky from his lips, and winks. "Daddy knows best," he calls playfully. Sleek black seal.

Harry says, "Tell her we'll try after supper but we've promised the kid a movie and probably can't. Maybe Friday." His father's face, disappointed and unaccusing, angers him so he explodes: "Goddammit Pop I have a family of my own to run! I can't do everything." He returns to his machine gratefully. And it fits right around him, purrs while he brushes a word from his mind ("Poconos"), makes loud rain when he touches the keys, is pleased he is back.

Janice is home when he comes back from work. The Falcon is in the garage. The little house is hazed by her cigarette smoke; a half-empty glass of vermouth sits on top of the television set and another on one of the shelves between the living room and the breakfast nook. Rabbit calls, "Janice!" Though the house is small and echoing, so that the click of the television knob, the unstoppering of a bottle, the creaking of Nelson's bedsprings can be heard anywhere, there is no answer. He hears steady tumbling water, climbs the stairs. The upstairs bathroom is packed with steam. Amazing, how hot women can stand water.

"Harry, you've just let a lot of cold air in."

She is shaving her legs in the tub and several small cuts are brightly bleeding. Though Janice was never a knockout, with something sullen and stunted and tight about her face, and a short woman in the decade of the big female balloons Hollywood sent up before it died, she always had nice legs and still does. Taut perky legs with a bony kneecap that Rabbit has always liked; he likes to see the bones in people. His wife is holding one soaped leg up as if for display and he sees through the steam the gray soap-curdled water slopping in and out and around her pussy and belly and bottom as she reaches to shave the ankle, and he is standing at the top of a stairway of the uncountable other baths he has heard her take or seen her have in the thirteen years of their marriage. He can keep count of these years because their marriage is six months older than their child. He asks, "Where's Nelson?"

"He's gone with Billy Fosnacht to Brewer to look at mini-bikes."

"I don't want him looking at mini-bikes. He'll get killed." The other child his daughter was killed. The world is quicksand. Find the straight path and stick to it.

"Oh Harry, it won't do any harm to look. Billy has one he rides all the time."

"I can't afford it."

"He's promised to earn half the money himself. I'll give him our half out of *my* money, if you're so uptight." Her money: her father gave her stocks years ago. And she earns money now. Does she need him at all? She asks, "Are you sure you closed the door? There's a terrible draft suddenly. There's not much privacy in this house, is there?"

"Well Jesus how much privacy do you think I owe you?"

"Well you don't have to stand there staring, you've seen me take a bath before."

"Well I haven't seen you with your clothes off since I don't know when. You're O.K."

"I'm just a cunt, Harry. There are billions of us now."

A few years ago she would never have said "cunt." It excites him, touches him like a breath on his cock. The ankle she is reaching to shave starts to bleed, suddenly, brightly, shockingly. "God," he tells her, "you are clumsy."

"Your standing there staring makes me nervous."

"Why're you taking a bath right now anyway?"

"We're going out to supper, remember? If we're going to make the movie at eight o'clock we ought to leave here at six. You should wash off your ink. Want to use my water?"

"It's all full of blood and little hairs."

"Harry, really. You've gotten so uptight in your old age."

Again, "uptight." Not her voice, another voice, another voice in hers.

Janice goes on, "The tank hasn't had time to heat enough for a fresh tub."

"O.K. I'll use yours."

His wife gets out, water spilling on the bathmat, her feet and buttocks steamed rosy. Her breasts sympathetically lift as she lifts her hair from the nape of her neck. "Want to dry my back?"

He can't remember the last time she asked him to do this. As he rubs, her smallness mixes with the absolute bigness naked women have. The curve that sways out from her waist to be swelled by the fat of her flank. Rabbit squats to dry her bottom, goosebumpy red. The backs of her thighs, the stray black hairs, the moss moist between. "O.*K.*," she says, and steps off. He stands to pat dry the down beneath the sweep of her upheld hair: Nature is full of nests. She asks, "Where do you want to eat?"

"Oh, anywhere. The kid likes the Burger Bliss over on West Weiser."

"I was wondering, there's a new Greek restaurant just across the bridge I'd love to try. Charlie Stavros was talking about it the other day."

"Yeah. Speaking of the other day—"

"He says they have marvellous grape leaf things and shish kebab Nelson would like. If we don't make him do something new he'll be eating at Burger Bliss the rest of his life."

"The movie starts at seven-thirty, you know."

"I *know*," she says, "that's why I took a bath *now*," and, a new Janice, still standing with her back to him, nestles her bottom against his fly, lifting herself on tiptoe and arching her back to make a delicate double damp spreading contact. His mind softens; his prick hardens. "Besides," Janice is going on, edging herself on tiptoes up and down like a child gently chanting to Banbury Cross, "the movie isn't just for Nelson, it's for *me*, for working so hard all week."

There was a question he was about to ask, but her caress erased it. She straightens, saying, "Hurry, Harry. The water will get cold." Two damp spots are left on the front of his suntans. The muggy bathroom has drugged him; when she opens the door to their bedroom, the contrast of cold air cakes him; he sneezes. Yet he leaves the door open while he undresses so he can watch her dress. She is practiced, quick; rapidly as a snake shrugs forward over the sand she has tugged her black pantyhose up over her legs. She nips to the closet for her skirt, to the bureau for her blouse, the frilly silver one, that he thought was reserved for parties. Testing the tub with his foot (too hot) he remembers.

"Hey Janice. Somebody said today your parents were in the Poconos. Last night you said your father was at the lot."

She halts in the center of their bedroom, staring into the bathroom. Her dark eyes darken the more; she sees his big white body, his spreading slack gut, his uncircumcised member hanging boneless as a rooster comb from its blond roots. She sees her flying athlete grounded, cuckolded. She sees a large white man a knife would slice like lard. The angelic cold strength of his leaving her, the anticlimax of his coming back and clinging: something in the combination that she cannot forgive, that justifies her. Her eyes must burn on him, for he turns his back and begins to step into her water: his buttocks merge with her lover's, she thinks how all men look innocent and vulnerable here, reverting to the baby they were. She says firmly, "They were in the Poconos but came back early. Mom always thinks at these resorts she's being snubbed," and without waiting for an answer to her lie runs downstairs.

While soaking in the pool tinged by her hair and blood Rabbit hears Nelson come into the house. Voices rise muffled through the ceiling. "What a crummy mini-bike," the child announces. "It's busted already."

Janice says, "Then aren't you glad it isn't yours?"

"Yeah, but there's a more expensive kind, really neat, a Gioconda, that Grandpa could get at discount for us so it wouldn't cost any more than the cheap one."

"Your father and I agree, two hundred dollars is too much for a toy."

"It's *not* a toy, Mom, it's something I could really learn about engines on. And you can get a license and Daddy could drive it to work some days instead of taking a bus all the time."

"Daddy likes taking the bus."

"I hate it!" Rabbit yells, "it stinks of *Ne*groes," but no voice below in the kitchen acknowledges hearing him.

Throughout the evening he has this sensation of nobody hearing him, of his spirit muffled in pulpy insulation, so he talks all the louder and more insistently. Driving the car (even with his flag decal the Falcon feels more like Janice's car than his, she drives it so much more) back down Emberly to Weiser, past the movie house and across the bridge, he says,

"Goddammit I don't see why we have to go back into Brewer to eat, I spend all frigging day in Brewer."

"Nelson agrees with me," Janice says. "It will be an interesting experiment. I've promised him there are lots of things that aren't gooey, it's not like Chinese food."

"We're going to be late for the movie, I'm sure of it."

"Peggy Fosnacht says—" Janice begins.

"That dope," Rabbit says.

"Peggy Fosnacht says the beginning is the most boring part. A lot of stars, and some symphony. Anyway there must be short subjects or at least those things that want you to go out into the lobby and buy more candy."

Nelson says, "I heard the beginning is real neat. There's a lot of cavemen eating meat that's really raw, he nearly threw up a guy said, and then you see one of them get really zapped with a bone. And they throw the bone up and it turns into a spaceship."

"Thank you, Mr. Spoil-It-All," Janice says. "I feel I've seen it now. Maybe you two should go to the movie and I'll go home to bed."

"The hell," Rabbit says. "You stick right with us and suffer for once."

Janice says, conceding, "Women don't dig science."

Harry likes the sensation, of frightening her, of offering to confront outright this faceless unknown he feels now in their lives, among them like a fourth member of the family. The baby that died? But though Janice's grief was worse at first, though she bent under it like a reed he was afraid might break, in the long years since, he has become sole heir to the grief. Since he refused to get her pregnant again the murder and guilt have become all his. At first he tried to explain how it was, that sex with her had become too dark, too *serious*, too kindred to death, to trust anything that might come out of it. Then he stopped explaining and she seemed to forget: like a cat who sniffs around in corners mewing for the drowned kittens a day or two and then back to lapping milk and napping in the wash basket. Women and nature forget. No need for science since they are what science seeks to know. Just thinking of the baby, remembering how he had been told of her death over a pay phone in a drugstore, puts a kink in his chest, a kink he still associates, dimly, with God. He prayed on the bus back, he remembers.

At Janice's directions he turns right off the bridge, at JIMBO's *Friendly* LOUNGE, and after a few blocks parks on Plum Street. He locks the car behind them. "This is pretty slummy territory," he complains to Janice. "A lot of rapes lately down here."

"Oh," she says, "the *Vat* prints nothing but rapes. You know what a rape usually is? It's a woman who changed her mind afterward."

"Watch how you talk in front of the kid."

"He knows more now than you ever will. That's nothing personal, Harry, it's just a fact. People are more sophisticated now than when you were a boy."

"How about when you were a girl?"

"I was very dumb and innocent, I admit it."

"But?"

"But nothing."

"I thought you were going to tell us how wise you are now."

"I'm not wise, but at least I've tried to keep my mind open."

Nelson, walking a little ahead of them but hearing too much anyway, points to the great Sunflower Beer clock on Weiser Square, which they can see across slate rooftops and a block of rubble on its way to being yet another parking lot. "It's twenty after six," he says. He adds, not certain his point was made, "At Burger Bliss they serve you right away, it's neat, they keep them warm in a big oven that glows purple."

"No Burger Bliss for you, baby," Harry says. "Try Pizza Paradise."

"Don't be ignorant," Janice says, "pizza is purely Italian." To Nelson she says, "We have plenty of time, there won't be anybody there this early."

"Where *is* it?" he asks.

"Right here," she says; she has led them without error.

The place is a brick row house, its red bricks painted oxblood red in the Brewer manner. A small un-neon sign advertises it, The Taverna. They walk up sandstone steps to the doorway, and a motherly mustached woman greets them, shows them into what once was a front parlor, now broken through to the room beyond, the kitchen behind swinging doors beyond that. A few center tables. Booths along the two walls. White walls bare but for some picture of an oval-faced yellow woman and baby with a candle flickering in front of it. Janice slides into one side of a booth and Nelson into the other and Harry, forced to choose, slides in beside Nelson, to help him with the menu, to find something on it enough like a hamburger. The tablecloth is a red checked cloth and the daisies in a blue glass vase are real flowers, soft, Harry notices, touching them. Janice was right. The place is nice. The only music is a radio playing in the kitchen; the only other customers are a couple talking so earnestly they now and then touch hands, immersed in some element where they cannot trust their eyes, the man red in the face as if choking, the woman stricken pale. They are Penn Park types, cool in their clothes, beige and pencil-gray, the right clothes insofar as any clothes can be right in this muggy river-bottom in the flood of July. Their faces have an edgy money look: their brows have that frontal clarity the shambling blurred poor can never duplicate. Though he can never now be one of them Harry likes their being here, in this restaurant so chaste it is *chic*. Maybe Brewer isn't as dead on its feet as it seems.

The menus are in hectographed handwriting. Nelson's face tightens, studying it. "They don't have any sandwiches," he says.

"Nelson," Janice says, "if you make a fuss out of this I'll never take you out anywhere again. Be a big boy."

"It's all in gobbledy-gook."

She explains, "Everything is more or less lamb. *Kebab* is when it's on a skewer. *Moussaka*, it's mixed with eggplant."

"I *hate* eggplant."

Rabbit asks her, "How do you know all this?"

"Everybody knows that much; Harry, you are so *provincial*. The two of you, sitting there side by side, determined to be miserable. Ugly Americans."

"You don't look all that Chinese yourself," Harry says, "even in your little Lord Fauntleroy blouse." He glances down at his fingertips and sees there an ochre smudge of pollen, from having touched the daisies.

Nelson asks, "What's *kalamaria?*"

"I don't know," Janice says.

"I want that."

"You don't know what you want. Have the *souvlakia*, it's the simplest. It's pieces of meat on a skewer, very well done, with peppers and onions between."

"I *hate* pepper."

Rabbit tells him, "Not the stuff that makes you sneeze, the green things like hollow tomatoes."

"I know," Nelson says. "I hate them. I know what a *pep*per is, Daddy; my *God*."

"Don't swear like that. When did you ever have them?"

"In a Pepperburger."

"Maybe you should take him to Burger Bliss and leave me here," Janice says.

Rabbit asks, "What are *you* going to have, if you're so fucking smart?"

"Daddy swore."

"Ssh," Janice says, "both of you. There's a nice kind of chicken pie, but I forget what it's called."

"You've been here before," Rabbit tells her.

"I want *melopeta,*" Nelson says.

Rabbit sees where the kid's stubby finger (Mom always used to point out, he has those little Springer hands) is stalled on the menu and tells him, "Dope, that's a dessert."

Shouts of greeting announce in the doorway a large family all black hair and smiles, initiates; the waiter greets them as a son and rams a table against a booth to make space for them all. They cackle their language, they giggle, they coo, they swell with the joy of arrival. Their chairs scrape, their children stare demure and big-eyed from under the umbrella of adult noise. Rabbit feels naked in his own threadbare little family. The Penn Park couple very slowly turn around, underwater, at the commotion, and then resume—she now blushing, he pale—contact, touching hands on the tablecloth, groping through the stems of wineglasses. The Greek flock settles to roost but there is one man left over, who must have entered with them but hesitates in the doorway. Rabbit knows him. Janice refuses to turn her head; she keeps her eyes on the menu, frozen so they don't seem to read. Rabbit murmurs to her, "There's Charlie Stavros."

"Oh, really?" she says, yet she still is reluctant to turn her head.

But Nelson turns his and loudly calls out, "Hi, Charlie!" Summers, the kid spends a lot of time at the lot.

Stavros, who has such bad and sensitive eyes his glasses are tinted lilac, focuses. His face breaks into the smile he must use at the close of a sale, a sly tuck in one corner of his lips making a dimple. He is a squarely marked-off man, Stavros, some inches shorter than Harry, some years younger, but with a natural reserve of potent gravity that gives him the presence and poise of an older person. His hairline is receding. His eyebrows go straight across. He moves deliberately, as if carrying something fragile within him; in his Madras checks and his rectangular thick hornrims and his deep squared sideburns he moves through the world with an air of having chosen it. His not having married, though he is in his thirties, adds to his quality of deliberation. Rabbit, when he sees him, always likes him more than he had intended to. He reminds him of the guys, close-set, slow, and never rattled, who were play-makers on the team. When Stavros, taking thought, moves around the obstacle of momentary indecision toward their booth, it is Harry who says, "Join us," though Janice, face downcast, has already slid over.

Charlie speaks to Janice. "The whole caboodle. Beautiful."

She says, "These two are being horrible."

Rabbit says, "We can't read the menu."

Nelson says, "Charlie, what's *kalamaria?* I want some."

"No you don't. It's little, like, octopuses cooked in their own ink."

"Ick," Nelson says.

"Nelson," Janice says sharply.

Rabbit says, "Sit yourself down, Charlie."

"I don't want to butt in."

"It'd be a favor. Hell."

"Dad's being grumpy," Nelson confides.

Janice impatiently pats the place beside her; Charlie sits down and asks her, "What *does* the kid like?"

"Hamburgers," Janice moans, theatrically. She's become an actress suddenly, every gesture and intonation charged to carry across an implied distance.

Charlie's squarish intent head is bowed above the menu. "Let's get him some *keftedes.* O.K., Nelson? Meatballs."

"Not with tomatoey goo on them."

"No goo, just the meat. A little mint. Mint's what's in Life-Savers. O.K.?"

"O.K."

"You'll love 'em."

But Rabbit feels the boy has been sold a slushy car. And he feels, with Stavros's broad shoulders next to Janice's, and the man's hands each sporting a chunky gold ring, that the table has taken a turn down a road Rabbit didn't choose. He and Nelson are in the back seat.

Janice says to Stavros, "Charlie, why don't you order for all of us? We don't know what we're doing."

Rabbit says, "*I* know what *I'm* doing. I'll order for myself. I want the"—he picks something off the menu at random —"the *païdakia.*"

"*Païdakia,*" Stavros says. "I don't think so. It's marinated lamb, you need to order it the day before, for at least six."

Nelson says, "Dad, the movie starts in forty minutes."

Janice explains, "We're trying to get to see this silly space movie."

Stavros nods as if he knows. There is a funny echo Rabbit's ears pick up. Things said between Janice and Stavros sound dead, duplicated. Of course they work together all day. Stavros tells them, "It's lousy."

"Why is it lousy?" Nelson asks anxiously. There is a look his face gets, bloating his lips and slightly sucking his eyes back into their sockets, that hasn't changed since his infancy, when his bottle would go dry.

Stavros relents. "Nellie, for you it'll be great. It's all toys. For me, it just wasn't sexy. I guess I don't find technology that sexy."

"Does everything *have* to be sexy?" Janice asks.

"It doesn't have to be, it tends to be," Stavros tells her. To Rabbit he says, "Have some *souvlakia.* You'll love it, and it's quick." And in an admirable potent little gesture, he moves his hand, palm outward as if his fingers had been snapped, without lifting his elbow from the table, and the motherly woman comes running to them.

"*Yasou.*"

"*Kale spera,*" she answers.

While Stavros orders in Greek, Harry studies Janice, her peculiar glow. Time has been gentle to her. As if it felt sorry for her. The something pinched and mean about her mouth, that she had even in her teens, has been relaxed by the appearance of other small wrinkles in her face, and her hair, whose sparseness once annoyed him, as another emblem of his poverty, she now brings down over her ears from a central parting in two smooth wings. She wears no lipstick and in certain lights her face owns a gypsy severity and the dignity present in newspaper photographs of female guerrilla fighters. The gypsy look she got from her mother, the dignity from the Sixties, which freed her from the need to look fluffy. Plain is beautiful enough. And now she is all circles in happiness, squirming on her round bottom and dancing her hands through arcs of exaggeration quick white in the candlelight. She tells Stavros, "If you hadn't shown up we would have starved."

"No," he says, a reassuring factual man. "They would have taken care of you. These are nice people."

"*These* two," she says, "are so American, they're helpless."

"Yeah," Stavros says to Rabbit, "I see the decal you put on your old Falcon."

"I told Charlie," Janice tells Rabbit, "*I* certainly didn't put it there."

"What's wrong with it?" he asks them both. "It's our flag, isn't it?"

"It's somebody's flag," Stavros says, not liking this trend and softly bouncing his fingertips together under his sheltered bad eyes.

"But not yours, huh?"

"Harry gets fanatical about this," Janice warns.

"I don't get fanatical, I just get a little sad about people who come over here to make a fat buck—"

"I was born here," Stavros quickly says. "So was my father."

"—and then knock the fucking flag," Rabbit continues, "like it's some piece of toilet paper."

"A flag is a flag. It's just a piece of cloth."

"It's more than just a piece of cloth to me."

"What is it to you?"

"It's—"

"The mighty Mississippi."

"It's people not finishing my sentences all the time."

"Just half the time."

"That's better than all the time like they have in China."

"Look. The Mississippi is very broad. The Rocky Mountains really swing. I just can't get too turned-on about cops bopping hippies on the head and the Pentagon playing cowboys and Indians all over the globe. That's what your little sticker means to me. It means screw the blacks and send the CIA into Greece."

"If we don't send somebody in the other side sure as hell will, the Greeks can't seem to manage the show by themselves."

"Harry, don't make yourself ridiculous, they invented civilization," Janice says. To Stavros she says, "See how little and tight his mouth gets when he thinks about politics."

"I don't *think* about politics," Rabbit says. "That's one of my Goddam precious American rights, not to think about politics. I just don't see why we're supposed to walk down the street with our hands tied behind our back and let ourselves be blackjacked by every thug who says he has a revolution going. And it really burns me up to listen to hotshot crap-car salesmen dripping with Vitalis sitting on their plumped-up asses bitching about a country that's been stuffing goodies into their mouth ever since they were born."

Charlie makes to rise. "I better go. This is getting too rich."

"Don't go," Janice begs. "He doesn't know what he's saying. He's sick on the subject."

"Yeah, don't go, Charlie, stick around and humor the madman."

Charlie lowers himself again and states in measured fashion, "I want to follow your reasoning. Tell me about the goodies we've been stuffing into Vietnam."

"Christ, exactly. We'd turn it into another Japan if they'd let us. That's all we want to do, make a happy rich country full of highways and gas stations. Poor old LBJ, Jesus with tears in his eyes on television, you must have heard him, he just about offered to make North Vietnam the fifty-first fucking state of the Goddam Union if they'd just stop throwing bombs. We're begging them to rig some elections, any elections, and they'd rather throw bombs. What more can we do? We're trying to give ourselves away, that's all our foreign policy is, is trying to give ourselves away to make little yellow people happy, and guys like you sit around in restaurants moaning, 'Jesus, we're rotten.' "

"I thought it was us and not them throwing the bombs."

"We've stopped; we stopped like all you liberals were marching for and what did it get us?" He leans forward to pronounce the answer clearly. "Not shit."

The whispering couple across the room look over in surprise; the family two booths away have hushed their noise to listen. Nelson is desperately blushing, his eyes sunk hot and sad in his sockets. "Not shit," Harry repeats more softly. He leans over the tablecloth, beside the trembling daisies. "Now I suppose you're going to say 'napalm.' That frigging magic word. They've been burying village chiefs alive and tossing mortars into hospitals for twenty years, and because of napalm they're candidates for the Albert F. Schweitzer peace prize. S, H, it." He has gotten loud again; it makes him rigid, the thoughts of the treachery and ingratitude befouling the flag, befouling him.

"Harry, you'll get us kicked out," Janice says; but he notices she is still happy, all in circles, a cookie in the oven.

"I'm beginning to dig him," Stavros tells her. "If I get your meaning," he says to Rabbit, "we're the big mama trying to make this unruly kid take some medicine that'll be good for him."

"That's right. You got it. We are. And most of 'em *want* to take the medicine, they're dying for it, and a few madmen in black pajamas would rather bury 'em alive. What's your theory? That we're in it for the rice? The Uncle Ben theory." Rabbit laughs and adds, "Bad old Uncle Ben."

"No," Stavros says, squaring his hands on the checked tablecloth and staring level-browed at the base of Harry's throat—gingerly with him, Harry notices, Why?—"my theory is it's a mistaken power play. It isn't that we want the rice, we don't want *them* to have it. Or the magnesium. Or the coastline. We've been playing chess with the Russians so long we didn't know we were off the board. White faces don't work in yellow countries any more. Kennedy's advisers who thought they could run the world from the dean's office pushed the button and nothing happened. Then Oswald voted Johnson in who was such a bonehead he thought all it took was a bigger thumb on the button. So the machine overheated, you got inflation and a falling market at one end and college riots at the other and in the middle forty thousand sons of American mothers killed by shit-smeared bamboo. People don't like having Sonny killed in the jungle any more. Maybe they never liked it, but they used to think it was necessary."

"And it isn't?"

Stavros blinks. "I see. You say war has to be."

"Yeah, and better there than here. Better little wars than big ones."

Stavros says, his hands on edge, ready to chop, "But you *like* it." His hands chop. "Burning up gook babies is right where you're at, friend." The "friend" is weak.

Rabbit asks him, "How did you do your Army bit?"

Stavros shrugs, squares his shoulders. "I was 4-F. Tricky ticker. I hear you sat out the Korean thing in Texas."

"I went where they told me. I'd still go where they told me."

"Bully for you. You're what made America great. A real gunslinger."

"He's silent majority," Janice says, "but he keeps making noise," looking at Stavros hopefully, for a return on her quip. God, she is dumb, even if her ass has shaped up in middle age.

"He's a normal product," Stavros says. "He's a typical good-hearted imperialist racist." Rabbit knows, from the careful level way this is pronounced, with that little tuck of a sold-car smile, that he is being flirted with, asked—his dim feeling is—for an alliance. But Rabbit is locked into his intuition that to describe any of America's actions as a "power play" is to miss the point. America is beyond power, it acts as in a dream, as a face of God. Wherever America is, there is freedom, and wherever America is not, madness rules with chains, darkness strangles millions. Beneath her patient bombers, paradise is possible. He fights back, "I don't follow this racist rap. You can't turn on television now without some black face spitting at you. Everybody from Nixon down is sitting up nights trying to figure out how to make 'em all rich without putting 'em to the trouble of doing any work." His tongue is reckless; but he is defending something infinitely tender, the star lit with his birth. "They talk about genocide when *they're* the ones planning it, they're the ones, the Negroes plus the rich kids, who want to pull it all down; not that they can't run squealing for a lawyer whenever some poor cop squints funny at 'em. The Vietnam war in my opinion—anybody want my opinion?—"

"Harry," Janice says, "you're making Nelson miserable."

"My opinion is, you have to fight a war now and then to

show you're willing, and it doesn't much matter where it is. The trouble isn't this war, it's this country. We wouldn't fight in Korea now. Christ, we wouldn't fight Hitler now. This country is so zonked out on its own acid, sunk so deep in its own fat and babble and filth, it would take H-bombs on every city from Detroit to Atlanta to wake us up and even then, we'd probably think we'd just been kissed."

"Harry," Janice asks, "do you want Nelson to die in Vietnam? Go ahead, tell him you do."

Harry turns to their child and says, "Kid, I don't want you to die anyplace. Your mother's the girl that's good at death."

Even he knows how cruel this is; he is grateful to her for not collapsing, for blazing up instead. "*Oh*," she says. "Oh. Tell him why he has no brothers or sisters, Harry. Tell him who refused to have another child."

"This is getting too rich," Stavros says.

"I'm glad you're seeing it," Janice tells him, her eyes sunk deep; Nelson gets that from her.

Mercifully, the food arrives. Nelson balks, discovering the meatballs drenched in gravy. He looks at Rabbit's tidily skewered lamb and says, "That's what I wanted."

"Let's swap, then. Shut up and eat," Rabbit says. He looks across to see that Janice and Stavros are having the same thing, a kind of white pie. They are sitting, to his printer's sense, too close, leaving awkward space on either side. To poke them into adjustment he says, "I think it's a swell country."

Janice takes it up, Stavros chewing in silence. "Harry, you've never *been* to any other country."

He addresses himself to Stavros. "Never had the desire to. I see these other countries on TV, they're all running like hell to be like us, and burning our Embassies because they can't make it fast enough. What other countries do *you* get to?"

Stavros interrupts his eating grudgingly to utter, "Jamaica."

"Wow," Rabbit says. "A real explorer. Three hours by jet to the lobby of some Hilton."

"They hate us down there."

"You mean they hate *you.* They never see *me*, I never go. Why do they hate us?"

"Same reason as everywhere. Exploitation. We steal their bauxite."

"Let 'em trade it to the Russkis for potatoes then. Potatoes and missile sites."

"We have missile sites in Turkey," Stavros says, his heart no longer in this.

Janice tries to help. "We've dropped two atom bombs, the Russians haven't dropped any."

"They didn't have any then or they would have. Here the Japanese were all set to commit hari-kari and we saved them from it; now look at 'em, happy as clams and twice as sassy, screwing us right and left. We fight their wars for them while you peaceniks sell their tinny cars."

Stavros pats his mouth with a napkin folded squarely and regains his appetite for discussion. "Her point is, we wouldn't be in this Vietnam mess if it was a white country. We wouldn't have gone in. We thought we just had to shout Boo and flash a few jazzy anti-personnel weapons. We thought it was one more Cherokee uprising. The trouble is, the Cherokees outnumber us now."

"Oh those fucking poor Indians," Harry says. "What were we supposed to do, let 'em have the whole continent for a campfire site?" Sorry, Tonto.

"If we had, it'd be in better shape than it is now."

"And we'd be nowhere. They were in the way."

"Fair enough," Stavros says. "Now you're in their way." He adds, "Paleface."

"Let 'em come," Rabbit says, and really is, at this moment, a defiant bastion. The tender blue flame has become cold fire in his eyes. He stares them down. He stares at Janice and she is dark and tense: an Indian. Massacre this squaw.

Then his son says, his voice strained upward through choked-down tears, "*Dad*, we're going to be *late* for the *mo*vie!"

Rabbit looks at his watch and sees they have four minutes to get there. The kid is right.

Stavros tries to help, fatherly like men who aren't fathers, who think kids can be fooled about essentials. "The opening part's the dullest, Nellie, you won't miss any of the space parts. You got to try some *baklava* for dessert."

"I'll miss the cave men," Nelson says, the choking almost complete, the tears almost risen.

"I guess we should go," Rabbit tells the two other adults.

"That's rude to Charlie," Janice says. "Really rude. Anyway I won't be able to stay awake during this in*ter*minable movie without coffee." To Nelson: "*Baklava* is really yummy. It's honey and flakes of thin dough, just the kind of dry thing you love. Try to be considerate, Nelson, your parents so rarely get to eat in a restaurant."

Torn, Rabbit suggests, "Or you could try that other stuff you wanted for the main deal, mellow patties or whatever."

The tears do come; the kid's tense face breaks. "You *promised*," he sobs, unanswerably, and hides his face against the white bare wall.

"Nelson, I am disappointed in you," Janice tells him.

Stavros says to Rabbit, tucking that pencil behind his ear again, "If you want to run now, she could get her coffee and I'll drop her off at the movie house in ten minutes."

"That's a possibility," Janice says slowly, her face opening cautiously, a dull flower.

Rabbit tells Stavros, "O.K., great. Thanks. You're nice to do that. You're nice to put up with us at all, sorry if I said anything too strong. I just can't stand to hear the U.S. knocked, I'm sure it's psychological. Janice, do you have money? Charlie, you tell her how much we owe."

Stavros repeats that masterful small gesture of palm outward, "you owe zilch. On me." There can be no argument. Standing, himself in a hurry to see the cave men (raw meat? a bone turning into a spaceship?), Rabbit experiences, among them here, in this restaurant where the Penn Park couple are paying their bill as if laying a baby to rest, keen family happiness: it prompts him to say to Janice, to cheer Nelson up further, "Remind me tomorrow to call your father about those baseball tickets."

Before Janice can intervene, Stavros says, everybody anxious now to please, "He's in the Poconos."

Janice thought when Charlie calls Harry "paleface" it's the end, from the way Harry looked over at her, his eyes a frightening blue, and then when Charlie let that slip about Daddy being away she knew it was; but somehow it isn't. Maybe the movie numbs them. It's so long and then that psychedelic section where he's landing on the planet before turning into a little old man in a white wig makes her head hurt, but she rides home resolved to have it out, to confess and dare him to make his move back, all he can do is run which might be a relief; she has a glass of vermouth in the kitchen to ready herself, but upstairs Nelson is shutting the door to his room and Harry is in the bathroom and when she comes out of the bathroom with the taste of toothpaste on top of the vermouth Harry is lying under the covers with just the top of his head showing. Janice gets in beside him and listens. His breathing is a sleeping tide. So she lies there awake like the moon.

In their ten though it became twenty minutes over the coffee together she had told Charlie she had thought it reckless of him to come to the restaurant when he had known she was bringing them and he said, in that way he has of going onto his dignity, his lips pushing out as if holding a lozenge and the hunch of his shoulders a bit gangsterish, that he thought that's what she wanted, that's why she told him she was going to talk them into it. At the time she thought silently, he doesn't understand women in love, just going to his restaurant, eating food that was him, had been enough an act of love for her, he didn't have to make it dangerous by showing up himself. It even coarsened it. Because once he was physically there all her caution dissolved, if instead of having coffee with her he had asked her to go to his apartment with him she would have done it and was even mentally running through the story she would have told Harry about suddenly feeling sick. But luckily he didn't ask, he finished the coffee and paid the whole bill and dropped her off under the stumpy marquee as promised. Men are strict that way, want to keep their promises to each other, women are beneath it, property. The way while making love Charlie sells her herself, murmuring about her parts, giving them the names Harry uses only in anger, she resisted at first but relaxed seeing for Charlie they were a language of love, his way of keeping himself up, selling her her own cunt. She doesn't panic as with Harry, knowing he can't hold it much longer, Charlie holds back forever, a thick sweet toy she can do anything with, her teddy bear. The fur on the back of his shoulders at first shocked her touch, something freakish, but no, that's the way many men still are. Cave men. Cave bears. Janice smiles in the dark.

In the dark of the car driving over the bridge along Weiser he asked her if Harry guessed anything. She said she thought nothing. Though something had been bugging him the last couple of days, her staying so late supposedly at the office.

"Maybe we should cool it a little."

"Oh, let him stew. His old line on me used to be I was useless, at first he was delighted I got a job. Now he thinks I neglect Nelson. I say to him, 'Give the boy a little room, he's thirteen and you're leaning on him worse than your own mother.' He won't even let him get a mini-bike because it's too dangerous supposedly."

Charlie said, "He sure was hostile to me."

"Not really. He's like that about Vietnam with everybody. It's what he really thinks."

"How can he think that crap? We-them, America first. It's dead."

She tried to imagine how. One of the nice things about having a lover, it makes you think about everything anew. The rest of your life becomes a kind of movie, flat and even rather funny. She answered at last, "Something is very real to him about it, I don't know what it is." She went on with difficulty, for a blurring, a halting, comes over her tongue, her head, whenever she tries to think, and one of the many beautiful things about Charlie Stavros is he lets her tumble it out anyway. He has given her not only her body but her voice. "Maybe he came back to me, to Nelson and me, for the old-fashioned reasons, and wants to live an old-fashioned life, but nobody does that any more, and he feels it. He put his life into rules he feels melting away now. I mean, I know he thinks he's missing something, he's always reading the paper and watching the news."

Charlie laughed. The blue lights of the bridge flickered on the backs of his hands parallel on the steering wheel. "I get it. You're his overseas commitment."

She laughed too, but it seemed a little hard of him to say, to make a joke of the marriage that was, after all, a part of her too. Sometimes Charlie didn't quite listen. Her father was like that: a hurry in their blood, wind in their ears. Getting ahead, you miss what the slow people see.

Stavros sensed the little wound and tried to heal it, patting her thigh as they arrived at the movie house. "Space odyssey," he said. "My idea of a space odyssey would be to get in the sack with your ass and ball for a week." And right here, with the light beneath the marquee slanting into the car and the agitated last late shreds of the audience buying their tickets, he ran his paw across her breasts and tucked his thumb into her lap. Heated and ruffled by this touch from him, guilty and late, she rushed into the movie house—its plum carpeting, its unnatural coldness, its display-casket of candies—and found Nelson and Harry down front, where they had had to sit because of her, because she had made them late so she could eat her lover's food, the great exploding screen close above them, their hair on fire, their ears translucent red. The backs of their heads, innocently alike, had sprung a rush of love within her, like coming, a push of pity that sent her scrambling across the jagged knees of strangers to the seat her husband and son had saved.

A car moves on the curved road outside. Rugs of light are hurled across the ceiling. The refrigerator below speaks to itself, drops its own ice into its own tray. Her body feels tense as a harp, she wants to be touched. She touches herself: hardly ever did it as a girl, after marrying Harry it seemed certainly wrong, marriage should make it never necessary, just turn to the other person and he would fix it. How sad it was with Harry now, they had become locked rooms to each other, they could hear each other cry but couldn't get in, not just the baby though that was terrible, the most terrible thing ever, but even that had faded, flattened, until it seemed it hadn't been her in that room but an image of her, and she had not been alone, there had been some man in the room with her, he was with her now, not Charlie but containing Charlie, everything you do is done in front of this man and how good to have him made flesh. She imagines it in her, like something you have swallowed. Only big, big. And slow, slow as sugar melts. Except now that she'd been with him so many times she could be quick in coming, sometimes asking him just to pound away and startling herself, coming, herself her toy, how strange to have to learn to play, they used to tell her, everybody, the gym teacher, the Episcopal minister, Mother even one awful embarrassing time, not to make your body a plaything when that's just what it was, she wonders if Nelson, his bedsprings creaking, his little jigger waiting for its hair, poor child, what would he think, what must he think, such a lonely life, sitting there alone at the TV when she comes home, his mini-bike, she's lost it. Though she flutters it faster she's lost it, her heat. How silly. How silly it all is. We're born and they try to feed us and change our diapers and love us and we get breasts and menstruate and go boy-crazy and finally one or two come forward to touch us and we can't wait to get married and have some babies and then stop having them and go man-crazy this time without even knowing it until you're in too deep the flesh grows more serious as we age and then eventually that phase must be over and we ride around in cars in flowered hats for a while to Tucson or seeing the leaves turn in New Hampshire and visit our grandchildren and then get into bed like poor Mrs. Angstrom, Harry is always after her to visit her but she doesn't see why she should she never had a good word to say for her when she was healthy, groping for words while her mouth makes spittle and her eyes trying to pop from her head trying to hear herself say something malicious, and then there's the nursing home or the hospital, poor old souls like when they used to visit her father's older sister, TVs going all up and down the hall and Christmas decorations dropping needles on the linoleum, and then we die and it wouldn't have mattered if we hadn't bothered to be born at all. And all the time there are wars and riots and history happening but it's not as important as the newspapers say unless you get caught in it. Harry seems right to her about that, Vietnam or Korea or the Philippines nobody cares about them yet they must be died for, it just is that way, by boys that haven't shaved yet, the other side has boys Nelson's age. How strange it is of Charlie to care so, to be so angry, as if he's a minority, which of course he is, her father used to talk of gang fights when he was in school, us against them, Springer an English name, Daddy very proud of that, then why, she used to ask herself at school, was she so dark, olive skin, never sunburned, hair that always frizzed up and never lay flat in bangs, never knew enough until recently to let it grow long in front and pin it back, his fucking madonna Charlie calls her blasphemous though there is an ikon in his bedroom, didn't have enough body in school, but she forgives those days now, sees she was being shaped, all those years, toward Charlie. His cunt. His rich cunt, though they were never rich just respectable, Daddy gave her a little stock to put away the time Harry was acting so irresponsible, the dividend checks come in, the envelopes with windows, she doesn't like Harry to see them, they make light of his working. Janice wants to weep, thinking of how hard Harry has worked these years. His mother used to say how hard he used to work practicing basketball, dribbling, shooting; whereas she said so spitefully Nelson has no aptitude. This is silly. This thinking is getting nowhere, there is tomorrow to face, must have it out with Harry, Charlie shrugs when she asks what to do, at lunch if Daddy isn't back from the Poconos they can go over to Charlie's apartment, the light used to embarrass her but she likes it best in the day now, you can see everything, men's bottoms so innocent, even the little hole like a purse drawn tight, the hair downy and dark, all the sitting they do, the world isn't natural for them any more: this is silly. Determined to bring herself off, Janice returns her hand and opens her eyes to look at Harry sleeping, all huddled into himself, stupid of him to keep her sex locked up all these years, his fault, all his fault, it was there all along, it was his job to call it out, she does everything for Charlie because he asks her, it feels holy, she doesn't care, you have to live, they put you here you have to live, you were made for one thing, women now try to deny it burning their bras but you were made for one thing, it feels like a falling, a falling away, a deep eye opening, a coming into the deep you, Harry wouldn't know about that, he never did dare dwell on it, racing ahead, he's too fastidious, hates sex really, she was there all along, there she is, oh: not quite. She knows he knows, she opens her eyes, she sees him lying on the edge of the bed, the edge of a precipice, they are on it together, they are about to fall off, she closes her eyes, she is about to fall off: there. Oh. *Oh.* The bed complains.

Janice sinks back. They say, she read somewhere, some doctors measuring your blood pressure when you do it, things taped to your head how can anybody concentrate, it's always best when you do it to yourself. Her causing the bed to shudder has stirred Harry half-awake; he heavily rolls over and loops his arm around her waist, a pale tall man going fat. She strokes his wrist with the fingers that did it. His fault. He is a ghost, white, soft. Tried to make a box for her to put her in like they put Rebecca in when the poor little baby died. The way she held it sopping wet against her chest already dead, she could feel it, and screamed a great red scream as if to make a hole to let life back in. The movie returns upon her, the great wheel turning against the black velvet in time with the glorious symphony that did lift her for all her confusion coming into the theater. Floating now like a ballerina among the sparse planets of her life, Daddy, Harry, Nelson, Charlie, she thinks of her coming without him as a betrayal of her lover, and furtively lifts her fingertips, with their nice smell of swamp, to her lips and kisses them, thinking, *You.*

Next day, Friday, the papers and television are full of the colored riots in York, snipers wounding innocent firemen, simple men on the street, what is the world coming to? The astronauts are nearing the moon's gravitational influence. A quick thunderstorm makes up in the late afternoon over Brewer, pelts shoppers and homebound workmen into the entranceways of shops, soaks Harry's white shirt before he and his father get to huddle in the Phoenix Bar. "We missed you last night," Earl Angstrom says.

"Pop, I *told* you we couldn't make it, we took the kid out to eat and then to a movie."

"O.K., don't bite my head off. I thought you left it more up in the air than that, but never mind, don't kill a man for trying."

"I said we *might*, was all. Did she act disappointed?"

"She didn't let on. Your mother's nature isn't to let on, you know that. She knows you have your problems."

"What problems?"

"How was the movie, Harry?"

"The kid liked it, I don't know, it didn't make much sense to me, but then I felt kind of sick on something I ate. I fell dead asleep soon as we got home."

"How did Janice like it? Did she seem to have a good time?"

"Hell, I don't know. At her age, are you supposed to have a good time?"

"I hope the other day, I didn't seem to be poking my nose in where it doesn't belong."

"Mom still raving about it?"

"A little bit. Now Mother, I tell her, now Mother, Harry's a big boy, Harry's a responsible citizen."

"Yeah," Rabbit admits, "maybe that's my problem," and shivers. With his shirt wet, it is cruelly cold in here. He signals for another daiquiri. The television, sound off, is showing film clips of cops in York stalking the streets in threes and fours, then cuts to a patrol in Vietnam, boys smudged with fear and fatigue, and Harry feels badly, that he isn't there with them. Then the television moves on to the big publicity-mad Norwegian who gave up trying to cross the Atlantic in a paper boat. Even if the TV sound were turned higher what he's saying would be drowned by the noise in the bar: the excitement of the thunderstorm plus its being Friday night.

"Think you could make it over this evening?" his father asks. "It doesn't have to be for long, just fifteen minutes or so. It would mean the world to her, with Mim as good as dead, hardly ever even writing a postcard."

"I'll talk to her about it," Harry says, meaning Janice, though he thinks of Mim whoring around on the West Coast, Mim that he used to take sledding on Jackson Road, snowflakes on her hood. He pictures her at parties, waiting with a face of wax, or lying beside a swimming pool freshly oiled while under the umbrella beside her some suety gangster with a cigar in the center of his face like a secondary prick pulls it from his mouth and guffaws. "But don't get her hopes up," he adds, meaning his mother. "We're sure to be over Sunday. I got to run."

The storm has passed. Sun pours through the torn sky, drying the pavement rapidly. Maplike stains: a pulped Kleenex retains an island of wet around it. Overweight bag-luggers and skinny Negro idlers emerge smiling from the shelter of a disused shoe store's entrance. The defaced BUS STOP sign, the wrappers spilled from the KEEP BREWER CLEAN can with its top like a flying saucer, the dimpled and rutted asphalt all glory, glistening, in the deluge having passed. The scattered handkerchiefs and horsetails of inky storm-cloud drift east across the ridge of Mt. Judge and the sky resumes the hazed, engendering, blank look of Pennsylvania humidity. And nervousness, that seeks to condense into anger, regathers in Rabbit.

Janice is not home when he arrives. Neither is Nelson. Coming up the walk he sees that, freshened by rain, their lawn looks greasy with crabgrass, spiky with plantain. The kid supposedly gets his dollar-fifty allowance in part for keeping it mowed but he hasn't since June. The little power mower, that had belonged to the Springers until they got one of those you ride, leans in the garage, a can of 3-in-1 beside one wheel. He oils it and sloshes in the gasoline—amber in the can, colorless in the funnel—and starts it up on the fourth pull. Its swath spits gummy hunks of wet grass, back and forth across the two square patches that form their front lawn. There is a larger lawn behind, where the clothes tree stands and where Nelson and he sometimes play catch with a softball worn down to its strings. It needs mowing too, but he wants Janice to find him out front, to give her a little guilty start to get them going.

But by the time she comes home, swinging down Vista spraying untarred grit and tucking the Falcon into the garage in that infuriating way of hers, just not quite far enough to close the door on the bumper, the blades of grass are mixing long shadows with their cut tips and Rabbit stands by their one tree, the spindly maple tethered to the earth, his palm sore from trimming the length of the walk with the hand-clippers.

"Harry," she says, "you're outdoors! How funny of you."

And it is true, Park Villas with its vaunted quarter-acre lots and compulsory barbecue chimneys does not tempt its residents outdoors, even the children in summer: in the snug brick neighborhood of Rabbit's childhood you were always outdoors, hiding in hollowed-out bushes, scuffling in the gravel alleys, secure in the closeness of windows from at least one of which an adult was always watching. Here, there is a prairie sadness, a barren sky raked by slender aerials. A sky poisoned by radio waves. A desolate smell from underground.

"Where the hell have you been?"

"Work, obviously. Daddy always used to say never to cut grass after rain, it's all lying down."

" 'Work, obviously.' What's obvious about it?"

"Harry, you're so strange. Daddy came back from the Poconos today and made me stay after six with Mildred's mess."

"I thought he came back from the Poconos days ago. You lied. Why?"

Janice crosses the cut grass and they stand together, he and she and the tree, the spindly planted maple that cannot grow, as if bewildered by the wide raw light. The kerosene scent of someone else's Friday evening barbecue drifts to them. Their neighbors in Penn Villas are strangers, transients—accountants, salesmen, supervisors, adjusters—people whose lives to them are passing cars and the shouts of unseen children. Janice's color heightens. Her body takes on a defiant suppleness. "I forget, it was a silly lie, you were just so angry over the phone I had to say something. It seemed the easiest thing to say, that Daddy was there; you know how I am. You know how confused I get."

"How much other lying do you do to me?"

"None. That I can remember right now. Maybe little things, how much things cost, the sort of things women lie about. Women like to lie, Harry, it makes things more fun." And, flirtatious, unlike her, she flicks her tongue against her upper lip and holds it there, like the spring of a trap.

She steps toward the young tree and touches it. He asks her, "Where's Nelson?"

"I arranged with Peggy for him to spend the night with Billy."

"With those dopes again. They give him ideas."

"At his age he's going to have ideas anyway."

"I half-promised Pop we'd go over tonight and visit Mom."

"I don't see why we should visit her. She's never liked me, she's done nothing but try to poison our marriage."

"Another question."

"Yes?"

"Are you fucking Stavros?"

"I thought women only *got* fucked."

Janice turns and choppily runs into the house, up the three steps, into the house with apple-green aluminum clapboards. Rabbit puts the mower back in the garage and enters by the side door into the kitchen. She is there, slamming pots around, making their dinner. He asks her, "Shall we go out to eat for a change? I know a nifty little Greek restaurant off Plum Street."

"That was just coincidence he showed up. I admit it was Charlie who recommended it, is there anything wrong with that? And you were certainly rude to him. You were incredible."

"I wasn't rude, we had a political discussion. I like Charlie. He's an O.K. guy, for a left-wing mealy-mouthed wop."

"You are really very strange lately, Harry. I think your mother's sickness is getting to you."

"In the restaurant, you seemed to know your way around the menu. Sure he doesn't take you there for lunch? Or on some of those late-work nights? You been working a lot of nights, and don't seem to get much done."

"You know nothing about what has to be done."

"I know your old man and Mildred Kroust used to do it themselves without all this overtime."

"Having the Toyota franchise is a whole new dimension. It's endless bills of lading, import taxes, customs forms." More fending words occur to Janice; it is like when she was little, making snow dams in the gutter. "Anyway, Charlie has lots of girls, he can have girls any time, single girls younger than me. They all go to bed now without even being asked, everybody's on the Pill, they just assume it." One sentence too many.

"How do you know?"

"He tells me."

"So you *are* chummy."

"Not very. Just now and then, when he's hung or needing a little mothering or something."

"Right, maybe he's scared of these hot young tits, maybe he likes older women, *mamma mia* and all that. These slick Mediterranean types need a lot of mothering."

It's fascinating to her, to see him circling in; she fights the rising in her of a wifely wish to collaborate, to help him find the truth that sits so large in her own mind she can hardly choose the words that go around it.

"Anyway," he goes on, "those girls aren't the boss's daughter."

Yes, that is what he'd think, it was what she thought those first times, those first pats as she was standing tangled in a net of numbers she didn't understand, those first sandwich lunches they would arrange when Daddy was out on the lot, those first five-o'clock whisky sours in the Atlas Bar down the street, those first kisses in the car, always a different car, one they had borrowed from the lot, with a smell of new car like a skin of glaze their touches were burning through. That was what she thought until he convinced her it was her, funny old clumsy her, Janice Angstrom née Springer, turned Springer again, in bud; it was her flesh being licked like ice cream, her time being stolen in moments compressed as diamonds, her nerves caught up in a hairfine watchspring cycle of pleasure that oscillated between them in tightening swift circles until it seemed a kind of frenzied sleep, a hypnosis so intense that later in her own bed she could not sleep at all, as if she had napped that afternoon. His apartment, they discovered, was only twelve minutes distant, if you drove the back way, by the old farmer's market that was now just a set of empty tin-roofed sheds.

"What good would my being the boss's daughter do him?"

"It'd make him feel he was climbing. All these Greeks or Polacks or whatever are on the make."

"I'd never realized, Harry, how full of racial prejudice you are."

"Yes or no about you and Stavros."

"No." But lying she felt, as when a child watching the snow dams melt, that the truth must push through, it was too big, too constant: though she was terrified and would scream, it was something she must have, her confession like a baby. She felt so proud.

"You dumb bitch," he says. He hits her not in the face but on the shoulder, like a man trying to knock open a stuck door. She hits him back, clumsily, on the side of the neck, as high as she can reach. Harry feels a flash of pleasure: sunlight in a tunnel. He hits her three, four, five times, unable to stop, boring his way to that sunlight, not as hard as he can hit, but hard enough for her to whimper; she doubles over so that his last punches are thrown hammerwise down into her neck and back, an angle he doesn't see her from that much—the chalk-white parting, the candle-white nape, the bra strap showing through the fabric of the back of the blouse. Her sobbing arises muffled and, astonished by a beauty expressed by her abasement, by a face that shines through her reduction to this craven faceless posture, he pauses. Janice senses that he will not hit her any more. She abandons her huddle, flops over to her side, and lets herself cry out loud—high-pitched, a startled noise pinched between sieges of windy gasping. Her face is red, wrinkled, newborn; in curiosity he drops to his knees to examine her. Her black eyes flash at this and she spits up at his face, but misjudges; the saliva falls back into her own face. For him there is only the faintest kiss of spray. Flecked with her own spit Janice cries, "I do, I *do* sleep with Charlie!"

"Ah, shit," Rabbit says softly, "of course you do," and bows his head into her chest, to protect himself from her scratching, while he half-pummels her sides, half-tries to embrace her and lift her.

"I love him. Damn you, Harry. We make love all the time."

"Good," he moans, mourning the receding of that light, that ecstasy of his hitting her, of knocking her open. Now she will become another cripple he must take care of. "Good for you."

"It's been going on for *months*," she insists, writhing and trying to get free to spit again, furious at his response. He pins her arms, which would claw, at her sides and squeezes her hard. She stares into his face. Her face is wild, still, frozen. She is seeking what will hurt him most. "I do things for him," she says, "I never do for you."

"Sure you do," he murmurs, wanting to have a hand free to stroke her forehead, to re-enclose her. He sees the gloss of her forehead and the gloss of the kitchen linoleum. Her hair wriggles outward into the spilled wriggles of the marbled linoleum pattern, worn where she stands at the sink. A faint sweetish smell beneath them, of the sluggish sink tie-in. She abandons herself to crying and softness and relief, and he has no trouble lifting her and carrying her in to the living-room sofa. He has zombie-strength: his shins shiver, his palm sore from the clipper handles is a crescent of bronze.

She sinks lost into the sofa's breadth.

He prompts her, "He makes better love than me," to keep her confession flowing, as a physician moistens a boil.

She bites her tongue, trying to think, surveying her ruins with an eye toward salvage. Impure desires—to save her skin, to be kind, to be exact—pollute her primary fear and anger. "He's different," she says. "I'm more exciting to him than to you. I'm sure it's just mostly our not being married."

"Where do you do it?"

Worlds whirl past and cloud her eyes—car seats, rugs, tree undersides seen through windshields, the beigy-gray carpeting in the narrow space between the three green steel desks and the safe and the Toyota cut-out, motel rooms with their cardboard panelling and scratchy bedspreads, his dour bachelor's apartment stuffed with heavy furniture and tinted relatives in silver frames. "Different places."

"Do you want to marry him?"

"No. *No.*" Why does she say this? The possibility opens an abyss. She would not have known this. A gate she had always assumed gave onto a garden gave onto emptiness. She makes to move closer to Harry, to drag him down closer to her; she is lying on the sofa, one shoe off, her bruises just beginning to smart, while he kneels on the carpet, having carried her here. He remains stiff when she pulls at him, he is dead, she has killed him.

He asks, "Was I so lousy to you?"

"Oh sweetie, no. You were good to me. You came back. You work in that dirty place. I don't know what got into me, Harry, I honestly don't."

"Whatever it was," he tells her, "it must be still there." He looks like Nelson, saying this, a mulling discontented hurt look, puzzling to pry something open, to get something out. She sees she will have to make love to him. A conflicted tide moves within her, desire for this pale and hairless stranger, abhorrence of this desire, fascination with the levels of betrayal possible.

He shies, afraid of failing her; he falls back from the sofa and sits on the floor and offers to talk, to strike a balance. "Do you remember Ruth?"

"The whore you lived with when you ran away."

"She wasn't a whore exactly."

"Whatever she was, what about her?"

"A couple of years ago, I saw her again."

"Did you sleep with her?"

"Oh God no. She had become very straight. That was the thing. We met on Weiser Street, she was shopping. She had put on so much weight I didn't recognize her, I think she recognized me first, something about the way this woman looked at me; and then it hit me. Ruth. She still had this great head of hair. By then she had gone by, I followed her for a while and then she ducked into Kroll's. I gave it an even chance, I waited there at the side entrance figuring if she came out of that one I'd say hello and if she went out one of the others O.K. I gave it five minutes. I really wasn't that interested." But in saying this, his heart beats faster as it had beat then. "Just as I was going away she came out lugging two shopping bags and looked at me and the first thing she said was, 'Let me alone.' "

"She loved you," Janice explains.

"She did and she didn't," he says, and loses her sympathy with this complacence. "I offered to buy her a drink but all she'd let me do is walk her up toward the parking lot where the old Acme used to be. She lived out toward Galilee, she told me. Her husband was a farmer and ran a string of school buses, I got the impression he was some guy older than she was, who'd had a family before. She told me they had three children, a girl and two boys. She showed me their pictures in a wallet. I asked how often she got into town and she said, 'As far as you're concerned, never.' "

"Poor Harry," Janice says. "She sounds awful."

"Well, she was, but still. She'd gotten heavy, as I said, she was sort of lost inside this other person who pretty much blended in with those other fat bag-luggers you see downtown, but at the same time, still, it was *her*."

"All right. You still love her," Janice says.

"No, I didn't, I don't. You haven't heard the worse thing she did then."

"I can't believe you never tried to get in touch with her after you came back to me. At least to see what she did about her . . . pregnancy."

"I felt I *shouldn't*." But he sees now, in his wife's dark and judging eyes, that the rules were more complicated, that there were some rules by which he should have. There were rules beneath the surface rules that also mattered. She should have explained this when she took him back.

She asks, "What was the worse thing?"

"I don't know if I should tell you."

"Tell me. Let's tell each other everything, then we'll take off all our clothes." She sounds tired. The shock of having given it all away must be sinking in. He talks to distract, as we joke with a loser at poker.

"You already said it. About the baby. I thought of that and asked her how old the girl was, her oldest child. She wouldn't tell me. I asked to see the wallet pictures again, to see if there was, you know, a resemblance. She wouldn't show them to me. She laughed at me. She was really quite nasty. She said something very strange."

"What?"

"I forget exactly. She looked me over and said I'd gotten fat. This from *her*. Then she said, 'Run along, Rabbit. You've had your day in the lettuce patch.' Or something like that. Nobody ever calls me Rabbit, was what sort of got me. This was two years ago. I think in the fall. I haven't seen her since."

"Tell me the truth now. These ten years, haven't you had any other women?"

He runs his mind backward, encounters a few dark places, a room in a Polish-American Club where Verity was having its annual blast, a skinny flat-chested girl with a cold, she had kept her bra and sweater on; and then a weird episode at the Jersey shore, Janice and Nelson off at the amusement park, him back from the beach in his trunks, a knock at the door of the cabin, a chunky colored girl, two skinny boys escorting her, offering herself for five or seven dollars, depending what he wanted done. He had had trouble understanding her accent, had made her repeat—with downcast eyes, as the boys with her sniggered—"screwin'," "suck-off." Frightened, he had quickly shut the flimsy door on them, locked it against a threat of rape, and jerked off facing the wall; the wall smelled of damp and salt. He tells Janice, "You know, ever since that happened to Becky, I haven't been that much for sex. It comes on, wanting it, and then something turns it off."

"Let me up."

Janice stands in front of the television set, the screen green ashes, a dead fire. Efficiently she undresses herself. Her dark-tipped breasts droop tubular and sway as she disengages her pantyhose. Her tan stops below her throat. Other summers they used to go the West Brewer pool some Sundays but the kid became too big to go with his parents so none go now. They haven't gone to the Shore since the Springers discovered the Poconos. Buggy brown lakes imprisoned among dark green trees: Rabbit hates it there and never goes, never goes anywhere, takes his vacation around the house. He used to daydream about going South, Florida or Alabama, to see the cotton fields and the alligators, but that was a boy's dream and died with the baby. He once saw Texas and that has to be enough. Tongue pinched between her lips, naked Janice unbuttons his shirt, fumbling. Numbly he takes over, completes the job. The pants, the shoes last. Socks. Air knows him, air of day still lingering, summer air tingling along the skin that never knows the light. He and Janice have not made love in the light for years. She asks him in the middle of it, "Don't you love *see*ing? I used to be so embarrassed."

In twilight they eat, still naked, salami sandwiches she makes, and drink whisky. Their house stays dark, though the others around them, that mirror it, turn on their lights. These neighboring lights, and the cars that pass along Vista Crescent, throw sliding soft witnesses into their room: the open shelves lunge like parallel swords, the driftwood lamp throws a rhinoceros-shadow, the school portrait of Nelson, in its cardboard frame on the mantel, from beneath the embalming tints of its color wash, smiles. To help them see when darkness comes, Janice turns on the television set without sound, and by the bluish flicker of module models pantomiming flight, of riot troops standing before smashed supermarkets, of a rowboat landing in Florida having crossed the Atlantic, of situation comedies and western melodramas, of great gray momentary faces unstable as quicksilver, they make love again, her body a stretch of powdery sand, her mouth a loose black hole, her eyes holes with sparks in them, his own body a barren landscape lit by bombardment, silently exploding images no gentler than Janice's playful ghostly touches, that pass through him and do him no harm. She inverts herself and pours out upon him the months of her new knowledge; her appetite frightens him, knowing he cannot fill it, any more than Earth's appetite for death can be satisfied. Her guilt became love; her love becomes rage. The first time was too quick but the second was sweet, with work and sweat in it, and the third time strainingly sweet, a work of the spirit almost purely, and the fourth time, because there was no fourth time, sad; straddling his thighs, her cunt revealed by the flickering touch of the television to be lopsidedly agape, she bows her head, her hair tickling his belly, and drops cold tears, starpricks, upon the slack flesh that has failed her.

"Jesus," he says, "I forgot. We were supposed to go over to Mom's tonight!"

He dreams of driving north with Charlie Stavros, in a little scarlet Toyota. The gear shift is very thin, a mere pencil, and he is afraid of breaking it as he shifts. Also, he is wearing golf shoes, which makes operating the pedals awkward. Stavros sits in the driver's seat and, with that stolid way of muttering, his square ringed hands masterfully gesturing, discusses his problem: Lyndon Johnson has asked him to be his Vice-President. They need a Greek. He would like to accept, but doesn't want to leave Brewer. So they are negotiating to have at least the summer White House moved to Brewer. They have lots of vacant lots they could build it on, Charlie explains. Rabbit is thinking, maybe this is his chance to get out of the printing plant and into a white-collar job. Services and software are where the future lies. He tells Stavros hopefully, "I can lick stamps." He shows him his tongue. They are on a superhighway heading north, into the deserted coal regions and, beyond that, the wilds of northern Pennsylvania. Yet here, in this region of woods and lakes, a strange white city materializes beside the highway; hill after hill of tall row houses white as bedsheets, crowding to the horizon, an enormous city, strange it seems to have no name. They part in a suburban region beside a drugstore and Stavros hands him a map; with difficulty Rabbit locates on it where they are. The metropolis, marked with a bull's-eye, is named, simply, The Rise.

The Rise, The Rise . . . the dream is so unpleasant he awakes, with a headache and an erection. His prick feels glassily thin and aches from all that work with Janice. The bed is empty beside him. He remembers they went to bed after two, when the television screen became a buzzing test-signal. He hears the sound of the vacuum cleaner downstairs. She is up.

He dresses in his Saturday clothes, patched chinos and apricot polo shirt, and goes downstairs. Janice is in the living room sweeping, pushing the silver tube back and forth. She glances over at him, looking old. Sex ages us. Priests are boyish, spinsters stay black-haired until after fifty. We others, the demon rots us out. She says, "There's orange juice on the table, and an egg in the pan. Let me finish this room."

From the breakfast table he surveys his house. The kitchen on one side, the living room on the other are visible. The furniture that frames his life looks Martian in the morning light: an armchair covered in synthetic fabric enlivened by a silver thread, a sofa of airfoam slabs, a low table hacked to imitate an antique cobbler's bench, a piece of driftwood that is a lamp, nothing shaped directly for its purpose, gadgets designed to repel repair, nothing straight from a human hand, furniture Rabbit has lived among but has never known, made of substances he cannot name, that has aged as in a department store window, worn out without once conforming to his body. The orange juice tastes acid; it is not even frozen orange juice but some chemical mix tinted orange.

He breaks his egg into the pan, sets the flame low, thinks guiltily of his mother. Janice turns off the vacuum, comes over, pours herself some coffee to sit opposite him with as he eats. Purple dents beneath her eyes. He asks her, "Are you going to tell him?"

"I suppose I must."

"Why? Wouldn't you like to keep him?"

"What are you saying, Harry?"

"Keep him, if he makes you happy. I don't seem to, so go ahead, until you've had your fill at least."

"Suppose I never have my fill?"

"Then I guess you should marry him."

"Charlie can never marry anybody."

"Who says?"

"He did once. I asked him why not and he wouldn't say. Maybe it has to do with his heart murmur. That was the only time we ever discussed it."

"What *do* you and he discuss? Except which way to do it next."

She might have risen to this taunt but doesn't. She is very flat, very honest and dry this morning, and this pleases him. A graver woman than he has known reveals herself. We contain chords someone else must strike. "We don't say much. We talk about funny little things, things we see from his windows, things we did as children. He loves to listen to me, when he was a boy they lived in the worst part of Brewer, a town like Mt. Judge looked marvellous to him. He calls me a rich bitch."

"The boss's daughter."

"Don't, Harry. You said that last night. You can't understand. It would sound silly, the things we talk about. He has a gift, Charlie does, of making everything exciting—the way food tastes, the way the sky looks, the customers that come in. Once you get past that defensiveness, that tough guy act, he's quite quick and, *lov*ing, in what he sees. He felt awful last night, after you left, that he had made you say more than you meant to. He hates to argue. He loves life. He really does, Harry. He loves life."

"We all do."

"Not really. I think our generation, the way we were raised, makes it hard for us to love life. Charlie does. It's like —daylight. You want to know something?"

He agrees, "Sure," knowing it will hurt.

"Daylight love—it's the best."

"O.*K*. Relax. I said, keep the son of a bitch."

"I don't believe you."

"Only one thing. Try to keep the kid from knowing. My mother already knows, the people who visit her tell her. It's all over town. Talk about daylight."

"*Let* it be," Janice says. She rises. "Goddam your mother, Harry. The only thing she's ever done for us is try to poison our marriage. Now she's drowning in the poison of her life. She's dying and I'm glad."

"Jesus, don't say that."

"Why not? She would, if it were me. Who did she want you to marry? Tell me, who would have been wonderful enough for you? Who?"

"My sister," he suggests.

"Let me tell you something else. At first with Charlie, whenever I'd feel guilty, so I couldn't relax, I'd just think of your mother, how she's not only treated me but treated *Nel*son, her own *grand*son, and I'd say to myself, O.K., fella, sock it to me, and I'd just *come*."

"O.K., O.K. Spare me the fine print."

"I'm sick, so sick, of sparing you things. There've been a lot of days"—and this makes her too sad to confess, so that a constraint slips like a net over her face, which goes ugly under the pull—"when I was sorry you came back that time. You were a beautiful brainless guy and I've had to watch that guy die day by day."

"It wasn't so bad last night, was it?"

"No. It was so good I'm angry. I'm all confused."

"You've been confused from birth, kid." He adds, "Any dying I've been doing around here, you've been helping it right along." At the same time, he wants to fuck her again, to see if she can turn inside out again. For some minutes last night she turned all tongue and his mouth was glued to hers as if in an embryo the first cell division had not yet occurred.

The phone rings. Janice plucks it from its carriage on the kitchen wall and says, "Hi, Daddy. How was the Poconos? No, I know you got back days ago, I'm just being funny. Of course he's here. Here he is." She holds it out to Rabbit. "For you."

Old Man Springer's voice is reedy, coaxing, deferential. "Harry, how's everything?"

"Not bad."

"You still game for the ball game? Janice mentioned you asked about the tickets to the Blasts today. They're in my hand, three right behind first base. The manager's been a client of mine for twenty years."

"Yeah, great. The kid spent the night at the Fosnachts, but I'll get him back. You want to meet at the stadium?"

"Let me pick you up, Harry. I'll be happy to pick you up in my car. That way we'll leave Janice yours." A note in his voice that didn't used to be there, gentle, faintly wheedling: nursing along an invalid. He knows too. The world knows. It'll be in the *Vat* next week. LINOTYPER'S WIFE LAYS LOCAL SALESMAN. *Greek Takes Strong Anti-Viet Stand.*

"Tell me, Harry," Springer wheedles on, "how is your mother's health? Rebecca and I are naturally very concerned. *Very* concerned."

"My father says it's about the same. It's a slow process, you know. They have drugs now that make it even slower. I've been meaning this week to get up to Mt. Judge to see her but we haven't managed."

"When you do, Harry, give her our love. Give her our love."

Saying everything twice: he probably swung the Toyota franchise because the Japs could understand him second time around.

"O.K., sure enough. Want Janice back?"

"No, Harry, you can keep her." A joke. "I'll be by twelve-twenty, twelve-thirty."

He hangs up. Janice is gone from the kitchen. He finds her in the living room crying. He goes and kneels beside the sofa and puts his arms around her but these actions feel like stage directions followed woodenly. A button is off on her blouse and the sallow curve of breast into the bra mixes with her hot breath in his ear. She says, "You can't understand, how good he was. Not sexy or funny or anything, just *good*."

"Sure I can. I've known some good people. They make you feel good."

"They make you feel everything you do and are *is* good. He never told me how dumb I am, every hour on the hour like you do, even though he's much smarter than you could ever imagine. He would have gone to college, if he hadn't been a Greek."

"Oh. Don't they let Greeks in now? The nigger quota too big?"

"You say such sick things, Harry."

"It's because nobody tells me how good I am," he says, and stands. The back of her neck is vulnerable beneath him. One good karate chop would do it.

The driveway crackles outside; it's much too early for Springer. He goes to the window. A blue Mustang. The passenger door swings open and Nelson gets out. On the other side appears Peggy Gring, wearing sunglasses and a miniskirt that flashes her big thighs like a card dealer's thumbs. Unhappiness—being deserted—has made her brisk, professional. She gives Rabbit hardly a hello and her sunglasses hide the eyes that he knows from school days are wall. The two women go into the kitchen. From the sound of Janice snuffling he guesses a confession is in progress. He goes outside to finish the yard work he began last night. All around him, in the backyards of Vista Crescent, to the horizons of Penn Villas with their barbecue chimneys and aluminum wash trees, other men are out in their yards; the sound of his mower is echoed from house to house, his motions of bending and pushing are carried outwards as if in fragments of mirror suspended from the hot blank sky. These his neighbors, they come with their furniture in vans and leave with the vans. They get together to sign futile petitions for better sewers and quicker fire protection but otherwise do not connect. Nelson comes out and asks him, "What's the matter with Mommy?"

He shuts off the mower. "What's she doing?"

"She's sitting at the table with Mrs. Fosnacht crying her eyes out."

"Still? I don't know, kid; she's upset. One thing you must learn about women, their chemistries are different from ours, they cry easier."

"Mommy almost never cries."

"So maybe it's good for her. Get lots of sleep last night?"

"Some. We watched an old movie about torpedo boats."

"Looking forward to the Blasts game?"

"Sure."

"But not much, huh?"

"I don't like sports as much as you do, Dad. It's all so competitive."

"That's life. Dog eat dog."

"You think? Why can't things just be nice? There's enough stuff for everybody to share."

"You think there is? Why don't you start then by sharing this lawnmowing? You push it for a while."

"You owe me my allowance." As Rabbit hands him a dollar bill and two quarters, the boy says, "I'm saving for a mini-bike."

"Good luck."

"Also, Dad—?"

"Yeah?"

"I think I should get a dollar twenty-five an hour for work. That's still under the federal minimum wage."

"See?" Rabbit tells him. "Dog eat dog."

As he washes up inside, pulling grass bits out of his cuffs and putting a Band-aid on the ball of his thumb (tender place; in high school they used to say you could tell how sexy a girl was by how fat she was here), Janice comes into the bathroom, shuts the door, and says, "I've decided to tell him. While you're at the ball game I'll tell him." Her face looks taut but pretty dried-out; patches of moisture glisten beside her nose. The tile walls amplify her sniffs. Peggy Gring's Mustang roars outside in leaving.

"Tell who what?"

"Tell Charlie. That it's all over. That you know."

"I said, keep him. Don't do anything for today at least. Calm down. Have a drink. See a movie. See that space movie again, you slept through the best parts."

"That's cowardly. No. He and I have always been honest with each other, I must tell him the truth."

"I think you're just looking for an excuse to see him while I'm tucked away at the ball park."

"You would think that."

"Suppose he asks you to sleep with him?"

"He wouldn't."

"Suppose he does, as a graduation present?"

She stares at him boldly: dark gaze tempered in the furnace of betrayal. It comes to him: growth is betrayal. There is no other route. There is no arriving somewhere without leaving somewhere. "I would," she says.

"Where are you going to find him?"

"At the lot. He stays on until six summer Saturdays."

"What reason are you going to give him? For breaking it off."

"Why, the fact that you know."

"Suppose he asks you why you told?"

"It's obvious why I told. I told because I'm your wife."

Tears belly out between her lids and the tension of her face breaks like Nelson's when a hidden anxiety, a D or a petty theft or a headache, is confessed. Harry denies his impulse to put his arm around her; he does not want to feel wooden again. She teeters, keeping her balance while sobbing, sitting on the edge of the bathtub, while the plastic showei curtain rustles at her shoulder.

"Aren't you going to stop me?" she brings out at last.

"Stop you from what?"

"From *see*ing him!"

Given this rich present of her grief, he can afford to be cruel. Coolly he says, "No, see him if you want to. Just as long as *I* don't have to see the bastard." And, avoiding the sight of her face, he sees himself in the cabinet mirror, a big pink pale man going shapeless under the chin, his little lips screwed awry in what wants to be a smile.

The gravel in the driveway crackles again. From the bathroom window he sees the boxy dun top of Springer's spandy new Toyota wagon. To Nelson he calls, "Grandpa's here. Let's go-o." To Janice he murmurs, "Sit tight, kid. Don't commit yourself to anything." To his father-in-law, sliding in beside him, across a spaghetti of nylon safety straps, Rabbit sings, "Buy me some pea-nuts and crack-er-jack . . ."

The stadium is on the southern side of Brewer, through a big cloverleaf, past the brick hulks of two old hosiery mills, along a three-lane highway where in these last years several roadside restaurants have begun proclaiming themselves as Pennsylvania Dutch, with giant plaster Amishmen and neon hex signs. GENUINE "*Dutch*" COOKING. *Pa. Dutch Smörgåsbord.* Trying to sell what in the old days couldn't be helped. Making a tourist attraction out of fat-fried food and a diet of dough that would give a pig pimples. They pass the country fairgrounds, where every September the same battered gyp stands return, and the farmers bring their stinking livestock, and Serafina the Egyptian Temptress will take off all her clothes for those yokels who put up a dollar extra. The first naked woman he saw was Serafina or her mother. She kept on her high heels and a black mask and bent way backwards; she spread her legs and kept a kind of token shimmy rhythm as she moved in a semi-circle so every straining head (luckily he was tall even then) could see a trace of her cleft, an exciting queasy-making wrinkle shabbily masked by a patch of hair that looked to him pasted-on. Rubbed threadbare? He didn't know. He couldn't imagine.

Springer is shaking his head over the York riots. "Sniper fire four nights in a row, Harry. What is the world coming to? We're so defenseless, is what strikes me, we're so defenseless against the violent few. All our institutions have been based on trust."

Nelson pipes up. "It's the only way they can get justice, Grandpa. Our laws defend property instead of people."

"They're defeating their own purposes, Nellie. Many a white man of good will like myself is being turned against the blacks. Slowly but surely he's being turned against them. It wasn't Vietnam beat Humphrey, it was law and order in the streets. That's the issue that the common man votes upon. Am I right or wrong, Harry? I'm such an old fogey I don't trust my own opinions any more."

One old geezer, Harry is remembering, at the side of the little stage, reached from behind and put his hand up on her pussy, shouting, "Aha!" She stopped her dance and stared out of the black mask. The tent went quiet; the geezer, surprisingly, found enough blood in himself to blush. *Aha.* That cry of triumph, as if he had snared a precious small animal, Harry never forgot. *Aha.* He slouches down and in answer to Springer says, "Things go bad. Food goes bad, people go bad, maybe a whole country goes bad. The blacks now have more than ever, but it feels like less, maybe. We were all brought up to want things and maybe the world isn't big enough to take all that wanting. I don't know. I don't know anything."

Old man Springer laughs; he snorts and snarls so his little gray mouse of a mustache merges with his nostril hairs. "Did you hear about Teddy Kennedy this morning?"

"What about him? No."

"Shut your ears, Nellie. I forgot you were in the car or I wouldn't have mentioned it."

"What, Grandpa? What did he do? Did somebody shoot him?"

"Apparently, Harry"—Springer talks out of the side of his mouth, as if to shield Nelson, yet so distinctly the child can easily hear—"he dumped some girl from Pennsylvania into one of those Massachusetts rivers. Murder as plain as my face." Springer's face, from the side, is a carving of pink bone, with rosy splotches where the cheekbones put most pressure, and a bump of red on the point where the nose turns. A hatchet face creased like an Indian's from a constant salesman's smile. One thing at least about setting type, there's a limit on how much ass you must kiss.

"Did they get him? Is he in jail, Grandpa?"

"Ah, Nelson, they'll never put a Kennedy in jail. Palms will be greased. Evidence will be suppressed. I call it a crying shame."

Rabbit asks, "What do you mean, dumped some girl?"

"They found her in his car upside down in the water beside some bridge, I forget the name, one of those islands they have up there. It happened last night and he didn't go to the police until they were about to nab him. And they call this a democracy, Harry, is the irony of it."

"What would you call it?"

"I'd call it a police state run by the Kennedys, is what I would call it. That family has been out to buy the country since those Brahmins up in Boston snubbed old Joe. And then he put himself in league with Hitler when he was FDR's man in London. Now they've got the young widow to marry a rich Greek in case they run out of American money. Not that she's the goodie-gumdrop the papers say, those two were a match. What's your opinion, Harry? Am I talking out of line? I'm such a back number now I don't trust to hear myself talk." *Aha.*

"I'd say," Harry says, "you're right with it. You should join the kids and buy yourself a bomb to throw."

Springer looks over from driving (the yellow parabolas of a McDonald's flash by; the tinsel spinners of a Mobil station break the noon sun into trinkets) to see if he has oversold. How timid, really, people who live by people must be. Earl Angstrom was right about that at least: better make your deals with things. Springer says, hedgily smiling, showing porcelain teeth beneath the gray blur, "I'll say this for the Kennedys, however, they don't get my dander up like FDR. There was a man, Harry, so mad he died of maggots in the brain. One thing to be said for the Kennedys, they didn't try to turn the economy upside down for the benefit of the poor, they were willing to ride along with the System as it's been handed down."

Nelson says, "Billy Fosnacht says when we grow up we're going to overthrow the System."

Springer can't hear, lost in his vision of executive madness and corruption. "He tried to turn it upside down for the benefit of the black and white trash, and when that didn't work for eight years he finagled the little Japanese into attacking Pearl Harbor so he had a war to bail him out of the Depression. That's why you have these wars, believe it or not, to bail the Democrats out of their crazy economics. LBJ, now, as soon as he got his four-year guarantee, went into Vietnam where nobody wanted us, just to get the coloreds up into the economy. LBJ, he was an FDR man. Truman, the same thing in Korea. History bears me out, every time, call me an old fogey if you want to: what's your angle on it, Nelson?"

"Last night on television," the boy says, "we watched an old movie about fighting the Japs in the Pacific, this little boat sank, and the captain or whatever he was swam miles with a broken back dragging this other guy."

"That was Kennedy," Springer says. "Pure propaganda. They made that movie because Old Joe owned a lot of those studios. He sank his money into the movies when all the honest businessmen who'd put this country on the map were losing their shirts. He was in close league, the story I heard, with those Jewish Communists out there."

Rabbit tells Nelson, "That's where your Aunt Mim is now, out there with those Communists."

"She's beautiful," Nelson tells his grandfather. "Have you ever seen my Aunt Mim?"

"Not as much as I'd have liked to, Nellie. She is a striking figure, however, I know you're right there. You're right to be proud of her. Harry, your silence disturbs me. Your silence disturbs me. Maybe I'm way off base. Way off. Tell me what *you* think of the state of the nation. With these riots everywhere, and this poor Polish girl, she comes from up near Williamsport, abused and drowned when the future President takes his pleasure. Pregnant, wouldn't surprise me. Nellie, you shouldn't be hearing any of this."

Harry stretches, cramped in the car, short of sleep. They

are near the stadium, and a little colored boy is waving them into a lot. "I think," he says, "about America, it's still the only place."

But something has gone wrong. The ball game is boring. The spaced dance of the men in white fails to enchant, the code beneath the staccato spurts of distant motion refuses to yield its meaning. Though basketball was his sport, Rabbit remembers the grandeur of all that grass, the excited perilous feeling when a high fly was hoisted your way, the homing-in on the expanding dot, the leathery smack of the catch, the formalized nonchalance of the heads-down trot in toward the bench, the ritual flips and shrugs and the nervous courtesies of the batter's box. There was a beauty here bigger than the hurtling beauty of basketball, a beauty refined from country pastures, a game of solitariness, of waiting, waiting for the pitcher to complete his gaze toward first base and throw his lightning, a game whose very taste, of spit and dust and grass and sweat and leather and sun, was America. Sitting behind first base between his son and his father-in-law, the sun resting on his thighs like a board, the rolled-up program like a baton in his hand, Rabbit waits for this beauty to rise to him, through the cheers and the rhythm of innings, the traditional national magic, tasting of his youth; but something is wrong. The crowd is sparse, thinning out from a cluster behind the infield to fistfuls of boys sprawling on the green seats sloped up from the outfield. Sparse, loud, hard: only the drunks, the bookies, the cripples, the senile, and the delinquents come out to the ball park on a Saturday afternoon. Their catcalls are coarse and unkind. "Ram it down his throat, Speedy!" "Kill that black bastard!" Rabbit yearns to protect the game from the crowd; the poetry of space and inaction is too fine, too slowly spun for them. And for the players themselves, they seem expert listlessly, each intent on a private dream of making it, making it into the big leagues and the big money, the own-your-own-bowling alley money; they seem specialists like any other, not men playing a game because all men are boys time is trying to outsmart. A gallant pretense has been abandoned, a delicate balance is being crushed. Only the explosions of orange felt on their uniforms, under the script *Blasts*, evoke the old world of heraldic local loyalties. Brewer versus Hazleton and who cares? Not Springer: as he watches, his lips absentmindedly move as if sorting out old accounts. Not Nelson: the screen of reality is too big for the child, he misses television's running commentary, the audacious commercials. His politely unspoken disappointment nags at Rabbit, prevents the game from rising and filling the scared hollow Janice's confession has left in him. The eight-team leagues of his boyhood have vanished with the forty-eight-star flag. The shortstops never chew tobacco any more. The game drags on, with a tedious flurry of strategy, of pinch-hitters and intentional walks, prolonging the end. Hazleton wins, 7–3. Old Man Springer sighs, getting up as if from a nap in an unnatural position. He wipes a fleck of beer from his mustache. " 'Fraid our boys didn't come through for you, Nellie," he says.

"That's O.K., Grampa. It was neat."

To Harry he says, needing to find something to sell, "That young Trexler is a comer though."

Rabbit is cross and groggy from two beers in the sun. He doesn't invite Springer into his house, just thanks him a lot for everything. The house is silent, like outer space. On the kitchen table is a sealed envelope, addressed "Harry." The letter inside, in Janice's half-formed hand, with its unsteady slant and miserly cramping, says

> Harry dear—
>
> I must go off a few days to think. Please don't try to find or follow me *please*. It is very important that we all respect each other as people and trust each other now. I was shocked by your idea that I keep a lover since I don't think this would be honest and it made me wonder if I mean anything to you at all. Tell Nelson I've gone to

the Poconos with Grandmom. Don't forget to give him lunch money for the playground.

Love,
Jan

"Jan"—her name from the years she used to work at Kroll's selling salted nuts in the smock with *Jan* stitched above the pocket in script. In those days some afternoons they would go to her friend's apartment up on Eighth Street. The horizontal rose rays as the sun set behind the great gray gasholder. The wonder of it as she let him slip off all her clothes. Underwear more substantial then: stocking snaps to undo, the marks of elastic printed on her skin. Jan. That name suspended in her these fifteen years; the notes she left for him around the house were simply signed "J."

"Where's Mom?" Nelson asks.

"She's gone to the Poconos," Rabbit says, pulling the note back toward his chest, in case the boy tries to read it. "She's gone with Mom-mom, her legs were getting worse in this heat. I know it seems crazy, but that's how things are sometimes. You and I can eat over at Burger Bliss tonight."

The boy's face—freckled, framed by hair that covers his ears, his plump lips buttoned shut and his eyes sunk in fear of making a mistake—goes rapt, seems to listen, as when he was three and flight and death were rustling above him. Perhaps his experience then shapes what he says now. Firmly he tells his father, "She'll be back."

Sunday dawns muggy. The seven o'clock news says there was scattered shooting again last night in York and the western part of the state. Edgartown police chief Dominick J. Arena is expected today formally to charge Senator Kennedy with leaving the scene of an accident. Apollo Eleven is in lunar orbit and the Eagle is being readied for its historic descent. Rabbit slept badly and turns the box off and walks around the lawn barefoot to shock the headache out of his skull. The houses of Penn Villas are still, with the odd Catholic car roaring off to mass. Nelson comes down around nine, and after making him breakfast Harry goes back to bed with a cup of coffee and the Sunday Brewer *Triumph*. Snoopy on the front page of the funny papers is lying dreaming on his doghouse and soon Rabbit falls asleep. The kid looked scared. The boy's face shouts, and a soundless balloon comes out. When he awakes, the electric clock says five of eleven. The second hand sweeps around and around; a wonder the gears don't wear themselves to dust. Rabbit dresses—fresh white shirt out of respect for Sunday—and goes downstairs the second time, his feet still bare, the carpeting fuzzy to his soles, a bachelor feeling. The house feels enormous, all his. He picks up the phone book and searches out

Stavros Chas 1204EisenhwerAv

He doesn't dial, merely gazes at the name and the number as if to see his wife, smaller than a pencil dot, crawling between the letters. He dials a number he knows by heart.

His father answers. "Yes?" A wary voice, ready to hang up on a madman or a salesman.

"Pop, hi; hey, I hope you didn't wait up or anything the other night, we weren't able to make it and I couldn't even get to a phone."

A little pause, not much, just enough to let him know they were indeed disappointed. "No, we figured something came up and went to bed about the usual time. Your mother isn't one to waste herself complaining, as you know."

"Right. Well, look. About today."

His voice goes hoarse to whisper, "Harry, you must come over today. You'll break her heart if you don't."

"I will, I will, but—"

The old man has cupped his mouth against the receiver, urging hoarsely, "This may be her last, you know. Birthday."

"We're coming, Pop. I mean, some of us are. Janice has had to go off."

"Go off how?"

"It's kind of complicated, something about her mother's legs and the Poconos, she decided last night she had to, I don't know. It's nothing to worry about. Everybody's all right, she's just not here. The kid's here though." To illustrate, he calls, "Nelson!"

There is no answer.

"He must be out on his bike, Pop. He's been right around all morning. When would you like us?"

"Whenever it suits you, Harry. Late afternoon or so. Come as early as you can. We're having roast beef. Your mother wanted to bake a cake but the doctor thought it might be too much for her. I bought a nice one over at the Half-A-Loaf. Butterscotch icing, didn't that used to be your favorite?"

"It's her birthday, not mine. What should I get her for a present?"

"Just your simple presence, Harry, is all the present she desires."

"Yeah, O.K. I'll think of something. Explain to her Janice won't be coming."

"As my father, God rest, used to say, It is to be regretted, but it can't be helped."

Once Pop finds that ceremonious vein, he tends to ride it. Rabbit hangs up. The kid's bike—a rusty Schwinn, been meaning to get him a new one, both fenders rub—is not in the garage. Nor is the Falcon. Only the oil cans, the gas can, the lawnmower, the jumbled garden hose (Janice must have used it last), a lawn rake with missing teeth, and the Falcon's snow tires are there. For an hour or so Rabbit swims around the house in a daze, not knowing who to call, not having a car, not wanting to go inside with the television set. He pulls weeds in the border beds where that first excited summer of their own house Janice planted bulbs and set in plants and shrubs. Since then they have done nothing, just watched the azaleas die and accepted the daffodils and iris as they came in and let the phlox and weeds fight as these subsequent summers wore on, nature lost in nature. He weeds until he begins to see himself as a weed and his hand with its ugly big moons on the fingernails as God's hand choosing and killing, then he goes inside the house and looks into the refrigerator and eats a carrot raw. He looks into the phone directory and looks up Fosnacht, there are a lot of them and it takes him a while to figure out M is the one, M for Margaret and just the initial to put off obscene calls, though if he were on that kick he'd soon figure out that initials were unattached women. "Peggy, hi; this is Harry Angstrom." He says his name with faint proud emphasis; they were in school together, and she remembers him when he was somebody. "I was just wondering, is Nelson over there playing with Billy? He went off on his bike a while ago and I'm wondering where to."

Peggy says, "He's not here, Harry. Sorry." Her voice is frosted with all she knows, Janice burbling into her ear yesterday. Then more warmly she asks, "How's everything going?" He reads the equation, Ollie left me; Janice left you: hello.

He says hastily, "Great. Hey, if Nelson comes by tell him I want him. We got to go to his grandmother's."

Her voice cools in saying goodbye, joins the vast glaring ice-face of all those who know. Nelson seems the one person left in the county who doesn't know: this makes him even more precious. Yet, when the boy returns, red-faced and damp-haired from hard pedalling, he tells his father, "I was at the Fosnachts."

Rabbit blinks and says, "O.K. After this, let's keep in better touch. I'm your mother and your father for the time being." They eat lunch, Lebanon baloney on stale rye. They walk up Emberly to Weiser and catch a 12 bus east into Brewer. It being Sunday, they have to wait twenty minutes under the cloudless colorless sky. At the hospital stop a crowd of visitors gets on, having done their duty, dazed, carrying away dead flowers and read books. Boats, white arrowheads tipping wrinkled wakes, are buzzing in the black river below the bridge. A colored kid leaves his foot in the aisle when Rabbit tries to get off; he steps over it. "Big feet," the boy remarks to his companion.

"Fat lips," Nelson, following, says to the colored boy.

They try to find a store open. His mother was always difficult to buy presents for. Other children had given their mothers cheerful junk: dime-store jewelry, bottles of toilet water, boxes of candy, scarves. For Mom that had been too much, or not enough. Mim always gave her something she had made: a woven pot holder, a hand-illustrated calendar. Rabbit was poor at making things so he gave her himself, his trophies, his headlines. Mom had seemed satisfied: lives more than things concerned her. But now what? What can a dying person desire? Grotesque prosthetic devices—arms, legs, battery-operated hearts—run through Rabbit's head as he and Nelson walk the dazzling, Sunday-stilled downtown of Brewer. Up near Ninth and Weiser they find a drugstore open. Thermos bottles, sunglasses, shaving lotion, Kodak film, plastic baby pants: nothing for his mother. He wants something big, something bright, something to get through to her. Realgirl Liquid Make-Up, Super Plenamins, Non-Smear polish remover, Nudit for the Legs. A rack of shampoo-in hair color, a different smiling cunt on every envelope: Snow Queen Blond, Danish Wheat, Killarney Russet, Parisian Spice, Spanish Black Wine. Nelson plucks him by the sleeve of his white shirt and leads to where a Sunbeam Clipmaster and a Roto-Shine Magnetic Electric Shoe Polisher nestle side by side, glossily packaged. "She doesn't wear shoes any more, just slippers," he says, "and she never cut her hair that I can remember. It used to hang down to her waist." But his attention is drawn on to a humidifier for $12.95. From the picture on the box, it looks like a fat flying saucer. No matter how immobile she gets, it would be there. Around Brewer, though, the summers are as humid as they can be anyway, but maybe in the winter, the radiators dry out the house, the wallpaper peels, the skin cracks; it might help. It would be there night and day, when he wasn't. He moves on to a Kantleek Water Bottle and a 2½-inch reading glass and dismisses both as morbid. His insides are beginning to feel sickly. The pain of the world is a crater all these syrups and pills a thousandfold would fail to fill. He comes to the Quikease Electric Massager with Scalp Comb. It has the silhouettes of naked women on the box, gracefully touching their shoulders, Lesbians, caressing the backs of their necks, where else the box leaves to the imagination, with what looks like a hair brush on a live wire. $11.95. Bedsores. It might help. It might make her laugh, tickle, buzz: it is life. Life is a massage. And it costs a dollar less than the humidifier. Time is ticking. Nelson tugs at his sleeve and wants a maple walnut ice cream soda. While the kid is eating it, Rabbit buys a birthday card to go with the massager. It shows a rooster crowing, a crimson sun rising, and green letters shouting on the outside *It's Great to Get Up in the A.M. . . .* and on the inside *. . . to Wish You a Happy Birthday, MA!* Ma. Am. God, what a lot of ingenious crap there is in the world. He buys it anyway, because the rooster is bright orange and jubilant enough to get through to her. Her eyes aren't dim necessarily but because her tongue gropes they could be. Play it safe.

The world outside is bright and barren. The two of them, father and son, feel sharply alone, Rabbit gripping his bulky package. Where is everybody? Is there life on Earth? Three blocks down the deserted street of soft asphalt the clock that is the face of a giant flower, the center of the Sunflower Beer sign, says they are approaching four. They wait at the same corner, opposite the Phoenix Bar, where Harry's father customarily waits, and take the 16A bus to Mt. Judge. They are the only passengers; the driver tells them mysteriously, "They're about down." Up they go through the City Park, past the World War II tank and the bandshell and the tennis court, around the shoulder of the mountain. On one side of them, gas stations and a green cliff; on the other, a precipice and, distantly, a viaduct. As the kid stares out of the window, toward the next mountain over, Rabbit asks him, "Where did you go this morning? Tell me the truth."

The boy answers, finally. "Eisenhower Avenue."

"To see if Mommy's car was there?"

"I guess."

"Was it?"

"Yop."

"D'you go in?"

"Nope. Just looked up at the windows awhile."

"Did you know the number to look at?"

"One two oh four."

"Yeah. That sounds right."

They get off at Central, beside the granite Baptist church, and walk up Jackson toward his parents' house. The streets haven't changed in his lifetime. They were built too close together for vacant lots and too solidly to tear down, of a reddish brick with purplish bruises in it, and a texture that as a child Rabbit thought of as chapped, like his lips in winter. Maples and horsechestnuts darken the stumpy front lawns, hedged by little wired barricades of barberry and box. The houses are semi-detached and heavy, their roofs are slate and their porches have brick walls and above each door of oak and bevelled glass winks a fanlight of sombre churchly colors. As a child Rabbit imagined that fanlight to be a child of the windows above the Lutheran altar and therefore of God, a mauve and golden seeing sentinel posted above where he and Pop and Mom and Mim came and went a dozen times a day. Now, entering with his son, still too much a son himself to knock, he feels his parents' place as stifling. Though the clock on the living room sideboard says only 4:20, darkness has come: dark carpets, thick drawn drapes, dead wallpaper, potted plants crowding the glass on the side that has the windows. Mom used to complain about how they had the inside half of a corner house; but when the Bolgers, their old neighbors, died, and their half went onto the market, they made no move to inquire after the price, and a young couple from Scranton bought it, the young wife pregnant and barefoot and the young husband something in one of the new electronics plants out along Route 422; and the Angstroms still live in the dark half. They prefer it. Sunlight fades. Space kills. They sent him, Harry, out in the world to shine, but hugged their own shadows here. Their neighbor house on the other side, across two cement sidewalks with a strip of grass between them, where lived the old Methodist Mom used to fight with about who would mow the grass strip, has had a FOR SALE sign up for a year. People now want more air and land than those huddled hillside neighborhoods can give them. The house smells to Rabbit of preservative: of odors filming other odors, of layers of time, of wax and aerosol and death; of safety.

A shape, a shade, comes forward from the kitchen. He expects it to be his father, but it is his mother, shuffling, in a bathrobe, yet erect and moving. She leans forward unsmiling to accept his kiss. Her wrinkled cheek is warm; her hand steadying itself on his wrist is knobbed and cold.

"Happy birthday, Mom." He hugs the massager against his chest; it is too early to offer it. She stares at the package as if he has put a shield between them.

"I'm sixty-five," she says, groping for phrases, so that her sentences end in the middle. "When I was twenty. I told my boy friend I wanted to be shot. When I was thirty." It is not so much the strange tremulous attempt of her lips to close upon a thought as the accompanying stare, an unblinking ungathering gaze into space that lifts her eyes out of any flow and frightens Rabbit with a sense of ultimate blindness, of a blackboard from which they will all be wiped clean.

"You told Pop this?"

"Not your dad. Another. I didn't meet your dad till later. This other one, I'm glad. He's not here to see me now."

"You look pretty good to me," Rabbit tells her. "I didn't think you'd be up."

"Nelson. How do I look. To you?" Thus she acknowledges the boy. She has always been testing him, putting him on the defensive. She has never forgiven him for not being another Harry, for having so much Janice in him. *Those little Springer hands.* Now her own hands, held forgotten in front of her bathrobe belt, constantly work in a palsied waggle.

"Nice," Nelson says. He is wary. He has learned that brevity and promptness of response are his best defense.

To take attention off the kid, Rabbit asks her, "*Should* you be up?"

She laughs, an astonishing silent thing; her head tips back, her big nose glints from the facets of its tip and underside, her hand stops waggling. "I know, the way Earl talks. You'd think from the way he wants me in bed. I'm laid out already. The doctor. Wants me up. I had to bake a cake. Earl wanted. One of those tasteless paps from the Half-A-Loaf. Where's Janice?"

"Yeah, about that. She's awfully sorry, she couldn't come. She had to go off with her mother to the Poconos, it took us all by surprise."

"Things can be. Surprising."

From upstairs Earl Angstrom's thin voice calls anxiously, with a wheedler's borrowed triumph, "They're down! Eagle has landed! We're on the moon, boys and girls! Uncle Sam is on the moon!"

"That's just. The place for him," Mom says, and with a rough gesture sweeps her distorted hand back toward her ear, to smooth down a piece of hair that has wandered loose from the bun she still twists up. Funny, the hair as it grays grows more stubborn. They say even inside the grave, it grows. Open coffins of women and find the whole thing stuffed like inside of a mattress. Pubic hair too? Funny it never needs to be cut. Serafina's looked threadbare, mangy. When he touches his mother's arm to help her up the stairs to look at the moon, the flesh above her elbow is disconcerting—loose upon the bone, as on a well-cooked chicken.

The set is in Mom's bedroom at the front of the house. It has the smell their cellar used to have when they had those two cats. He tries to remember their names. Pansy. And Willy. Willy, the tom, got in so many fights his belly began to slosh and he had to be taken to the Animal Rescue. There is no picture of the moon on the tube, just crackling voices while cardboard cut-outs simulate what is happening, and electronic letters spell out who in the crackle of men is speaking.

". . . literally thousands of little one and two foot craters around the area," a man is saying in the voice that used to try to sell them Shredded Ralston between episodes of Tom Mix. "We see some angular blocks out several hundred feet in front of us that are probably two feet in size and have angular edges. There is a hill in view just about on the ground track ahead of us. Difficult to estimate, but might be a half a mile or a mile."

A voice identified as Houston says, "Roger, Tranquillity. We copy. Over." The voice has that Texas authority. As if words were invented by them, they speak so lovingly. When Rabbit was stationed at Fort Hood in '53, Texas looked like the moon to him, brown land running from his knees level as a knife, purple rumpled horizon, sky bigger and barer than he could believe, first time away from his damp green hills, last time too. Everybody's voice was so nice and gritty and loving, even the girls in the whorehouse. *Honeh. You didn't pay to be no two-timer.*

A voice called Columbia says, "Sounds like a lot better than it did yesterday. At that very low sun angle, it looked rough as a cob then." As a what? The electronic letters specify: MIKE COLLINS SPEAKING FROM COMMAND MODULE ORBITING MOON.

Tranquillity says, "It really was rough, Mike, over the targeted landing area. It was extremely rough, cratered and large numbers of rocks that were probably some many larger than five or ten feet in size." Mom's room has lace curtains aged yellowish and pinned back with tin daisies that to an infant's eyes seemed magical, rose-and-thorns wallpaper curling loose from the wall above where the radiator safety valve steams, a kind of plush armchair that soaks up dust. When he was a child this chair was downstairs and he would sock it to release torrents of swirling motes into the shaft of afternoon sun; these whirling motes seemed to him worlds, each an earth, with him on one of them, unthinkably small, unbearably. Some light used to get into the house in late afternoon, between the maples. Now the same maples have thronged that light solid, made the room cellar-dim. The bedside table supports an erect little company of pill bottles and a Bible. The walls hold tinted photographs of himself and Mim in high school, taken he remembers by a pushy pudgy little blue-jawed crook who called himself a Studio and weaseled his way into the building every spring and made them line up in the auditorium and wet-comb their hair so their parents couldn't resist two weeks later letting them take in to the homeroom the money for an 8 by 10 tinted print and a sheet of wallet-sized grislies of themselves; now this crook by the somersault of time has become a donor of selves otherwise forever lost: Rabbit's skinny head pink in its translucent blond whiffle, his ears out from his head an inch, his eyes unreally blue as marbles, even his lower lids youthfully fleshy; and Miriam's face plump between the shoulder-length shampoo-shining sheaves rolled under in Rita Hayworth style, the scarlet tint of her lipstick pinned like a badge on the starched white of her face. Both children smile out into space, through the crook's smudged lens, from that sweat-scented giggling gym toward their mother bedridden some day.

Columbia jokes, "When in doubt, land long."

Tranquillity says, "Well, we did."

And Houston intervenes, "Tranquillity, Houston. We have a P twenty-two update for you if you're ready to copy. Over."

Columbia jokes again: "At your service, sir."

Houston, unamused, a city of computers working without sleep, answers, "Right, Mike. P one one zero four thirty two eighteen; P two one zero four thirty-seven twenty-eight and that is four miles south. This is based on a targeted landing site. Over."

Columbia repeats the numbers.

Tranquillity says, "Our mission timer is now reading nine zero four thirty-four forty-seven and static."

"Roger, copy. Your mission timer is now static at—say again the time."

"Nine zero four thirty-four forty-seven."

"Roger, copy, Tranquillity. That gravity align looked good. We see you recycling."

"Well, no. I was trying to get time sixteen sixty-five out and somehow it proceeded on the six-twenty-two before I could do a BRP thirty-two enter. I want to log a time here and then I'd like to know whether you want me to proceed on torquing angles or to go back and re-enter again before torquing. Over."

"Rog, Buzz. Stand by."

Nelson and his grandfather listen raptly to these procedures; Mary Angstrom turns impatiently—or is it that her difficulty of motion makes all gestures appear impatient?—and makes her shuffling way out into the landing and down the stairs again. Rabbit, heart trembling in its hollow, follows. She needs no help going down the stairs. In the garishly bright kitchen she asks, "Where did you say. Janice was?"

"In the Poconos with her mother."

"Why should I believe that?"

"Why shouldn't you?"

She stoops over, waveringly, to open the oven and look in, her tangled wire hair making a net of light. She grunts, stands, and states, "Janice. Stays out of my way. These days."

In his frightened, hypnotized condition, Rabbit can only, it seems, ask questions. "Why would she do that?"

His mother stares and stares, only a movement of her tongue between her parted lips betraying that she is trying to speak. "I know too much," she at last brings out, "about her."

Rabbit says, "You know only what a bunch of pathetic old gossips tell you about her. And stop bugging Pop about it, he comes into work and bugs me." Since she does not fight back, he is provoked to go on. "With Mim out turning ten tricks a day in Las Vegas I'd think you'd have more to worry about than poor Janice's private life."

"She was always," his mother brings out, "spoiled."

"Yes and Nelson too I suppose is spoiled. How would you describe me? Just yesterday I was sitting over at the Blasts game thinking how lousy I used to be at baseball. Let's face it. As a human being I'm about C minus. As a husband I'm about zilch. When Verity folds I'll fold with it and have to go on welfare. Some life. Thanks, Mom."

"Hush," she says, expressionless, "you'll make. The cake fall," and like a rusty jackknife she forces herself to bend over and peer into the gas oven.

"Sorry Mom, but Jesus I'm tired lately."

"You'll feel better when. You're my age."

The party is a success. They sit at the kitchen table with the four places worn through the enamel in all those years.

It is like it used to be, except that Mom is in a bathrobe and Mim has become Nelson. Pop carves the roast beef and then cuts up Mom's piece in small bits for her; her right hand can hold a fork but cannot use a knife. His teeth slipping down, he proposes a toast in New York State wine to "my Mary, an angel through thick and thin"; Rabbit wonders what the thin was. Maybe this is it. When she unwraps her few presents, she laughs at the massager. "Is this. To keep me hopping?" she asks, and has her husband plug it in, and rests it, vibrating, on the top of Nelson's head. He needs this touch of cheering up. Harry feels Janice's absence gnawing at him. When the cake is cut the kid eats only half a piece, so Rabbit has to eat double so not to hurt his mother's feelings. Dusk thickens: over in West Brewer the sanitorium windows are burning orange and on this side of the mountain the shadows sneak like burglars into the narrow concrete space between this house and the unsold one. Through the papered walls, from the house of the young barefoot couple, seeps the dull bass percussion of a rock group, making the matched tins (cookies, sugar, flour, coffee) on Mom's shelf tingle in their emptiness. In the living room the glass face of the mahogany sideboard shivers. Nelson's eyes begin to sink, and the buttoned-up cupid-curves of his mouth smile in apology as he slumps forward into the cold enamel of the table. His elders talk about old times in the neighborhood, people of the Thirties and Forties, once so alive you saw them every day and never thought to take even a photograph. The old Methodist refusing to mow his half of the grass strip. Before him the Zims with that pretty daughter the mother would shriek at every breakfast and supper. The man down the street who worked nights at the pretzel plant and who shot himself one dawn with nobody to hear it but the horses of the milk wagon. They had milk wagons then. The streets were soft dust. Nelson fights sleep. Rabbit asks him, "Want to head home?"

"Negative, Pop." He drowsily grins at his own wit.

Rabbit extends the joke. "The time is twenty-one hours. We better rendezvous with our spacecraft."

But the spacecraft is empty: a long empty box in the blackness of Penn Villas, slowly spinning in the void, its border beds half-weeded. The kid is frightened to go home. So is Rabbit. They sit on Mom's bed and watch television in the dark. They are told the men in the big metal spider sitting on the moon cannot sleep, so the moon-walk has been moved up several hours. Men in studios, brittle and tired from killing time, demonstrate with actual-size mockups what is supposed to happen; on some channels men in space suits are walking around, laying down tinfoil trays as if for a cookout. At last it happens. The real event. Or is it? A television camera on the leg of the module comes on: an abstraction appears on the screen. The announcer explains that the blackness in the top of the screen is the lunar night, the blackness in the lower left corner is the shadow of the spacecraft with its ladder, the whiteness is the surface of the moon. Nelson is asleep, his head on his father's thigh; funny how kids' skulls grow damp when they sleep. Like bulbs underground. Mom's legs are under the blankets; she is propped up on pillows behind him. Pop is asleep in his chair, his breathing a distant sad sea, touching shore and retreating, touching shore and retreating, an old pump that keeps going; lamplight sneaks through a crack in the windowshade and touches the top of his head, his sparse hair mussed into lank feathers. On the bright box something is happening. A snaky shape sneaks down from the upper left corner; it is a man's leg. It grows another leg, eclipses the bright patch that is the surface of the moon. A man in clumsy silhouette has interposed himself among these abstract shadows and glare. He says something about "steps" that a crackle keeps Rabbit from understanding. Electronic letters travelling sideways spell out MAN IS ON THE MOON. The voice, crackling, tells Houston that the surface is fine and powdery, he can pick it up with his toe, it adheres to his boot like powdered charcoal, that he sinks in only a fraction of an inch, that it's easier to move around than in the simulations on the earth. From behind him, Rabbit's mother's hand with difficulty reaches out, touches the back of his skull, stays there, awkwardly tries to massage his scalp, to ease away thoughts of the trouble she knows he is in. "I don't know, Mom," he abruptly admits. "I know it's happened, but I don't feel anything yet."

II. JILL

"It's different but it's very pretty out here."
—NEIL ARMSTRONG, *July 20, 1969*

DAYS, pale slices between nights, they blend, not exactly alike, transparencies so lightly tinted that only stacked all together do they darken to a fatal shade. One Saturday in August Buchanan approaches Rabbit during the coffee break. They are part of the half-crew working the half-day; hence perhaps this intimacy. The Negro wipes from his lips the moisture of the morning whisky enjoyed outside in the sunshine of the loading platform, and asks, "How're they treatin' you, Harry?"

"They?" Harry has known the other man by sight and name for years but still is not quite easy, talking to a black; there always seems to be some joke involved, that he doesn't quite get.

"The world, man."

"Not bad."

Buchanan stands there blinking, studying, jiggling up and down on his feet engagingly. Hard to tell how old they are. He might be thirty-five, he might be sixty. On his upper lip he wears the smallest possible black mustache, smaller than a type brush. His color is ashy, without any shine to it, whereas the other shop Negro, Farnsworth, looks shoe-polished and twinkles among the printing machinery, under the steady shadowless light. "But not good, huh?"

"I'm not sleeping so good," Rabbit does confess. He has an itch, these days, to confess, to spill, he is so much alone.

"Your old lady still shackin' up across town?"

Everybody knows. Niggers, coolies, derelicts, morons. Numbers writers, bus conductors, beauty shop operators, the entire brick city of Brewer. VERITY EMPLOYEE NAMED CUCKOLD OF WEEK. *Angstrom Accepts Official Horns from Mayor.* "I'm living alone," Harry admits, adding, "with the kid."

"How about that," Buchanan says, lightly rocking. "How about that?"

Rabbit says weakly, "Until things straighten out."

"Gettin' any tail?"

Harry must look startled, for Buchanan hastens to explain, "Man has to have tail. Where's your dad these days?" The question flows from the assertion immediately, though it doesn't seem to follow.

Rabbit says, puzzled, offended, but because Buchanan is a Negro not knowing how to evade him, "He's taking two weeks off so he can drive my mother back and forth to the hospital for some tests."

"Yeass." Buchanan mulls, the two pushed-out cushions of his mouth appearing to commune with each other through a hum; then a new thought darts out through them, making his mustache jig. "Your dad is a real pal to you, that's a wonderful thing. That is a truly wonderful thing. I never had a dad like that, I knew who the man was, he was around town, but he was never my dad in the sense your dad is your dad. He was never my pal like that."

Harry hangs uncertainly, not knowing if he should commiserate or laugh. "Well," he decides to confess, "he's sort of a pal, and sort of a pain in the neck."

Buchanan likes the remark, even though he goes through peppery motions of rejecting it. "Oh, never say that now. You just be grateful you have a dad that cares. You don't know, man, how lucky you have it. Just 'cause your wife's gettin' her ass looked after elsewhere don't mean the whole world is come to some bad end. You should be havin' your tail, is all. You're a big fella."

Distaste and excitement contend in Harry; he feels tall and pale beside Buchanan, and feminine, a tingling target of fun and tenderness and avarice mixed. Talking to Negroes makes him feel itchy, up behind the eyeballs, maybe because theirs look so semi-liquid and yellow in the white and sore. Their whole beings seem lubricated on pain. "I'll manage," he says reluctantly, thinking of Peggy Fosnacht.

The end-of-break bell rings. Buchanan snaps his shoulders into a hunch and out of it as if rendering a verdict. "How about it, Harry, steppin' out with some of the boys tonight," he says. "Come on into Jimbo's lounge around nine, ten, see what develops. Maybe nothin'. Maybe sumpthin'. You're just turnin' old, the way you're goin' now. Old and fat and finicky, and that's no way for a nice big man to go." He sees that Rabbit's instincts are to refuse; he holds up a quick palm the color of silver polish and says, "Think about it. I like you, man. If you don't show, you don't show. No sweat."

All Saturday the invitation hums in his ears. Something in what Buchanan said. He was lying down to die, had been lying down for years. His body had been telling him to. His eyes blur print in the afternoons, no urge to run walking even that stretch of tempting curved sidewalk home, has to fight sleep before supper and then can't get under at night, can't even get it up to jerk off to relax himself. Awake with the first light every morning regardless, another day scraping his eyes. Without going much of anywhere in his life he has somehow seen everything too often. Trees, weather, the molding trim drying its cracks wider around the front door, he notices every day going out, house made of green wood. No belief in an afterlife, no hope for it, too much more of the same thing, already it seems he's lived twice. When he came back to Janice that began the second time for him; poor kid is having her first time now. Bless that dope. At least she had the drive to get out. Women, fire in their crotch, won't burn out, begin by fighting off pricks, end by going wild hunting for one that still works.

Once last week he called the lot to find out if she and Stavros were reporting for work or just screwing around the clock, Mildred Kroust answered, she put him on to Janice, who whispered, "Harry, Daddy doesn't know about us, don't ever call me here, I'll call you back." And she had called him late that afternoon, at the house, Nelson in the other room watching *Gilligan's Island*, and said cool as you please, he hardly knew her voice, "Harry, I'm sorry for whatever pain this is causing you, truly sorry, but it's very important that at this point in our lives we don't let guilt feelings motivate us. I'm trying to look honestly into myself, to see who I am, and where I should be going. I want us both, Harry, to come to a decision we can live with. It's the year nineteen sixty-nine and there's no reason for two mature people to smother each other to death simply out of inertia. I'm searching for a valid identity and I suggest you do the same." After some more of this, she hung up. Her vocabulary had expanded, maybe she was watching a lot of psychiatric talk shows. The sinners shall be justified. Screw her. Dear Lord, screw her. He is thinking this on the bus.

He thinks, *Screw her*, and at home has a beer and takes a bath and puts on his good summer suit, a light gray sharkskin, and gets Nelson's pajamas out of the drier and his toothbrush out of the bathroom. The kid and Billy have arranged for him to spend the night. Harry calls up Peggy to check it out. "Oh absolutely," she says, "I'm not going anywhere, why don't you stay and have dinner?"

"I can't I don't think."

"Why not? Something else to do?"

"Sort of." He and the kid go over around six, on an empty bus. Already at this hour Weiser has that weekend up-tempo, cars hurrying faster home to get out again, a very fat man with orange hair standing under an awning savoring a cigar as if angels will shortly descend, an expectant shimmer on the shut storefronts, girls clicking along with heads big as rose-bushes, curlers wrapped in a kerchief. Saturday night. Peggy meets him at the door with an offer of a drink. She and Billy live in an apartment in one of the new eight-story buildings in West Brewer overlooking the river, where there used to be a harness racetrack. From her living room she has a panorama of Brewer, the concrete eagle on the skyscraper Court House flaring his wings above the back of the Owl Pretzels sign. Beyond the flowerpot-red city Mt. Judge hangs smoky-green, one side gashed by a gravel pit like a roast beginning to be carved. The river coal black.

"Maybe just one. I gotta go somewhere."

"You said that. What kind of drink?" She is wearing a clingy palish-purple sort of Paisley mini that shows a lot of heavy leg. One thing Janice always had, was nifty legs. Peggy has a pasty helpless look of white meat behind the knees.

"You have daiquiri mix?"

"I don't know, Ollie used to keep things like that, but when we moved I think it all stayed with him." She and Ollie Fosnacht had lived in an asbestos-shingled semi-detached some blocks away, not far from the county mental hospital. Ollie lives in the city now, near his music store, and she and the kid have this apartment, with Ollie in their view if they can find him. She is rummaging in a low cabinet below some empty bookcases. "I can't see any, it comes in envelopes. How about gin and something?"

"You have bitter lemon?"

More rummaging. "No, just some tonic."

"Good enough. Want me to make it?"

"If you like." She stands up, heavy-legged, lightly sweating, relieved. Knowing he was coming, Peggy had decided against sunglasses, a sign of trust to leave them off. Her walleyes are naked to him, her face has this helpless look, turned full toward him while both eyes seem fascinated by something in the corners of the ceiling. He knows only one eye is bad but he never can bring himself to figure out which. And all around her eyes this net of white wrinkles the sunglasses usually conceal.

He asks her, "What for you?"

"Oh, anything. The same thing. I drink everything."

While he is cracking an ice tray in the tiny kitchenette, the two boys have snuck out of Billy's bedroom. Rabbit wonders if they have been looking at dirty photographs. The kind of pictures kids used to have to pay an old cripple on Plum Street a dollar apiece for you can buy a whole magazine full of now for seventy-five cents, right downtown. The Supreme Court, old men letting the roof cave in. Billy is a head taller than Nelson, sunburned where Nelson takes a tan after his mother, both of them with hair down over their ears, the Fosnacht boy's blonder and curlier. "Mom, we want to go downstairs and run the mini-bike on the parking lot."

"Come back up in an hour," Peggy tells them, "I'll give you supper."

"Nelson had a peanut butter sandwich before we left," Rabbit explains.

"Typical male cooking," Peggy says. "Where're you going this evening anyway, all dressed up in a suit?"

"Nowhere much. I told a guy I might meet him." He

doesn't say it is a Negro. He should be asking her out, is his sudden frightened feeling. She is dressed to go out; but not so dolled-up it can't appear she plans to stay home tonight. He hands her her g.-and-t. The best defense is to be offensive. "You don't have any mint or limes or anything."

Her plucked eyebrows lift. "No, there are lemons in the fridge, is all. I could run down to the grocery for you." Not entirely ironical: using his complaint to weave coziness.

Rabbit laughs to retract. "Forget it, I'm just used to bars, where they have everything. At home all I ever do is drink beer."

She laughs in answer. She is tense as a schoolteacher facing her first class. To relax them both he sits down in a loose leather armchair that says *pfsshhu.* "Hey, this is nice," he announces, meaning the vista, but he spoke too early, for from this low chair the view is flung out of sight and becomes all sky. A thin bright wash, stripes like fat in bacon.

"You should hear Ollie complain about the rent." Peggy sits down not in another chair but on the flat grille where the radiator breathes beneath the window, opposite and above him, so he sees a lot of her legs, shiny skin stuffed to the point of shapelessness. Still, she is showing him what she has, right up to the triangle of underpants, which is one more benefit of being alive in 1969. Miniskirts and those magazines: well, hell, we've always known women had crotches, why not make it legal? A guy at the shop brought in a magazine that, honestly, was all cunts, in blurred bad four-color but cunts, upside-down, backwards, the girls attached to them rolling their tongues in their mouths and fanning their hands on their bellies and otherwise trying to hide how silly they felt. Homely things, really, cunts. Without the Supreme Court that might never have been made clear.

"Hey, how is old Ollie?"

Peggy shrugs. "He calls. Usually to cancel his Sunday with Billy. You know he never was the family man you are."

"How does he spend his time?"

"Oh," Peggy says, and awkwardly turns her body so Rabbit sees pricked out in windowlight the tonic bubbles in her drink, which is surprisingly near drunk, "he rattles around Brewer with a bunch of creeps. Musicians, mostly. They go to Philadelphia a lot, and New York. Last winter he went skiing at Aspen and told me all about it, including the girls. He came back so brown, I cried for days. I could never get him outdoors, when we had the place over on Franklin Street. How do *you* spend *your* time?"

"I work. I mope around the house with the kid. We look at the boob tube and play catch in the backyard."

"Do you mope for *her*, Harry?" With a clumsy shrug of her hip the woman moves off her radiator perch, her blue eyes staring wildly above his head, so he thinks she is launching herself at him and flinches. The net of wrinkles around her eyes seems a net flung at his head. But she floats past him and, clattering, refills her drink. "Want another?"

"No thanks, I'm still working on this one. I gotta go in a minute."

"So soon," she croons unseen, as if remembering the beginning of a song in her tiny kitchenette. From far below their windows arises the razzing, coughing sound of the boys on the mini-bike. The noise swoops and swirls, a rude buzzard. Beyond it across the river hangs the murmur of Brewer traffic, constant like the sea; an occasional car toots, a wink of phosphorescence. From the kitchenette, as if she had been baking the thought in the oven, Peggy calls, "She's not worth it." Then her body is at his back, her voice upon his head. "I didn't know," she says, "you loved her so much. I don't think Janice knew it either."

"Well, you get used to somebody. Anyway, it's an insult. With a spic like that. You should hear him run down the U.S. government."

"Harry, you know what I think. I'm sure you know what I think."

He doesn't. He has no idea. She seems to think he's been reading her underpants.

"I think she's treated you horribly. The last time we had lunch together, I told her so. I said, 'Janice, your attempts to justify yourself do not impress me. You've left a man who came back to you when you needed him, and you've left your son at a point in his development when it's immensely important to have a stable home setting.' I said that right to her face."

"Actually the kid goes over to the lot pretty much and sees her there. She and Stavros take him out to eat. In a way it's like he gained an uncle."

"You're so for*giv*ing, Harry! Ollie would have *strang*led me; he's still immensely jealous. He's always asking me who my boy friends are."

He doubts she has any, and sips his drink. Although in this county women with big bottoms usually don't go begging. Dutchmen love bulk. He says, "Well, I don't know if I did such a great job with Janice. She has to live too."

"Well Harry, if that's your reasoning, we *all* have to live." And from the way she stands there in front of him, if he sat up straight her pussy would be exactly at his nose. Tickling hair: he might sneeze. He sips the drink again, and feels the tasteless fluid expand his inner space. He might sit up at any minute, if she doesn't watch out. From the hair on her head probably a thick springy bush, though you can't always tell, some of the cunts in the magazine just had wisps at the base of their bellies, hardly an armpit's worth. Dolls. She moves away saying, "Who'll hold families together, if everybody has to live? Living is a compromise, between doing what *you* want and doing what *oth*er people want."

"What about what poor old God wants?"

The uncalled-for noun jars her from the seductive pose she has assumed, facing out the window, her backside turned to him. The dog position. Tip her over a chair and let her fuss herself with her fingers into coming while he does it from behind. Janice got so she preferred it, more animal, she wasn't distracted by the look on his face, never was one for wet kisses, when they first started going together complained she couldn't breathe, he asked her if she had adenoids. Seriously. No two alike, a billion cunts in the world, snowflakes. Touch them right they melt. What we most protect is where we want to be invaded. Peggy leaves her drink on the sill like a tall jewel and turns to him with her deformed face open. Since the word has been sprung on her, she asks, "Don't you think God is people?"

"No, I think God is everything that isn't people. I guess I think that. I don't think enough to know what I think." In irritation, he stands.

Big against the window, a hot shadow, palish-purple edges catching the light ebbing from the red city, the dim mountain, Peggy exclaims. "Oh, you think with"—and to assist her awkward thought she draws his shape in the air with two hands, having freed them for this gesture—"your whole person."

She looks so helpless and vague there seems nothing for Harry to do but step into the outline of himself she has drawn and kiss her. Her face, eclipsed, feels large and cool. Her lips bumble on his, the spongy wax of gumdrops, yet narcotic, not quite tasteless: as a kid Rabbit loved bland candy like Dots; sitting in the movies he used to plow through three nickel boxes of them, playing with them with his tongue and teeth, playing, playing before giving himself the ecstasy of the bite. Up and down his length she bumps against him, straining against his height, touching. The strange place on her where nothing is, the strange place higher where some things are. Her haunches knot with the effort of keeping on tiptoe. She pushes, pushes: he is a cunt this one-eyed woman is coldly pushing up into. He feels her mind gutter out; she has wrapped them in a clumsy large ball of darkness.

Something scratches on the ball. A key in a lock. Then the door knocks. Harry and Peggy push apart, she tucks her hair back around her spread-legged eyes and runs heavily to the door and lets in the boys. They are red-faced and furious. "Mom, the fucking thing broke down again," Billy tells his mother. Nelson looks over at Harry. The boy is near tears. Since Janice left, he is silent and delicate: an eggshell full of tears.

"It wasn't my fault," he calls huskily, injustice a sieve in his throat. "Dad, he says it was my fault."

"You baby, I didn't say that exactly."

"You did. He did, Dad, and it wasn't."

"All I said was he spun out too fast. He always spins out too fast. He flipped on a loose stone, now the headlight is bent under and it won't start."

"If it wasn't such a cheap one it wouldn't break all the time."

"It's not a cheap one it's the best one there is almost and anyway you don't even have any—"

"I wouldn't take one if you gave it to me—"

"So who are you to talk."

"Hey, easy, easy," Harry says. "We'll get it fixed. I'll pay for it."

"Don't pay for it, Dad. It wasn't anybody's fault. It's just he's so spoiled."

"You shrimp," Billy says, and hits him, much the same way that three weeks ago Harry hit Janice, hard but seeking a spot that could take it. Harry separates them, squeezing Billy's arm so the kid clams up. This kid is going to be tough some day. Already his arm is stringy.

Peggy is just bringing it all into focus, her insides shifting back from that kiss. "Billy, these things will happen if you insist on playing so dangerously." To Harry she says, "*Damn* Ollie for getting it for him, I think he did it to spite me. He knows I hate machines."

Harry decides Billy is the one to talk to. "Hey. Billy. Shall I take Nelson back home, or do you want him to spend the night anyway?"

And both boys set up a wailing for Nelson to spend the night. "Dad you don't have to come for me or anything, I'll ride my bike home in the morning first thing, I left it here yesterday."

So Rabbit releases Billy's arm and gives Nelson a kiss somewhere around the ear and tries to find the right eye of Peggy's to look into. "Okey-doak. I'll be off."

She says, "Must you? Stay. Can't I give you supper? Another drink? It's early yet."

"This guy's waiting," Rabbit lies, and makes it around her furniture to the door.

Her body chases him, her vague eyes shining in their tissue-paper sockets, and her lips have that loosened look kissed lips get; he resists the greedy urge to buy another box of Dots. "Harry," she begins, and seems to fall toward him, after a stumble, though they don't touch.

"Yeah?"

"I'm usually here. If—you know."

"I know. Thanks for the g.-and-t. Your view is great." He reaches then and pats, not her ass exactly, the flank at the side of it, too broad, too firm, alive enough under his palm, it turns out, to make him wonder, when her door closes, why he is going down the elevator, and out.

It is too early to meet Buchanan. He walks back through the West Brewer side streets toward Weiser, through the dulling summer light and the sounds of distant games, of dishes rattled in kitchen sinks, of television muffled to a murmur mechanically laced with laughter and applause, of cars driven by teenagers laying rubber and shifting down. Children and old men sit on the porch steps beside the lead-colored milk-bottle boxes. Some stretches of sidewalk are brick; these neighborhoods, the oldest in West Brewer, close to the river, are cramped, gentle, barren. Between the few trees, city trees that never knew an American forest, they brought them in from China and Brazil, there is a rigid flourishing of hydrants, meters, and signs, some of them, virtual billboards in white on green, directing motorists to superhighways whose number is blazoned on the federal shield or on the commonwealth keystone; from these obscure West Brewer byways, sidewalks and asphalt streets rumpled comfortably as old clothes, one can be arrowed toward Philadelphia, Baltimore, Washington the national capital, New York the headquarters of commerce and fashion. Or in the other direction can find Pittsburgh, Chicago, mountains of snow, a coastline of sun. But beneath these awesome metal insignia of vastness and motion fat men in undershirts loiter, old ladies move between patches of gossip with the rural waddle of egg-gatherers, dogs sleep curled beside the cooling curb, and children with hockey sticks and tape-handled bats diffidently chip at whiffle balls and wads of leather, whittling themselves into the next generation of athletes and astronauts. Rabbit's eyes sting in the dusk, in this smoke of his essence, these harmless neighborhoods that have gone to seed. So much love, too much love, it is our madness, it is rotting us out, exploding us like dandelion polls. He stops at a corner grocery for a candy bar, an Oh Henry, then at the Burger Bliss on Weiser, dazzling in its lake of parking space, for a Lunar Special (double cheeseburger with an American flag stuck into the bun) and a vanilla milkshake, that tastes toward the bottom of chemical sludge.

The interior of Burger Bliss is so bright that his fingernails, with their big mauve moons, gleam and the coins he puts down in payment seem cartwheels of metal. Beyond the lake of light, unfriendly darkness. He ventures out past a dimmed drive-in bank and crosses the bridge. High slender arc lamps on giant flower stems send down a sublunar light by which the hurrying cars all appear purple. There are no other faces but his on the bridge. From the middle, Brewer seems a web, to which glowing droplets adhere. Mt. Judge is one with the night. The luminous smudge of the Pinnacle Hotel hangs like a star.

Gnats bred by the water brush Rabbit's face; Janice's desertion nags him from within, a sore spot in his stomach. Ease off beer and coffee. Alone, he must take care of himself. Sleeping alone, he dreads the bed, watches the late shows, Carson, Griffin, cocky guys with nothing to sell but their brass. Making millions on sheer gall. American dream. When he first heard the phrase as a kid he pictured God lying sleeping, the quilt-colored map of the U.S. coming out of his head like a cloud. Peggy's embrace drags at his limbs. Suit feels sticky. Jimbo's Friendly Lounge is right off the Brewer end of the bridge, a half-block down from Plum. Inside it, all the people are black.

Black to him is just a political word but these people really are, their faces shine of blackness turning as he enters, a large soft white man in a sticky gray suit. Fear travels up and down his skin, but the music of the great green-and-mauve-glowing jukebox called Moonmood slides on, and the liquid of laughter and tickled muttering resumes flowing; his entrance was merely a snag. Rabbit hangs like a balloon waiting for a dart; then his elbow is jostled and Buchanan is beside him.

"Hey, man, you made it." The Negro has materialized from the smoke. His overtrimmed mustache looks wicked in here.

"You didn't think I would?"

"Doubted it," Buchanan says. "Doubted it severely."

"It was your idea."

"Right. Harry, you are right. I'm not arguing, I am rejoicing. Let's fix you up. You need a drink, right?"

"I don't know, my stomach's getting kind of sensitive."

"You need two drinks. Tell me your poison."

"Maybe a daiquiri?"

"Never. That is a lady's drink for salad luncheons. Rufe, you old rascal."

"Yazzuh, yazzuh," comes the answer from the bar.

"Do a Stinger for the man."

"Yaz-*zuh*."

Rufe has a bald head like one of the stone hatchets in the Brewer Museum, only better polished. He bows into the marine underglow of the bar and Buchanan leads Rabbit to a booth in the back. The place is deep and more complicated than it appears from the outside. Booths recede and lurk: darkwood cape-shapes. Along one wall, Rufe and the lowlit bar; behind and above it, not only the usual Pabst and Bud and Miller's gimcracks bobbing and shimmering, but two stuffed small deer-heads, staring with bright brown eyes that will never blink. Gazelles, could they have been gazelles? A space away, toward a wall but with enough room for a row of booths behind, a baby grand piano, painted silver with one of those spray cans, silver in circular swirls. In a room obliquely off the main room, a pool table: colored boys all arms and legs spidering around the idyllic green felt. The presence of any game reassures Rabbit. Where any game is being played a hedge exists against fury. "Come meet some soul," Buchanan says. Two shadows in the booth are a man and a woman. The man wears silver circular glasses and a little pussy of a goatee and is young. The woman is old and wrinkled and smokes a yellow cigarette that requires much sucking in and holding down and closing of the eyes and sighing. Her brown eyelids are gray, painted blue. Sweat shines below the base of her throat, on the slant bone between her breasts, as if she had breasts, which she does not, though her dress, the blood-color of a rooster's comb, is cut deep, as if she did. Before they are introduced she says "Hi" to Harry, but her eyes slit to pin him fast in the sliding of a dream.

"This man," Buchanan is announcing, "is a co-worker of mine, he works right beside his daddy at Ver-i-ty Press, an expert lino-typist," giving syllables an odd ticking equality, a put-on or signal of some sort? "But not only that. He is an ath-e-lete of renown, a basketball player bar none, the Big O of Brewer in his day."

"Very beautiful," the other dark man says. Round specs tilt, glint. The shadow of a face they cling to feels thin in the darkness. The voice arises very definite and dry.

"Many years ago," Rabbit says, apologizing for his bulk, his bloated pallor, his dead fame. He sits down in the booth to hide.

"He has the hands," the woman states. She is in a trance. She says, "Give old Babe one of those hands, white boy." A-prickle with nervousness, wanting to sneeze on the sweetish smoke, Rabbit lifts his right hand up from his lap and lays it on the slippery table. Innocent meat. Distorted paw. Reminds him of, on television, that show with chimpanzees synchronized with talk and music, the eerie look of having just missed a correct design.

The woman touches it. Her touch reptilian cool. His eyes lift, brooding. Above the glistening bone her throat drips jewels, a napkin of rhinestones or maybe real diamonds; Cadillacs after all, alligator shoes, they can't put their money into real estate like whites, Springer's thrifty Toyotas not to the point. His mind is racing with his pulse. She has a silver sequin pasted beside one eye. Accent the ugly until it becomes gorgeous. Her eyelashes are great false crescents. That she has taken such care of herself leads him to suspect she will not harm him. His pulse slows. Her touch slithers nice as a snake. "Do dig that thumb," she advises the air. She caresses his thumb's curve. Its thin-skinned veined ball. Its colorless moon nail. "That thumb means sweetness and light. It is an indicator of pleasure in Sagittarius and Leo." She gives one knuckle an affectionate pinch.

The Negro not Buchanan (Buchanan has hustled to the bar to check on the Stinger) says, "Not like one of them usual little sawed-off nuggers these devils come at you with, right?"

Babe answers, not yielding her trance, "No, sir. This thumb here is extremely plausible. Under the right signs it would absolutely function. Now these knuckles here, they aren't so good, I don't get much music out of these knuckles." And she presses a chord on them, with fingers startlingly hard and certain. "But this here thumb," she goes back to caressing it, "Is a real enough heartbreaker."

"All these Charlies is heartbreakers, right? Just cause they don't know how to shake their butterball asses don't mean they don't get Number One in, they gets it in real mean, right? The reason they so mean, they has so much religion, right? That big white God go tells 'em, Screw that black chick, and they really wangs away 'cause God's right there slappin' away at their butterball asses. Cracker spelled backwards is fucker, right?"

Rabbit wonders if this is how the young Negro really talks, wonders if there is a real way. He does not move, does not even bring back his hand from the woman's inspection, her touches chill as teeth. He is among panthers.

Buchanan, that old rascal, bustles back and sets before Rabbit a tall pale glass of poison and shoves in so Rabbit has to shove over opposite the other man. Buchanan's eyes check around the faces and guess it's gotten heavy. Lightly he says, "This man's wife, you know what? That woman, I never had the pleasure of meeting her, not counting those Verity picnics where Farnsworth, you all know Farnsworth now—?"

"Like a father," the young man says, adding, "Right?"

"—gets me so bombed out of my mind on that barrel beer I can't remember anybody by face or name, where was I? Yes, that woman, she just upped and left him the other week, left him flat to go chasing around with some other gentleman, something like a Spaniard, didn't you say Harry?"

"A Greek."

Babe clucks. "Honey, now what did he have you didn't? He must of had a thumb long as this badmouth's tongue." She nudges her companion, who retrieves from his lips this shared cigarette, which has grown so short it must burn, and sticks out his tongue. Its whiteness shocks Rabbit; a mouthful of luminous flesh. Though fat and pale, it does not look very long. This man, Rabbit sees, is a boy; the patch of goatee is all he can grow. Harry does not like him. He likes Babe, he thinks, even though she has dried hard, a prune on the bottom of the box. In here they are all on the bottom of the box. This drink, and his hand, are the whitest thing around. Not to think of the other's tongue. He sips. Too sweet, wicked. A thin headache promptly begins.

Buchanan is persisting, "Don't seem right to me, healthy big man living alone with nobody now to comfort him."

The goatee bobs. "Doesn't bother me in the slightest. Gives the man time to think, right? Gets the thought of cunt off his back, right? Chances are he has some hobby he can do, you know, like woodwork." He explains to Babe, "You know, like a lot of these peckerwoods have this clever thing they can do down in their basements, like stamp collecting, right? That's how they keep making it big. Cleverness, right?" He taps his skull, whose narrowness is padded by maybe an inch of tight black wool. The texture reminds Rabbit of his mother's crocheting, if she had used tiny metal thread. Her blue bent hands now. Even in here, family sadness pokes at him, makes sore holes.

"I used to collect baseball cards," he tells them. He hopes to excite enough rudeness from them so he can leave. He remembers the cards' bubble-gum smell, their silken feel from the powdered sugar. He sips the Stinger.

Babe sees him make a face. "You don't have to drink that piss." She nudges her neighbor again. "Let's have one more stick."

"Woman, you must think I'm made of hay."

"I know you're plenty magical, that's one thing. Off that uptight shit, the ofay here needs a lift and I'm nowhere near spaced enough to pee-form."

"Last drag," he says, and passes her the tiny wet butt.

She crushes it into the Sunflower Beer ashtray. "This roach is hereby dead." And holds her thin hand palm up for a hit.

Buchanan is clucking. "Mother-love, go easy on yourself," he tells Babe.

The other Negro is lighting another cigarette; the paper is twisted at the end and flares, subsides. He passes it to her saying, "Waste is a sin, right?"

"Hush now. This honeyman needs to loosen up, I hate to see 'em sad, I always have, they aren't like us, they don't have the insides to accommodate it. They's like little babies that way, they passes it off to someone else." She is offering Rabbit the cigarette, moist end toward him.

He says, "No thanks, I gave up smoking ten years ago."

Buchanan chuckles, with thumb and forefinger smooths his mustache sharper.

The boy says, "They're going to live forever, right?"

Babe says, "This ain't any of that nicotine shit. This weed is kindness itself."

While Babe is coaxing him, Buchanan and the boy diagonally discuss his immortality. "My daddy used to say, Down home, you never did see a dead white man, any more'n you'd see a dead mule."

"God's on their side, right? God's white, right? He doesn't

want no more Charlies up there to cut into his take, he has it just fine the way it is, him and all those black angels out in the cotton."

"Your mouth's gonta hurt you, boy. The man is the lay of the land down here."

"Whose black ass you hustling, hers or yours?"

"You just keep your smack in the heel of your shoe."

Babe is saying, "You suck it in as far as it'll go and hold it down as long as you absolutely can. It needs to mix with *you.*"

Rabbit tries to comply, but coughing undoes every puff. Also he is afraid of getting "hooked," of being suddenly jabbed with a needle, of starting to hallucinate because of something dropped into his Stinger. AUTOPSY ORDERED IN FRIENDLY LOUNGE DEATH. *Coroner Notes Strange Color of Skin.*

Watching him cough, the boy says, "He *is* beautiful. I didn't know they still came with all those corners. Right out of the crackerbox, right?"

This angers Rabbit enough to keep a drag down. It burns his throat and turns his stomach. He exhales with the relief of vomiting and waits for something to happen. Nothing. He sips the Stinger but now it tastes chemical like the bottom of that milkshake. He wonders how he can get out of here. Is Peggy's offer still open? Just to feel the muggy kiss of summer night on the Brewer streets would be welcome. Nothing feels worse than other people's good times.

Babe asks Buchanan, "What'd you have in mind, Buck?" She is working on the joint now and the smoke includes her eyes.

The fat man's shrug jiggles Rabbit's side. "No big plans," Buchanan mutters. "See what develops. Woman, way you're goin', you won't be able to tell those black keys from the white."

She plumes smoke into his face. "Who owns who?"

The boy cuts in. "Ofay doesn't dig he's a john, right?"

Buchanan, his smoothness jammed, observes, "That mouth again."

Rabbit, tired of this, asks loudly, "What else shall we talk about?" and twiddles his fingers at Babe for the joint. Inhaling still burns, but something is starting to mesh. He feels his height above the others as a good, a lordly, thing.

Buchanan is probing the other two. "Jill in tonight?"

Babe says, "Left her back at the place."

The boy asks, "On a nod, right?"

"You stay away, hear, she got herself clean. She's on no nod, just tired from mental confusion, from fighting her signs."

"Clean," the boy says, "what's clean? White is clean, right? Cunt is clean, right? Shit is clean, right? There's nothin' not clean the law don't go pointing its finger at it, right?"

"Wrong," Babe says. "Hate is not clean. A boy like you with hate in his heart, he needs to wash."

"Wash is what they said to Jesus, right?"

"Who's Jill?" Rabbit asks.

"Wash is what Pilate said he thought he might go do, right? Don't go saying clean to me, Babe, that's one darkie bag they had us in too long."

Buchanan is still delicately prying at Babe. "She coming in?"

The other cuts in, "She'll be in, can't keep that cunt away; put locks on the doors, she'll ooze in the letter slot."

Babe turns to him in mild surprise. "Now you loves little Jill."

"You can love what you don't like, right?"

Babe hangs her head. "That poor baby," she tells the tabletop, "just going to hurt herself and anybody standing near."

Buchanan speaks slowly, threading his way. "Just thought, man might like to meet Jill."

The boy sits up. Electricity, reflected from the bar and the streets, spins around his spectacle rims. "Gonna match 'em up," he says, "you're gonna cut yourself in on an all-honky fuck. You can out-devil these devils any day, right? You could of out-niggered Moses on the hill."

He seems to be a static the other two put up with. Buchanan is still prying at Babe across the table. "Just thought," he shrugs, "two birds with one stone."

A tear falls from her creased face to the tabletop. Her hair is done tight back like a schoolgirl's, a ribbon in back, a part straight as a knife on her skull. It must hurt, with kinky hair. "Going to take herself down all the way, it's in her signs, can't slip your signs."

"Who's that voodoo supposed to boogaboo?" the boy asks. "Whitey here got so much science he don't even need to play the numbers, right?"

Rabbit asks, "Is Jill white?"

The boy tells the two others angrily, "Cut the crooning, she'll be here, Christ, where else would she go, right? We're the blood to wash her sins away, right? Clean. Shit, that burns me. There's no dirt made that cunt won't swallow. With a smile on her face, right? Because she's *clean.*" There seems to be not only a history but a theology behind his anger. Rabbit sees this much, that the other two are working to fix him up with this approaching cloud, this Jill, who will be pale like the Stinger, and poisonous.

He announces, "I think I'll go soon."

Buchanan swiftly squeezes his forearm. "What you want to do that for, Br'er Rabbit? You haven't achieved your objective, friend."

"My only objective was to be polite." *Ooze through the letter slot*: haunted by this image and the smoke inside him, he feels he can lift up from the booth, pass across Buchanan's shoulders like a shawl, and out the door. Nothing can hold him, not Mom, not Janice. He could slip a posse dribbling, Tothero used to flatter him.

"You going to go off half-cocked," Buchanan warns.

"You ain't heard Babe play," the other man says.

He stops rising. "Babe plays?"

She is flustered, stares at her thin ringless hands, fiddles, mumbles. "Let him go. Let the man run. I don't want him to hear me."

The boy teases her. "Babe now, what sort of bad black act you putting on? He wants to hear you do your thing. Your darkie thing, right? You did the spooky card-reading bit and now you can do the banjo bit and maybe you can do the hot momma bit afterwards but it doesn't look like it right now, right?"

"Ease off, nigger," she says, face still bent low. "Sometime you going to lean too hard."

Rabbit asks her shyly, "You play the piano?"

"He gives me bad vibes," Babe confesses to the two black men. "Those knuckles of his aren't too good. Bad shadows in there."

Buchanan surprises Harry by reaching and covering her thin bare hands with one of his broadened big pressman's hands, a ring of milk blue jade on one finger, battered bright copper on another. His other arm reaches around Harry's shoulders, heavy. "Suppose you was him," he says to Babe, "how would that make you feel?"

"Bad," she says. "As bad as I feel anyway."

"Play for me Babe," Rabbit says in the lovingness of pot, and she lifts her eyes to his and lets her lips pull back on long yellow teeth and gums the color of rhubarb stems. "Men," Babe gaily drawls. "They sure can retail the shit." She pushes herself out of the booth, hobbling in her comb-red dress, and crosses through a henscratch of applause to the piano painted as if by children in silver swirls. She signals to the bar for Rufe to turn on the blue spot and bows stiffly, once, grudging the darkness around her a smile and, after a couple of runs to burn away the fog, plays.

What does Babe play? All the good old ones. All show tunes. "Up a Lazy River," "You're the Top," "Thou Swell,"

"Summertime," you know. There are hundreds, thousands. Men from Indiana wrote them in Manhattan. They flow into each other without edges, flowing under black bridges of chords thumped six, seven times, as if Babe is helping the piano to remember a word it won't say. Or spanking the silence. Or saying, *Here I am, find me, find me.* Her hands, all brown bone, hang on the keyboard hushed like gloves on a table; she gazes up through blue dust to get herself into focus, she lets her hands fall into another tune: "My Funny Valentine," "Smoke Gets in Your Eyes," "I Can't Get Started," starting to hum along with herself now, lyrics born in some distant smoke, decades when Americans moved within the American dream, laughing at it, starving on it, but living it, humming it, the national anthem everywhere. Wise guys and hicks, straw boaters and bib overalls, fast bucks, broken hearts, penthouses in the sky, shacks by the railroad tracks, ups and downs, rich and poor, trolley cars, and the latest news by radio. Rabbit had come in on the end of it, as the world shrank like an apple going bad and America was no longer the wisest hick town within a boat ride of Europe and Broadway forgot the tune, but here it all still was, in the music Babe played, the little stairways she climbed and came tap-dancing down, twinkling in black, and there is no other music, not really, though Babe works in some Beatles songs, "Yesterday" and "Hey Jude," doing it rinky-tink, her own style of ice to rattle in the glass. As Babe plays she takes on swaying and leaning backwards; at her arms' ends the standards go root back into ragtime. Rabbit sees circus tents and fireworks and farmers' wagons and an empty sandy river running so slow the sole motion is catfish sleeping beneath the golden skin.

The boy leans forward and murmurs to Rabbit, "You want ass, right? You can have her. Fifty gets you her all night, all ways you can think up. She knows a lot."

Sunk in her music, Rabbit is lost. He shakes his head and says, "She's too good."

"Good, man; she got to live, right? This place don't pay her shit."

Babe has become a railroad, prune-head bobbing, napkin of jewels flashing blue, music rolling through crazy places, tunnels of dissonance and open stretches of the same tinny thin note bleeding itself into the sky, all sad power and happiness worn into holes like shoe soles. From the dark booths around voices call out in a mutter "Go Babe" and "Do it, do it." The spidery boys in the adjacent room are frozen around the green felt. Into the mike that is there no bigger than a lollipop she begins to sing, sings in a voice that is no woman's voice at all and no man's, is merely human, the words of Ecclesiastes. A time to be born, a time to die. A time to gather up stones, a time to cast stones away. Yes. The Lord's last word. There is no other word, not really. Her singing opens up, grows enormous, frightens Rabbit with its enormous black maw of truth yet makes him overjoyed that he is here; he brims with joy, to be here with these black others, he wants to shout love through the darkness of Babe's noise to the sullen brother in goatee and glasses. He brims with this itch but does not spill. For Babe stops. As if suddenly tired or insulted Babe breaks off the song and shrugs and quits.

That is how Babe plays.

She comes back to the table stooped, trembling, nervous, old.

"That was beautiful, Babe," Rabbit tells her.

"It was," says another voice. A small white girl is standing there prim, in a white dress casual and dirty as smoke.

"Hey. Jill," Buchanan says.

"Hi Buck. Skeeter, hi."

So Skeeter is his name. He scowls and looks at the cigarette of which there is not even butt enough to call a roach.

"Jilly-love," Buchanan says, standing until his thighs scrape the table edge, "allow me to introduce. Harry the Rabbit Angstrom, he works at the printing plant with me, along with his daddy."

Jill asks, "Where is his daddy?," still looking at Skeeter, who will not look at her.

"Jilly, you go sit in here where I am," Buchanan says. "I'll go get a chair from Rufe."

"Down, baby," Skeeter says. "I'm splitting." No one offers to argue with him. Perhaps they are all as pleased as Rabbit to see him go.

Buchanan chuckles, he rubs his hands. His eyes keep in touch with all of them, even though Babe seems to be dozing. He says to Jill, "How about a beverage? A 7Up? Rufe can make a lemonade even."

"Nothing," Jill says. Teaparty manner. Hands in lap. Thin arms. Freckles. Rabbit scents in her a perfume of class. She excites him.

"Maybe she'd like a real drink," he says. With a white woman here he feels more in charge. Negroes, you can't blame them, haven't had his advantages. Slave ships, cabins, sold down the river, Ku Klux Klan, James Earl Ray: Channel 44 keeps having these documentaries all about it.

"I'm under age," Jill tells him politely.

Rabbit says, "Who cares?"

She answers, "The police."

"Not up the street they wouldn't mind so much," Buchanan explains, "if the girl halfway acted the part, but down here they get a touch fussy."

"The fuzz is fussy," Babe says dreamily. "The fuzz is our fussy friends. The fuzzy motherfuckers fuss."

"Don't, Babe," Jill begs. "Don't pretend."

"You let your old black mamma have a buzz on," Babe says. "Don't I take good care of you mostly?"

"How would the police know if this kid has a drink?" Rabbit asks, willing to be indignant.

Buchanan makes his high short wheeze. "Friend Harry, they'd just have to turn their heads."

"There're cops in here?"

"Friend"—and from the way he sidles closer Harry feels he's found another father—"if it weren't for po-lice spies, poor Jimbo's wouldn't sell two beers a night. Po-lice spies are the absolute backbone of local low life. They got so many plants going, that's why they don't dare shoot in riots, for fear of killing one of their own."

"Like over in York."

Jill asks Rabbit, "Hey. You live in Brewer?" He sees that she doesn't like his being white in here, and smiles without answering. Screw you, little girl.

Buchanan answers for him. "Lady, does he live in Brewer? If he lived any more in Brewer he'd be a walking advertisement. He'd be the Owl Pretzel owl. I don't think this fella's ever gotten above Twelfth Street, have you Harry?"

"A few times. I was in Texas in the Army, actually."

"Did you get to fight?" Jill asks. Something scratchy here, but maybe like a kitten it's the way of making contact.

"I was all set to go to Korea," he says. "But they never sent me." Though at the time he was grateful, it has since eaten at him, become the shame of his life. He had never been a fighter but now there is enough death in him so that in a way he wants to kill.

"Now Skeeter," Buchanan is saying, "he's just back from Vietnam."

"That's why he so rude," Babe offers.

"I couldn't tell if he was rude or not," Rabbit confesses.

"That's nice," Buchanan says.

"He was rude," Babe says.

Jill's lemonade arrives. She is still girl enough to look happy when it is set before her: cakes at the teaparty. Her face lights up. A crescent of lime clings to the edge of the glass; she takes it off and sucks and makes a sour face. A child's plumpness has been drained from her before a woman's bones could grow and harden. She is the reddish type of fair; her hair hangs dull, without fire, almost flesh-color, or the color of the flesh of certain soft trees, yews or cedars. Small soft ears peep through dearly, pale chips of eggshell; Harry feels protective, timidly. In her tension of small bones she reminds him of Nelson. He asks her, "What do you do, Jill?"

"Nothing much," she says. "Hang around." It had been square of him to ask, pushing. The blacks fit around her like shadows.

"Jilly's a poor soul," Babe volunteers, stirring within her buzz. "She's fallen on evil ways." And she pats Rabbit's hand as if to say, *Don't you fall upon these ways.*

"Young Jill," Buchanan clarifies, "has run away from her home up there in Connecticut."

Rabbit asks her, "Why would you do that?"

"Why not? Let freedom ring."

"Can I ask how old you are?"

"You can ask."

"I'm asking."

Babe hasn't let go of Rabbit's hand; with the fingernail of her index finger she is toying with the hairs on the back of his fist. It makes his teeth go cold, for her to do that. "Not so old you couldn't be her daddy," Babe says.

He is beginning to get the drift. They are presenting him with this problem. He is the consultant honky. The girl, too, unwilling as she is, is submitting to the interview. She inquires of him, only partly parrying, "How old are *you?*"

"Thirty-six."

"Divide by two."

"Eighteen, huh? How long've you been on the run? Away from your parents."

"Her daddy dead," Buchanan interposes softly.

"Long enough, thank you." Her face pales, her freckles stand out sharply: blood-dots that have dried brown. Her dry little lips tighten; her chin drifts toward him. She is pulling rank. He is Penn Villas, she is Penn Park. Rich kids make all the trouble.

"Long enough for what?"

"Long enough to do some sick things."

"Are you sick?"

"I'm cured."

Buchanan interposes, "Babe helped her out."

"Babe is a beautiful person," Jill says. "I was really a mess when Babe took me in."

"Jilly is my sweetie," Babe says, as suddenly as in playing she moves from one tune to another, "Jilly is my baby-love and I'm her mamma-love," and takes her brown hands away from Harry's to encircle the girl's waist and hug her against the rooster-comb-red of her dress; the two are women, though one is a prune and the other a milkweed. Jill pouts in pleasure. Her mouth is lovable when it moves, Rabbit thinks, the lower lip bumpy and dry as if chapped, though this is not winter but the humid height of summer.

Buchanan is further explaining. "Fact of it is, this girl hasn't got no place regular to go. Couple weeks ago, she comes in here, not knowing I suppose the place was mostly for soul, a little pretty girl like this get in with some of the brothers they would tear her apart limb by sweet limb"—he has to chuckle—"so Babe takes her right away under her wing. Only trouble with that is"—the fat man rustles closer, making the booth a squeeze—"Babe's place is none too big, and anyways . . ."

The child flares up. "Anyways I'm not welcome." Her eyes widen; Rabbit has not seen their color before, they have been shadowy, moving slowly, as if their pink lids are tender or as if, rejecting instruction and inventing her own way of moving through the world, she has lost any vivid idea of what to be looking for. Her eyes are green. The dry tired green, yet one of his favorite colors, of August grass.

"Jilly-love," Babe says, hugging, "you the most welcome little white baby there could be."

Buchanan is talking only to Rabbit, softer and softer. "You know, those things happen over York way, they could happen here, and how could we protect"—the smallest wave of his hand toward the girl lets the sentence gracefully hang; Harry is reminded of Stavros's gestures. Buchanan ends chuckling: "We be so busy keepin' holes out of our own skins. Dependin' where you get caught, being black a bad ticket both ways!"

Jill snaps, "I'll be all right. You two stop it now. Stop trying to sell me to this creep. I don't want him. He doesn't want me. Nobody wants me. That's all right. I don't want anybody."

"Everybody wants somebody," Babe says. "I don't mind your hangin' around my place, some gentlemen mind, is all."

Rabbit says, "Buchanan minds," and this perception astonishes them; the two blacks break into first shrill, then jingling, laughter, and another Stinger appears on the table between his hands, pale as lemonade.

"Honey, it's just the visibility," Babe then adds sadly. "You make us ever so visible."

A silence grows like the silence when a group of adults is waiting for a child to be polite. Sullenly Jill asks Rabbit, "What do *you* do?"

"Set type," Rabbit tells her. "Watch TV. Sit around."

"Harry here," Buchanan explains, "had a nasty shock the other day. His wife for no good reason upped and left him."

"No reason at all?" Jill asks. Her mouth pouts forward, vexed and aggressive, yet her spark of interest dies before her breath is finished with the question.

Rabbit thinks. "I think I bored her. Also, we didn't agree politically."

"What about?"

"The Vietnam war. I'm all for it."

Jill snatches in her breath.

Babe says, "I knew those knuckles looked bad."

Buchanan offers to smooth it over. "Everybody at the plant is for it. We think, you don't hold 'em over there, you'll have those black pajama fellas on the streets over here."

Jill says to Rabbit seriously, "You should talk to Skeeter about it. He says it was a fabulous trip. He loved it."

"I wouldn't know about that. I'm not saying it's pleasant to fight in or be caught in. I just don't like the kids making the criticisms. People say it's a mess so we should get out. If you stayed out of every mess you'd never get into anything."

"Amen," Babe says. "Life is generally shit."

Rabbit goes on, feeling himself get rabid, "I guess I don't much believe in college kids or the Viet Cong. I don't think they have any answers. I think they're minorities trying to bring down everything that halfway works. Halfway isn't all the way but it's better than no way."

Buchanan smooths on frantically. His upper lip is bubbling with sweat under his slit of a mustache. "I agree ninety-nine per cent. Enlightened self-interest is the phrase I like. The way I see, enlightened self-interest's the best deal we're likely to get down here. I don't buy pie in the sky whoever is slicing it. These young ones like Skeeter, they say All power to the people, you look around for the people, the only people around is *them*."

"Because of Toms like you," Jill says.

Buchanan blinks. His voice goes deeper, hurt. "I ain't no Tom, girl. That kind of talk doesn't help any of us. That kind of talk just shows how young you are. What I am is a man trying to get from Point A to Point B, from the cradle to the grave hurting the fewest people I can. Just like Harry here, if you'd ask him. Just like your Daddy, God rest his soul."

Babe says, hugging the stubbornly limp girl, "I just likes Jilly's spunk, she's less afraid what to do with her life than fat old smelly you, sittin' there lickin' yourself like an old cigar end." But while talking she keeps her eyes on Buchanan as if his concurrence is to be desired. Mothers and fathers, they turn up everywhere.

Buchanan explains to Jill with a nice levelness, "So that is the problem. Young Harry here lives in this fancy big house over in the fanciest part of West Brewer, all by himself, and never gets any tail."

Harry protests. "I'm not that alone. I have a kid with me."

"Man has to have tail," Buchanan is continuing.

"Play, Babe," a dark voice shouts from a dark booth. Rufe bobs his head and switches on the blue spot. Babe sighs and offers Jill what is left of Skeeter's joint. Jill shakes her head and gets out of the booth to let Babe out. Rabbit thinks the girl is leaving and discovers himself glad when she sits down again, opposite him. He sips his Stinger and she chews the ice from her lemonade while Babe plays again. This time the boys in the poolroom softly keep at their game. The clicking and the liquor and the music mix and make the space inside him very big, big enough to hold blue light and black faces and "Honeysuckle Rose" and stale smoke sweeter than alfalfa and this apparition across the way, whose wrists and forearms are as it were translucent and belonging to another order of creature; she is not yet grown. Her womanliness is attached to her, it floats from her like a little zeppelin he can almost see. And his inside space expands to include beyond Jimbo's the whole world with its arrowing wars and polychrome races, its continents shaped like ceiling stains, its strings of gravitational attraction attaching it to every star, its glory in space as of a blue marble swirled with clouds; everything is warm, wet, still coming to birth but himself and his home, which remains a strange dry place, dry and cold and emptily spinning in the void of Penn Villas like a cast-off space capsule. He doesn't want to go there but he must. He must. "I must go," he says, rising.

"Hey, hey," Buchanan protests. "The night hasn't even got itself turned around to get started yet."

"I ought to be home in case my kid can't stand the kid he's staying with. I promised I'd visit my parents tomorrow, if they didn't keep my mother in the hospital for more tests."

"Babe will be sad, you sneaking out. She took a shine to you."

"Maybe that other guy she took a shine to will be back. My guess is Babe takes a shine pretty easy."

"Don't you get nasty."

"No, I love her, Jesus. Tell her. She plays like a whiz. This has been a terrific change of pace for me." He tries to stand, but the table edge confines him to a crouch. The booth tilts and he rocks slightly, as if he is already in the slowly turning cold house he is heading toward. Jill stands up with him, obedient as a mirror.

"One of these times," Buchanan continues beneath them, "maybe you can get to know Babe better. She is one good egg."

"I don't doubt it." He tells Jill, "Sit down."

"Aren't you going to take me with you? They want you to."

"Gee. I hadn't thought to."

She sits down.

"Friend Harry, you've hurt the little girl's feelings. Nasty must be your middle name."

Jill says, "Far as creeps like this are concerned, I have no feelings. I've decided he's queer anyway."

"Could be," Buchanan says. "It would explain that wife."

"Come on, let me out of the booth. I'd *like* to take her—"

"Then help yourself, friend. On me."

Babe is playing "Time After Time." *I tell myself that I'm.*

Harry sags. The table edge is killing his thighs. "O.K., kid. Come along."

"I wouldn't dream of it."

"You'll be bored," he feels in honesty obliged to add.

"You've been had," she tells him.

"Jilly now, be gracious for the gentleman." Buchanan hastily pushes out of the booth, lest the combination tumble, and lets Harry slide out and leans against him confidentially. Geezers. His breath rises bad, from under the waxed needles. "Problem is," he explains, the last explaining he will do tonight, "it don't look that good, her being in here, under age and all. The fuzz now, they aren't absolutely unfriendly, but they hold us pretty tight to the line, what with public opinion the way it is. So it's not that healthy for anybody. She's a poor child needs a daddy, is the simple truth of it."

Rabbit asks her, "How'd he die?"

Jill says, "Heart. Dropped dead in a New York theater lobby. He and my mother were seeing *Hair*."

"O.K. Let's shove." To Buchanan Rabbit says, "How much for the drinks? Wow. They're just hitting me."

"On us," is the answer, accompanied by a wave of a palm the color of silver polish. "On the black community." He has to wheeze and chuckle. Struggling for solemnity: "This is real big of you, man. You're a big man."

"See you at work Monday."

"Jilly-love, you be a good girl. We'll keep in touch."

"I bet."

Disturbing, to think that Buchanan works. We all work. Day selves and night selves. The belly hungers, the spirit hungers. Mouths munch, cunts swallow. Monstrous. Soul. He used to try to picture it when a child. A parasite like a tapeworm inside. A sprig of mistletoe hung from our bones, living on air. A jellyfish swaying between our lungs and our liver. Black men have more, bigger. Cocks like eels. Night feeders. Their touching underbelly smell on buses, their dread of those clean dry places where Harry must be. He wonders if he will be sick. Poison in those Stingers, on top of moonburgers.

Babe shifts gears, lays out six chords like six black lead

slugs slapping into the tray, and plays, "There's a Small Hotel." *With a wishing well.*

With this Jill, then, Rabbit enters the street. On his right, toward the mountain, Weiser stretches sallow under blue street lights. The Pinnacle Hotel makes a tattered blur, the back of the Sunflower Beer clock shows yellow neon petals; otherwise the great street is dim. He can remember when Weiser with its five movie marquees and its medley of neon outlines appeared as gaudy as a carnival midway. People would stroll, children between them. Now the downtown looks deserted, sucked dry by suburban shopping centers and haunted by rapists. LOCAL HOODS ASSAULT ELDERLY, last week's *Vat* had headlined. In the original version of the head LOCAL had been BLACK.

They turn left, toward the Running Horse bridge. River moisture soothes his brow. He decides he will not be sick. Never, even as an infant, could stand it; some guys, Ronnie Harrison for one, liked it, throw up after a few beers or before a big game, joke about the corn between their teeth, but Rabbit needed to keep it down, even at the cost of a bellyache. He still carries from sitting in Jimbo's the sense of the world being inside him; he will keep it down. The city night air. The ginger of tar and concrete baked all day, truck traffic lifted from it like a lid, space between the headlights. Infrequent headlights stroke this girl, catching her white legs and thin dress as she hangs on the curb hesitant.

She asks, "Where's your car?"

"I don't have any."

"That's impossible."

"My wife took it when she left me."

"You didn't have two?"

"No." This is really a rich kid.

"I have a car," she says.

"Where is it?"

"I don't know."

"How can you not know?"

"I used to leave it on the street up near Babe's place off of Plum, I didn't know it was somebody's garage entrance, and one morning they had taken it away."

"And you didn't go after it?"

"I didn't have the money for any fine. And I'm scared of the police, they might check me out. The staties must have a bulletin on me."

"Wouldn't the simplest thing for you be to go back to Connecticut?"

"Let's not have any editorials," she says.

"What didn't you like about it?"

"It was all ego. Sick ego."

"Something pretty egotistical about running away, too. Your mother must be miserable."

The girl makes no answer, but crosses the street, from Jimbo's to the beginning of the bridge. Rabbit has to follow. "What kind of car was it?"

"A white Porsche."

"Wow."

"My father gave it to me for my seventeenth birthday."

"My father-in-law runs the Toyota agency in town."

They keep arriving at this place, where a certain symmetry snips their exchanges short. Having crossed the bridge, they stand on a little pond of sidewalk squares where in this age of cars few feet tread. The bridge was poured in the Thirties—sidewalks, broad balustrades, and lamp plinths—of reddish rough concrete; above them an original light standard, iron fluted and floral toward the top, marks stately but unlit the entrance to the bridge, illumined since recently with cold bars of violet on tall aluminum stems rooted in the center of the walkway. Her white dress is unearthly in this light. A man's name is embedded in a bronze plaque, illegible. Jill asks impatiently, "Well, how shall we do?"

He assumes she means transportation. He is too shaky still, too full of smoke and Stinger, to look beyond that. The way to the center of Brewer, where taxis prowl and doze, feels blocked. In the gloom beyond Jimbo's neon nimbus, brown shadows, local hoods, giggle in doorways, watching. Rabbit says, "Let's walk across the bridge and hope for a bus. The last one comes around eleven, maybe on Saturdays it's later. Anyway, if none comes at all, it's not too far to walk to my place. My kid does it all the time."

"I love walking," she says. She touchingly adds, "I'm strong. You mustn't baby me."

The balustrade was poured in an X-pattern echoing rail fences; these Xs click past his legs not rapidly enough. The gritty breadth he keeps touching runs tepid. Flecks as if of rock salt had been mixed into it. Not done that way any more, not done this color, reddish, the warmth of flesh, her hair also, cut cedar color, lifting as she hurries to keep up.

"What's the rush?"

"Don't you hear them?"

Cars thrust by, rolling balls of light before them. An anvil-drop below, to the black floor of the river: white shards, boat shapes. Behind them, pattering feet, the press of pursuit. Rabbit dares stop and peek backwards. Two brown figures are chasing them. Their shadows shorten and multiply and lengthen and simplify again as they fly beneath the successive mauve angels, in and out of isthmuses of shadow; one is brandishing something white in his hand. It glitters. Harry's heart jams; he wants to make water. The West Brewer end of the bridge is forever away. LOCAL MAN STABBED DEFENDING UNKNOWN GIRL. He squeezes her arm and tries to make her run. Her skin is smooth and narrow yet tepid like the balustrade. She pants, "Cut it out," and pulls away. He turns and finds, unexpectedly, what he had forgotten was there, courage; his body fits into the hardshell blindness of meeting a threat, rigid, only his eyes soft spots, himself a sufficient shield. *Kill.*

The Negroes halt under the near purple moon and back a step, frightened. They are young, their bodies liquid. He is bigger than they. The white flash in the hand of one is not a knife but a pocketbook of pearls. The bearer shambles forward with it. His eyewhites and the pearls look lavender in the light. "This yours, lady?"

"Oh. Yes."

"Babe sent us after."

"Oh. Thank you. Thank her."

"We scare somebody?"

"Not me. Him."

"Yeah."

"Dude scared us too."

"Sorry about that," Rabbit volunteers. "Spooky bridge."

"O.K."

"O.K., Chuck." Their mauve eyeballs roll; their purple hands flip as their legs in the stitched skin of Levis seek the rhythm of leaving. They giggle together; and also at this moment two giant trailer trucks pass on the bridge, headed in opposite directions: their rectangles thunderously overlap and, having clapped the air between them, hurtle each on its way, corrosive and rumbling. The bridge trembles. The Negro boys have disappeared. Rabbit walks on with Jill.

The pot and brandy and fear in him enhance the avenue he knows too well. No bus comes. Her dress flutters in the corner of his eye as he tries, his skin stretched and his senses shuffling and circling like a cloud of gnats, to make talk. "Your home was in Connecticut."

"A place called Stonington."

"Near New York?"

"Near enough. Daddy used to go down Mondays and come

back Fridays. He loved to sail. He said about Stonington it was the only town in the state that faces the open sea, everything else is on the Sound."

"And he died, you said. My mother—she has Parkinson's Disease."

"Look, do you like to talk this much? Why don't we just walk? I've never been in West Brewer before. It's nice."

"What's nice about it?"

"Everything. It doesn't have a glorious past like the city does. So it's not so disappointed. Look at that, Burger Bliss. Isn't it beautiful, all goldy and plasticky with that purple fire inside?"

"That's where I ate tonight."

"How was the food?"

"Awful. Maybe I taste everything too much, I should start smoking again. My kid loves the place."

"How old did you say he was?"

"Thirteen. He's small for his age."

"That still makes him thirteen."

"Yeah. I try not to ride him."

"What would you ride him about?"

"Oh. He's bored by things I used to love. I don't think he's having much fun. He never goes outdoors."

"Hey. What's your name?"

"Harry."

"Hey, Harry. Would you mind feeding me?"

"Sure, I mean No. At home? I don't know what we have in the icebox. Refrigerator."

"I mean over there, at the burger place."

"Oh, sure. Terrific. I'm sorry. I assumed you ate."

"Maybe I did, I tend to forget material details like that. But I don't think so. All I feel inside is lemonade."

She selects a Cashewburger for 85¢, and a strawberry milkshake. In the withering light she devours the burger, and he orders her another. She smiles apologetically. She has small inturned teeth, grayish and spaced with hairline gaps. Nice. "Usually I try to rise above eating."

"Why?"

"It's so ugly. Don't you think, it's one of the uglier things we do?"

"It has to be done."

"That's your philosophy, isn't it?" Even in this garishly lit place her face has about it something shadowy and elusive, something prematurely aged or still to be formed. Finished, she wipes her fingers one by one on a paper napkin and says decisively, "Thank you very much." He pays. She clutches the purse, but what is in it? Credit cards? Diagrams for the revolution?

He has had coffee, to keep himself awake. Be up all night fucking this poor kid. Upholding the honor of middle-aged squares. Different races. In China, they used to tell in the Army, the women put razor blades in their cunts in case the Japanese tried rape; Rabbit's scrotum shrivels at the thought. Enjoy the walk. They march down Weiser, the store windows dark but for burglar lights, the Acme parking lot empty but for scattered neckers, the movie marquee changed from 2001 to TRUE GRIT. Short enough to get it all on. They cross the street at a blinking yellow to Emberly Avenue, which then becomes Emberly Drive, which becomes Vista Crescent. The development is dark. "Talk about spooky," she says.

"I think it's the flatness," he says. "The town I grew up in, no two houses were on the same level."

"There's such a smell of plumbing somehow."

"Actually, the plumbing is none too good."

This smoky creature at his side has halved his weight. He floats up the steps to the porchlet, knees vibrating. Her profile by his shoulder is fine and cool as the face on the old dime. The key to the door of three stepped windows nearly flies out of his hand, it feels so magical. Whatever he expects when he flicks on the inside hall light, it is not the same old furniture, the fake cobbler's bench, the sofa and the silverthread chair facing each other like two bulky drunks too tired to go upstairs, the blank TV screen in its box of metal painted with wood grain, the see-through shelves with nothing on them.

"Wow," Jill says. "This is really tacky."

Rabbit apologizes, "We never really picked out the furniture, it just kind of happened. Janice was always going to do different curtains."

Jill asks, "Was she a good wife?"

His answer is nervous; the question plants Janice back in the house, quiet in the kitchen, crouching at the head of the stairs, listening. "Not too bad. Not much on organizational ability, but until she got mixed up with this other guy at least she kept plugging away. She used to drink too much but got that under control. We had a tragedy about ten years ago that sobered her up I guess. Sobered me up too. A baby died."

"How?"

"An accident."

"That's sad. Where do we sleep?"

"Why don't you take the kid's room, I guess he won't be back. The kid he's staying with, he's a real spoiled jerk, I told Nelson if it got too painful he should just come home. I probably should have been here to answer the phone. What time is it? How about a beer?"

Penniless, she is wearing a little wristwatch that must have cost a hundred at least. "Twelve-ten," she says. "Don't you want to sleep with me?"

"Huh? That's not your idea of bliss, is it? Sleeping with a creep?"

"You are a creep, but you just fed me."

"Forget it. On the white community. Ha."

"And you have this sweet funny family side. Always worrying about who needs you."

"Yeah, well it's hard to know sometimes. Probably nobody

if I could face up to it. In answer to your question, sure I'd like to sleep with you, if I won't get hauled in for statutory rape."

"You're really scared of the law, aren't you?"

"I try to keep out of its way is all."

"I promise you on a Bible—do you have a Bible?"

"There used to be one somewhere, that Nelson got for going to Sunday school, when he did. We've kind of let all that go. Just promise me."

"I promise you I'm eighteen. I'm legally a woman. I am not bait for a black gang. You will not be mugged or blackmailed. You may fuck me."

"Somehow you're making me almost cry."

"You're awfully scared of me. Let's take a bath together and then see how we feel about it."

He laughs. "By then I guess I'll feel pretty gung-ho about it."

She is serious, a serious small-faced animal sniffing out her new lair. "Where's the bathroom?"

"Take off your clothes here."

The command startles her; her chin dents and her eyes go wide with fright. No reason he should be the only scared person here. Rich bitch calling his living room tacky. Standing on the rug where he and Janice last made love, Jill skins out of her clothes. She kicks off her sandals and strips her dress upward. She is wearing no bra. Her tits tug upward, drop back, give him a headless stare. She is wearing bikini underpants, black lace, in a pattern too fine to read. Not pausing a moment for him to drink her in, she pulls the elastic down with two thumbs, wriggles, and steps out. Where Janice had a springy triangle encroaching on the insides of her thighs when she didn't shave, Jill has scarcely a shadow, amber fuzz dust darkened toward the center to an upright dainty mane. The horns of her pelvis like starved cheekbones. Her belly a child's, childless. Her breasts in some lights as she turns scarcely exist. Being naked elongates her neck: a true ripeness there, in the unhurried curve from base of skull to small of back, and in the legs, which link to the hips with knots of fat and keep a plumpness all the way down. Her ankles are less slim than Janice's. But, hey, she is naked in this room, his room. This really strange creature, too trusting. She bends to pick up her clothes. She treads lightly on his carpet, as if watchful for tacks. She stands an arm's-length from him, her mouth pouting prim, a fleck of dry skin on the lower lip. "And you?"

"Upstairs." He undresses in his bedroom, where he always does; in the bathroom on the other side of the partition, water begins to cry, to sing, to splash. He looks down and has nothing of a hard-on. In the bathroom he finds her bending over to test the temperature mix at the faucet. A tuft between her buttocks. From behind she seems a boy's slim back wedged into the upside-down valentine of a woman's satin rear. He yearns to touch her, to touch the satin symmetry, and does. It stings his fingertips like glass we don't expect is there. Jill doesn't deign to flinch or turn at his touch, testing the water to her satisfaction. His cock stays small but has stopped worrying.

Their bath is all too gentle, silent, liquid, and pure. They are each attentive: he soaps and rinses her breasts as if their utter cleanness challenges him to make them even cleaner; she kneels and kneads his back as if a year of working weariness were in it. She blinds him in drenched cloth; she counts the gray hairs (six) in the hair of his chest. Still even as they stand to dry each other and he looms above her like a Viking he cannot shake the contented impotence of his sensation that they are the ends of spotlight beams thrown on the clouds, that their role is to haunt this house like two bleached creatures on a television set entertaining an empty room.

She glances at his groin. "I don't turn you on exactly, do I?"

"You do, you do. Too much. It's still too strange. I don't even know your last name."

"Pendleton." She drops to her knees on the bathroom rug and takes his penis into her mouth. He backs away as if bitten. "Wait."

Jill looks up at him crossly, looks up the slope of his slack gut, a cranky puzzled child with none of the answers in the last class of the day, her mouth slick with forbidden candy. He lifts her as he would a child, but she is longer than a child, and her armpits are scratchy and deep; he kisses her on the mouth. No gumdrops, her lips harden and she twists her thin face away, saying into his shoulder, "I don't turn anybody on, much. No tits. My mother has nifty tits, maybe that's my trouble."

"Tell me your trouble," he says, and leads her by the hand toward the bedroom.

"Oh, Jesus, one of those. Trouble-shooters. From the look of it you're in worse shape than me, you can't even respond when somebody takes off their clothes."

"First times are hard, you need to absorb somebody a little first." He darkens the room and they lie on the bed. She offers to embrace him again, sharp teeth and knees anxious to have it done, but he smooths her onto her back and massages her breasts, plumping them up, circling. "These aren't your trouble," he croons. "These are lovely." Down below he feels himself easily stiffening, clotting: cream in the freezer. CLINIC FOR RUNAWAYS OPENED. *Fathers Do Duty On Nights Off.*

Relaxing, Jill grows stringy; tendons and resentments come to the surface. "You should be fucking my mother, she really is good with men, she thinks they're the be-all and end-all. I know she was playing around, even before Daddy died."

"Is that why you ran away?"

"You wouldn't believe if I really told you."

"Tell me."

"A guy I went with tried to get me into heavy drugs."

"That's not so unbelievable."

"Yeah, but his reason was crazy. Look, you don't want to hear this crap. You're up now, why don't you just give it to me?"

"Tell me his reason."

"You see, when I'd trip, I'd see, like, you know—God. He never would. He just saw pieces of like old movies, that didn't add up."

"What kind of stuff did he give you? Pot?"

"Oh, no, listen, pot is just like having a Coke or something. Acid, when he could get it. Strange pills. He'd rob doctors' cars to get their samples and then mix them to see what happened. They have names for all these pills, purple hearts, dollies, I don't know what all. Then after he stole this syringe he'd inject stuff, he wouldn't even know what it was half the time, it was wild. I would never let him break my skin. I figured, anything went in by the mouth, I could throw it up, but anything went in my veins, I had no way to get rid of it, it could kill me. He said that was part of the kick. He was really freaked, but he had this, you know, power over me. I ran."

"Has he tried to follow you?" A freak coming up the stairs. Green teeth, poisonous needles. Rabbit's penis has wilted, listening.

"No, he's not the type. Toward the end I don't think he knew me from Adam really, all he was thinking about was his next fix. Junkies are like that. They get to be bores. You think they're talking to you or making love or whatever, and then you realize they're looking over your shoulder for the next fix. You realize you're nothing. He didn't need me to find God for him, if he met God right on the street he'd've tried to hustle Him for money enough for a couple bags."

"What did he look like?"

"Oh, about five-ten, brown hair down to his shoulders, slightly wavy when he brushed it, a neat build. Even after smack had pulled all the color from him he had a wonderful frame. His back was really marvellous, with long sloping shoulders and all these ripply little ribby bumps behind, you know, here." She touches him but is seeing the other. "He had been a runner in junior high."

"I meant God."

"Oh, God. He changed. He was different every time. But you always knew it was Him. Once I remember something like the inside of a big lily, only magnified a thousand times, a sort of glossy shining funnel that went down and down. I can't talk about it." She rolls over and kisses him on the mouth feverishly. His inability to respond seems to excite her; she gets up in a crouch and like a raccoon drinking water kisses his chin, his chest, his navel, goes down and stays. Her mouth nibbling is so surprising he fights the urge to laugh; her fingers on the hair of his thighs tickle like the threat of ice on his skin. The hair of her head makes a tent on his belly. He pushes at her but she sticks at it: might as well relax. The ceiling. The garage light shining upwards shows a stained patch where chimney flashing let the rain in. Must turn the garage light off. Though maybe a good burglar preventive. These junkies around steal anything. He wonders how Nelson made out. Asleep, boy sleeps on his back, mouth open, frightening; skin seems to tighten on the bone like in pictures of Buchenwald. Always tempted to wake him, prove he's O.K. Missed the eleven o'clock news tonight. Vietnam death count, race riots probably somewhere. Funny man, Buchanan. No plan, exactly, just feeling his way, began by wanting to sell him Babe, maybe that's the way to live. Janice in bed got hot like something cooking but this kid stays cool, a prep-school kid applying what she knows. It works.

"That's nice," she says, stroking the extent of his extended cock, glistening with her spittle.

"You're nice," he tells her, "not to lose faith."

"I like it," she tells him, "making you get big and strong."

"Why bother?" he asks. "I'm a creep."

"Want to come into me?" the girl asks. But when she lies on her back and spreads her legs, her lack of self-consciousness again strikes him as sad, and puts him off, as does the way she winces when he seeks to enter; so that he grows small. Her blurred face widens its holes and says with a rising inflection, "You don't *like* me."

While he fumbles for an answer, she falls asleep. It is the answer to a question he hadn't thought to ask: was she tired? Of course, just as she was hungry. A guilty grief expands his chest muscles and presses on the backs of his eyes. He gets up, covers her with a sheet. The nights are growing cool, August covers the sun's retreat. The cold moon. Scraped wallpaper. Pumice stone under a flash bulb. Footprints stay for a billion years, not a fleck of dust blows. The kitchen linoleum is cold on his feet. He switches off the garage light and spreads peanut butter on six Saltines, making three sandwiches. Since Janice left, he and Nelson shop for what they like, keep themselves stocked in salt and starch. He eats the crackers sitting in the living room, not in the silverthread chair but the old brown mossy one, that they've had since their marriage. He chews and stares at the uninhabited aquarium of the television screen. Ought to smash it, poison, he read somewhere the reason kids today are so crazy they were brought up on television, two minutes of this, two minutes of that. Cracker crumbs adhere to the hair of his chest. Six gray. Must be more than that. What did Janice do for Stavros she didn't do for him? Only so much you can do. Three holes, two hands. Is she happy? He hopes so. Poor mutt, he somehow squelched her potential. Let things bloom. The inside of a great lily. He wonders if Jesus will be waiting for Mom, a man in a nightgown at the end of a glossy chute. He hopes so. He remembers he must work tomorrow, then remembers he mustn't, it is Sunday. Sunday, that dog of a day. Ought to go to church but he can't get himself up to believe it. Ruth used to mock him and church, in those days he could get himself up for anything. Ruth and her chicken farm, wonders if she can stand it. Hopes so. He pushes himself up from the fat chair, brushes crumbs from his chest hair. Some fall and catch further down. Wonder why it was made so curly there, springy, they could stuff mattresses with it, if people would shave, like nuns and wigs. Upstairs, the body in his bed sinks his heart like a bar of silver. He had forgotten she was on his hands. Bad knuckles. The poor kid, she stirs and tries to make love to him again, gives him a furry-mouthed French kiss and falls asleep at it again. A day's work for a day's lodging. Puritan ethic. He masturbates, picturing Peggy Fosnacht. What will Nelson think?

Jill sleeps late. At quarter of ten Rabbit is rinsing his cereal bowl and coffee cup and Nelson is at the kitchen screen door, red-faced from pumping his bicycle. "Hey, Dad!"

"Shh."

"Why?"

"Your noise hurts my head."

"Did you get drunk last night?"

"What sort of talk is that? I never get drunk."

"Mrs. Fosnacht cried after you left."

"Probably because you and Billy are such brats."

"She said you were going to meet somebody in Brewer." She shouldn't be telling kids things like that. These divorced women, turn their sons into little husbands: cry, shit, and change Tampax right in front of them. "Some guy I work with at Verity. We listened to some colored woman play the piano and then I came home."

"We stayed up past twelve o'clock watching a wicked neat

movie about guys landing somewhere in boats that open up in front, some place like Norway—"

"Normandy."

"That's right. Were you there?"

"No, I was your age when it happened."

"You could see the machine gun bullets making the water splash up all in a row, it was a blast."

"Hey, try to keep your voice down."

"Why, Dad? Is Mommy back? Is she?"

"No. Have you had any breakfast?"

"Yeah, she gave us bacon and French toast. I learned how to make it, it's easy, you just smash some eggs and take bread and fry it, I'll make you some sometime."

"Thanks. Mom-mom Angstrom used to make it."

"I hate her cooking. Everything tastes greasy. Didn't you used to hate her cooking, Dad?"

"I liked it. It was the only cooking I knew."

"Billy Fosnacht says she's dying, is she?"

"She has a disease. But it's very slow. You've seen how she is. She may get better. They have new things for it all the time."

"I hope she does die, Dad."

"No you don't. Don't say that."

"Mrs. Fosnacht tells Billy you should say everything you feel."

"I'm sure she tells him a lot of crap."

"Why do you say crap? I think she's nice, once you get used to her eyes. Don't you like her, Dad? She thinks you don't."

"Peggy's O.K. What's on your schedule? When was the last time you went to Sunday school?"

The boy circles around to place himself in his father's view. "There's a reason I rushed home. Mr. Fosnacht is going to take Billy fishing on the river in a boat some guy he knows owns and Billy asked if I could come along and I said I'd have to ask you. O.K., Dad? I had to come home anyway to get a bathing suit and clean pants, that fucking mini-bike got these all greasy."

All around him, Rabbit hears language collapsing. He says weakly, "I didn't know there was fishing in the river."

"They've cleaned it up, Ollie says. At least above Brewer. He says they stock it with trout up around Lengel's Island."

Ollie, is it? "That's hours from here. You've never fished. Remember how bored you were with the ball game we took you to."

"That was a boring game, Dad. Other people were playing it. This is something you do yourself. Huh, Dad? O.K.? I got to get my bathing suit and I said I'd be back on the bicycle by ten-thirty." The kid is at the foot of the stairs: stop him.

Rabbit calls, "What am I going to do all day, if you go off?"

"You can go visit Mom-mom. She'd rather see just you anyway." The boy takes it that he has secured permission, and pounds upstairs. His scream from the landing freezes his father's stomach. Rabbit moves to the foot of the stairs to receive Nelson in his arms. But the boy, safe on the next-to-bottom step, halts there horrified. "Dad, something moved in your bed!"

"My bed?"

"I looked in and saw it!"

Rabbit offers, "Maybe it was just the air-conditioner fan lifting the sheets."

"*Dad.*" The child's pallor begins to recede as some flaw in the horror of this begins to dawn. "It had long hair, and I saw an arm. Aren't you going to call the police?"

"No, let's let the poor old police rest, it's Sunday. It's O.K., Nelson, I know who it is."

"You do?" The boy's eyes sink upon themselves defensively as his brain assembles what information he has about long-haired creatures in bed. He is trying to relate this contraption of half-facts to the figure of his father looming, a huge riddle in an undershirt, before him. Rabbit offers, "It's a girl who's run away from home and I somehow got stuck with her last night."

"Is she going to live here?"

"Not if you don't want me to," Jill's voice composedly calls from the stairs. She has come down wrapped in a sheet. Sleep has made her more substantial, her eyes are fresh wet grass now. She says to the boy, "I'm Jill. You're Nelson. Your father talks about you all the time."

She advances toward him in her sheet like a little Roman senator, her hair tucked under behind, her forehead shining. Nelson stands his ground. Rabbit is struck to see that they are nearly the same height. "Hi," the kid says. "He does?"

"Oh, yes," Jill goes on, showing her class, becoming no doubt her own mother, a woman pouring out polite talk in an unfamiliar home, flattering vases, curtains. "You are *very* much on his mind. You're very fortunate, to have such a protective father."

The kid looks over with parted lips. Christmas morning. He doesn't know what it is, but he wants to like it, before it's unwrapped.

Tucking her sheet about her tighter, Jill moves them into the kitchen, towing Nelson along on the thread of her voice. "You're lucky, you're going on a boat. I love boats. Back home we had a twenty-two-foot sloop."

"What's a sloop?"

"It's a sailboat with one mast."

"Some have more?"

"Of course. Schooners and yawls. A schooner has the big mast behind, a yawl has the big one up front. We had a yawl once but it was too much work, you needed another man really."

"You used to sail?"

"All summer until October. Not only that. In the spring

we all used to have to scrape it and caulk it and paint it. I liked that almost the best, we all used to work at it together, my parents and me and my brothers."

"How many brothers did you have?"

"Three. The middle one was about your age. Thirteen?"

He nods silently.

"He was my favorite. Is my favorite."

A bird outside hoarsely weeps in sudden agitation. Cat? The refrigerator purrs.

Nelson abruptly volunteers, "I had a sister once but she died."

"What was her name?"

His father has to answer for him. "Rebecca."

Still Jill doesn't look toward him, but concentrates on the boy. "May I eat breakfast, Nelson?"

"Sure."

"I don't want to take the last of your favorite breakfast cereal or anything."

"You won't. I'll show you where we keep them. Don't take the Rice Krispies, they're a thousand years old and taste like floor fluff. The Raisin Bran and Alphabits are O.K., we bought them this week at the Acme."

"Who does the shopping, you or your father?"

"Oh—we share. I meet him on the parking lot after work sometimes."

"When do you see your mother?"

"A lot of times. Weekends sometimes I stay over in Charlie Stavros's apartment. He has a real gun in his bureau. It's O.K., he has a license. I can't go over there this weekend because they've gone to the Shore."

"Where's the shore?"

Delight that she is so dumb creases the corners of Nelson's mouth. "In New Jersey. Everybody calls it just the Shore. We used to go to Wildwood sometimes but Dad hated the traffic too much."

"That's one thing I miss," Jill says, "the smell of the sea. Where I grew up, the town is on a peninsula, with sea on three sides."

"Hey, shall I make you some French toast? I just learned how."

Jealousy, perhaps, makes Rabbit impatient with this scene: his son in spite of his smallness bony and dominating and alert, Jill in her sheet looking like one of those cartoon figures, Justice or Liberty or Mourning Peace. He goes outside to bring in the Sunday *Triumph*, sits reading the funnies in the sunshine on the porchlet steps until the bugs get too bad, comes back into the living room and reads at random about the Egyptians, the Phillies, the Onassises. From the kitchen comes sizzling and giggling and whispering. He is in the Garden Section (*Scorn not the modest goldenrod, dock, and tansy that grow in carefree profusion in fields and roadside throughout these August days; carefully dried and arranged, they will form attractive bouquets to brighten the winter months around the corner*) when the kid comes in with milk on his mustache and, wide-eyed, pressingly, with a new kind of energy, asks, "Hey Dad, can she come along on the boat? I've called up Billy and he says his father won't mind, only we have to hurry up."

"Maybe *I* mind."

"*Dad*. Don't." And Harry reads his son's taut face to mean, *She can hear. She's all alone. We must be nice to her, we must be nice to the poor, the weak, the black. Love is here to stay.*

Monday, Rabbit is setting the *Vat* front page. WIDOW, SIXTY-SEVEN, RAPED AND ROBBED. *Three Black Youths Held.*

Police authorities revealed Saturday that they are holding for questioning two black minors and Wendell Phillips, 19, of 42B Plum Street, in connection with

the brutal assault of an unidentified sywsfyz kmlhs
the brutal assault of an unidentified elderly white woman late Thursday night.

The conscienceless crime, the latest in a series of similar incidents in the Third Ward, aroused residents of the neighborhood to organize a committee of protest which appeared before Friday's City Council session.

Nobody Safe

''Nobody's safe on the st

''Nobody's safe on the streets any more,'' said committee spokesman Bernard Vogel to VAT reporters.

''Nobody's safe not even in our own homes.''

Through the clatter Harry feels a tap on his shoulder and looks around. Pajasek, looking worried. "Angstrom, telephone."

"Who the hell?" He feels obliged to say this, as apology for being called at work, on Verity time.

"A woman," Pajasek says, not placated.

Who? Jill (last night her hair still damp from the boat ride tickled his belly as she managed to make him come) was in trouble. They had kidnapped her, the police, the blacks. Or Peggy Fosnacht was calling up to offer supper again. Or his mother had taken a turn for the worse and with her last heartbeats had dialled this number. He is not surprised she would want to speak to him instead of his father, he has never doubted she loves him most. The phone is in Pajasek's little office, three walls of frosted glass, on the desk with the parts catalogues (these old Mergenthalers are always breaking down) and the spindled dead copy. "Hello?"

"Hi, sweetie. Guess who."

"Janice. How was the Shore?"

"Crowded and muggy. How was it here?"

"Pretty good."

"So I hear. I hear you went out in a boat."

"Yeah, it was the kid's idea, he got me invited by Ollie. We went up the river as far as Lengel's Island. We didn't catch much, the state put some trout in but I guess the river's still too full of coal silt. My nose is so sunburned I can't touch it."

"I hear you had a lot of people in the boat."

"Nine or so. Ollie runs around with this musical crowd. We had a picnic up at the old camp meeting ground, near Stogey's Quarry, you know, where that witch lived so many years. Ollie's friends all got out guitars and played. It was nice."

"I hear *you* brought a guest too."

"Who'd you hear that from?"

"Peggy told me. Billy told her. He was all turned-on about it, he said Nelson brought a girl friend."

"Beats a mini-bike, huh?"

"Harry, I don't find this amusing. Where did you find this girl?"

"Uh, she's a go-go dancer in here at the shop. For the lunch hour. The union demands it."

"*Where*, Harry?"

Her weary dismissive insistence pleases him. She is growing in confidence, like a child at school. He confesses, "I sort of picked her up in a bar."

"Well. How long is she going to stay?"

"I haven't asked. These kids don't make plans the way we used to, they aren't so scared of starving. Hey, I got to get back to the machine. Pajasek doesn't like our being called here, by the way."

"I don't intend to make a practice of it. I called you at work because I didn't want Nelson to overhear. Harry, now are you listening to me?"

"Sure, to who else?"

"I want that girl out of my home. I don't want Nelson exposed to this sort of thing."

"What sort of thing? You mean the you and Stavros sort of thing?"

"Charlie is a mature man. He has lots of nieces and nephews so he's very understanding with Nelson. This girl sounds like a little animal out of her head with dope."

"That's how Billy described her?"

"After she talked to Billy Peggy called up Ollie for a better description."

"And that was his description. Gee. They got along famously at the time. She was better-looking than those two old crows Ollie had along, I tell ya."

"Harry, you're horrible. I consider this a very negative development. I suppose I have no control over how you dispose of your sexual needs, but I will not have my son corrupted."

"He's not corrupted, she's got him to help with the dishes, that's more than we could ever do. She's like a sister to him."

"And what is she to you, Harry?" When he is slow to answer, she repeats, her voice taunting, aching, like her mother's, "Harry, what is she to you? A little wifey?"

He thinks and tells her, "Come on back to the house, I'm sure she'll go."

Now Janice thinks. Finally she states: "If I come back to the house, it'll be to take Nelson away."

"Try it," he says, and hangs up.

He sits a minute in Pajasek's chair to give the phone a chance to ring. It does. He picks it up. "Yeah?"

Janice says, near tears, "Harry, I don't like to tell you this, but if you'd been adequate I would never have left. You drove me to it. I didn't know what I was missing but now that I have it I know. I refuse to accept all the blame, I really do."

"O.K. No blame assigned. Let's keep in touch."

"I want that girl away from my son."

"They're getting along fine, relax."

"I'll sue you. I'll take you to court."

"Fine. After the stunts you've been pulling, it'll at least give the judge a laugh."

"That's my house legally. At least half of it is."

"Tell me which my half is, and I'll try to keep Jill in it."

Janice hangs up. Maybe using Jill's name had hurt. He doesn't wait for another ring this time, and leaves the cubicle of frosted glass. The trembling in his hands, which feel frightened and inflated, merges with the clatter of the machines; as his body sweat is lost in the smell of oil and ink. He resettles himself at his machine and garbles three lines before he can put her phone call in the back of his mind. He supposes Stavros can get her legal advice. But, far from feeling Stavros as one of the enemy camp, he counts on him to keep this madwoman, his wife, under control. Through her body, they have become brothers.

Jill through the succession of nights adjusts Rabbit's body to hers. He cannot overcome his fear of using her body as a woman's—her cunt *stings*, is part of it; he never forces his way into her without remembering those razor blades—but she, beginning the damp-haired night after the boat ride, perfects ways with her fingers and mouth to bring him off. Small curdled puddles of his semen then appear on her skin, and though easily wiped away leave in his imagination a mark like an acid-burn on her shoulders, her throat, the small of her back; he has the vision of her entire slender fair flexible body being eventually covered with these invisible burns, like a napalmed child in the newspapers. And he, on his side, attempting with hands or mouth to reciprocate, is politely dissuaded, pushed away, reassured she has already come, serving him, or merely asked for the mute pressure of a thigh between hers and, after some few minutes during which he can detect no spasm of relief, thanked. The August nights are sticky and close; when they lie on their backs the ceiling of heavy air seems a foot above their faces. A car, loud on the soft tar and loose gravel, slides by. A mile away across the river a police siren bleats, a new sound, more frantic than the old rising and falling cry. Nelson turns on a light, makes water, flushes the toilet, turns out the light with a *snap* close to their ears. Had he been listening? Could he ever be watching? Jill's breath saws in her throat. She is asleep.

He finds her when he comes back from work sitting and reading, sitting and sewing, sitting and playing Monopoly with Nelson. Her books are spooky: yoga, psychiatry, zen, plucked from racks at the Acme. Except to shop, she reluctantly goes outdoors, even at night. It is not so much that the police of several states are looking for her—they are looking as well for thousands like her—as that the light of common day, and the sights and streets that have been the food of Rabbit's life, seem to strike her as poisonous and too powerful. They rarely watch television, since she leaves the room when they turn the set on, though when she's in the kitchen he sometimes sneaks himself a dose of six o'clock news. Instead, in the evenings, she and Nelson discuss God, beauty, meaning.

"Whatever men make," she says, "what they felt when they made it is there. If it was made to make money, it will smell of money. That's why these houses are so ugly, all the corners they cut are still in them. All the savings. That's why the cathedrals are so lovely; nobles and ladies in velvet and ermine dragged the stones up the ramps. Think of a painter. He stands in front of the canvas with a color on his brush. Whatever he feels when he makes the mark—if he's tired or bored or happy and proud—will be there. The same color, but we'll feel it. Like fingerprints. Like handwriting. Man is a mechanism for turning things into spirit and turning spirit into things."

"What's the point?" Nelson asks.

"The point is ecstasy," she says. "Energy. Anything that is good is in ecstasy. The world is what God made and it doesn't stink of money, it's never tired, too much or too little, it's always exactly full. The second after an earthquake, the stones are calm. Everywhere is *play*, even in thunder or an avalanche. Out on my father's boat I used to look up at the stars and there seemed to be invisible strings between them, tuned absolutely right, playing thousands of notes I could almost hear."

"Why can't we hear them?" Nelson asks.

"Because our egos make us deaf. Our egos make us blind. Whenever we think about ourselves, it's like putting a piece of dirt in our eye."

"There's that thing in the Bible."

"That's what He meant. Without our egos the universe would be absolutely clean, all the animals and rocks and spiders and moon-rocks and stars and grains of sand absolutely doing their thing, unself-consciously. The only consciousness would be God's. Think of it, Nelson, like this: matter is the mirror of spirit. But it's three-dimensional, like an enormous room, a ballroom. And inside it are these tiny *other* mirrors tilted this way and that and throwing the light back the wrong way. Because to the big face looking in, these little mirrors are just dark spots, where He can't see Himself."

Rabbit is entranced to hear her going on like this. Her voice, laconic and dry normally, moves through her sentences as through a memorized recitation, pitched low, an underground murmur. She and Nelson are sitting on the floor with the Monopoly board between them, houses and hotels and money, the game has been going on for days. Neither gives any sign of knowing he has come into the room and is towering above them. Rabbit asks, "Why doesn't He just do away with the spots then? I take it the spots are us."

Jill looks up, her face blank as a mirror in this instant. Remembering last night, he expects her to look burned around the mouth; it had been like filling a slippery narrow-mouthed pitcher from an uncontrollable faucet. She answers, "I'm not sure He's noticed us yet. The cosmos is so large and our portion of it so small. So small and recent."

"Maybe we'll do the erasing ourselves," Rabbit offers helpfully. He wants to help, to hold his end up. Never too late for education. With Janice and Old Man Springer you could never have this kind of conversation.

"There is that death-wish," Jill concedes.

Nelson will talk only to her. "Do you believe in life on other planets? I don't."

"Why Nelson, how ungenerous of you. Why not?"

"I don't know, it's silly to say—"

"Say it."

"I was thinking, if there was life on other planets, they would have killed our moon men when they stepped out of the space ship. But they didn't, so there isn't."

"Don't be dumb," Rabbit says. "The moon is right down our block. We're talking about life in systems billions of light years away."

"No, I think the moon was a good test," Jill says. "If nobody bothered to defend it, it proves how little God is content with. Miles and miles of gray dust."

Nelson says, "One guy at school I know says there's people on the moon but they're smaller than atoms, so even when they grind the rocks up they won't find them. He says they have whole cities and everything. We breathe them in through our nostrils and they make us think we see flying saucers. That's what this one guy says."

"I myself," Rabbit says, still offering, drawing upon an

old *Vat* feature article he set, "have some hopes for the inside of Jupiter. It's gas, you know, the surface we see. A couple of thousand miles down inside the skin there might be a mix of chemicals that could support a kind of life, something like fish."

"It's your Puritan fear of waste makes you want that," Jill tells him. "You think the other planets must be *used* for something, must be *farmed*. Why? Maybe the planets were put there just to teach men how to count up to seven."

"Why not just give us seven toes on each foot?"

"A kid at school," Nelson volunteers, "was born with an extra finger. The doctor cut it off but you can still see where it was."

"Also," Jill says, "astronomy. Without the planets the night sky would have been one rigid thing, and we would never have guessed at the third dimension."

"Pretty thoughtful of God," Rabbit says, "if we're just some specks in His mirror."

Jill waves his point away blithely. "He does everything," she says, "by the way. Not because it's what He has to do."

She can be blithe. After he told her once she ought to go outdoors more, she went out and sunbathed in just her bikini underpants, on a blanket beside the barbecue, in the view of a dozen other houses. When a neighbor called up to complain, Jill justified herself, "My tits are so small, I thought they'd think I was a boy." Then after Harry began giving her thirty dollars a week to shop with, she went and redeemed her Porsche from the police. Its garage parking fees had quadrupled the original fine. She gave her address as Vista Crescent and said she was staying the summer with her uncle. "It's a nuisance," she told Rabbit, "but Nelson ought to have a car around, at his age, it's too humiliating not to. Everybody in America has a car except you." So the Porsche came to live by their curb. Its white is dusty and the passenger-side front fender is scraped and one convertible top snap is broken. Nelson loves it so much he nearly cries, finding it there each morning. He washes it. He reads the manual and rotates the tires. That crystalline week before school begins, Jill takes him for drives out into the country, into the farmland and the mountains of Brewer County; she is teaching him how to drive.

Some days they return after Rabbit is home an hour from work. "Dad, it was a blast. We drove way up into this mountain that's a hawk refuge and Jill let me take the wheel on the twisty road coming down, all the way to the highway. Have you ever heard of shifting down?"

"I do it all the time."

"It's when you go into a lower gear instead of braking. It feels neat. Jill's Porsche has about five gears and you can really zoom around curves because the center of gravity is so low."

Rabbit asks Jill, "You sure you're handling this right? The kid might kill somebody. I don't want to be sued."

"He's very competent. And responsible. He must get that from you. I used to stay in the driver's seat and let him just steer but that's more dangerous than giving him control. The mountain was really quite deserted."

"Except for hawks, Dad. There must be a billion. They sit on all these pine trees waiting for the guys to put out whole carcasses of cows and things. It's really grungy."

"Well," Rabbit says, "hawks got to live too."

"That's what I keep telling him," Jill says. "God is in the tiger as well as in the lamb."

"Yeah. God really likes to chew himself up."

"You know what you are?" Jill asks, her eyes the green of a meadow, her hair a finespun amber tangle dissolving into windowlight; a captured idea is fluttering in her head. "You are cynical."

"Just middle-aged. Ideas used to grab me too. It's not that you get better ideas, the old ones just get tired. After a while you see that even dollars and cents are just an idea. Finally the only thing that matters is putting some turds in the toilet bowl once a day. They stay real, somehow. Somebody came up to me and said, 'I'm God,' I'd say, 'Show me your badge.' "

Jill dances forward, on fire with some fun and wickedness the day has left in her, and gives him a hug that dances off, a butterfly hug. "I think you're beautiful. Nelson and I both think so. We often talk about it."

"You do? That's the only thing you can think of to do, talk about me?" He means to be funny, to keep her mood alive, but her face stops, hovers a second; and Nelson's tells him he has struck something. What they do. In that little car. Well, they don't need much space, much contact: young bodies. The kid's faint mustache, black hairs; her amber mane, the softest flame. Bodies not sodden yet like his. At that keen age the merest touch. Their brother-sister shyness, touching hands in the flicker of wet glass at the sink. If she'd offer to give hairy old heavy him a blow job the first night, what wouldn't she do? Bring the kid along, somebody has to. Why not? Chief question facing these troubled times. Why not.

Though he doesn't pursue this guilt he has startled from her, that night he does make her take him squarely, socks it into her, though she offers her mouth and her cunt is so tight it sears. She is frightened when he doesn't lose his hardness; he makes her sit up on him and pulls her easily torn satin hips down, the pelvis bones starved, and she sucks in breath sharply and out of pained astonishment pitched like delight utters, "You're wombing me!" He tried to picture it. A rosy-black floor in her somewhere, never knows where he is, in among kidneys, intestines, liver. His fair silver girl with flesh-colored hair and cloudy innards floats upon him, stings him, sucks him up like a cloud, falls, forgives him. Love of her, surprising him, coats him with distaste and confusion, so that he quickly sleeps, only his first dreams jostled when she gets from bed to go wash, check on Nelson, talk to God, take a pill, whatever else she needs to do to fill the wound where his seared cock was. How sad, how strange. We make companions out of air and hurt them, so they will defy us, completing creation.

Harry's father sidles up to him at the coffee break. "How's every little thing, Harry?"

"Not bad."

"I hate like hell to nag like this, you're a grown man with your own miseries, I know that, but I'd be appreciative as hell if you'd come over some evenings and talk to your mother. She hears all sorts of malicious folderol about you and Janice now, and it would help settle her down if you could put her straight. We're no moralists, Harry, you know that; your mother and I tried to live by our own lights and to raise the two children God was good enough to give us by those same lights, but I know damn well it's a different world now, so we're no moralists, me and Mary."

"How is her health, generally?"

"Well, that's another of these problematical things, Harry. They've gone ahead and put her on this new miracle drug, they have some name for it I can never remember, L-dopa, that's right, L-dopa, it's still in the experimental stage I guess, but there's no doubt in a lot of cases it works wonders. Trouble is, also it has these side effects they don't know too much about, depression in your mother's case, some nausea and lack of appetite; and nightmares, Harry, nightmares that wake her up and she wakes me up so I can hear her heart beating, beating like a tom-tom. I never heard that before, Harry, another person's heart in the room as clear as footsteps, but that's what these L-dopa dreams do for her. But there's no doubt, her talk comes easier, and her hands don't shake that way they have so much. It's hard to know what's right, Harry. Sometimes you think, Let Nature take its course, but then you wonder, What's Nature and what isn't? Another side effect"—he draws closer, glancing around and then glancing down as his coffee slops in the paper cup and burns his fingers—"I shouldn't mention it but it tickles me, your mother says this new stuff she's taking, whatever you call it, makes her feel, how shall I say?"—he glances around again, then confides to his son—"lovey-dovey. Here she is, just turned sixty-five, lying in bed half the day, and gets these impulses so bad she says she can hardly stand it, she says she won't watch television, the commercials make it worse. She says she has to laugh at herself. Now isn't that a helluva thing? A good woman like that. I'm sorry to talk your ear off, I live alone with it too much, I suppose, what with Mim on the other side of the country. Christ knows it isn't as if you don't have your problems too."

"I don't have any problems," Rabbit tells him. "Right now I'm just holding my breath to when the kid gets back into school. His state of mind's pretty well stabilized, I'd say. One of the reasons, you know, I don't make it over to Mt. Judge as often as I should, Mom was pretty rough on Nelson when he was little and the kid is still scared of her. On the other hand I don't like to leave him alone in the house, with all these robberies and assaults all over the county, they come out into the suburbs and steal anything they can get their hands on. I was just setting an item, some woman in Perley, they stole her vacuum cleaner and a hundred feet of garden hose while she was upstairs going to the bathroom."

"It's these God, damn, blacks, is what it is." Earl Angstrom lowers his voice so it turns husky, though Buchanan and Farnsworth always take their coffee break outside in the alley, with Boonie and the other drinkers. "I've always called 'em black and they call themselves blacks now and that suits me fine. They can't do a white man's job, except for a few, and take even Buck, he's never made head of makeup though he's been here the longest; so they have to rob and kill, the ones that can't be pimps and prizefighters. They can't cut the mustard and never could. This country should have taken whosever advice it was, George Washington if memory serves, one of the founding fathers, and shipped 'em all back to Africa when we had a chance. Now, Africa wouldn't take 'em. Booze and Cadillacs and white pussy, if you'll pardon my saying so, have spoiled 'em rotten. They're the garbage of the world, Harry. American Negroes are the lowest of the low."

"O.K., O.K." To see his father passionate about anything disagrees with Rabbit. He shifts to the most sobering subject they have between them: "Does she mention me much? Mom."

The old man licks spittle from his lips, sighs, slumps confidingly lower, glancing down at the cooled scummed coffee in his hands. "All the time, Harry, every minute of the day. They tell her things about you and she raves against the Springers; oh, how she carries on about that family, especially the women of it. Apparently, the Mrs. is saying you've taken up with a hippie teenager, that's what drove Janice out of the house in the first place."

"No, Janice went first. I keep inviting her back."

"Well, whatever the actualities of the case are, I know you're trying to do the right thing. I'm no moralist, Harry, I know you young people nowadays have more tensions and psychological pressures than a man my age could tolerate. If I'd of had the atomic bomb and these rich-kid revolutionaries to worry about, I'd no doubt just have put a shotgun to my head and let the world roll on without me."

"I'll try to get over. I ought to talk to her," Rabbit says. He looks past his father's shoulder to where the yellow-faced wall clock jumps to within a minute of 11:10, the end of the coffee break. He knows that in all this rolling-on world his mother is the only person who knows him. He remembers from the night we touched the moon the nudge delivered out of her dying, but doesn't want to open himself to her until he understands what is happening inside him enough to protect it. She has something happening to her, death and L-dopa, and he has something happening to him, Jill. The girl has been living with them three weeks and is learning to keep house and to give him a wry silent look, saying *I know you*, when he offers to argue about Communism or kids today or any of the other sore spots where he feels rot beginning and black madness creeping in. A little wry green look that began the night he hurt her upwards and touched her womb.

His father is more with him than he suspects, for the old man draws still closer and says, "One thing it's been on my mind to say, Harry, forgive me talking out of turn, but I hope you're taking all the precautions, knock up one of these minors, the law takes a very dim view. Also, they say they're dirty as weasels and giving everybody the clap." Absurdly, as the clock ticks the last minute and the end-of-break bell rasps, the old man claps.

In his harsh white after-work shirt he opens the front door of the apple-green house and hears guitar music from above. Guitar chords slowly plucked, and two high small voices moving through a melody. He is drawn upstairs. In Nelson's room, the two are sitting on the bed, Jill up by the pillows in a yoga position that displays the crotch of her black lace underpants. A guitar is cradled across her thighs. Rabbit has never seen the guitar before; it looks new. The pale wood shines like a woman oiled after a bath. Nelson sits beside Jill in jockey shorts and T-shirt, craning his neck to read from the sheet of music on the bedspread by her ankles. The boy's legs, dangling to the floor, look suddenly sinewy, long, beginning to be shaded with Janice's dark hair, and Rabbit notices that the old posters of Brooks Robinson and Orlando Cepeda and Steve McQueen on a motorcycle have been removed from the boy's walls. Paint has flaked where the Scotch tape was. They are singing, ". . . must a man wa-alk down"; the delicate thread breaks when he enters, though they must have heard his footsteps on the stairs as warning. The kid's being in his underclothes is O.K.: far from dirty as a weasel, Jill has gotten Nelson to take a shower once a day, before his father's homecoming, which she has made, perhaps because her own father came home to Stonington only on Fridays, a ceremony.

"Hey, Dad," Nelson says, "this is neat. We're singing harmony."

"Where did you get the guitar?"

"We hustled."

Jill nudges the boy with a bare foot, but not quick enough to halt the remark.

Rabbit asks him, "How do you hustle?"

"We stood on streetcorners in Brewer, mostly at Weiser and Seventh, but then we moved over to Cameron when a pig car slowed down to look us over. It was a gas, Dad. Jill would stop these people and tell 'em I was her brother, our mother was dying of cancer and our father had lit out, and we had a baby brother at home. Sometimes she said a baby sister. Some of the people said we should apply to welfare, but enough gave us a dollar or so so finally we had the twenty dollars Ollie promised was all he'd charge us for a forty-four dollar guitar. And he threw in the music free after Jill talked to him in the back room."

"Wasn't that nice of Ollie?"

"Harry, it really was. Don't look like that."

He says to Nelson, "I wonder what they talked about."

"Dad, there was nothing dishonest about it, these people we stopped felt better afterwards, for having got us off their conscience. Anyway, Dad, in a society where power was all to the people money wouldn't exist anyway, you'd just be given what you need."

"Well hell, that's the way your life is now."

"Yeah, but I have to beg for everything, don't I? And I never did get a mini-bike."

"Nelson, get some Goddam clothes on and stay in your room. I want to talk to Jill a second."

"If you hurt her, I'll kill you."

"If you don't shut up, I'll make you live with Mommy and Charlie Stavros."

In their bedroom, Rabbit carefully closes the door and in a soft shaking voice tells Jill, "You're turning my kid into a beggar and a whore just like yourself," and, after waiting a second for her to enter a rebuttal, slaps her thin disdainful face with its prim lips and its green eyes drenched so dark in defiance their shade is as of tree leaves, a shuffling concealing multitude, a microscopic forest he wants to bomb. His slap feels like slapping plastic; stings his fingers, does no good. He slaps her again, gathers the dry flesh of her hair into his hand to hold her face steady, feels cold fury when she buckles and tries to slither away but, after a fist to the side of her neck, lets her drop onto the bed.

Still shielding her face, Jill hisses up at him, strangely hisses out of her little inturned teeth, until her first words come. They are calm and superior. "You know why you did that, you just wanted to hurt me, that's why. You just wanted to have that kick. You don't give a shit about me and Nelson hustling. What do you care about who begs and who doesn't, who steals and who doesn't?"

A blankness in him answers when she asks; but she goes on. "What have the pig laws ever done for you except screw you into a greasy job and turn you into such a gutless creep you can't even keep your idiotic wife?"

He takes her wrist. It is fragile. Chalk. He wants to break it, to feel it snap; he wants to hold her absolutely quiet in his arms for the months while it will heal. "Listen. I earn my money one fucking dollar at a time and you're living on it and if you want to go back bumming off your nigger friends, go. Get out. Leave me and my kid alone."

"You creep," she says, "you baby-killing creep."

"Put another record on," he says. "You sick bitch. You rich kids playing at life make me sick, throwing rocks at the poor dumb cops protecting your daddy's loot. You're just playing, baby. You think you're playing a great game of happy cunt but let me tell you something. My poor dumb mutt of a wife throws a better piece of ass backwards than you can manage frontwards."

"Backwards is right, she couldn't stand facing you."

He squeezes her chalk wrist tighter, telling her, "You have no juice, baby. You're all sucked out and you're just eighteen. You've tried everything and you're not scared of nothing and you wonder why it's all so dead. You've had it handed to you, sweet baby, that's why it's so dead. Fucking Christ you think you're going to make the world over you don't have a fucking clue what makes people run. Fear. That's what makes us poor bastards run. You don't know what fear is, do you, poor baby? That's why you're so dead." He squeezes her wrist until he can picture the linked curved bones in it bending ghostly as in an X ray; and her eyes widen a fraction, a hair-space of alarm he can see only because he is putting it there.

She tugs her wrist free and rubs it, not lowering her eyes from his. "People've run on fear long enough," Jill says. "Let's try love for a change."

"Then you better find yourself another universe. The moon is cold, baby. Cold and ugly. If you don't want it, the Commies do. They're not so fucking proud."

"What's that noise?"

It is Nelson crying, outside the door, afraid to come in. It had been the same way with him and Janice, their fights: just when they were getting something out of them, the kid would beg them to stop. Maybe he imagined that Becky had been killed in just such a quarrel, that this one would kill him. Rabbit lets him in and explains, "We were talking politics."

Nelson squeezes out in the spaces between his sobs. "Daddy, why do you disagree with everybody?"

"Because I love my country and can't stand to have it knocked."

"If you loved it you'd want it better," Jill says.

"If it was better *I'd* have to be better," he says seriously, and they all laugh, he last.

Thus, through lame laughter—she still rubs her wrists, the hand he hit her with begins to hurt—they seek to reconstitute their family. For supper Jill cooks a filet of sole, lemony, light, simmered in sunshine, skin flaky brown; Nelson gets a hamburger with wheatgerm sprinkled on it to remind him of a Nutburger. Wheatgerm, zucchini, water chestnuts, celery salt, Familia: these are some of the exotic items Jill's shopping brings into the house. Her cooking tastes to him of things he never had: candlelight, saltwater, health fads, wealth, class. Jill's family had a servant, and it takes her some nights to understand that dirtied dishes do not clear and clean themselves by magic, but have to be carried and washed. Rabbit, still, Saturday mornings, is the one to vacuum the rooms, to bundle his shirts and the sheets for the laundry, to sort out Nelson's socks and underwear for the washer in the basement. He can see, what these children cannot, dust accumulate, deterioration advance, chaos seep in, time conquer. But for her cooking he is willing to be her servant, part-time. Her cooking has renewed his taste for life. They have wine now with supper, a California white in a half-gallon jug. And always a salad: salad in Brewer County cuisine tends to be a brother of sauerkraut, fat with creamy dressing, but Jill's hands toss lettuce in a glowing film invisible as health. Where Janice would for dessert offer some doughy goodie from the Half-A-Loaf, Jill concocts designs of fruit. And her coffee is black nectar compared to the watery tar Janice used to serve. Contentment makes Harry motionless; he watches the dishes be skimmed from the table, and resettles expansively in the living room. When the dishwashing machine is fed and chugging contentedly, Jill comes into the living room, sits on the tacky carpet, and plays the guitar. What does she play? "Farewell, Angelina, the sky is on fire," and a few others she can get through a stanza of. She has maybe six chords. Her fingers on the frets often tighten on strands of her hanging hair; it must hurt. Her voice is a thin instrument that quickly cracks. "All my tri-als, Lord, soon be o-over," she sings, quitting, looking up for applause.

Nelson applauds. Small hands.

"Great," Rabbit tells her and, mellow on wine, goes on, in apology for his life, "no kidding, I once took that inner light trip and all I did was bruise my surroundings. Revolution, or whatever, is just a way of saying a mess is fun. Well, it *is* fun, for a while, as long as somebody else has laid in the supplies. A mess is a luxury, is all I mean."

Jill has been strumming for him, between sentences, part helping him along, part poking fun. He turns on her. "Now you tell us something. You tell us the story of your life."

"I've had no life," she says, and strums. "No man's daughter, and no man's wife."

"Tell us a story," Nelson begs. From the way she laughs, showing her spaced gray teeth and letting her thin cheeks go dimply, they see she will comply.

"This is the story of Jill and her lover who was ill," she announces, and releases a chord. It's as if, Rabbit thinks, studying the woman-shape of the guitar, the notes are in there already, waiting to fly from the dovecote of that round hole. "Now Jill," Jill goes on, "was a comely lass, raised in the bosom of the middle class. Her dad and mother each owned a car, and on the hood of one was a Mercedes star. I don't know how much longer I can go on rhyming." She strums quizzically.

"Don't try it," Rabbit advises.

"Her upbringing"—emphasis on the "ging"—"was orthodox enough—sailing and dancing classes and *français* and all that stuff."

"Keep rhyming, Jill," Nelson begs.

"Menstruation set in at age fourteen, but even with her braces off Jill was no queen. Her knowledge of boys was con*fined* to boys who played tennis and whose parents with her parents *dined*. Which suited her perfectly *well*, since having observed her parents drinking and chatting and getting and spending she was in no great hurry to become old and fat and *swell*. Ooh, that was a stretch."

"Don't rhyme on my account," Rabbit says. "I'm getting a beer, anybody else want one?"

Nelson calls, "I'll share yours, Dad."

"Get your own. I'll get it."

Jill strums to reclaim their attention. "Well, to make a boring story short, one summer"—she searches ahead for a rhyme, then adds, "after her daddy died."

"Uh-oh," Rabbit says, returning with two beers.

"She met a boy who became her psycho-physical guide."

Rabbit pulls his tab and tries to hush the *pff*.

"His name was Freddy—"

He sees there is nothing to do but yank it, which he does so quickly the beer foams through the keyhole.

"And the nicest thing about him was that *she* was ready." Strum. "He had nice brown shoulders from being a lifeguard, and his bathing suit held something sometimes soft and sometimes hard. He came from far away, from romantic Rhode Island across Narragansett Bay."

"Hey," Rabbit *olés*.

"The only bad thing was, inside, the nice brown lifeguard had already died. Inside there was an old man with a dreadful need, for pot and hash and LSD and speed." Now her strumming takes a different rhythm, breaking into the middle on the offbeat.

"He was a born loser, though his teeth were pearly white, and he fucked sweet virgin Jill throughout one sandy night. She fell for him"—*strum*—"and got deep into his bag of being stoned; she freaked out nearly every time the bastard telephoned. She went from popping pills to dropping acid, then" —she halts and leans forward staring at Nelson so hard the boy softly cries, "Yes?"

"He lovingly suggested shooting heroin."

Nelson looks as if he will cry: the way his eyes sink in and his chin develops another bump. He looks, Rabbit thinks, like a sulky girl. He can't see much of himself in the boy, beyond the small straight nose.

The music runs on.

"Poor Jill got scared; the other kids at school would tell her not to be a self-destructive fool. Her mother, still in mourning, was being kept bus-*ee*, by a divorced tax lawyer from nearby Wester-lee. Bad Freddy was promising her Heaven above, when all Jill wanted was his mundane love. She wanted the feel of his prick, not the prick of the needle; but Freddy would beg her, and stroke her, and sweet-talk and wheedle."

And Rabbit begins to wonder if she has done this before, that rhyme was so slick. What *has*n't this kid done before?

"She was afraid to *die*"—strum, strum, pale orange hair thrashing—"he asked her *why*. He said the world was rotten and insane; she said she had no cause to complain. He said racism was rampant, hold out your arm; she said no white man but him had ever done her any harm. He said the first shot will just be beneath the skin; she said okay, lover, put that shit right in." Strum strum *strum*. Face lifted toward them, she is a banshee, totally bled. She speaks the next line. "It was hell."

St-r-r-um. "He kept holding her head and patting her ass, and saying relax, he'd been to life-saving class. He asked her, hadn't he shown her the face of God, she said, Yes; thank you, but she would have been happy to settle for less. She saw that her lover with his brown skin and white teeth was death; she feared him and loved him with every frightened breath. So what did Jill do?"

Silence hangs on the upbeat.

Nelson blurts, "What?"

Jill smiles. "She ran to the Stonington savings bank and generously withdrew. She hopped inside her Porsche and drove away, and that is how come she is living with you two creeps today."

Both father and son applaud. Jill drinks deep of the beer as a reward to herself. In their bedroom, she is still in the mood, artistic elation, to be rewarded. Rabbit says to her, "Great song. But you know what I didn't like about it?"

"What?"

"Nostalgia. You miss it. Getting stoned with Freddy."

"At least," she says, "I wasn't just playing, what did you call it, happy cunt?"

"Sorry I blew my stack."

"Still want me to go?"

Rabbit, having sensed this would come, hangs up his pants, his shirt, puts his underclothes in the hamper. The dress she has dropped on the floor he drapes on a hook in her half of the closet, her dirty panties he puts in the hamper. "No. Stay."

"Beg me."

He turns, a big tired man, slack-muscled, who has to rise and set type in eight hours. "I beg you to stay."

"Take back those slaps."

"How can I?"

"Kiss my feet."

He kneels to comply. Annoyed at such ready compliance,

which implies pleasure, she stiffens her feet and kicks so her toenails stab his cheek, dangerously near his eyes. He pins her ankles to continue his kissing. Slightly doughy, matronly ankles. Green veins on her insteps. Nice remembered locker room taste. Cheap vanilla.

"Your tongue between my toes," she says; her voice cracks timidly, issuing the command. When again he complies, she edges forward on the bed and spreads her legs. "Now here." She knows he enjoys this, but asks it anyway, to see what she can make of him, this strange man. His head, with its stubborn old-fashioned short haircut—the enemy's uniform, athlete and soldier; bone above the ears, dingy blond silk thinning on top—feels large as a boulder between her thighs. The excited warmth of singing her song, ebbing, unites with the distant warmth of his tongue lapping. A spark kindles, a green sprig lengthens in the desert she has willed within her. "A little higher," Jill says, then, her voice quite softened and crumbling, "Faster."

One day after work as he and his father are walking down Pine Street toward their before-bus drink at the Phoenix Bar, a dapper thickset man with sideburns and hornrims intercepts them. "Hey. Angstrom." Both father and son halt, blink. In the tunnel of sunshine, after their day of work, they generally feel hidden.

Harry recognizes Stavros. He is wearing a suit of little slate-gray checks on a ground of greenish threads. He looks a touch thinner, more brittle, his composure more of an effort. Maybe he is just tense for this encounter. Harry says, "Dad, I'd like you to meet a friend of mine. Charlie Stavros, Earl Angstrom."

"Pleased to meet you, Earl."

The old man ignores the extended square hand and speaks to Harry. "Not the same Stavros that's ruined my daughter-in-law?"

Stavros tries for a quick sale. "Ruined. That's pretty strong. Humored is more how I'd put it." His try for a smile ignored, Stavros turns to Harry. "Can we talk a minute? Maybe have a drink down at the corner. Sorry to butt in like this, Mr. Angstrom."

"Harry, what is your preference? You want to be left alone with this scum or shall we brush him off?"

"Come on, Dad, what's the point?"

"You young people may have your own ways of working things out, but I'm too old to change. I'll get on the next bus. Don't let yourself be talked into anything. This son of a bitch looks slick."

"Give my love to Mom. I'll try to get over this weekend."

"If you can, you can. She keeps dreaming about you and Mim."

"Yeah, some time could you give me Mim's address?"

"She doesn't have an address, just care of some agent in Los Angeles, that's the way they do it now. You were thinking of writing her?"

"Maybe send her a postcard. See you tomorrow."

"Terrible dreams," the old man says, and slopes to the curb to wait for the 16A bus, cheated of his beer, the thin disappointed back of his neck reminding Harry of Nelson.

Inside the Phoenix it is dark and cold; Rabbit feels a sneeze gathering between his eyes. Stavros leads the way to a booth and folds his hands on the Formica tabletop. Hairy hands that have held her breasts. Harry asks, "How is she?"

"She? Oh hell, in fine form."

Rabbit wonders if this means what it seems. The tip of his tongue freezes on his palate, unable to think of a delicate way to probe. He says, "They don't have a waitress in the afternoon. I'll get a daiquiri for myself, what for you?"

"Just soda water. Lots of ice."

"No hootch?"

"Never touch it." Stavros clears his throat, smooths back the hair above his sideburns with a flat hand that is, nevertheless, slightly trembling. He explains, "The medicos tell me it's a no-no."

Coming back with their drinks, Rabbit asks, "You sick?"

Stavros says, "Nothing new, the same old ticker. Janice must have told you, heart murmur since I was a kid."

What does this guy think, he and Janice sat around discussing him like he was their favorite child? He does remember Janice crying out he couldn't marry, expecting him, Harry, her husband, to sympathize. Oddly, he had. "She mentioned something."

"Rheumatic fever. Thank God they've got those things licked now, before I was twelve I caught every bug they made." Stavros shrugs. "They tell me I can live to be a hundred, if I take care of the physical plant. You know," he says, "these doctors. There's still a lot they don't know."

"I know. They're putting my mother through the wringer right now."

"Jesus, you ought to hear Janice go on about your mother."

"Not so enthusiastic, huh?"

"Not so at all. She needs some gripe, though, to keep herself justified. She's all torn up about the kid."

"She left him with me and there he stays."

"In court, you know, you'd lose him."

"We'd see."

Stavros makes a small chopping motion around his glass full of soda bubbles (poor Peggy Fosnacht; Rabbit should call her) to indicate a new angle in their conversation. "Hell," he says, "I can't take him in. I don't have the room. As it is now, I have to send Janice out to the movies or over to her parents when my family visits. You know I just don't have a mother,

I have a *grand*mother. She's ninety-three, speaking of living forever."

Rabbit tries to imagine Stavros's room, which Janice described as full of tinted photographs, and instead imagines Janice nude, tinted, Playmate of the month, posed on a nappy Greek sofa, nappy mustard color, with scrolling arms, her body twisted at the hips just enough to hide her gorgeous big black bush. The crease of the centerfold cuts across her navel and one hand dangles a rose. The vision makes Rabbit for the first time hostile. He asks Stavros, "How do you see this all coming out?"

"That's what I wanted to ask *you*."

Rabbit asks, "She going sour on you?"

"No, Jesus, *au contraire*. She's balling me ragged."

Rabbit sips, swallows that, probes for another nerve. "She miss the kid?"

"Nelson, he comes over to the lot some days and she sees him weekends anyhow, I don't know as she saw much more of him before. I don't know as how motherhood is Janice's best bag anyway. What she doesn't much care for is the idea of her baby just out of diapers shacking up with this hippie."

"She's not a hippie, especially; unless everybody that age is. And I'm the one shacking up."

"How is she at it?"

"She's balling me ragged," Rabbit tells him. He is beginning to get Stavros's measure. At first, meeting him on the street so suddenly, he felt toward him like a friend, met through Janice's body. Then first coming into the Phoenix he felt him as a sick man, a man holding himself together against odds. Now he sees him as a type he never liked, the competitor. The type that sits on the bench doing the loudmouth bit until the coach sends them in with a play or with orders to foul. Brainy cute close-set little playmakers. O.K. So Rabbit is competing again. What he has to do is hang loose and let Stavros make the move.

Stavros hunches his square shoulders infinitesimally, has some soda, and asks, "What do you see yourself doing with this hippie?"

"She has a name. Jill."

"What's Jill's big picture, do you know?"

"No. She has a dead father and a mother she doesn't like, I guess she'll go back to Connecticut when her luck runs thin."

"Aren't you being, so to speak, her luck?"

"I'm part of her picture right now, yeah."

"And she of yours. You know, your living with this girl gives Janice an open-and-shut divorce case."

"You don't scare me, somehow."

"Do I understand that you've assured Janice that all she has to do is come back and the girl will go?"

Rabbit begins to feel it, where Stavros is pressing for the opening. The tickle above his nose is beginning up again. "No," he says, praying not to sneeze, "you don't understand that." He sneezes. Six faces at the bar look around; the little Schlitz spinner seems to hesitate. They are giving away refrigerators and ski weekends in Chile on the TV.

"You don't want Janice back now?"

"I don't know."

"You would like a divorce so you can keep living the good life? Or marry the girl, maybe, even? Jill. She'll break your balls, Sport."

"You think too fast. I'm just living day by day, trying to forget my sorrow. I've been left, don't forget. Some slick-talking kinky-haired peacenik-type Japanese-car salesman lured her away, I forget the son-of-a-bitch's name."

"That isn't exactly the way it was. She came pounding on my door."

"You let her in."

Stavros looks surprised. "What else? She had put herself

out on a limb. Where could she go? My taking her in made the least trouble for everybody."

"And now it's trouble?"

Stavros fiddles his fingertips as if cards are in them; if he loses this trick, can he take the rest? "Her staying on with me gives her expectations we can't fulfill. Marriage isn't my thing, sorry. For anybody."

"Don't try to be polite. So now you've tried her in all positions and want to ship her back. Poor old Jan. So dumb."

"I don't find her dumb. I find her—unsure of herself. She wants what every normal chick wants. To be Helen of Troy. There've been hours when I gave her some of that. I can't keep giving it to her. It doesn't hold up." He becomes angry; his square brow darkens. "What do *you* want? You're sitting there twitching your whiskers watching me squirm, so how about it? If I kick her out, will you pick her up?"

"Kick her out and see. She can always go live with her parents."

"Her mother drives her crazy."

"That's what mothers are for." Rabbit pictures his. There is a depth of suffering, of toothsore reality, beneath this finagle, that makes it silly, worse than silly, evil. His bladder gets a touch of that guilty sweetness it had when as a child he was running to school late, beside the slime-rimmed gutter water that ran down from the ice plant. He tries to explain. "Listen, Stavros. You're the one in the wrong. You're the one screwing another man's wife. If you want to pull out, pull out. Don't try to commit me to one of your fucking coalition governments."

"Back to that," Stavros says.

"Right. You intervened, not me."

"I didn't intervene, I performed a rescue."

"That's what all us hawks say." He is eager to argue about Vietnam, but Stavros keeps to the less passionate subject.

"She was desperate, fella. Christ, hadn't you taken her to bed in ten years?"

"I resent that."

"Go ahead. Resent it."

"She was no worse off than a million wives." A billion cunts, how many wives? Five hundred million? "We had relations. They didn't seem so bad to me."

"All I'm saying is, I didn't cook this up, it was delivered to me hot. I didn't have to talk her into anything, she was pushing all the way. I was the first chance she had. If I'd been a one-legged milkman, I would have done."

"You're too modest."

Stavros shakes his head. "She's some tiger."

"Stop it, you're giving me a hard-on."

Stavros studies him squarely. "You're a funny guy."

"Tell me what it is you don't like about her now."

His merely interested tone relaxes Stavros's shoulders an inch. The man measures off a little cage in front of his lapels. "It's just too—confining. It's weight I don't need. I got to keep light, on an even keel. Between you and me, I'm not going to live forever."

"You just told me you might."

"The odds are not."

"You know, you're just like me, the way I used to be. Everybody now is like the way I used to be."

"She's had her kicks for the summer, let her come back. Tell the hippie to move on, that's what she wants to hear anyway."

Rabbit sips the dregs of his second daiquiri. It is delicious, to let this silence lengthen, widen: he will not promise to take Janice back. The game is on ice. He says at last, because continued silence would have been unbearably rude, "Just don't know. Sorry to be so vague."

Stavros takes it up quickly. "She on anything?"

"Who?"

"This nympho of yours."

"On something?"

"You know. Pills. Acid. She can't be on horse or you wouldn't have any furniture left."

"Jill? No, she's kicked that stuff."

"Don't you believe it. They never do. These flower babies, dope is their milk."

"She's fanatic against. She's been there and back. Not that this is any of your business." Rabbit doesn't like the way the game has started to slide; there is a hole he is trying to plug and can't.

"How about Nelson? Is he acting different?"

"He's growing up." The answer sounds evasive. Stavros brushes it aside.

"Drowsy? Nervous? Taking naps at odd times? What do they do all day while you're playing hunt and peck? They must do *some*thing, fella."

"She teaches him how to be polite to scum. Fella. Let me pay for your bilge water."

"So what have I learned?"

"I hope nothing."

But Stavros has sneaked in for that lay-up and the game is in overtime. Rabbit hurries to get home, to see Nelson and Jill, to sniff their breaths, look at their pupils, whatever. He has left his lamb with a viper. But outside the Phoenix, in the hazed sunshine held at its September tilt, traffic is snarled, and the buses are caught along with everything else. A movie is being made. Rabbit remembers it mentioned in the *Vat* (BREWER MIDDLE AMERICA? *Gotham Filmmakers Think So*) that Brewer had been chosen for a location by some new independent outfit; none of the stars' names meant anything to him, he forgot the details. Here they are. An arc of cars and trucks mounted with lights extends halfway into Weiser Street, and a crowd of locals with rolled-up shirtsleeves and bag-lugging grannies and Negro delinquents straggles into the rest of the street to get a closer look, cutting down traffic to one creeping lane. The cops that should be unsnarling the tangle are ringing the show, protecting the moviemakers. So tall, Rabbit gets a glimpse from a curb. One of the boarded-up stores near the old Baghdad that used to show M-G-M but now is given over to skin flicks (*Sepia Follies*, *Honeymoon in Swapland*) has been done up as a restaurant front; a tall salmon-faced man with taffy hair and a little bronze-haired trick emerge from this pretend-restaurant arm in arm and there is some incident involving a passerby, another painted actor who emerges from the crowd of dusty real people watching, a bumping-into, followed by laughter on the part of the first man and the woman and a slow resuming look that will probably signal when the film is all cut and projected that they are going to fuck. They do this several times. Between times everybody waits, wisecracks, adjusts lights and wires. The girl, from Rabbit's distance, is impossibly precise: her eyes flash, her hair hurls reflections like a helmet. Even her dress scintillates. When someone, a director or electrician, stands near her, he looks dim. And it makes Rabbit feel dim, dim and guilty, to see how the spotlights carve from the sunlight a yet brighter day, a lurid pastel island of heightened reality around which the rest of us—technicians, policemen, the straggling fascinated lake of spectators including himself—are penumbral ghosts, suppliants ignored.

Local Excavations
Unearth Antiquities

As Brewer renews itself, it discovers more about itself.

The large-scale demolition and reconstruction now taking place in the central

city continues uncovering numerous artifacts of the ''olden times'' which yield interesting insights into our city's past.

An underground speakeasy complete with wall murals emerged to light during the creation of a parking lot at M ing the creation of a parking lot at Muriel and Greeley Streets.

Old-timers remembered the hideaway as the haunt of ''Gloves'' Naugel and other Prohibition figures, as also the training-ground for musicians like ''Red'' Wenrich of sliding trombone fame who went on to become household names on a nationwide scale.

Also old sign-boards are common. Ingeniously shaped in the forms of cows, beehives, boots, mortars, plows, they advertise ''dry goods and notions,'' leatherwork, drugs, and medicines, produce of infinite variety. Preserved underground, most are still easily legible and date from the nineteenth century.

Amid the old fieldstone foundations, metal tools and grindstones come to light.

Arrowheads are not uncommon.

Dr. Klaus Schoerner, vice-president of the Brewer Historical Society, spent a

At the coffee break, Buchanan struts up to Rabbit. "How's little Jilly doing for you?"

"She's holding up."

"She worked out pretty fine for you, didn't she?"

"She's a good girl. Mixed-up like kids are these days, but we've gotten used to her. My boy and me."

Buchanan smiles, his fine little mustache spreading an em, and sways a half-step closer. "Little Jill's still keeping you company?"

Rabbit shrugs, feeling pasty and nervous. He keeps giving hostages to fortune. "She has nowhere else to go."

"Yes, man, she must be working out real fine for you." Still he doesn't walk away, go outside to the platform for his whisky. He stays and, still smiling but letting a pensive considerate shadow slowly subdue his face, says, "You know, friend Harry, what with Labor Day coming on, and the kids going back to school, and all this inflation you see everywhere, things get a bit short. In the financial end."

"How many children do you have?" Rabbit asks politely. Working with him all these years, he never thought Buchanan was married.

The plump ash-gray man rocks back and forth on the balls of his feet. "Oh . . . say five, that's been counted. They look to their daddy for support, and Labor Day finds him a little embarrassed. The cards just haven't been falling for old Lester lately."

"I'm sorry," Rabbit says. "Maybe you shouldn't gamble."

"I am just tickled to death little Jilly's worked out to fit your needs," Buchanan says. "I was thinking, twenty would sure help me by Labor Day."

"Twenty dollars?"

"That is all. It is miraculous, Harry, how far I've learned to make a little stretch. Twenty little dollars from a friend to a friend would sure make my holiday go easier all around. Like I say, seeing Jill worked out so good, you must be feeling pretty good. Pretty generous. A man in love, they say, is a friend to all."

But Rabbit has already fished out his wallet and found two tens. "This is just a loan," he says, frightened, knowing he is lying, bothering by that sliding again, that sweet bladder running late to school. The doors will be shut, the principal Mr. Kleist always stands by the front doors, with their rattling chains and push bars rubbed down to the yellow of brass, to snare the tardy and clap them into his airless office, where the records are kept.

"My children bless you," Buchanan says, folding the bills away. "This will buy a world of pencils."

"Hey, whatever happened to Babe?" Rabbit asks. He finds,

with his money in Buchanan's pocket, he has new ease; he has bought rights of inquiry.

Buchanan is caught off guard. "She's still around. She's still doing her thing as the young folks say."

"I wondered, you know, if you'd broken off connections."

Because he is short of money. Buchanan studies Rabbit's face, to make certain he knows what he is implying. Pimp. He sees he does, and his mustache broadens. "You want to get into that nice Babe, is that it? Tired of white meat, want a drumstick? Harry, what would your Daddy say?"

"I'm just asking how she was. I liked the way she played."

"She sure took a shine to you, I know. Come up to Jimbo's some time, we'll work something out."

"She said my knuckles were bad." The bell rasps. Rabbit tries to gauge how soon the next touch will be made, how deep this man is into him; Buchanan sees this and playfully, jubilantly slaps the palm of the hand Rabbit had extended, thinking of his knuckles. The slap tingles. Skin.

Buchanan says, "I *like* you, man," and walks away. A plum-pudding-colored roll of fat trembles at the back of his neck. Poor diet, starch. Chitlins, grits.

**fascinating hour with the VAT reporter,
chatting informally concerning Brewer's easliest days as a trading post with
er's earliest days as a trading post with
the Indian tribes along the Running
Horse River.**

**He showed us a pint of log huts
He showed us a print of log huts
etched when the primitive settlement
bore the name of Greenwich, after
Greenwich, England, home of the famed
observatory.**

**Also in Dr. Kleist's collection were
many fascinating photos of Weiser
Street when it held a few rude shops
and inns. The most famous of these inns
was the Goose and Feathers, where
George Washington and his retinue**

tarried one night on their way west to suppress the Whisky Rebellion in 1720. suppress the Whisky Rebellion in 1799.
The first iron mine in the vicinity was the well-known Oriole Furnace, seven miles south of the city. Dr. Kleist owns a collection of original slag and spoke enthusiastically about the methods whereby these early ironmakers produced a sufficiently powerful draft in

Pajasek comes up behind him. "Angstrom. Telephone." Pajasek is a small tired bald man whose bristling eyebrows increase the look of pressure about his head, as if his forehead is being pressed over his eyes, forming long horizontal folds. "You might tell the party after this you have a home number."

"Sorry, Ed. It's probably my crazy wife."

"Could you get her to be crazy on your private time?"

Crossing from his machine to the relative quiet of the frosted-glass walls is like ascending through supportive water to the sudden vacuum of air. Instantly, he begins to struggle. "Janice, for Christ's sake, I told you not to call me here. Call me at home."

"I don't want to talk to your little answering service. Just the thought of her voice makes me go cold all over."

"Nelson usually answers the phone. She never answers it."

"I don't want to hear her, or see her, or hear about her. I can't describe to you, Harry, the disgust I feel at just the thought of that person."

"Have you been on the bottle again? You sound screwed-up."

"I am sober and sane. And satisfied, thank you. I want to know what you're doing about Nelson's back-to-school clothes. You realize he's grown three inches this summer and nothing will fit."

"Did he, that's terrific. Maybe he won't be such a shrimp after all."

"He will be as big as my father and my father is no shrimp."

"Sorry, I always thought he was."

"Do you want me to hang up right now? Is that what you want?"

"No, I just want you to call me someplace else than at work."

She hangs up. He waits in Pajasek's wooden swivel chair, looking at the calendar, which hasn't been turned yet though this is September, and the August calendar girl, who is holding two ice cream cones so the scoops cover just where her nipples would be, one strawberry and one chocolate, *More Than Enough!* being the caption, until the phone rings.

"What were we saying?" he asks.

"I must take Nelson shopping for school clothes."

"O.K., come around and pick him up any time. Set a day."

"I will not come near that house, Harry, as long as that girl is in it. I won't even go near Penn Villas. I'm sorry, it's an absolute physical revulsion."

"Maybe you're pregnant, if you're so queasy. Have you and Chas been taking precautions?"

"Harry, I don't know you any more. I said to Charlie, I can't believe I lived twelve years with that man, it's as if it never happened."

"Thirteen. Nelson is thirteen."

She begins to cry. "You never forgave me for that, did you?"

"I did, I did. Relax. I'll send Nelson over to your love nest to go shopping. Name the day."

"Send him to the lot Saturday morning. I don't like him coming to the apartment, it seems too terrible when he leaves."

"Does it have to be Saturday? There was some talk of Jill driving us both down to Valley Forge, the kid and I've never seen it."

"Are you poking fun of me? Why do you think this is all so funny, Harry? This is *life*."

"I'm not, we were. Seriously."

"Well, tell her you can't. You two send Nelson over and stay in bed. Only send him with some money, I don't see why I should pay for his clothes."

"Buy everything at Kroll's and charge it."

"Kroll's has gone terribly downhill, you know it has. There's a nice little new shop now up near Perley, past that submarine place that used to be Chinese."

"Open another charge account. Tell him you're Springer Motors and offer a Toyota for security."

"Harry, you mustn't be so hostile. You sent me off myself. You said, that night, I'll never forget it, it was the shock of my life, 'See him if you want to, just so I don't have to see the bastard.' Those were your words."

"Hey, that reminds me, I did see him the other day."

"Who?"

"Chas. Your dark and swarthy lover."

"How?"

"He ambushed me after work. Waiting in the alley with a dagger. *Oog*, I said, you got me, you Commie rat."

"What did he want?"

"Oh, to talk about you."

"What about me? Harry, are you lying, I can't tell any more. *What* about me?"

"Whether or not you were happy."

She makes no comeback, so he goes on, "We concluded you were."

"Right," Janice says, and hangs up.

the days before the Bessemer furnace.
Old faded photographs of Weiser
Street show a prosperous-appearing
avenue of tasteful, low brick buildings
with horsedrawn trolly tracks promi-
with horse-drown trolley traks prami-

with horsed-rawn trolleyyyfff etaoin etaoinshrdlu etaoinshrdlucmfwpvbgkqjet

He asks her, "What did you and the kid do today?"

"Oh, nothing much. Hung around the house in the morning, took a drive in the afternoon."

"Where to?"

"Up to Mt. Judge."

"The town?"

"The mountain. We had a Coke in the Pinnacle Hotel and watched a softball game in the park for a while."

"Tell me the truth. Do you have the kid smoking pot?"

"Whatever gave you that idea?"

"He's awfully fascinated with you, and I figure it's either pot or sex."

"Or the car. Or the fact that I treat him like a human being instead of a failed little athlete because he's not six feet six. Nelson is a very intelligent sensitive child who is very upset by his mother leaving."

"I know he's intelligent, thanks, I've known the kid for years."

"Harry, do you want me to leave, is that it? I will if that's what you want. I could go back to Babe except she's having a rough time."

"What kind of rough time?"

"She's been busted for possession. The pigs came into the Jimbo the other night and took about ten away, including her and Skeeter. She says they asked for a bigger payoff and the owner balked. The owner is white, by the way."

"So you're still in touch with that crowd."

"You don't want me to be?"

"Suit yourself. It's your life to fuck up."

"Somebody's been bugging you, haven't they?"

"Several people."

"Do whatever you want to with me, Harry. I can't be anything in your real life."

She is standing before him in the living room, in her cut-off jeans and peasant blouse, her hands held at her sides slightly lifted and open, like a servant waiting for a tray. Her fingers are red from washing his dishes. Moved to gallantry, he confesses, "I need your sweet mouth and your pearly ass."

"I think they're beginning to bore you."

He reads this in reverse: he bores her. Always did. He attacks: "O.K., what *about* sex, with you and the kid?"

She looks away. She has a long nose and long chin, and that dry moth mouth that he feels, seeing it in repose, when she is not watching him, as absentmindedly disdainful, as above him and wanting to flutter still higher. Summer has put only a few freckles on her, and these mostly on her forehead, which bulges gently as a milk pitcher. Her hair is kinky from being so much in those little tiny braids hippies make. "He likes me," she answers, except it is no answer.

He tells her. "We can't do that trip to Valley Forge tomorrow. Janice wants Nelson to go shopping with her for school clothes, and I should go see my mother. You can drive me if you want, or I can take the bus."

He thinks he is being obliging, but she gives him her blank dead-grass stare and says, "You remind me of my mother sometimes. She thought she owned me too."

Saturday morning, she is gone. But her clothes still hang like rags in the closet. Downstairs on the kitchen table lies a note in green magic marker: *Out all day. Will drop Nelson at the lot.* ☮ ♡ X J. So he takes the bus. The lawns in Mt. Judge, patches of grass between cement walks, are burned; spatterings of leaves here and there in the maples are already turned gold. There is that scent in the air, of going back to school, of beginning again and reconfirming the order that exists. He wants to feel good, he always used to feel good at every turning of the year, every vacation or end of vacation, every new sheet on the calendar: but his adult life has proved to have no seasons, only changes of weather, and the older he gets, the less weather interests him. How can the planet keep turning and turning and not get so bored it explodes?

The house next to his old house still has the FOR SALE sign up. He tries his front door but it is locked; he rings, and after a prolonged shuffle and rumble within Pop comes to the door. Rabbit asks, "What's this locked door business?"

"Sorry, Harry, there've been so many burglaries in town lately . . . We had no idea you were coming."

"Didn't I promise?"

"You've promised before. Not that your mother and I can blame you, we know your life is difficult these days."

"It's not so difficult. In some ways it's easier. She upstairs?"

Pop nods. "She's rarely down any more."

"I thought this new stuff was working."

"It does in a way, but she's so depressed she lacks the will. Nine-tenths of life is will, my father used to say it, and the longer I live the more I see how right he was."

The disinfected scent of the house is still oppressive, but Harry goes up the stairs two at a time; Jill's disappearance has left him vigorous with anger. He bursts into the sick-room, saying, "Mom, tell me your dreams."

She has lost weight. The bones have shed all but the minimum connective tissue; her face is strained over the bones with an expression of far-seeing, expectant sweetness. Her voice emerges from this apparition more strongly than before, with less hesitation between words.

"I'm tormented something cruel at night, Harry. Did Earl tell you?"

"He mentioned bad dreams."

"Yes, bad, but not so bad as not being able to sleep at all. I know this room so well now, every object. At night even that innocent old bureau and that—poor shapeless armchair—they."

"They what?" He sits on the bed to take her hand, and fears the swaying under his weight will jostle and break her bones.

She says, "They want. To suffocate me."

"Those things do?"

"All things—do. They crowd in, in the queerest way, these simple homely bits of furniture I've. Lived with all my life. Dad's asleep in the next room, I can hear him snore. No cars go by. It's just me and the streetlamp. It's like being—under water. I count the seconds I have breath left for. I figure I can go forty, thirty, then it gets down to ten."

"I don't know breathing was affected by this."

"It isn't. It's all my mind. The things I have in my mind, Hassy, it reminds me of when they clean out a drain. All that hair and sludge mixed up with a rubber comb somebody went and dropped down years ago. Sixty years ago in my case."

"You don't feel that about your life, do you? I think you did a good job."

"A good job at what? We don't even know what we're trying to do, is the humor of it."

"Have a few laughs," he offers. "Have a few babies."

She takes him up on that. "I keep dreaming about you and Mim. Always together. When you haven't been together since you got out of school."

"What do Mim and I do, in these dreams?"

"You look up at me. Sometimes you want to be fed and I can't find the food. Once I remember looking into the icebox and. A man was in it frozen. A man I never knew, just one. Of those total strangers dreams have. Or else the stove won't light. Or I can't locate where Earl put the food when he came home from shopping, I know he. Put it somewhere. Silly things. But they become so important. I wake up screaming at Earl."

"Do Mim and I say anything?"

"No, you just look up like children do. Slightly frightened but sure I'll save. The situation. This is how you look. Even when I can see you're dead."

"Dead?"

"Yes. All powdered and set out in coffins. Only still standing up, still waiting for something from me. You've died because I couldn't get the food on the table. A strange thing about these dreams, come to think of it. Though you look up at me from a child's height. You look the way you do now. Mim all full of lipstick, with one of those shiny miniskirts and boots zippered up to her knee."

"Is that how she looks now?"

"Yes, she sent us a publicity picture."

"Publicity for what?"

"Oh, you know. For herself. You know how they do things now. I didn't understand it myself. It's on the bureau."

The picture, eight by ten, very glossy, with a diagonal crease where the mailman bent it, shows Mim in a halter and bracelets and sultan pants, her head thrown back, one long bare foot—she had big feet as a child, Mom had to make the shoe salesmen go deep into the stockroom—up on a hassock. Her eyes from the way they've reshaped them do not look like Mim at all. Only something about the nose makes it Mim. The kind of lump on the end, and the nostrils: the way as a baby they would tuck in when she started to cry is the way they tuck in now when they tell her to look sexy. He feels in this picture less Mim than the men posing her. Underneath, the message pale in ballpoint pen, she had written, *Miss you all Hope to come East soon Love Mim.* A slanting cramped hand that hadn't gone past high school. Jill's message had been written in splashy upright private-school semi-printing, confident as a poster. Mim never had that.

Rabbit asks, "How old is Mim now?"

Mom says, "You don't want to hear about my dreams."

"Sure I do." He figures it: born when he was six, Mim would be thirty now: she wasn't going anywhere, not even in harem costume. What you haven't done by thirty you're not likely to do. What you have done you'll do lots more. He says to his mother: "Tell me the worst one."

"The house next door has been sold. To some people who want to put up an apartment building. The Scranton pair have gone into partnership with them and then. These two walls go up, so the house doesn't get any light at all, and I'm in a hole looking up. And dirt starts to come down on me, cola cans and cereal boxes, and then. I wake up and know I can't breathe."

He tells her, "Mt. Judge isn't zoned for high-rise."

She doesn't laugh. Her eyes are wide now, fastened on that other half of her life, the night half, the nightmare half that now is rising like water in a bad cellar and is going to engulf her, proving that it was the real half all along, that daylight was an illusion, a cheat. "No," she says, "that's not the worst. The worst is Earl and I go to the hospital for tests. All around us are tables the size of our kitchen table. Only instead of set for meals each has a kind of puddle on it, a red puddle mixed up with crumpled bedsheets so they're shaped like. Children's sandcastles. And connected with tubes to machines with like television patterns on them. And then it dawns on me these are each people. And Earl keeps saying, so proud and pleased he's brainless, 'The government is paying for it all. The government is paying for it.' And he shows me the paper you and Mim signed to make me one of—you know, *them.* Those puddles."

"That's not a dream," her son says. "That's how it is."

And she sits up straighter on the pillows, stiff, scolding. Her mouth gets that unforgiving downward sag he used to fear more than anything, more than vampires, more than polio, more than thunder or God or being late for school. "I'm ashamed of you," she says. "I never thought I'd hear a son of mine so bitter."

"It was a joke, Mom."

"Who has so much to be grateful for," she goes on implacably.

"For what? For exactly what?"

"For Janice's leaving you, for one thing. She was always. A damp washrag."

"And what about Nelson, huh? What happens to him now?" This is her falsity, that she forgets what time creates, she still sees the world with its original four corners, her and Pop and him and Mim sitting at the kitchen table. Her tyrant love would freeze the world.

Mom says, "Nelson isn't my child, you're my child."

"Well, he exists anyway, and I have to worry about him. You just can't dismiss Janice like that."

"She's dismissed you."

"Not really. She calls me up at work all the time. Stavros wants her to come back."

"Don't you let her. She'll. Smother you, Harry."

"What choices do I have?"

"Run. Leave Brewer. I never knew why you came back. There's nothing here any more. Everybody knows it. Ever since the hosiery mills went south. Be like Mim."

"I don't have what Mim has to sell. Anyway she's breaking Pop's heart, whoring around."

"He wants it that way, your father has always been looking. For excuses to put on a long face. Well, he has me now, and I satisfy him. Let the dead bury the dead. Don't say no to life, Hassy. Bitterness never helps. I'd rather have a postcard from you happy than. See you sitting there like a lump."

Always these demands and impossible expectations. These harsh dreams. "Hassy, do you ever pray?"

"Mostly on buses."

"Pray for rebirth. Pray for your own rebirth."

His cheeks flame; he bows his head. He feels she is asking him to kill Janice, to kill Nelson. Freedom means murder. Rebirth means death. A lump, he silently resists, and she looks aside with the corner of her mouth worse bent. She is still trying to call him forth from her womb, can't she see he is an old man? An old lump whose only use is to stay in place to keep the lumps on top of him from tumbling.

Pop comes upstairs and tunes in the Phillies game on television. "They're a much sounder team without that Allen," he says. "He was a bad egg, Harry, I say that without prejudice; bad eggs come in all colors."

After a few innings, Rabbit leaves.

"Can't you stay for at least the game, Harry? I believe there's a beer still in the refrigerator, I was going to go down to the kitchen anyway to make Mother some tea."

"Let him go, Earl."

To protect the electrical wires, a lot of the maples along Jackson Road have been mutilated, the center of their crowns cut out. Rabbit hadn't noticed this before, or the new sidewalk squares where they have taken away the little surface gutters that used to trip you roller skating. He had been roller skating when Kenny Leggett, an older boy from across the street, who later became a five-minute miler, a county conference marvel, but that was later, this day he was just a bigger boy who had hit Rabbit with an icy snowball that winter, could have taken out an eye if it had hit higher, this day he just tossed across Jackson Road the shout, "Harry, did you hear on the radio? The President is dead." He said "The President," not "Roosevelt"; there had been no other President for them. The next time this would happen, the President would have a name: as he sat at the deafening tall machine one Friday after lunch his father sneaked up behind him and confided, "Harry, it just came over the radio, engraving had it on. Kennedy's been shot. They think in the head." Both men dead of violent headaches. Their smiles fade in the field of stars. We grope on, under bullies and accountants. On the bus, Rabbit prays as his mother told him to do: *Make the L-dopa work, give her pleasanter dreams, keep Nelson more or less pure, don't let Stavros turn too hard on Janice, help Jill find her way home. Keep Pop healthy. Me too. Amen.*

The bus goes around the side of the mountain. The gas station with the Dayglo spinners, the distance-hazed viaduct in the valley. He waits to change from the 16A bus to the 12 in the doorway of the roasted-peanut place on Weiser. PIG ATROCITIES STIR CAMDEN, a headline in the rack reads. The bus comes and pulls him across the bridge. The day whines at the windows, a September brightness empty of a future: the lawns smitten flat, the black river listless and stinking. HOBBY HEAVEN. BUTCH CSSDY & KID. He walks down Emberly toward Vista Crescent among sprinklers twirling in unison, under television aerials raking the same four o'clock garbage from the sky.

The dirty white Porsche is in the driveway, halfway into the garage, the way Janice used to do it, annoyingly. Jill is in the brown armchair, in her slip. From the slumped way she sits he sees she has no underpants on. She answers his questions groggily, with a lag, as if they are coming to her through a packing of dirty cotton, of fuzzy memories accumulated this day.

"Where'd you go so early this morning?"

"Out. Away from creeps like you."

"You drop the kid off?"

"Sure."

"When'd you get back?"

"Just now."

"Where'd you spend all day?"

"Maybe I went to Valley Forge anyway."

"Maybe you didn't."

"I did."

"How was it?"

"Beautiful. A gas, actually. He was a beautiful dude."

"Describe one room."

"You go in a door, and there's a four-poster bed, and a little tasselled pillow, and on it it says, 'George Washington slept here.' On the bedside tables you can still see the pills he took, to make himself sleep, when the redcoats had got him all uptight. The walls have some kind of lineny stuff on them, and all the chairs have ropes across the arms so you can't sit down on them. That's why I'm sitting on this one. Because it didn't. O.K.?"

He hesitates among the many alternatives she seems to be presenting. Laughter, anger, battle, surrender. "O.K. Sounds interesting. I'm sorry we couldn't go."

"Where did you go?"

"I went to visit my mother, after doing the housework around here."

"How is she?"

"She talks better, but seems frailer."

"I'm sorry. I'm sorry she has that disease. I guess I'll never meet your mother, will I?"

"Do you want to? You can see my father any time you want, just be in the Phoenix Bar at four-fifteen. You'd like him, he cares about politics. He thinks the System is shit."

"And I'll never meet your wife."

"Why would you want to? What is this?"

"I don't know, I'm interested. Maybe I'm falling for you."

"Jesus, don't do that."

"You don't think much of yourself, do you?"

"Once the basketball stopped, I suppose not. My mother by the way told me I should let Janice screw herself and leave town."

"What'd you say to that?"

"I said I couldn't."

"You're a creep."

Her lack of underpants and his sense that she has already been used today, and his sense of this unique summer, this summer of the moon, slipping away forever, lead him to ask, blushing for the second time this afternoon, "You wouldn't want to make love, would you?"

"Fuck or suck?"

"Whichever. Fuck." For he has come to feel that she gives him the end of her with teeth in it as a way of keeping the other for some man not yet arrived, some man more real to her than himself.

"What about Nelson?" she asks.

"He's off with Janice, she may keep him for supper. He's no threat. But maybe you're too tired. From all that George Washington."

Jill stands and pulls her slip to her shoulder and holds it there, a crumpled bag containing her head, her young body all there below, pale as a candlestick, the breasts hardened drippings. "Fuck me," she says coolly, tossing her slip toward the kitchen, and, when under him and striving, continues, "I want you to fuck all the shit out of me, all the shit and dreariness of this shit-dreary world, hurt me, clean me out, I want you to be all of my insides, sweetheart, right up to my throat, yes, oh yes, bigger, more, shoot it all out of me, sweet oh sweet sweet creep." Her eyes dilate in surprise. This green is just a rim, around pupils whose pure black is muddied with his shadow. "You've gotten little."

It is true: all her talk, her wild wanting it, have scared him down to nothing. She is too wet; something has enlarged her. And the waxen solidity of her young body, her buttocks spheres too perfect, feels alien to him: he grasps her across a distance clouded with Mom's dry warm bones and Janice's dark curves, Janice's ribs crescent above where the waist dipped. He senses winds playing through her nerve-ends, feels her moved by something beyond him, of which he is only a shadow, a shadow of white, his chest a radiant shield crushing her. She disengages herself and kneels to tongue his belly. They play with each other in a fog. The furniture dims around them. They are on the scratchy carpet, the television screen a mother-planet above them. Her hair is in his mouth. Her ass is two humps under his eyes. She tries to come against his face but his tongue isn't that strong. She rubs her clitoris against his chin upside down until he hurts. Elsewhere she is nibbling him. He feels gutted, silly, limp. At last he asks her to drag her breasts, the tough little tips, across his genitals, that lie cradled at the join of his legs. In this way he arouses himself, and attempts to satisfy her, and does, though by the time she trembles and comes they are crying over secrets far at their backs, in opposite directions, moonchild and earthman. "I love you," he says, and the fact that he doesn't makes it true. She is sitting on him, still working like some angry mechanic who, having made a difficult fit, keeps testing it.

In the small slipping sound they make he hears their mixed liquids, imagines in the space of her belly a silver machine, spider-shaped, spun from the threads of their secretions, carefully spinning. This links them. He says, surrendering, "Oh cry. Do." He pulls her down to him, puts their cheeks together, so their tears will mix.

Jill asks him, "Why are you crying?"

"Why are you?"

"Because the world is so shitty and I'm part of it."

"Do you think there's a better one?"

"There must be."

"Well," he considers, "why not?"

By the time Nelson comes home, they have both taken baths, their clothes are on, the lights are on. Rabbit is watching the six o'clock news (the round-up tally on summer riots, the week's kill figures in Vietnam, the estimate of traffic accidents over the coming Labor Day weekend) and Jill is making lentil soup in the kitchen. Nelson spreads over the floor and furniture the unwrapped loot of his day with Janice: snappy new Jockey shorts, undershirts, stretch socks, two pairs of slacks, four sports shirts, a corduroy jacket, wide neckties, even cufflinks to go with a lavender dress shirt, not to mention new loafers and basketball sneakers.

Jill admires: "Groovy, groovier, grooviest. Nelson, I just pity those eighth-grade girls, they'll be at your mercy."

He looks at her anxiously. "You know it's square. I didn't want to, Mom made me. The stores were disgusting, all full of materialism."

"What stores did she go to?" Rabbit asked. "How the hell did she pay for all this junk?"

"She opened charge accounts everywhere, Dad. She bought herself some clothes too, a really neat thing that looks like pajamas only it's O.K. to wear to parties if you're a woman, and stuff like that. And I got a suit, kind of grayey-green with checks, really cool, that we can pick up in a week when they make the alterations. Doesn't it feel funny when they measure you?"

"Do you remember, who was the name on the accounts? Me or Springer?"

Jill for a joke has put on one of his new shirts and tied her hair in a tail behind with one of his wide new neckties. To show herself off she twirls. Nelson, entranced, can scarcely speak. At her mercy.

"The name on her driver's license, Dad. Isn't that the right one?"

"And the address here? All those bills are going to come here?"

"Whatever's on the driver's license, Dad. Don't go heavy on *me*, I told her I just wanted blue jeans. And a Che Guevara sweatshirt, only there aren't any in Brewer."

Jill laughs. "Nelson, you'll be the best-dressed radical at West Brewer Junior High. Harry, these neckties are *silk!*"

"So it's war."

"Dad, *don't*. It wasn't my *fault*."

"I know that. Forget it. You needed the clothes, you're growing."

"And Mom really looked neat in some of the dresses."

He goes to the window, rather than continue to be heavy on the kid. He sees his own car, the old Falcon, slowly pull out. He sees for a second the shadow of Janice's head, the way she sits at the wheel hunched over, you'd think she'd be more relaxed with cars, having grown up with them. She had been waiting, for what? For him to come out? Or was she just looking at the house, maybe to spot Jill? Or homesick. By a tug of tension in one cheek he recognizes himself as smiling, seeing that the flag decal is still on the back window, she hasn't let Stavros scrape it off.

III. SKEETER

"We've been raped, we've been raped!"
—BACKGROUND VOICE ABOARD SOYUZ 5

ONE day in September Rabbit comes home from work to find another man in the house. The man is a Negro. "What the hell," Rabbit says, standing in the front hall beside the three chime tubes.

"Hell, man, it's revolution, right?" the young black says, not rising from the mossy brown armchair. His glasses flash two silver circles; his goatee is a smudge in shadow. He has let his hair grow out so much, into such a big ball, that Rabbit didn't recognize him at first.

Jill rises, quick as smoke, from the chair with the silver threads. "You remember Skeeter?"

"How could I forget him?" He goes forward a step, his hand lifted ready to be shaken, the palm tingling with fear; but since Skeeter makes no move to rise, he lets it drop back to his side, unsullied.

Skeeter studies the dropped white hand, exhaling smoke from a cigarette. It is a real cigarette, tobacco. "I like it,"

Skeeter says. "I like your hostility, Chuck. As we used to say in Nam, it is my meat."

"Skeeter and I were just talking," Jill says; her voice has changed, it is more afraid, more adult. "Don't I have any rights?"

Rabbit speaks to Skeeter. "I thought you were in jail or something."

"He is out on bail," Jill says, too hastily.

"Let him speak for himself."

Wearily Skeeter corrects her. "To be precise, I am way out on bail. I have jumped the blessed thing. I am, as they would say, de*sir*ed by the local swine. I have become one hot item, right?"

"It would have been two years," Jill says. "Two years for nothing, for not hurting anybody, not stealing anything, for nothing, Harry."

"Did Babe jump bail too?"

"Babe is a lady," Skeeter goes on in this tone of weary mincing precision. "She makes friends easy, right? I have no friends. I am known far and wide for my lack of sympathetic qualities." His voice changes, becomes falsetto, cringing. "Ah is one *baad* niggeh." He has many voices, Rabbit remembers, and none of them exactly his.

Rabbit tells him, "They'll catch you sooner or later. Jumping bail makes it much worse. Maybe you would have gotten off with a suspended sentence."

"I have one of those. Officialdom gets bored with handing them out, right?"

"How about your being a Vietnam veteran?"

"How a*bout* it? I am also black and unemployed and surly, right? I seek to undermine the state, and Ol' Massah State, he cottons on."

Rabbit contemplates the set of shadows in the old armchair, trying to feel his way. The chair has been with them ever since their marriage, it comes from the Springers' attic. This nightmare must pass. He says, "You talk a cool game, but I think you panicked, boy."

"Don't boy me."

Rabbit is startled; he had meant it neutrally, one athlete calling to another. He tries to amend: "You're just hurting yourself. Go turn yourself in, the day won't make that much difference."

Skeeter stretches luxuriously in the chair, yawns, inhales and exhales. "It dawns upon me," he says, "that you have a white gentleman's concept of the police and their exemplary works. There is nothing, let me repeat no thing, that gives them more pleasurable sensations than pulling the wings off of witless poor black men. First the fingernails, then the wings. Truly, they are constituted for that very sacred purpose. To keep me off your back and under your smelly feet, right?"

"This isn't the South," Rabbit says.

"Hee-yah! Friend Chuck, have you ever considered running for po-litical office, there can't be a county clerk left who believes the sweet things you do. The news is, the South is everywhere. We are fifty miles from the Mason-Dixon line where we sit, but way up in Detroit they are shooting nigger boys like catfish in a barrel. The news is, the cotton is in. Lynching season is on. In these Benighted States, everybody's done become a cracker." A brown hand delicately gestures from the shadows, then droops. "Forgive me, Chuck. This is just too simple for me to explain. Read the papers."

"I do. You're crazy."

Jill horns in. "The System is rotten, Harry. The laws are written to protect a tiny elite."

"Like people who own boats in Stonington," he says.

"Score one," Skeeter calls, "right?"

Jill flares. "What of it, I ran away from it, I reject it, I *shit* on it, Harry, where you're still loving it, you're eating it, you're eating my shit. My father's. Everybody's. Don't you see how you're *used?*"

"So now you want to use me. For *him.*"

She freezes, white. Her lips thin to nothing. "Yes."

"You're crazy. I'd be risking jail too."

"Harry, just a few nights, until he can hustle up a stake. He has family in New Orleans, he'll go there. Skeeter, right?"

"Right, sugar. Oh so right."

"It isn't just the pot bust, the pigs think he's a dealer, they say he pushes, they'll crucify him. Harry. They will."

Skeeter softly croons the start of "That Old Rugged Cross."

"Well, does he? Push."

Skeeter grins under his great ball of hair. "What can I get for you, Chuck? Goof balls, jolly beans, red devils, purple hearts. They have so much Panama Red in Philly right now they're feeding it to cows. Or want to sniff a little scag for a real rush?" From the gloom of the chair he extends his pale palms cupped as if heaped with shining poison.

So he is evil. Rabbit in his childhood used to lift, out of the same curiosity that made him put his finger into his belly-button and then sniff it, the metal waffle-patterned lid on the backyard cesspool, around the corner of the garage from the basketball hoop. Now this black man opens up under him in the same way: a pit of scummed stench impossible to see to the bottom of.

Harry turns and asks Jill, "Why are you doing this to me?"

She turns her head, gives him that long-chinned profile, a medallion to wear into battle. "I was stupid," she says, "to think you might trust me. You shouldn't have said you loved me."

Skeeter hums "True Love," the old Crosby–Grace Kelly single.

Rabbit re-asks, "Why?"

Skeeter rises from the chair. "Jesus deliver me from puking uptight honky lovers. She's doing it because I been screwing her all afternoon, right? If I go, she comes with me, hey Jill honey, right?"

She says, again thin-lipped, "Right."

Skeeter tells her, "I wouldn't take you on a bet, you poor cock-happy bitch. Skeeter splits alone." To Rabbit he says, "Toodle-oo, Chuck. Goddam green pickles, but it's been fun to watch you squirm." Standing, Skeeter seems frail, shabby in blue Levis and a colorless little Army windbreaker from which the insignia have been unstitched. His ball of hair has shrunk his face.

"Toodle-oo," Rabbit agrees, with relief in his bowels, and turns his back.

Skeeter declines to go so simply. He steps closer, he smells spicy. He says, "Throw me out. I want you to touch me."

"I don't want to."

"Do it."

"I don't want to fight you."

"I screwed your bitch."

"Her decision."

"And a lousy little cunt she was, too. Like putting your prick in a vise."

"Hear him, Jill?"

"Hey. Rabbit. That's what they used to call you, right? Your mamma's a whore, right? She goes down on old black winos behind the railroad station for fifty cents, right? If they don't have fifty cents she does it free because she likes it, right?"

Remote Mom. The quilty scent of her room, medicine, bedwarmth. Of all those years when she was well he can only remember her big bones bent above the kitchen table with its four worn places; she is not sitting down, she has already eaten, she is feeding him supper, he has come home from practice late, it is after dark, the windows are glazed from within.

"Your daddy's a queer, right? You must be too to take all this shit. Your wife couldn't stand living with a queer, it was like being balled by a mouse, right? You're a mouse down there, hey, ain't that right, gimme a feel." He reaches and Rabbit bats his hand away. Skeeter dances, delighted. "Nothin' there, right? Hey. Rabbit. Jill says you believe in God. I got news for you. Your God's a pansy. Your white God's queerer than the Queen of Spades. He sucks off the Holy Ghost and makes his son watch. Hey. Chuck. Another thing. Ain't no Jesus. He was a faggot crook, right? They bribed the Romans to get his carcass out of the tomb 'cause it smelled so bad, right?"

"All you're showing me," Rabbit says, "is how crazy you are." But a creeping sweetness, rage, is filling him solid. Sunday school images, a dead man whiter than lilies, the lavender rocks where he was betrayed by a kiss, are being packed into him.

Skeeter dances on, he is wearing big creased Army boots. He bumps Harry's shoulder, tugs the sleeve of his white shirt. "Hey. Wanna know how I know? Wanna know? Hey. I'm the real Jesus. I am *the* black Jesus, right? There is none other, no. When I fart, lightning flashes, right? Angels scoop it up in shovels of zillion-carat gold. Right? Kneel down, Chuck. Worship me. I am Jesus. Kiss my balls, they are the sun and the moon, right, and my pecker's a comet whose head is the white-hot heart of the glory that never does fail!" And, his head rolling like a puppet's, Skeeter unzips his fly and prepares to display this wonder.

Rabbit's time has come. He is packed so solid with anger and fear he is seeing with his pores. He wades toward the boy deliciously and feels his fists vanish, one in the region of the belly, the other below the throat. He is scared of the head, whose glasses might shatter and slash. Skeeter curls up and drops to the floor dry as a scorpion and when Rabbit pries at him he has no opening, just abrasive angles shaking like a sandpaper machine. Rabbit's hands start to hurt. He wants to pry this creature open because there is a soft spot where he can be split and killed; the curved back is too tough, though knuckles slammed at the hole of the ear do produce a garbled whimper.

Jill is screaming and with her whole weight pulling the tail of his shirt and in the ebb of his sweetness Rabbit discovers his hands and forearms somehow clawed. His enemy is cringing on the floor, the carpet that cost them eleven dollars a yard and was supposed to wear longer than the softer loop for fifteen that Janice wanted (she always said it reminded her of the stuff they use in miniature golf courses), cringing expertly, knees tucked under chin and hands over head and head tucked under the sofa as far as it will go. His Levis are rumpled up and it shocks Rabbit to see how skinny his calves and ankles are, iridescent dark spindles. Humans made of a new material. Last longer, wear more evenly. And Jill is sobbing, "Harry, no more, no more," and the door chime is saying its three syllables over and over, a scale that can't get anywhere, that can't get over the top.

The door pops open. Nelson is there, in his spiffy new school clothes, fishbone-striped sport shirt and canary-yellow slacks. Billy Fosnacht is behind him, a hairy head taller. "Hey," Skeeter says from the floor, "it's Babychuck, right?"

"Is he a burglar, Dad?"

"We could hear the furniture being smashed and everything," Billy says. "We didn't know what to do."

Nelson says, "We thought if we kept ringing the bell it would stop."

Jill tells him, "Your father lost all control of himself."

Rabbit asks, "Why should I always be the one to have control of myself?"

Getting up as if from a bin of dust, one careful limb at a time, Skeeter says, "That was to get us acquainted, Chuck. Next time I'll have a gun."

Rabbit taunts, "I thought at least I'd see some nice karate chops from basic training."

"Afraid to use 'em. Break you in two, right?"

"Daddy, who is he?"

"He's a friend of Jill's called Skeeter. He's going to stay here a couple days."

"He is?"

Jill's voice has asked.

Rabbit sifts himself for the reason. Small scraped places smart on his knuckles; overstimulation has left a residue of nausea; he notices through the haze that still softly rotates around him that the endtable was upset and that the lamp whose base is driftwood lies on the carpet awry but not smashed. The patient fidelity of these things bewilders him. "Sure," he says. "Why not?"

Skeeter studies him from the sofa, where he sits bent over, nursing the punch to his stomach. "Feeling guilty, huh Chuck? A little tokenism to wash your sins away, right?"

"Skeeter, he's being generous," Jill scolds.

"Get one thing straight, Chuck. No gratitude. Anything you do, do for selfish reasons."

"Right. The pleasure I get in pounding you around." But in fact he is terrified at having taken this man in. He will have to sleep with him in the house. The tint of night, Skeeter will sneak to his side with a knife shining like the moon. He will get the gun as he has promised. FUGITIVE FROM JUSTICE HOLDS FAMILY AT GUNPOINT. *Mayor Vows, No Deals.* Why has he invited this danger? To get Janice to rescue him. These thoughts flit by in a flash. Nelson has taken a step toward the black man. His eyes are sunk in their sockets with seriousness. Wait, wait. He is poison, he is murder, he is black.

"Hi," Nelson says, and holds out his hand.

Skeeter puts his skinny fingers, four gray crayons, as thick at the tips as in the middle, in the child's hand and says, "Hi there, Babychuck." He nods over Nelson's shoulder toward Billy Fosnacht. "Who's your gruesome friend?"

And everybody, everybody laughs, even Billy, even Skeeter contributes a cackle, at this unexpected illumination, that Billy *is* gruesome, with his father's skinny neck and big ears and his mother's mooncalf eyes and the livid festerings of adolescence speckling his cheeks and chin. Their laughter makes a second wave to reassure him they are not laughing at him, they are laughing in relief at the gift of truth, they are rejoicing in brotherhood, at having shared this moment, giggling and cackling; the house is an egg cracking because they are all hatching together.

But in bed, the house dark and Billy gone home, Skeeter breathing exhausted on the sofa downstairs, Rabbit repeats his question to Jill: "Why have you done this to me?"

Jill snuffles, turns over. She is so much lighter than he, she irresistibly rolls down to his side. Often in the morning he wakes to find himself nearly pushed from the bed by this inequality, her sharp little elbows denting his flesh. "He was so pathetic," she explains. "He talks tough but he really has nothing, he really does want to become the black Jesus."

"Is that why you let him screw you this afternoon? Or didn't you?"

"I didn't really."

"He lied?"

Silence. She slides an inch deeper into his side of the bed. "I don't think it counts when you just let somebody do it to you and don't do anything back."

"You don't."

"No, it just happens on the surface, a million miles away."

"And how about with me? Is it the same way, you don't feel anything, it's so far away. So you're really a virgin, aren't you?"

"Shh. Whisper. No, I do feel things with you."

"What?"

She nudges closer and her arm encircles his thick waist. "I feel you're a funny big teddy bear my Daddy has given me. He used to bring home these extravagant Steiff toys from Schwarz's in New York, giraffes six feet high that cost five hundred dollars, you couldn't do anything with them, they'd just stand around taking up space. Mother hated them."

"Thanks a lot." Sluggishly he rolls over to face her.

"Other times, when you're over me, I feel you're an angel. Piercing me with a sword. I feel you're about to announce something, the end of the world, and you say nothing, just pierce me. It's beautiful."

"Love me?"

"Please, Harry. Since that God thing I went through I just can't focus that way on anybody."

"Is Skeeter out of focus for you too?"

"He's horrible. He really is. He feels all scaly, he's so bitter."

"Then why in holy hell—?"

She kisses him to stop his voice. "Shh. He'll hear." Sounds travel freely down the stairs, through the house of thin partitions. The rooms are quadrants of one rustling heart. "Because I must, Harry. Because whatever men ask of me, I must give, I'm not interested in holding anything for myself. It all melts together anyway, you see."

"I don't see."

"I think you do. Otherwise why did you let him stay? You had him beaten. You were killing him."

"Yeah, that was nice. I thought I was out of shape worse than I am."

"Yet now he's here." She flattens her body against his; it feels transparent. He can see through her to the blue window beyond, moonlit, giving onto the garage roof, composition shingling manufactured with a strange shadow-line, to give an illusion of thickness. She confesses, in such a whisper it may be only a thought he overhears, "He frightens me."

"Me too."

"Half of me wanted you to kick him out. More than half."

"Well," and he smiles unseen, "if he is the next Jesus, we got to keep on His good side." Her body broadens as if smiling. It has grown plain that the betrayals and excitements of the day must resolve into their making love now. He encloses her skull in his hands, caressing the spinelike ridges behind the seashell curve of her ears, palming the broad curve of the whole, this cup, sealed upon a spirit. Knowing her love is coming, he sees very clearly, as we see in the etched hour before snow. He amends, "Also, Janice has been doing some things out of the way, so I have to do things out of the way."

"To pay her back."

"To keep up with her."

The item was narrow-measure:

Sentenced for Possession

Eight local men and one woman were given six-month sentences for possession of marijuana Thursday.

The defendants appearing before Judge Milton F. Schoffer had been apprehended in a police raid on Jimbo's Lounge, Weiser Street, early in the morning of August 29.

The female among them, Miss Beatrice Greene, a well-known local entertainer under her nom de plume of "Babe," had her sentence suspended, with one

year's probation, as were four of the men. Two minors were remanded to juvenile court.

A tenth defendant, Hubert H. Farnsworth, failed to appear in court and forfieted bail. A war-
court and forfeited bail. A war-
ant has been issued for his ar-
rest.
ant has been issued for his arrest.

The proprietor of Jimbo's, Mr. Timothy Cartney of Penn

Rabbit's ears can sense now when Pajasek is coming up behind him with a phone call. Something weary and menacing in his step, and then his breath has a sarcastic caress. "Angstrom, maybe we should move your lino into my office. Or install a phone jack out here."

"I'll give her hell, Ed. This is the last time."

"I don't like a man's private life to interfere with his work."

"I don't either. I tell you, I'll tell her."

"Do that, Harry. Do that for good old Verity. We have a team here, we're in a highly competitive game, let's keep up our end, what do you say?"

Behind the frosted walls he says into the phone, "Janice, this is the last time. I won't come to the phone after this."

"I won't be calling you after this, Harry. After this all our communications will be through lawyers."

"How come?"

"How come? How *come!*"

"How come. Come on. Just give me information, can you? I got to get back to the machine."

"Well, for one reason how come, you've let me sit over here without ever once calling me back, and for another you've taken a darkie into the house along with that hippie, you're in*cred*ible, Harry, my mother always said it, 'He means no harm, he just has less moral sense than a skunk,' and she was right."

"He's just there a couple days, it's a funny kind of emergency."

"It must be funny. It must be hilarious. Does your mother know? So help me, I have a mind to call and tell her."

"Who told you, anyway? He never goes out of the house."

He hopes by his reasonable tone to bring hers down; she does unwind a notch. "Peggy Fosnacht. She said Billy came home absolutely bug-eyed. He said the man was on the living room floor and the first thing he said was to insult Billy."

"It wasn't meant as an insult, it was meant to be pleasant."

"Well I wish *I* could be pleasant. I wish it very much. I've seen a lawyer and we're filing a writ for immediate custody of Nelson. The divorce will follow. As the guilty party you can't remarry for two years. Absolutely, Harry. I'm sorry. I thought we were more mature than this, I *hated* the lawyer, the whole thing is too ugly."

"Yeah, well, the law is. It serves a ruling elite. More power to the people."

"I think you've lost your mind. I honestly do."

"Hey, what did you mean, I let you sit over there? I thought that was what you wanted. Isn't Stavros still doing the sitting with you?"

"You might at least have fought a *little*," she cries, and gasps for breath between sobs. "You're so weak, you're so wishy-washy," she manages to bring out, but then it becomes pure animal sound, a kind of cooing or wheezing, as if all the air is running out of her, so he says, "We'll talk later, call me at home," and hangs up to plug the leak.

Park, expressed shock and strong disapproval of drug use over the telephone to VAT inquiries.

Cartney was not in the building at the time of the arrests.

Rumors have prevailed for some time concerning the sale

of this well-known nightspot and gathering place to a ''black capitalist'' syndicate.

During the coffee break Buchanan comes over. Rabbit touches his wallet, wondering if the touch will go up. Escalation. Foreign aid. Welfare. He'll refuse if it does. If he asks more than twenty, let them riot in the streets. But Buchanan holds out two ten dollar bills, not the same two, but just as good. "Friend Harry," he says, "never let it be said no black man pays his debts. I'm obliged to you a thousand and one times over, them two sawbucks turned the cards right around. Would you believe two natural full houses in a row? I couldn't believe it myself, nobody could, those fools all stayed the second time like there was no tomorrow." He wads the money into Rabbit's hand, which is slow to close.

"Thanks, uh, Lester. I didn't really—"

"Expect to get it back?"

"Not so soon."

"Well, sometimes one man's in need, sometimes another man is. Spread it around, isn't that what the great ones teach us?"

"I guess they do. I haven't talked to many great ones lately."

Buchanan chuckles politely and rocks back and forth on his heels, estimating, rolling a toothpick in his lips, beneath the mustache no thicker than a toothpick. "I hear tell you're so hard up over at your place you're taking in boarders."

"Oh. That. It's just temporary, it wasn't my idea."

"I believe that."

"Uh—I'd rather it didn't get around."

"That's just what I'd rather."

Change the subject, somehow. "How's Babe now? Back in business?"

"What kind of business you think she's in?"

"You know, singing. I meant after the bust and court sentence. I just set the news item."

"I know what you meant. I know exactly. Come on down to Jimbo's, any night of the week, get better acquainted. Babe's estimation of you has shot way up, I tell you that. Not that she didn't take a shine in the first place."

"Yeah, O.K., great. Maybe I'll get down sometime. If I can get a babysitter." The idea of ever going into Jimbo's again frightens him, as does the idea of leaving Nelson, Jill, and Skeeter alone in the house. He is sinking into an underworld he used to see only from a bus. Buchanan squeezes his arm.

"We'll set something up," the Negro promises. "Oh, yeass." The hand squeezes tighter, as if pressing fingerprints through the screen of Harry's blue workshirt. "Jer-ome asked me to express an especial gratitude."

Jerome?

The yellow-faced clock ticks, the end-of-break buzzer rasps. The last to return to his machine, Farnsworth passes between the brightly lit makeup tables, a man so black he twinkles. He bobs his shaved head, wipes the whisky from his lips, and throws Harry a dazzling grin. Brothers in paternity.

He gets off the bus early, on the other side of the bridge, and walks along the river through the old brick neighborhoods burdened with great green highway signs. Peggy Fosnacht's buzzer buzzes back and when he gets off the elevator she is at the door in a shapeless blue bathrobe. "Oh, *you*," she says. "I thought it would be Billy having lost his key again."

"You alone?"

"Yes, but Harry, he'll be back from school any minute."

"I only need a minute." She leads him in, pulling her bathrobe tighter about her body. He tries to wrap his errand in a little courtesy. "How've you been?"

"I'm managing. How have you been?"

"Managing. Just."

"Would you like a drink?"

"This early in the day?"

"I'm having one."

"No, Peggy, thanks. I can only stay a minute. I got to see what's cooking back at the ranch."

"Quite a lot, I hear."

"That's what I wanted to say something about."

"Please sit down. I'm getting a crick in my neck." Peggy takes a sparkling glass of beaded fluid from the sill of the window that overlooks Brewer, a swamp of brick sunk at the foot of its mountain basking westward in the sun. She sips, and her eyes slide by. "You're offended by my drinking. I just got out of the bathtub. That's often how I spend my afternoons, after spending the morning with the lawyers or walking the streets looking for a job. Everybody wants younger secretaries. They must wonder why I keep my sunglasses on. I come back and take off all my clothes and get into the tub and ever so slowly put a drink inside me and watch the steam melt the ice cubes."

"It sounds nice. What I wanted to say—"

She is standing by the window with one hip pushed out; the belt of her bathrobe is loose and, though she is a shadow against the bright colorless sky, he can feel with his eyes as if with his tongue the hollow between her breasts that would still be dewy from her bath.

She prompts, "What you wanted to say—"

"Was to ask you a favor: could you kind of keep it quiet about the Negro staying with us that Billy saw? Janice called me today and I guess you've already told her, that's O.K. if you could stop it there, I don't want everybody to know. Don't tell Ollie, if you haven't already, I mean. There's a legal angle or I wouldn't bother." He lifts his hands helplessly; it wasn't worth saying, now that he's said it.

Peggy steps toward him, stabbingly, too much liquor or trying to keep the hip out seductively or just the way she sees, two of everything, and tells him, "She must be an awfully good lay, to get you to do this for her."

"The girl? No, actually, she and I aren't usually on the same wavelength."

She brushes back her hair with an approximate flicking motion that lifts the bathrobe lapel and exposes one breast; she is drunk. "Try another wavelength."

"Yeah, I'd love to, but right now, the fact is, I'm running too scared to take on anything else, and anyway Billy's about to come home."

"Sometimes he hangs around Burger Bliss for hours. Ollie thinks he's getting bad habits."

"Yeah, how *is* old Ollie? You and he getting together at all?"

She lets her hand down from her hair; the lapel covers her again. "Sometimes he comes by and fucks me, but it doesn't seem to bring us any closer."

"Probably it does, he just doesn't express it. He's too embarrassed at having hurt you."

"That's how *you* would be, but Ollie isn't like that. It would never enter his head to feel guilty. It's the artist in him, you know he really can play almost any instrument he picks up. But he's a cold little bastard."

"Yeah, I'm kind of cold too." He has stood in alarm, since she has come closer another clumsy step.

Peggy says, "Give me your hands." Her eyes fork upon him, around him. Her face unchanging, she reaches down and lifts his hands from his sides and holds them to her chest. "They're warm." He thinks, *Cold heart*. She inserts his left hand into her bathrobe and presses it around a breast. He thinks of spilling guts, of a cow's stomach tumbling out; elastically she overflows his fingers, her nipple a clot, a gumdrop stuck to his palm. Her eyes are closed—veins in her lids, crow's feet at the corners—and she is intoning, "You're not cold, you're warm, you're a warm man, Harry, a good man. You've been hurt and I want you to heal, I want to help you heal, do whatever you want with me." She is talking as if to herself, rapidly, softly, but has brought him so close he hears it all; her breath beats at the base of his throat. Her heartbeat is sticking to his palm. The skin of her brow is vexed and the piece of her body her bathrobe discloses is lumpy and strange, blind like the brow of an ox, but eased by liquor she has slid into that state where the body of the other is her own body, the body of secretive self-love that the mirror we fill and the bed we warm alone give us back; and he is enclosed in this body of love of hers and against all thought and wish he thickens all over tenderly and the one-eyed rising beneath his waist begins.

He protests "I'm not good" but is also sliding; he relaxes the hand that is holding her breast to give it air to sway in.

She insists "You're good, you're lovely" and fumbles at his fly; with the free hand he pulls aside the lapel of the bathrobe so the other breast is free and the bathrobe belt falls unknotted.

An elevator door sucks shut in the hall. Footsteps swell toward their door. They spring apart; Peggy wraps the robe around herself again. He keeps on his retinas the afterimage of a ferny triangle, broader than his palm, beneath a belly whiter than crystal, with silvery stretch-marks. The footsteps pass on by. The lovers sigh with relief, but the spell has been broken. Peggy turns her back, reknots her belt. "You're keeping in touch with Janice," she says.

"Not really."

"How did you know I told her about the black?"

Funny, everybody else has no trouble saying "black." Or hating the war. Rabbit must be defective. Lobotomy. A pit opens where guilt gnaws, at the edge of his bladder. He must hurry home. "She called me to say a lawyer was starting divorce proceedings."

"Does that upset you?"

"I guess. Sort of. Sure."

"I suppose I'm dumb, I just never understood why you put up with Janice. She was never enough for you, never. I love Janice, but she is about the most childish, least sensitive woman I've ever known."

"You sound like my mother."

"Is that bad?" She whirls around; her hair floats. He has never seen Peggy so suddenly soft, so womanly frontal. Even her eyes he could take. In play, mocking the pressure of Billy impending at his back, he rubs the back of his hand across her nipples. Nibs and Dots.

"Maybe you're right. We should try out our wavelengths."

Peggy flushes, backs off, looks stony, as if an unexpected mirror has shown her herself too harshly. She pulls the blue terrycloth around her so tight her shoulders huddle. "If you want to take me out to dinner some night," she says, "I'm around," adding irritably, "but don't count your chickens."

Hurry, hurry. The bus takes forever to come, the walk down Emberly is endless. Yet his house, third from the end of Vista Crescent, low and new and a sullen apple-green on the quarter-acre of lawn scraggly with plantain, is intact, and all around it the unpopulated stretches of similar houses hold unbroken the intensity of duplication. That the blot of black inside his house is unmirrored fools him into hoping it isn't there. But, once up the three porch steps and through the door of three stepped windows, Rabbit sees, to his right, in the living room, from behind—the sofa having been swung around—a bushy black sphere between Jill's cone of strawberry gold and Nelson's square-cut mass of Janice-dark hair. They are watching television. Skeeter seems to have reinstated the box. The announcer, ghostly pale because the adjustment is too bright and mouthing as rapidly as a vampire because there is too much news between too many commercials, enunciates, ". . . after a five-year exile spent in Communist Cuba, various African states, and Communist China, landed in Detroit today and was instantly taken into custody by waiting FBI men. Elsewhere on the racial front, the U.S. Commission on Civil Rights sharply charged that the Nixon Administration has made quote a major retreat unquote pertaining to school integration in the southern states. In Fayette Mississippi three white Klansmen were arrested for the attempted bombing of the supermarket owned by newly elected black mayor of Fayette Charles Evers brother of the slain civil rights leader. In New York City Episcopal spokesmen declined to defend further their controversial decision to grant two hundred thousand dollars toward black church leader James Forman's demand of five hundred million dollars in quote reparations unquote from the Christian churches in America for quote three centuries of indignity and exploitation unquote. In Hartford Connecticut and Camden New Jersey an uneasy peace prevails after last week's disturbances within the black communities of these cities. And now, an important announcement."

"Hello, hello," Rabbit says, ignored.

Nelson turns and says, "Hey Dad. Robert Williams is back in this country."

"Who the hell is Robert Williams?"

Skeeter says, "Chuck baby, he's a man going to fry your ass."

"Another black Jesus. How many of you are there?"

"By many false prophets," Skeeter tells him, "you shall know my coming, right? That's the Good Book, right?"

"It also says He's come and gone."

"Comin' again, Chuck. Gonna fry your ass. You and Nixon's, right?"

"Poor old Nixon, even his own commissions beat on him. What the hell can he do? He can't go into every ghetto and fix the plumbing himself. He can't give every copped-out junkie a million dollars and a Ph.D. Nixon, who's Nixon? He's just a typical flatfooted Chamber of Commerce type who lucked his way into the hot seat and is so dumb he thinks it's good luck. Let the poor bastard alone, he's trying to bore us to death so we won't commit suicide."

"Nixon, shit. That honky was put there by the cracker vote, right? Strom Stormtrooper is his very bag. He is Herod, man, and all us black babies better believe it."

"Black babies, black leaders, Jesus am I sick of the word black. If I said white one-eightieth as often as you say black you'd scream yourself blue. For Chrissake, forget your skin."

"I'll forget it when you forget it, right?"

"Lord I'd love to forget not only your skin but everything inside it. I thought three days ago you said you were getting out in three days."

"Dad, *don't*." The kid's face is tense. Mom was right, too delicate, too nervous. Thinks the world is going to hurt him, so it will. The universal instinct to exterminate the weak.

Jill rises to shield the other two. Three on one: Rabbit is exhilarated. Faking and dodging, he says before she can speak, "Tell the darker of your boy friends here I thought he promised to pull out when he got a stake. I have twenty bucks here to give him. Which reminds me of something else."

Skeeter interrupts, addressing the air. "I *love* him when he gets like this. He is the Man."

And Jill is saying her piece. "Nelson and I refuse to live with this quarrelling. Tonight after supper we want to have an organized discussion. There's a crying need for education in this household."

"Household," Rabbit says, "I'd call it a refugee camp." He persists in what he has been reminded of. "Hey, Skeeter. Do you have a last name?"

"X," Skeeter tells him. "42X."

"Sure it's not Farnsworth?"

Skeeter's body sheds its shell, hangs there outfeinted a second, before regathering hardness. "That SuperTom," he says definitively, "is not the slightest relation of mine."

"The *Vat* had your last name as Farnsworth."

"The *Vat*," Skeeter pronounces mincingly, "is a Fascist rag."

Having scored, you put your head down and run back up the floor; but with that feeling inside, of having made a mark that can't be rubbed out. "Just wondering," Rabbit smiles. He stretches out his arms as if from wall to wall. "Who wants a beer besides me?"

After supper, Nelson washes the dishes and Skeeter dries. Jill tidies up the living room for their discussion; Rabbit helps her swing the sofa back into place. On the shelves between the living room and the breakfast nook that he and Janice had kept empty Rabbit notices now a stack of tired paperbacks, their spines chafed and biased by handling. *The Selected Writings of W. E. B. Du Bois, The Wretched of the Earth, Soul on Ice, The Life and Times of Frederick Douglass,* others, history, Marx, economics, stuff that makes Rabbit feel sick, as when he thinks about what surgeons do, or all the plumbing and gas lines there are under the street. "Skeeter's books," Jill explains. "I went into Jimbo's today for them, and his clothes. Babe had them."

"Hey Chuck," Skeeter calls from the sink, through the shelves, "know where I got those books? Over in Nam, at the Longbinh base bookstore. They love us to read, that crazy Army of yours. Teach us how to read, shoot, dig pot, sniff scag, black man's best friend, just like they say!" He snaps his towel, *pap!*

Rabbit ignores him and asks Jill, "You went in there? It's full of police, they could easy tail you."

Skeeter shouts from the kitchen, "Don't you worry Chuck, those poor pigs've bigger niggers than me to fry. You know what happened over in York, right? Brewer's gone to make that look like the Ladies Aid ball!" *Pap!*

Nelson washing beside him asks, "Will they shoot every white person?"

"Just the big old ugly ones, mostly. You stay away from that gruesome Billy and stick next to me, Babychuck, you'll be all right."

Rabbit pulls down a book at random and reads,

> Government is for the people's progress and not for the comfort of an aristocracy. The object of industry is the welfare of the workers and not the wealth of the owners. The object of civilization is the cultural progress of the mass of workers and not merely of an intellectual elite.

It frightens him, as museums used to frighten him, when it was part of school to take trips there and to see the mummy rotting in his casket of gold, the elephant tusk filed into a hundred squinting Chinamen. Unthinkably distant lives, abysses of existence, worse than what crawls blind on ocean floors. The book is full of Skeeter's underlinings. He reads,

> Awake, awake, put on thy strength, O Zion! Reject the weakness of missionaries who teach neither love nor brotherhood, but chiefly the virtues of private profit from capital, stolen from your land and labor. Africa, awake! Put on the beautiful robes of Pan-African socialism.

Rabbit replaces the book feeling better. There are no such robes. It is all crap. "What's the discussion about?" he asks, as they settle around the cobbler's bench.

Jill says nervously, blushing, "Skeeter and Nelson and I were talking about it today after school and agreed that since there seems to be such a painful communications problem—"

"Is that what it is?" Rabbit asks. "Maybe we communicate too well."

"—a structured discussion might be helpful and educational."

"Me being the one who needs to be educated," Rabbit says.

"Not necessarily." The care with which Jill speaks makes Rabbit feel pity; *we are too much for her*, he thinks. "You're older than we are and we respect your experience. We all agree, I think, that your problem is that you've never been given a chance to formulate your views. Because of the competitive American context, you've had to convert everything into action too rapidly. Your life has no reflective content; it's all instinct, and when your instincts let you down, you have nothing to trust. That's what makes you cynical. Cynicism, it has been said, is tired pragmatism. Pragmatism suited a certain moment here, the frontier moment, it did the work, very wastefully and ruthlessly, but it did it."

"On behalf of Daniel Boone," Rabbit says, "I thank you."

"It's wrong," Jill goes on gently, "when you say Americans are exploiters, to forget that the first things they exploit are themselves. You," she says, lifting her face, her eyes and freckles and nostrils a constellation, "you've never given yourself a chance to think, except on techniques, basketball and printing, that served a self-exploitative purpose. You carry an old God with you, and an angry old patriotism. And now an old wife." He takes breath to protest, but her hand begs him to let her finish. "You accept these things as sacred not out of love or faith but fear; your thought is frozen because the first moment when your instincts failed, you raced to the conclusion that everything is nothing, that zero is the real answer. That is what we Americans think, it's win or lose, all or nothing, kill or die, because we've never created the leisure in which to take thought. But now, you see, we must, because action is no longer enough, action without thought is violence. As we see in Vietnam."

He at last can speak. "There was violence in Vietnam before we ever heard of the place. You can see by just the way I'm sitting here listening to this crap I'm a pacifist basically." He points at Skeeter. "*He's* the violent son of a bitch."

"But you *see*," Jill says, her voice lulling and nagging, with just a teasing ragged hem showing of the voice she uses in bed, "the reason Skeeter annoys and frightens you is he's opaque, you don't know a thing about his history, I don't mean his personal history so much as the history of his race, how he got here. Things that threaten you like riots and welfare have jumped into the newspapers out of nowhere for you. So for tonight we thought we would just talk a little, have a kind of seminar, about Afro-American history."

"Please, Dad," Nelson says.

"Jesus. O.K. Hit me. We were beastly to the slaves so why do so few American Negroes want to give up their Cadillacs and, excuse the expression, colored televisions and go back to Africa?"

"Dad, *don't*."

Skeeter begins. "Let's forget the slavery, Chuck. It was forever ago, everybody used to do it, it was a country kind of thing, right? Though I must say, the more it began to smell like shit, the tighter you held on to it, right?"

"We had more country."

"Easy, sit back. No arguments, right? You had cotton come along, right? Anybody but darkies die working those cotton swamps, right? Anyhoo, you had this war. You had these crazies up North like Garrison and Brown agitating and down South a bunch of supercrackers like Yancy and Rhett who thought they could fatten their own pie by splitting, funny thing is"—he chuckles, wheezes, Rabbit pictures him with a shaved head and sees Farnsworth—"they didn't, the Confederacy sent 'em away on a ship and elected all play-it-safes to office! Same up North with cats like Sumner. Come to the vote, people scared of the man with the idea, right? Do you know, suppose you don't, dude called Ruffin, bright as could be, invented modern agriculture or next thing to it, hated the Yankees so much he pulled the string on the first cannon at Sumter and shot himself in the head when the South lost? Wild men. Beautiful, right? So any*hoo*, Lincoln got this war, right, and fought it for a bunch of wrong reasons—what's so sacred about a *Union*, just a power trust, right?—and for another wrong reason freed the slaves, and it was done. God bless America, right? So here I begin to get mad."

"Get mad, Skeeter," Rabbit says. "Who wants a beer?"

"Me, Dad."

"Half a one."

Jill says, "I'll split it with him."

Skeeter says, "That stuff rots the soul. Mind if I burn some good Red?"

"It's not legal."

"Right. But everybody does it. All those swish cats over in Penn Park, you think they have a martini when they come home at night? That's yesterday. They blow grass. Sincerely, it is more in than chewing gum. Over in Nam, it was the fighting boy's candy."

"O.K. Light up. I guess we've gone this far."

"There is far to go," Skeeter says, rolling his joint, from a rubber pouch he produces from within the sofa, where he sleeps, and thin yellow paper, licking it rapidly with that fat pale tongue, and twisting the ends. When he lights it, the twisted end flames. He sucks in hungrily, holds it in as if about to dive very deep, and then releases the sweet used smoke with a belch. He offers the wet end to Rabbit. "Try?"

Rabbit shakes his head, watching Nelson. The kid's eyes are bird-bright, watching Skeeter. Maybe Janice is right, he's letting the kid see too much. Still, he didn't do the leaving. And life is life, God invented it, not him. But he looks at Nelson fearful that his presence in the room will be construed as a blessing. He says to Skeeter, "Get on with your song. Lincoln won the war for the wrong reasons."

"And then he was shot, right?" Skeeter passes the joint to Jill. As she takes it her eyes ask Rabbit, *Is this what you want?* She holds it the way the experts do, not like a tobacco cigarette, something for Fred Astaire to gesture with, but reverently as food, with as many fingers as she can get around it, feeding the wet end to herself like a nipple. Her thin face goes peaceful, puts on the fat of dreams. Skeeter is saying, "So then you had these four million freed slaves without property or jobs in this economy dead on its feet thinking the halleluiah days had come. Green pastures, right? Forty acres and a mule, right? Goddam green pickles Chuck, that was the most pathetic thing, the way those poor niggers jumped for the bait. They taught themselves to read, they broke their backs for chickenshit, they sent good men to the fuckhead Yoo Ess Senate, they set up legislatures giving Dixie the first public schools it ever had, how about that now, there's a fact for your eddi-cayshun, right? Jill honey, hand that stick back, you gonna blow yourself to the moon, that is uncut Red. And all this here while, Chuck and Babychuck, the crackers down there were frothing at the mouth and calling our black heroes baboons. Couldn't do much else as long as the Northern armies hung around, right? Baboons, monkeys, apes: these hopeful sweet blacks trying to make men of themselves, thinking they'd been called to be men at last in these the Benighted States of Amurri-ka." Skeeter's face is shedding its shell of scorn and writhing as if to cry. He has taken his glasses off. He is reaching toward Jill for the marijuana cigarette, keeping his eyes on Rabbit's face. Rabbit is frozen, his mind racing. Nelson. Put him to bed. Seeing too much. His own face as he listens to Skeeter feels weak, shapeless, slipping. The beer tastes bad, of malt. Skeeter wants to cry, to yell. He is sitting on the edge of the sofa and making gestures so brittle his arms might snap off. He is crazy. "So what did the South do? They said baboon and lynched and whipped and cheated the black man of what pennies he had and thanked their white Jesus they didn't have to feed him any more. And what did the North do? It copped out. It pulled out. It had put on all that muscle for the war and now it was wading into the biggest happiest muck of greed and graft and exploitation and pollution and slum-building and Indian-killing this poor old whore of a planet has ever been saddled with, right? Don't go sleepy on me Chuck, here comes the interesting part. The Southern assholes got together with the Northern assholes and said, Let's us do a deal. What's all this about democracy, let's have here a dollar-cracy. Why'd we ever care, free versus slave? Capital versus labor, that's where it's at, right? This poor cunt of a country's the biggest jampot's ever come along so let's eat it, friend. You screw your black labor and we'll screw our immigrant honky and Mongolian idiot labor and, *whoo-hee!* Halleluiah, right? So the Freedman's Bureau was trashed and the military governors were chased back by crackers on horses who were very big on cutting up colored girls with babies inside 'em and Tilden was cheated out of the Presidency in the one bony-fidey swindle election you can find admitted in every honky history book. Look it up, right? And that was the revolution of 1876. Far as the black man goes, that's the '76 that hurt, the one a hundred years before was just a bunch of English gents dodging taxes." Skeeter has put his glasses back on; the glass circles glitter behind a blueness of smoke. His voice has settled for irony again. "So let's all sing America the Beautiful, right? North and West, robber barons and slums. Down South, one big nigger barbecue. Hitler bless his sweet soul leastways tried to keep the ovens out of sight. Down Dixieway, every magnolia had a rope. Man, they passed laws if a nigger sneezed within three miles of a white.ass his balls were chewed off by sawtoothed beagles. Some nigger didn't hop off the sidewalk and lick up the tobacco juice whenever the town trash spit, he was tucked into a chain gang and peddled to the sheriff's brother-in-law cheaper than an alligator egg. And if he dared ask for the vote the Fifteenth Amendment had flat-out given him, why, they couldn't think up ways to skin him slowly enough, they couldn't invent enough laws to express their dis-approbation, better for a poor black man to go stick his head up Great-aunt Lily's snatch than try to stick it in a polling booth. Right? Chuck, I got to hand it to you, you had it all ways. The South got slavery back at half the price, it got control of Congress back by counting the black votes that couldn't be cast, the North got the cotton money it needed for capital, and everybody got the fun of shitting on the black man and then holding their noses. You believe any of this?"

"I believe all of it," Rabbit says.

"Do you believe, do you believe I'm so mad just telling this if I had a knife right now I'd poke it in your throat and watch that milk-white blood come out and would love it, oh, would I love it." Skeeter is weeping. Tears and smoke mix on the skin of his face.

"O.K., O.K.," Rabbit says.

"Skeeter, don't cry," Nelson says.

"Skeeter, it was too rich, I'm going to lose it," Jill says and stands. "I'm dizzy."

But Skeeter will talk only to Harry. "What I want to say to you," he says, "what I want to make ever so clear, Chuck, is you had that chance. You could have gone some better road, right? You took that greedy turn, right? You sold us out, right? You sold yourselves out. Like Lincoln said, you paid in blood, sword for the lash and all that, and you didn't lift us up, we held out our hands, man, we were like faithful dogs waiting for that bone, but you gave us a kick, you put us down, you put us down."

"Skeeter, please don't ever give me any more of that whatever it was, ever, ever," Jill says, drifting away.

Skeeter controls his crying, lifts his face darkened in streaks like ashes wetted down. "It wasn't just us, you sold yourselves out, right? You really had it here, you had it all, and you took that greedy mucky road, man, you made yourself the asshole of the planet. Right? To keep that capitalist thing rolling you let those asshole crackers have their way and now you's all asshole crackers, North and South however you look there's assholes, you lapped up the poison and now it shows, Chuck, you say America to you and you still get bugles and stars but say it to any black or yellow man and you get hate, right? Man the world does hate you, you're the big pig keeping it all down." He jabs blearily with his skinny finger, and hangs his head.

From upstairs, discreet as the noise a cat makes catching a bird, comes a squeezed heaving noise, Jill being sick.

Nelson asks, "Dad, shouldn't you call a doctor?"

"She'll be O.K. Go to bed. You have school tomorrow."

Skeeter looks at Rabbit; his eyeballs are fiery and rheumy. "I said it, right?"

"Trouble with your line," Rabbit tells him, "it's pure self-pity. The real question is, Where do you go from here? We all got here on a bad boat. You talk as if the whole purpose of this country since the start has been to frustrate Negroes. Hell, you're just ten per cent. The fact is most people don't give a damn *what* you do. This is the freest country around, make it if you can, if you can't, die gracefully. But Jesus, stop begging for a free ride."

"Friend, you are wrong. You are white but wrong. We fascinate you, white man. We are in your dreams. We are technology's nightmare. We are all the good satisfied nature you put down in yourselves when you took that mucky greedy turn. We are what has been left *out* of the industrial revolution, so we are the *next* revolution, and don't you know it? You know it. Why else you so scared of me, Rabbit?"

"Because you're a spook. I'm going to bed."

Skeeter rolls his head loosely, touches it dubiously. In the light from the driftwood lamp his round mass of hair is seen as insubstantial, his skull narrow as the bone handle of a knife. He brushes at his forehead as if midges are there. He says, "Sweet dreams. I'm too spaced to sleep right now, I got just to sit here, nursing the miseries. Mind if I play the radio if I keep it low?"

"No."

Upstairs, Jill, a sudden warm wisp in his arms, begs with rapid breath, "Get him out of here, Harry, don't let him stay, he's no good for me, no good for any of us."

"You brought him here." He takes her talk as the exaggerating that children do, to erase their fears by spelling them out; and indeed in five minutes she is dead asleep, motionless. The electric clock burns beyond her head like a small moon's skeleton. Downstairs, a turned-down radio faintly scratches. And shortly Rabbit too is asleep. Strangely, he sleeps soundly, with Skeeter in the house.

"Harry, how about a quick one?" His father tells the bartender, as always, "Let's make it a Schlitz."

"Whisky sour," he says. Summer is over, the air-conditioning in the Phoenix has been turned off. He asks, "How's Mom doing?"

"As good as can be hoped, Harry." He nudges a conspiratorial inch closer. "That new stuff really seems to do the job, she's on her feet for hours at a time now. For my money, though, the sixty-four-thousand-dollar question is what the long-range effects will be. The doctor, he's perfectly honest about it. He says to her when we go on in to the hospital, 'How's my favorite guinea pig?' "

"What's the answer?" Rabbit abruptly asks.

His father is startled. "Her answer?"

"Anybody's."

His father now understands the question and shrugs his narrow shoulders in their clean white shirt. "Blind faith," he suggests. In a mutter he adds, "One more bastard under the ground."

On the television above the bar men are filing past a casket, but the sound is turned off and Rabbit cannot tell if it is Everett Dirksen's lying-in-state in Washington or Ho Chi Minh's ceremonies in Hanoi. Dignitaries look alike, always dressed in mourning. His father clears his throat, breaks the silence. "Janice called your mother last night."

"Boy, I think she's cracking up, she's on the phone all the time. Stavros must be losing his muscle."

"She was very disturbed, she said you'd taken a colored man into your house."

"I didn't exactly take him, he kind of showed up. Nobody's supposed to know about it. I think he's Farnsworth's son."

"That can't be, Jerry's never married to my knowledge."

"They don't marry generally, right? They weren't allowed to as slaves."

This bit of historical information makes Earl Angstrom grimace. He takes, what for him, with his boy, is a tough line. "I must say, Harry, I'm not too happy about it either."

The funeral (the flag on the coffin has stars and stripes, so it must be Dirksen's) vanishes, and flickering in its place are shots of cannons blasting, of trucks moving through the desert, of planes soundlessly batting through the sky, of soldiers waving. He cannot tell if they are Israeli or Egyptian. He asks, "How happy is Mom about it?"

"I must say, she was very short with Janice. Suggested if she wanted to run your household she go back to it. Said she had no right to complain. I don't know what all else. I couldn't bear to listen, when women get to quarrelling, I head for the hills."

"Janice talk about lawyers?"

"Your mother didn't mention it if she did. Between you and me, Harry, she was so upset it scared me. I don't believe she slept more than two, three hours; she took twice the dose of Seconal and still it couldn't knock her out. She's worried and, pardon my crust for horning in where I have no business, Harry, so am I."

"Worried about what?"

"Worried about this new development. I'm no nigger-hater, I'm happy to work with 'em and I have for twenty years, if needs be I'll live next to 'em though the fact is they haven't cracked Mt. Judge yet, but get any closer than that, you're playing with fire, in my experience."

"What experience?"

"They'll let you down," Pop says. "They don't have any feeling of obligation. I'm not blaming a soul, but that's the fact, they'll let you down and laugh about it afterwards. They're not like white men and there's no use saying they are. You asked me what experience, I don't want to go into stories, though there's plenty I could tell, just remember I was raised in the Third Ward when it was more white than black, we mixed it up in every sense. I know the people of this county. They're good-natured people. They like to eat and drink and like to have their red-light district and their numbers, they'll elect the scum to political office time and time again; but they don't like seeing their women desecrated."

"Who's being desecrated?"

"Just that menagerie over there, the way you're keeping

it, is a desecration. Have you heard from your neighbors what they think about it yet?"

"I don't even know my neighbors."

"That black boy shows his face outside, you'll get to know them, you'll get to know them as sure as I'm standing here trying to be a friend and not a father. The day when I could whip sense into you is long by, Harry, and anyway you gave us a lot less trouble than Mim. Your mother always says you let people push you around and I always answer her, Harry knows his way around, he lands on his feet; but I'm beginning to see she may be right. Your mother may be all crippled up but she's still hard to fool, ask the man who's tried."

"When did you try?"

But this secret—had Pop played Mom false?—stays dammed behind those loose false teeth the old man's mouth keeps adjusting, pensively sucking. Instead he says, "Do us a favor, Harry, I hate like hell to beg, but do us a favor and come over tonight and talk about it. Your mother stiff-armed Janice but I know when she's been shook."

"Not tonight, I can't. Maybe in a couple of days, things'll clear up."

"Why not, Harry? We promise not to grill you or anything, Lord, I wouldn't ask for myself, it's your mother's state of mind. You know"—and he slides so close their white sleeves touch and Rabbit smells the sour fog of his father's breath—"she's having the adventure now we're all going to have to have."

"Stop asking, Pop. I can't right now."

"They've gotcha in their clutches, huh?"

He stands straight, decides one whisky sour will do, and answers, "Right."

That night after supper they discuss slavery. Jill and Skeeter have done the dishes together, Rabbit has helped Nelson with his homework. The kid is into algebra this year but can't quite manage that little flip in his head whereby a polynomial cracks open into two nice equalities of *x*, one minus and one plus. Rabbit had been good at math, it was a game with limits, with orderly movements and a promise of completion at the end. The combination always cracked open. Nelson is tight about it, afraid to let go and swing, a smart kid but tight, afraid of maybe that thing that got his baby sister: afraid it might come back for him. They have half an hour before *Laugh-In*, which they all want to watch. Tonight Skeeter takes the big brown chair and Rabbit the one with silver threads. Jill and Nelson sit on the airfoam sofa. Skeeter has some books; they look childishly bright under his thin brown hands. School days. *Sesame Street*.

Skeeter says to Rabbit, "Chuck, I been thinking I sold out the truth last night when I said your slavery was a country thing. The fact upon reflection appears to be that your style of slavery was uniquely and e-specially bad, about the worst indeed this poor blood-soaked globe has ever seen." Skeeter's voice as he speaks exerts a steady pressure, wind rattling a dead tree. His eyes never deviate to Nelson or Jill.

Rabbit, a game student (in high school he used to get B's), asks, "What was so bad about it?"

"Let me guess what you think. You think it wasn't so bad on the plantations, right? What with banjos and all the fritters you could eat and Ol' Massah up at the big house instead of the Department of Welfare, right? Those niggers were savages anyway, their chuckleheads pure bone, and if they didn't like it, well, why didn't they just up and die in their chains like the noble old redman, right?"

"Yeah. Why didn't they?"

"I love that question. Because I have the answer. The reason is, old Tonto was so primitive farmwork made no sense to him, he was on the moon, right?, and just withered away. Now the black man, he was from West Africa, where they had agriculture. Where they had social organization. How do you think those slaves got to the coast from a thousand miles away? Black men arranged it, they wouldn't cut the white men in, they kept the pie all for themselves. Organization men, right?"

"That's interesting."

"I'm glad you said that. I am grateful for your interest."

"He meant it," Jill intercedes.

"Swallow your tongue," Skeeter says without looking toward her.

"Swallow your tongue yourself," Nelson intervenes. Rabbit would be proud of the boy, but he feels that Nelson's defense of Jill, like Skeeter's attack, are automatic: parts of a pattern the three have developed while he is away working.

"The readings," Jill prompts.

Skeeter explains. "Little Jilly and I, today, been talking, and her idea is, to make our nights more structured, right? We'd read aloud a few things, otherwise I'm apt to do all the talking, that is until you decide to dump me on the floor again."

"Let me get a beer then."

"Puts pimples on your belly, man. Let me light up some good Tijuana brass and pass it over, old athlete like you shouldn't be getting a beer gut, right?"

Rabbit neither agrees nor moves. He glances at Nelson: the kid's eyes are sunk and shiny, frightened but not to the point of panic. He is learning, he trusts them. He frowns over to stop his father looking at him. Around them the furniture—the fire place that never holds a fire, the driftwood base like a corpse lying propped on one arm—listens. A quiet rain has begun at the windows, sealing them in. Skeeter holds his lips pinched to seal into himself the first volumes of sweet smoke, then exhales, sighing, and leans back into the chair, vanishing between the brown wings but for the glass-and-silver circles of his spectacles. He says, "He was property, right? From Virginia on, it was profit and capital absolutely. The King of England, all he cared about was tobacco cash, right? Black men just blots on the balance sheet to him. Now the King of Spain, he knew black men from way back; those Moors had run his country and some had been pretty smart. So south of the border a slave was property but he was also other things. King of Spain say, That's my subject, he has legal rights, right? Church say, That's an everlasting immortal soul there: baptize him. Teach him right from wrong. His marriage vows are sacred, right? If he rustles up the bread to buy himself free, you got to sell. This was all written in the law down there. Up here, the law said one thing: no rights. No rights. This is no man, this is one warm piece of animal meat, worth one thousand Yoo Hess Hay coldblooded clams. Can't let it marry, that might mess up selling it when the market is right. Can't let it go and testify in court, that might mess up Whitey's property rights. There was no such thing, *no* such, believe me, as the father of a slave child. That was a legal fact. Now how could the law get that way? Because they did believe a nigger was a piece of shit. And they was scared of their own shit. Man, those crackers were sick and they knew it absolutely. All those years talkin' about happy Rastus chompin' on watermelon they was scared shitless of uprisings, *up*risings, Chuck, when there hadn't been more than two or three the whole hundred years and those not amounted to a bucket of piss. They was scared rigid, right? Scared of blacks learning to read, scared of blacks learning a trade, scared of blacks on the job market, there was no place for a freedman to go, once he *was* freed, all that talk about free soil, the first thing the free-soil convention in Kansas said was we don't want no black faces here, keep 'em away from our eyeballs. The thing about these Benighted States all around is that it was never no place like other places where this happens because that happens, and some men have more luck than others so let's push a little here and give a little here; no, sir, this place was never such a place it was a *dream*, it was a state of mind from those poor fool pilgrims on, right? Some white man see a black man he don't see a man he sees a *symbol*, right? All these people around here are walking around inside their own *heads*, they don't even know if you kick somebody else it *hurts*, Jesus won't even tell 'em because the Jesus they brought over on the boats was the meanest most de-balled Jesus the good Lord ever let run around scaring people. Scared, *scared*. I'm scared of you, you scared of me, Nelson scared of us both, and poor Jilly here so scared of everything she'll run and hide herself in dope again if we don't all act like big daddies to her." He offers the smoking wet-licked reefer around. Rabbit shakes his head no.

"Skeeter," Jill says, "the selections." A prim clubwoman calling the meeting to order. "Thirteen minutes to *Laugh-In*," Nelson says. "I don't want to miss the beginning, it's neat when they introduce themselves."

"Ree-ight," Skeeter says, fumbling at his forehead, at that buzzing that seems sometimes there. "Out of this book here." The book is called *Slavery;* the letters are red, white, and blue. It seems a small carnival under Skeeter's slim hand. "Just for the fun of it, to give us something more solid than my ignorant badmouthing, right? You know, like a happening. Chuck, this gives you pretty much a pain in the ass, right?"

"No, I like it. I like learning stuff. I have an open mind."

"He turns me on, he's so true to life," Skeeter says, handing the book to Jill. "Baby, you begin. Where my finger is, just the part in little type." He announces, "These are old-time speeches, dig?"

Jill sits up straight on the sofa and reads in a voice higher than her natural voice, a nice-girl-school–schooled voice, with riding lessons in it, and airy big white-curtained rooms; territory even above Penn Park.

"*Think*," she reads, "*of the nation's deed, done continually and afresh. God shall hear the voice of your brother's blood, long crying from the ground; His justice asks you even now, 'America, where is thy brother?' This is the answer which America must give: 'Lo, he is there in the rice-swamps of the South, in her fields teeming with cotton and the luxuriant cane. He was weak and I seized him; naked and I bound him; ignorant, poor and savage, and I over-mastered him. I laid on his feebler shoulders my grievous yoke. I have chained him with my fetters; beat him with my whip. Other tyrants had dominion over him, but my finger was on his human flesh. I am fed with his toil; fat, voluptuous on his sweat, and tears, and blood. I stole the father, stole also the sons, and set them to toil; his wife and daughters are a pleasant spoil to me. Behold the children also of thy servant and his handmaidens—sons swarthier than their sire. Askest thou for the African? I have made him a beast. Lo, there Thou hast what is thine.*' " She hands the book back blushing. Her glance at Rabbit says, *Bear with us. Haven't I loved you?*

Skeeter is cackling. "Green pickles, that turns me on. A pleasant spoil to me, right? And did you dig that beautiful bit about the sons swarthier than their sire? Those old Yankee sticks were really bugged, one respectable fuck would have stopped the abolition movement cold. But they weren't getting it back home in the barn so they sure gave hell to those crackers getting it out in the slave shed. Dark meat is soul meat, right? That was Theodore Parker, here's another, the meanest mouth in the crowd, old William Lloyd. Nellie, you try this. Just where I've marked. Just read the words slow, don't try for any expression."

Gaudy book in hand, the boy looks toward his father for rescue. "I feel stupid."

Rabbit says, "Read, Nelson. I want to hear it."

He turns for help elsewhere. "Skeeter, you promised I wouldn't have to."

"I said we'd see how it *went.* Come on, your Daddy likes it. He has an open mind."

"You're just poking fun of everybody."

"Let him off," Rabbit says. "I'm losing interest."

Jill intervenes. "Do it, Nelson, it'll be fun. We won't turn on *Laugh-In* until you do."

The boy plunges in, stumbling, frowning so hard his father wonders if he doesn't need glasses. "*No matter,*" he reads, "*though every party should be torn by dis-*, dis—"

Jill looks over his shoulder. "Dissensions."

"*—every sest—*"

"Sect."

"*—every sect dashed into fragments, the national compact dissolved—*"

Jill says, "Good!"

"Let him ride," Skeeter says, his eyes shut, nodding.

Nelson's voice gains confidence. "*—the land filled with the horrors of a civil and a servile war—still, slavery must be buried in the grave of infantry—*"

"Infamy," Jill corrects.

"*—in-fa-my, beyond the possibility of a rez, a razor—*"

"A resurrection."

"*If the State cannot survive the anti-slavery agitation, then let the State perish. If the Church must be cast down by the strugglings of Humanity, then let the Church fall, and its fragments be scattered to the four winds of heaven, never more to curse the earth. If the American Union cannot be maintained, except by immolating*—what's that?"

"Sacrificing," Jill says.

Rabbit says, "I thought it meant burn."

Nelson looks up, uncertain he should continue.

The rain continues at the windows, gently, gently nailing them in, tighter together.

Skeeter's eyes are still closed. "Finish up. Do the last sentence, Babychuck."

"*If the Republic must be blotted out from the roll of nations, by proclaiming liberty to the captives, then let the Republic sink beneath the waves of oblivion, and a shout of joy, louder than the voice of many waters, fill the universe at its extinction.* I don't understand what any of this stuff means."

Skeeter says, "It means, More Power to the People, Death to the Fascist Pigs."

Rabbit says, "To me it means, Throw the baby out with the bath." He remembers a tub of still water, a kind of dust on its dead surface. He relives the shock of reaching down through it to pull the plug. He loops back into the room where they are sitting now, within the rain.

Jill is explaining to Nelson, "He's saying what Skeeter says. If the System, even if it works for most people, has to oppress some of the people, then the whole System should be destroyed."

"Do I say that? No." Skeeter leans forward from the mossy brown wings, reaching a trembling thin hand toward the young people, all parody shaken from his voice. "That'll come anyway. That big boom. It's not the poor blacks setting the bombs, it's the offspring of the white rich. It's not injustice pounding at the door, it's impatience. Put enough rats in a cage the fat ones get more frantic than the skinny ones cause they feel more *squeezed*. No. We must look past that, past the violence, into the next stage. That it's gonna blow up we can as*sume*. That's not interesting. What comes next is what's interesting. There's got to be a great *calm*."

"And you're the black Jesus going to bring it in," Rabbit mocks. "From A.D. to A.S. After Skeeter. I should live so long. All Praise Be Skeeter's Name."

He offers to sing but Skeeter is concentrating on the other two, disciples. "People talk revolution all the time but revolution's not interesting, right? Revolution is just one crowd taking power from another and that's bullshit, that's just power, and power is just guns and gangsters, and that's boring bullshit, right? People say to me Free Huey, I say Screw Huey, he's just Agnew in blackface. World forgets gangsters like that before they're dead. No. The problem is really, when the gangsters have knocked each other off, and taken half of everybody else with them, to make use of the *space*. After the Civil War ended, there was space, only they let it fill up with that same old greedy muck, only worse, right? They turned that old dog-eat-dog thing into a divine law."

"That's what we need, Skeeter," Rabbit says. "Some new divine laws. Why doncha go up to the top of Mt. Judge and have 'em handed to you on a tablet?"

Skeeter turns that nicely carved knife-handle of a face to him slowly, says slowly, "I'm no threat to you, Chuck. You're *set*. Only thing I could do to you is kill you and that matters less than you think, right?"

Jill delicately offers to make peace. "Didn't we pick out something for Harry to read?"

"Fuck it," Skeeter says. "That won't swing now. He's giving off ugly vibes, right? He's not ready. He is immature."

Rabbit is hurt, he had only been kidding. "Come on, I'm ready, give me my thing to read."

Skeeter asks Nelson, "What say, Babychuck? Think he's ready?"

Nelson says, "You must read it right, Dad. No poking fun."

"Me? Who'd I ever poke fun of?"

"Mommy."

Skeeter gives him the book open to a page. "Just a little bit. Just read where I've marked."

Soft red crayon. Those Crayola boxes that used to remind him of bleachers with every head a different color. This strange return. "*I believe, my friends and fellow citizens,*"

Rabbit reads thrillingly, "*we are not prepared for this suffrage. But we can learn. Give a man tools and let him commence to use them, and in time he will learn a trade. So it is with voting. We may not understand it at the start, but in time we shall learn to do our duty*."

The rain makes soft applause.

Skeeter tips his narrow head and smiles at the two children on the sofa. "Makes a pretty good nigger, don't he?"

Nelson says, "Don't, Skeeter. He didn't poke fun so you shouldn't."

"Nothing wrong with what I said, that's what the world needs, pretty good niggers, right?"

To show Nelson how tough he is, Rabbit tells Skeeter, "This is all bleeding-heart stuff. It'd be like me bellyaching that the Swedes were pushed around by the Finns in the year Zilch."

Nelson cries, "We're missing *Laugh-In!*"

They turn it on. The cold small star expands, a torrent of stripes snaps into a picture, Sammy Davis Jr. is being the little dirty old man, tapping along behind the park bench, humming that aimless sad doodling tune. He perks up, seeing there is someone sitting on the bench. It is not Ruth Buzze but Arte Johnson, the white, the real little dirty old man. They sit side by side and stare at each other. They are like one man looking into a crazy mirror. Nelson laughs. They all laugh: Nelson, Jill, Rabbit, Skeeter. Kindly the rain fastens them in, a dressmaker patting and stitching all around the house, fitting its great wide gown.

Skeeter asks him another night, "You want to know how a Ne-gro feels?"

"Not much."

"Dad, don't," Nelson says.

Jill, silent, abstracted, passes Rabbit the joint. He takes a tentative puff. Has hardly held a cigarette in ten years, scared to inhale. Nearly sick after the other time, in Jimbo's. You suck and hold it down. Hold it down.

"Ee-magine," Skeeter is saying, "being in a glass box, and every time you move toward something, your head gets bumped. Ee-magine being on a bus, and everybody movin' away, 'cause your whole body's covered with pustulatin' scabs, and they're scared to get the disease."

Rabbit exhales, lets it out. "That's not how it is. These black kids on buses are pushy as hell."

*

"You've set so much type the world is lead, right? You don't hate nobody, right?"

"Nobody." Serenely. Space is transparent.

"How you feel about those Penn Park people?"

"Which ones?"

"All those ones. All those ones live in those great big piecrust mock-Two-door houses with His and Hers Caddies parked out by the hydrangea bushes. How about all those old farts down at the Mifflin Club with all those iron gates that used to own the textile mills and now don't own anything but a heap of paper keeps 'em in cigars and girl friends? How about those? Let 'em settle in before you answer."

Rabbit pictures Penn Park, the timbered gables, the stucco, the weedless lawns plumped up like pillows. It was on a hill. He used to imagine it on the top of a hill, a hill he could never climb, because it wasn't a real hill like Mt. Judge. And he and Mom and Pop and Mim lived near the foot of this hill, in the dark next to the Bolgers, and Pop came home from work every day too tired to play catch in the backyard, and Mom never had jewelry like other women, and they bought day-old bread because it was a penny cheaper, and Pop's teeth hurt to keep money out of the dentist's hands, and now Mom's dying was a game being played by doctors who drove Caddies and had homes in Penn Park. "I hate them," he tells Skeeter.

The black man's face lights up, shines. "Deeper."

Rabbit fears the feeling will be fragile and vanish if he looks at it but it does not; it expands, explodes. Timbered gables, driveway pebbles, golf clubs fill the sky with debris. He remembers one doctor. He met him early this summer by accident, coming up on the porch to visit Mom, the doctor hurrying out, under the fanlight that sees everything, in a swank cream raincoat though it had just started to sprinkle, that kind of dude, who produces a raincoat from nowhere when proper, all set up, life licked, tweed trousers knife-sharp over polished strapped shoes, hurrying to his next appointment, anxious to get away from this drizzling tilted street. Pop worrying his teeth like an old woman in the doorway, performing introductions, "our son Harry," pathetic pride. The doctor's irritation at being halted even a second setting a prong of distaste on his upper lip behind the clipped mustache the color of iron. His handshake also metal, arrogant, it pinches Harry's unready hand and says, *I am strong, I twist bodies to my will. I am life, I am death.* "I hate those Penn Park motherfuckers," Harry amplifies, performing for Skeeter, wanting to please him. "If I could push the red button to blow them all to Kingdom Come"—he pushes a button in mid-air—"I would." He pushes the button so hard he can see it there.

"Ka-boom, right?" Skeeter grins, flinging wide his sticklike arms.

*

"But it is," Rabbit says. "Everybody knows black pussy is beautiful. It's on posters even, now."

Skeeter asks, "How you think all this mammy shit got

started? Who you think put all those hog-fat churchified old women at the age of thirty in Harlem?"

"Not me."

"It *was* you. Man, you is just who it was. From those breeding cabins on you made the black girl feel sex was shit, so she hid from it as quick as she could in the mammy bit, right?"

"Well, tell 'em it's not shit."

"They don't believe me, Chuck. They see I don't count. I have no muscle, right? I can't protect my black women, right? 'Cause you don't let me be a man."

"Go ahead. Be one."

Skeeter gets up from the armchair with the silver threads and circles the imitation cobbler's bench with a wary hunch-backed quickness and kisses Jill where she sits on the sofa. Her hands, after a startled jerk, knit together and stay in her lap. Her head does not pull back nor strain forward. Rabbit cannot see, around the eclipsing orb of Skeeter's Afro, Jill's eyes. He can see Nelson's eyes. They are warm watery holes so dark, so stricken he would like to stick pins into them, to teach the child there is worse. Skeeter straightens from kissing, wipes the Jill-spit from his mouth. "A pleasant spoil. Chuck, how do you like it?"

"I don't mind. If she doesn't."

Jill has closed her eyes, her mouth open on a small bubble.

"She *does* mind it," Nelson protests. "Dad, don't *let* him!"

Rabbit says to Nelson, "Bedtime, isn't it?"

*

Physically, Skeeter fascinates Rabbit. The lustrous pallor of the tongue and palms and the soles of the feet, left out of the sun. Or a different kind of skin? White palms never tan either. The peculiar glinting lustre of his skin. The something so very finely turned and finished in the face, reflecting light at a dozen polished points: in comparison white faces are blobs: putty still drying. The curious greased grace of his gestures, rapid and watchful as a lizard's motions, free of mammalian fat. Skeeter in his house feels like a finely made electric toy; Harry wants to touch him but is afraid he will get a shock.

*

"O.K.?"

"Not especially." Jill's voice seems to come from further away than beside him in the bed.

"Why not?"

"I'm scared."

"Of what? Of me?"

"Of you and him together."

"We're not together. We hate each other's guts."

She asks, "When are you kicking him out?"

"They'll put him in jail."

"Good."

The rain is heavy above them, beating everywhere, inserting itself in that chimney flashing that always leaked. He pictures a wide brown stain on the bedroom ceiling. He asks, "What's with you and him?"

She doesn't answer. Her lean cameo profile is lit by a flash. Seconds pass before the thunder arrives.

He asks shyly, "He getting into you?"

"Not that way any more. He says that's not interesting. He wants me another way now."

"What way can that be?" Poor girl, crazy suspicious.

"He wants me to tell him about God. He says he's going to bring some mesc for me."

The thunder follows the next flash more closely.

"That's crazy." But exciting: maybe she can do it. Maybe he can get music out of her like Babe out of the piano.

"He is crazy," Jill says. "I'll never be hooked again."

"What can I do?" Rabbit feels paralyzed, by the rain, the thunder, by his curiosity, by his hope for a break in the combination, for catastrophe and deliverance.

The girl cries out but thunder comes just then and he has to ask her to repeat it. "All you care about is your *wife*," she shouts upward into the confusion in heaven.

*

Pajasek comes up behind him and mumbles about the phone. Rabbit drags himself up. Worse than a liquor hang-over, must stop, every night. Must get a grip on himself. Get a grip. Get angry. "Janice, for Chrissake—"

"It isn't Janice, Harry. It's me. Peggy."

"Oh. Hi. How's tricks? How's Ollie?"

"Forget Ollie, don't ever mention his name to me. He hasn't been to see Billy in weeks or contributed *an*ything to his keep, and when he finally does show up, you know what he brings? He's a genius, you'll never guess."

"Another mini-bike."

"A puppy. He brought us a Golden Retriever puppy. Now what the hell can we do with a puppy with Billy off in school and me gone from eight to five every day?"

"You got a job. Congratulations. What do you do?"

"I type tape for Brewer Fealty over at Youngquist, they're putting all their records on computer tape and not only is the work so boring you could scream, you don't even know when you've made a mistake, it comes out just holes in this tape, all these premium numbers."

"It sounds nifty. Peggy, speaking of work, they don't appreciate my being called here."

Her voice retreats, puts on dignity. "Pardon *me*. I wanted to talk to you when Nelson wasn't around. Ollie has promised Billy to take him fishing next Sunday, not *this* Sunday, and I wondered, since it doesn't look as if you'll ever ask me, if you'd like to have dinner Saturday when you bring him over."

Her open bathrobe, that pubic patch, the silver stretch-marks, don't count your chickens. Meaning do count your chickens. "That might be great," he says.

"Might be."

"I'll have to see, I'm kind of tied up these days—"

"Hasn't that man gone yet? Kick him out, Harry. He's taking incredible advantage of you. Call the police if he won't go. Really, Harry, you're much too passive."

"Yeah. Or something." Only after shutting the office door behind him and starting to walk through the solid brightness toward his machine does he feel the marijuana clutch at him, drag at his knees like a tide. Never again. Let Jesus come at him another way.

*

"Tell us about Vietnam, Skeeter." The grass is mixing with his veins and he feels very close, very close to them all: the driftwood lamp, Nelson's thatch of hair an anxious tangle, Jill's bare legs a touch unshaped at the ankles. He loves them. All. His voice moves in and out behind their eyes. Skeeter's eyes roll red toward the ceiling. Things are pouring for him through the ceiling.

"Why you want to be told?" he asks.

"Because I wasn't there."

"Think you should have been there, right?"

"Yes."

"Why would that be?"

"I don't know. Duty. Guilt."

"No sir. You want to have been there because that is where it was at, right?"

"O.K."

"It was the best place," Skeeter says, not quite as a question.

"Something like that."

Skeeter goes on, gently urging, "It was where you would have felt not so de-balled, right?"

"I don't know. If you don't want to talk about it, don't. Let's turn on television."

"*Mod Squad* will be on," Nelson says.

Skeeter explains: "If you can't fuck, dirty pictures won't do it for you, right? And then if you can, they don't do it either."

"O.K., don't tell us anything. And try to watch your language in front of Nelson."

*

At night when Jill turns herself to him in bed he finds the unripe hardness of her young body repels him. The smoke inside him severs his desires from his groin, he is full of flitting desires that prevent him from directly answering her woman's call, a call he helped create in her girl's body. Yet in his mind he sees her mouth defiled by Skeeter's kiss and feels her rotting with his luminous poison. Nor can he forgive her for having been rich. Yet through these nightly denials, these quiet debasements, he feels something unnatural strengthening within him that may be love. On her side she seems, more and more, to cling to him; they have come far from that night when she went down on him like a little girl bobbing for apples.

*

This fall Nelson has discovered soccer; the junior high school has a team and his small size is no handicap. Afternoons Harry comes home to find the child kicking the ball, sewn of black-and-white pentagons, again and again against the garage door, beneath the unused basketball backboard. The ball bounces by Nelson, Harry picks it up, it feels bizarrely seamed in his hands. He tries a shot at the basket. It misses clean. "The touch is gone," he says. "It's a funny feeling," he tells his son, "when you get old. The brain sends out the order and the body looks the other way."

Nelson resumes kicking the ball, vehemently, with the side of his foot, against a spot on the door already worn paintless. The boy has mastered that trick of trapping the ball to a dead stop under his knees.

"Where are the other two?"

"Inside. Acting funny."

"How funny?"

"You know. The way they act. Dopey. Skeeter's asleep on the sofa. Hey, Dad."

"What?"

Nelson kicks the ball once, twice, hard as he can, until it gets by him and he has worked up nerve to tell. "I hate the kids around here."

"What kids? I never see any. When I was a kid, we were all over the streets."

"They watch television and go to Little League and stuff."

"Why do you hate them?"

Nelson has retrieved the ball and is shuffling it from one foot to the other, his feet clever as hands. "Tommy Frankhauser said we had a nigger living with us and said his father said it was ruining the neighborhood and we'd better watch out."

"What'd you say to that?"

"I said he better watch out himself."

"Did you fight?"

"I wanted to but he's a head taller than me even though we're in the same grade and he just laughed."

"Don't worry about it, you'll shoot up. All us Angstroms are late bloomers."

"I hate them, Dad, I *hate* them!" And he heads the ball so it bounces off the shadow-line shingles of the garage roof.

"Mustn't hate anybody," Harry says, and goes in.

Jill is in the kitchen, crying over a pan of lamb chops. "The flame keeps getting too big," she says. She has the gas turned down so low the little nipples of blue are sputtering. He turns it higher and Jill screams, falls against him, presses her face into his chest, peeks up with eyes amusement has dyed deep green. "You smell of ink," she tells him. "You're all ink, so clean, just like a new newspaper. Every day, a new newspaper comes to the door."

He holds her close; her tears tingle through his shirt. "Has Skeeter been feeding you anything?"

"No, Daddy. I mean lover. We stayed in the house all day and watched the quizzes, Skeeter hates the way they always have Negro couples on now, he says it's tokenism."

He smells her breath and, as she has promised, there is nothing, no liquor, no grass, just a savor of innocence, a faint tinge of sugar, a glimpse of a porch swing and a beaded pitcher. "Tea," he says.

"What an elegant little nose," she says, of his, and pinches it. "That's right. Skeeter and I had iced tea this afternoon." She keeps caressing him, rubbing against him, making him sad. "You're elegant all over," she says. "You're an enormous snowman, twinkling all over, except you don't have a carrot for a nose, you have it here."

"Hey," he says, hopping backwards.

Jill tells him urgently, "I like you there better than Skeeter, I think being circumcised makes men ugly."

"Can you make the supper? Maybe you should go up and lie down."

"I hate you when you're so uptight," she tells him, but without hate, in a voice swinging as a child wandering home swings a basket, "can I cook the supper, I can do anything, I can fly, I can make men satisfied, I can drive a white car, I can count in French up to any number; look!"—she pulls her dress way up above her waist—"I'm a Christmas tree!"

But the supper comes to the table badly cooked. The lamb chops are rubbery and blue near the bone, the beans crunch underdone in the mouth. Skeeter pushes his plate away. "I can't eat this crud. I ain't that primitive, right?"

Nelson says, "It tastes all right, Jill."

But Jill knows, and bows her thin face. Tears fall onto her plate. Strange tears, less signs of grief than chemical condensations: tears she puts forth as a lilac puts forth buds. Skeeter keeps teasing her. "Look at me, woman. Hey you cunt, look me in the eye. What do you see?"

"I see you. All sprinkled with sugar."

"You see Him, right?"

"Wrong."

"Look over at those drapes, honey. Those ugly homemade drapes where they sort of blend into the wallpaper."

"He's not there, Skeeter."

"Look at me. *Look.*"

They all look. Since coming to live with them, Skeeter has aged; his goatee has grown bushy, his skin has taken on a captive's taut glaze. He is not wearing his glasses tonight.

"Skeeter, He's not there."

"Keep looking at me, cunt. What do you see?"

"I see—a chrysalis of mud. I see a black crab. I just thought, an angel is like an insect, they have six legs. Isn't that true? Isn't that what you want me to say?"

*

Skeeter tells them about Vietnam. He tilts his head back as if the ceiling is a movie screen. He wants to do it justice but is scared to let it back in. "It was where it was coming to an end," he lets out slowly. "There was no roofs to stay under, you stood out in the rain like a beast, you slept in holes in the ground with the roots poking through, and, you know, you could do it. You didn't die of it. That was interesting.

It was like you learned there was life on another world. In the middle of a recon action, a little old gook in one of them hats would come out and try to sell you a chicken. There were these little girls pretty as dolls selling you smack along the road in those little cans the press photogs would throw away, right? It was very complicated, there isn't any net"—he lifts his hand—"to grab it all in."

Colored fragments pour down toward him through the hole in the ceiling. Green machines, an ugly green, eating ugly green bushes. Red mud pressed in patterns to an ooze by Amtrac treads. The emerald of rice paddies, each plant set there with its reflection in the water pure as a monogram. The white of human ears a guy from another company had drying under his belt like withered apricots, white. The black of the *ao dai* pajamas the delicate little whores wore, so figurine-fine he couldn't believe he could touch them though this clammy guy in a white suit kept pushing, saying, "Black GI, number one, biggest pricks, Viet girls like suck." The red, not of blood, but of the Ace of Diamonds a guy in his company wore in his helmet for luck. All that luck-junk, peace-signs of melted lead, love beads, beads spelling LOVE, HORSESHIT, MOTHER, BURY ME DEEP, Ho Chi Minh sandals cut from rubber tires for tiny feet, Tao crosses, Christian crosses, the cross-shaped bombs the Phantoms dropped on the trail up ahead, the X's your laces wore into your boots over the days, the shiny green body bags tied like mail sacks, sun on red dust, on blue smoke, sun caught in shafts between the canopies of the jungle where dinks with Russian rifles waited quieter than orchids, it all tumbles down on him, he is overwhelmed. He knows he can never make it intelligible to these three ofays that worlds do exist beyond these paper walls.

"Just the sounds," Skeeter says. "When one of them Unfriendly mortar shells hits near your hole it is as if a wall were there that was big and solid, twenty feet thick of noise, and you is just a gushy bug. There is feet up there just as soon step on you as not, it doesn't matter, right? It does blow your mind. And the dead, the dead are so weird, they are so—*dead.* Like a stiff chewed mouse the cat fetches up on the lawn. I mean, they are so out of it, so peaceful, there is no word for it, this same grunt last night he was telling you about his girl back in Oshkosh, making it so real you had to jack off, and the VC trip a Claymore and his legs go this way and he goes the other. It was bad. They used to say, 'A world of hurt,' and that is what it was."

Nelson asks, "What's a grunt?"

"A grunt is a leg. An eleven bush, right? He is an ordinary drafted soldier who carries a rifle and humps the boonies. The green machine is very clever. They put the draftees out in the bush to get blown and the re-ups sit back at Longbinh tellin' reporters the body count. They put old Charlie Company on some bad hills, but they didn't get me to re-up. I'd had a bushel, right?"

"I thought I was Charlie," Rabbit says.

"I thought the Viet Cong was," Nelson says.

"You are, they are, so was I, everybody is. I was Company C for Charlie, Second Battalion, 28th Infantry, First Division. We messed around all up and down the Dongnai River." Skeeter looks at the blank ceiling and thinks, I'm not doing it, I'm not doing it justice, I'm selling it short. The holy quality is hardest to get. "The thing about Charlie is," he says, "he's everywhere. In Nam, it's all Charlies, right? Every gook's a Charlie, it got so you didn't mind greasing an old lady, a little kid, they might be the ones planted punji stakes at night, they might not, it didn't matter. A lot of things didn't matter. Nam must be the only place in Uncle Sam's world where black-white doesn't matter. Truly. I had white boys die for me. The Army treats a black man truly swell, black body can stop a bullet as well as any other, they put us right up there, and don't think we're not grateful, we are indeed, we hustle to stop those bullets, we're so happy to die alongside

Whitey." The white ceiling still is blank, but beginning to buzz, beginning to bend into space; he must let the spirit keep lifting him along these lines. "One boy I remember, *hate* the way you make me bring it back, I'd give one ball to forget this, hit in the dark, VC mortars had been working us over since sunset, we never should have been in that valley, lying there in the dark with his guts spilled out, I couldn't see him, hustling my ass back from the perimeter, I stepped on his insides, felt like stepping on a piece of Jell-O, worse, he screamed out and died right then, he hadn't been dead to then. Another time, four of us out on recon, bunch of their AK-47s opened up, had an entirely different sound from the M-16, more of a cracking sound, dig?, not so punky. We were pinned down. Boy with us, white boy from Tennessee, never shaved in his life and ignorant as Moses, slithered away into the bush and wiped 'em out, when we picked him up bullets had cut him in two, impossible for a man to keep firing like that. It was bad. I wouldn't have believed you could see such bad things and keep your eyeballs. These poor unfriendlies, they'd call in the napalm on 'em just up ahead, silver cans tumbling over and over, and they'd come out of the bush right at you, burning and shooting, spitting bullets and burning like a torch in some parade, come tumbling right into your hole with you, they figured the only place to get away from the napalm was inside our perimeter. You'd shoot 'em to shut off their noise. Little boys with faces like the shoeshine back at base. It got so killing didn't feel so bad, it never felt *good*, just necessary, like taking a piss. Right?"

"I don't much want to hear any more," Nelson says. "It makes me feel sick and we're missing Samantha."

Jill tells him, "You must let Skeeter tell it if he wants to. It's good for Skeeter to tell it."

"It happened," Rabbit tells him. "If it didn't happen, I wouldn't want you to be bothered with it. But it happened, so we got to take it in. We got to deal with it somehow."

*

"Schlitz."

"I don't know. I feel lousy. A ginger ale."

"Harry, you're not yourself. How's it going? D'ya hear anything from Janice?"

"Nothing, thank God. How's Mom?"

The old man nudges closer, as if to confide an obscenity. "Frankly, she's better than a month ago anybody would have dared to hope."

*

Now Skeeter does see something on the ceiling, white on white, but the whites are different and one is pouring out of a hole in the other. "Do you know," he asks, "there are two theories of how the universe was done? One says, there was a Big Bang, just like in the Bible, and we're still riding that, it all came out of nothing all at once, like the Good Book say, right? And the funny thing is, all the evidence backs it up. Now the other, which I prefer, says it only seems that way. Fact is, it says, there is a steady state, and though it is true everything is expanding outwards, it does not thin out to next to nothingness on account of the reason that through strange holes in this nothingness new somethingness comes pouring in from exactly nowhere. Now that to me has the ring of truth."

Rabbit asks, "What does that have to do with Vietnam?"

"It is the local hole. It is where the world is redoing itself. It is the tail of ourselves we are eating. It is the bottom you have to have. It is the well you look into and are frightened by your own face in the dark water down there. It is as they say Number One and Number Ten. It is the end. It is the beginning. It is beautiful, men do beautiful things in that mud. It is where God is pushing through. He's coming, Chuck, and Babychuck, and Ladychuck, let Him in. Pull down, shoot to kill, Chaos is His holy face. The sun is burning through. The moon is turning red. The moon is a baby's head bright red between his momma's legs."

Nelson screams and puts his hands over his ears. "I *hate* this, Skeeter. You're scaring me. I don't want God to come, I want Him to stay where He is. I want to grow up like *him*"—his father, Harry, the room's big man—"average and ordinary. I *hate* what you say about the war, it doesn't sound beautiful it sounds horrible."

Skeeter's gaze comes down off the ceiling and tries to focus on the boy. "Right," he says. "You still want to live, they still got you. You're still a slave. Let go. Let go, boy. Don't be a slave. Even *him*, you know, your Daddychuck, is learning. He's learning how to die. He's one slow learner but he takes it a day at a time, right?" He has a mad impulse. He lets it lift him. He goes and kneels before the child where he sits on the sofa beside Jill. Skeeter kneels and says, "Don't keep the Good Lord out, Nellie. One little boy like you put his finger in the dike, take it out. Let it come. Put your hand on my head and promise you won't keep the Good Lord out. Let Him come. Do that for old Skeeter, he's been hurtin' so long."

Nelson puts his hand on Skeeter's orb of hair. His eyes widen, at how far his hand sinks down. He says, "I don't want to hurt you, Skeeter. I don't want anybody to hurt anybody."

"Bless you, boy." Skeeter in his darkness feels blessing flow down through the hand tingling in his hair like sun burning through a cloud. Mustn't mock this child. Softly, stealthily, parting vines of craziness, his heart approaches certainty.

Rabbit's voice explodes. "Shit. It's just a dirty little war that has to be fought. You can't make something religious out of it just because you happened to be there."

Skeeter stands and tries to comprehend this man. "Trouble with you," he sees, "you still cluttered up with common sense. Common sense is bullshit, man. It gets you through the days all right, but it keeps you from *knowing*. You just don't *know*, Chuck. You don't even know that now is all the time there is. What happens to you, is all that happens, right? You are it, right? You. Are. It. I've come down"—he points to the ceiling, his finger a brown crayon—"to tell you that, since along these two thousand years somewhere you've done gone and forgotten again, right?"

Rabbit says, "Talk sense. Is our being in Vietnam wrong?"

"Wrong? Man, how can it be wrong when that's the way it is? These poor Benighted States just being themselves, right? Can't stop bein' yourself, somebody has to do it for you, right? Nobody that big around. Uncle Sam wakes up one morning, looks down at his belly, sees he's some cockroach, what can he do? Just keep bein' his cockroach self, is all. Till he gets stepped on. No such shoe right now, right? Just keep doing his cockroach thing. I'm not one of these white lib-er-als like that cracker Fulldull or Charlie McCarthy a while back gave all the college queers a hard-on, think Vietnam some sort of mistake, we can fix it up once we get the cave men out of office, it is *no* mistake, right, any President comes along falls in love with it, it is lib-er-al-ism's very wang, dingdong pussy, and fruit. Those crackers been lickin' their mother's ass so long they forgotten what she looks like frontwards. What is lib-er-alism? Bringin' joy to the world, right? Puttin' enough sugar on dog-eat-dog so it tastes good all over, right? Well now what could be nicer than Vietnam? We is keepin' that coast open. Man, what is we all about if it ain't keepin' things open? How can money and jizz make their way if we don't keep a few cunts like that open? Nam is an act of love, right? Compared to Nam, beatin' Japan was flat-out ugly. We was ugly fuckers then and now we is truly a civilized spot." The ceiling agitates; he feels the gift of tongues descend to him. "We is *the* spot. Few old fools like the late Ho may not know it, we is what the world is begging *for*. Big beat, smack, black cock, big-assed cars and billboards, we is into *it*. Jesus come down, He come down here. These other countries, just bullshit places, right? We got the *ape* shit, right? Bring down Kingdom Come, we'll swamp the world in red-hot real American blue-green ape shit, right?"

"Right," Rabbit says.

Encouraged, Skeeter sees the truth: "Nam," he says, "Nam the spot where our heavenly essence is pustulatin'. Man don't like Vietnam, he don't like America."

"Right," Rabbit says. "*Right.*"

The two others, pale freckled faces framed in too much hair, are frightened by this agreement. Jill begs, "Stop. Everything hurts." Skeeter understands. Her skin is peeled, the poor girl is wide open to the stars. This afternoon he got her to drop some mescaline. If she'll eat mesc, she'll snort smack. If she'll snort, she'll shoot. He has her.

Nelson begs, "Let's watch television."

Rabbit asks Skeeter, "How'd you get through your year over there without being hurt?"

These white faces. These holes punched in the perfection of his anger. God is pouring through the white holes of their faces; he cannot stanch the gushing. It gets to his eyes. They had been wicked, when he was a child, to teach him God was a white man. "I *was* hurt," Skeeter says.

*

BEATITUDES OF SKEETER

(*written down in Jill's confident, rounded, private-school hand, in green felt pen, playfully one night, on a sheet of Nelson's notebook filler*)

Power is bullshit.
Love is bullshit.
Common sense is bullshit.
Confusion is God's very face.
Nothing is interesting save eternal sameness.
There is no salvation, 'cepting through Me.

Also from the same night, some drawings by her, in crayons Nelson found for her; her style was cute, linear, arrested where some sophomore art class had left it, yet the resemblances were clear. Skeeter of course was the spade. Nelson, his dark bangs and side-sheaves exaggerated, the club, on a stem of a neck. Herself, her pale hair crayoned in the same pink as her sharp-chinned face, the heart. And Rabbit, therefore, the diamond. In the center of the diamond, a tiny pink nose. Sleepy small blue eyes with worried eyebrows. An almost invisible mouth, lifted as if to nibble. Around it all, green scribbles she had to identify with an affectionate pointing arrow and a balloon: "in the rough."

*

One of these afternoons, when Nelson is home from soccer practice and Harry is home from work, they cram into Jill's Porsche and drive out into the county. Rabbit has to have the front seat; Nelson and Skeeter squeeze into the baggage area behind. Skeeter scuttles blinking from the doorway to the curb and inside the car says, "Man, been so long since I been out in the air, it hurts my lungs." Jill drives urgently, rapidly, with the arrogance of the young; Rabbit keeps slapping his foot on the floor, where there is no brake. Jill's cool profile smiles. Her little foot in a ballet slipper feeds gas halfway through curves, pumps up speed enough just to pinch them past a huge truck—a raging, belching house on wheels—before another hurtling the other way scissors them into oblivion, on a straight stretch between valleys of red earth and pale corn stubble. The country is beautiful. Fall has lifted that heavy Pennsylvania green, the sky is cleared of the suspended summer milk, the hills edge into shades of amber and flaming orange that in another month will become the locust-husk tint that crackles underfoot in hunting season. A brushfire haze floats in the valleys like fog on a river's skin. Jill stops the car beside a whitewashed fence and an apple tree. They get out into a cloud of the scent of fallen apples, overripe. At their feet apples rot in the long dank grass that banks a trickling ditch, the grass still powerfully green; beyond the fence a meadow has been scraped brown by grazing, but for clumps where burdock fed by cowdung grows high as a man. Nelson picks up an apple and bites on the side away from wormholes. Skeeter protests, "Child, don't put your mouth on that garbage!" Had he never seen a fruit eaten in nature before?

Jill lifts her dress and jumps the ditch to touch one of the rough warm whitewashed slats of the fence and to look between them into the distance, where in the dark shelter of trees a sandstone farmhouse glistens like a sugar cube soaked in tea and the wide gaunt wheel of an old farm wagon, spokes stilled forever, waits beside a rusty upright that must be a pump. Her eyes go blind to the green. She remembers rusty cleats that waited for the prow line of visiting boats on docks in Rhode Island and along the Sound, the whole rusty neglected salt-bleached barnacled look of things built where the sea laps, summer sun on gull-gray wood, docks, sheds, metal creaking with the motion of the water, very distant from this inland overripeness, and says, "Let's go."

And they cram back into the little car, and again there are the trucks, and the gas stations, and the "Dutch" restaurants with neon hex signs, and the wind and the speed of the car drowning out all smells and sounds and thoughts of a possible other world. The open sandstone country south of Brewer, the Amish farms printed on the trimmed fields like magazine covers, becomes the ugly hills and darker valleys north of the city, where the primitive iron industry had its day and where the people built of brick, tall narrow-faced homes with gables and dormers like a buzzard's shoulders, perched on domed lawns behind spiked retaining walls. The soft flowerpot-red of Brewer hardens up here, ten miles to the north, to a red dark like dried blood. Though it is not yet the coal regions, the trees feel darkened by coal dust. Rabbit begins to remember accounts, a series run in the *Vat*, of strange murders, axings and scaldings and stranglings committed in these pinched valleys with their narrow main streets of dried-blood churches and banks and Oddfellows' halls, streets that end with, as a wrung neck, a sharp turn over abandoned railroad tracks into a sunless gorge where a stream the color of tarnished silver is now and then crossed by a damp covered bridge that rattles as it swallows you.

Rabbit and Nelson, Skeeter and Jill, crushed together in the little car, laugh a lot during this drive, laugh at nothing, at the silly expression on the face of a hick as they barrel past, at pigs dignified as statesmen in their pens, at the names on mailboxes (Hinnershitz, Focht, Schtupnagel), at tractor-riding men so fat nothing less wide than a tractor seat would hold them. They even laugh when the little car, though the gas gauge stands at ½, jerks, struggles, slows, stops as if braked. Jill has time only to bring it to the side of the road, out of traffic. Rabbit gets out to look at the engine, but the works of this machine are not open and tall and transparent as with a Linotype, but are tangled and greasy and closed. The starter churns but the engine will not turn over. The chain of explosions that works by faith is jammed. He leaves the hood up to signal an emergency. Skeeter, crouching down in the back, calls, "Chuck, know what you're doin' with that hood, you're callin' down the fucking fuzz!"

Rabbit tells him, "You better get out of the back. We get hit from behind, you've had it. You too Nelson. Out."

It is the most dangerous type of highway, three-lane. The commuter traffic out from Brewer shudders past in an avalanche of dust and noise and carbon monoxide. No Good Samaritans stop. The Porsche has stalled atop an embankment seeded with that feathery finespun ground-cover the state uses to hold steep soil: crown vetch. Below, swifts are skimming a shorn cornfield. Rabbit and Nelson lean against the fenders and watch the sun, an hour above the horizon, fill the field with stubble-shadows, ridges subtle as those of corduroy. Jill wanders off and gathers a baby bouquet of those tiny daisylike flowers that bloom in the fall, on stems so thin they form a cirrus hovering an inch or two above the earth. Jill offers the bouquet to Skeeter, to lure him out. He reaches to bat the flowers from her hand; they scatter and fall in the grit of the roadside. His voice comes muffled from within the Porsche. "You honky cunt, this all a way to turn me in, nothing wrong with this fucking car, right?"

"It won't go," she says; one flower rests on the toe of one ballet slipper. Her face has shed expression.

Skeeter's voice whines and snarls in its metal shell. "Knew I should never come out of that house. Jill honey, I know why. Can't stay off the stuff, right? No will at all, right? Easier than having any will, hand old Skeeter over to the law, hey, right?"

Rabbit asks her, "What's he saying?"

"He's saying he's scared."

Skeeter is shouting, "Get them dumb honkies out of the way, I'm making a run for it. How far down on the other side of that fence?"

Rabbit says, "Smart move, you'll really stick out up here in the boondocks. Talk about a nigger in the woodpile."

"Don't you nigger me, you honky prick. Tell you one thing, you turn me in I'll get you all greased if I have to send to Philly to do it. It's not just me, we're everywhere, hear? Now you fuckers get this car to *go*, hear me? Get it to *go*."

Skeeter issues all this while crouched down between the leather backs of the bucket seats and the rear window. His panic is disgusting and may be contagious. Rabbit lusts to pull him out of his shell into the sunshine, but is afraid to reach in; he might get stung. He slams the Porsche door shut on the churning rasping voice, and at the rear of the car slams down the hood. "You two stay here. Calm him down, keep him in the car. I'll walk to a gas station, there must be one up the road."

He runs for a while, Skeeter's venomous fright making his own bladder burn. After all these nights together betrayal is the Negro's first thought. Maybe natural. Running to keep that black body pinned back there. Turtle on its back. Like running late to school. Skeeter has become a duty. Late, late. Then an antique red flying horse sign suspended above sunset-dyed fields. It is an old-fashioned garage, an unfathomable work space redolent of oil, the walls precious with wrenches, fan belts, peen hammers, parts. An old Coke machine, the kind that dispenses bottles, purrs beside the hydraulic lift. The mechanic, a weedy young man with a farmer's drawl and black palms, drives him in a jolting tow truck back up the highway. The side window is broken; air whistles there, hungrily gushes.

*

"Seized up," is the mechanic's verdict. He asks Jill, "When'd you last put oil in it?"

"Oil? Don't they do it when they put the gas in?"

"Not unless you ask."

"You dumb mutt," Rabbit says to Jill.

Her mouth goes prim and defiant. "Skeeter's been driving the car too."

Skeeter, as the mechanic poked under the hood, uncurled from behind the seats and straightened in the air, his glasses orange discs in the last of the sun. Rabbit asks him, "How far've you been taking this crate?"

"Oh," the black man says, fastidious in earshot of the mechanic, "here and there. Never recklessly. I wasn't aware," he minces on, "the automobile was your property."

"It's just," he says lamely, "the waste. The carelessness."

Jill asks the mechanic, "Can you fix it in an hour? My little brother here has homework to do."

The mechanic speaks only to Rabbit. "The enchine's destroyed. The pistons have fused to the cylinders. The nearest place to fix a car like this is probably Pottstown."

"Can we leave it with you until we arrange to have somebody come for it?"

"I'll have to charge a dollar a day for the parking."

"Sure. Swell."

"And that'll be twenty for the towing."

He pays out the twenty Buchanan gave him. The mechanic tows the Porsche back to the garage. They ride with him, Jill and Harry in the cab ("Careful now," the mechanic says as Jill slides over, "I don't want to get grease on that nice white dress"), Skeeter and Nelson in the little car, dragged backwards at a slant. At the garage, the mechanic phones for a cab to take them into West Brewer. Skeeter disappears behind a smudged door and flushes the toilet repeatedly. Nelson settles to watching the mechanic unhitch the car and listens to him talk about "enchines." Jill and Harry walk outside. Crickets are shrilling in the dark cornfields. A quarter-moon, with one sick eye, scuds above the flying horse sign. The outer lights are switched off. He notices something white on her slipper. The little flower that fell has stuck there. He stoops and hands it to her. She kisses it to thank him, then, silently lays it to rest in a trash barrel full of wiped oil towels and punctured cans. "Don't get your dress greasy." Car tires crackle; an ancient Fifties Buick, with those tailfins patterned on B-19s, pulls into their orbit. The driver is fat and chews gum. On the way back to Brewer, his head bulks as a pyramid against the oncoming headlights, motionless but for the tremor of chewing. Skeeter sits beside him. "Beautiful day," Rabbit calls forward to him.

Jill giggles. Nelson is asleep on her lap. She toys with his hair, winding it around her silent fingers.

"Fair for this time of the year," is the slow answer.

"Beautiful country up here. We hardly ever get north of the city. We were driving around sightseeing."

"Not too many sights to see."

"The engine seized right up on us, I guess the car's a real mess."

"I guess."

"My daughter here forgot to put any oil in it, that's the way young people are these days, ruin one car and on to the next. Material things don't mean a thing to 'em."

"To some, I guess."

Skeeter says sideways to him, "Yo' sho' meets a lot ob nice folks hevin' en acci-dent lahk dis, a lot ob naas folks way up no'th heah."

"Yes, well," the driver says, and that is all he says until he says to Rabbit, having stopped on Vista Crescent, "Eighteen."

"Dollars? For ten miles?"

"Twelve. And I got to go back twelve now."

Rabbit goes to the driver's side to pay, while the others run into the house. The man leans out and asks, "Know what you're doing?"

"Not exactly."

"They'll knife you in the back every time."

"Who."

The driver leans closer; by street-lamplight Rabbit sees a wide sad face, sallow, a whale's lipless mouth clamped in a melancholy set, a horseshoe-shaped scar on the meat of his nose. His answer is soft: "Jigaboos."

Embarrassed for him, Rabbit turns away and sees—Nelson is right—a crowd of children. They are standing across the Crescent, some with bicycles, watching this odd car unload. This phenomenon on the bleak terrain of Penn Villas alarms him: as if growths were to fester on the surface of the moon.

*

The incident—his skin daring the sun again—emboldens Skeeter. Rabbit comes home from work to find him and Nelson shooting baskets in the driveway. Nelson bounces the ball to his father and Rabbit's one-handed set from twenty feet out swishes. Pretty. "Hey," Skeeter crows, so all the homes in Penn Villas can hear, "where'd you get that funky old style of shooting a basketball? You were tryin' to be comical, right?"

"Went in," Nelson tells him.

"Shit, boy, a one-armed dwarf could have blocked it. T'get that shot off you need a screen two men thick, right? You gotta jump and shoot, jump and shoot, right?" He demonstrates; his shot misses but looks right: the ball held high, a back-leaning ascent into the air, a soft release that would arch over any defender. Rabbit tries it, but finds his body heavy, the effort of lifting jarring. The ball flies badly. Says Skeeter, "You got a white man's lead gut, but I adore those hands." They scrimmage one on one; Skeeter is quick and slick, slithering by for the layup on the give-and-go to Nelson again and again. Rabbit cannot stop him, his breath begins to ache in his chest, but there are moments when the ball and his muscles and the air overhead and the bodies competing with his all feel taut and unified and defiant of gravity. Then the October chill bites into his sweat and he goes into the house. Jill has been sleeping upstairs. She sleeps more and more lately, a dazed evading sleep that he finds insulting. When she comes downstairs, in that boring white dress, brushing back sticky hair from her cheeks, he asks roughly, "Dja do anything about the car?"

"Sweet, what would I do?"

"You could call your mother."

"I can't. She and Stepdaddy would make a thing. They'd come for me."

"Maybe that's a good idea."

"Stepdaddy's a creep." She moves past him, not focusing,

into the kitchen. She looks into the refrigerator. "You didn't shop."

"That's your job."

"Without a car?"

"Christ, you can walk up to the Acme in five minutes."

"People would see Skeeter."

"They see him anyway. He's outside horsing around with Nelson. And evidently you've been letting him drive all around Pennsylvania." His anger recharges itself: *lead gut.* "Goddammit, how can you just run an expensive car like that into the ground and just let it *sit?* There's people in the world could live for ten years on what that car cost."

"Don't, Harry. I'm weak."

"O.K. I'm sorry." He tugs her into his arms. She rocks sadly against him, rubbing her nose on his shirt. But her body when dazed has an absence, an unconnectedness, that feels disagreeable against his skin. He itches to sneeze.

Jill is murmuring, "I think you miss your wife."

"That bitch. Never."

"She's like all you people, caught in this society. She wants to be alive while she is alive."

"Don't you?"

"Sometimes. But I know it's not enough. It's how they get you. Let me go now. You don't like holding me, I can feel it. I just remembered, some frozen chicken livers behind the ice cream. But they take forever to thaw."

*

Six o'clock news. The pale face caught behind the screen sternly says, unaware that his head, by some imperfection in reception at 26 Vista Crescent, is flattened, and his chin rubbery and long, says, "Chicago. Two thousand five hundred Illinois National Guardsmen remained on active duty today in the wake of a day of riots staged by members of the extremist faction of the Students for a Democratic Society.

Windows were smashed, cars overturned, policemen assaulted by the young militants whose slogan is"—sad, stern pause; the bleached face lifts toward the camera, the chin stretches, the head flattens like an anvil—"Bring the War Home." Film cuts of white-helmeted policemen flailing at nests of arms and legs, of long-haired girls being dragged, of sudden bearded faces shaking fists that want to rocket out through the television screen; then back to clips of policemen swinging clubs, which seems balletlike and soothing to Rabbit. Skeeter, too, likes it. "Right on!" he cries. "Hit that crazy dude again!" In the commercial break he turns and explains to Nelson, "It's beautiful, right?"

Nelson asks, "Why? Aren't they protesting the war?"

"Sure as a hen has balls they are. What those crackers protesting is they gotta wait twenty years to get their daddy's share of the pie. They want it *now.*"

"What would they do with it?"

"Do, boy? They'd *eat* it, that's what they'd do."

The commercial—an enlarged view of a young woman's mouth—is over. "Meanwhile, within the courtroom, the trial of the Chicago Eight continued on its turbulent course. Presiding Judge Julius J. Hoffman, no relation to Defendant Abbie Hoffman, several times rebuked Defendant Bobby Seale, whose outbursts contained such epithets as"—again, the upward look, the flattened head, the disappointed emphasis—"pig, fascist, and racist." A courtroom sketch of Seale is flashed.

Nelson asks, "Skeeter, do you like *him?*"

"I do not much cotton," Skeeter says, "to establishment niggers."

Rabbit has to laugh. "That's ridiculous. He's as full of hate as you are."

Skeeter switches off the set. His tone is a preacher's, ladylike. "I am by no means full of hate. I am full of love, which is a dynamic force. Hate is a paralyzing force. Hate freezes.

Love strikes and liberates. Right? Jesus liberated the money-changers from the temple. The new Jesus will liberate the new money-changers. The old Jesus brought a sword, right? The new Jesus will also bring a sword. He will be a living flame of love. Chaos is God's body. Order is the Devil's chains. As to Robert Seale, any black man who has John Kennel Badbreath and Leonard Birdbrain giving him fund-raising cocktail parties is one house nigger in my book. He has gotten into the power bag, he has gotten into the publicity bag, he has debased the coinage of his soul and is thereupon as they say irrelevant. We black men came here without names, we are the future's organic seeds, seeds have no names, right?"

"Right," Rabbit says, a habit.

Jill's chicken livers have burned edges and icy centers.

*

Eleven o'clock news. A gauzy-bearded boy, his face pressed so hard against the camera the focus cannot be maintained, screams, "Off the pigs! All power to the people!"

An unseen interviewer mellifluously asks him, "How would you describe the goals of your organization?"

"Destruction of existing repressive structures. Social control of the means of production."

"Could you tell our viewing audience what you mean by 'means of production'?"

The camera is being jostled; the living room, darkened otherwise, flickers. "Factories. Wall Street. Technology. All that. A tiny clique of capitalists is forcing pollution down our throats, and the SST and the genocide in Vietnam and in the ghettos. All that."

"I see. Your aim, then, by smashing windows, is to curb a runaway technology and create the basis for a new humanism."

The boy looks off-screen blearily, as the camera struggles

to refocus him. "You being funny? You'll be the first up against the wall, you—" And the blip showed that the interview had been taped.

Rabbit says, "Tell me about technology."

"Technology," Skeeter explains with exquisite patience, the tip of his joint glowing red as he drags, "is horseshit. Take that down, Jilly."

But Jill is asleep on the sofa. Her thighs glow. They sing.

Skeeter goes on, "We are all at work at the mighty labor of forgetting everything we know. We are sewing the apple back on the tree. Now the Romans had technology, right? And the barbarians saved them from it. The barbarians were their saviors. Since we cannot induce the Eskimos to invade us, we have raised a generation of barbarians ourselves, pardon me, *you* have raised them, Whitey has raised them, the white American middle-class and its imitators the world over have found within themselves the divine strength to generate millions of subhuman idiots that in less benighted ages only the aristocracies could produce. The last Merovingian princes were dragged about in ox carts gibbering and we are now blessed with motorized gibberers. It is truly written, we shall blow our minds, and dedicate the rest to Chairman Mao. Right?"

Rabbit argues, "That's not fair. These kids have some good points. The war aside, what about pollution?"

"I am getting weary," Skeeter says, "of talking with white folk. You are defending your own. These rabid children, as surely as Agnew Dei, desire to preserve the status quo against the divine plan and the divine wrath. They are Antichrist. They perceive God's face in Vietnam and spit upon it. False prophets: by their proliferation you know the time is nigh. Public shamelessness, ingenious armor, idiocy revered, the laws of bribery and protection the only actual laws: we are Rome. And I am the Christ of the new Dark Age. Or if not me, then someone exactly like me, whom later ages will suppose to have been me. Do you believe?"

"I believe." Rabbit drags on his own joint, and feels his world expand to admit new truths as a woman spreads her legs, as a flower unfolds, as the stars flee one another. "I do believe."

*

Skeeter likes Rabbit to read to him from *The Life and Times of Frederick Douglass.* "You're just gorgeous, right? You're gone to be our big nigger tonight. As a white man, Chuck, you don't amount to much, but niggerwise you groove." He has marked sections in the book with paper clips and a crayon.

Rabbit reads, "*The reader will have noticed that among the names of slaves that of Esther is mentioned. This was the name of a young woman who possessed that which was ever a curse to the slave girl—namely, personal beauty. She was tall, light-colored, well formed, and made a fine appearance. Esther was courted by 'Ned Roberts,' the son of a favorite slave of Colonel Lloyd, and who was as fine-looking a young man as Esther was a woman. Some slaveholders would have been glad to have promoted the marriage of two such persons, but for some reason Captain Anthony disapproved of their courtship. He strictly ordered her to quit the society of young Roberts, telling her that he would punish her severely if he ever found her again in his company. But it was impossible to keep this couple apart. Meet they would and meet they did.* Then we skip." The red crayon mark resumes at the bottom of the page; Rabbit hears drama entering his voice, early morning mists, a child's fear. "*It was early in the morning, when all was still, and before any of the family in the house or kitchen had risen. I was, in fact, awakened by the heart-rendering shrieks and piteous cries of poor*

Esther. My sleeping-place was on the dirt floor of a little rough closet which opened into the kitchen—"

Skeeter interrupts, "You can smell that closet, right? Dirt, right, and old potatoes, and little bits of grass turning yellow before they can grow an inch, right? Smell that, he *slept* in there."

"Hush," Jill says.

"*—and through the cracks in its unplaned boards I could distinctly see and hear what was going on, without being seen. Esther's wrists were firmly tied, and the twisted rope was fastened to a strong iron staple in a heavy wooden beam above, near the fireplace. Here she stood on a bench, her arms tightly drawn above her head. Her back and shoulders were perfectly bare. Behind her stood old master, cowhide in hand, pursuing his barbarous work with all manner of harsh, coarse, and tantalizing epithets. He was cruelly deliberate, and protracted the torture as one who was delighted with the agony of his victim. Again and again he drew the hateful scourge through his hand, adjusting it with a view of dealing the most pain-giving blow his strength and skill could inflict. Poor Esther had never before been severely whipped. Her shoulders were plump and tender. Each blow, vigorously laid on, brought screams from her as well as blood. 'Have mercy! Oh, mercy!' she cried. 'I won't do so no more.' But her piercing cries seemed only to increase his fury.*" The red mark stops but Rabbit sweeps on to the end of the chapter. "*The whole scene, with all its attendant circumstances, was revolting and shocking to the last degree, and when the motives for the brutal castigation are known, language has no power to convey a just sense of its dreadful criminality. After laying on I dare not say how many stripes, old master untied his suffering victim. When let down she could scarcely stand. From my heart I pitied her, and child as I was, and new to such scenes, the shock was tremendous. I was terrified,* *hushed, stunned, and bewildered. The scene here described was often repeated, for Edward and Esther continued to meet, notwithstanding all efforts to prevent their meeting.*"

Skeeter turns to Jill and slaps her sharply, as a child would, on the chest. "Don't hush me, you cunt."

"I wanted to hear the passage."

"How'd it turn you on, cunt?"

"I liked the way Harry read it. With feeling."

"Fuck your white feelings."

"Hey, easy," Rabbit says, helplessly, seeing that violence is due.

Skeeter is wild. Keeping his one hand on her shoulder as a brace, with the other he reaches to her throat and rips the neck of her white dress forward. The cloth is tough; Jill's head snaps far forward before the rip is heard. She recoils back into the sofa, her eyes expressionless; her little tough-tipped tits bounce in the torn V.

Rabbit's instinct is not to rescue her but to shield Nelson. He drops the book on the cobbler's bench and puts his body between the boy and the sofa. "Go upstairs."

Nelson, stunned, bewildered, has risen to his feet; he moans, "He'll *kill* her, Dad." His cheeks are flushed, his eyes are sunk.

"No he won't. He's just high. She liked it."

"Oh shit, shit," the child repeats in desperation; his face caves into crying.

"Hey there Babychuck," Skeeter calls. "You want to whip me, right?" Skeeter hops up, does a brittle bewitched dance, strips off his shirt so violently one cuff button flies off and strikes the lampshade. His skinny chest, naked, is stunning in its articulation: every muscle sharp in its attachment to the bone, the whole torso carved in a jungle wood darker than shadow and more dense than ivory. Rabbit has never seen such a chest except on a crucifix. "What's next?" Skeeter shouts.

"Wanna whup my bum, right? Here it is!" His hands have undone his fly button and are on his belt, but Nelson has fled the room. His sobbing comes downstairs, diminishing.

"O.K., that's enough," Rabbit says.

"Read a little bitty bit more," Skeeter begs.

"You get carried away."

"That damn child of yours, thinks he owns this cunt."

"Stop calling her a cunt."

"Man, wasn't this Jesus gave her one." Skeeter cackles.

"You're horrible," Jill tells him, drawing the torn cloth together.

He flips one piece aside. "Moo."

"Harry, help me."

"Read the book, Chuck, I'll be good. Read me the next paper clip."

Above them, Nelson's footsteps cross the floor. If he reads, the boy will be safe. "*Alas,* that the one?"

"That'll do. Little Jilly, you love me, right?"

"*Alas, this immense wealth, this gilded splendor, this profusion of luxury, this exemption from toil, this life of ease, this sea of plenty, were not the pearly gates they seemed—*"

"You're my pearly gate, girl."

"*The poor slave, on his hard pine plank, scantily covered with his thin blanket, slept more soundly than the feverish voluptuary who reclined upon his downy pillow. Food to the indolent is poison, not sustenance. Lurking beneath the rich and tempting viands were invisible spirits of evil, which filled the self-deluded gormandizer with aches and pains, passions uncontrollable, fierce tempers, dyspepsia, rheumatism, lumbago, and gout, and of these the Lloyds had a full share.*"

Beyond the edge of the page Skeeter and Jill are wrestling; in gray flashes her underpants, her breasts are exposed. Another flash, Rabbit sees, is her smile. Her small gray teeth bare in silent laughter; she is liking it, being raped. Seeing him spying, Jill starts, struggles angrily out from under, hugs the rags of her dress around her, and runs from the room. Her footsteps flicker up the stairs. Skeeter blinks at her flight; he resettles the great pillow of his head with a sigh. "Beautiful," is the sigh. "One more, Chuck. Read me the one where he fights back." His brown chest melts into the beige sofa; its airfoam is covered in a plaid of green and tan and red that have rubbed and faded to a single shade hardly worth naming.

"You know, I gotta get up and go to work tomorrow."

"You worried about your little dolly? Don't you worry about that. The thing about a cunt, man, it's just like a Kleenex, you use it and throw it away." Hearing silence, he says, "I'm just kidding, right? To get your goat, O.K.? Come on, let's put it back together, the next paper clip. Trouble with you, man, you're all the time married. Woman don't like a man who's nothin' but married, they want some soul that keeps 'em guessing, right? Woman stops guessing, she's dead."

Rabbit sits on the silverthread chair to read. "*Whence came the daring spirit necessary to grapple with a man who, eight-and-forty hours before, could, with the slightest word, have made me tremble like a leaf in a storm, I do not know; at any rate, I was resolved to fight, and what was better still, I actually was hard at it. The fighting madness had come upon me, and I found my strong fingers firmly attached to the throat of the tyrant, as heedless of consequences, at the moment, as if we stood equals before the law. The very color of the man was forgotten. I felt supple as a cat, and was ready for him at every turn. Every blow of his was parried, though I dealt no blows in return. I was strictly on the defensive, preventing him from injuring me, rather than trying to injure him. I flung him on the ground several times when he meant to have hurled me there. I held him so firmly by the throat that his blood followed my nails. He held me, and I held him.*"

"Oh I love it, it grabs me, it kills me," Skeeter says, and he gets up on one elbow so his body confronts the other man's. "Do me one more. Just one more bit."

"I gotta get upstairs."

"Skip a couple pages, go to the place I marked with double lines."

"Why doncha read it to yourself?"

"It's not the same, right? Doin' it to yourself. Every school kid knows that, it's not the same. Come on, Chuck. I been pretty good, right? I ain't caused no trouble, I been a faithful Tom, give the Tom a bone, read it like I say. I'm gonna take off all my clothes, I want to hear it with my pores. Sing it, man. Do it. Begin up a little, where it goes *A man without force*." He prompts again, "*A man without force*," and is fussing with his belt buckle.

"*A man without force*," Rabbit intently reads, "*is without the essential dignity of humanity. Human nature is so constituted, that it cannot honor a helpless man, though it can pity him, and even this it cannot do long if signs of power do not arise*."

"Yes," Skeeter says, and the blur of him is scuffling and slithering, and a patch of white flashes from the sofa, above the white of the printed page.

"*He can only understand*," Rabbit reads, finding the words huge, each one a black barrel his voice echoes in, "*the effect of this combat on my spirit, who has himself incurred something, or hazarded something, in repelling the unjust and cruel aggressions of a tyrant. Covey was a tyrant and a cowardly one withal. After resisting him, I felt as I had never felt before*."

"Yes," Skeeter's voice calls from the abyss of the unseen beyond the rectangular island of the page.

"*It was a resurrection from the dark and pestiferous tomb of slavery, to the heaven of comparative freedom. I was no longer a servile coward, trembling under the frown of a brother worm of the dust, but my long-cowed spirit was roused to an attitude of independence. I had reached a point at which I was* not afraid to die." Emphasis.

"Oh yes. Yes."

"*This spirit made me a freeman in* fact, *though I still remained a slave in* form. *When a slave cannot be flogged, he is more than half free.*"

"A-men."

"*He has a domain as broad as his own manly heart to defend, and he is really 'a power on earth.'* "

"Say it. Say it."

"*From this time until my escape from slavery, I was never fairly whipped. Several attempts were made, but they were always unsuccessful. Bruised I did get, but the instance I have described was the end of the brutification to which slavery had subjected me.*"

"Oh, you do make one lovely nigger," Skeeter sings.

Lifting his eyes from the page, Rabbit sees there is no longer a patch of white on the sofa, it is solidly dark, only moving in a whispering rhythm that wants to suck him forward. His eyes do not dare follow down to the hand the live line of reflected light lying the length of Skeeter's rhythmic arm. Long as an eel, feeding. Rabbit stands and strides from the room, dropping the book as if hot, though the burning eyes of the stippled Negro on the cover are quick to follow him across the hard carpet, up the varnished stairs, into the white realm where an overhead frosted fixture burns on the landing. His heart skips. He has escaped. Narrowly.

*

Light from the driftwood lamp downstairs floods the little maple from underneath, its leaves red like your fingers on a flashlight face. Its turning head half-fills their bedroom window. In bed Jill turns to him pale and chill as ice. "Hold me," she says. "Hold me, hold me, hold me," so often and level it frightens him. Women are crazy, they contain this ancient craziness, he is holding wind in his arms. He feels she wants to be fucked, any way, without pleasure, but to pin her down. He would like to do this for her but he cannot pierce the fright, the disgust between them. She is a mermaid gesturing beneath the skin of the water. He is floating rigid to keep himself from sinking in terror. The book he has read aloud torments him with a vision of bottomless squalor, of dead generations, of buried tortures and lost reasons. Rising, working, there is no reason any more, no reason for anything, no reason why not, nothing to breathe but a sour gas bottled in empty churches, nothing to rise by; he lives in a tight well whose dank sides squeeze and paralyze him, no, it is Jill tight against him, trying to get warm, though the night is hot. He asks her, "Can you sleep?"

"No. Everything is crashing."

"Let's try. It's late. Shall I get another blanket?"

"Don't leave me for even a second. I'll fall through."

"I'll turn my back, then you can hug me."

Downstairs, Skeeter flicks the light off. Outside, the little maple vanishes like a blown-out flame. Within himself, Rabbit completes his motion into darkness, into the rhythmic brown of the sofa. Then terror returns and squeezes him shut like an eyelid.

*

Her voice sounds tired and wary, answering. "Brewer Fealty, Mrs. Fosnacht. May I help you?"

"Peggy? Hi, it's Harry Angstrom."

"So it is." A new sarcastic note. "I *don't* believe it!" Overexpressive. Too many men.

"Hey, remember you said about Nelson and Billy going fishing this Sunday and inviting me for Saturday dinner?"

"Yes, Harry, I do remember."

"Is it too late? For me to accept?"

"Not at all. What's brought this about?"

"Nothing special. Just thought it might be nice."

"It will be nice. I'll see you Saturday."

"Tomorrow," he clarifies. He would have talked on, it was his lunch hour, but she cuts the conversation short. Press of work. Don't count your chickens.

*

After work as he walks home from the bus stop on Weiser, two men accost him, at the corner where Emberly Avenue becomes a Drive, beside a red-white-and-blue mailbox. "Mr. Angstrom?"

"Sure."

"Might we talk to you a minute? We're two of your neighbors." The man speaking is between forty and fifty, plump, in a gray suit that has stretched to fit him, with those narrow lapels of five years ago. His face is soft but pained. A hard little hook nose at odds with the puffy patches below his eyes. His chin is two damp knobs set side by side, between them a dimple where the whiskers hide from the razor. He has that yellow Brewer tint and an agile sly white-collar air. An accountant, a schoolteacher. "My name is Mahlon Showalter, I live on the other side of Vista Crescent, the house, you probably noticed, with the new addition in back we added on last summer."

"Oh, yeah." He recalls distant hammering but had not noticed; he really only looks at Penn Villas enough to see that it isn't Mt. Judge: that is, it is nowhere.

"I'm in computers, the hardware end," Showalter says. "Here's my card." As Rabbit glances at the company name on it Showalter says, "We're going to revolutionize business in this town, file that name in your memory. This here is Eddie Brumbach, he lives around the further crescent, Marigold, up from you."

Eddie presents no card. He is black-haired, shorter and

younger than Harry. He stands the way guys in the Army used to, all buttoned in, shoulders tucked back, an itch for a fight between their shoulder blades. Only in part because of his brush cut, his head looks flattened on top, like the heads on Rabbit's television set. When he shakes hands, it reminds him of somebody else. Who? One side of Brumbach's face has had a piece of jawbone removed, leaving a dent and an L-shaped red scar. Gray eyes like dulled tool tips. He says with ominous simplicity, "Yessir."

Showalter says, "Eddie works in the assembly shop over at Fessler Steel."

"You guys must have quit work early today," Rabbit says.

Eddie tells him, "I'm on night shift this month."

Showalter has a way of bending, as if dance music is playing far away and he wants to cut in between Rabbit and Eddie. He is saying, "We made a decision to talk to you, we appreciate your patience. This is my car here, would you like to sit in it? It's not too comfortable, standing out like this."

The car is a Toyota; it reminds Harry of his father-in-law and gets a whole set of uneasy feelings sliding. "I'd just as soon stand," he says, "if it won't take long," and leans on the mailbox to make himself less tall above these men.

"It won't take long," Eddie Brumbach promises, hitching his shoulders and coming a crisp step closer.

Showalter dips his shoulder again as if to intervene, looks sadder around the eyes, wipes his soft mouth: "Well no, it needn't. We don't mean to be unfriendly, we just have a few questions."

"Friendly questions," Rabbit clarifies, anxious to help this man, whose careful slow voice is pure Brewer; who seems, like the city, bland and broad and kind, and for the time being depressed.

"Now some of us," Showalter goes on, "were discussing, you know, the neighborhood. Some of the kids have been telling us stories, you know, about what they see in your windows."

"They've been looking in my windows?" The mailbox blue is hot; he stops leaning and stands. Though it is October the sidewalk reflects flinty and a translucent irritability rests upon the pastel asphalt rooftops, the spindly young trees, the low houses like puzzles assembled of wood and cement and brick and fake-fieldstone siding. He is trying to look through these houses to his own, to protect it.

Brumbach bristles, thrusts himself into Rabbit's attention. "They haven't had to look in any windows, they've had what's going on pushed under their noses. And it don't smell good."

Showalter intervenes, his voice wheedling like a woman's, buttering over. "No now, that's putting it too strong. But it's true, I guess, there hasn't been any particular secret. They've been coming and going in that little Porsche right along, and I notice now he plays basketball with the boy right out front."

"He?"

"The black fella you have living with you," Showalter says, smiling as if the snag in their conversation has been discovered, and all will be clear sailing now.

"And the white girl," Brumbach adds. "My younger boy came home the other day and said he saw them screwing right on the downstairs rug."

"Well," Rabbit says, stalling. He feels absurdly taller than these men, he feels he might float away while trying to make out the details of what the boy had seen, a little framed rectangle hung in his head like a picture too high on the wall. "That's the kind of thing you see, when you look in other people's windows."

Brumbach steps neatly in front of Showalter, and Rabbit remembers who his handshake had been reminiscent of: the doctor giving Mom the new pills. *I twist bodies to my will. I am life, I am death.* "Listen, brother. We're trying to raise children in this neighborhood."

"Me too."

"And that's something else. What kind of pervert are you bringing up there? I feel sorry for the boy, it's the fact, I do. But what about the rest of us, who are trying to do the best we can? This is a decent white neighborhood," he says, hitting "decent" weakly but gathering strength for, "that's why we live here instead of across the river over in Brewer where they're letting 'em run wild."

"Letting who run wild?"

"You know fucking well who, read the papers, these old ladies can't even go outdoors in broad daylight with a pocketbook."

Showalter, supple, worried, sidles around and intrudes himself. "White neighborhood isn't exactly the point, we'd welcome a self-respecting black family, I went to school with blacks and I'd work right beside one any day of the week, in fact my company has a recruitment program, the trouble is, their own leaders tell them not to bother, tell them it's a sellout, to learn how to make an honest living." This speech has slid further than he had intended; he hauls it back. "If he acts like a man I'll treat him like a man, am I way out of line on that, Eddie?"

Brumbach puffs up so his shirt pocket tightens on his cigarette pack; his forearms bend at his sides as if under the pull of their veins. "I fought beside them in Vietnam," he says. "No problems."

"Hey that's funny you're a Viet veteran too, this guy we're kind of talking about—"

"No problems," Brumbach goes on, "because we all knew the rules."

Showalter's hands glide, flutter, touch his narrow lapels in a double downward caress. "It's the girl and the black together," he says quickly, to touch it and get away.

Brumbach says, "Christ those boogs love white ass. You should have seen what went on around the bases."

Rabbit offers, "That was yellow ass, wasn't it?"

Showalter tugs at his arm and takes him aside, some steps from the mailbox. Harry wonders if anybody ever mails a letter in it, he passes it every day and it seems mysterious as a fire hydrant, waiting for its moment that may never come. He never hears it clang. In Mt. Judge people were always mailing Valentines. Showalter says, "Don't keep riding him."

Rabbit calls over to Brumbach, "I'm not riding you, am I?"

Showalter tugs harder, so Harry has to bend his ear to the man's little beak and soft unhappy mouth. "He's not that stable. He feels very threatened. It wasn't my idea to get after you, I said to him, The man has his rights of privacy."

Rabbit tries to play the game, whispers. "How many more in the neighborhood feel like him?"

"More than you'd think. I was surprised myself. These are reasonable good people, but they have blind spots. I believe if they didn't have children, if this wasn't a children's neighborhood, it'd be more live and let live."

But Rabbit worries they are being rude to Brumbach. He calls over, "Hey, Eddie. I tell you what."

Brumbach is not pleased to be called in; he had wanted Showalter to settle. Rabbit sees the structure: one man is the negotiations, the other is the muscle. An age of specialization and collusion. Brumbach barks, "What?"

"I'll keep my kid from looking in your windows, and you keep yours from looking in mine."

"We had a name over there for guys like you. Wiseass. Sometimes just by mistake they got fragged."

"I'll tell you what else," Rabbit says. "As a bonus, I'll try to remember to draw the curtains."

"You better do fucking more than pull the fucking curtains," Brumbach tells him, "you better fucking barricade the whole place."

Out of nowhere a mail truck, red, white, and blue, with a canted windshield like a display case, squeaks to a stop at the curb; hurriedly, not looking at any of them, a small man in gray unlocks the mailbox front and scoops a torrent, hundreds it seems, of letters into a gray sack, locks it shut, and drives away.

Rabbit goes close to Brumbach. "Tell me what you want. You want me to move out of the neighborhood."

"I want you to move the black out."

"It's him and the girl together you don't like, suppose he stays and the girl goes?"

"The black goes."

"He goes when he stops being my guest. Have a nice supper."

"You've been warned."

Rabbit asks Showalter, "You hear that threat?"

Showalter smiles, he wipes his brow, he is less depressed. He has done what he could. "I told you," he says, "not to ride him. We came to you in all politeness. I want to repeat, it's the circumstances of what's going on, not the color of anybody's skin. There's a house vacant abutting me and I told the realtor, I said as plain as I say to you, 'Any colored family, with a husband in the house, can get up the equity to buy it at the going market price, let them have it by all means. By all means.' "

"It's nice to meet a liberal," Rabbit says, and shakes his hand. "My wife keeps telling me I'm a conservative."

And, because he likes him, because he likes anybody who fought in Vietnam where he himself should have been fighting, had he not been too old, too old and fat and cowardly, he offers to shake Brumbach's hand too.

The cocky little man keeps his arms stiff at his sides. Instead he turns his head, so the ruined jaw shows. The scar is not just a red L, Rabbit sees, it is an ampersand, complicated by white lines where skin was sewn and overlapped to repair a hole that would always be, that would always repel eyes. Rabbit makes himself look at it. Brumbach's voice is less explosive, almost regretful, sad in its steadiness. "I earned this face," he says. "I got it over there so I could have a decent life here. I'm not asking for sympathy, a lot of my buddies made out worse. I'm just letting you know, after what I seen and done, no wiseass is crowding me in my own neighborhood."

*

Inside the house, it is too quiet. The television isn't going. Nelson is doing homework at the kitchen table. No, he is reading one of Skeeter's books. He has not gotten very far. Rabbit asks, "Where are they?"

"Sleeping. Upstairs."

"Together?"

"I think Jill's on your bed, Skeeter's in mine. He says the sofa stinks. He was awake when I got back from school."

"How did he seem?"

Though the question touches a new vein, Nelson answers promptly. For all the shadows between them, they have lately grown toward each other, father and son. "Jumpy," he answers, into the book. "Said he was getting bad vibes lately and hadn't slept at all last night. I think he had taken some pills or something. He didn't seem to see me, looking over my head, kind of, and kept calling me Chuck instead of Babychuck."

"And how's Jill?"

"Dead asleep. I looked in and said her name and she didn't move. Dad—"

"Spit it out."

"He *gives* her things." The thought is too deep in him to get out easily; his eyes sink in after it, and his father feels him digging, shy, afraid, lacking the right words, not wanting to offend his father.

Harry prompts, "Things."

The boy rushes into it. "She never laughs any more, or takes any interest in anything, just sits around and sleeps. Have you looked at her skin, Dad? She's gotten so pale."

"She's naturally fair."

"Yeah, I know, but it's more than that, she looks *sick*, Dad. She doesn't eat hardly anything and throws up sometimes anyway. Dad, don't let him keep doing it to her, whatever it is. Stop him."

"How can I?"

"You can kick him out."

"Jill's said she'll go with him."

"She won't. She hates him too."

"Don't you like Skeeter?"

"Not really. I know I should. I know you do."

Do I? Surprised, he promises Nelson, "I'll talk to him. But you know, people aren't property, I can't control what they want to do together. We can't live Jill's life for her."

"We *could*, if you wanted to. If you cared at all." This is as close as Nelson has come to defiance; Rabbit's instinct is to be gentle with this sprouting, to ignore it.

He points out simply, "She's too old to adopt. And you're too young to marry."

The child frowns down into the book, silent.

"Now tell me something."

"O.K." Nelson's face tenses, prepared to close; he expects to be asked about Jill and sex and himself. Rabbit is glad to disappoint him, to give him a little space here.

"Two men stopped me on the way home and said kids had been looking in our windows. Have you heard anything about this?"

"Sure."

"Sure what?"

"Sure they do."

"Who?"

"All of them. Frankhauser, and that slob Jimmy Brumbach, Evelyn Morris and those friends of hers from Penn Park, Mark Showalter and I guess his sister Marilyn though she's awful little—"

"When the hell do they do this?"

"Different times. When they come home from school and I'm at soccer practice, before you get home, I hang around out front. I guess sometimes they come back after dark."

"They see anything?"

"I guess sometimes."

"They talk to you about it? Do they tease you?"

"I guess. Sometimes."

"You poor kid. What do you tell 'em?"

"I tell 'em to fuck off."

"Hey. Watch your language."

"That's what I tell 'em. You asked."

"And do you have to fight?"

"Not much. Just sometimes when they call me something."

"What?"

"Something. Never mind, Dad."

"Tell me what they call you."

"Nigger Nellie."

"Huh. Nice kids."

"They're just kids, Dad. They don't mean anything. Jill says ignore them, they're ignorant."

"And do they kid you about Jill?"

The boy turns his face away altogether. His hair covers his neck, yet even from the back he would not be mistaken for a girl: the angles in the shoulders, the lack of brushing in the hair. The choked voice comes: "I don't want to talk about it any more Dad."

"O.K. Thanks. Hey. I'm sorry. I'm sorry you have to live in the mess we all make."

Surprisingly, the choked voice resumes. "Gee I wish Mom would come back. Jesus, but I wish it!" Nelson thumps the back of the kitchen chair and then rests his forehead where his fist struck; Rabbit ruffles his hair, helplessly, on his way past, to the refrigerator to get a beer.

*

The nights close in earlier now. After the six o'clock news there is darkness. Rabbit says to Skeeter, "I met another veteran from Vietnam today."

"Shit, the world's filling up with Viet veterans so fast there won't be nobody else soon, right? Never forget, got into a lighthouse up near Tuy Hoa, white walls all over, everybody been there one time or another and done their drawings. Well, what blew my mind, absolutely, was somebody, Charlie or the unfriendlies, Arvin never been near this place till we handed it to 'em, somebody on that other side had done a whole wall's worth of Uncle Ho himself, Uncle Ho being buggered, Uncle Ho shitting skulls, Uncle Ho doing this and that, it was downright disrespectful, right? And I says to myself, those poor dinks being screwed the same as us, we is all in the grip of crazy old men thinkin' they can still make history happen. History isn't going to happen any more, Chuck."

"What is going to happen?" Nelson asks.

"A bad mess," Skeeter answers, "then, most probably, Me."

Nelson's eyes seek his father's, as they do now when Skeeter's craziness shows. "Dad, shouldn't we wake up Jill?"

Harry is into his second beer and his first joint; his stockinged feet are up on the cobbler's bench. "Why? Let her sleep. Don't be so uptight."

"No suh," Skeeter says, "the boy has a good plan there, where is that fucking little Jill? I do feel horny."

Nelson asks, "What's horny?"

"Horny is what I feel," Skeeter answers. "Babychuck, go

drag down that no-good cunt. Tell her the menfolk needs their vittles."

"Dad—"

"Come on, Nellie, quit nagging. Do what he asks. Don't you have any homework? Do it upstairs, this is a grown-up evening."

When Nelson is gone, Rabbit can breathe. "Skeeter, one thing I don't understand, how do you feel about the Cong? I mean are they right, or wrong, or what?"

"Man by man, or should I say gook by gook, they are very beautiful, truly. So brave they must be tripping, and a lot of them no older than little Nellie, right? As a bunch, I never could dig what they was all about, except that we was white or black as the case may be, and they was yellow, and had got there first, right? Otherwise I can't say they made a great deal of sense, since the people they most liked to castrate and string up and bury in ditches alive and make that kind of scene with was yellow like them, right? So I would consider them one more facet of the confusion of false prophecy by which you may recognize My coming in this the fullness of time. However. However, I confess that politics being part of this boring power thing do not much turn me on. Things human turn me on, right? You too, right, Chuck? Here she is."

Jill has drifted in. Her skin looks tight on her face.

Rabbit asks her, "Hungry? Make yourself a peanut butter sandwich. That's what we had to do."

"I'm not hungry."

Trying to be Skeeter, Rabbit goads her. "Christ, you should be. You're skinny as a stick. What the hell kind of piece of ass are you, there's nothing there any more. Why you think we keep you here?"

She ignores him and speaks to Skeeter. "I'm in need," she tells him.

"Shee-yut, girl, we're all in need, right? The whole world's in need, isn't that what we done agreed on, Chuck? The whole benighted world is in need of Me. And Me, I'm in need of something else. Bring your cunt over here, white girl."

Now she does look toward Rabbit. He cannot help her. She has always been out of his class. She sits down on the sofa beside Skeeter and asks him gently, "What? If I do it, will you do it?"

"Might. Tell you what, Jill honey. Let's do it for the man."

"What man?"

"*The* man. That man. Victor Charlie over there. He wants it. What you think he's keepin' us here for? To *breed*, that's what for. Hey. Friend Harry?"

"I'm listening."

"You like being a nigger, don't ya?"

"I do."

"You want to be a good nigger, right?"

"Right." The sad rustling on the ceiling, of Nelson in his room, feels far distant. Don't come down. Stay up there. The smoke mixes with his veins and his lungs are a branching tree.

"Okay," Skeeter says. "Now here's how. You is a big black man sittin' right there. You is chained to that chair. And I, I is white as snow. Be-hold." And Skeeter, with that electric scuttling suddenness, stands, and pulls off his shirt. In the room's deep dusk his upper half disappears. Then he scrabbles at himself at belt-level and his lower half disappears. Only his glasses remain, silver circles. His voice, disembodied, is the darkness. Slowly his head, a round cloud, tells against the blue light from the streetlamp at the end of the Crescent. "And this little girl here," he calls, "is black as coal. An ebony virgin torn from the valley of the river Niger, right? Stand up, honey, show us your teeth. Turn clean around." The black shadows of his hands glide into the white blur Jill is, and guide it upward, as a potter guides a lump of clay upward on the humming wheel, into a vase. She keeps rising, smoke from the vase. Her dress is being lifted over her head. "Turn around, honey, show us your rump." A soft slap gilds the darkness, the whiteness revolves. Rabbit's eyes, enlarged, can sift out shades of light and dark, can begin to model the bodies six feet from him, across the cobbler's bench. He can see the dark crack between Jill's buttocks, the faint dent her hip muscle makes, the shadowy mane between her starved-cheek hipbones. Her belly looks long. Where her breasts should be, black spiders are fighting: he sorts these out as Skeeter's hands. Skeeter is whispering to Jill, murmuring, while his hands flutter like bats against the moon. He hears her say, in a voice sifted through her hair, a sentence with the word "satisfy" in it.

Skeeter cackles: forked lightning. "Now," he sings, and his voice has become golden hoops spinning forward, an auctioneer who is a juggler, "we will have a demon-stray-shun of o-bee-deeyance, from this little coal-black lady, who has been broken in by expert traders working out of Nashville, Tennessee, and who is guaranteed by them ab-so-lutily to give no trouble in the kitchen, hallway, stable, *or* bedroom!" Another soft slap, and the white clay dwindles; Jill is kneeling, while Skeeter still stands. A most delicate slipping silvery sound touches up the silence now; but Rabbit cannot precisely see. He needs to see. The driftwood lamp is behind him. Not turning his head, he gropes and switches it on.

Nice.

What he sees reminds him in the first flash of the printing process, an inked plate contiguous at some few points to white paper. As his eyes adjust, he sees Skeeter is not black, he is a gentle brown. These are smooth-skinned children being gently punished, one being made to stand and the other to kneel. Skeeter crouches and reaches down a long hand, fingernails like baby rose petals, to shield Jill's profile from the glare. Her eyelids remain closed, her mouth remains open, her breasts cast no shadow they are so shallow, she is feminine most in the swell of her backside spread on her propping heels and in the white lily of a hand floating beside his balls as if to receive from the air a baton. An inch or two of Skeeter is unenclosed by her face, a purplish inch bleached to lilac, below his metallic pubic explosion, the shape and texture of his goatee. Keeping his protective crouch, Skeeter turns his face sheepishly toward the light; his eyeglasses glare opaquely and his upper lip lifts in imitation of pain. "Hey man, what's with that? Cut that light."

"You're beautiful," Rabbit says.

"O.K., strip and get into it, she's full of holes, right?"

"I'm scared to," Rabbit confesses: it is true, they seem not only beautiful but in the same vision an interlocked machine that might pull him apart.

Though the slap of light left her numb, this confession pierces Jill's trance; she turns her head, Skeeter's penis falling free, a bright string of moisture breaking. She looks at Harry, past him; as he reaches to switch off the light mercifully, she screams. In the corner of his vision, he saw it too: a face. At the window. Eyes like two cigarette burns. The lamp is out, the face is vanished. The window is a faintly blue rectangle in a black room. Rabbit runs to the front door and opens it. The night air bites. October. The lawn looks artificial, lifeless, dry, no-color: a snapshot of grass. Vista Crescent stretches empty but for parked cars. The maple is too slender to hide anyone. A child might have made it across the front of the house along the flowerbeds and be now in the garage. The garage door is up. And, if the child is Nelson, a door from the garage leads into the kitchen. Rabbit decides not to look, not to give chase; he feels that there is no space for him to step into, that the vista before him is a flat, stiff, cold photograph. The only thing that moves is the vapor of his breathing. He closes the door. He hears nothing move in the kitchen. He tells the living room, "Nobody."

"Bad," Skeeter says. His penis is quite relaxed, a whip between his legs as he squats. Jill is weeping on the floor; face down, she has curled her naked body into a knot. Her bottom forms the top half of a valentine heart, only white; her flesh-colored hair fans spilled over the sullen green carpet. Rabbit and Skeeter together squat to pick her up. She fights it, she makes herself roll over limply; her hair streams across her face, clouds her mouth, adheres like cobwebs to her chin and throat. A string as of milkweed spittle is on her chin; Rabbit wipes her chin and mouth with his handkerchief and, for weeks afterward, when all is lost, will take out this handkerchief and bury his nose in it, in its imperceptible spicy smell.

*

Jill's lips are moving. She is saying, "You promised. You promised." She is talking to Skeeter. Though Rabbit bends his big face over hers, she has eyes only for the narrow black face beside him. There is no green in her eyes, the black pupils have eclipsed the irises. "It's such dumb hell," she says, with a little whimper, as if to mock her own complaint, a Connecticut housewife who knows she exaggerates. "Oh Christ," she adds in an older voice and shuts her eyes. Rabbit touches her; she is sweating. At his touch, she starts to shiver. He wants to blanket her, to blanket her with his body if there is nothing else, but she will talk only to Skeeter. Rabbit is not there for her, he only thinks he is here.

Skeeter asks down into her, "Who's your Lord Jesus, Jill honey?"

"You are."

"I am, right?"

"Right."

"You love me more'n you love yourself?"

"Much more."

"What do you see when you look at me, Jill honey?"

"I don't know."

"You see a giant lily, right?"

"Right. You promised."

"Love my cock?"

"Yes."

"Love my jism, sweet Jill? Love it in your veins?"

"Yes. Please. Shoot me. You promised."

"I your Savior, right? Right?"

"You promised. You must. Skeeter."

"O.K. Tell me I'm your Savior."

"You are. Hurry. You did promise."

"O.K." Skeeter explains hurriedly. "I'll fix her up. You go upstairs, Chuck. I don't want you to see this."

"I want to see it."

"Not this. It's bad, man. Bad, bad, bad. It's shit. Stay clean, you in deep enough trouble on account of me without being party to this, right? Split. I'm begging, man."

Rabbit understands. They are at war. They have taken a hostage. Everywhere out there, there are unfriendlies. He checks the front door, staying down below the three windows echoing the three chime-tones. He sneaks into the kitchen. Nobody is there. He slips the bolt across, in the door that opens from the garage. Sidling to make his shadow narrow, he climbs upstairs. At Nelson's door he listens for the sound of unconscious breathing. He hears the boy's breath rasp, touching bottom. In his own bedroom, the streetlamp prints negative spatters of the maple leaves on his wallpaper. He gets into bed in his underwear, in case he must rise and run; as a child, in summer, he would have to sleep in his underwear when the wash hadn't dried on the line. Rabbit listens to the noises downstairs—clicking, clucking kitchen noises, of a pan being put on the stove, of a bit of glass clinking, of footsteps across the linoleum, the sounds that have always made him sleepy, of Mom up, of the world being tended to. His thoughts begin to dissolve, though his heart keeps pounding, waves breaking on Jill's white valentine, stamped on his retinas like the sun. Offset versus letterpress, offset never has the bite of the other, looks greasy, the wave of the future. She slips into bed beside him; her valentine nestles cool against his belly and silken limp cock. He has been asleep. He asks her, "Is it late?"

Jill speaks very slowly. "Pretty late."

"How do you feel?"

"Better. For now."

"We got to get you to a doctor."

"It won't help."

He has a better idea, so obvious he cannot imagine why he has never thought of it before. "We got to get you back to your father."

"You forget. He's dead."

"Your mother, then."

"The car's dead."

"We'll get it out of hock."

"It's too late," Jill tells him. "It's too late for you to try to love me."

He wants to answer, but there is a puzzling heavy truth in this that carries him under, his hand caressing the inward dip of her waist, a warm bird dipping toward its nest.

Sunshine, the old clown, rims the room. The maple has so many leaves fallen morning light slants in baldly. A headache grazes his skull, his dream (Pajasek and he were in a canoe, paddling upstream, through a dark green country; their destination felt to be a distant mountain striped and folded like a tablecloth. "When can I have my silver bullet?"

Rabbit asked him. "You promised." "Fool," Pajasek told him. "Stupid." "You know so much more," Rabbit answered, nonsensically, and his heart opened in a flood of light) merges with the night before, both unreal. Jill sleeps dewily beside him; at the base of her throat, along her hairline, sweat has collected and glistens. Delicately, not to disturb her, he takes her wrist and turns it so he can see the inside of her freckled arm. They might be bee-stings. There are not too many. He can talk to Janice. Then he remembers that Janice is not here, and that only Nelson is their child. He eases from the bed, amused to discover himself in underwear, like a kid at camp whose pajamas have been knotted and soaked.

After breakfast, while Jill and Skeeter sleep, he and Nelson rake and mow the lawn, putting it to bed for the winter. He hopes this will be the last mowing, though in fact the grass, parched in high spots, is vigorously green where a depression holds moisture, and along a line from the kitchen to the street—perhaps the sewer connection is broken and seeping, that is why it flows sluggishly. And the leaves—he calls to Nelson, who has to shut off the razzing mower to listen, "How the hell does such a skinny little tree produce so many leaves?"

"They aren't all *its* leaves. They blow in from the other trees."

And he looks, and sees that his neighbors have trees, saplings like his, but some already as tall as the housetops. Someday Nelson may come back to this, his childhood neighborhood, and find it strangely dark, buried in shade, the lawns opulent, the homes venerable. Rabbit hears children calling in other yards, and sees across several fences and driveways kids having a Saturday scrimmage, one voice piping, "I'm free, I'm free," and the ball obediently floating. This isn't a bad neighborhood, he thinks, this could be a nice place if you gave it a chance. And around the other houses men with rakes and mowers mirror him. He asks Nelson, before the boy restarts the mower, "Aren't you going to visit your mother today?"

"Tomorrow. Today she and Charlie were driving up to the Poconos, to look at the foliage. They went with some brother of Charlie's and his wife."

"Boy, she's moving right in." A real Springer. He smiles to himself, perversely proud. The legal stationery must be on the way. And then him, yes, he can join that army, of Brewer geezers. Human garbage, Pop used to say. He better enjoy Vista Crescent while he has it. He resumes raking, and listens for the mower's razzing to resume. Instead, there is the lurch and rattle of the starter, repeated, and Nelson's voice calling, "Hey Dad. I think it's out of gas."

A Saturday, then, of small sunlit tasks, acts of caretaking and commerce. He and Nelson stroll with the empty five-gallon can up to Weiser and get it filled at the Getty station. Returning, they meet Jill and Skeeter emerging from the house, dressed to kill. Skeeter wears stovepipe pants, alligator shoes, a maroon turtleneck and a peach-colored cardigan. He looks like the newest thing in golf pros. Jill has on her white dress and a brown sweater of Harry's; she suggests a cheerleader, off to the noon pep rally before the football game. Her face, though thin, and the skin of it thin and brittle like isinglass, has a pink flush; she seems excited, affectionate. "There's some salami and lettuce in the fridge for you and Nelson to make lunch with if you want. Skeeter and I are going into Brewer to see what we can do about this wretched car. And we thought we might drop in on Babe. We'll be back late this after. Maybe you should visit your mother this afternoon, I feel guilty you never do."

"O.K., I might. You O.K.?" To Skeeter: "You have carfare?"

In his clothes Skeeter puts on a dandy's accent; he thrusts out his goatee and says between scarcely parted teeth, "Jilly is loaded. And if we run short, your name is good credit, right?" Rabbit tries to recall the naked man of last night, the dangling penis, the jutting heels, the squat as by a jungle fire, and cannot; it was another terrain.

Serious, a daylight man, he scolds: "You better get back before Nelson and I go out around six. I don't want to leave the house empty." He drops his voice so Nelson won't hear. "After last night, I'm kind of spooked."

"What happened last night?" Skeeter asks. "Nothin' spooky that I can remember, we'se all jest folks, livin' out life in these Benighted States." He has put on all his armor, nothing will get to him.

Rabbit tests it: "You're a *baad* nigger."

Skeeter smiles in the sunshine with angelic rows of teeth; his spectacles toss halos higher than the TV aerials. "Now you're singing my song," he says.

Rabbit asks Jill, "You O.K. with this crazyman?"

She says lightly, "He's my sugar daddy," and puts her arm through his, and linked like that they recede down Vista Crescent, and vanish in the shuffle of picture windows.

Rabbit and Nelson finish the lawn. They eat, and toss a football around for a while, and then the boy asks if he can go off and join the scrimmage whose shouts they can hear, he knows some of the kids, the same kids who look into windows but that's O.K., Dad; and really it does feel as though all can be forgiven, all will sink into Saturday's America like rain into earth, like days into time. Rabbit goes into the house and watches the first game of the World Series, Baltimore out-classing the Mets, for a while, and switches to Penn State out-classing West Virginia at football, and, unable to sit still any longer with the bubble of premonition swelling inside him, goes to the phone and calls his home. "Hi Pop, hey. I thought of coming over this after but the kid is outside playing a game and we have to go over to Fosnachts tonight anyhow, so can she wait until tomorrow? Mom. Also I ought to get hot on changing the screens around to storm windows, it felt chilly last night."

"She can wait, Harry. Your mother does a lot of waiting these days."

"Yeah, well." He means it's not his fault, he didn't invent old age. "When is Mim coming in?"

"Any day now, we don't know the exact day. She'll just arrive, is how she left it. Her old room is ready."

"How's Mom sleeping lately? She still having dreams?"

"Strange you should ask, Harry. I always said, you and your mother are almost psychic. Her dreams are getting worse. She dreamed last night we buried her alive. You and me and Mim together. She said only Nelson tried to stop it."

"Gee, maybe she's warming up to Nelson at last."

"And Janice called us this morning."

"What about? I'd hate to have Stavros's phone bill."

"Difficult to say, what about. She had nothing concrete that we could fathom, she just seems to want to keep in touch. I think she's having terrible second thoughts, Harry. She says she's exceedingly worried about you."

"I bet."

"Your mother and I spent a lot of time discussing her call; you know our Mary, she's never one to admit when she's disturbed–"

"Pop, there's somebody at the door. Tell Mom I'll be over tomorrow, absolutely."

There had been nobody at the door. He had suddenly been unable to keep talking to his father, every word of the old man's dragging with reproach. But having lied frightens him now; "nobody" has become an evil presence at the door. Moving through the rooms stealthily, he searches the house for the kit Skeeter must use to fix Jill with. He can picture it from having watched television: the syringe and tourniquet and the long spoon to melt the powder in. The sofa cushions divulge a dollar in change, a bent paperback of *Soul on Ice*, a pearl from an earring or pocketbook. Jill's bureau drawers upstairs conceal nothing under the underwear but a box of Tampax, a packet of hairpins, a half-full card of Enovid pills, a shy little tube of ointment for acne. The last place he thinks to look is the downstairs closet, fitted into an ill-designed corner beside the useless fire place, along the wall of stained pine where the seascape hangs Janice bought at Kroll's complete with frame, one piece in fact with its frame, a single shaped sheet of plastic, Rabbit remembers from hanging it on the nail. In this closet, beneath the polyethylene bags holding their winter clothes, including the mink stole old man Springer gave Janice on her twenty-first birthday, there is a squat black suitcase, smelling new, with a combination lock. Packed so Skeeter could grab it and run from the house in thirty seconds. Rabbit fiddles with the lock, trying combinations at random, trusting to God to make a very minor miracle, then, this failing, going at it by system, beginning 111, 112, 113, 114, and then 211, 212, 213, but never hits it, and the practical infinity of numbers opens under him dizzyingly. Some dust in the closet starts him sneezing. He goes outdoors with the Windex bottle for the storm windows.

This work soothes him. You slide up the aluminum screen, putting the summer behind you, and squirt the inside window with the blue spray, give it those big square swipes to spread it thin, and apply the tighter rubbing to remove the film and with it the dirt; it squeaks, like birdsong. Then slide the winter window down from the slot where it has been waiting since April and repeat the process; and go inside and repeat the process, twice: so that at last four flawless transparencies permit outdoors to come indoors, other houses to enter yours. The mirror is two-way.

Toward five o'clock Skeeter and Jill return. They are jubilant. Through Babe they found a man willing to give them six hundred dollars for the Porsche. He drove them up-county, he examined the car, and Jill signed the registration over to him.

"What color was he?" Rabbit asks.

"He was green," Skeeter says, showing him ten-dollar bills fanned in his hand, lettuce yellowed by fingering.

Rabbit asks Jill, "Why'd you split it with *him?*"

Skeeter says, "I dig hostility. You want your cut, right?" His lips push, his glasses glint.

Jill laughs it off. "Skeeter's my partner in crime," she says.

"You want my advice, what you should do with that money?" Rabbit says. "You should get a train ticket back to Stonington."

"The trains don't run any more. Anyway, I thought I'd buy some new dresses. Aren't you tired of this ratty old white one? I had to pin it up in the front and wear this sweater over it."

"It suits you," he says.

She takes up the challenge in his tone. "Something bugging you?"

"Just your sloppiness."

"Would you like me to leave? I could now."

His arms go numb as if injected; his hands feel heavy, his palms, tingling, swell. Her nibbling mouth, her apple hardness, the sea-fan of her flesh-colored hair on their pillows in the morning light, her white valentine of packed satin. "No," he begs, "don't go yet."

"Why not?"

"You're under my skin." The phrase feels unnatural on his lips, puffs them like a dry wind in passing; it must have been spoken for Skeeter, for Skeeter cackles appreciatively.

"Chuck, you're learning to be a loser. I love it. The Lord loves it. Losers gonna grab the earth, right?"

Nelson returns from the football game with a bruised upper

lip, his smile lopsided and happy. "They give you a hard time?" Rabbit asks.

"No, it was fun. Skeeter, you ought to play next Saturday, they asked about you and I said you used to be a quarterback for Brewer High."

"Quarterback, shit, I was *full*back, I was so small they couldn't find me."

"I don't mind being small, it makes you quicker."

"O.K.," his father says, "see how quick you can take a bath. And for once in your life brush your hair."

Festively, Jill and Skeeter see them off to the Fosnachts. Jill straightens Rabbit's tie, Skeeter dusts his shoulders like a Pullman porter. "Just think, honey," Skeeter says to Jill, "our little boy's all growed up, his first date."

"It's just dinner," Rabbit protests. "I'll be back for the eleven o'clock news."

"That big honky with the sideways eyes, she may have something planned for dessert."

"You stay as late as you want," Jill tells him. "We'll leave the porch light on and won't wait up."

"What're *you* two going to do tonight?"

"Jes' read and knit and sit cozy by the fire," Skeeter tells him.

"Her number's in the book if you need to get ahold of me. Under just M."

"We won't," Jill tells him.

Nelson unexpectedly says, "Skeeter, lock the doors and don't go outside unless you have to."

The Negro pats the boy's brushed hair. "Wouldn't dream of it, chile. Ol' tarbaby, he just stay right here in his briar patch."

"Dad, we shouldn't go."

"Don't be dumb." They go. Orange sunlight stripes with long shadows the spaces of flat lawn between the low houses. As Vista Crescent curves, the sun moves behind them and

Rabbit is struck, seeing their elongated shadows side by side, by how much like himself Nelson walks: the same loose lope below, the same faintly tense alertness of the head and shoulders above. In shadow the boy, like himself, is tall as the giant at the top of the beanstalk, treading the sidewalk on telescoping legs. Rabbit turns to speak. Beside him, the boy's overlong black hair bounces as he strides to keep up, lugging his pajamas and toothbrush and change of underwear and sweater in a paper grocery bag for tomorrow's boat ride. Rabbit finds there is nothing to say, just mute love spinning down, love for this extension of himself downward into time when he will be in the grave, love cool as the flame of sunlight burning level among the stick-thin maples and fallen leaves, themselves flames curling.

And from Peggy's windows Brewer glows and dwindles like ashes in a gigantic hearth. The river shines blue long after the shores turn black. There is a puppy in the apartment now, a fuzzy big-pawed Golden that tugs at Rabbit's hand with a slippery nipping mouth; its fur, touched, is as surprising in its softness as ferns. Peggy has remembered he likes daiquiris; this time she has mix and the electric blender rattles with ice before she brings him his drink, half froth. She has aged a month: a pound or two around her waist, two or three more gray hairs showing at her parting. She has gathered her hair back in a twist, rather than letting it straggle around her face as if she were still in high school. Her face looks pushed-forward, scrubbed, glossy. She tells him wearily, "Ollie and I may be getting back together."

She is wearing a blue dress, secretarial, that suits her more than that paisley that kept riding up her pasty thighs. "That's good, isn't it?"

"It's good for Billy." The boys, once Nelson arrived, went down the elevator again, to try to repair the mini-bike in the basement. "In fact, that's mostly the reason; Ollie is worried about Billy. With me working and not home until dark, he hangs around with that bad crowd up toward the bridge. You know, it's not like when we were young, the temptations they're exposed to. It's not just cigarettes and a little feeling up. At fourteen now, they're ready to go."

"Billy's fourteen now? I guess he is," Harry says, brushing froth from his lips and wishing she would come away from the window so he could see all of the sky. "I guess they figure they might be dead at eighteen."

"Janice says you like the war."

"I don't like it; I defend it. I wasn't thinking of that, they have a lot of ways to die now we didn't have. Anyway, it's nice about you and Ollie, if it works out. A little sad, too."

"Why sad?"

"Sad for me. I mean, I guess I blew my chance, to—"

"To what?"

"To cash you in."

Bad phrase, too harsh, though it had been an apology. He has lived with Skeeter too long. But her blankness, the blankness of her silhouette as Peggy stands in her habitual pose against the windows, suggested it. A blank check. A woman is blank until you fuck her. Everything is blank until you fuck it. Us and Vietnam, fucking and being fucked, blood is wisdom. Must be some better way but it's not in nature. His silence is leaden with regret. She remains blank some seconds, says nothing. Then she moves into the space around him, turns on lamps, lifts a pillow into place, plumps it, stoops and straightens, turns, takes light upon her sides, is rounded into shape. A lumpy big woman but not a fat one, clumsy but not gross, sad with evening, with Ollie or not Ollie, with being thirty-six and knowing nothing. He and Peggy Gring sat in the same classrooms since first grade; she had seen him when he was good, had sat in those hot bleachers screaming, when he was a hero, naked and swift and lean. She has seen him come to nothing. She plumps down in the chair beside his, brushes at the ghost of the hairdo she no longer has, and says, "I've been cashed in a lot lately."

"You mean with Ollie?"

"Others. Guys I meet at work. Ollie minds. That may be why he wants back in."

"If Ollie minds, you must be telling him. So you must want him back in too."

She looks into the bottom of her glass; there is nothing there but ice. "And how about you and Janice?"

"Janice who? Let me get you another drink."

"Wow. You've become a gentleman."

"Slightly."

As he puts her gin-and-tonic into her hand, he says, "Tell me about those other guys."

"They're O.K. I'm not that proud of them. They're human. I'm human."

"You do it but don't fall in love?"

"Apparently. Is that terrible?"

"No," he says. "I think it's nice."

"You think a lot of things are nice lately."

"Yeah. I'm not so uptight."

The boys come back upstairs. They complain the new headlight they bought doesn't fit. Peggy feeds them, a casserole of chicken legs and breasts, poor dismembered creatures simmering. Rabbit wonders how many animals have died to keep his life going, how many more will die. A barnyard full, a farmful of thumping hearts, seeing eyes, racing legs, all stuffed squawking into him as into a black sack. No avoiding it: life does want death. To be alive is to kill. Dinner inside them, they stuff themselves on television: Jackie Gleason, *My Three Sons*, *Hogan's Heroes*, *Petticoat Junction*, *Mannix*. An orgy. Nelson is asleep on the floor, radioactive light beating on his closed lids and open mouth. Rabbit carries him into Billy's room, while Peggy tucks her own son in.

"Mom, I'm not sleepy." "It's past bedtime." "It's Saturday night." "You have a big day tomorrow." "When is *he* going home?" He must think Harry has no ears. "When he wants to." "What are you going to do?" "Nothing that's any of your business." "*Mom.*" "Shall I listen to your prayers?" "When he's out of the room." "You say them to yourself tonight."

Harry and Peggy return to the living room and watch the week's news roundup. The weekend commentator is fairer-haired and less severe in expression than the weekday one. He says there has been some good news this week. American deaths in Vietnam were reported the lowest in three years, and one twenty-four-hour period saw no American battle deaths at all. The Soviet Union made headlines this week, agreeing with the U.S. to ban atomic weapons from the world's ocean floors, agreeing with Red China to hold talks concerning their sometimes bloody border disputes, and launching Soyuz 6, a linked three-stage space spectacular bringing closer the day of permanent space stations. In Washington, Hubert Humphrey endorsed Richard Nixon's handling of the Vietnam war and Lieutenant General Lewis B. Hershey, crusty and controversial head for twenty-eight years of this nation's selective service system, was relieved of his post and promoted to four-star general. In Chicago, riots outside the courtroom and riotous behavior within continued to characterize the trial of the so-called Chicago Eight. In Belfast, Protestants and British troops clashed. In Prague, Czechoslovakia's revisionist government, in one of its sternest moves, banned citizens from foreign travel. And preparations were under way: for tomorrow's Columbus Day parades, despite threatened protests from Scandinavian groups maintaining that Leif Ericson and not Columbus was the discoverer of America, and for Wednesday's Moratorium Day, a nationwide outpouring of peaceful protest. "Crap," says Rabbit. Sports. Weather. Peggy rises awkwardly from her chair to turn it off. Rabbit rises, also stiff. "Great supper," he tells her. "I guess I'll get back now."

The television off, they stand rimmed by borrowed light: the bathroom door down the hall left ajar for the boys, the apartment-house corridor a bright slit beneath the door leading out, the phosphorescence of Brewer through the windows. Peggy's body, transected and rimmed by those remote fires, does not quite fit together; her arm jerks up from darkness and brushes indifferently at her hair and seems to miss. She shrugs, or shudders, and shadows slip from her. "Wouldn't you like," she asks, in a voice not quite hers, originating in the dim charged space between them, and lighter, breathier, "to cash me in?"

Yes, it turns out, yes he would, and they bump, and fumble, and unzip, and she is gumdrops everywhere, yet stately as a statue, planetary in her breadth, a contour map of some snowy land where he has never been; not since Ruth has he had a woman this big. Naked, she makes him naked, even kneeling to unlace his shoes, and then kneeling to him in the pose of Jill to Skeeter, so he has glided across a gulf, and stands where last night he stared. He gently unlinks her, lowers her to the floor, and tastes earth, salt swamp, between her legs. Her thighs part easily, she grows wet readily, she is sadly unclumsy at this, she has indeed been to bed with many men. In the knowing way she handles his prick he feels their presences, feels himself competing, is put off, goes soft. She leaves off and comes up and presses the gumdrop of her tongue between his lips. Puddled on the floor, they keep knocking skulls and ankle bones on the furniture legs. The puppy, hearing their commotion, thinks they want to play and thrusts his cold nose and scrabbling paws among their sensitive flesh; his fern-furry busy bustlingness tickles and hurts. This third animal among them re-excites Rabbit; observing this, Peggy leads him down her hall, the dark crease between her buttocks snapping tick-tock with her walk.

Holding her rumpled dress in front of her like a pad, she pauses at the boy's door, listens, and nods. Her hair has gone loose. The puppy for a while whimpers at their door, claws the floor as if to dig there; then is eclipsed by the inflammation of their senses, falls silent under the thunder of their blood. Harry is afraid with this unknown woman, of timing her wrong, but she tells him, "One sec." Him inside her, she does something imperceptible, relaxing and tensing the muscles of her vagina, and announces, "Now." She comes one beat ahead of him, a cool solid thump of a come that lets him hit home without fear of hurting her: a fuck innocent of madness. Then slides in that embarrassment of afterwards —of returning discriminations, of the other re-emerging from the muddle, of sorting out what was hers and what was yours, and who gets credit. He hides his face in the hot cave at the side of her neck. "Thank you."

"Thank you yourself," Peggy Fosnacht says, and, what he doesn't especially like, hugs his bottom to give her one more deep thrust before he softens. Both Jill and Janice too ladylike for that. Still, he is at home.

Until she says, "Would you mind rolling off? You're squeezing the breath out of me."

"Am I so heavy?"

"After a while."

"Actually, I better go."

"Why? It's only midnight."

"I'm worried about what they're doing back at the house."

"Nelson's here. The others, what do you care?"

"I don't know. I care."

"Well they don't care about you and you're in bed with someone who does."

He accuses her: "You're taking Ollie back."

"Have any better ideas? He's the father of my child."

"Well that's not my fault."

"No, nothing's your fault," and she tumbles around him, and they make solid sadly skillful love again, and they talk and he dozes a little, and the phone rings. It shrills right beside his ear. A woman's arm elastic and warm reaches across his face to pluck it silent. Peggy's. She listens, and hands it to him with an expression he cannot read. There is a clock beside the telephone; its luminous hands say one-twenty. "Hey. Chuck? Better get your ass over here. It's bad. Bad."

"Skeeter?" His throat hurts, just speaking. Fucking Peggy has left him dry.

The voice at the other end hangs up.

Rabbit kicks out of the bedcovers and hunts in the dark for his clothes. He remembers. The living room. The boys' door opens as he runs down the hall naked. Nelson's astonished face takes in his father's nakedness. He asks, "Was it Mom?"

"Mom?"

"On the phone."

"Skeeter. Something's gone wrong at the house."

"Should I come?"

They are in the living room, Rabbit stooping to gather his clothes scattered over the floor, hopping to get into his underpants, his suit pants. The puppy, awake again, dances and nips at him.

"Better stay."

"What can it be, Dad?"

"No idea. Maybe the cops. Maybe Jill getting sicker."

"Why didn't he talk longer?"

"His voice sounded funny, I'm not sure it was our phone."

"I'm coming with you."

"I told you to stay here."

"I *must*, Dad."

Rabbit looks at him and agrees, "O.K. I guess you must."

Peggy in blue bathrobe is in the hall; more lights are on.

Billy is up. His pajamas are stained yellow at the fly, he is pimply and tall. Peggy says, "Shall I get dressed?"

"No. You're great the way you are." Rabbit is having trouble with his tie: his shirt collar has a button in the back that has to be undone to get the tie under. He puts on his coat and stuffs the tie into his pocket. His skin is tingling with the start of sweat and his penis murmuringly aches. He has forgotten to do the laces of his shoes and as he kneels to do them his stomach jams into his throat.

"How will you get there?" Peggy asks.

"Run," Rabbit answers.

"Don't be funny, it's a mile and a half. I'll get dressed and drive you."

She must be told she is not his wife. "I don't want you to come. Whatever it is, I don't want you and Billy to have to see it."

"Mo-*om*," Billy protests from the doorway. But he is still in stained pajamas whereas Nelson is dressed, but for bare feet. His sneakers are in his hand.

Peggy yields. "I'll get you my car keys. It's the blue Mustang, the fourth slot in the line against the wall. Nelson knows. No, Billy. You and I will stay here."

Rabbit takes the keys, which come into his hand as cold as if they have been in the refrigerator. "Thanks a lot. Or have I said that before? Sorry about this. Great dinner, Peggy."

"Glad you liked it."

"We'll let you know what's what. It's probably nothing, the son of a bitch is probably just stoned out of his mind."

Nelson has put his socks and sneakers on. "Let's *go*, Dad. Thank you very much, Mrs. Fosnacht."

"You're both very welcome."

"Thank Mr. Fosnacht if I can't go on the boat; I probably can't."

Billy is still trying. "Mo-*om*, let me."

"No."

"Mom, you're a bitch."

Peggy slaps her son: pink leaps up on his cheek in stripes like fingers, and the child's face hardens beyond further controlling. "Mom, you're a whore. That's what the bridge kids say. You'll lay anybody."

Rabbit says, "You two take it easy," and turns; they flee, father and son, down the hall, down the steel stairwell, not waiting for an elevator, to a basement of parked cars, a polychrome lake caught in a low illumined grotto. Rabbit blinks to realize that even while he and Peggy were heating their little mutual darkness a cold fluorescent world surrounded them in hallways and down stairwells and amid unsleeping pillars upholding their vast building. The universe is unsleeping, neither ants nor stars sleep, to die will be to be forever wide awake. Nelson finds the blue Mustang for him. Its dashlights glow green at ignition. Almost silently the engine comes to life, backs them out, sneaks them along through the stained grotto wall. In a corner by the brickwork of a stairwell the all-chrome mini-bike waits to be repaired. An asphalt exitway becomes a parking lot, becomes a street lined with narrow houses and great green signs bearing numbers, keystones, shields, the names of unattainable cities. They come onto Weiser; the traffic is thin, sinister. The stoplights no longer regulate but merely wink. Burger Bliss is closed, though its purple oven glows within, plus a sallow residue of ceiling tubes to discourage thieves and vandals. A police car nips by, bleating. The Acme lot at this hour has no horizon. Are the few cars still parked on it abandoned? Or lovers? Or ghosts in a world so thick with cars their shadows like leaves settle everywhere? A whirling light, insulting in its brilliance, materializes in Rabbit's rear-view mirror and as it swells acquires the overpowering grief of a siren. The red bulk of a fire engine plunges by, sucking the Mustang toward the center of the street, where the trolley-track bed used to be. Nelson cries, "Dad!"

"Dad what?"

"Nothing, I thought you lost control."

"Never. Not your Dad."

The movie marquee, unlit and stubby, is announcing, BACK BY REQST—2001. All these stores along Weiser have burglar lights on and a few, a new defense, wear window grilles.

"Dad, there's a glow in the sky."

"Where?"

"Off to the right."

He says, "That can't be us. Penn Villas is more ahead."

But Emberly Avenue turns right more acutely than he had ever noticed, and the curving streets of Penn Villas do deliver them toward a dome of rose-colored air. People, black shapes, race on silent footsteps, and cars have run to a stop diagonally against the curbs. Down where Emberly meets Vista Crescent, a toy policeman stands, rhythmically popping into brightness as the twirling fire-engine lights pass across him: painted tin. Harry parks where he can drive no further and runs down Vista, after Nelson. Fire hoses lie across the asphalt, some deflated like long canvas trouser legs and some fat as cobras, jetting hissingly from their joints. The gutter gnashes with swirling black water and matted leaves; around the sewer drain, a whirlpool widens out from the clogged center. Two houses from their house, they enter an odor akin to leafsmoke but more acrid and bitter, holding paint and tar and chemicals; one house away, the density of people stops them. Nelson sinks into the crowd and vanishes. Rabbit shoulders after him, apologizing, "Excuse me, this is my house, pardon me, my house." He says this but does not yet believe it. His house is masked from him by heads, by searchlights and upward waterfalls, by rainbows and shouts, by something magisterial and singular about the event that makes it as hard to see as the sun. People, neighbors, part to let him through. He sees. The garage is gone; the charred studs still stand, but the roof has collapsed and the shingles smolder with spurts of blue-green flame amid the drenched wreckage on the cement floor. The handle of the power mower pokes up intact. The rooms nearest the garage, the kitchen and the bedroom above it, the bedroom that had been his and Janice's and then his and Jill's, flame against the torrents of water. Flame sinks back, then bursts out again, through roof or window, in tongues: dragon's taunts. The apple-green aluminum clapboards do not themselves burn; rather, they seem to shield the fire from the water. Abrupt gaps in the shifting weave of struggling elements let shreds show through of the upstairs wallpaper, of the kitchen shelves; then shut at a breath of wind. He scans the upstairs window for Jill's face, but glimpses only the stained ceiling. The roof above, half the roof, is a field of smoke, smoke bubbling up and coming off the shadow-line shingles in serried billows that look combed. Smoke pours out of Nelson's windows, but that half of the house is not yet aflame, and may be saved. Indeed, the house burns spitefully, spitting, stinkingly: the ersatz and synthetic materials grudge combustion its triumph. Once in boyhood Rabbit saw a barn burn in the valley beyond Mt. Judge; it was a torch, an explosion of hay outstarring the sky with embers. Here there is no such display.

There is space around him. The spectators, the neighbors, in honor of his role, have backed off. Months ago Rabbit had seen that bright island of moviemakers and now he is at the center of this bright island and still feels peripheral, removed, nostalgic, numb. He scans the firelit faces and does not see Showalter or Brumbach. He sees no one he knows.

The crowd stirs, *ooh*. He expects to see Jill at the window, ready to leap, her white dress translucent around her body. But the windows let only smoke escape, and the drama is on the ground. A policeman is struggling with a slight lithe figure; Harry thinks eagerly, *Skeeter*, but the struggle pivots, and it is Nelson's white face. A fireman helps pin the boy's arms. They bring him away from the house, to his father. Seeing his father, Nelson clamps shut his eyes and draws his lips back in a snarl and struggles so hard to be free that the two men holding his arms seem to be wildly operating pump handles. "She's *in* there, Dad!"

The policeman, breathing hard, explains, "Boy tried to get into the house. Says there's a girl in there."

"I don't know, she must have gotten out. We just got here."

Nelson's eyes are frantic; he screeches everything. "Did Skeeter *say* she was with *him?*"

"No. He just said things were bad."

In listening, the fireman and policeman loosen their grip, and Nelson breaks away to run for the front door again. Heat must meet him, for he falters at the porchlet steps, and he is seized again, by men whose slickers make them seem beetles. This time, brought back, Nelson screams up at Harry's face: "You fucking asshole, you've let her die. I'll kill you. I'll kill *you.*" And, though it is his son, Harry crouches and gets his hands up ready to fight. But the boy cannot burst the grip of the men. He tells them in a voice less shrill, arguing for his release, "I know she's in there. She was always begging him to do something to help her and he never would. Him and Skeeter did it. Skeeter is a Negro who lives with us. Let me go, please. Please let me go. Just let me get her out, I know I can. I *know* I can. She'd be upstairs asleep. She'd be easy to lift. Dad, I'm sorry. I'm sorry I swore at you. I didn't mean it. Tell them to let me. Tell them about Jill. Tell them to get her out."

Rabbit asks the firemen, "Wouldn't she have come to the window?"

The fireman, an old rodent of a man, with tufty eyebrows

and long yellow teeth, ruminates as he talks. "Girl asleep in there, smoke might get to her before she properly woke up. People don't realize what a deadly poison smoke is. That's what does you in, the smoke not the fire." He asks Nelson, "O.K. to let go, sonny? Act your age now, we'll send men up the ladder."

One beetle-backed fireman chops at the front door. The glass from the three panes shatters and tinkles on the flagstones. Another fireman emerges from the other side of the roof and with his ax picks a hole above the upstairs hall, about where Nelson's door would be. Something invisible sends him staggering back. A violet flame shoots up. A cannonade of water chases him back over the roof ridge.

"They're not doing it right, Dad," Nelson moans. "They're not getting her. I know where she is and they're not *get*ting her, Dad!" And the boy's voice dies in a shuddering. When Rabbit reaches toward him he pulls away and hides his face. The back of his head feels soft beneath the hair: an overripe fruit.

Rabbit reassures him, "Skeeter would've gotten her out."

"He *would*n't of, Dad! He wouldn't *care*." And his head falls forward from Harry's touch.

A policeman is beside them. "You Angstrom?" He is one of the new style of cops, collegiate-looking: pointed nose, smooth chin, sideburns cut to a depth Rabbit still thinks of as antisocial.

"Yes."

The cop takes out a notebook. "How many persons were in residence here?"

"Four. Me and the kid—"

"Name?"

"Nelson."

"Any middle initial?"

"F for Frederick." The policeman writes slowly and speaks

so softly he is hard to hear against the background of crowd murmur and fire crackle and water being hurled. Harry has to ask, "What?"

The cop repeats, "Name of mother?"

"Janice. She's not living here. She lives over in Brewer."

"Address?"

Harry remembers Stavros's address, but gives instead, "Care of Frederick Springer, 89 Joseph Street, Mt. Judge."

"And who is the girl the boy mentioned?"

"Jill Pendleton, of Stonington, Connecticut. Don't know the street address."

"Age?"

"Eighteen or nineteen."

"Family relationship?"

"None."

It takes the cop a very long time to write this one word. Something is happening to a corner of the roof; the crowd noise is rising, and a ladder is being lowered through an intersection of searchlights.

Rabbit prompts: "The fourth person was a Negro we called Skeeter. *S-k*-double *e-t-e-r*."

"Black male?"

"Yes."

"Last name?"

"I don't know. Could be Farnsworth."

"Spell please."

Rabbit spells it and offers to explain. "He was just here temporarily."

The cop glances up at the burning ranch house and then over at the owner. "What were you doing here, running a commune?"

"No, Jesus; listen. I'm a conservative. I voted for Hubert Humphrey."

The cop studies the house. "Any chance this black is in there now?"

"Don't think so. He was the one that called me, it sounded as if from a phone booth."

"Did he say he'd set the fire?"

"No, he didn't even say there was a fire, he just said things were bad. He said the word 'bad' twice."

"Things were bad," the cop writes, and closes his notepad. "We'll want some further interrogation later." Reflected firelight gleams peach-color off of the badge in his cap. The corner of the house above the bedroom is collapsing; the television aerial, that they twice adjusted and extended to cut down ghosts from their neighbors' sets, tilts in the leap of flame and slowly swings downward like a skeletal tree, still clinging by some wires or brackets to its roots. Water vaults into what had been the bedroom. A lavish cumulus of yellow smoke pours out, golden-gray, rich as icing squeezed from the sugary hands of a pastry cook.

The cop casually allows, "Anybody in there was cooked a half-hour ago."

Two steps away, Nelson is bent over to let vomit spill from his mouth. Rabbit steps to him and the boy allows himself to be touched. He holds him by the shoulders; it feels like trying to hold out of water a heaving fish that wants to go back under, that needs to dive back under or die. His father brings back his hair from his cheeks so it will not be soiled by vomit; with his fist he makes a feminine knot of hair at the back of the boy's hot soft skull. "Nellie, I'm sure she got out. She's far away. She's safe and far away."

The boy shakes his head *No* and retches again; Harry holds him for minutes, one hand clutching his hair, the other around his chest. He is holding him up from drowning. If Harry were to let go, he would drown too. He feels precariously heavier than his bones, seems to move across the surface of this event, that pulls like Jupiter, propped by struts that may break. Policemen, spectators, watch him struggle with Nelson but do not intervene. Finally a cop, not the interrogating one, does approach and in a calm Dutch voice asks, "Shall we have a car take the boy somewhere? Does he have grandparents in the county?"

"Four of them," Rabbit says. "Maybe he should go to his mother."

"*No!*" Nelson says, and breaks loose to face them. "You're not getting me to go until we know where Jill is." His face shines with tears but is sane: he waits out the next hour standing by his father's side.

The flames are slowly smothered, the living-room side of the house is saved. The interior of the kitchen side seems a garden where different tints of smoke sprout; formica, vinyl, nylon, linoleum each burn differently, yield their curdling compounds back to earth and air. Firemen wet down the wreckage and search behind the gutted walls. Now the upstairs windows stare with searchlights, now the lower. A skull full of fireflies. Yet still the crowd waits, held by a pack sense of smell; death is in heat. A signal Rabbit never noticed has fetched an ambulance; it arrives with a tentative sigh of its siren. Scarlet lights do an offbeat dance on its roof. A strange container, a green rubber bag or sheet, is taken into the house, and brought back by three grim men in slickers. The ambulance receives the shapeless package, is shut with that punky sound only the most expensive automobile doors make, and—again, the tentative sigh of a siren just touched—pulls away. The crowd thins after it. The night overflows with the noise of car motors igniting and revving up.

Nelson says, "Dad."

"Yeah."

"That was her, wasn't it?"

"I don't know. Maybe."

"It was *some*body."

"I guess."

Nelson rubs his eyes; the gesture leaves swipes of ash, Indian markings. The child seems harshly ancient.

"I need to go to bed," he says.

"Want to go back to the Fosnachts?"

"No." As if in apology he explains, "I hate Billy." Further qualifying, he adds, "Unless you do." Unless you want to go back and fuck Mrs. Fosnacht again.

Rabbit asks him, "Want to see your mother?"

"I can't, Dad. She's in the Poconos."

"She should be back by now."

"I don't want to see her now. Take me to Mom-mom's."

There is in Rabbit an engine murmuring, *Undo, undo,* that wants to take them back to this afternoon, beginning with the moment they left the house, and not do what they did, not leave, and have it all unhappen, and Jill and Skeeter still there, in the house still there. Beneath the noise of this engine the inner admission that it did happen is muffled; he sees Nelson through a gauze of shock and dares ask, "Blame me, huh?"

"Sort of."

"You don't think it was just bad luck?" And though the boy hardly bothers to shrug Harry understands his answer: luck and God are both up there and he has not been raised to believe in anything higher than his father's head. Blame stops for him in the human world, it has nowhere else to go.

The firemen of one truck are coiling their hoses. A policeman, the one who asked after Nelson, comes over. "Angstrom? The chief wants to talk to you where the boy can't hear."

"Dad, ask him if that was Jill."

The cop is tired, stolid, plump, the same physical type as —what was his name?—Showalter. Kindly patient Brewerites. He lets out the information, "It was a body."

"Black or white?" Rabbit asks.

"No telling."

Nelson asks, "Male or female?"

"Female, sonny."

Nelson begins to cry again, to gag as if food is caught in his throat, and Rabbit asks the policeman if his offer is still good, if a cruiser might take the boy to his grandparents' house in Mt. Judge. The boy is led away. He does not resist; Rabbit thought he might, might insist on staying with his father to the end. But the boy, his hair hanging limp and his tears flowing unchecked, seems relieved to be at last in the arms of order, of laws and limits. Nelson doesn't even wave from the window of the silver-blue West Brewer cruiser as it U-turns in Vista Crescent and heads away from the tangle of hoses and puddles and red reflections. The air tastes sulphuric. Rabbit notices that the little maple was scorched on the side toward the house; its twigs smolder like cigarettes.

As the firemen wind up their apparatus, he and the police chief sit in the front of an unmarked car. Harry's knees are crowded by the radio apparatus on the passenger's side. The chief is a short man but doesn't look so short sitting down, with his barrel chest crossed by a black strap and his white hair crew-cut close to his scalp and his nose which was once broken sideways and has accumulated broken veins in the years since. He says, "We have a death now. That makes it a horse of another color."

"Any theories how the fire started?"

"I'll ask the questions. But yes. It was set. In the garage. I notice a power mower in there. Can of gas to go with it?"

"Yeah. We filled the can just this afternoon."

"Tell me where you were this evening."

He tells him. The chief talks on his car radio to the West Brewer headquarters. In less than five minutes they call back. But in the total, unapologetic silence the chief keeps during these minutes, a great lump grows in Rabbit, love of the law. The radio sizzles its words like bacon frying: "Mrs. Fosnacht confirms suspect's story. Also a minor boy in dwelling as additional witness."

"Check," the chief says, and clicks off.

"Why would I burn my own house down?" Rabbit asks.

"Most common arsonist is owner," the chief says. He studies Rabbit thoughtfully; his eyes are almost round, as if somebody took a stitch at the corner of each lid. "Maybe the girl was pregnant by you."

"She was on the Pill."

"Tell me about her."

He tries, though it is hard to make it seem as natural as it felt. Why did he permit Skeeter to move in on him? Well, the question was more, Why not? He tries, "Well, when my wife walked out on me, I kind of lost my bearings. It didn't seem to matter, and anyway he would have taken Jill with him, if I'd kicked him out. I got so I didn't mind him."

"Did he terrorize you?"

He tries to make these answers right. Out of respect for the law. "No. He entertained us." Harry begins to get mad. "Some law I don't know about against having people live with you?"

"Law against harboring," the chief says, neglecting to write on his pad. "Brewer police report a Hubert Johnson out on default on a possession charge."

Rabbit's silence is not what he wants. He makes it clearer what he wants. "You in ignorance over the existence of this indictment and defiance of court?" He makes it even clearer. "Shall I accept your silence as a profession of ignorance?"

"Yes." It is the only opening. "Yes, I knew nothing about Skeeter, not even his last name. You say it's Johnson. I thought it was Farnsworth."

"His present whereabouts, any ideas?"

"No idea. His call came through from it sounded like a phone booth but I couldn't swear to it."

The cop puts his broad hand over the notebook as if across the listening mouth of a telephone receiver. "Off the record. We've been watching this place. He was a little fish, a punk. We hoped he would lead us to something bigger."

"What bigger? Dope?"

"Civil disturbance. The blacks in Brewer are in touch with

Philly, Camden, Newark. We know they have guns. We don't want another York here, now do we?" Again, Rabbit's silence is not what he wants. He repeats, "Now do we?"

"No, of course not. I was just thinking. He talked as if he was beyond revolution, he was kind of religious-crazy, not gun-crazy."

"Any idea why he set this fire?"

"I don't think he did. It isn't his style."

The pencil is back on the notebook. "Screw style," the chief says. "I want facts."

"I don't have any more facts than I've told you. Some people in the neighborhood were upset because Skeeter was living with us, two men stopped me on the street yesterday and complained about it, I can give you their names if you want."

The pencil hovers. "They complained. Any specific threats of arson?"

&. "Nothing that specific."

The chief makes a notation, it looks like *n.c.*, and turns the notebook page. "The black have sexual relations with the girl?"

"Look, I was off working all day. I'd come back and we'd cook supper and help the kid with his homework and sit around and talk. It was like having two more kids in the house, I don't know what they did every minute. Are you going to arrest me, or what?"

A fatherly type himself, the chief takes a smiling long time answering. Rabbit sees that his nose wasn't broken by accident, somewhere in the alleys of time he had asked for it. His snow-soft hair is cut evenly as a powderpuff, with a pink dent above the ears where the police cap bites. His smile broadens enough to crease his cheek. "Strictly speaking," he says, "this isn't my beat. I'm acting on behalf of my esteemed colleague the sheriff of Furnace Township, who rolled over and went back to sleep. Offhand I'd say we're doing a good enough business in the jails without putting solid citizens like you in there. We'll have some more questions later." He flips the notebook shut and flips the radio on to put out a call, "All cars, Brewer police copy, be on the lookout, Negro, male, height approx five-six, weight approx one-twenty-five, medium dark-skinned, hair Afro, name Skeeter, that is Sally, Katherine, double Easter—" He does not turn his head when Rabbit opens the car door and walks away.

So again in his life the net of law has slipped from him. He knows he is criminal, yet is never caught. Sickness sinks through his body like soot. The firemen wet down the smoking wreckage, the clot of equipment along Vista Crescent breaks up and flows away. The house is left encircled in its disgrace with yellow flashers on trestles warning people off. Rabbit walks around the lawn, so lately a full stage, sodden and pitted by footprints, and surveys the damage.

The burning was worse on the back side: the fixtures of the bedroom bathroom dangle in space from stems of contorted pipe. The wall that took the bed headboard is gone. Patches of night-blue sky show through the roof. He looks in the downstairs windows and sees, by flashing yellow light, as into a hellish fun house, the sofa and the two chairs, salted with fallen plaster, facing each other across the cobbler's bench. The driftwood lamp is still upright. On the shelves giving into the breakfast nook, Skeeter's books squat, soaked and matted. Where the kitchen was, Harry can see out through the garage to an N of charred 2 by 4s. The sky wants to brighten. Birds—birds in Penn Villas, where? there are no trees old enough to hold them—flicker into song. It is cold now, colder than in the heart of the night, when the fire was alive. The sky pales in the east, toward Brewer. Mt. Judge develops an outline in the emulsion of pre-dawn gray. A cloud of birds migrating crosses the suburb southward, toward Weiser and the tall madhouse and beyond. The soot is settling on Harry's bones. His eyelids feel like husks. In his weariness he hallucinates; as in the seconds before we sleep, similes seem living organisms. The freshening sky above Mt. Judge is Becky, the child that died, and the sullen sky to the west, the color of a storm sky but flawed by stars, is Nelson, the child that lives. And he, he is the man in the middle.

He walks up to his battered front door, brushes away the glass shards, and sits down on the flagstone porchlet. It is warm, like a hearth. Though none of his neighbors came forward to speak to him, to sparkle on the bright screen of his disaster, the neighborhood presents itself to his gaze unapologetically, naked in the gathering light, the pastel roof shingles moist in patches echoing the pattern of rafters, the backyard bathing pools and swing sets whitened by dew along with the grass. A half-moon rests cockeyed in the blanched sky like a toy forgotten on a floor. An old man in a noisy green raincoat, a geezer left behind as a watchman, walks over and speaks to him. "This your home, huh?"

"This is it."

"Got some other place to go?"

"I suppose."

"Body a loved one?"

"Not exactly."

"That's good news. Cheer up, young fella. Insurance'll cover most of it."

"Do I have insurance?"

"Had a mortgage?"

Rabbit nods, remembering the little slippery bankbook, imagining it burned.

"Then you had insurance. Damn the banks all you will, they look after their own, you'll never catch them damn Jews short."

This man's presence begins to seem strange. It has been months since anything seemed as strange as this man's presence. Rabbit asks him, "How long you staying here?"

"I'm on duty till eight."

"Why?"

"Fire procedure. Prevent looting." The two of them look wonderingly at the dormant houses and cold lawns of Penn Villas. As they look, a distant alarm rings and an upstairs light comes on, sallow, dutiful. Still, looting these days is everywhere. The geezer asks him, "Anything precious in there, you might want to take along?" Rabbit doesn't move. "You better go get some sleep, young fella."

"What about you?" Rabbit asks.

"Fella my age doesn't need much. Sleep long enough soon enough. Anyway, I like the peacefulness of these hours, have ever since a boy. Always up, my dad, he was a great boozer and a late sleeper, used to wallop the bejesus out of me if I made a stir mornings. Got in the habit of sneaking out to the birds. Anyway, double-hour credit, time outdoors on this shift. Don't always put it in, go over a certain amount, won't get any social security. Kill you with kindness, that's the new technique."

Rabbit stands up, aching; pain moves upward from his shins through his groin and belly to his chest and out. A demon leaving. Smoke, mist rise. He turns to his front door; swollen by water, axed, it resists being opened. The old man tells him, "It's my responsibility to keep any and all persons out of this structure. Any damage you do yourself, you're the party responsible."

"You just told me to take out anything precious."

"You're responsible, that's all I'm saying. I'm turning my back. Fall through the floor, electrocute yourself, don't call for help. Far as I'm concerned, you're not there. See no evil is the way I do it."

"That's the way I do it too." Under pressure the door pops open. Splintered glass on the other side scrapes white arcs into the hall floor finish. Rabbit begins to cry from smoke and the smell. The house is warm, and talks to itself; a swarm of small rustles and snaps arises from the section on his left; settling noises drip from the charred joists and bubble up from the drenched dark rubble where the floor had been. The bed's metal frame has fallen into the kitchen. On his right, the living room is murky but undamaged. The silver threads of the Lustrex chair gleam through an acid mist of fumes; the television set's green blank waits to be turned on. He thinks of taking it, it is the one resaleable item here, but no, it is too heavy to lug, he might drop himself through the floor, and there are millions like it. Janice once said we should drop television sets into the jungle instead of bombs, it would do as much good. He thought at the time the idea was too clever for her; even then Stavros was speaking through her.

She always loved that dumb bench. He remembers her kneeling beside it early in their marriage, rubbing it with linseed oil, short keen strokes, a few inches at a time, it made him feel horny watching. He takes the bench under his arm and, discovering it to be so light, pulls the driftwood lamp loose from its socket and takes that too. The rest the looters and insurance adjusters can have. You never get the smell of smoke out. Like the smell of failure in a life. He remembers the storm windows, Windexing their four sides, and it seems a fable that his life was ever centered on such details. His house slips from him. He is free. Orange light in long stripes, from sun on the side of him opposite from the side the sun was on when he and Nelson walked here a long night ago, stretches between the low strange houses as he walks down Vista Crescent with the table and the lamp tugging under his arms. Peggy's Mustang is the only car still parked along the curb: a boat the ebb has stranded. He opens the door, pushes the seat forward to put the bench in the back, and finds someone there. A Negro. Asleep. "What the hell," Rabbit says.

Skeeter awakes blind and gropes for his glasses on the rubber floor. "Chuck baby," he says, looking up with twin circles of glass. His Afro is flattened on one side. Bad fruit. "All by yourself, right?"

"Yeah." The little car holds a concentration of that smell which in the mornings would spice the living room, give it animal substance, sleep's sweetness made strong.

"How long's it been light?"

"Just started. It's around six. How long've you been here?"

"Since I saw you and Babychuck pull in. I called you from a booth up on Weiser and then watched to see if you'd go by. The car wasn't you but the head was, right, so I snuck along through the backyards and got in after you parked. The old briar patch theory, right? Shit if I didn't fall asleep. Hey get in man, you're lettin' in the wind."

Rabbit gets in and sits in the driver's seat, listening without turning his head, trying to talk without moving his mouth. Penn Villas is coming to life; a car just passed. "You ought to know," he says, "they're looking for you. They think you set it."

"Count on the fuzz to fuck up. Why would I go burn my own pad?"

"To destroy evidence. Maybe Jill—what do you call it?—O.D.'d."

"Not on the scag she was getting from me, that stuff was so cut sugar water has more flash. Look, Chuck, that up at your house was honky action. Will you believe the truth, or shall I save my breath for the pigpen?"

"Let's hear it."

Skeeter's voice, unattached to his face, is deeper than Harry remembers, with a hypnotic rasping lilt that reminds him of chidhood radio. "Jill sacked out early and I made do with the sofa, right? Since getting back on the stuff she wasn't putting out any of her own, and anyway I was pretty spaced and beat, we went twice around the county unloading that bullshit car. Right? So I wake up. There was this rattling around. I placed it coming from the kitchen, right? I was thinkin' it was Jill coming to bug me to shoot her up again, instead there was this *whoosh* and soft *woomp,* reminded me of an APM hitting in the bush up the road, only it wasn't up any road, I say to myself *The war is come home.* Next thing there's this slam of a door, garage door from the rumble of it, and I flip to the window and see these two honky cats makin' tail across the lawn, across the street, into between those houses there, and disappear, right? They had no car I could see. Next thing, I smell smoke."

"How do you know these were white men?"

"Shit, you know how honkies run, like with sticks up their ass, right?"

"Could you identify them if you saw them again?"

"I ain't identifying Moses around here. My skin is fried in this county, right?"

"Yeah," Rabbit says. "Something else you should know. Jill is dead."

The silence from the back seat is not long. "Poor bitch, doubt if she knows the difference."

"Why didn't you get her out?"

"Hell, man, there was *heat*, right? I thought lynching time had come, I didn't know there wasn't twelve hundred crackers out there, I was in no shape to take care of some whitey woman, let Whitey take care of his own."

"But nobody stopped you."

"Basic training, right? I eluded as they say my pursuers."

"They didn't want to hurt you. It was me, they were trying to tell *me* something. People around here don't lynch, don't be crazy."

"Crazy, you've been watching the wrong TV channel. How about those cats in Detroit?"

"How about those dead cops in California? How about all this Off the Pigs crap you brothers have been pushing? I should take you in. The Brewer cops would love to see you, they love to re-educate crazy coons."

Two more cars swish by; from the height of a milk truck the driver looks down curiously. "Let's drive," Skeeter says.

"What's in it for me?"

"Nothing much, right?"

The Mustang starts at a touch. The motor is more silent than their tires swishing in the puddles along Vista Crescent, past the apple-green ruin and the man in the green raincoat dozing on the doorstep. Rabbit heads out the curved streets to where they end, to where they become truck tracks between muddy house foundations. He finds a lost country lane. Tall rows of poplars, a neglected potholed surface. Skeeter sits up. Rabbit waits for the touch of metal on the back of his neck. A gun, a knife, a needle: they always have something. Poison darts. But there is nothing, nothing but the fluctuating warmth of Skeeter's breathing on the back of his neck. Into this reticence of steel Rabbit reads not poverty of means but positive love. "How could you let her die?" he asks.

"Man, you want to talk guilt, we got to go back hundreds of years."

"I don't *feel* guilty," Rabbit says.

"Goddam green pickles, Chuck, then just don't. But don't pull that long face on me neither. Everybody stuck inside his own skin, might as well make himself at home there, right?"

"Tell you what. I'll drive you ten miles south and you take it from there."

"That's cutting it fine, but let's say sold. One embarrassment as they say remains. We brothers call it bread."

"You just got six hundred for selling her car."

"That sly bitch, she took it with her, I don't have it. My wallet back in that sofa, every mothering thing, right?"

"How about that black suitcase in the closet?"

"Say. You been snooping, or what?"

"I have maybe thirty dollars," Rabbit says. "You can have that. But then that's quits. I'll keep this ride from the cops but then that's it. Like you said, you've had it in this county."

"I shall return," Skeeter promises, "only in glory."

"When you do, leave me out of it."

Miles pass. A hill, a cluster of sandstone houses, a cement factory, a billboard pointing to a natural cave, another with a great cutout of a bearded Amishman. Skeeter in yet another of his voices, the one that sounds most like a white man and therefore in Rabbit's ears most human, asks, "How'd Babychuck take it, Jill's being wasted?"

"About like you'd expect."

"Broken up, right?"

"Broken up."

"Tell him, there's a ton of cunt in the world."

"I'll let him figure that out himself."

They come to a corner where two narrow roads meet in sunlight. On the far side of a tan cut cornfield a whitewashed stone house sends up smoke. A wooden arrow at the intersection says Galilee 2. Otherwise it could be nowhere. A jet trail smears in the sky. Pennsylvania spreads south silently, through green and brown. A dry stone conduit underlies the road here; a roadside marker is a metal keystone rusted blank. Rabbit empties his wallet into Skeeter's pink palm and chokes off the impulse to apologize for its not being more. He wonders now what would be proper. A Judas kiss? They have not touched since the night they wrestled and Harry won. He holds out his hand to shake farewell. Skeeter studies it as if like Babe he will tell a fortune, takes it into both his slick narrow hands, tips it so the meaty pink creases are skyward, contemplates, and solemnly spits into the center. His saliva being as warm as skin, Harry at first only knows it has happened by seeing: moisture full of bubbles like tiny suns. He chooses to take the gesture as a blessing, and wipes his palm dry on his pants. Skeeter tells him, "Never did figure your angle."

"Probably wasn't one," is the answer.

"Just waiting for the word, right?" Skeeter cackles. When

he laughs there is that complexity about his upper lip white men don't have, a welt in the center, a genial seam reminding Rabbit of the stitch of flesh that holds the head of your cock to the shaft. As Harry backs the Mustang around in the strait intersection, the young black waits by a bank of brown weed stalks. In the rear view mirror, Skeeter looks oddly right, blends right in, even with the glasses and goatee, hanging empty-handed between fields of stubble where crows settle and shift, gleaning.

COL. EDWIN E. ALDRIN, JR.: *Now you're clear. Over toward me. Straight down, to your left a little bit. Plenty of room. You're lined up nicely. Toward me a little bit. Down. O.K. Now you're clear. You're catching the first hinge. The what hinge? All right, move. Roll to the left. O.K., now you're clear. You're lined up on the platform. Put your left foot to the right a little bit. O.K., that's good. More left. Good.*

NEIL ARMSTRONG: *O.K., Houston, I'm on the porch.*

IV. MIM

RABBIT is at his machine. His fingers feather, the matrices rattle on high, the molten lead comfortably steams at his side.

ARSON SUSPECTED IN PENN VILLAS BLAZE

Out-of-Stater Perishes

West Brewer police are still collecting testimony from neighbors in connection with the mysterious fire that destroyed the handsome Penn Villas residence of Mr. and Mrs. Harold Angstrom.

A guest in the home, Mill Jiss

A guest in the home, Miss Jill Pendleton, 18, of Stonington, Connecticut, perished of smoke inhalation and burns. Rescue attempts by valiant firemen were to no avail.

Miss Pendleton was pronounced dead on arrival at the Sister of Mercy Homeopathic Sisters of Mercy Homeopathic Hospital in Brewer.

A man reported seen in the vicinity of the dwelling, Hubert Johnson last of Plum Street, is being sought for questioning. Mr. Johnson is also known as ''Skeeter'' and sometimes gives his last name as Farnsworth.

Furnance Township fire chief Raymond ''Buddy'' Fessler told VAT reporters, ''The fire was set I'm pretty sure, but we have no evidence of a Molotov cocktail or anything of that nature. This was not a bombing in the ordinary sense.''

Neighbors are baffled by the event, reporting nothing unusual about the home but the skulking presence of a black man thought

Pajasek taps him on the shoulder.

"If that's my wife," Rabbit says. "Tell her to bug off. Tell her I'm dead."

"It's nobody on the phone, Harry. I need to have a word with you privately. If I may."

That "if I may" is what puts the chill into Harry's heart. Pajasek is imitating somebody higher up. He shuts his frosted-glass door on the clatter and with a soft thump sits at his desk; he slowly spreads his fingers on the mass of ink-smirched papers there. "More bad news, Harry," he says. "Can you take it?"

"Try me."

"I hate like Jesus to put this into you right on top of your misfortune with your home, but there's no use stalling. Nothing stands still. They've decided up top to make Verity an offset plant. We'll keep an old flatbed for the job work, but the *Vat* said either go offset or have them print in Philly. It's been in the cards for years. This way, we'll be geared up to take other periodicals, there's some new sheets starting up in Brewer, a lot of it filth in my book but people buy it and the law allows it, so there you are." From the way he sighs, he thinks he's made his point. His forehead, seen from above, is global; the worried furrows retreat to the horizon of the skull, where the brass-pale hair begins, wisps brushed straight back.

Rabbit tries to help him. "So no linotypers, huh?"

Pajasek looks up startled; his eyebrows arch and drop and there is a moment of spherical smoothness, with a long clean highlight from the fluorescent tubes overhead. "I thought I made that point. That's part of the technical picture, that's where the economy comes. Offset, you operate all from film, bypass hot metal entirely. Go to a cathode ray tube, Christ, it delivers two thousand lines a minute, that's the whole *Vat* in seven minutes. We can keep a few men on, retrain them to the computer tape, we've worked the deal out with the union, but this is a sacrifice, Harry, from the management point of view. I'm afraid you're far down the list. Nothing to do with your personal life, understand me—strictly seniority. Your Dad's secure, and Buchanan, Christ, let him go we'd have every do-good outfit in the city on our necks, it's not the way *I'd* do things. If they'd come to me I would have told them, that man is half-soused from eleven o'clock on every morning, they're all like that, I'd just as soon have a moron with mittens on as long he was white—"

"O.K.," Rabbit says. "When do I knock off?"

"Harry, this hurts me like hell. You learned the skill and now the bottom's dropping out. Maybe one of the Brewer dailies can take you on, maybe something in Philly or up in Allentown, though what with papers dropping out or doubling up all over the state there's something of a glut in the trade right now."

"I'll survive. What did Kurt Schrack do?"

"Who he?"

"You know. The *Schockelschtuhl* guy."

"Christ, him. That was back in B.C. As I remember he bought a farm north of here and raises chickens. If he's not dead by now."

"Right. Die I guess would be the convenient thing. From the management point of view."

"Don't talk like that, Harry, it hurts me too much. Give me credit for some feelings. You're a young buck, for Chrissake, you got the best years still ahead of you. You want some fatherly advice? Get the hell out of the county. Leave the mess behind you. Forget that slob you married, no offense."

"No offense. About Janice, you can't blame her, I wasn't that great myself. But I can't go anywhere, I got this kid."

"Kid, schmid. You can't live your life that way. You got to reason outwards from Number One. To you, you're Number One, not the kid."

"That's not how it feels, exactly," Rabbit begins, then sees from the sudden gleaming globe of Pajasek's head bent to study the smirched slips on his desk that the man doesn't really want to talk, he wants Harry to go. So Rabbit asks, "So when do I go?"

Pajasek says, "You'll get two months pay plus the benefits you've accumulated, but the new press is coming in this weekend, faster than we thought. Everything moves faster nowadays."

"Except me," Rabbit says, and goes. His father, in the bright racket of the shop, swivels away from his machine and gives him the thumbs down sign questioningly. Rabbit nods, thumbs down. As they walk down Pine Street together after work, feeling ghostly in the raw outdoor air after their day's immersion in fluorescence, Pop says, "I've seen the handwriting on the wall all along, whole new philosophy operating at the top now at Verity, one of the partner's sons came back from business school somewhere full of beans and crap. I said to Pajasek, 'Why keep me on, I have less than a year before retirement?' and he says, 'That's the reason.' I said to him, 'Why not let me go and give my place to Harry?' and he says, 'Same reason.' He's running scared himself, of course. The whole economy's scared. Nixon's getting himself set to be the new Hoover, these moratorium doves'll be begging for LBJ to come back before Tricky Dick's got done giving their bank accounts a squeeze!"

Pop talks more than ever now, as if to keep Harry's mind cluttered; he clings to him like sanity. It has been a dreadful three days. All Sunday, on no sleep, he drove back and forth through Brewer between Mt. Judge and Penn Villas, through the municipal headache of the Columbus Day parade. The monochrome idyll of early morning, Skeeter dwindling to a brown dot in brown fields, became a four-color nightmare of martial music, throbbing exhaustion, bare-thighed girls twirling bolts of lightning, iridescent drummers pounding a tattoo on the taut hollow of Harry's stomach, cars stalled in the side-streets, Knights of Columbus floats, marching veterans, American flags. Between entanglements with this monster celebration, he scavenged in warm ashes and trucked useless stained and soaked furniture, including a charred guitar, to the garage at the back of the Jackson Road place. He found no wallet in the sofa, and no black bag in the closet. Jill's bureau had been along the wall of which only charred 2 by 4s remained, yet he prodded the ashes for a scrap of the six hundred dollars. Back on Jackson Road, insurance investigators were waiting for him, and the sheriff of Furnace Township, a little apple-cheeked old man, in suspenders and a soft felt hat, who was mostly interested in establishing that his failure to be present at the fire could in no way be held against him. He was quite deaf, and every time someone in the room spoke he would twirl around and alertly croak, "Let's put *that* on the record too! I want everything out in the open, everything on the record!"

Worst of all, Harry had to talk to Jill's mother on the telephone. The police had broken the news to her and her tone fluctuated between a polite curiosity about how Jill came to be living in this house and a grieved anger seeking its ceiling, a flamingo in her voice seeking the space to flaunt its vivid wings but cramped in a closet of partial comprehension. "She was staying with me, yes, since before Labor Day," Rabbit told her, over the downstairs phone, in the dark living room, smelling of furniture polish and Mom's medicine. "Before that she had been bumming around in Brewer with a crowd of Negroes who hung out at a restaurant they've closed down since. I thought she'd be better off with me than with them."

"But the police said there *was* a Negro."

"Yeah. He was a friend of hers. He kind of came and went." Each time he was made to tell this story, he reduced the part Skeeter played, beginning with having to lie about driving him south that morning, until the young black man has become in his backwards vision little more substantial than a shadow behind a chair. "The cops say he might have set the fire but I'm sure he didn't."

"How are you sure?"

"I just am. Look, Mrs.—"

"Aldridge." And this, of all things, her second husband's name, set her to crying.

He fought through her sobbing. "Look, it's hard to talk now, I'm dead beat, my kid's in the next room, if we could talk face to face, I could maybe explain—"

The flamingo tested a wing. "*Explain!* Can you explain her back to life?"

"No, I guess not."

The politeness returned. "My husband and I are flying to Philadelphia tomorrow morning and renting a car. Perhaps we should meet."

"Yeah. I'd have to take off from work, except for the lunch hour."

"We'll meet at the West Brewer police station," the distant voice said with surprising firmness, a sudden pinch of authority. "At noon."

Rabbit had never been there before. The West Brewer Borough Hall was a brick building with white trim, set diagonally on a plot of grass and flower beds adjacent to the tall madhouse, itself really an addition to the original madhouse, a granite mansion built a century ago by one of Brewer's iron barons. All this land had belonged to that estate. Behind the neoclassic town hall stretched a long cement-block shed with a corrugated roof; some doors were open and Rabbit saw trucks, a steamroller, the spidery black machine that tars roads, the giant arm that lifts a man in a basket to trim branches away from electric wires. These appliances of a town's housekeeping seemed to Harry part of a lost world of blameless activity; he felt that he would never be allowed to crawl back into that world. Inside the town hall, there were wickets where people could pay their utilities bills, paneled doors labelled in flaking gold Burgess and Assessor and Clerk. Gold arrows pointed downstairs to the Police Department. Rabbit saw too late he could have entered this half-basement from the side, saving himself the gaze of ten town employees. The cop behind the green-topped counter looked familiar, but it took a minute for the sideburns to register. The collegiate type. Harry was led down a hall past mysterious rooms; one brimmed with radio equipment, another with filing cabinets, a third gave on a cement stairway leading still further down. The dungeon. Jail. Rabbit wanted to run down into this hole and hide but was led into a fourth room, with a dead green table and metal folding chairs. The broken-nosed chief was in here and a woman who, though hollow with exhaustion and slow-spoken with pills, was Connecticut. She had more edge, more salt to her manner, than Pennsylvania women. Her hair was not so much gray as grayed; her suit was black. Jill's pensive thin face must have come from her father, for her mother had quite another kind, a roundish eager face with pushy lips that when she was happy must be greedy. Rabbit flicked away the impression of a peppy little dog: wideset brown eyes, a touch of jowl, a collar of pearls at her throat. *Nifty tits,* Jill had said, but her mother's cupped and braced bosom, excessive for her height, which was Jill's, struck Rabbit in this moment of sexless and sorrowing encounter as a militant prow, part of a uniform's padding. He regretted that he had not enough praised Jill here, her boyish chest with its shallow faint shadows, where she had felt to herself shy and meager, and yet had been soft enough in his mouth, quite soft enough, and abundant, as grace is abundant, that we do not measure, but take as a presence, that abounds. In his mist, he heard the chief grunt introductions: Mr. and Mrs. Aldridge. Rabbit remembered in Jill's song the tax lawyer from Westerly, but the man remained blank for him; he had eyes only for the woman, for this wrong-way reincarnation of Jill. She had Jill's composure, less fragilely; even her despairing way of standing with her hands heavy at her sides, at a loss, was Jill's. Rabbit wondered, Has she come from identifying the remains? What was left but blackened bones? Teeth. A bracelet. A flesh-colored swatch of hair. "Hey," he said to her, "I'm sick about this."

"Yee-s." Her bright eyes passed over his head. "Over the phone, I was so stupid, you mentioned explaining."

Had he? What had he wanted to explain? That it was not his fault. Yet Nelson thought it was. For taking her in? But she was unsheltered. For fucking her? But it is all life, sex, fire, breathing, all combination with oxygen, we shimmer at all moments on the verge of conflagration, as the madhouse windows tell us. Rabbit tried to remember. "You had asked about Skeeter, why I was sure he hadn't set the fire."

"Yes. Why were you?"

"He loved her. We all did."

"You all used her?"

"In ways."

"In your case"—strange precision, clubwoman keeping a meeting within channels, the vowels roughened by cigarettes and whisky, weathered in the daily sunslant of cocktails—"as a concubine?"

He guessed at what the word meant. "I never forced it," he said. "I had a house and food. She had herself. We gave what we had."

"You are a beast." Each word was too distinct; the sentence had been lying in her mind and had warped and did not quite fit.

"O.K., sure," he conceded, refusing to let her fly, to let that flamingo fury escape her face and scream. The blank man behind her coughed and shifted weight, preparing to be embarrassed. Harry's guts felt suspended and transparent, as before a game. He was matched against this woman in a way he was never matched with Jill. Jill had been too old for him, too wise, having been born so much later. This little pug, her salt hair and money and rasping clubwoman voice aside, was his generation, he could understand what she wanted. She wanted to stay out of harm's way. She wanted to have some fun and not be blamed. At the end she wanted not to have any apologizing to do to any heavenly committee. Right now she wanted to tame the ravenous miracle of her daughter being cast out and destroyed. Mrs. Aldridge touched her cheeks in a young gesture, then let her hands hang heavy beside her hips.

"I'm sorry," she said. "There are always . . . circumstances. I wanted to ask, were there any . . . effects."

"Effects?" He was back with blackened bones, patterns of teeth, melted bracelets. He thought of the bracelets girls in high school used to wear, chains with name-tags, Dorene, Margaret, Mary Ann.

"Her brothers asked me . . . some memento . . ."

Brothers? She had said. Three. One Nelson's age.

Mrs. Aldridge stepped forward, bewildered, hoping to be helpful. "There was a car."

"They sold the car," Rabbit said, too loudly. "She ran it without oil and the engine seized up and she sold it for junk."

His loudness alarmed her. He was still indignant, about the waste of that car. She took a step backward, protesting, "She loved the car."

She didn't love the car, she didn't love anything we would have loved, he wanted to tell Mrs. Aldridge, but maybe she knew more than he, she was there when Jill first saw the car, new and white, her father's gift. Rabbit at last found in his mind an "effect." "One thing I did find," he told Mrs. Aldridge, "her guitar. It's pretty well burned, but—"

"Her guitar," the woman repeated, and perhaps having forgotten that her daughter played brought her eyes down, made her round face red and brought the man over to comfort her, a man blank like men in advertisements, his coat impeccable and in the breast pocket a three-folded maroon handkerchief. "I have *noth*ing," she wailed, "she didn't even leave me a *note* when she *left*." And her voice had shed its sexy roughness, become high and helpless; it was Jill again, begging, *Hold me, help me, I'm all shit inside, everything is crashing in.*

Harry turned from the sight. The chief, leading him out the side door, said, "Rich bitch, if she'd given the girl half a reason to stay home she'd be alive today. I see things like this every week. All our bad checks are being cashed. Keep your nose clean, Angstrom, and take care of your own." A coach's paternal punch on the arm, and Harry was sent into the world.

"Pop, how about a quick one?"

"Not today, Harry, not today. We have a surprise for you at home. Mim's coming."

"You sure?" The vigil for Mim is months old; she keeps sending postcards, always with a picture of a new hotel on them.

"Yep. She called your mother this morning, she's in New York, I talked to your mother this noon. I should have told you but you've had so much on your mind I thought, Might as well save it. Things come in bunches, that's the mysterious truth. We get numb and the Lord lets us have it, that's how His mercy works. You lose your wife, you lose your house, you lose your job. Mim comes in the same day your mother couldn't sleep a wink for nightmares, I bet she's been downstairs all day trying to tidy up if it kills her, you wonder what's next." But he has just said it: Mom's death is next. The number 16A bus joggles, sways, smells of exhaust. The Mt. Judge way, there are fewer Negroes than toward West Brewer. Rabbit sits on the aisle; Pop, by the window, suddenly hawks and spits. The spittle runs in a weak blur down the dirty glass. "Goddammit, but that burns me," he explains, and Rabbit sees they have passed a church, the big gray Presbyterian at Weiser and Park: on its steps cluster some women in overcoats, two young men with backwards collars, nuns and schoolchildren carrying signs and unlit candles protesting the war. This is Moratorium Day. "I don't have much use for Tricky Dick and never have," Pop is explaining, "but the poor devil, he's trying to do the decent thing over there, get us out so the roof doesn't fall in until after we leave, and these queer preachers so shortsighted they can't see across the pulpit go organizing these parades that all they do is convince the little yellow Reds over there they're winning. If I were Nixon I'd tax the bejesus out of the churches, it'd take some of the burden off the little man. Old Cushing up there in Boston must be worth a hundred million just by his lonesome."

"Pop, all they're saying is they want the killing to stop."

"They've got you too, have they? Killing's not the worst thing around. Rather shake the hand of a killer than a traitor."

So much passion, where he now feels none, amuses Harry, makes him feel protected, at home. It has been his salvation, to be home again. The same musty teddy-bear smells from the carpet, the same embrace of hot air when you open the cellar door, the same narrow stairs heading up off the living room with the same loose baluster that lost its dowel and has to be renailed again and again, drying out in the ebb of time; the same white-topped kitchen table with the four sets of worn spots where they used to eat. An appetite for boyish foods has returned: for banana slices on cereal, for sugar doughnuts though they come in boxes with cellophane windows now instead of in waxpaper bags, for raw carrots and cocoa, at night. He sleeps late, so he has to be waked for work; in Penn Villas, in the house where Janice never finished making curtains, he would be the one the sun would usually rouse first. Here in Mt. Judge familiar gloom encloses him. The distortions in Mom's face and speech, which used to distress him during his visits, quickly assimilate to the abiding reality of her presence, which has endured all these years he has been absent, remains the same half of the sky, the same door that seals him in—like the cellar bulkhead out back, of two heavy halves. As a child he used to crouch on the cement steps beneath them and listen to the rain. The patter above seemed to be shaping his heart, pitting his consciousness lovingly and mixing its sound with the brusque scrape and stride of Mom working in the kitchen. She still, for spells, can work in the kitchen. Harry's being home, she claims, is worth a hundred doses of L-dopa.

The one disturbing element, new and defiant of assimilation, is Nelson. Sullen, grieving, strangely large and loutish sprawled on the caneback davenport, his face glazed by some television of remembrance: none of them quite know what to do about him. He is not Harry, he is sadder than Harry ever was, yet he demands the privileges and indulgence of Harry's place. In the worn shadows of the poorly lit half-house on Jackson Road, the Angstroms keep being startled by Nelson's ungrateful presence, keep losing him. "Where's

Nellie?" "Where did the kid get to?" "Is the child upstairs or down?" are questions the other three often put to one another. Nelson stays in his temporary room—Mim's old room—for hours of listening to rock-pop-folk turned down to a murmur. He skips meals without explaining or apologizing, and is making a scrapbook of news items the Brewer papers have carried about their fire. Rabbit discovered this scrapbook yesterday, snooping in the boy's room. Around the clippings the boy had drawn with various colors of ballpoint flowers, peace signs, Tao crosses, musical notes, psychedelic rainbows, those open-ended swirling doodles associated with insanity before they became commercial. Also there are two Polaroid snaps of the ruin; Billy took them Monday with a new camera his father had given him. The photos, brownish and curling, show a half-burned house, the burned half dark like a shadow but active in shape, eating the unburned half, the garage studs bent like matchsticks in an ashtray. Looking at the photographs, Rabbit smells ash. The smell is real and not remembered. In Nelson's closet he finds the source, a charred guitar. So that is why it wasn't in the garage when he looked for it, to give to Jill's mother. She is back in Connecticut now, let the poor kid keep it. His father can't reach him, and lives with him in his parents' house as an estranged, because too much older, brother.

He and his father see, walking up Jackson Road, a strange car parked in front of number 117, an indigo Toronado with orange-on-blue New York plates. His father's lope accelerates; "There'se Mim!" he calls, and it is. She is upstairs and comes to the head of the stairs as they enter beneath the fanlight of stained glass; she descends and stands with them in the murky little foyer. It is Mim. It isn't. It has been years since Rabbit has seen her. "Hi," Mim says, and kisses her father dryly, on the cheek. They were never even when the children were little much of a family for kissing. She would kiss her brother the same way, dismissingly, but he holds her, wanting to feel the hundreds of men who have held her before, this his sister whose diapers he changed, who used to hold his thumb when they'd go for Sunday walks along the quarry, who once burst out *oh I love you* sledding with him, the runners whistling on the dark packed slick, the street waxy with snow still falling. Puzzled by his embrace, Mim kisses him again, another peck on the same cheek, and then firmly shrugs his arms away. A competence in that. She felt lean, not an ounce extra but all woman, swimming must do it, in hotel pools, late hours carve the fat away and swimming smooths what's left. She appears to wear no makeup, no lipstick, except for her eyes, which are inhuman, Egyptian, drenched in peacock purple and blue, not merely outlined but re-created, and weighted with lashes he expects to stick fast when she blinks. These marvellously masked eyes force upon her pale mouth all expressiveness; each fractional smile, sardonic crimping, attentive pout, and abrupt broad laugh follows its predecessor so swiftly Harry imagines a coded tape is being fed into her head and producing, rapid as electronic images, this alphabet of expressions. Her nose, her one flaw, that kept her off the screen, that perhaps kept her from fame, is still long, with that mortifying faceted lump at the end, exactly like Mom's nose, but now that Mim is thirty and never going to be a model beauty seems less a flaw, indeed saves her face from mere expertness and gives it, between the peacock eyes and the actressy-fussy mouth, a lenient homeliness. And this, Rabbit guesses, would extend her appeal for men, though now she would get barroom criers, with broken careers and marriages, who want plain warmth, rather than comers who need an icy showpiece on their arm. In the style of the Sixties her clothes are clownish: bell-bottom slacks striped horizontally as if patched from three kinds of gingham; a pinstripe blouse, mannish but for the puff sleeves; shoes that in color and shape remind him of Donald Duck's bill; and hoop earrings three inches across. Even in high school Mim had liked big earrings; they made her look like a gypsy or Arab then, now, with the tan, Italian. Or Miami Jewish. Her hair is expensively tousled honey-white, which doesn't offend him; not since junior high has she worn it the color it was, the mild brown she once called, while he leaned in her doorway watching her study herself in the mirror, "Protestant rat."

Pop busies his hands, touching her, hanging up his coat, steering her into the dismal living room. "When did you get here? Straight from the West Coast? You fly straight to Idlewild, they do it non-stop now, don't they?"

"Dad, they don't call it Idlewild any more. I flew in a couple days ago, I had some stuff in New York to do before I drove down. Jersey was breathtaking, once you got past the oil tanks. Everything still so green."

"Where'd you get the car, Mim? Rent it from Hertz?" The old man's washed-out eyes sparkle at her daring, at her way with the world.

Mim sighs. "A guy lent it to me." She sits in the caneback rocker and puts her feet up on the very hassock that Rabbit as a child had once dreamed about: he dreamed it was full of dollar bills to solve all their problems. The dream had been so vivid he had tested it; the stitched scar of his incision still shows. The stuffing had been disagreeable fibre deader than straw.

Mim lights a cigarette. She holds it in the exact center of her mouth, exhales twin plumes around it, frowns at the snuffed match.

Pop is enchanted by the routine, struck dumb. Rabbit asks her, "How does Mom seem to you?"

"Good. For someone who's dying."

"She make sense to you?"

"A lot of it. The guy who doesn't make much sense to me

is you. She told me what you've been doing. Lately."

"Harry's had a hell of a time lately," Pop chimes in, nodding as if to mesh himself with this spinning wheel, his dazzling daughter. "Today in at Verity, get this, they gave him his notice. They kept me on and canned a man in his prime. I saw the handwriting on the wall but I didn't want it to be me who'd tell him, it was their meatloaf, let them deliver it, bastards, a man gives them his life and gets a boot in the fanny for his pains."

Mim closes her eyes and lets a look of weary age wash over her and says, "Pop, it's fantastic to see you. But don't you want to go up and look in on Mom for a minute? She may need to be led to the pot, I asked her but with me she could be shy still."

Pop rises quickly, obliging; yet then he stands in a tentative crouch, offering to say away her brusqueness. "You two have a language all your own. Mary and I, we used to marvel, I used to say to her, There couldn't ever have been a brother and a sister closer than Harry and Miriam. These other parents used to tell us, you know, about kids fighting, we didn't know what they were talking about, we'd never had an example. I swear to God above we never heard a loud word between the two of you. A lot of boys, all of six when Mim arrived, might have resented, you know, settled in with things pretty much his own way up to then, crowding the nest: not Harry. Right from the start, right from that first summer, we could trust you alone with him, alone in the house, Mary and I off to a movie, about the only way to forget your troubles in those days, go off to a motion picture." He blinks, gropes among these threads for the one to pull it all tight. "I swear to God, we've been lucky," he says, then weakens it by adding, "when you look at some of the things that can happen to people," and goes up; his tears spark as he faces the bulb burning at the head of the stairs, before cautiously returning his eyes to the treads.

Did they ever have a language of their own? Rabbit can't remember it, he just remembers them being here together, in this house season after season, for grade after grade of school, setting off down Jackson Road in the aura of one holiday after another, Hallowe'en, Thanksgiving, Christmas, Valentine's Day, Easter, in the odors and feel of one sports season succeeding another, football, basketball, track; and then him being out and Mim shrunk to a word in his mother's letters; and then him coming back from the Army and finding her grown up, standing in front of the mirror, ready for boys, maybe having had a few, tinting her hair and wearing hoop earrings; and then Janice took him off; and then both of them were off and the house empty of young life; and now both of them are here again. The smoke from her cigarette seems what the room needs, has needed a long time, to chase these old furniture and sickness smells away. He is sitting on the piano stool; he perches forward and reaches toward her. "Gimme a weed."

"I thought you stopped."

"Years ago. I don't inhale. Unless it's grass."

"Grass yet. You've been living it up." She fishes in her purse, a big bright patchy bag that matches her slacks, and tosses him a cigarette. It is menthol, with a complicated filter tip. Death is easily fooled. If the churches don't work, a filter will do.

He says, "I don't know what I've been doing."

"I would say so. Mom talked to me for an hour. The way she is now, that's a lot of talking."

"What d'ya think of Mom now? Now that you have all this perspective."

"She's a great woman. With nowhere to put it."

"Well, is where you put it any better?"

"It involves less make-believe."

"I don't know, you look pretty fantastic to me."

"Thanks."

"What'd she say? Mom."

"Nothing you don't know, except Janice calls her a lot."

"I knew that. She's called a couple times since Sunday, I can't stand it to talk to her."

"Why not?"

"She's too wild. She doesn't make any sense. She says she's getting a divorce but never starts it, she says she'll sue me for burning her house and I tell her I only burned my half. Then she says she'll come get Nelson but never comes, I wish the hell she would."

"What does it mean to you, her being wild like this?"

"I think she's losing her buttons. Probably drinking like a fish."

Mim turns her profile to blunt the cigarette in the saucer serving as an ashtray on the carpet. "It means she wants back in." Mim knows things, Rabbit realizes proudly. Wherever you go in some directions, Mim has been there. The direction where she hasn't been is the one that has Nelson in it, and the nice hot slap of the slug being made beside your left hand. But these are old directions, people aren't going that way any more. Mim repeats, "She wants you back."

"People keep telling me that," Rabbit says, "but I don't see much evidence. She can find me if she wants to."

Mim crosses her pants legs, aligns the stripes, and lights another cigarette. "She's trapped. Her love for this guy is the biggest thing she has, it's the first step out she's taken since she drowned that baby. Let's face it, Harry. You kids back here in the sticks still believe in ghosts. Before you screw you got to square it with old Jack Frost, or whatever you call him. To square skipping out with herself she has to make it a big deal. So. Remember as kids those candy jars down at Spottsie's you reached inside of to grab the candy and then you couldn't get your fist out? If Janice lets go to pull her hand out she'll have no candy. She wants it out, but she wants the candy too; no, that's not exactly it, she wants the *idea* of what she's made out of the candy in her own mind. So. Somebody has to break the jar for her."

"I don't want her back still in love with this spic."

"That's how you have to take her."

"The son of a bitch, he even has the nerve, sitting there in these snappy suits, he must make three times what I do just cheating people, he has the fucking nerve to be a dove. One night we all sat in this restaurant with him and me arguing across the table about Vietnam and them playing touch-ass side by side. You'd like him, actually, he's your type. A gangster."

Patiently Mim is sizing him up: one more potential customer at the bar. "Since when," she asks, "did you become such a war lover? As I remember you, you were damn glad to wriggle out of that Korean thing."

"It's not all war I love," he protests, "it's *this* war. Because nobody else does. Nobody else understands it."

"Explain it to me, Harry."

"It's a, it's a kind of head fake. To keep the other guy off balance. The world the way it is, you got to do something like that once in a while, to keep your options, to keep a little space around you." He is using his arms to show her his crucial concept of space. "Otherwise, he gets so he can read your every move and you're dead."

Mim asks, "You're sure there is this other guy?"

"Sure I'm sure." The other guy is the doctor who shakes your hand so hard it hurts. *I know best.* Madness begins in that pinch.

"You don't think there might just be a lot of little guys trying to get a little more space than the system they're under lets them have?"

"Sure there are these little guys, billions of 'em"—billions, millions, too much of everything—"but then also there's this big guy trying to put them all into a big black bag. He's crazy, so so must we be. A little."

She nods like a type of doctor herself. "That fits," she says. "Be crazy to keep free. The life you been leading lately sounds crazy enough to last you a while."

"What did I do wrong? I was a fucking Good Samaritan. I took in these orphans. Black, white, I said Hop aboard. Irregardless of color or creed, Hop aboard. Free eats. I was the fucking Statue of Liberty."

"And it got you a burned-down house."

"O.K. That's other people. That's their problem, not mine. I did what felt right." He wants to tell her everything, he wants his tongue to keep pace with this love he feels for this his sister; he wants to like her, though he feels a forbidding denseness in her, of too many conclusions reached, a wall dead beyond marring. He tells her, "I learned some things."

"Anything worth knowing?"

"I learned I'd rather fuck than be blown."

Mim removes a crumb, as of tobacco but the cigarette is filtered, from her lower lip. "Sounds healthy," she says. "Rather unAmerican, though."

"And we used to read books. Aloud to each other."

"Books about what?"

"I don't know. Slaves. History, sort of."

Mim in her red-striped clown costume laughs. "You went back to school," she says. "That's sweet." She used to get better marks than he did, even after she began with boys: As and Bs against his Bs and Cs. Mom at the time told him girls had to be smarter, just to pull even. Mim asks, "So what'd you learn from these books?"

"I learned"—he gazes at a corner of a room, wanting to get this right: he sees a cobweb above the sideboard, gesturing in some ceiling wind he cannot feel—"the country isn't perfect." Even as he says this he realizes he doesn't believe it, any more than he believes at heart that he will die. He is tired of explaining himself. "Speaking of sweet," he says, "how is *your* life?

"*Ça va.* That's French for, It goes."

"Somebody keeping you, or is it a new one every night?"

She looks at him and considers. A glitter of reflexive anger snipes at her mask of eye makeup. Then she exhales and relaxes, seeming to conclude, Well he's my brother. "Neither. I'm a career girl, Harry. I perform a service. I can't describe it to you, the way it is out there. They're not bad people. They have rules. They're not very interesting rules, nothing like Stick your hand in the fire and make it up to Heaven. They're more like, Ride the exercise bicycle the morning after. The men believe in flat stomach muscles and sweating things out. They don't want to carry too much fluid. You could say they're puritans. Gangsters are puritans. They're narrow and hard because off the straight path you don't live. Another rule they have is, Pay for what you get because anything free has a rattlesnake under it. They're survival rules, rules for living in the desert. That's what it is, a desert. Look out for it, Harry. It's coming East."

"It's here. You ought to see the middle of Brewer, it's all parking lots."

"But the things that grow you can eat, and the sun is still some kind of friend. Out there, we hate it. We live underground. All the hotels are underground with a couple of the windows painted blue. We like it best at night, about three in the morning, when the big money comes to the crap table. Beautiful faces, Harry. Hard and blank as chips. Thousands flow back and forth without any expression. You know what I'm struck by back here, looking at the faces? How soft they are. God they're soft. You look so soft to me, Harry. You're soft still standing and Pop's soft curling under. If we don't get Janice propped back under you you're going to curl under too. Come to think of it, Janice is not soft. She's hard as a nut. That's what I never liked about her. I bet I'd like her now. I should go see her."

"Sure. Do. You can swap stories. Maybe you could get her

a job on the West Coast. She's pretty old but does great things with her tongue."

"That's quite a hang-up you have there."

"Nobody's perfect. How about you? You have some specialty, or just take what comes?"

She sits up. "She really hurt you, didn't she?" And eases back. She stares at Harry interested. Perhaps she didn't expect in him such reserves of resentful energy. The living room is dark though the noises that reach them from outside say that children are still playing in the sun. "You're soft," she says, lulling, "like slugs under fallen leaves. Out there, Harry, there are no leaves. People grow these tan shells. I have one, look." She pulls up her pinstripe blouse and her belly is brown. He tries to picture the rest and wonders if her pussy is tinted honey-blonde to match the hair on her head. "You never see them out in the sun but they're all tan, with flat stomach muscles. Their one flaw is, they're still soft inside. They're like those chocolates we used to hate, those chocolate creams, remember how we'd pick through the Christmas box they'd give us at the movie theater, taking out only the square ones and the caramels in cellophane? The other ones we hated, those dark brown round ones on the outside, all ooky inside. But that's how people are. It embarrasses everybody but they need to be milked. Men need to be drained. Like boils. Women too for that matter. You asked me my specialty and that's it, I milk people. I let them spill their insides on me. It can be dirty work but usually it's clean. I went out there wanting to be an actress and that's in a way what I got, only I take on the audience one at a time. In some ways it's more intimate. So. Tell me some more about your life."

"Well I was nursemaid to this machine but now they've retired the machine. I was nursemaid to Janice but she upped and left."

"We'll get her back."

"Don't bother. Then I was nursemaid to Nelson and he hates me because I let Jill die."

"She let herself die. Speaking of that, that's what I do like about these kids: they're trying to kill it. Even if they kill themselves in the process."

"Kill what?"

"The softness. Sex, love; me, mine. They're doing it in. I have no playmates under thirty, believe it. They're burning it out with dope. They're going to make themselves hard clean through. Like, oh, cockroaches. That's the way to live in the desert. Be a cockroach. It's too late for you, and a little late for me, but once these kids get it together, they'll be no killing them. They'll live on poison."

Mim stands; he follows. For all that she was a tall girl and is enlarged by womanhood and makeup, her forehead comes to his chin. He kisses her forehead. She tilts her face up, slime-blue eyelids shut, to be kissed again. Pop's loose mouth under Mom's chiselled nose. He tells her, "You're a cheerful broad," and pecks her dry cheek. Perfumed stationery. A smile in her cheek pushes his lips. She is himself, with the combination jiggled.

She gives him a sideways hug, patting the fat around his waist. "I swing," Mim confesses. "I'm no showboat like Rabbit Angstrom, but in my quiet way I swing." She tightens the hug, and linked like that they walk to the foot of the stairs, to go up and console their parents.

Next day, Thursday, when Pop and Harry come home, Mim has Mom and Nelson downstairs at the kitchen table, having tea and laughing. "Dad," Nelson says, the first time since Sunday morning he has spoken to his father without first being spoken to, "did you know Aunt Mim worked at Disneyland once? Do Abraham Lincoln for him, please do it again."

Mim stands. Today she wears a knit dress, short and gray; in black tights her legs show skinny and a little knock-kneed, the same legs she had as a kid. She wobbles forward as to a lectern, removes an imaginary piece of paper from a phantom breast pocket, and holds it wavering a little below where her eyes would focus if they could see. Her voice as if on rustling tape within her throat emerges: "Fow-er scow-er and seven yaars ago—"

Nelson is falling off the chair laughing; yet his careful eyes for a split second check his father's face, to see how he takes it. Rabbit laughs, and Pop emits an appreciative snarl, and even Mom: the bewildered foolish glaze on her features becomes intentionally foolish, amused. Her laughter reminds Rabbit of the laughter of a child who laughs not with the joke but to join the laughter of others, to catch up and be human among others. To keep the laughter swelling Mim sets out two more cups and saucers in the jerky trance of a lifesize Disney doll, swaying, nodding, setting one cup not in its saucer but on the top of Nelson's head, even to keep the gag rolling pouring some hot water not in the teacup but onto the table; the water runs, steaming, against Mom's elbow. "Stop, you'll scald her!" Rabbit says, and seizes Mim, and is shocked by the tone of her flesh, which for the skit has become plastic, not hers, flesh that would stay in any position you twisted it to. Frightened, he gives her a little shake, and she becomes human, his efficient sister, wiping up, swishing her tail from table to stove, taking care of them all.

Pop asks, "What kind of work did Disney have you do, Mim?"

"I wore a little Colonial get-up and led people through a replica of Mt. Vernon." She curtseys and with both hands in artificial unison points to the old gas stove, with its crusty range and the crazed mica window in the oven door. "The Fa-ther of our Coun-try," she explains in a sweet, clarion, idiot voice, "was himself nev-er a fa-ther."

"Mim, you ever get to meet Disney personally?" Pop asks.

Mim continues her act. "His con-nu-bi-al bed, which we see before us, measures five feet four and three-quarter inches from rail to rail, and from head-board to foot-board is two inch-es under sev-en feet, a gi-ant's bed for those days, when most gentle-men were no bigger than warm-ing pans. Here"—she plucks a plastic fly swatter off the fly-specked wall—"you see a warm-ing pan."

"If you ask me," Pop says to himself, having not been answered, "it was Disney more than FDR kept the country from going under to the Commies in the Depression."

"The ti-ny holes," Mim is explaining, holding up the fly-swatter, "are de-signed to let the heat e-scape, so the fa-ther of our coun-try will not suf-fer a chill when he climbs into bed with his be-lov-ed Mar-tha. Here"—Mim gestures with two hands at the Verity Press giveaway calendar on the wall, turned to October, a grinning jack-o-lantern—"is Mar-tha."

Nelson is still laughing, but it is time to let go, and Mim does. She pecks her father on the forehead and asks him, "How's the Prince of Pica today? Remember that, Daddy? When I thought pica was the place where they had the leaning tower."

"North of Brewer somewhere," Nelson tells her, "I forget the exact place, there's some joint that calls itself the Leaning Tower of Pizza." The boy waits to see if this is funny, and though the grown-ups around the table laugh obligingly, he decides that it wasn't, and shuts his mouth. His eyes go wary again. "Can I be excused?"

Rabbit asks sharply, "Where're you going?"

"My room."

"That's Mim's room. When're you going to let her have it?"

"Any time."

"Whyncha go outdoors? Kick the soccer ball around, do something positive, for Chrissake. Get the self-pity out of your system."

"Let. Him alone," Mom brings out.

Mim intercedes. "Nelson, when will you show me your famous mini-bike?"

"It's not much good, it keeps breaking down." He studies her, his possible playmate. "You can't ride it in clothes like that."

"Out West," she says, "everybody rides motorcycles in trendy knits."

"Did you ever ride a motorcycle?"

"All the time, Nelson. I used to be the den mother for a pack of Hell's Angels. We'll ride over and look at your bike after supper."

"It's not the kid's bike, it's somebody else's," Rabbit tells her.

"It'll be dark after supper," Nelson tells Mim.

"I love the dark," she says. Reassured, he clumps upstairs, ignoring his father. Rabbit is jealous. Mim has learned, these years out of school, what he has not: how to manage people.

Mom lifts her teacup, sips, sets it down. A perilous brave performance. She is proud of something; he can tell by the way she sits, upright, her neck cords stretched. Her hair has been brushed tight about her head. Tight and almost glossy. "Mim," she says, "went calling today."

Rabbit asks, "On who?"

Mim answers. "On Janice. At Springer Motors."

"Well." Rabbit pushes back from the table, his chair legs scraping. "What did the little mutt have to say for herself?"

"Nothing. She wasn't there."

"Where was she?"

"He said seeing a lawyer."

"Old Man Springer said that?" Fear slides into his stomach, nibbling. The law. The long white envelope. Yet he likes the idea of Mim going over there and standing in one of her costumes in front of the Toyota cut-out, a gaudy knife into the heart of the Springer empire. Mim, their secret weapon.

"No," she tells him, "not Old Man Springer. Stavros."

"You saw Charlie there? Huh. How does he look? Beat?"

"He took me out to lunch."

"Where?"

"I don't know, some Greek place in the black district."

Rabbit has to laugh. People dead and dying all around him, he has to let it out. "Wait'll he tells her that."

Mim says, "I doubt he will."

Pop is slow to follow. "Who're we talking about, Mim? That slick talker turned Janice's head?"

Mom's face gropes; her eyes stretch as if she is strangling yet her mouth struggles with happiness. In suspense they all fall silent. "Her lover," she pronounces. A sick feeling stabs Rabbit.

Pop says, "Well I've kept my trap shut throughout this mess, don't think Harry there wasn't a temptation to meddle but I kept my peace, but a lover in my book is somebody who loves somebody through thick and thin and from all I hear this spic is just after the ass. The ass and the Springer name. Pardon the expression."

"I think," Mom says, faltering though her face still shines. "It's nice. To know Janice has."

"An ass," Mim finally completes for her. And it seems to Rabbit wicked that these two, Pop and Mim, are corrupting Mom on the edge of the grave. Coldly he asks Mim, "What'd you and Chas talk about?"

"Oh," Mim says, "things." She shrugs her knitted hip off the kitchen table, where she has been perched as on a bar stool. "Did you know, he has a rheumatic heart? He could kick off at any minute."

"Fat chance," Rabbit says.

"That type of operator," Pop says, snarling his teeth back into place, "lives to be a hundred, while they bury all the decent natural Americans. Don't ask me why it works that way, the Lord must have His reasons."

Mim says, "I thought he was sweet. And quite intelligent. And *much* nicer about you all than you are about him. He was very thoughtful about Janice, he's probably the first person in thirty years to give her some serious attention as a *per*son. He sees a lot in her."

"Must use a microscope," Rabbit says.

"And *you*," Mim says, turning, "he thinks you're about the biggest spook he's ever met. He can't understand why if you want Janice back you don't come and get her back."

Rabbit shrugs. "I don't believe in force. I don't like contact sports."

"I did tell him, what a gentle brother you were."

"Never hurt a fly if he could help it, used to worry me," Pop says. "As if we'd had a girl and didn't know it. Isn't that the truth, Mother?"

Mom gets out, "Never. All boy."

"In that case, Charlie says," Mim goes on.

Rabbit interrupts: " 'Charlie' yet."

"In that case, he said, why is he for the war?"

"Fuck," Rabbit says. He is more tired and impatient than he knew. "Anybody with any sense at all is for the damn war. They want to fight, we *got* to fight. What's the alternative? What?"

Mim tries to ride down her brother's rising anger. "His theory is," she says, "you like any disaster that might spring you free. You liked it when Janice left, you liked it when your house burned down."

"And I'll like it even more," Rabbit says, "when you stop seeing this greasy creep."

Mim gives him the stare that has put a thousand men in their place. "Like you said. He's my type."

"A gangster, right. No wonder you're out there screwing yourself into the morgue. You know where party chicks like you wind up? In coroners' reports, when you take too many sleeping pills when the phone stops ringing, when the gangsters find playmates in not such baggy condition. You're in big trouble, Sis, and the Stavroses of the world are going to be no help. They've put you where you are."

"Mo-om," Mim cries, out of old instinct appealing to the frail cripple nodding at the kitchen table. "Tell Harry to lay *off*." And Rabbit remembers, it's a myth they never fought; they often did.

When Pop and Harry return from work the next day, Harry's last on the job, the Toronado with New York plates is not in front of the house. Mim comes in an hour later, after Rabbit has put the supper chops in the oven; when he asks her where she's been, she drops her big stripey bag on the old davenport and answers, "Oh, around. Revisiting the scenes of my childhood. The downtown is really sad now, isn't it? All black-topped parking lots and Afro-topped blacks. And linoleum stores. I did one nice thing, though. I stopped at that store on lower Weiser with the lefty newspapers for sale and bought a pound of peanuts. Believe it or not Brewer is the only place left you can get good peanuts in the shell. Still warm." She tosses him the bag, wild; he grabs it left-handed and as they talk in the living room he cracks peanuts. He uses a flowerpot for the shells.

"So," he says. "You see Stavros again?"

"You told me not to."

"Big deal, what I tell you. How was he? Still clutching his heart?"

"He's touching. Just the way he carries himself."

"Boo hoo. You analyze me some more?"

"No, we were selfish, we talked about ourselves. He saw right through me. We were halfway into the first drink and he looks me up and down through those tinted glasses and says, 'You work the field don't you?' Gimme a peanut."

He tosses a fistful overhanded; they pelt her on the chest. She is wearing a twitchy little dress that buttons down the front and whose pattern imitates lizardskin. When she puts her feet up on the hassock he sees clear to the crotch of her pantyhose. There are three schools: those who wear underpants under, those who wear them over, and those who wear none. Mim looks to be of the third school. She acts lazy and soft; her eyes have relented, though the makeup shines as if freshly applied. "That's all you did?" he asks. "Eat lunch."

"Th-that's all, f-f-folks."

"What're you tryin' to prove? I thought you came East to help Mom."

"To help her help *you*. How can I help *her*, I'm no doctor."

"Well, I really appreciate your help, fucking my wife's boy friend like this."

Mim laughs at the ceiling, showing Harry the horseshoe curve of her jaw's underside, the shining white jugular bulge. As if cut by a knife the laugh ends. She studies her brother gravely, impudently. "If you had a choice, who would you rather went to bed with him, her or me?"

"Her. Janice, I can always have too, I mean it's possible; but you, never."

"I know," Mim gaily agrees. "Of all the men in the world, you're the only one off bounds. You and Pop."

"And how does that make me seem?"

She focuses hard on him, to get the one-word answer. "Ridiculous."

"That's what I thought. Hey, Jesus. Did you really give Stavros a bang today? Or're you just getting my goat? Where would you go? Wouldn't Janice miss him at the office?"

"Oh—he could say he was out on a sale or something," Mim offers, bored now. "Or he could tell her to mind her own business. That's what European men do." She stands, touches all the buttons in the front of her lizardskin dress to make sure they're done. "Let's go visit Mom." Mim adds, "Don't fret. Years ago, I made it a rule never to be with a guy more than three times. Unless there was some percentage in getting involved."

That night Mim gets them all dressed and out to dinner, at the smörgåsbord diner south toward the ball park. Though Mom's head waggles and she has some trouble cutting the crust of her apple pie, she manages pretty well and looks happy: how come he and Pop never thought of getting her out of the house? He resents his own stupidity, and tells Mim in the hall, as they go in to their beds—she is back in her old room, Nelson sleeps with him now—"You're just little Miss Fix-It, aren't you?"

"Yes," she snaps, "and you're just big Mister Muddle." She begins undoing her buttons in front of him, and closes her door only after he has turned away.

Saturday morning she takes Nelson in her Toronado over to the Fosnachts; Janice has arranged with Mom that she and Peggy will do something all day with the boys. Though it takes twenty minutes to drive from Mt. Judge to West Brewer, Mim is gone all morning and comes back to the house after two. Rabbit asks her, "How was it?"

"What?"

"No, seriously. Is he that great in the sack, or just about average in your experience? My theory for a while was there must be something wrong with him, otherwise why would he latch on to Janice when he can have all these new birds coming up?"

"Maybe Janice has wonderful qualities."

"Let's talk about him. Relative to your experience." He

imagines that all men have been welded into one for her, faces and voices and chests and hands welded into one murmuring pink wall, as once for him the audience at those old basketball games became a single screaming witness that was the world. "To your wide experience," he qualifies.

"Why don't you tend your own garden instead of hopping around nibbling at other people's?" Mim asks. When she turns, her body becomes a gate, of horizontal stripes, her ass barred in orange.

"I have no garden," he says.

"Because you didn't tend it at all. Everybody else has a life they try to fence in with some rules. You just do what you feel like and then when it blows up or runs down you sit there and pout."

"Christ," he says, "I went to work day after day for ten years."

Mim tosses this off. "You felt like it. It was the easiest thing to do."

"You know, you're beginning to remind me of Janice."

She turns; the gate opens. "Charlie told me Janice is fantastic. A real wild woman."

Sunday Mim stays home all day. They go for a drive in Pop's old Chevy, out to the quarry, where they used to walk. The fields that used to be dusted white with daisies and then yellow with goldenrod are housing tracts now; of the quarry only the great gray hole in the ground remains. The Oz-like tower of sheds and chutes where the cement was processed is gone, and the mouth of the cave where children used to hide and frighten themselves is sealed shut with bulldozed dirt and rusted sheets of corrugated iron. "Just as well," Mom pronounces. "Awful things. Used to happen there. Men and boys." They eat at the aluminum diner out on Warren Street, with a view of the viaduct, and this meal out is less successful than the last. Mom refuses to eat. "No appetite," she says, yet Rabbit and Mim think it is because the booths are close and the place is bright and she doesn't want people to see her fumble. They go to a movie. The movie page of the *Vat* advertises: *I Am Curious Yellow, Midnight Cowboy*, a double bill of *Depraved* and *The Circus* (Girls Never Played Games Like This Before!), a Swedish X-film titled *Yes*, and *Funny Girl. Funny Girl* sounds like more of the same but it has Barbra Streisand; there will be music. They make it late to the 6:30 show. Mom falls asleep and Pop gets up and walks around in the back of the theater and talks to the usher in a penetrating whine until one of the scattered audience calls out "*Shh.*" On the way out, the lights on, a trio of hoods give Mim such an eye Rabbit gives them back the finger. Blinking in the street, Mom says, "That was nice. But really Fanny. Was very ugly. But stylish. And a gangster. She always knew Nick Arnstein was a gangster. Everybody. Knew it."

"Good for her," Mim says.

"It isn't the gangsters who are doing the country in," Pop says. "If you ask me it's the industrialists. The monster fortunes. The Mellons and the DuPonts, those are the cookies we should put in jail."

Rabbit says, "Don't get radical, Pop."

"I'm no radical," the old man assures him, "you got to be rich to be radical."

Monday, a cloudy day, is Harry's first day out of work. He is awake at seven but Pop goes off to work alone. Nelson goes with him; he still goes to school in West Brewer and switches buses on Weiser. Mim leaves the house around eleven, she doesn't say where to. Rabbit scans the want ads in the Brewer *Triumph*. Accountant. Administrative Trainee. Apprentice Spray Painter. Auto Mechanic. Bartender. The world is full of jobs, even with Nixon's Depression. He skips down through Insurance Agents and Programmers to a column of Salesmen and then turns to the funnies. Goddam "Apartment 3-G": he feels he's been living with those girls for years now, when is he going to see them with their clothes off? The artist keeps teasing him with bare shoulders in bathrooms, naked legs in the foreground with the crotch coming just at the panel edge, glimpses of bra straps being undone. He calculates: after two months' pay from Verity he has thirty-seven weeks of welfare and then he can live on Pop's retirement. It is like dying now, they don't let you fall though, they keep you up forever with transfusions, otherwise you'll be an embarrassment to them. He skims the divorce actions and doesn't see himself and goes upstairs to Mom.

She is sitting up in the bed, her hands quiet on the quilted coverlet, an inheritance from her own mother. The television is also quiet. Mom stares out of the window at the maples. They have dropped leaves enough so the light in here seems harsh. The sad smell is more distinct: fleshly staleness mingled with the peppermint of medicine. To spare her the walk down the hall they have put a commode over by the radiator. To put a little bounce into her life, he sits down heavily on the bed. Her eyes with their film of clouding pallor widen; her mouth works but produces only saliva. "What's up?" Harry loudly asks. "How's it going?"

"Bad dreams," she brings out. "L-dopa does things. To the system."

"So does Parkinson's Disease." This wins no response. He tries, "What do you hear from Julia Arndt? And what's-er-name, Mamie Kellog? Don't they still come visiting?"

"I've outlasted. Their interest."

"Don't you miss their gossip?"

"I think. It scared them when. It all came true."

He tries, "Tell me one of your dreams."

"I was picking scabs. All over my body. I got one off and underneath. There were bugs, the same. As when you turn over a rock."

"Wow. Enough to make you stay awake. How do you like Mim's being here?"

"I do."

"Still full of sauce, isn't she?"

"She tries to be. Cheerful."

"Hard as nails, I'd say."

"Inch by inch," Mom says.

"Huh?"

"That was on one of the children's programs. Earl leaves the set on and makes me watch. Inch by inch."

"Yeah, go on."

"Life is a cinch. Yard by yard, life is hard."

He laughs appreciatively, making the bed bounce more. "Where do you think I went wrong?"

"Who says. You did?"

"Mom. No house, no wife, no job. My kid hates me. My sister says I'm ridiculous."

"You're. Growing up."

"Mim says I've never learned any rules."

"You haven't had to."

"Huh. Any decent kind of world, you wouldn't need all these rules."

She has no ready answer for this. He looks out of her windows. There was a time—the year after leaving, five years after—when this homely street, with its old-fashioned high crown, its sidewalk blocks tugged up and down by maple roots, its retaining walls of sandstone and railings of painted iron and two-family brickfront houses whose siding imitates gray rocks, excited Rabbit with the magic of his own existence. These mundane surfaces had given witness to his life; this chalice had held his blood; here the universe had centered, each downtwirling maple seed of more account than galaxies. No more. Jackson Road seems an ordinary street anywhere. Millions of such American streets hold millions of lives, and let them sift through, and neither notice nor mourn, and fall into decay, and do not even mourn their own passing but instead grimace at the wrecking ball with the same gaunt façades that have outweathered all their winters. However steadily Mom communes with these maples, the branches' misty snake-shapes as inflexibly fixed in these two windows as the leading of stained glass, they will not hold back her fate by the space of a breath; nor, if they are cut down tomorrow to widen Jackson Road at last, will her staring, that planted them within herself, halt their vanishing. And the wash of new light will extinguish even her memory of them. Time is our element, not a mistaken invader. How stupid, it has taken him thirty-six years to begin to believe that. Rabbit turns his eyes from the windows and says, to say something, "Having Mim home sure makes Pop happy"; but in his silence Mom, head rolling on the pillow, her nostrils blood-red in contrast with the linen, has fallen asleep.

He goes downstairs and makes himself a peanut butter sandwich. He pours himself a glass of milk. He feels the whole house as balanced so that his footsteps might shake Mom and tumble her into the pit. He goes into the cellar and finds his old basketball and, more of a miracle still, a pump with the air needle still screwed into the nozzle. In their frailty things keep faith. The backboard is still on the garage but years have rusted the hoop and loosened the bolts, so the first hard shots tilt the rim sideways. Nevertheless he keeps horsing around and his touch begins to come back. Up and soft, up and soft. Imagine it just dropping over the front of the rim, forget it's a circle. The day is very gray so the light is nicely even. He imagines he's on television; funny, watching the pros on the box how you can tell, from just some tone of their bodies as they go up, if the shot will go in. Mim comes out of the house, down the back steps, down the cement walk, to him. She is wearing a plain black suit, with wide boxy lapels, and a black skirt just to the knee. An outfit a Greek would like. Classic widow. He asks her, "That new?"

"I got it at Kroll's. They're outlandishly behind the coasts, but their staid things are half as expensive."

"You see friend Chas?"

Mim puts down her purse and removes her white gloves and signals for the ball. He used to spot her ten points at Twenty-one when he was in high school. As a girl she had speed and a knock-kneed moxie at athletics, and might have done more with it if he hadn't harvested all the glory already. "Friend Janice too," she says, and shoots. It misses but not by much.

He bounces it back. "More arch," he tells her. "Where'd you see Jan?"

"She followed us to the restaurant."

"You fight?"

"Not really. We all had martinis and *retsina* and got pretty well smashed. She can be quite funny about herself now, which is a new thing." Her grease-laden eyes squint at the basket. "She says she wants to rent an apartment away from Charlie so she can have Nelson." This shot, the ball hits the crotch and every loose bolt shudders looser.

"I'll fight her all the way on that."

"Don't get uptight. It won't come to that."

"Oh it won't. Aren't you a fucking little know-it-all?"

"I try. One more shot." Her breasts jog her black lapels as she shoves the dirty ball into the air. A soft drizzle has started. The ball swishes the net, if the net had been there.

"How could you give Stavros his bang if Janice was there?"

"We sent her back to her father."

He had meant the question to be rude, not for it to be answered. "Poor Janice," he says. "How does she like being out-tarted?"

"I said, don't get uptight. I'm flying back tomorrow. Charlie knows it and so does she."

"Mim. You can't, so soon. What about them?" He gestures at the house. From the back, it has a tenement tallness, a rickety hangdog wood-and-tar-shingle backside mismatched to its solid street face. "You'll break their hearts."

"They know. My life isn't here, it's there."

"You have nothing there but a bunch of horny hoods and a good chance of getting V.D."

"Oh, we're clean. Didn't I tell you? We're all obsessed with cleanliness."

"Yeah. Mim. Tell me something else. Don't you ever get tired of fucking? I mean"—to show the question is sincere, not rude—"I'd think you would."

She understands and is sisterly honest. "Actually, no. I don't. As a girl I would have thought you would but now being a woman I see you really don't. It's what we do. It's what people do. Of course, there are times, but even then, there's something nice. People want to be nice, haven't you noticed? They don't like being shits, that much; but you have to find some way out of it for them."

Her eyes in their lassos of paint seem, outdoors, younger—her irises gold near the pupil, brown eyes that came from somewhere far back in the family—than they have a right to be. "Well, good," he says weakly; he wants to take her hand, to be led. As her brother, once, he had been afraid she would fall in the quarry if he let go and he had let go and she had fallen and now says it's all right, all things must fall. She laughs and goes on, "Of course I was never squeamish like you. Remember how you hated food that was mixed up, when the pea-juice touched the meat or something? And that time I told you all food had to be mushed like vomit before you could swallow it, you hardly ate for a week."

"I don't remember that. Stavros is really great, huh?"

Mim picks up her white gloves from the grass. "He's nice." She slaps her palm with the gloves, studying her brother. "One other thing you should know," she says.

"What?" He braces for the worst, the hit that will leave nothing there.

"It's raining." And in the darkening drizzle she sprints,

still knock-kneed and speedy, up the walk through their narrow backyard, up the stairs of their spindly back porch. He hugs the ball and follows.

In his parents' house Rabbit not only reverts to peanut butter sandwiches and cocoa and lazing in bed when the sounds of Pop and Nelson leaving have died; he finds himself faithfully masturbating. The room itself demands it: a small long room he used to imagine as a railway car being dragged through the night. Its single window gives on the sunless passageway between the houses. As a boy in this room he could look across the space of six feet at the drawn shade of the room that used to be little Carolyn Zim's. The Zims were night owls. Some nights, though he was three grades ahead of her, Carolyn would go to bed later than he, and he would strain to see in the chinks of light around her shade the glimmer of her undressing. And by pressing his face to the chill glass by his pillow he could look at a difficult diagonal into Mr. and Mrs. Zim's room and one night glimpsed a pink commotion that may have been intercourse. But nearly every morning the Zims could be heard at breakfast fighting and Mom used to wonder how long they would stay together. People that way plainly wouldn't be having intercourse. In those days this room was full of athletes, mostly baseball players, their pictures came on school tablet covers, Musial and Dimag and Luke Appling and Rudy York. And for a while there had been a stamp collection, weird to remember, the big blue album with padded covers and the waxpaper mounts and the waxpaper envelopes stuffed with a tumble of Montenegro and Sierra Leone cancelleds. He imagined then he would travel to every country in the world and send Mom a postcard from every one, with these stamps. He was in love with the idea of travelling, with running, with geography, with Parcheesi and Safari and all board games where you roll the dice and move; the sense of a railroad car was so vivid he could almost see his sallow overhead light, tulip-shaped, tremble and sway with the motion. Yet travelling became an offense in the game he got good at.

The tablet covers were pulled from the wall while he was in the Army. The spots their tacks left were painted over. The tulip of frosted glass was replaced by a fluorescent circle that buzzes and flickers. Mom converted his room to her junk room: an old push-treadle Singer, a stack of *Reader's Digests* and *Family Circles*, a bridge lamp whose socket hangs broken like a chicken's head by one last tendon, depressing pictures of English woods and Italian palaces where he has never been, the folding cot from Sears where Nelson slept while Mim was here. When Mim left Tuesday, Nelson moved back to her room, abandoning his father to memories and fantasies. He always has to imagine somebody, masturbating. As he gets older real people aren't exciting enough. He tried imagining Peggy Fosnacht, because she had been recent, and good, all gumdrops; but remembering her reminds him that he has done nothing for her, has not called her since the fire, has no desire to, left her Mustang in the basement and had Nelson give her the key, scared to see her, blames her, she seduced him, the low blue flame that made her want to be fucked spread and became the fire. From any thought of the fire his mind darts back singed. Nor can he recall Janice; but for the bird-like dip of her waist under his hand in bed she is all confused mocking darkness where he dare not insert himself. He takes to conjuring up a hefty coarse Negress, fat but not sloppy fat, muscular and masculine, with a trace of a mustache and a chipped front tooth. Usually she is astraddle him like a smiling Buddha, slowly rolling her ass on his thighs, sometimes coming forward so her big cocoa-colored breasts swing into his face like boxing gloves with sensitive tips. He and this massive whore have just shared a joke, in his fantasy; she is laughing and good humor is rippling through his chest; and the room they are in is no ordinary room but a kind of high attic, perhaps a barn, with distant round windows admitting dusty light and rafters from which ropes hang, almost a gallows. Though she is usually above him, and he sometimes begins on his back, imagining his fingers are her lips, for the climax he always rolls over and gives it to the bed. He has never been able to shoot off lying on his back; it feels too explosive, too throbbing, too blasphemous upwards. God is on that side of him, spreading His feathered wings as above a crib. Better turn and pour it into Hell. You nice big purple-lipped black cunt. Gold tooth.

When this good-humored goddess of a Negress refuses, through repeated conjuration, to appear vividly enough, he tries imagining Babe. Mim, during her brief stay, told him offhand, at the end of his story, that what he should have done was sleep with Babe; it had been all set up, and it was what his subconscious wanted. But Babe in his mind has stick fingers cold as ivory, and there is no finding a soft hole in her, she is all shell. And the puckers on her face have been baked there by a wisdom that withers him. He has better luck making a movie that he is not in, imagining two other people, Stavros and Mim. How did they do it? He sees her scarlet Toronado barrelling up the steepness of Eisenhower Avenue, stopping at 1204. The two of them get out, the red doors slam punkily, they go in, go up, Mim first. She would not even turn for a preliminary kiss; she would undress swiftly. She would stand in noon windowlight lithe and casual, her legs touching at the knees, her breasts with their sunken nipples and bumpy aureoles (he has seen her breasts, spying) still girlish and undeveloped, having never nursed a child. Stavros would be slower in undressing, stolid, nursing his heart, folding his pants to keep the crease for when he returns to the lot. His back would be hairy: dark whirlpools on his shoulder blades. His cock would be thick and ropily veined, ponderous but irresistible in rising under Mim's deft teasing; he hears their wisecracking voices die; he imagines afternoon clouds dimming the sepia faces of the ancestral

Greeks on the lace-covered tables; he sees the man's clotted cock with the column of muscle on its underside swallowed by Mim's rat-furred vagina (no, she is not honey-blonde here), sees her greedy ringless fingers press his balls deeper up, up into her ravenous stretched cunt; and himself comes. As a boy, he had felt it as a space-flight, a squeezed and weightless spinning over onto his head, but now it is a mundane release as of anger, a series of muffled shouts into the safe bedsheet, rocks thrown at a boarded window. In the stillness that follows he hears a tingling, a submerged musical vibration slowly identifiable as the stereo set of the barefoot couple next door, in the other half of the house.

One night while he is letting his purged body drift in listening Jill comes and bends over and caresses him. He turns his head to kiss her thigh and she is gone. But she has wakened him; it was her presence, and through this rip in her death a thousand details are loosed; tendrils of hair, twists of expression, her frail voice quavering into pitch as she strummed. The minor details of her person that slightly repelled him, her small gray teeth, her doughy legs, the apple smoothness of her valentine bottom, the something prim and above-it-all about her flaky mouth, the unwashed dress she perferred to wear, now return and become the body of his memory. Times return when she merged on the bed with moonlight, her young body just beginning to learn to feel, her nerve endings still curled in like fernheads in the spring, green, a hardness that repelled him but was not her fault, the gift of herself was too new to give, her angel of a body that took orders like a dog, that licked and would have loved, was waiting to learn the words by hearing them spoken, wanting to uncurl. Pensive moments of her face return to hurt him. A daughterly attentiveness he had bid her hide. Why? He had retreated into deadness and did not wish her to call him out. He was not ready, he had been hurt. Let black Jesus have her, he had been converted to a hardness of heart, a billion cunts and only one him. He tries to picture, what had been so nice, Jill and Skeeter as he actually saw them once in hard lamplight, but in fantasy now Rabbit rises from the chair to join them, to be a father and lover to them, and they fly apart like ink and paper whirling to touch for an instant. She is touching him again as he lies in his boyhood bed and this time he does not make the mistake of turning his face, he very carefully brings his hand up from his side to touch the ends of her hair where it must hang. Waking to find his hand in empty mid-air he cries; grief rises in him out of a parched stomach, a sore throat, singed eyes; remembering her daughterly blind grass-green looking to him for more than shelter he blinds himself, leaves stains on the linen that need not be wiped, they will be invisible in the morning. Yet she had been here, her very breath and presence. He must tell Nelson in the morning. On this resolve he relaxes, lets his room, with hallucinatory shuddering, be coupled to an engine and tugged westward toward the desert, where Mim is now.

"That bitch," Janice said. "How many times did you screw her?"

"Three times," Charlie said. "That ended it. It's one of her rules."

This ghost of conversation haunts Janice this night she cannot sleep. Harry's witch of a sister has gone back to whoring but her influence is left behind in Charlie like a poison, a touch of disease. They had it so perfect. Lord they had never told her, not her mother or father or the nurses at school, only the movies had tried to tell her but they couldn't show it, at least not until recently, how perfect it could be. Sometimes she comes just thinking about him and then other times they last forever together, it is beautiful how slow he can be, murmuring all the time to her, selling her herself. They call it a piece of ass and she never understood why until Charlie, it wasn't on her front so much where she used to get mad at Harry because he couldn't make their bones touch or give her the friction she needed long enough so then he ended blaming her for not being with him, it was deeper inside, where the babies happened, where everything happens, she remembers how, was it with Nelson or poor little Becky, they said push and it was embarrassing like forcing it when you haven't been regular, but then the pain made her so panicky she didn't care what came out, and what came out was a little baby, all red-faced and cross as if it had been interrupted doing something else in there inside her. Stuff up your ass, she had hated to hear people say it, what men did to each other in jail or in the Army where the only women are yellow women screaming by the roadside with babies in their arms and squatting to go to the bathroom anywhere, disgusting, but stuffed was what she felt, and with Charlie there it is again, it is a piece of ass she is giving him, he is remaking her from the bottom up, another expression she had hated, the whole base of her feels made new, mud made radiant. Yet afterwards, when she tries to say this, how he remakes her (sometimes she feels like hot iron on an anvil the way he pounds), he gives that lovable shrug and pretends it was something anybody could do, a trick like that little trick he does with matches to amuse his nephews, making them pick the last one up, instead of the sad truth which is that nobody else in the whole wide (Harry was always worrying about how wide the world was, caring about things like how far stars are and the moon shot and the way the Communists wanted to put everybody in a big black bag so he couldn't breathe) world but Charlie could do that for her, she was made for him from the beginning of time without exaggeration. When she tries to describe this to him, how unique they are and sacred, he measures a space of silence with his wonderful hands, just the way his thumbs are put together takes the breath out of her, and slips the question like a cloak from his shoulders.

"How *could* you *do* that to me?"

He shrugged. "I didn't do it to you. I did it to her. I screwed her."

"Why? Why?"

"Why not? Relax. It wasn't that great. She was cute as hell at lunch, but as soon as we got into bed her thermostat switched off. Like handling white rubber."

"Oh, Charlie. Talk to me, Charlie. Tell me why."

"Don't lean on me, tiger."

She had made him make love to her. She had done everything for him. She had worshipped him, she had wanted to cry out her sorrow that there wasn't more she could do, that bodies were tools shaped for too many purposes. Though she had extracted her lover's semen from him, she failed to extract testimony that his sense of their love was as absolute as her own. Terribly—complainingly, preeningly—she had said, "You know I've given up the world for you."

He had sighed, "You can get it back."

"I've destroyed my husband. He's in all the newspapers."

"He doesn't mind."

"I've dishonored my parents."

He had turned his back. With Harry it had been usually she who turned her back. He is hard to snuggle against, too big; it is like clinging to a rock slippery with hair. He had, for him, apologized: "Tiger, I'm bushed. I've felt rotten all day."

"Rotten how?"

"Deep down rotten. Shaky rotten."

And feeling him slip toward oblivion had so enraged her she had hurled herself naked from bed, had shrieked at him the words he had taught her in love, knocked a dead great-aunt from a bureau top, announced that any decent man would at least have *offered* to marry her now knowing she wouldn't accept, did things to the peace of the apartment that now reverberate in her insomnia, make the darkness shudder between pulses of the headlights that tirelessly pass below on Eisenhower Avenue. The view from the back of Charlie's apartment is an unexpected one, of a bend in the Running Horse River like a cut in fabric, of the elephant-colored gas tanks in the boggy land beside the dump, and, around a church with twin blue domes she never knew was there, a little cemetery with iron crosses instead of stones. The traffic out front never ceases. Janice has lived near Brewer all her life but never in it before, and thought all places went to sleep like people, and was surprised how this city always rumbles with traffic, like her heart which even through dreams keeps pouring out its love.

She awakes. The curtains at the window are silver. The moon is a cold stone above Mt. Judge. The bed is not her bed, then she remembers it has been her bed since, when? July it was. For some reason she sleeps with Charlie on her left; Harry was always on her right. The luminous hands of the electric clock by Charlie's bedside put the time at after two. Charlie is lying face up in the moonlight. She touches his cheek and it is cold. She puts her ear to his mouth and hears no breathing. He is dead. She decides this must be a dream.

Then his eyelids flutter as if at her touch. His eyeballs in the faint cold light seem unseeing, without pupils. Moonlight glints in a dab of water at the far corner of the far eye. He groans, and Janice realizes this is what has waked her. A noise not freely given but torn from some heavy mechanism of restraint deep in his chest. Seeing that she is up on an elbow watching, he says, "Hi, tiger. It hurts."

"What hurts, love? Where?" Her breath rushes from her throat so fast it burns. All the space in the room, from the corners in, seems a crystal a wrong move from her will shatter.

"Here." He seems to mean to show her but cannot move his arms. Then his whole body moves, arching upward as if twitched by something invisible outside of him. She glances around the room for the unspeaking presence tormenting them, and sees again the lace curtains stamped, interwoven medallions, on the blue of the streetlamp, and against the reflecting blue of the bureau mirror the square blank silhouettes of framed aunts, uncles, nephews. The groan comes again, and the painful upward arching: a fish hooked deep, in the heart.

"Love, is there any pill?"

He makes words through his teeth. "Little white. Top shelf. Bathroom cabinet."

The crowded room pitches and surges with her panic. The floor tilts beneath her bare feet; the nightie she put on after making her bad scene taps her burning skin scoldingly. The bathroom door sticks. One side of the frame strikes her shoulder, hard. She cannot find the light cord, her hand flailing in the darkness; then she strikes it and it leaps from her touch and while she waits for it to swing back down out of the blackness Charlie groans again, the worst yet, the tightest-sounding. The cord finds her fingers and she pulls; the light pounces on her eyes, she feels them shrink so rapidly it hurts yet she doesn't take the time to blink, staring for the little white pills. She confronts in the cabinet a sick man's wealth. All the pills are white. No, one is aspirin; another is yellow and transparent, those capsules that hold a hundred little bombs to go off against hayfever. Here: this one must be it; though the little jar is unlabelled the plastic squeeze lid looks important. There is tiny red lettering on each pill but she can't take the time to read it, her hands shake too much, they must be right; she tilts the little jar into her palm and five hurry out, no, six, and she wonders how she can be wasting time counting and tries to slide some back into the tiny round glass mouth but her whole body is beating so hard her joints have locked to hold her together. She looks for a glass and sees none and takes the square top of the Water Pik and very stupidly lets the faucet water run to get cold, wetting her palm in turning it off, so the pills there blur and soften and stain the creased skin they are cupped in. She has to hold everything, pills and slopping Water Pik lid, in one hand to free the other to close the bathroom door to keep the light caged away from Charlie. He lifts his large head a painful inch from the pillow and studies the pills melting in her hand and gets out, "Not those. *Little* white." He grimaces as if to laugh. His head sinks back. His throat muscles go rigid. The noise he makes now is up an octave, a woman's noise. Janice sees she does not have time to go back and search again, he is being tuned too high. She sees that they are beyond chemicals; they are pure spirits, she must make a miracle. Her body feels leaden on her bones, she remembers Harry telling her she has the touch of death. But a pressure from behind like a cuff on the back of her head pitches her forward with a keening cry pitched like his own and she presses herself down upon his body that has been so often pressed upon hers; he has become a great hole nothing less large than she wild with love can fill. She wills her heart to pass through the walls of bone and give its rhythm to his. He grits his teeth "Christ" and strains upward against her as if coming and she presses down with great calm, her body a sufficiency, its warmth and wetness and pulse as powerful as it must be to staunch this wound that is an entire man, his length and breadth loved, his level voice loved and his clever square hands loved and his whirlpools of hair loved and his buffed fingernails loved and the dark gooseflesh bag of his manhood loved and the frailty held within him like a threat and lock against her loved. She is a gateway of love gushing from higher ground; she feels herself dissolving piece by piece like a little mud dam in a sluice. She feels his heart kick like pinned prey and keeps it pinned. Though he has become a devil, widening now into a hole wider than a quarry and then gathering into a pain-squeezed upper thrust as pointed and cold as an icicle she does not relent; she widens herself to hold his edges in, she softens herself to absorb the spike of his pain. She will not let him leave her. There is a third person in the room, this person has known her all her life and looked down upon her until now; through this other pair of eyes she sees she is weeping, hears herself praying, *Go, Go,* to the devil thrashing inside this her man. "Go!" she utters aloud.

Charlie's body changes tone. He is dead. No, at his mouth she eavesdrops on the whistle of his breathing. Sudden sweat soaks his brow, his shoulders, his chest, her breasts, her cheek where it was pressed against his cheek. His legs relax. He grunts, "O.K." She dares slide from him, tucking the covers, which she had torn down to bare his chest, back up to his chin.

"Shall I get the real pills now?"

"In a minute. No immediate need now: nitroglycerin. What you brought me was Coricidin. Cold pills."

She sees that his grimace had meant to be laughter, for he does smile now. Harry is right. She is stupid.

To ease the hurt look from her face Stavros tells her, "Rotten feeling. Pressure worse than a fist. You can't breathe, move anything makes it worse, you feel your own heart. Like some animal skipping inside you. Crazy."

"I was scared to leave you."

"You did great. You brought me back from nowhere."

She knows this is true. The mark upon her as a giver of death has been erased. As in fucking, she has been rendered transparent, then filled solid with peace. As if after fucking, she takes playful inventory of his body, feels the live sweat on his broad skin, traces a finger down the line of his nose.

He repeats, "Crazy," and sits up in bed, cooling himself, gasping safe on the shore. She snuggles at his side and lets her tears out like a child. Absently, still moving his arms gingerly, he fumbles with the ends of her hair as it twitches on his shoulder.

She asks, "Was it me? My throwing that fit about Harry's sister? I could have killed you."

"Never." Then he admits, "I need to keep things orderly or they get to me."

"My being here is disorderly," she says.

"Never mind," he says, not quite denying, and tugs her hair so her head jerks.

Janice gets up and fetches the right pills. They had been there all along, on the top shelf; she had looked on the middle shelf. He takes one and shows her how he puts it under his tongue to dissolve. As it dissolves he makes that mouth she loves, lips pushed forward as if concealing a lozenge. When she turns off the light and gets into bed beside him, he rolls on his side to give her a kiss. She does not respond, she is too full of peace. Soon the soft rhythm of his unconscious breathing rises from his side of the bed. On her side, she cannot sleep. Awake in every nerve she floats in a space purged of obstacles and illusions. The traffic continues down below. She and Charlie float motionless above Brewer; he sleeps on the wind, his heart hollow. Next time she might not be able to keep him up. Miracles are granted but we must not lean on them. This love that has blown through her has been a miracle, the one thing worthy of it remaining is to leave. Spirits are insatiable but bodies get enough. She has had enough, he has had enough; more might be too much. She might begin to kill. He calls her tiger. Toward six the air brightens. She sees his square broad forehead, the thinning hair dry and tangled before its morning combing, the nose so shapely a kind of feminine vanity seems to be bespoken, the mouth even in sleep slightly pouting, a snail-shine of saliva released from one corner. Angel, buzzard, Janice sees that in the vast volume of her love she has renounced the one possible imperfection, its object. Her own love engulfs her; she sinks down through its purity swiftly fallen, all feathers.

Mom has the phone by her bed; downstairs Rabbit hears it ring, then hears it stop, but some time passes before she makes him understand it is for him. She cannot raise her voice above a kind of whimper now, but she has a cane, an intimidating knobby briar Pop brought home one day from the Brewer Salvation Army store. She taps on the floor with it until attention comes up the stairs. She is quite funny with it, waving it around, thumping. "All my life," she says. "What I wanted. A cane."

He hears the phone ring twice and then only slowly the tapping of the cane sinks in; he is vacuuming the living room rug, trying to get some of the fustiness up. In Mom's room, the smell is more powerful, the perverse vitality of rot. He has read somewhere that what we smell are just tiny fragments of the thing itself tickling a plate in our nose, a subtler smoke. Everything has its cloud, a flower's bigger than a rock's, a dying person's bigger than ours. Mom says, "For you." The pillows she is propped on have slipped so she sits at a slant. He straightens her and, since the word "Janice" begins with a sound difficult for her throat muscles to form, she is slow to make him understand who it is.

He freezes, reaching for the phone. "I don't want to talk to her."

"Why. Not."

"O.K., O.K." It is confusing, having to talk here, Janice's voice filling his ear while Mom and her rumpled bed fill his vision. Her blue-knuckled hands clasp and unclasp; her eyes, open too wide, rest on him in a helpless stare, the blue irises ringed with a thin white circle like a sucked Life-Saver. "Now what?" he says to Janice.

"You could at least not be rude right away," she says.

"O.K., I'll be rude later. Let me guess. You're calling to tell me you've finally gotten around to getting a lawyer."

Janice laughs. It's been long since he heard it, a shy noise that tries to catch itself halfway out, like a snagged yo-yo. "No," she says, "I haven't gotten around to that yet. Is that what you're waiting for?" She is harder to bully now.

"I don't know what I'm waiting for."

"Is your mother there? Or are you downstairs?"

"Yes. Up."

"You sound that way. Harry—Harry, are you there?"

"Sure. Where else?"

"Would you like to meet me anyplace?" She hurries on, to make it business. "The insurance men keep calling me, I guess we owned the house jointly, they say you won't fill out any of the forms. They say we ought to be making some decisions. I mean about the house. Daddy already is trying to sell it for us."

"Typical."

"And then there's Nelson."

"You don't have room for him. You and your spic."

His mother looks away, shocked; studies her hands, and by an effort of will stops their idle waggling. Janice has taken a quick high breath. He cannot bump her off the line today. "That's another thing, sweetie. I've moved out. It's all decided, everything's fine. I mean, that way. With Charlie and me. I'm calling from my parents' place, I've spent the last two nights here. Harry?"

"I'm listening. I'm right here. What do you think, I'm going to run away?"

"You have before. I was talking to Peggy yesterday on the phone, she and Ollie are back together, and *he* had heard you had gone off to some other state, a newspaper in Baltimore had given you a job."

"Fat chance."

"And Peggy said she hadn't heard from you at all. I think she's hurt."

"Why should she be hurt?"

"She told me why."

"Yeah. She would. Hey. This is a lot of fun chatting, but did you have anything definite you want to say? You want Nelson to come live with the Springers, is that it? I suppose he might as well, he's—" he is going to confess that the boy is unhappy, but his mother is listening and it would hurt her feelings. Considering her condition, she has really put herself out for Nelson this time.

Janice understands, and asks, "Would you like to see me? I mean, would it make you too mad, looking at me?"

And he laughs; his own laugh is unfamiliar in his ears. "It might," he says, meaning it might not.

"Oh, let's," she says. "You want to come here? Or shall I come there?" She understands his silence, and confirms, "We need a third place. Maybe this is stupid, but what about the Penn Villas house? We can't go in, but we need to look at it and decide what to do, I mean somebody's offering to buy it, the bank talked to Daddy the other day."

"O.K. I got to make Mom lunch now. How about two?"

"And I want to give you something," Janice is going on, while Mom is signalling her need to be helped to the commode; her blue hand tightens white around the gnarled handle of the cane.

"Don't let her wriggle," is her advice, when he hangs up,

"her way. Around you." Sitting on the edge of the bed, Mom thumps the floor with her cane for emphasis, drawing an arc with the tip as illustration.

After putting the lunch dishes in the drainer Harry prepares for a journey. For clothes, he decides on the suntans he is wearing and has worn for two weeks straight, and a fresh white shirt as in his working days, and an old jacket he found in a chest in the attic: his high school athletic jacket. It carries MJ in pistachio green on an ivory shield on the back, and green sleeves emerge from V-striped shoulders. The front zips. Zipped, it binds across his chest and belly, but he begins that way, walking down Jackson Road under the chill maples; when the bus lets him out at Emberly, the warmer air of this lower land lets him unzip, and he walks jauntily flapping along the curving street where the little ranch houses have pumpkins on their porchlets and Indian corn on their doors.

His own house sticks out from way down Vista Crescent: black coal in a row of candies. His station wagon is parked there. The American flag decal is still on the back window. It looks aggressive, fading.

Janice gets out of the driver's seat and stands beside the car looking lumpy and stubborn in a charcoal-gray loden coat he remembers from winters past. He had forgotten how short she is, how the dark hair has thinned back from the tight forehead, with that oily shine that puts little bumps along the hairline. She has abandoned the madonna hairdo, wears her hair parted way over on one side, unflatteringly. But her mouth seems less tight; her lips have lost the crimp in the corners and seem much readier to laugh, with less to lose, than before. His instinct, crazy, is to reach out and pet her—do something, like tickle behind her ear, that you would do to a dog; but they do nothing. They do not kiss. They do not shake hands. "Where'd you resurrect that old Jock jacket?" He had forgotten that was what they called themselves: the Mt. Judge Jocks. Janice says, "I'd forgotten what awful school colors we had. Ick. Like one of those fake ice creams."

"I found it in an old trunk in my parents' attic. They've kept all that stuff. It still fits."

"Fits who?"

"A lot of my clothes got burned up." This note of apology because he sees she is right, it was an ice cream world he made his mark in. Yet she too is wearing something too young for her, with a hairdo reverting to adolescence, parted way over like those South American flames of the Forties. Chachacha.

She digs into a side pocket of the loden coat awkwardly. "I said I had a present for you. Here." What she hands him twinkles and dangles. The car keys.

"Don't you need it?"

"Not really. I can drive one of Daddy's. I don't know why I ever thought I did need it, I guess at first I thought we might escape to somewhere. Go out west. Canada. I don't know. We never even considered it."

He asks, "You're gonna stay at your parents'?"

Janice looks up past the jacket to him, seeking his face. "I can't stand it, really. Mother nags so. You can see she's been primed not to say anything to me, but it keeps coming out, she keeps using the phrase 'public opinion.' As if she's a Gallup poll. And Daddy. For the first time, he seems pathetic to me. Somebody is opening a Datsun agency in one of the shopping centers and he feels really personally threatened. I thought," Janice says, her dark eyes resting on his face lightly, ready to fly if what she sees there displeases her, "I might get an apartment somewhere. Maybe in Peggy's building. So Nelson could walk to school in West Brewer again. I'd have Nelson, of course." Her eyes dart away.

Rabbit says, "So the car is sort of a swap."

"More of a peace offering."

He makes the peace sign, then transfers it to his head, as horns. She is too dumb to get it. He tells her, "The kid is pretty miserable, maybe you ought to take him. Assuming you're through with Whatsisname."

"We're through."

"Why?"

Her tongue flicks between her lips, a mannerism that once struck him as falsely sensual but seems inoffensive now, like licking a pencil. "Oh," Janice says. "We'd done all we could together. He was beginning to get jittery. Your sweet sister didn't help, either."

"Yeah. I guess we were sort of hard on him." The "we"—him, her, Mim, Mom; ties of blood, of time and guilt, family ties. He does not ask her for more description. He has never understood exactly about women, why they have to menstruate for instance, or why they feel hot some times and not others, and how close the tip of your prick comes to their womb or whether the womb is a hollow place without a baby in it or what, and instinct disposes him to consign Stavros to that same large area of feminine mystery. He doesn't want to bring back any lovelight into her eyes, that are nice and quick and hard on him, the prey.

Perhaps she had prepared to tell him more, how great her love was and how pure it will remain, for she frowns as if checked by his silence. She asks him, "Why is Nelson miserable? Do you think."

He gestures at the burned green shell. "My clothes weren't the only thing went up in that."

"The girl. Were she and Nelson close?"

"She was sort of a sister. He keeps losing sisters."

"Poor baby boy."

Janice turns and they look together at where they lived. Some agency, the bank or the police or the insurance company, has put up a loose fence of posts and wire around it, but children have freely approached, picking the insides clean, smashing the windows, storm windows and all, in the half that still stands. Some person has taken the trouble to bring a spray can of yellow paint and has hugely written NIGGER on the side. Also the word KILL. The two words don't go together, so it is hard to tell which side the spray can had been on. Maybe there had been two spray cans. Demanding equal time. On the broad stretch of aluminum clapboards below the windows, where in spring daffodils come up and in summer phlox goes wild, yellow letters spell in half-script, *Pig Power is Clean Power.* Also there is a peace sign and a swastika, apparently from the same can. And other people, borrowing charred sticks from the rubble, have come along and tried to edit and add to these slogans and symbols, making Pig into Black and Clean into Cong. It all adds up no better than the cluster of commercials TV stations squeeze into the chinks between programs. A clown with a red spray can has scrawled between two windows TRICK OR TREAT.

Janice asks, "Where was she sleeping?"

"Upstairs. Where we did."

"Did you love her?" For this her eyes leave his face and contemplate the trampled lawn. He remembers that this gray coat originally had a hood.

He confesses to her, "Not like I should have. She was sort of *too* nice." Saying this makes him feel guilty, he imagines how hurt Jill would be hearing it, so to right himself he accuses Janice: "If you'd stayed in there, she'd still be alive."

Her eyes lift quickly. "No you don't. Don't try to pin *that* rap on me, Harry Angstrom. Whatever happened in there was your trip." Her trip drowns babies; his burns girls. They were made for each other. She offers to bring the truth into neutral. "Peggy says the Negro was doping her, that's what Billy says Nelson told him."

"She wanted it, he said. The Negro."

"Strange, he got away."

"Underground Railroad."

"Did you help him? Did you see him after the fire?"

"Slightly. Who says I did?"

"Nelson."

"How did he know?"

"He guessed."

"I drove him south into the county and let him off in a cornfield."

"I hope he's not ever going to come back. I don't want him, I mean, I wouldn't want him if—" Janice lets the thought die, premature.

Rabbit feels heightened and frozen by this giant need for tact; he and she seem to be slowly revolving, afraid of jarring one another away. "He promised he won't." Only in glory.

Relieved, Janice gestures toward the half-burned house. "It's worth a lot of money," she says. "The insurance company wants to settle for eight thousand. Some man talked to Daddy and offered nineteen-five. I guess the lot is worth seven or eight by itself, this is becoming such a fashionable area."

"I thought Brewer was dying."

"Only in the middle."

"Let's sell the bastard."

"Let's."

They shake hands. He twirls the car keys in front of her face. "Lemme drive you back to your parents'."

"Do we have to go there?"

"You could come to my place and visit Mom. She'd love to see you. She can hardly talk now."

"Let's save that," Janice says. "Could we just drive around?"

"Drive around? I'm not sure I still know how to drive."

"Peggy says you drove her Mustang."

"Gee. A person doesn't have many secrets in this county."

As they drive out Weiser toward the city, she asks, "Can your mother manage the afternoon alone?"

"Sure. She's managed a lot of them."

"I'm beginning to like your mother, she's quite nice to me, over the phone."

"She's mellowing." They cross the bridge and drive up Weiser in Brewer, past the Wallpaper Boutique, the roasted peanut newsstand, the expanded funeral home, the great stores with the façades where the pale shadow of the neon sign for the last owner underlies the hopeful bright sign the new owners have put up, the new trash disposal cans with tops like flying saucers, the blank marquees of the deserted movie palaces. They pass Pine Street and the Phoenix Bar. He announces, "I ought to be out scouting printshops for a job, maybe move to another city. Baltimore might be a good idea."

Janice says, "You look better since you stopped work. Your color is better. Wouldn't you be happier in an outdoor job?"

"They don't pay. Only morons work outdoors any more."

"I would keep working at Daddy's. I think I should."

"What does that have to do with me? You're going to get an apartment, remember?"

She doesn't answer again. Weiser is climbing too close to the mountain, to Mt. Judge and their homes. He turns left on Summer. Brick three-stories with fanlights; optometrists' and chiropractors' signs. A limestone church with a round window. He announces, "We could buy a farm."

She makes the connection. "Because Ruth did."

"That's right, I'd forgotten," he lies, "this was her street." Once he ran along this street toward the end and never got there.

To take his mind off Ruth, Janice asks, "How did you like Peggy?"

"Yeah, how about that? She's gotten to be quite a good lay."

"But you didn't go back."

"Couldn't stomach it, frankly. It wasn't her, she was great. But all this fucking, everybody fucking, I don't know, it just makes me too sad. It's what makes everything so hard to run."

"You don't think it's what *makes* things run? Human things."

"There must be something else."

She doesn't answer.

"No? Nothing else?"

Instead of answering, she says, "Ollie is back with her now, but she doesn't seem especially happy."

It is easy in a car; the STOP signs and corner groceries flicker by, brick and sandstone merge into a running screen. At the end of Summer Street he thinks there will be a brook, and then a dirt road and open pastures; but instead the city street broadens into a highway lined with hamburger diners, and drive-in sub shops, and a miniature golf course with big plaster dinosaurs, and food-stamp stores and motels and gas stations that are changing their names, Humble to Getty, Atlantic to Arco. He has been here before.

Janice says, "Want to stop?"

"I ate lunch. Didn't you?"

"Stop at a motel," she says.

"You and me?"

"You don't have to *do* anything, it's just we're wasting gas this way."

"Cheaper to waste gas than pay a motel, for Chrissake. Anyway don't they like you to have luggage?"

"They don't care. Anyway I think I did put a suitcase in the back, just in case."

He turns and looks and there it is, the tatty old brown one still with the hotel label on from the time they went to the Shore, *Wildwood Cabins*. The same suitcase she must have packed to run to Stavros with. "Say," he says. "You're full of sexy tricks now, aren't you?"

"Forget it, Harry. Take me home. I'd forgotten about you."

"These guys who run motels, don't they think it's fishy if you check in before suppertime? What time is it, two-thirty."

"Fishy? What's fishy, Harry? God, you're a prude. Everybody knows people screw. It's how we all got here. When're you going to grow up, even a little bit?"

"Still, to march right in with the sun pounding down—"

"Tell him I'm your wife. Tell him we're exhausted. It's the truth, actually. I didn't sleep two hours last night."

"Wouldn't you rather go to my parents' place? Nelson'll be home in an hour."

"Exactly. Who matters more to you, me or Nelson?"

"Nelson."

"Nelson or your mother?"

"My mother."

"You are a sick man."

"There's a place. Like it?"

Safe Haven Motel the sign says, with slats strung below it claiming

QUEEN SIZE BEDS
ALL COLOR TVS
SHOWER & BATH
TELEPHONES
"MAGIC FINGERS"

A neon VACANCY sign buzzes dull red. The office is a little brick tollbooth; there is a drained swimming pool with a green tarpaulin over it. At the long brick façade bleakly broken by doorways several cars already park; they seem to be feeding, metal cattle at a trough. Janice says, "It looks crummy."

"That's what I like about it," Rabbit says. "They might take us."

But as he says this, they have driven past. Janice asks, "Seriously, haven't you ever done this before?"

He tells her, "I guess I've led a kind of sheltered life."

"Well, it's by now," she says, of the motel.

"I could turn around."

"Then it'd be on the wrong side of the highway."

"Scared?"

"Of what?"

"Me." Racily Rabbit swings into a Garden Supplies parking lot, spewing gravel, brakes just enough to avoid a collision with oncoming traffic, crosses the doubled line, and heads back the way they came. Janice says, "If you want to kill yourself, go ahead, but don't kill me; I'm just getting to like being alive."

"It's too late," he tells her. "You'll be a grandmother in a couple more years."

"Not with you at the wheel."

But they cross the double line again and pull in safely. The VACANCY sign still buzzes. Ignition off. Lever at P. The sun shimmers on the halted asphalt. "You can't just *sit* here," Janice hisses. He gets out of the car. Air. Globes of ether, pure nervousness, slide down his legs. There is a man in the little tollbooth, along with a candy bar machine and a rack of black-tagged keys. He has wet-combed silver hair, a string tie with a horseshoe clasp, and a cold. Placing the registration card in front of Harry, he pats his chafed nostrils with a blue bandana. "Name and address and license plate number," he says. He speaks with a Western twang.

"My wife and I are really bushed," Rabbit volunteers. His ears are burning; the blush spreads downward, his undershirt feels damp, his heart jars his hand as it tries to write, *Mr. and Mrs. Harold Angstrom.* Address? Of course, he must lie. He writes unsteadily, *26 Vista Crescent, Penn Villas, Pa.* The junk mail and bills have been getting to him from that address. Wonderful service, the postal. Put yourself in one of those boxes, sorted from sack to sack, finally there you go, *plop,* through the right slot out of millions. Supernatural, that it works. Young punk revolutionaries, let them try to get the mail through, through rain and sleet and dark of night. The man with the string tie patiently leans on his formica desk while Rabbit's thoughts race and his hand jerks. "License plate number, that's the one that counts," he peaceably drawls. "Show me a suitcase or pay in advance."

"No kidding, she is my wife."

"Must be on honeymoon straight from haah school."

"Oh, this." Rabbit looks down at his peppermint-and-cream Mt. Judge athletic jacket, and fights the creeping return of his blush. "I haven't worn this for I don't know how many years."

"Looks to still fit," the man says, tapping the blank space for the plate number. "Ah'm in no hurry if you're not," he says.

Harry goes to the show window of the little house and studies the license plate and signals for Janice to show the suitcase. He lifts an imaginary suitcase up and down by the handle and she doesn't understand. Janice sits in their car, mottled and dimmed by window reflections, like some dubious modern product extravagantly wrapped, in a metal package rich with waste space. He pantomimes unpacking; he draws a rectangle in the air; he exclaims, "God, she's dumb!" and she belatedly understands, reaching back and lifting the bag into view through the layers of glass between them. The man nods; Harry writes his plate number (U20-692) on the card and is given a numbered key (17). "Toward the back," the man says, "more quaat away from the road."

"I don't care if it's quiet, we're just going to sleep," Rabbit says; key in hand, he bursts into friendliness. "Where're you from, Texas? I was stationed there with the Army once, Fort Hood, near El Paso."

The man inserts the card into a rack, looking through the lower half of his bifocals, and clucks his tongue. "You ever get up around Santa Fe?"

"Nope. Never. Sorry I didn't."

"That's my idea of a *goood* place," the man tells him.

"I'd like to go someday. I really would. Probably never will, though."

"Don't say that, young buck like you."

"I'm not so young."

"You're yungg," the man absentmindedly insists, and this is so nice of him, this and giving him the key, people are so nice generally, that Janice asks him as he gets back into the car what he's grinning about. "And what took so long?"

"We were talking about Santa Fe. He advised me to go."

The door numbered 17 gives on a room surprisingly long, narrow but long. The carpet is purple, and bits of backlit cardboard here and there undercut the sense of substance, as in a movie lobby. The bathroom is at the far end, the walls are of cement-block painted rose, imitation oils of the ocean are trying to adorn them, two queen-sized beds look across the narrow room at a television set. Rabbit takes off his shoes and turns on the set and gets on one bed. A band of light appears, expands, jogs itself out of diagonal twitching stripes into *The Dating Game*. A colored girl from Philly is trying to decide which of three men to take her out on a date; one man is black, another is white, the third is yellow. The color is such that the Chinese man is orange and the colored girl looks bluish. The reception has a ghost so when she laughs there are many, many teeth. Janice turns it off. Like him she is in stocking feet. They are burglars. He protests, "Hey. That was interesting. She couldn't see them behind that screen so she'd have to tell from their voices what color they were. If she cared."

"You *have* your date," Janice tells him.

"We ought to get a color television, the pro football is a lot better."

"Who's this we?"

"Oh—me and Pop and Nelson and Mom. And Mim."

"Why don't you move over on that bed?"

"You *have* your bed. Over there."

She stands there, firm-footed on the wall-to-wall carpet without stockings, nice-ankled. Her dull wool skirt is just short enough to show her knees. They have boxy edges. Nice. She asks, "What is this, a put-down?"

"Who am I to put you down? The swingingest broad on Eisenhower Avenue."

"I'm not so sure I like you any more."

"I didn't know I had that much to lose."

"Come on. Shove over."

She throws the old charcoal loden coat over the plastic chair beneath the motel regulations and the fire inspector's certificate. Being puzzled darkens her eyes on him. She pulls off her sweater and as she bends to undo her skirt the bones of her shoulders ripple in long quick glints like a stack of coins being spilled. She hesitates in her slip. "Are you going to get under the covers?"

"We could," Rabbit says, yet his body is as when a fever leaves and the nerves sink down like veins of water into sand. He cannot begin to execute the energetic transitions contemplated: taking off his clothes, walking that long way to the bathroom. He should probably wash in case she wants to go down on him. Then suppose he comes too soon and they are back where they've always been. Much safer to lie here enjoying the sight of her in her slip; he had been lucky to choose a little woman, they keep their shape better than big ones. She looked older than twenty at twenty but doesn't look that much older now, at least angry as she is, black alive in her eyes. "You can get in but don't expect anything, I'm still pretty screwed up." Lately he has lost the ability to masturbate; nothing brings him up, not even the image of a Negress with nipples like dowel-ends and a Hallowe'en pumpkin instead of a head.

"I'll say," Janice says. "Don't expect anything from me either. I just don't want to have to shout between the beds."

With heroic effort Rabbit pushes himself up and walks the

length of the rug to the bathroom. Returning naked, he holds his clothes in front of him and ducks into the bed as if into a burrow, being chased. He feels particles of some sort bombarding him. Janice feels skinny, strange, snaky-cool, the way she shivers tight against him immediately; the shock on his skin makes him want to sneeze. She apologizes: "They don't heat these places very well."

"Be November pretty soon."

"Isn't there a thermostat?"

"Yeah. I see it. Way over in the corner. You can go turn it up if you want."

"Thanks. The man should do that."

Neither moves. Harry says, "Hey. Does this remind you of Jeanette's bed?" Jeanette was the girl who when they were all working at Kroll's had an apartment in Brewer she let Harry and Janice use.

"Not much. That had a view."

They try to talk, but out of sleepiness and strangeness it only comes in spurts. "So," Janice says after a silence wherein nothing happens. "Who do you think you are?"

"Nobody," he answers. He snuggles down as if to kiss her breasts but doesn't; their presence near his lips drugs him. All sorts of winged presences exert themselves in the air above their covers.

Silence resumes and stretches, a ballerina in the red beneath his eyelids. He abruptly asserts, "The kid really hates me now."

Janice says, "No he doesn't." She contradicts herself promptly, by adding, "He'll get over it." Feminine logic: smother and outlast what won't be wished away. Maybe the only way. He touches her low and there is moss, it doesn't excite him, but it is reassuring, to have that patch there, something to hide in.

Her body irritably shifts; him not kissing her breasts or anything, she puts the cold soles of her feet on the tops of his. He sneezes. The bed heaves. She laughs. To rebuke her, he asks innocently, "You always came with Stavros?"

"Not always."

"You miss him now?"

"No."

"Why not?"

"You're here."

"But don't I seem sad, sort of?"

"You're making me pay, a little. That's all right."

He protests, "I'm a mess," meaning he is sincere: which perhaps is not a meaningful adjustment over what she had said. He feels they are still adjusting in space, slowly twirling in some gorgeous ink that filters through his lids as red. In a space of silence, he can't gauge how much, he feels them drift along sideways deeper into being married, so much that he abruptly volunteers, "We must have Peggy and Ollie over sometime."

"Like hell," she says, jarring him, but softly, an unexpected joggle in space. "You stay away from her now, you had your crack at it."

After a while he asks her—she knows everything, he realizes—"Do you think Vietnam will ever be over?"

"Charlie thought it would, just as soon as the big industrial interests saw that it was unprofitable."

"God, foreigners are dumb," Rabbit murmurs.

"Meaning Charlie?"

"All of you." He feels, gropingly, he should elaborate. "Skeeter thought it was the doorway into utter confusion. There would be this terrible period, of utter confusion, and then there would be a wonderful stretch of perfect calm, with him ruling, or somebody exactly like him."

"Did you believe it?"

"I would have liked to, but I'm too rational. Confusion is just a local view of things working out in general. That make sense?"

"I'm not sure," Janice says.

"You think Mom ever had any lovers?"

"Ask her."

"I don't dare."

After another while, Janice announces, "If you're not going to make love, I might as well turn my back and get some sleep. I was up almost all night worrying about this—reunion."

"How do you think it's going?"

"Fair."

The slither of sheets as she rotates her body is a silver music, sheets of pale noise extending outward unresisted by space. There was a grip he used to have on her, his right hand cupping her skull through her hair and his left hand on her breasts gathering them together, so the nipples were an inch apart. The grip is still there. Her ass and legs float away. He asks her, "How do we get out of here?"

"We put on our clothes and walk out the door. But let's have a nap first. You're talking nonsense already."

"It'll be so embarrassing. The guy at the desk'll think we've been up to no good."

"He doesn't care."

"He does, he *does* care. We could stay all night to make him feel better, but nobody else knows where we are. They'll worry."

"Stop it, Harry. We'll go in an hour. Just shut up."

"I feel so guilty."

"About what?"

"About everything."

"Relax. Not everything is your fault."

"I can't accept that."

He lets her breasts go, lets them float away, radiant debris. The space they are in, the motel room long and secret as a burrow, becomes all interior space. He slides down an inch on the cool sheet and fits his microcosmic self limp into the curved crevice between the polleny offered nestling orbs of her ass; he would stiffen but his hand having let her breasts go comes upon the familiar dip of her waist, ribs to hip bone, where no bones are, soft as flight, fat's inward curve, slack, his babies from her belly. He finds this inward curve and slips along it, sleeps. He. She. Sleeps. O.K.?

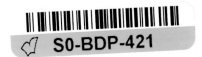

HORST HEGEWALD-KAWICH

mon chiot

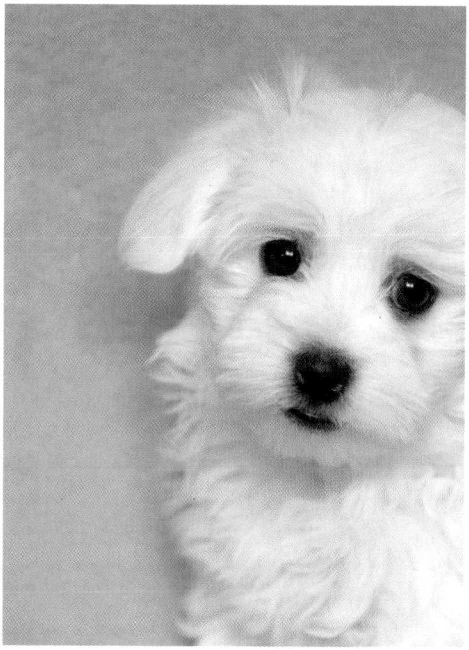

• MARABOUT •

SOMMAIRE

1 Typiquement chien

2 La vie rêvée du chiot

Bienvenue à la maison

3

Une alimentation saine

4

5 Soins et santé

6 Éducation et activité

La communication

7

En cas de problème

8

Annexes

Typiquement chien

Le chien est souvent l'ami le plus fidèle et le plus fiable de son maître. Il ne le critique pas et répond à ses attentes. Sa seule exigence : que l'homme apprenne à connaître et à comprendre sa nature.

Ce que tous les chiens ont en commun

Même si des milliers d'années de cohabitation entre l'homme et le chien ont modifié le comportement de nos compagnons, ils conservent une bonne part de leur héritage venu du loup.

L'ASCENDANCE DU CHIEN *(Canis familiaris)* et sa parenté avec le loup *(Canis lupus)* sont désormais établies scientifiquement grâce à de récentes analyses génétiques qui ont écarté les derniers doutes.

Cela fait des milliers d'années que l'homme, qui vivait alors encore de la chasse et de la cueillette, a commencé à domestiquer le loup, sans doute en élevant des louveteaux qui ont donné naissance au chien au cours des millénaires.

Il ne s'agissait alors pas uniquement d'apprivoiser des loups, mais de « créer » le chien, au moyen de sélections ciblées parmi des loups élevés isolément. Les raisons semblent d'abord en avoir été uniquement sociales car ces premiers « chiens-loups » n'étaient d'aucune utilité.

On est parfaitement en droit de croire que les femmes et les enfants de nos ancêtres trouvaient alors les louveteaux tout aussi mignons que nous trouvons aujourd'hui les chiots.

Pour élever les louveteaux, il fallait du lait. Or, les animaux utiles comme les vaches ou les chèvres n'existaient pas encore. Par conséquent, ce sont sans doute les femmes qui allaitaient les louveteaux, en plus de leurs enfants.

L'empreinte de l'homme

L'élevage de louveteaux isolés de leurs congénères a peu à peu créé par empreinte des liens sociaux forts centrés autour de l'homme. Les louveteaux se sont éloignés de leurs cousins sauvages qui sont devenus des étrangers pour eux. Aujourd'hui encore, le chien occupe une place à part parmi les animaux domestiques : aucun autre ne se concentre aussi exclusivement sur l'homme dans son comportement social et ne développe un tel attachement et une telle fidélité envers nous. C'est ce qui en fait un partenaire si agréable.

Les louveteaux sont aussi turbulents dans leurs jeux que le sont les chiots.

La première année

Les chiens sont des animaux extrêmement intelligents, dotés d'une très grande sensibilité et capacité d'adaptation et dont le comportement social ressemble à celui de l'homme.
Les mécanismes de ce comportement social inné doivent cependant être entraînés et consolidés, surtout pendant les 16 premières semaines. Pour cela, il est important que le chiot rencontre régulièrement des congénères, de son âge et plus âgés, ou d'autres hommes et qu'il apprenne à connaître les environnements les plus divers. En effet, c'est à cet âge que les bases de son futur comportement social sont jetées et la première année est la plus importante dans la vie d'un chien. Son caractère se développe, sa nature définitive prend forme, résultat de ses prédispositions innées et de l'environnement façonné par l'homme.
Jusqu'à sa maturité sexuelle, le chiot traverse les phases de développement suivantes :

- phase végétative (1re et 2e semaines)
- phase de transition (3e semaine)
- phase d'imprégnation (4e à 7e semaine)
- phase de socialisation (8e à 12e semaine)
- phase de hiérarchisation (13e à 16e semaine)
- phase d'ordre dans la meute (5e et 6e mois), suivie de la phase de puberté.

1 **« Amour fraternel » :** Les jeux en commun font naître un fort sentiment d'appartenance entre les chiots, même s'ils y font parfois preuve d'une extrême rudesse.

2 **Entraînement à la vie :** Les bagarres et luttes permettent aux chiots de tester en s'amusant les rôles sociaux de chacun et leur capacité à s'imposer. Les jeux de combat leur donnent l'occasion de s'exercer sans risque à des comportements essentiels pour leur survie.

Le chiot du haut veut en imposer et témoigne clairement d'un comportement de domination.

Toutes les expériences positives et négatives vécues par le chien au cours de ces différentes phases le marquent d'une empreinte quasi innée. Les processus d'apprentissage de la première année fusionnent les comportements innés et acquis (appris) du jeune chien pour produire un caractère bon et équilibré ou mauvais et faible. Les occasions passées ne peuvent alors plus être rattrapées.

La nature du chien

« La nature d'un chien est la somme de ses comportements innés et acquis, ainsi que de ses états internes du moment avec lesquels il réagit à son environnement. »
Cela comprend plus précisément son attachement à son maître, son comportement envers les hommes et les chiens étrangers et sa tendance à la domination. Son tempérament et sa vitalité, sa capacité à apprendre et sa motivation jouent également un rôle important.
Il faut y ajouter son intelligence instinctive (talents innés propres à certaines races, comme la surveillance d'un troupeau pour le border collie), ainsi que l'intelligence du travail (ce dont le chien est capable pour exécuter un travail ou un exercice sportif) et l'intelligence adaptative qui lui permet d'appliquer correctement et de combiner ce qu'il a appris, par exemple en tant que chien de chasse ou chien policier, pour venir à bout des situations les plus diverses. Enfin, l'intelligence sociale du chien détermine son rapport à l'homme.

Les points communs au chien et au loup

Bien que la plupart des races actuelles de chiens ne ressemblent plus guère au loup, on reconnaît encore leur proche parenté à divers aspects physiques, aux sens et instincts héréditaires et aux organes. De même, de nombreux comportements du chien viennent de ceux du loup, et sont donc des comportements naturels – même si certaines de leurs manifestations s'avèrent parfois importunes. Malgré ces points communs, il importe de bien réaliser que nos chiens ne sont plus des loups depuis longtemps du fait de la domestication et sous l'effet du milieu dans lequel ils vivent désormais depuis longtemps.

Les ressemblances physiques : Les chiens ont le pied léger et se déplacent à différentes allures pas toujours faciles à distinguer. Ils peuvent aussi en changer très rapidement et ce sont des chasseurs, des sauteurs ou, pour certains, des grimpeurs habiles. Leur squelette (321 os) est mobile car les os sont reliés les uns aux autres par des articulations, des muscles et des tendons. Les chiens sont digitigrades et marchent sur quatre doigts. Le cinquième, qui correspond à notre pouce, est situé plus haut sur la face interne du métatarse. Quant au cinquième doigt de l'arrière-main, l'ergot, il ressemble à une griffe de loup mais n'a aucune fonction et les éleveurs raisonnables le coupent dès la naissance pour éviter tout risque de blessure.

La dentition naturelle des chiens forme un ciseau dans lequel les dents de la mâchoire supérieure (sauf les molaires postérieures) recouvrent la face externe de la rangée de dents inférieure.

Les sélections successives ont donné naissance à des décalages ou prognathismes chez certaines races : les chiens bégus ont les incisives inférieures qui dépassent des supérieures, tandis que chez les grignards, les incisives inférieures sont très en arrière des supérieures, au point de toucher parfois le palais.

Un chien adulte a 42 dents, les chiots ont 28 dents de lait et les dents définitives poussent entre le 4e et le 6e mois.

Les organes internes : Comme sa dentition, les organes digestifs du chien sont ceux d'un carnivore. Son estomac notamment est beaucoup plus gros que celui d'un herbivore, tandis que son tube digestif est très court. Par ailleurs, c'est aussi un charognard, au grand regret de beaucoup de propriétaires de chiens. Le cœur d'un chien en bonne santé est conçu pour fonctionner en régime continu mais ne récupère pas aussi vite que chez le loup après un effort. Les poumons eux aussi sont ceux d'un chasseur et très performants.

La peau et les poils : Le pelage du chien lui sert à compenser les différences de température en cas de froid ou de chaleur excessifs. En effet, il ne

LE SAVIEZ-VOUS ?

400 millions de chiens vivent dans la rue.

Parmi les 600 millions de chiens du monde, près de 400 millions sont contraints de vivre dans la rue dans des conditions indignes, sans personne de référence et à demi sauvages. En Allemagne par exemple, 5,3 millions de chiens sont officiellement recensés, mais 80 000 d'entre eux environ, « sans maître », sont pris en charge chaque année par les refuges pour animaux. Un bien triste bilan pour le fidèle et si sympathique compagnon de l'homme.

C'est aujourd'hui scientifiquement avéré, sans doute possible : **le chien descend du loup.** Tous les propriétaires de chiens devraient en être conscients.

possède ni glandes sudoripares, ni pores cutanés, et doit abaisser sa température corporelle en haletant en cas de trop grosse chaleur. Parmi les multiples types de pelage créés par l'homme, le poil court à duvet, tel notamment celui du berger allemand, est celui qui ressemble le plus à celui du loup et le mieux adapté à toutes les zones climatiques.

Des sens particulièrement développés

L'homme n'est supérieur au chien que pour le goût, nous avons le dessous pour tous les autres sens. Notre avantage gustatif est facile à expliquer : après tout, l'estomac du chien et du loup est conçu pour absorber des aliments naturels et le lapin à la crème d'estragon ou le canard à l'orange ne figurent pas au menu dans la nature. D'autres études scientifiques aux résultats stupéfiants ont mis en évidence chez certains chiens de véritables dons de télépathie : ils avertissent leurs maîtres avant une crise d'épilepsie ou d'hypoglycémie et annoncent les tremblements de terre plusieurs jours à l'avance. De même, leur sens de l'orientation ou leur compréhension de l'état psychique de leur maître sont pour nous une source constante d'étonnement.

L'odorat: Les odeurs sont composées de molécules extrêmement fines qui flottent en suspension dans l'air ou adhérent aux objets. Pour les percevoir, le berger allemand possède 220 millions de cellules olfactives, tandis que le teckel n'en a « que » 125 millions et que l'homme se contente de cinq millions environ. Ce don héréditaire exceptionnel que possèdent les chiens a parfois été amélioré par l'élevage et la sélection pour le spécialiser, notamment chez les chiens de chasse et de piste.

L'odorat joue aussi un rôle essentiel pour la compréhension des chiens entre eux (communication olfactive). En effet, contrairement à notre monde d'impressions visuelles, le chien perçoit son environnement sous forme d'images olfactives intenses qu'il stocke dans sa mémoire. Cette mémoire olfactive lui permet notamment de s'orienter et la facilité avec laquelle il retrouve le chemin de la maison grâce à son nez tient souvent du miracle à nos yeux.

Se lécher les commissures des lèvres est un geste de salutation affectueuse pour les chiens.

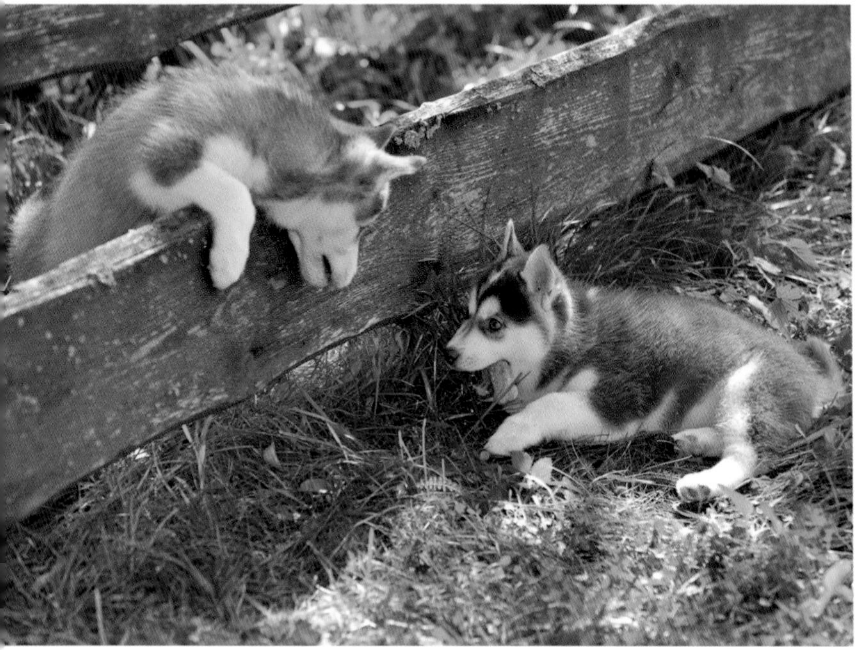

La curiosité et la volonté de découvrir sont les principaux mobiles de l'apprentissage pour les chiots. Observer et renifler tout ce qui les entoure les stimule et les rend plus autonomes.

C'est pourquoi il est très important de solliciter et d'entraîner chaque jour le flair des chiots (› page 105).

La vue : Comme son ancêtre le loup, le chien perçoit parfaitement les mouvements, même si cette faculté ne lui sert plus depuis longtemps – depuis qu'il ne vit plus de la chasse. Il voit le moindre mouvement de très loin, même celui des animaux les plus rapides ou les objets qui roulent et se déplacent. Chez la plupart des chiens, le mouvement est un stimulus qui déclenche aussitôt l'instinct de proie ou de poursuite (› page 129), ce qui peut s'avérer dangereux avec la circulation lorsqu'un chien pas encore éduqué n'est pas tenu en laisse.

Les chiens ne distinguent pas les couleurs aussi nettement que l'homme car il importe peu à un « prédateur » de connaître la couleur de sa proie. En revanche, une couche réfléchissante au fond de l'œil donne au chien comme au loup une bonne vision crépusculaire. Il perçoit essentiellement un spectre de couleurs allant du jaune au vert et au bleu, mais les objets que nous voyons comme verts lui paraissent incolores et le rouge lui apparaît jaune.

L'ouïe : La forme naturelle des oreilles du chien est la forme relevée héritée du loup. Les oreilles pivotent individuellement comme un capteur radar et peuvent localiser et identifier des bruits de toutes les directions. Le chien entend également les ultrasons (sons de plus de 20 000 hertz), par exemple le trottinement d'une souris. Il est donc très supérieur à l'homme en ce qui concerne la perception de sons très faibles. Les éleveurs ont aujourd'hui créé d'autres formes d'oreilles, comme par exemple les oreilles semi-dressées du collie ou les oreilles tombantes de nombreuses races de chiens de chasse. La réduction des oreilles et de la queue par coupage (castration) telle qu'elle a été longtemps pratiquée, notamment chez les boxers, est désormais interdite en France, même s'il existe malheureusement encore des « amoureux des chiens » qui trouvent du plaisir à posséder des animaux ainsi mutilés, que cela ne gêne pas de voir leur protégé limité dans sa communication avec ses congénères comme avec son maître et qui font couper leur chien à l'étranger ou y acquièrent un chien déjà « coupé ».

Le toucher : Ce sens permet au chien de ressentir les contacts, la température et la douleur. L'animal porte sur les joues, la gorge et le menton, les sourcils et la « moustache » des poils tactiles, ou vibrisses, aux extrémités nerveuses extrêmement sensibles. Son toucher est particulièrement développé au niveau du mufle, des lèvres, de la langue et des coussinets des pattes. Il est particulièrement mis à contribution lorsque le chien joue avec des congénères, lèche ou donne des coups de pattes. Il peut ainsi apprendre alors qu'il est encore un chiot à reconnaître, par exemple que son partenaire a mal, pour adapter à l'avenir son comportement lors des jeux et des bagarres.

Les fameux instincts

Tout ce que le chien entreprend de faire toute la journée est déclenché et déterminé par ses instincts innés.

Les principaux instincts du chien sont :

- L'instinct de meute, important pour la soumission et l'obéissance.
- L'instinct de proie, nécessaire à la chasse.
- L'instinct alimentaire, essentiel à la survie.

MON ANIMAL DOMESTIQUE

Comment se forme le caractère du chiot ?

Analysez le développement de votre chiot dans toutes les situations. Consignez vos résultats et notez les modifications positives ou négatives de son caractère avant d'essayer de les élucider.

Début du test :

- ○ Quelle est la force de l'attachement que porte le chiot à chaque membre de la famille ?
- ○ Comment se comporte-t-il envers les étrangers et les chiens qu'il ne connaît pas ?
- ○ Se soumet-il docilement ?
- ○ Quelle est la force de son tempérament et de sa vitalité ?
- ○ Comment peut-il être motivé à quel jeu ?

Résultat du test :

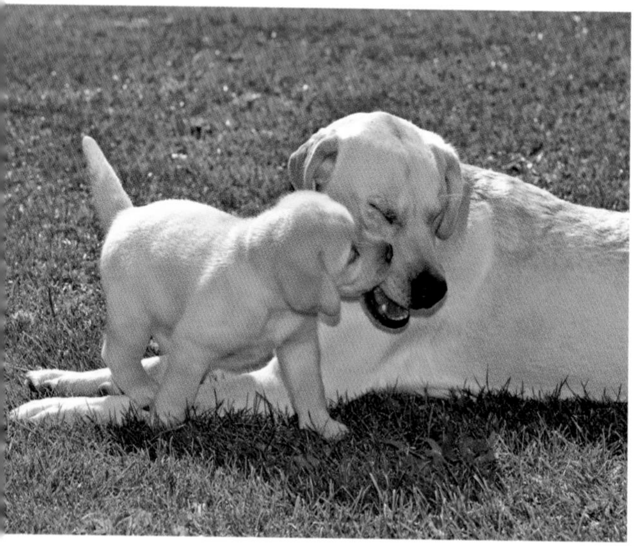

La mère ne veut pas toujours ce que veut son petit. Elle le lui fait savoir clairement.

- L'instinct de curiosité, mobile de l'apprentissage.
- L'instinct d'agression, qui se manifeste chez les chiens de garde et de défense. Il n'est en revanche pas souhaitable chez les chiens de famille et doit être réprimé dès l'éducation du chiot.
- L'instinct de fuite, qui peut sauver la vie du chien.
- L'instinct sexuel, qui assure la préservation de l'espèce.
- L'instinct de sommeil, qui permet au chien de se détendre.
- L'instinct de soins corporels, qui maintient l'animal en bonne santé et contribue à des comportements de confort, par exemple lorsque le chien s'étire ou se secoue.
- L'instinct maternel, indispensable chez les chiennes pour élever leurs petits.
- L'instinct d'élimination, qui doit être régulé pendant l'éducation du chiot pour le rendre propre.

Tous ces instincts ou pulsions sont hérités du loup, ils sont pour la plupart encore essentiels à la survie des chiens et peuvent être déclenchés à tout moment par le stimulus correspondant. L'éducation peut freiner ces instincts ou, au contraire, les renforcer, mais en aucun cas les inhiber complètement. Certains de ces instincts, comme par exemple l'instinct sexuel, ne se développent que chez le chien adulte ; d'autres, comme l'instinct de proie, sont déjà parfaitement développés chez le chiot mais ne s'éveillent complètement qu'avec le succès (capture de la proie). Toujours en ce qui concerne l'instinct de proie, il est déclenché par un stimulus typique, par exemple un lapin, et place le chien dans une « disposition instinctive » avant de susciter l'« action instinctive » correspondante, à savoir la poursuite du lapin, qui se termine éventuellement par l'« acte final » et la « satisfaction de l'instinct », la capture et le dépeçage de la proie.

La rapidité de réaction d'un chien à un stimulus dépend de son seuil de stimulation du moment : s'il est bas, l'animal réagira littéralement « à la toux d'une puce », alors que s'il est, au contraire, élevé, le chien sera difficile à stimuler. Chez un même chien, le seuil de stimulation ne dépend pas uniquement du caractère, mais peut varier selon les cas. Pour en savoir plus sur les instincts du chien, voir les chapitres suivants.

Les races de chiens

Qui n'a jamais eut le coup de foudre pour une race et un adorable chiot ? Dans les pages qui suivent, vous pouvez voir à quoi ressemblera votre chouchou à l'âge adulte et quelles sont ses qualités.

LORSQUE L'HOMME a commencé à découvrir l'utilité et les différentes possibilités d'emploi du chien, il a aussi commencé à accoupler uniquement les chiens qui répondaient le mieux à ses exigences. La force, la vitesse, l'endurance et la santé étaient alors les plus prisées. En même temps, les apparences se sont diversifiées sous l'égide de l'homme, grâce à la variabilité interespèce héritée du loup et parce que toutes sortes de chiens ont été créées, aussi bien des chiens de grande taille que des chiens nains ou des chiens au pelage de différentes couleurs – qui n'auraient pas survécu seuls dans la nature. Il n'était pas encore question de races, uniquement de sélection par croisement de différentes variétés de chiens, ce que l'on appelle aujourd'hui des bâtards.

L'élevage ciblé

Ce n'est qu'au début du XIXe siècle, ou pour certaines races récentes au début du XXe siècle, que l'élevage en race pure a débuté avec l'accouplement de chiens de même race ou de même variété à l'ascendance garantie. Pour cela, on a commencé à tenir des livres d'élevage et à établir des arbres généalogiques, les standards établis définissant l'aspect préconisé pour chaque race. Dès la deuxième moitié du XIXe siècle cependant, on a noté les effets néfastes des unions consanguines sur les chiens ainsi élevés et remarqué que les bâtards étaient souvent épargnés par les maladies génétiques propres à certaines races : c'est ce qu'on appelle l'hétérosis ou vitalité des croisements.
On n'a plus aujourd'hui que rarement recours à l'élevage par croisement pour obtenir un idéal de beauté ou certains standards de race – à mon avis nuisibles aux animaux. La pratique connaît en revanche de grands succès pour élever des animaux d'utilité et accroître leur vitalité.

ASTUCE

Fédérations et associations

La Fédération Cynologique Internationale (FCI) existe depuis 1911. En France, la Société Centrale Canine (SCC) lui est affiliée, ainsi que 147 associations de races spécialisées (❯ Adresses utiles, page 141). Il existe aujourd'hui 339 races de chiens reconnues.

D'un seul coup d'œil : portraits de races

West Highland White Terrier

Les ancêtres du « westie » étaient des terriers cairns bruns. La variante blanche, le West Highland White Terrier, a été créée pour mieux la différencier des lapins et des renards à la chasse. Le « westie » fait aujourd'hui partie des chiens domestiques et de famille les plus appréciés. Il est parfois un peu têtu mais se rattrape avec son charme si particulier. Contrairement aux autres terriers, il est très peu agressif.

Cavalier King Charles Spaniel

Sa beauté séduit de plus en plus depuis quelque temps. Il présente aussi toutes les qualités d'un chien de famille spécialement adapté à la ville. Le Cavalier King Charles Spaniel est facile à élever et aime jouer avec les enfants.

▲
Carlin

Une forte personnalité dont le fan-club ne cesse de croître. Veiller à ce qu'il ait un museau suffisamment développé.

▲
Teckel

On lui donnerait le bon Dieu sans confession, mais il n'est pas pour autant tombé de la dernière pluie. Il doit être systématiquement éduqué dès son plus jeune âge pour ne pas qu'il prenne la direction de la « meute » homme-chien. Il joue parfois les « faux durs » envers les enfants.

Schnauzer miniature ▶

Il n'a rien à envier au teckel pour la roublardise. Fonceur intrépide, c'est aussi un bon gardien même s'il peut alors aboyer très fort.

▲
Chihuahua

Le plus petit chien du monde a aussi une personnalité dont il faut tenir compte. Il est éveillé et attentif.

West Highland White Terrier

Le « westie » serait issu du terrier cairn brun roux et aurait été créé après que le chien favori de la famille Malcolm of Poltalloch a été pris par erreur pour un renard et tué pendant une chasse. Le poil d'un blanc éclatant du westie le rend plus reconnaissable. Il est très à la mode depuis les années 1970, à tel point que des « reproducteurs » sans scrupule ont gagné des fortunes au détriment de la qualité de la race. Veillez par conséquent à l'acheter chez un éleveur sérieux. Ce petit chien toujours prêt à jouer, mais sûr de lui, est aussi une forte personnalité. Son entretien est difficile car il doit régulièrement être tondu. Chien de famille idéal pour les enfants, il convient aussi aux débutants et aux personnes âgées.

Cavalier King Charles Spaniel

Chiens favoris des rois d'Angleterre, ils ressemblent au King Charles Spaniel dont le museau est cependant plus long et qui est un peu plus grand. Le Cavalier King Charles Spaniel est un chien idéal pour la ville, il connaît actuellement une popularité croissante à laquelle on doit un élevage de masse à grand renfort d'unions consanguines, ce qui a entraîné une forte recrudescence des maladies cardiaques mortelles. Lors de l'achat, vérifier les antécédents médicaux sur plusieurs générations. Chien gai et amical, il est affectueux et très attaché à son maître. Il aime les promenades mais reste volontiers à la maison par mauvais temps. Convient aux personnes âgées et aux éleveurs débutants.

Teckel, basset

Encore très utilisé comme chien d'utilité à la chasse, il était appelé « chien de blaireau » ou « chien de terrier » au Moyen Âge, un nom qui en dit long sur son utilité. L'élevage en race pure ne date que de 1888. Le teckel existe avec trois types de poils : poil court, poil long et poil dur et en trois tailles : teckel, teckel nain et teckel kaninchen. Il est intéressant de noter que la taille n'est pas mesurée au garrot comme pour toutes les autres races de chiens, mais à la poitrine, derrière les pattes antérieures. Le teckel est très éveillé, attachant et intelligent. Il doit être traité avec fermeté et cohérence pour ne pas qu'il prenne la direction des opérations. Il rivalise depuis des années avec le berger allemand comme chien le plus apprécié.

Carlin

Le carlin est arrivé de Chine en Europe au XVIIe siècle. Ses ancêtres auraient été créés il y a 2400 ans à partir de dogues pour accompagner les prêtres bouddhistes. Introduit en Hollande par la Compagnie néerlandaise des Indes orientales, il a d'abord été le compagnon des aristocrates et des rois, mais cela fait longtemps qu'il est devenu le chien d'agrément idéal et qu'on le voit aussi courir et sauter en haletant drôlement dans toutes les sociétés. Il est joueur, amical et intelligent. Il peut facilement être éduqué mais est parfois un peu borné. Pour l'achat, choisir un éleveur qui ne tienne pas à un museau trop court afin qu'il puisse respirer librement. Le carlin est un compagnon idéal pour les personnes âgées qui aiment les chiens et les éleveurs débutants.

Chihuahua

Son origine n'est pas attestée avec précision, mais le plus petit chien du monde passe pour avoir déjà existé au temps des Aztèques, du moins sa variante à poil court. Les premiers ont dû arriver en Amérique en 1519 avec les conquérants espagnols : les Aztèques auraient considéré les sujets bleus comme sacrés et sacrifié les roux lors des crémations.
Le chihuahua est affectueux, câlin, éveillé et attentif. Lors des rencontres avec de gros chiens, il affiche parfois une certaine tendance à la mégalomanie et ne tient alors plus compte d'aucune règle du savoir-vivre canin s'il n'a pas été suffisamment socialisé pendant la phase d'imprégnation.
Il n'aime ni être mouillé, ni avoir froid et s'énerve facilement en présence d'enfants trop entreprenants. Il convient bien aux personnes âgées et aux éleveurs débutants.

Schnauzer miniature

Le schnauzer miniature est la copie en miniature du grand schnauzer et était autrefois un grand chasseur de rats.
Il est exposé comme une race à part entière depuis 1899. C'est aujourd'hui un chien de compagnie apprécié. Malheureusement, l'élevage de masse lui vaut parfois une certaine faiblesse de caractère ou des maladies congénitales, mais les sujets de bonne lignée sont des compagnons sûrs d'eux et des gardiens intrépides, bien que parfois bruyants. Il s'entend bien avec les enfants et les autres chiens et met beaucoup d'empressement à s'intégrer à sa famille. Les schnauzers en général perdent très peu de poils mais leur pelage a besoin de soins réguliers (tontes). S'il est élevé avec fermeté, ce sera un compagnon idéal pour les personnes âgées et les éleveurs débutants.

Berger australien

Il fait partie du « top ten » des races les plus appréciées en Amérique. Plein de tempérament, il a besoin de mouvement et d'activités qui le stimulent.

Caniche

Chien de chasse créé pour la chasse aquatique, il a donné naissance à de nombreuses races de chiens de chasse et de berger.

Cocker américain

Il a aussi été en son temps un chien « à la mode », ce qui n'étonnera personne tant il est mignon. La race en a cependant souffert du fait de « reproducteurs » irresponsables. Heureusement, il est aujourd'hui produit par des éleveurs sérieux et soucieux de qualité.

Cocker anglais

Ci-dessus une variante noire de cocker. Le cocker américain est issu du cocker anglais.

Labrador Retriever

C'est aujourd'hui le chien de famille et d'enfants numéro un. Il a les nerfs solides et un caractère équilibré. Il montre un désir de plaire à son maître prononcé. Les attaches familiales fortes sont particulièrement importantes pour ce chien.

Parson Russell Terrier

Le Parson Russel et son petit frère plus court sur pattes, le terrier Jack Russel, sont à réserver aux maîtres sportifs qui peuvent leur offrir suffisamment d'activité.

Golden Retriever

Ci-dessus un sujet au poil presque blanc. Comme le labrador retriever, le golden retriever est un nageur passionné et il aime rapporter.

Berger australien ou Australian Shepherd

Les éleveurs de moutons de plusieurs pays émigrés aux États-Unis ont apporté avec eux leurs chiens de berger qui se sont croisés avec les chiens sauvages australiens, ou dingos, et les collies, venus d'Australie aux États-Unis avec les importations de moutons, pour donner naissance au berger australien. Il fait aujourd'hui partie des races les plus appréciées aux États-Unis. Sportif de talent, il envahit aussi depuis quelques années nos terrains de sport canin. Il est endurant et plein de tempérament, il se montre amical envers l'homme et pacifique envers les autres animaux. Il apprend facilement et très volontiers, mais a besoin d'être sollicité par les activités correspondantes et de beaucoup de mouvement. C'est le chien de famille parfait pour les débutants sportifs.

Caniche

Cette race de chiens de chasse est très ancienne mais son origine est mal connue. On sait seulement que c'était un excellent chien de chasse, particulièrement dans l'eau. Il a donné naissance à de nombreuses autres races de chiens de chasse et de berger. Malgré ses « coiffures » parfois originales, c'est aujourd'hui l'un des chiens de compagnie les plus appréciés. Il existe en quatre tailles : grand ou caniche royal, moyen, nain et toy. Le caniche a été très à la mode entre 1950 et 1970 et la race a alors extrêmement souffert de l'élevage de masse. Elle se remet aujourd'hui grâce à de bons éleveurs. Le caniche apprend tout, il aime la marche, est très robuste et veut tout faire avec son maître. Il doit être tondu régulièrement mais ne perd pas de poils. C'est le chien idéal pour les éleveurs débutants.

Cocker spaniel

La race descend de chiens de chasse espagnols, comme l'indique l'appellation « spaniel ». Les cockers spaniels auraient chassé la bécasse au XIXe siècle. Ils pouvaient fouiller, donner de la voix lorsqu'ils étaient sur les traces du gibier, rapporter et indiquer aux chasseurs le gibier abattu. Aujourd'hui, ils ne sont presque plus élevés que comme chien de compagnie. Les races de cocker les plus connues sont le cocker anglais et le cocker américain qui en descend. Elles sont toutes les deux vivantes et joueuses en famille, amicales et ouvertes. Les cockers sont faciles à éduquer mais il importe de montrer de la fermeté sans dureté. Ils ont besoin de beaucoup d'activité et prennent un grand plaisir au sport canin sans exagération. C'est un chien pour les éleveurs débutants et sportifs.

Labrador Retriever

Il a le pelage noir, blond ou brun. Outre ses qualités de chasseur, c'est un excellent chien antidrogue, mais surtout chien guide d'aveugles. Il est attachant, a les nerfs solides, est patient et aime jouer avec les enfants, ne braconne et ne rôde pas. Il a besoin d'une éducation ferme, mais sans violence. Les labradors ont tendance au surpoids et à la goinfrerie, mais un excès de graisse les rend moins mobiles et ennuyeux. Dans sa région d'origine, le sud de Terre-Neuve, il était utilisé pour le travail aquatique, d'où son amour de l'eau. C'est un compagnon très facile, même pour les éleveurs débutants.

Golden Retriever

Cette race a été créée par Lord Tweedmouth en 1868 par croisement entre un labrador jaune, un tweed-water spaniel, un setter irlandais et un Saint-Hubert couleur sable, toutes races dont descend donc le Golden Retriever. De nature semblable à celle du labrador, c'est un chien de famille à bonne capacité d'adaptation, moins polyvalent cependant que le labrador. Moins audacieux que ce dernier, c'est comme lui un nageur et un rapporteur passionné qui a besoin de beaucoup d'activité et de l'éducation correspondante. Chien à la mode, la race a souffert de l'élevage de masse, mais les sujets de bonne lignée conviennent parfaitement aux éleveurs débutants.

Parson Russel Terrier

Jusqu'à 1980, les terriers de chasse blancs et colorés n'ont été élevés que pour leur utilité, comme le voulait leur inventeur, le révérend Parson Russell. La race est aujourd'hui produite selon les prescriptions d'un standard très précis. Le « pasteur chasseur » du Devon, dans l'ouest de l'Angleterre, préférait le type à poil dur, haut sur pattes pour accompagner les chasseurs à cheval et assez petit pour traquer les renards dans leurs terriers. La plus petite variante, aux pattes plus courtes, est reconnue sous le nom de terrier Jack Russel. Les deux races ont un caractère indépendant et une volonté farouche de s'imposer qui n'en font pas les meilleurs chiens de compagnie. Ce ne sont pas des chiens pour éleveurs débutants, ni pour les maîtres âgés qui recherchent la paix.

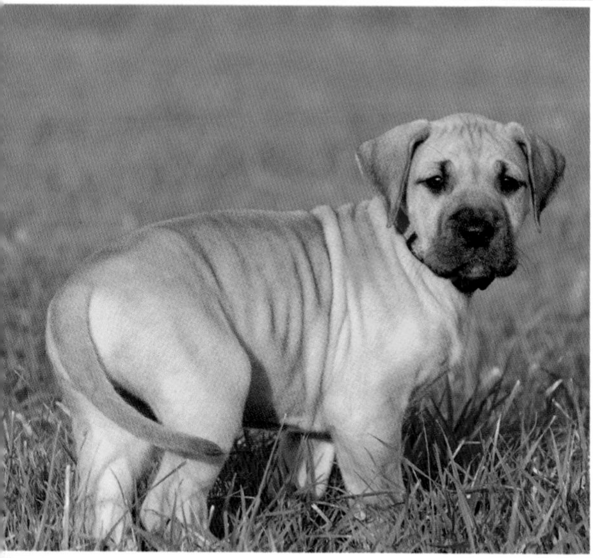

Dogue allemand

Il atteint une hauteur au garrot de plus de 80 centimètres. Les dogues sont d'un bon naturel, ils ont besoin de fortes attaches familiales et de beaucoup de mouvement, ce ne sont pas des chiens pour les « pantouflards ».

Dogue allemand

Rares sont aujourd'hui ceux qui peuvent se permettre d'élever un chien aussi somptueux, mais tellement gros, le plus souvent pour de simples raisons de place.

Collie à poil long

Il est connu dans le monde entier pour avoir incarné « Lassie ». C'est un chien de berger intelligent qui exige beaucoup d'activité. Très sensible, il a tout particulièrement besoin d'un maître compréhensif. Il aime le sport, notamment les exercices d'agility, d'obéissance ou de gymnastique canine.

▲ **Terrier Airedale**

Ce terrier à fort tempérament aime apprendre et est facile à éduquer. Il a besoin de beaucoup de sorties et d'une activité ciblée. Un chien pour personnes actives.

▲ **Berger allemand**

Aussi mignons que soient ces deux chiots et même si le berger allemand compte parmi les races les plus appréciées, il ne convient pas aux éleveurs débutants et ne deviendra un vrai « policier » qu'avec une éducation attentive et une bonne formation.

Boxer allemand ▶

C'est un boute-en-train plein d'énergie qui a impérativement besoin d'une activité raisonnable, par exemple le sport canin. Chien attachant, joueur et ami des enfants, il convient également aux éleveurs débutants.

▲ **Bouvier bernois**

L'autorité du bernois adulte émane déjà des chiots. Éduqué avec amour, c'est un merveilleux chien de famille.

Dogue allemand, Danois

Les premiers Germains chassaient déjà le sanglier avec des chiens de type dogue. Réservé ensuite à la noblesse, on a vu des meutes entières de ces molosses accompagner les chasses à courre à la laie. Élevé par Bismarck au rang d'emblème de l'empire, il n'est plus élevé depuis que comme imposant chien de compagnie et cela fait plusieurs dizaines d'années que les sélections visent uniquement la douceur. S'il est éduqué systématiquement, le dogue allemand est équilibré et affectueux envers ses maîtres et leurs enfants. Il aime la vie de famille mais a besoin de beaucoup d'espace, le chenil le rendrait malade. Les sujets de bonne lignée sont de superbes chiens pour éleveurs expérimentés.

Collie

Le collie à poil long était au départ un robuste chien de berger écossais, originaire des régions froides du nord de l'Écosse. Chien d'utilité, il avait alors des pattes et un museau plus courts que ceux de la race élégante qu'il est devenu aujourd'hui. Il n'a commencé à devenir à la mode qu'au milieu du XIXe siècle avec le croisement d'un setter et d'un barzoi qui en a fait un chien d'exposition. L'élevage de masse a depuis presque détruit la race, mais on retrouve aujourd'hui de bons éleveurs. Le collie est un chien intelligent attiré par la vie de famille, facile à élever, avec un instinct de garde et de protection inné, mais qui exige beaucoup d'activité. Son pelage long et somptueux demande beaucoup de soin, mais il convient aussi aux éleveurs débutants.

Berger allemand

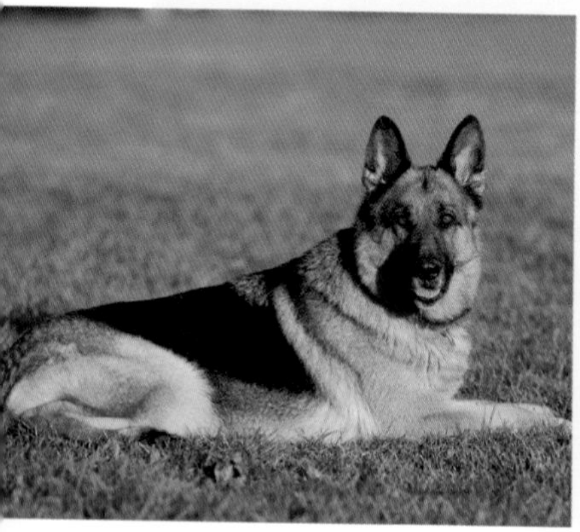

L'une des races les plus polyvalentes en ce qui concerne l'utilité. Il est notamment employé comme chien de berger, chien de protection, chien policier, chien guide d'aveugles, chien d'aide aux handicapés ou chien d'avalanche et n'a encore été détrôné par aucun dispositif technique dans l'armée comme chien antidrogue, chien anti-explosifs ou pour la recherche de cadavres. Éduqué systématiquement, il s'intègre bien à la famille et convient aux maîtres en mesure d'occuper abondamment son corps et son esprit au quotidien. Il s'entend parfaitement avec les enfants responsables. Sa vigilance et son instinct de protection sont innés et n'ont pas besoin d'être spécialement éveillés par des exercices de stimulation. Il convient moins aux éleveurs débutants.

Terrier Airedale

La race est née dans le Yorkshire, en Angleterre, issue d'otterhound, de bull-terrier, de setter Gordon et de collie noir et feu à partir desquels le premier éleveur, Wilfried Holmes, a créé un chien polyvalent, fringant et indifférent au mauvais temps. Pendant les deux guerres mondiales, le terrier Airedale a également fait ses preuves en tant que chien de secours et de liaison. D'un fort tempérament, c'est un chien vigilant aux bonnes qualités de protection et facile à élever. Il a besoin d'une éducation ferme et d'exercices réguliers qui le stimulent intellectuellement. Son poil demande beaucoup de soin, il doit être tondu régulièrement. C'est un vrai clown, parfois jusqu'à un âge avancé, qui procure beaucoup de plaisir à son maître, un chien pour éleveurs déjà expérimentés ayant le sens de l'humour.

Bouvier bernois

Il fait partie des plus beaux chiens de ferme et son métier principal est la garde. Il gagne aujourd'hui rapidement en popularité, alors même que la race a failli disparaître à la fin du XIXe siècle et a été sauvée in extremis par un éleveur du nom de Franz Schertenleib qui a découvert les derniers sujets restants dans la région de Berne. Dans les années 1930, les sélections en ont accru les mensurations, ce qui a affaibli le caractère de certaines lignées. Le bouvier bernois est aujourd'hui un « garde d'enfants » idéal, affectueux et fiable, méfiant envers les étrangers. Il aime les promenades et la vie au grand air, mais n'est pas un passionné de sport ou de marche. Une éducation systématique suffit à en faire un chien domestique ou de ferme agréable et docile.

Boxer

L'un des ancêtres classiques du boxer, le Bullenbeißer ou « mordeur de taureaux », était utilisé en Allemagne et en Hollande pour la chasse au cerf et au sanglier. Le boxer, sous son apparence actuelle, est issu de croisements entre le Bullenbeißer brabançon et de races bavaroises ou étrangères à partir desquels un chien de service et d'utilité acceptable a été développé vers 1860. Le boxer passe pour être amical et joueur, mais il défend aussi sérieusement ses maîtres s'il le faut. Sa patience avec les enfants est infinie. Son humeur se lit sur son visage. Il a besoin d'être éduqué avec amour, mais fermement, et de beaucoup d'activité, mais il convient alors aussi aux éleveurs débutants.

D'AUTRES RACES DE CHIENS D'UN SEUL COUP D'ŒIL

	Qualités	Besoins en exercices
Saint-Bernard	Naturel, bon et fidèle s'il est de bonne lignée, patient envers les enfants, instinct de protection suffisant.	Pas beaucoup de marche, mais suffisamment de mouvement.
Border Collie	Boute-en-train plein d'énergie et très intelligent. Caractère souple, facilement soumis et sympathique.	L'agility et le sport régulier ne suffisent pas à satisfaire son intelligence et sa volonté de travail.
Terrier de Boston	Inoffensif et amical, mais sûr de lui.	Apprend très rapidement tous les tours.
Dalmatien	Compagnon agréable au fort tempérament qui ne passe pas inaperçu.	Accompagner pendant des heures son maître à vélo ou à cheval rend un dalmatien heureux.
Bouledogue français	Souple, câlin, tendre, toujours drôle et peu exigeant.	Ne réclame pas de longues promenades, mais veut être toujours là.
Hovawart	Bon gardien. Distingue le bien du mal, même sans y avoir été formé.	Éducation systématique et suffisamment de mouvement.
Petit épagneul de Münster	Vivant, attachant, docile. Aime les enfants.	Chien de chasse polyvalent, a besoin d'activités de remplacement s'il est élevé par un particulier.
Kromfohrländer	Joyeux et attachant, mais pas soumis pour autant.	Activité, bon chien pour l'agility.
Berger blanc suisse	Plus doux et plus sensible que le berger allemand. Grandes qualités de chien de compagnie.	Doit être systématiquement éduqué, après quoi il a besoin de sport et d'activités ludiques.
Loulou nain	Joyeux, intelligent et sûr de lui, il porte à son maître un amour immodéré.	Aucune activité particulière, il se contente d'être là et de monter la garde.

Soins	Convient à...
Poil long qui nécessite un certain soin.	Il recherche la proximité de l'homme et tomberait malade en chenil.
Poil soyeux facile à soigner.	Superbe chien qui devrait rester entre les mains des bergers.
Ne perd pas ses poils et ne sent pas le chien.	Pour tous ceux qui cherchent un chien pas trop gros, mais quand même un « vrai chien ».
Pelage facile à soigner, mais les poils se piquent dans tous les textiles.	Il convient aux sportifs qui aiment bouger et se déplacer dans la nature.
Poil d'entretien facile, les bouledogues aiment les massages à la brosse.	Pour tous les âges.
Poil court et lisse d'entretien facile mais assez long.	Il a besoin de place et d'attaches familiales avec beaucoup de grand air.
Poil souple et agréable, d'entretien facile.	Pour les amoureux de la nature actifs, de préférence les chasseurs.
Ne nécessite aucun soin particulier.	Il aime les personnes actives qui lui confient des missions à remplir.
Poil lisse, long ou court, qui demande des soins réguliers.	Il lui faut des caractères fermes et conséquents qui disposent du temps suffisant.
Poil long aux nombreuses teintes superbes qui nécessite beaucoup de soins.	Convient à tous les âges, à condition d'habiter en milieu rural, car c'est un gardien zélé qui aboie très fort.

2.

La vie rêvée du chiot

Homme et chien : une association idéale. À condition que chacun des deux se sente compris par l'autre. Un accord parfait auquel il n'est pas si difficile de parvenir.

Les droits fondamentaux du chien de famille

La bonne volonté seule ne suffit pas pour qu'un chien se sente traité comme il le mérite. Il est essentiel de tenir compte de son caractère et de sa nature avant même l'acquisition.

POUR RÉPONDRE aux besoins d'un chien, il faut d'abord les connaître. Il n'est pourtant pas rare de voir les exigences de l'animal et les dépenses qu'elles impliquent sous-estimées, même par les plus fervents amoureux des animaux. Il importe donc de s'informer précisément dès le départ de tout ce que cela représente avant d'accueillir un chien chez soi.

Avant l'achat : à quoi faut-il penser ?

Commencer par mettre les choses au point avec les autres membres de la famille pour être sûr que tous sans exception approuvent l'acquisition d'un chien et que, par exemple, aucun n'est allergique aux poils de chien.

Si vous êtes locataire, il vous faut une autorisation du propriétaire pour élever un chien. Si vous êtes propriétaire, vous devrez généralement avoir aussi l'accord des autres copropriétaires.

Beaucoup de temps, de patience et de connaissances sont nécessaires pour élever un chien sans problème. Avant l'achat, il importe notamment de bien réfléchir si vous, mais aussi le reste de la famille, pourrez répondre aux exigences de la race qui vous intéresse éventuellement pour de simples raisons esthétiques.

Le temps. Quelle que soit la race choisie, penser au temps requis pour son élevage : les différents chiens exigent plus ou moins d'attention, de soins et d'activités éducatives ou spécifiques toute la journée. Outre au moins deux sorties quotidiennes (d'une demi-heure chacune), prévoir de réserver plusieurs heures par jour à son compagnon. Et ne pas croire qu'un petit chien demande moins de temps : grand ou petit, tous les chiens exigent la même attention, en plus des besoins spécifiques aux différentes races

Rien de meilleur au monde pour un chiot qu'une séance de jeu turbulente, de préférence avec son maître comme partenaire.

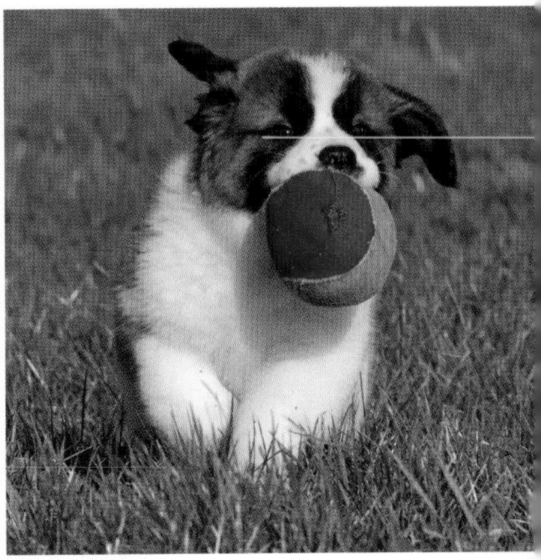

L'argent. La charge financière que représente l'élevage d'un chien n'est pas négligeable : les taxes mensuelles prélevées par certains pays ou certaines communes peuvent atteindre plus de 100 euros, auxquels il faut ajouter l'assurance responsabilité civile, la nourriture, les vaccinations annuelles, les accessoires, les cotisations aux associations canines, les cours des écoles pour chiens et les frais vétérinaires imprévus en cas de blessure ou de maladie (❯ Le saviez-vous ?, page 37).

Les vacances. Même sans aller à l'étranger, il n'est pas toujours possible d'emmener son chien avec soi à l'hôtel et si c'est le cas (penser à le demander avant de partir), il faut souvent compter avec certaines restrictions. Je déconseille les voyages en avion avec un chiot : outre le stress qu'ils représentent pour l'animal, ce sont des entreprises difficiles et onéreuses. Si vous choisissez de laisser votre compagnon à la maison, il vous faudra trouver une personne de confiance pour s'en occuper ou assumer les frais d'une bonne pension pour chiens – une solution que l'on ne saurait cependant imposer à un chiot qui vient d'arriver dans une famille.

Que faut-il offrir au chien ?

Pour l'équilibre du chien, il faut lui offrir les éléments suivants, et ce dans l'ordre qui suit :

- activité et mouvement
- cohérence et discipline
- amour et sympathie

L'activité et le mouvement qu'elle implique, ou l'activité supplémentaire sous forme de jeu, doivent représenter la principale occupation du chiot avec sa personne de référence (❯ à partir de la page 36).

La cohérence et la discipline ont pour but de fixer des règles et des limites éducatives au chien.

L'amour et la sympathie sont très importants pour le chien, mais il ne s'agit pas de « faire du zèle » en le câlinant et le dorlotant sans cesse. Mieux vaut lui montrer votre amour en lui apportant les soins appropriés et en répondant à ses besoins. Il ressentira l'affection et l'attention de son maître sous la forme d'un encouragement positif lorsqu'il a accompli quelque chose de difficile.

À quoi le chien a-t-il droit ?

Il va de soi que tout chien a droit à une alimentation saine, un logis propre et des soins appropriés selon ses besoins

◀ *Malgré tous les signes d'une merveilleuse amitié, le chiot et l'enfant doivent apprendre la bonne attitude l'un envers l'autre. Pour cela, les parents sont mis à contribution.*

(❯ chapitres 4 et 5). Mais il a aussi droit à son intégrité corporelle et à des contacts sociaux.

Un bon « chef de meute ». Tout chien souhaite comme « compagnons de meute » des hommes qui connaissent et aiment les animaux, sous la direction desquels il peut trouver protection et sécurité et qui s'attirent ainsi sa reconnaissance et son « respect ». De nombreux maîtres ne parviennent cependant pas à faire reconnaître leur domination par leur ami à quatre pattes car ils l'identifient trop à une personne et mesurent ses besoins à ceux des hommes (❯ page 96). Ils ne connaissent pas la nature de leur chien et ne savent pas ce dont il est capable, de sorte qu'ils ne peuvent pas répondre à ses besoins. Le chien doit être considéré comme un être vivant aux exigences propres qui a le droit de voir ces exigences respectées. Une « personnalisation » trop poussée du chiot et le manque d'éducation cohérente ouvrent la voie à de futurs conflits. L'animal ne sait alors plus dans quelle catégorie classer son maître, il ne se retrouve dans aucune structure hiérarchique et dès son plus jeune âge, il prend conscience de l'échec de l'homme à montrer les qualités de chef requises par le désordre qui règne dans la « meute homme-chien ». Son instinct de meute inné le pousse alors à prendre petit à petit la direction des opérations et il y parvient au plus tard avec sa maturité sexuelle. Le chien n'agit pas ainsi pour, comme on pourrait le supposer chez l'homme, « faire carrière », il est forcé par son instinct à assumer la direction pour assurer la survie de la meute. Or, à son grand désarroi, il est alors puni par son maître pour des actes qui lui paraissent nécessaires en

TEST

Est-ce le chien qui me convient ?

Le désir de chien s'empare rapidement de tous à la vue d'un adorable chiot. Avant de se décider, mieux vaut cependant bien réfléchir pour être sûr de pouvoir l'élever dans le respect de ses besoins.

	oui	non
1. Tous les membres de la famille sont-ils d'accord avec l'arrivée d'un chien à la maison ? Certains sont-ils allergiques aux poils de chien ?	○	○
2. Disposez-vous d'assez de place ? Avez-vous l'autorisation de votre propriétaire pour élever un chien ?	○	○
3. Aurez-vous le temps et l'envie de faire deux à trois promenades tous les jours et par tous les temps ?	○	○
4. Savez-vous que le chien adulte ne devra jamais rester seul plus de deux à trois heures d'affilée par jour ?	○	○
5. Possédez-vous les connaissances et disposez-vous d'assez de temps pour l'éducation et l'activité du chien ?	○	○
6. Connaissez-vous quelqu'un pour s'occuper du chien lorsque vous serez en vacances ou malade ?	○	○
7. Êtes-vous prêt à assumer tous les coûts liés à un chien, notamment les factures du vétérinaire ?	○	○
8. Votre mode de vie actuel vous permettra-t-il d'élever un chien pendant dix à quinze ans ?	○	○

SOLUTION : Si vous avez répondu « oui » à toutes les questions, le chien est l'animal qu'il vous faut. Il se sentira bien chez vous car vous assumerez la pleine responsabilité de ses besoins. En revanche, à partir d'un seul « non », vous devriez réfléchir avant d'adopter un chien.

Son rêve le plus cher : un chien

Notre fille de dix ans Mélanie souhaite plus que tout avoir un chien, alors que nous ne sommes pas tellement enthousiastes à cette idée. Que représente vraiment l'acquisition d'un chien pour les parents et à quoi devons-nous faire attention pour ne pas nous tromper en le choisissant ?

LES ENFANTS QUI VEULENT UN CHIEN ont généralement une certaine idée de tout ce qu'ils pourront faire avec lui. Ils se voient en rêve jouer avec lui, faire les fous, se promener ou lui apprendre des tours. Vous, ses parents, semblez sur le point d'acquérir un chiot « pour votre fille » alors que vous n'êtes pas vraiment intéressés par les chiens. N'oubliez pas cependant que c'est vous, en tant qu'adulte, qui assumerez l'entière responsabilité de l'animal, de ses soins et de son éducation. S'il va de soi que votre fille devra assumer certaines tâches pour apprendre la responsabilité et nouer un lien solide avec le chien, vous ne devrez en aucun cas lui laisser l'entière responsabilité de son compagnon sans aucun contrôle : c'est beaucoup trop demander à un enfant de dix ans.

Se tester

Mon conseil : testez-vous et votre enfant pour être sûr qu'il ne s'agit pas d'un simple désir passager de sa part et que vous vous accommoderez d'un chien. Pour cela, empruntez par exemple un chien que vous connaissez pour un week-end et, si tout se passe bien, proposez à ses maîtres de le garder pendant qu'ils sont en vacances. Ou alors proposez à un refuge pour animaux de promener des chiens pendant quelques semaines. Si vous et votre fille passez le test avec succès et que tous avez désormais envie d'un chien, il ne reste plus qu'à choisir celui qui vous convient.

Choisir le bon chien

Votre fille rêve sans doute d'une certaine race de chiens. Avant tout, vous devez cependant vous assurer que le comportement de cette race correspond à vos attentes et surtout que vous pourrez répondre à son besoin d'activité. Le chien de famille ou d'enfants par excellence n'existe pas, rien ne vaut donc l'avis d'un spécialiste qui vous aidera à choisir celui qu'il vous faut. Les chiots plaisent toujours aux amoureux des animaux, mais saurez-vous l'éduquer pour en faire un chien de famille bien élevé ? Peut-être aussi avez-vous fait la connaissance d'un chien plus âgé dans un refuge pour animaux ? Dans ce cas, il importe de prendre en compte son apparence, mais aussi son caractère et, là encore, les conseils d'un spécialiste s'avèrent souvent plus que payants.

tant que « chef », et donc évidents. En effet, et contrairement à l'homme, le chien adopte une attitude cohérente correspondant au rang supérieur qu'il occupe désormais dans la meute. Par conséquent, si son rôle de « patron » lui impose de discipliner un membre humain de la meute et si ses premiers avertissements ne sont pas entendus, il peut arriver qu'il emploie les dents, comportement que l'homme interprète comme inopportun et qui peut l'amener à consulter un spécialiste avec le chien « caractériel ». Heureusement, nos chiens sont capables d'adaptation et ces cas extrêmes ne sont pas systématiques. En revanche, si les victimes sont des enfants, le moindre incident est de trop. Un grand nombre de chiens souffre aujourd'hui de ne pas être compris et vit à huis clos sous la tyrannie amoureuse de leurs maîtres qui les réduit au rang d'homme. C'est pourtant à la personne de référence du chiot qu'il revient de s'informer suffisamment sur les besoins propres à la race souhaitée pour être sûre de pouvoir y répondre pendant toute la vie de l'animal. Le maître doit être en mesure de transformer l'attitude innée, purement instinctive et pas toujours opportune du chiot, en un comportement positif, au moyen d'une éducation systématique et cohérente, mais aussi patiente et affectueuse. En effet, le futur caractère du chiot restera marqué de manière décisive par la qualité de sa personne de référence.

Il est aujourd'hui impossible d'élever un chien selon ses besoins sans connaître les acquis de la recherche comportementale moderne et tout éleveur se doit d'acquérir ces connaissances. En effet, un chiot pris en charge par des hommes qui maîtrisent les règles de la compréhension mutuelle prendra confiance, nouera des attaches fortes et trouvera sa place dans sa famille humaine sans problème (❯ à partir de la page 93).

Conseil : les châtiments corporels ne renforcent en rien le rôle de chef de l'homme par rapport à l'animal (❯ à partir de la page 122).

Ces deux teckels se connaissent bien et se font entièrement confiance, leur comportement l'un envers l'autre fait presque penser à des « câlins ». ▶

Beaucoup de chiens de famille ne travaillent pas. Pourtant, ils ont besoin de **sollicitations physiques et intellectuelles** pour rester en bonne santé et mener une existence digne d'être vécue.

La proximité avec l'homme. Les chiens domestiques dépendent totalement de l'homme. Pendant des siècles, les chiens ont accompagné l'homme presque jour et nuit à la chasse, pour garder les troupeaux ou dans les nombreuses autres activités pour lesquelles ils avaient été élevés mais aujourd'hui, la plupart d'entre eux, et pas seulement les chiens de compagnie ou d'agrément, passe la majeure partie de sa vie chez nous à attendre. Même les chiens de service et d'utilité ne sont plus guère employés aux travaux spécifiques à leur race, mais rabaissés au rang de chiens de luxe, et patientent généralement toute la journée, ou presque, en attendant l'heure de faire un petit tour sans aucun intérêt au coin de la rue en tirant le plus souvent leur maître dénué de toute imagination.

Les paniers en osier donnent à tous les chiots envie de les mordiller.

Le mouvement et l'activité. Selon les races et les aptitudes pour lesquelles ils ont été élevés, les chiens ont plus ou moins besoin de se dépenser physiquement par des activités appropriées et de mouvement en liberté. La plupart des maîtres ont cependant tort lorsqu'ils affirment que si leur chien a tant besoin de mouvement, c'est uniquement parce qu'il descend d'un prédateur à pied.

La promenade classique est effectuée plusieurs fois par jour, mais le chien n'en profite guère puisqu'il doit rester en laisse la plupart du temps, sans la moindre possibilité de « travailler ». S'il pouvait courir librement et explorer les environs avec son maître, flairer la piste de gibier ou les marquages laissés par d'autres chiens, uriner au pied des arbres ou déterrer les souris, c'est alors qu'une promenade lui ferait plaisir. Bien entendu, de telles libertés supposent discipline et obéissance, ainsi qu'un attachement fort à son maître.

Certains maîtres tentent aussi de répondre au besoin de marche soi-disant énorme du chien en l'attachant à leur vélo pour de longues courses monotones, ce qui tourne parfois à la torture pour l'animal. Les chiens ainsi entraînés développent un corps d'athlète, ils n'en continuent pas moins de manquer d'activité raisonnable : les

chiens d'aujourd'hui ne souffrent pas du manque de mouvement, mais du manque d'activité. En effet, les tâches correspondant à la nature du chien et visant à le satisfaire par des activités appropriées ne doivent pas uniquement favoriser et solliciter la santé physique, mais aussi son intellect (❯ chapitre 6).
Les chiens ont le besoin instinctif de s'occuper et le satisfont de différentes manières. Les loups et les chiens sauvages passent dix à douze heures par jour à chercher de la nourriture. Ils se déplacent toujours dans un but et selon des règles précises. Aucun chien ne marche ni ne court uniquement pour s'entraîner physiquement, ou alors il souffre de troubles du comportement dus au fait qu'il passe le plus clair de son temps enfermé dans un espace réduit ou enchaîné.

Les chiots eux aussi ressentent déjà le besoin impérieux de s'occuper, ce qui développe leur intelligence. Pour cela, proposer au chiot dès son plus jeune âge de petites tâches qu'il peut accomplir avec succès et qui le sollicitent. Il doit également avoir régulièrement l'occasion de contacts sociaux avec d'autres chiens, par exemple lors de rencontres entre chiots et/ou chiens spécialement organisées par les écoles pour chiens et les associations canines, sur les terrains de jeux pour chiens ou lors de promenades communes. Outre la confirmation de son comportement social par le jeu avec d'autres chiens, il ne saurait trouver de meilleures occasions de mouvement sain et adapté.

LE SAVIEZ-VOUS ?

Élever un chien coûte cher

Quelques exemples de frais d'entretien pendant la durée de vie moyenne (douze ans) d'un chien : l'alimentation, avec une dépense quotidienne de 3 euros, revient à 13000 euros en douze ans; les taxes annuelles de 50 euros environ représentent 600 euros; l'assurance responsabilité civile à 150 euros par an grève le budget de 1800 euros; compter 1000 euros environ pour les seuls frais de vétérinaire courants et les vaccinations régulières, sans maladie grave, ainsi que 1000 euros pour les cotisations aux associations canines et les cours; les accessoires tels que laisse, collier, panier, gamelles et divers ustensiles de toilette se montent à 500 euros environ pour les modèles les plus simples. En douze ans, le total est de 18000 euros, soit une somme considérable...

Tout pour les chiens !

Un lit douillet, la « vaisselle » appropriée pour manger et boire, des ustensiles de toilette adaptés, des jouets contre l'ennui et, bien sûr, un collier et une laisse pour les sorties, tel est l'équipement de base du chiot.

L'ENTRÉE D'UN CHIOT dans une famille doit se dérouler avec le moins de heurts possible. Pour cela, penser à s'équiper de tout le nécessaire avant même son arrivée. Demandez conseil dans un bon magasin animalier, vous pourrez y tester vous-même la qualité des accessoires.

Un lit où se sentir bien

On trouve un grand choix de lits pour chiens dans les boutiques spécialisées : les tapis en polyester doux et souple qui absorbent l'humidité conviennent surtout aux grands chiens, étalés sur un sol froid ou dans la voiture, les grands coussins garnis de billes de polystyrène ou de mousse sont beaucoup plus confortables. Les chiens d'aujourd'hui aiment leur bien-être, spécialement les chiots, et préfèrent dans tous les cas les lits bien chauds et douillets dans des matières souples et douces. Les corbeilles en plastique dur ou en osier doivent donc être garnies d'une couverture ou rembourrées, sans quoi elles sont parfaitement inconfortables. Les paniers classiques en osier font par ailleurs entendre des craquements souvent très gênants au moindre mouvement de l'animal, sans compter que les baguettes de saule tressées incitent de nombreux chiens, même adultes, à les ronger. Quant aux corbeilles ou paniers aux bords de différentes hauteurs, ils doivent être parfaitement adaptés à la taille du chien. On trouve des lits moelleux garnis de mousse dans toutes les tailles et tous les modèles à des prix modiques. Penser cependant que le chiot atteindra sa taille adulte vers huit à douze mois et aura alors besoin d'un plus grand lit – mais si vous le lui achetez dès le départ pour faire des économies, il risque de s'y sentir perdu et de ne pas y être à l'aise, sans compter qu'il serait dommage de le voir ronger un lit de trop grande qualité. On peut cependant se contenter provisoirement pour le « bébé » d'une petite caisse ouverte à l'avant ou d'un carton bien stable

ASTUCE

La qualité se paie

Évitez les économies mal placées pour les accessoires de votre chien. Les produits de qualité sont généralement plus chers, mais souvent aussi plus durables et plus sûrs. Les colliers par exemple doivent pouvoir être fermés facilement, les laisses être équipées de solides mousquetons et les coussins supporter plus d'un lavage.

garni d'une couverture matelassée, ou encore d'une caisse pour chien aux multiples utilisations (› page 43). Les petits chiens, surtout ceux à poil court, aiment dormir à l'abri dans une « caverne » où ils peuvent se blottir avec délice (› photo ci-contre).

Le bon emplacement. Comme les hommes, les chiens ont besoin d'un endroit où se retirer, par exemple lorsqu'ils en ont assez de faire les fous avec les enfants ou veulent manger tranquillement. Les endroits où le chien dort et prend ses repas doivent par ailleurs être interdits aux enfants tant que leur supériorité n'est pas reconnue par le chien au même titre que les adultes. Le lit doit être placé à un endroit calme et à l'écart des courants d'air, mais d'où le chien peut encore suffisamment embrasser du regard le reste de la pièce. Les chiens ne dorment généralement pas très profondément pendant la journée, ils perçoivent donc tout ce qui se passe autour d'eux. Par conséquent, le lit ne doit en aucun cas être placé dans l'entrée car les allées et venues seraient source de stress pour le chien. Les gamelles non plus, car certains chiens défendent leur table, même vide, et plus d'un homme en a déjà fait la douloureuse expérience. Pendant la journée, les grands chiens restent pour la plupart couchés sur le sol à des endroits stratégiques de la maison et ne font usage de leur couche plus moelleuse que la nuit. On peut cependant étaler une couverture à l'endroit qu'ils préfèrent, surtout si le sol est dallé. Tous les chiens apprécient le confort et cherchent sans cesse à l'améliorer. Ils aiment notamment les positions en hauteur et sont tentés par une place sur le canapé. En revanche, s'ils la défendent contre leur maître, c'est le signe qu'ils ne tiennent pas ce dernier en très haute estime et il importe alors de prendre sans tarder des mesures contre cette attitude dominatrice.

Bien à l'abri

1 **La caisse :** elle est indispensable pendant la première phase d'éducation. Bien stable, le chiot peut y être logé en toute sécurité et elle est également idéale pour le transport.

2 **La niche dôme :** très appréciée des chiots et des petits chiens adultes, elle leur offre une « grotte » chaude et douillette où dormir. Veiller à en choisir une avec coussin intérieur amovible et lavable.

Un lit chaud et douillet contribue à la qualité de vie du chiot.

Des gamelles adaptées

Elles existent dans les modèles les plus divers. Les moins chères sont en plastique et plutôt déconseillées car elles sont trop légères et le chien peut les pousser à travers toute la maison lorsqu'il mange. Les plus stables sont celles en céramique, qui sont aussi plus lourdes, et donc difficiles à nettoyer. Les gamelles en acier inoxydable doivent être équipées d'un anneau en caoutchouc antidérapant. Je recommande pour ma part les supports pour deux gamelles en acier inoxydable à hauteur réglable (lavables au lave-vaisselle, › page 68), en sachant que les gamelles doivent être plates plutôt que profondes.

Le bon emplacement. Dresser la table du chien à un endroit calme qui lui est accessible en permanence.

Collier, laisse et sifflet

Le collier. Les plus conseillés sont réglables et dans des matières souples qui « grandissent avec » le chiot pendant un à deux mois. Le collier doit être suffisamment large pour recouvrir au moins deux vertèbres cervicales du chiot. Les chiens sont aussi sensibles que les hommes au niveau des cervicales de sorte que, si vous ne parvenez pas à faire perdre l'habitude de tirer au chiot, mieux vaut l'habituer au harnais pour des raisons de santé, cela réduira la pression sur son larynx et ses cervicales.

La laisse. Elle doit être adaptée à la taille et à la vitalité du chiot, longue de trois mètres environ, la plus fine possible et totalement indéchirable. Elle ne doit en aucun cas représenter un poids supplémentaire à traîner pour le chiot. L'entraînement à la laisse commence dès l'arrivée du chiot à la maison, des laisses de longueurs différentes pour l'éducation ultérieure et la formation sont présentées au chapitre 6.

Le sifflet. À deux tons, il peut servir à appeler le chien à grande distance. Il ne répondra cependant pas de lui-même au coup de sifflet, mais doit être dressé en conséquence.

Les ustensiles de toilette

Parmi les accessoires de base indispensables à tous les chiens, quel que soit leur type de poil, figurent un peigne adapté à la longueur du poil, un peigne anti-puces et une brosse à poils durs. Certains pelages exigent des outils plus spécifiques, tels que ciseaux à tondre ou rasoirs électriques. Votre éleveur ou vendeur spécialisé vous conseillera

L'équipement de base d'un seul coup d'œil

Laisse et collier

Le collier réglable plat, en cuir ou nylon, fait partie de l'équipement de base, comme la fine laisse de 10 mètres pour retenir le chien en terrain découvert et la laisse de 3 mètres pour faire un tour.

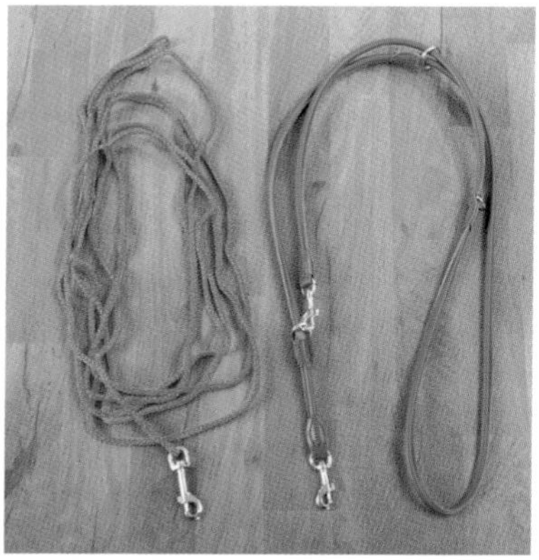

Lit et gamelles

Un lit doux et souple adapté à la taille du chien ne doit en aucun cas manquer. Pour les gamelles, les supports stables à hauteur réglable sont particulièrement conseillés (› photo page 68).

Soins et jeux

Les principaux ustensiles de toilette sont : une brosse (adaptée à la longueur du poil), un peigne, une pince à tiques et une pince à épiler. Une petite balle renforce la motivation du chiot à jouer.

MON ANIMAL DOMESTIQUE

Quel type de joueur est mon chiot ?

Quels sont les jeux qui motivent le plus votre chien, et ceux qui l'attirent moins ? Pour le savoir, proposez-lui différents jeux et testez son comportement. Est-il un joueur actif, plutôt calme, ou encore peureux ?

Début du test :

○ Type de joueur extrême : le chiot s'excite facilement, il est très actif, combatif ou dominateur lorsqu'il joue.

○ Type flegmatique : le chiot joue calmement, il est équilibré, parfois un peu pataud et s'arrête de jouer dès qu'il cesse d'être motivé.

○ Type peureux : il est facile à freiner et à impressionner lorsqu'il joue, il se soumet très facilement à un partenaire plus dominateur.

Résultat du test :

les brosses ou peignes les plus adaptés à votre chien (› chapitre 5). Enfin, une serviette spéciale chien particulièrement absorbante pour l'essuyer, par exemple après une promenade sous la pluie, est une acquisition souvent très utile.

Les jouets

Pour les jeux avec l'homme les plus appréciés et les plus adaptés au chien, l'offre se compose des objets suivants :

Les jeux de chasse. Pour les jeux de chasse classiques avec un chiot, les balles en caoutchouc dur adaptées à la taille de l'animal sont plus résistantes et plus faciles à nettoyer que les balles en caoutchouc classiques ou les balles de tennis. Sans compter que ces dernières abîment les dents du chien et peuvent nuire à sa santé car elles sont enduites d'un produit imperméabilisant pour pouvoir être jouées plus longtemps. Parmi les proies-jouets sonores, le « hérisson qui couine » est un grand classique qui a depuis longtemps fait ses preuves pour les jeunes chiots : il ne roule pas aussi vite qu'une balle et produit des cris rappelant ceux d'une petite proie qui constituent une motivation supplémentaire pour les bébés chiens. En ce qui concerne les autres jouets « couineurs », veiller à ce que leur forme rappelant celle d'une balle n'incite pas trop le chien à leur courir après ou à les attraper. Le « kong » à lancer au bout d'un cordon solide fait également partie de l'équipement de base. Du fait de sa forme particulière, il ne repart pas toujours dans la même direction après avoir touché le sol comme une balle, ce qui en fait un jouet très apprécié des chiens qui aiment apporter car il est plus difficile à attraper. Un dummy qui flotte et un autre qui peut être rempli de nourriture (› page 105) conviennent également aux jeux éducatifs.

Les jeux à tirer et à mordre. Pour l'aider à mesurer ses forces avec un jeu à tirer et à mordre, commencer par proposer au chiot un tissu souple en guise de proie, puis plus tard un petit boudin en jute ou une corde à nœuds colorée à tirer du commerce (› chapitre 6).

Les jeux pour maîtres célibataires. Les boutiques spécialisées proposent aujourd'hui toutes sortes de jouets qui permettent au chien de s'occuper seul.

La caisse

Une caisse stable est très utile pour loger le chien en toute sécurité. La surveillance totale que requièrent les chiots, surtout les premières semaines, rend nécessaire de les enfermer de temps en temps dans la caisse pour pouvoir se livrer à d'autres occupations : bien à l'abri, ils ne peuvent ni faire de dégâts, ni vous empêcher de travailler. La caisse est également très pratique pour l'apprentissage de la propreté (› chapitre 3) et peut être utilisée pour les transports en voiture avec les dispositifs de sécurité adéquats.

La caisse doit être juste assez grande pour permettre au chiot de s'étirer confortablement lorsqu'il est couché, de se lever ou de s'asseoir. La garnir de sa couverture dont il connaît l'odeur et sur laquelle il dort depuis la séparation d'avec sa mère et ses frères et sœurs. Une autre couverture sur la caisse la transforme en « caverne » où il fait bon dormir. Pour éviter d'acheter deux fois une caisse, en choisir une de la taille du futur chien adulte et y placer une séparation pour en limiter la surface à la taille du chiot.

Son jouet favori motive toujours un chien, il est souvent « respecté » et exempt de morsures.

Bienvenue à la maison

Qu'un chiot soit mignon ou pas, l'essentiel est qu'il vous convienne, à vous et à votre mode de vie. Aussi, mieux vaut prendre le temps nécessaire pour choisir le chien de vos rêves.

Deux amis qui s'entendent bien

Pour mettre toutes les chances de son côté et développer une longue et merveilleuse relation homme-chien, il importe de choisir son compagnon avec son cœur autant qu'avec sa raison et de bien se préparer.

L'HOMME ET LE CHIEN doivent se convenir mutuellement pour une cohabitation harmonieuse. Pourtant, la plupart des amoureux des chiens rêvent de « leur » compagnon alors même que ses exigences, propres à sa race, ne conviennent pas à leurs conditions de vie. Dans ce cas, les problèmes sont souvent inévitables.

À chacun son mode de vie

Prenons l'exemple du border collie : un superbe chien, très intelligent, mais qui a besoin d'une activité physique et intellectuelle extrême. Un maître déjà âgé ou plus très actif ne sera certainement pas heureux avec lui, de même qu'un homme jeune et sportif avec un bouledogue anglais qui se satisfait pleinement de la devise de Churchill « No sports ! » ne sera pas franchement ravi de son « paresseux », à moins d'apprécier ses autres avantages. Pour trouver le chiot qui convient à votre famille et être sûr de pouvoir l'élever dans le respect de ses besoins, il est essentiel de s'informer sur les comportements spécifiques des différentes races.

Pour cela, étudier les groupes de races de la FCI, la confédération internationale des éleveurs de chiens qui classe près de 330 races en 10 groupes (❯ page 50).

Si vous cherchez un chien pour une famille ou pour une personne âgée, vous devriez trouver votre bonheur dans le groupe 9, celui des chiens d'agrément et de compagnie. Si vous préférez un plus gros chien de famille – et si vous disposez de la place correspondante, envisagez les races reconnues comme dotées d'un bon naturel, par exemple le labrador retriever, l'eurasien ou un brave terre-neuve moins demandeur de mouvement. Pour les personnes sportives et actives, l'offre est déjà beaucoup plus large entre les nombreuses

Qui peut résister à un aussi mignon bébé ?

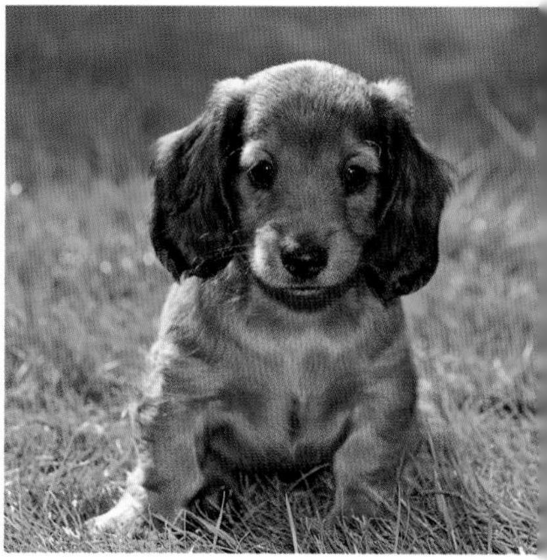

TEST

Dominant ou soumis ?

Pour tester le caractère et la nature du chiot, le maintenir couché sur le dos et l'empêcher de bouger avec une main sur le poitrail (› photos pages 48-49). Attention à ne pas confondre un comportement soumis et la simple peur : la soumission envers un supérieur est parfaitement normale.

	oui	non
1. Le chiot ne témoigne aucune résistance, reste détendu et vous lèche peut-être même la main.	○	○
2. Il se défend un court instant, mais reste calme et détendu.	○	○
3. Il persiste à se défendre, gigote et semble tendu.	○	○
4. Il persiste à se défendre, grogne et mord.	○	○
5. Il se fige et tire la queue entre les pattes.	○	○

RÉSULTATS ET INTERPRÉTATION : Selon ce que vous observez chez votre chiot et les réactions constatées parmi celles proposées, son caractère peut être défini comme suit, si vous avez répondu oui aux questions :

1. Caractère bien formé, chiot bien socialisé, il se soumet.
2. Caractère formé, chiot très socialisé qui se soumet après un peu d'insistance.
3. Chiot moyennement socialisé qui réagit avec assez d'indifférence. Il pourra développer un caractère dominateur en l'absence d'éducation adéquate.
4. Chiot dominant qui fixe lui-même les règles du jeu, mal socialisé.
5. Chiot craintif, pas assez formé à l'homme et mal socialisé.

races de travail, notamment les chiens de chasse, les chiens de berger ou les terriers qui tous ont besoin de beaucoup d'activité, de mouvement et d'une éducation systématique et cohérente.
Si vous trouvez un chiot bâtard qui vous plaît, essayez de savoir de quelles races il est issu, c'est le seul moyen de prévoir les surprises que vous réserve sinon ce sympathique inconnu en matière d'apparence, de taille et de caractère. Si vous évitez ensuite les trop graves erreurs d'élevage, il ne vous posera sans doute aucun problème particulier.

Le chiot d'éleveur

Si vous avez une prédilection pour une race donnée, vous ne pourrez éviter de passer par un éleveur dont il faudra alors contrôler soigneusement le sérieux et la qualité. En effet, sous l'appellation d'« éleveur » se cachent aussi des brebis galeuses uniquement intéressées par le profit. Ils produisent des chiens souvent malades et atteints de tares congénitales, proposés sur Internet ou dans les journaux à un prix réduit par rapport à ceux des éleveurs sérieux, et trouvent donc toujours des acheteurs naïfs qui croient faire une affaire. Les chiots sont souvent transportés en vrac depuis la République tchèque ou la Pologne et livrés aux revendeurs ou directement à des particuliers : les acheteurs ne voient ni la mère, ni l'élevage ; ils ne peuvent pas choisir leur chiot car on leur fait miroiter qu'il n'en reste qu'un de disponible et que les autres « sont partis comme des petits pains » ; les chiens ont souvent moins de huit semaines et sont tellement stressés qu'ils tombent gravement malades dès leur arrivée dans leur nouveau foyer car ils sont trop jeunes et leurs défenses immunitaires pas assez développées ; il est parfois impossible de savoir s'ils ont été ou non correctement vaccinés, mais les déficiences les plus graves et les maladies chroniques n'apparaissent souvent que lorsque le chien grandit. Mieux vaut donc éviter ces offres peu sérieuses.

Comment reconnaître un bon éleveur : Il est généralement affilié à une confédération par l'intermédiaire de son association de race et en suit les directives d'élevage. En France, la plus grande de ces associations est la Société Centrale Canine (SCC). Pour être admis à l'élevage, des tests de caractère et des examens de santé visant à détecter certaines maladies spécifiques de la race sont prescrits, ainsi que des examens supplémentaires pour les chiens de travail. Les éleveurs qui agissent délibérément à l'encontre de ces directives se voient refuser les papiers de leurs petits et sont parfois même exclus de leur association. Les confédérations tiennent des livres d'élevage pour chaque race et peuvent suivre l'ascendance d'un chien sur de nombreuses générations. Les chiots de ces élevages reconnus sont vendus par un service spécialisé.

Pour choisir un chiot, mieux vaut se faire soi-même une idée sur place. L'élevage et ses environs donnent-ils l'impression d'être propres et soignés ? L'éleveur ne doit pas avoir plus d'une ou deux chiennes en âge de procréer et ne pas élever plus de deux portées par an. Ses chiens ne doivent pas être confinés dans un chenil, mais vivre aussi chez lui. Il doit continuer de s'occuper « gratuitement » des vieilles chiennes qui ne servent plus à la reproduction. Le père des chiots ne peut que rarement être vu car c'est généralement la chienne qui est amenée au chien, et pas le contraire. Un bon éleveur s'informera précisément des conditions de vie et du logement des acheteurs, il demandera souvent à les rencontrer avec leur famille pour se rendre compte de ce qui attend son chiot. Les bébés doivent déjà avoir été en contact avec des étrangers, notamment avec des enfants, avant même leur huitième semaine. De nombreux éleveurs ont dans leur jardin un petit terrain de jeu réservé aux chiots avec différents jouets qui leur permettent d'apprendre à connaître leur corps ou de s'entraîner au courage et à l'habileté. Enfin, de petites excursions dans le voisinage avec la maman chien ou de courts trajets en voiture enrichissent leur « trésor d'expériences positives ».

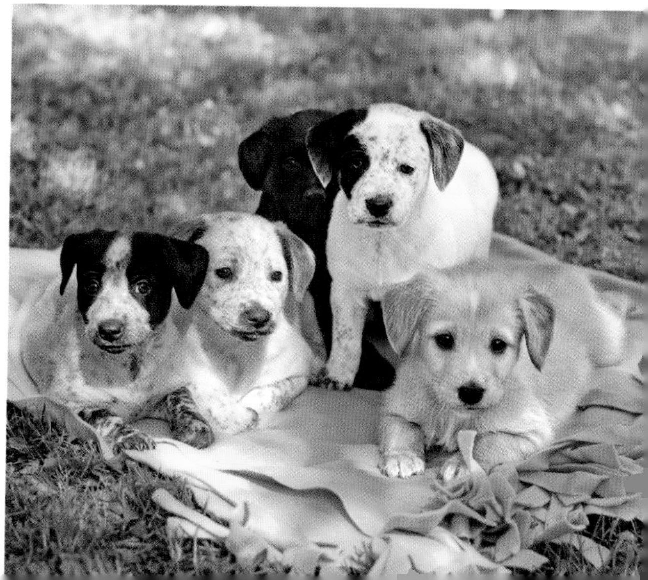

Pas de choix sans embarras : lequel adopter ? Le mieux est de se faire conseiller par un spécialiste des chiens.

Pour tester un chiot

1 **Dominant :** Le chiot est maintenu avec douceur pour l'empêcher de bouger. Un chiot dominant grogne et mord.

2 **Détendu :** Un chiot socialisé au caractère bien formé ne se défend pas mais reste parfaitement détendu. Cette soumission n'est cependant en aucun cas un signe de peur.

3 **Pour le porter :** Passer une main sous l'avant du corps du chiot et l'autre sous son arrière-train : il ne peut rien se passer.

Les papiers. Le chiot ne doit pas être donné avant huit semaines, il doit être vacciné, vermifugé et identifié par une micropuce ou un tatouage. L'éleveur présente le pedigree des parents et le procès-verbal d'enregistrement de portée, il garantit l'envoi ultérieur de l'arbre généalogique du chiot par un contrat de vente en bonne et due forme et fournit à l'acheteur le carnet de vaccination et un calendrier des vermifugations.

Le chiot de particulier

Il arrive parfois que des particuliers proposent des chiots. Il s'agit généralement de bâtards car aucune preuve de leur ascendance ne peut être apportée, ce qui ne signifie pas pour autant qu'ils comportent des défauts. Le risque est cependant assez élevé car les parents chiens n'ont pas été officiellement admis à l'élevage après un examen, mais le bébé est né par hasard. Ces animaux sont parfois proposés sur Internet ou dans les journaux comme des bâtards « élevés avec amour » mais attention ! Les vendeurs n'ont pas tous que de bonnes intentions, certains misent délibérément sur la compassion et croisent des chiens pour obtenir des races soi-disant nouvelles aux noms de fantaisie et gagner ainsi beaucoup d'argent. Ce sont généralement de jolies petites races qui sont croisées pour tromper les profanes ignorants. Ces chiens n'ont évidemment jamais de papiers.
Si vous êtes malgré tout intéressé par un tel chiot, demandez conseil à un spécialiste pour l'examiner.

Le chiot de refuge

Les refuges pour animaux proposent parfois des petits chiens aux particuliers. Dans ce cas, essayer de s'informer pour savoir ce que le chiot a vécu depuis sa naissance. Vous devez être parfaitement conscient qu'il n'a peut-être pas passé ses premières semaines dans des conditions optimales pour bien grandir et qu'il a peut-être reçu

une imprégnation négative au cours de cette période essentielle (› page 8). Avec de la compréhension, beaucoup d'amour et de patience, un chiot de refuge peut néanmoins se développer et devenir un formidable chien de famille. Toutefois, si vous choisissez d'adopter un chiot de refuge, ne pas le faire pour des raisons de prix mais en étant toujours parfaitement conscient que, malgré les petits problèmes qui risquent de se poser, vous offrez à un chien la chance d'une vie heureuse.

Les points à contrôler

La maman chien et les chiots doivent se montrer spontanés et amicaux envers l'homme, tous doivent avoir l'air propre et en bonne santé. Ne pas acheter de chiot dont vous ne pouvez voir la mère, ni si vous ne pouvez rendre visite aux chiots, s'ils ont peur et se cachent. De même, l'achat est déconseillé lorsque les chiots sont apathiques, ne peuvent être motivés pour rien et paraissent malades (› Astuce, page 49). Ne pas les acheter par pitié s'ils sont souillés de crottes, s'ils sentent l'urine ou si leur ventre est gonflé par les vers – nous sommes encore beaucoup trop nombreux à nous laisser attendrir par ces pauvres créatures et à encourager ainsi les « producteurs de chiens » sans scrupule. Un bon éleveur saura vous conseiller le chiot qui vous convient le mieux : un bébé timide ne serait pas heureux dans une famille

ASTUCE

Un chiot en bonne santé

Il suit d'un regard éveillé ce qui se passe autour de lui et il est facile à motiver. Son poil est luisant et collé au corps, ses yeux clairs ne coulent pas. La gueule, le museau, les yeux, les oreilles et l'anus sont propres. Il aime bouger, a une démarche harmonieuse, mange avec appétit sans être trop gros.

aux enfants trop actifs, tandis qu'un petit « combattant » sûr de lui et têtu ne tarderait pas à faire tourner en bourrique des maîtres pas assez fermes.
Si vous avez le choix, ne prenez ni le plus grand, ni le plus petit, ni le plus effronté, ni le plus timide (❯ Test, page 48).
Si vous craignez de ne pas pouvoir choisir le chiot qui convient le mieux à votre famille, n'hésitez surtout pas à vous faire conseiller par un bon spécialiste des chiens, c'est une décision judicieuse qui se paiera cher par de nombreuses années de cohabitation harmonieuse avec votre compagnon à quatre pattes !

Chien ou chienne ?

Le sexe ne joue pas un très grand rôle, les éleveurs les plus expérimentés vous le diront, ce qui compte c'est une éducation systématique et de l'amour. La facilité avec laquelle un chien ou une chienne peut être élevé dépend de sa personnalité, pas de son sexe.
Il est impossible d'affirmer en bloc que les chiennes sont plus faciles à élever et plus rapidement formées, car cela dépend en grande partie du talent du maître.

Dans la plupart des races, les mâles sont plus grands, plus forts et plus imposants. Ils ont plus tendance à se comporter en dominateurs et à s'imposer dans leurs rapports avec les autres chiens. Enfin, les mâles sont souvent plus sûrs d'eux que les femelles, surtout chez les chiens de service et d'uti-

LE SAVIEZ-VOUS ?

Les dix groupes de races de chiens reconnues

Les races de chiens reconnues par la FCI sont classées selon le système suivant : groupe 1 : chiens de berger et de bouvier (sauf bouvier suisse) ; groupe 2 : chiens de type pinscher, schnauzer, molossoïdes, bouvier suisse ; groupe 3 : terriers de grande et petite taille, terriers de type bull et terriers nains ; groupe 4 : teckels (aussi appelés bassets) ; groupe 5 : spitzs et chiens de type primitif, chiens nordiques de traîneau, de chasse, de garde et de berger, y compris les spitzs asiatiques et les chiens de type primitif avec un épi linéaire sur le dos (une ligne de poils qui pousse à contre-poil) ; groupe 6 : chiens courants, chiens de recherche au sang et races apparentées ; groupe 7 : chiens d'arrêt ; groupe 8 : chiens rapporteurs, leveurs et chiens d'eau ; groupe 9 : chiens d'agrément et de compagnie ; groupe 10 : lévriers, à poil long, dur ou court. Outre ces groupes, plus d'une centaine de races ne sont pas reconnues par la FCI.

Entre chien et chienne, il n'y a **pas de grandes différences de caractère.** La facilité avec laquelle un chien peut être dirigé dépend surtout de son éleveur.

lité (par exemple le berger allemand, le dobermann, le rottweiler). Certains éleveurs affirment et répètent que, contrairement aux chiennes qui ne sont que deux fois par an en chaleur pendant deux à quatre semaines, les chiens sont en rut toute l'année et toujours très intéressés par toutes les « dames chiens » qui passent. Je pense pour ma part qu'il y a là confusion avec certains « messieurs du sexe fort » en ce qui concerne le sexe féminin humain. En effet, les chiens mâles mènent en général une existence paisible et équilibrée toute l'année, ils se montrent parfaitement amicaux et joueurs avec les chiennes en dehors des périodes de chaleurs de ces dernières. C'est uniquement lorsqu'une chienne émet des signaux sexuels sous forme de puissantes odeurs qu'elle éveille l'intérêt sexuel des mâles, mais un attrait permanent de ces derniers serait contre nature. Les meutes de loups ou de chiens sauvages, sans compter les élevages mixtes, vivraient sinon dans un stress sexuel permanent, toute vie de groupe paisible serait impossible. Si vous deviez élever une chienne non castrée, ce que pour ma part je déconseille formellement, il vous reviendra de choisir soigneusement les trajets de vos promenades quotidiennes pendant ses chaleurs (❯ Castration, page 90) pour éviter qu'elle ne rende sexuellement fous tous les mâles du quartier attirés par la trace odorante qu'elle laisse alors derrière elle telle une traînée de feu; elle ne devra pas non plus rester seule au jardin pendant ses chaleurs car les mauvais sujets ne manquent pas dans le voisinage qui ne dorment pas et les chiennes recherchent le contact avec un mâle pendant l'œstrus (au plus fort des chaleurs). Toutes mes chiennes depuis quarante ans ont été castrées et ont mené une existence équilibrée, sans être soumises au moindre stress sexuel.

Jeux de chiots : invitation à une bagarre pour jouer.

L'arrivée du chiot

C'est à peine croyable mais pourtant vrai : les premières heures et les premiers jours avec votre nouveau petit compagnon marquent à jamais votre future cohabitation. Aussi, prenez le temps et laissez les choses se mettre tranquillement en place...

C'EST LE GRAND JOUR : vous allez chercher votre nouveau chiot. Tout est prêt pour l'accueillir, tout le nécessaire est là (› page 38).

Le transport à la maison

Le plus souvent, le nouveau membre de la famille n'habite pas la porte à côté, mais pas non plus à l'autre bout du monde, et vous allez le chercher en voiture. Pour un trajet qui ménage le chiot et le détende, certains points doivent être respectés :

- Même si vous avez l'habitude de conduire, contentez-vous cette fois du rôle de passager pour pouvoir vous occuper suffisamment du chiot.
- Prévoir d'arriver à la maison avant la tombée de la nuit pour laisser au chiot suffisamment le temps d'explorer son nouvel environnement.
- Le chiot ne doit plus avoir été nourri au moins cinq heures avant le départ pour qu'il ne soit pas malade pendant le trajet.
- Ne pas laisser le chien tout seul dans sa caisse ou à l'arrière d'un break : s'il garde un souvenir angoissé de ce premier trajet, il n'aimera plus la voiture par la suite.
- S'asseoir sur le siège arrière avec le chiot dans les bras et placer à côté de soi un panier garni d'une couverture imprégnée de l'odeur de sa mère et de ses frères et sœurs dans lequel le coucher une fois qu'il est endormi.
- Garder à portée de main une serviette et du papier absorbant en cas de « petit accident ».
- Si le trajet dure plus d'une heure, faire une pause toutes les heures, sauf si le chiot ne se réveille pas.
- Pendant les pauses, se promener quelques minutes avec le chiot en laisse pour qu'il puisse se soulager.
- On reconnaît que le chien se sent mal à son halètement et à un écoulement aqueux des crocs. Dans ce cas, le faire aussitôt descendre de voiture et le promener jusqu'à ce qu'il retrouve un comportement normal.

L'arrivée dans une nouvelle maison

Une fois arrivé à la maison, sortir le chiot et lui montrer tout de suite l'endroit où il devra « faire ses petites affaires » par la suite. Mon truc : je demande quelques crottes à l'éleveur et les dépose aux futures « toilettes » du nouveau venu, l'odeur familière le motive à « se vider » à cet endroit plutôt qu'à un autre. Offrir au bébé de l'eau et

Les coussins pour chiens sont garnis de flocons de mousse. Ils offrent au chiot un confort et une douceur merveilleux.

attendre dehors jusqu'à ce qu'il ait au moins uriné, ne le rentrer qu'ensuite.

Le calme : La dernière chose dont le chiot a besoin, c'est d'un comité d'accueil enthousiaste et d'enfants trop bruyants. Il a besoin avant tout de calme et il ne doit pas en manquer pendant quelques jours.

La découverte : La première fois, laisser le chiot découvrir la maison sans le déranger. Au bout d'un moment, lorsque la fatigue le gagne, le coucher dans son panier ou dans la caisse avec laquelle il s'est déjà familiarisé pendant le trajet et le laisser dormir. Dès qu'il se réveille, l'amener à ses « toilettes » et attendre qu'il se soulage, le complimenter alors joyeusement. Il est temps de lui donner son premier repas, identique à ceux auxquels il a été habitué chez l'éleveur ou à son premier domicile. S'il n'a pas encore fait de crottes, le sortir de nouveau après le repas.

La prise de contact : Les premiers jours, les enfants ne doivent pas trop jouer avec le chiot qui serait sinon complètement dépassé par les événements. Il doit prendre contact de lui-même et a besoin d'un peu de temps pour faire connaissance avec ses maîtres et s'adapter à eux.

L'apprentissage d'un nouveau rythme : Les étapes sont les suivantes : où trouver de l'eau, où manger, où dormir et surtout, comment se déroulent les journées dans la nouvelle « meute » ?

Elles constituent autant de nouvelles impressions que le bébé chien doit assimiler en toute tranquillité. Dès qu'il a fait connaissance avec son environnement, il supporte les visiteurs et les amis. Ne pas oublier qu'il dort parfois beaucoup pendant cette phase et faire en sorte que les enfants ne l'en empêchent pas, il pourrait en résulter un chien nerveux souffrant de troubles du comportement.

Offrez au bébé chien **du temps et du calme** pour se familiariser avec son nouvel environnement.

La construction d'une relation : Les premières semaines, le chiot ne doit nouer d'attaches solides qu'avec sa personne de référence et les membres de sa famille. Par conséquent, ne pas le laisser à des étrangers ou à des enfants, même un court instant. Il lui faudra quelques mois pour connaître sa place, la voisine pourra alors le surveiller quelques heures de temps en temps ou d'autres enfants et des amis venir jouer avec lui – sous la surveillance de son maître.

Les premières nuits : Elles constituent un événement clé pour le chiot et sont liées à la propreté nocturne, en même temps que le début de l'entraînement. Mon expérience : les « nouveau-nés » passent leurs deux ou trois premières nuits dans mon lit. Cela leur permet, d'une part, de s'attacher étroitement à moi et, d'autre part, je les ai plus facilement sous la main la nuit pour leur apprendre la propreté : dès qu'ils quittent leur position de repos, je les porte dans le jardin à leurs « toilettes ». Les maîtres qui ne sont pas disposés à se donner cette peine ou refusent absolument de prendre le chien dans leur lit s'exposent souvent à des mois d'attente avant que le chiot ne soit propre. Au bout de quelques jours, le chiot dort près de mon lit dans un panier ou une bassine dont il ne peut sortir seul : son agitation m'indique qu'il « doit ». En effet, les chiens sont des animaux naturellement propres et il leur répugne de souiller leur couche. L'important pour le maître est de se réveiller et de répondre à leur besoin. Le nouveau lit ne doit pas être suffisamment grand pour permettre au chiot de se soulager à un endroit et de continuer à dormir au sec un peu plus loin (› page 38). Le placer tout près de son lit pour que le bébé sente la proximité de son maître. Avec une surveillance systématique, un chiot fait ses nuits au bout d'une à deux semaines. Il importe cependant de tou-

Le meilleur moyen de tester qui a la poigne la plus ferme.

jours le faire sortir dès son réveil. Une fois qu'il a dormi toute la nuit « sans fuites » pendant une semaine et si vous souhaitez qu'il dorme à l'avenir à un autre endroit de la chambre ou de la maison, déplacer sa corbeille de cinquante centimètres par jour jusqu'à l'endroit voulu. Attention cependant, n'avancer que s'il a eu une bonne nuit la veille.

La propreté

Les premières semaines, vous devrez avoir le chiot en permanence sous les yeux. En fin de compte, il n'est autorisé à bouger librement que dans la pièce où vous vous tenez et pouvez le surveiller en faisant autre chose – comme si c'était un enfant qui se déplace à quatre pattes. Si pour une raison ou pour une autre vous ne pouvez provisoirement plus le surveiller, le mettre pendant ce temps dans un carton où il pourra dormir ou dans sa caisse où il trouvera quelques friandises. Il ne tardera pas à s'endormir et vous n'aurez plus besoin de l'avoir sous les yeux en permanence, d'autant plus que vous l'entendrez se réveiller s'il veut sortir. L'expérience permet également d'acquérir une certaine connaissance des moments où le chiot doit se soulager : juste après avoir mangé ou bu, lorsqu'il se réveille ou qu'il a dû passer un peu plus longtemps dans sa caisse. Dans ce cas, sortir au plus vite pour qu'il fasse ses besoins. De même, s'il interrompt brusquement un jeu et flaire intensément le sol, s'accroupit en faisant le dos rond et tourne sur lui-même, prenez-le dans vos bras en protestant d'un « Non ! » énergique et portez-le aussitôt dehors, c'est le signe qu'il se prépare à faire une crotte.

CHECK-LIST

Les dangers à éviter

Imaginez que vous avez un enfant en âge de marcher à quatre pattes. Le comportement à adopter est le même avec un chiot qui arrive dans une famille :

1. Retirer tous les objets placés à une hauteur que le chien peut atteindre.
2. Mettre en sûreté les câbles sous tension qui courent à travers la pièce.
3. Empêcher l'accès aux escaliers avec des grilles à cet effet (disponibles en animalerie).
4. Conserver en sûreté les produits chimiques tels que produits nettoyants, engrais, produit anti-escargots ou autres agents de destruction de nuisibles et médicaments.
5. Veiller à laisser hors de portée du chiot les petits objets qui traînent tels que jouets (legos, billes, perles, etc.), balles de ping-pong, aiguilles ou objets pointus.
6. Les plantes d'intérieur ou d'extérieur toxiques pour les chiens sont notamment : la rose de Noël, l'if, la trompette des anges, la digitale, le cytise, le colchique, l'hyacinthe, le buis, le laurier-cerise, le thuya, le muguet, le gui, les solanacées (belladone), le laurier-rose, les jonquilles, le fusain, le rhododendron, le pied-d'alouette, le marronnier, la grande ciguë, le perce-neige, le houx et le genévrier.
7. Protéger les étangs de jardin et les soupiraux avec une clôture, ainsi que les massifs et les jeunes arbres ou arbrisseaux précieux : aucune plante n'est à l'abri des dents de lait d'un jeune chiot entreprenant.
8. Vérifier que la clôture du jardin est suffisamment sûre pour empêcher les évasions.
9. Placer la cage des cochons d'Inde, hamsters ou oiseaux hors de portée du bébé chien pour lui éviter la simple tentation de harceler ses habitants et lui permettre de s'habituer lentement aux autres animaux avec lesquels il vit.

Les occasions ne manquent pas de porter un chiot dans son jeune âge, il doit néanmoins se servir essentiellement de ses pattes pour marcher.

Il fait parfois pipi plus rapidement selon l'urgence et il arrive que vous ne puissiez le faire sortir à temps. Si vous le prenez sur le fait, lui faire entendre un « Non ! » ferme et le porter immédiatement à l'extérieur. En revanche, s'il s'est laissé aller en votre absence, ne tenir aucun compte du petit accident. Le taper ou lui mettre le nez dans sa « commission » ne ferait que détruire la confiance qu'il a en vous car il ne ferait pas de lien entre la punition et son acte. Par conséquent, mieux vaut au début faire sortir le bébé un court instant toutes les heures par mesure de précaution. Vous apprendrez ainsi très rapidement à connaître son rythme et pourrez vous organiser en conséquence avec le temps.

Ce qu'un chiot doit apprendre

Son nom : Les noms à deux syllabes terminés par une voyelle comme « a », « é » ou « ou » sont les plus faciles à prononcer. Le nom doit cependant convenir au chien. Commencer par toujours le prononcer sur un ton agréable en l'associant à une friandise ou une caresse, et il ne tardera pas à y répondre. En revanche, ne pas prononcer son nom en même temps que des mots réprobateurs comme « non » ou « pfff » pour lui faire abandonner un comportement inopportun sur un ton énergique, il risquerait de lui donne un sens négatif.

Le collier : Un bon éleveur habitue ses chiots au collier avant de les donner. En règle générale cependant, le bébé chien ne se trouve en contact avec cet objet désagréable qu'au moment du départ. La première fois, associer le collier à un bon repas et le laisser au chien toute la journée – mais pas la nuit. Donner une friandise au chiot à chaque fois que vous lui remettez son collier et au bout de quelques jours, il s'y sera habitué et vous ne le lui mettrez plus que pour la promenade ou éventuellement pour le dresser.

La première sortie

Beaucoup de maîtres veulent promener leur chiot dès les premiers jours. Or, les chiots les plus inexpérimentés refusent alors d'avancer, sont pris de panique et veulent à tout prix rentrer à la maison. Les deux premières semaines, il suffit au chiot de découvrir le jardin ou l'endroit où il doit faire ses besoins sur la pelouse en bas de l'immeuble. Ce n'est que lorsqu'il s'y sentira suffisamment en sûreté qu'il s'intéressera à son environnement. De même pour se promener avec un chiot, ne pas marcher d'un pas rapide, mais le laisser donner libre cours à sa curiosité : il doit accumuler les expériences. C'est en général chez son maître qu'un petit chien apprend à connaître l'environnement, les bruits de la circulation, les odeurs de la rue, les étrangers et, bien sûr, les autres chiens... on comprend qu'un petit tour au coin de la rue suffise amplement. Une autre astuce : avant la première vaccination, aller voir le vétérinaire une ou deux fois avec le chiot sans raison particulière, il lui offrira une friandise sans le soumettre à aucun traitement et lors de la visite suivante, la peur du chiot se sera envolée.

MON ANIMAL DOMESTIQUE

Comment se développe un chiot

Un journal est très utile pour se souvenir, mais aussi pour surveiller la bonne croissance du chiot. Pour cela, noter régulièrement tous les changements observés.

Début du test :

○ Photographier le chiot toutes les semaines debout, assis ou pendant différentes activités.
○ Mesurer toutes les semaines sa taille, sa longueur, son tour de poitrine et de cou.
○ Le peser toutes les semaines et comparer la progression de son poids avec les chiffres donnés pages 71-72. Noter tous les changements et toutes les particularités dans un journal.

Résultat du test :

Questions-réponses : **Acclimatation**

À quelles autres astuces peut-on avoir recours pour que notre chiot reste propre la nuit ?

Donnez-lui son dernier repas, eau comprise, avant 18 heures. Jusqu'à 22 heures, il doit pouvoir se soulager toutes les heures. Sortir pour la dernière fois avant de vous coucher et ne lui donner de nouveau à boire que le lendemain matin.

Un chiot peut-il s'entendre avec d'autres animaux domestiques ?

Quelques problèmes peuvent se poser pour l'habituer à des animaux qui habitent déjà la maison. Les petits animaux comme les lapins nains, hamsters, etc. font partie du tableau de chasse du chien, rien ne garantit donc qu'il domine durablement son instinct de chasse et les tolère. Mieux vaut placer les cages hors de sa portée afin qu'il puisse s'y habituer lentement. En revanche, la cohabitation avec un chat ne pose que rarement problème, on voit même souvent de grandes amitiés se développer entre les deux. Les chats apprennent en général tout seuls à tenir compte du chiot, contentez-vous de freiner ce dernier s'il fait mine de courir après le chat les premiers jours.

Puis-je laisser mon chiot de 12 semaines un long moment tout seul à la maison ?

Non, car il n'est pas encore propre. Par ailleurs, il doit d'abord apprendre à rester seul dans une autre pièce. Pour cela, fermez la porte derrière vous comme par inadvertance pendant les travaux ménagers et ne tenez pas compte de ses protestations éventuelles. Attendez pour le « libérer » qu'il se tienne tranquille un court instant. Ouvrez alors la porte, mais continuez de l'ignorer : il doit comprendre qu'il peut vous faire confiance et que vous reviendrez toujours. Vous pouvez aussi utiliser la caisse (› page 43) dans laquelle placer quelque chose à ronger pendant que vous allez, par exemple, à la cave : à votre retour, ignorez le chiot et ne le plaignez pas, ne le laissez sortir de la caisse sans dire un mot que 10 minutes plus tard.

J'ai acheté pour notre chiot une caisse pour les trajets en voiture, mais il refuse obstinément d'y entrer. Quelle est mon erreur ?

Donnez au chiot ses repas dans la caisse pendant quelques jours en plaçant la gamelle de nourriture tout au fond. Laissez la porte ouverte jusqu'à ce qu'il entre et sorte sans problème. Placez sa couverture habituelle dans la caisse et cacher une ou deux friandises dans les plis. S'il se couche de lui-même sur la couverture pour se reposer, laissez d'abord la porte de la caisse ouverte. Attendre qu'il se comporte de manière parfaitement naturelle avec la caisse pour

y placer une friandise qu'il convoite tout particulièrement et pendant qu'il se régale, fermez la porte et mettez la caisse dans la voiture. Restez cohérent et faites preuve de patience.

L'éleveur ne veut pas donner ses chiots avant 12 semaines. Trouvez-vous cela normal ?

Le meilleur moment pour donner un chiot est entre la 8e et la 9e semaine, car c'est pendant la phase de socialisation, qui se termine à la 14e semaine, qu'il doit apprendre à connaître son nouvel environnement sans sa mère ni ses frères et sœurs. S'il manque cette imprégnation, il se peut qu'il ait plus tard des problèmes avec les étrangers.

En guise de salutation, notre chiot fait à chaque fois une petite flaque. Comment lui faire perdre cette habitude ?

On appelle ce comportement urination de soumission. Ce sont surtout les chiens les plus soumis qui le montrent. La cause peut en être une faiblesse de caractère innée, une première éducation trop grossière ou une domination trop forte de l'homme qui le salue. Reprenez-vous et imposez-vous moins, parlez notamment moins fort. Avant que le chiot ne se soumette, appelez-le et donnez-lui rapidement une friandise sans dire un mot, puis ignorez-le en vous détournant. Avec le temps, il prendra de l'assurance. Demandez aux visiteurs de ne pas tenir compte de lui et de ne pas lui parler. S'il lui arrive encore de faire une petite flaque, ignorez-le complètement et ne le laissez pas regarder pendant que vous nettoyez les dégâts.

Qu'appelle-t-on un chien dominant ?

L'attitude d'un chien dominant est amicale, mais pas racoleuse. Il n'est pas non plus hostile ou agressif. Il exprime calme et maîtrise de soi et il est reconnu comme supérieur par ses congénères et les chiens moins dominants qui se soumettent. Il tient la tête et la queue dressées. Certains éleveurs croient que leur chien est dominant parce qu'il n'en fait qu'à sa tête lorsqu'il est tenu en laisse, fait preuve d'agression ou n'obéit à aucun ordre, mais un tel chien est le plus souvent simplement mal élevé. Un chien dominant n'a pas besoin de s'imposer par la voix ou l'expression corporelle.

Quand faut-il utiliser un harnais plutôt qu'un collier ?

Je conseille les harnais pour les chiens nains, ceux à l'encolure très épaisse ou ceux qui ont des problèmes de gorge. Je préfère cependant un collier souple pendant l'éducation et la formation car les signaux sont transmis plus clairement par une laisse et un collier que par un harnais.

Une alimentation saine

Comment nourrir son compagnon à quatre pattes pour être sûr de lui offrir une longue vie en pleine santé ? Dans ce chapitre, je vous fais part du résultat de mes trente ans d'expériences positives.

On reconnaît un chien à ce qu'il mange

À quoi ressemble le chien modèle : nerveux, musclé, ni trop gras, ni trop maigre, le poil épais et luisant, l'œil clair et brillant. Une alimentation équilibrée y est pour beaucoup.

NOUS DÉCIDONS NOUS-MÊMES de ce que nous mangeons, mais nos chiens, eux, dépendent de ce que nous choisissons pour eux et de nos connaissances en la matière.

L'alimentation naturelle

Le chien est un animal carnivore. Sa dentition est celle d'un carnassier, conçue essentiellement pour capturer et dépecer des proies. Son alimentation naturelle s'oriente donc vers celle des prédateurs, auxquels la chair des proies fournit des protéines et des matières grasses, les os du calcium, le sang du sodium, le foie et les reins des vitamines liposolubles, l'intestin et son contenu des vitamines hydrosolubles. Le loup, l'ancêtre de nos chiens, se nourrit aussi de fruits, de graminées, de racines, de feuilles, ainsi que des excréments d'autres animaux et d'autres déchets.

Trop de céréales nuit : L'organisme du chien est adapté à une alimentation riche en protéines, soit essentiellement de la viande. Un régime alimentaire mixte à forte proportion de céréales a souvent pour conséquence, en raison d'une stimulation insuffisante des céréales sur la muqueuse intestinale, une production d'acide chlorhydrique insuffisante, ce qui entraîne des troubles digestifs à la suite d'une fermentation défectueuse car la digestion des aliments n'est pas assez intensive. C'est pourquoi je recommande de ne jamais servir des céréales à votre chien en même temps qu'un repas carné.

Les aliments préparés

Selon l'industrie des aliments pour animaux, près de 30 % des maîtres donnent à leur chien des aliments préparés, secs ou humides en boîtes. La qualité diffère selon les fabricants mais il s'agit

Ronger et grignoter fait plaisir, mais fait aussi du bien lorsque les premières petites dents sortent et que les gencives démangent.

Parfaitement concentrés : il se passe quelque chose qui pourrait être intéressant.

toujours d'aliments complets contenant tous les éléments dont le chien a besoin. Les produits de mauvaise qualité contiennent surtout des céréales et la qualité des protéines, désignées par l'appellation « sous-produits animaux », ne peut en être vérifiée. En règle générale, plus les différents composants sont indiqués précisément avec leur pourcentage, meilleure sera la qualité. Il s'agit cependant toujours d'aliments conservés à base de produits cuits ayant subi un processus de transformation intensif. Il leur manque la vitalité des produits frais. C'est pourquoi, en ce qui me concerne, je nourris mes chiens depuis plus de trente ans avec de la viande crue, des os, des légumes et les compléments correspondants.

Les repas maison

Les loups ne mangent pas que la viande, mais aussi la peau et les poils de leurs proies. Ce type d'alimentation naturelle est, bien sûr, irréalisable pour la majeure partie des propriétaires de chiens actuels, notamment pour des raisons esthétiques. Il convient alors de composer à partir d'aliments naturels un régime dont la composition se rapproche le plus possible de celui d'un « canidé sauvage ». Les éléments de base en sont les suivants :

- viande
- os ou équivalent
- légumes
- compléments alimentaires

La viande seule nuirait à la santé du chien car elle contient beaucoup de phosphore et très peu de calcium. Or, les chiens ont besoin de plus de calcium que de phosphore dans leur alimentation (rapport 1:1,2). Par conséquent, un apport supplémentaire de calcium est nécessaire, en plus des os en quantités raisonnables (❯ Les os, page 64). Les viandes les plus adaptées au chien sont le bœuf, l'agneau, le cheval, le gibier et le poisson ; la viande maigre et musculeuse est très digeste et a une teneur en protéines élevée ; la viande de tête ou viande pour ragoût est plus grasse et contient plus de tissu conjonctif ; la volaille (chair musculaire) est très peu grasse pour une qualité de protéines élevée. Les abats (foie, cœur, reins, rate, poumons, panse) contiennent en plus des vitamines spécifiques et des oligo-éléments mais ne doivent pas constituer plus de 5 % de la proportion de viande par repas car ils sont très riches en phosphore ; le foie peut entraîner un excédent de vitamine A, tandis que la panse est très indigeste, peu protéinée mais avec une forte proportion de tissu conjonctif. On trouve dans le commerce de la viande en morceaux congelée, de différentes sortes ou mélangée, qui peut être servie au chien tiède avec l'eau de décongélation.

ASTUCE

Nourrir un chiot en voyage

Pendant les vacances et en voyage, il est généralement impossible de préparer soi-même les repas de son chien. Par conséquent, je conseille plutôt d'emmener des aliments secs que des boîtes, car ils sont plus pratiques. Habituez le chien à son nouveau régime quelques jours avant le départ.

Condition de base en matière de prévention et de santé : **un chiot doit recevoir une alimentation équilibrée** pour se développer parfaitement.

Attention ! Ne jamais donner de viande de porc crue à votre compagnon car elle peut contenir le virus de la maladie d'Aujeszki, mortelle pour le chien.

Les os fournissent au chien du calcium, mais aussi de nombreux minéraux. Un chien aux dents saines tolère parfaitement les « gros os de poitrine » de veau ou d'agneau crus et charnus. On peut les remplacer ou compléter, pour les chiots ou les chiens âgés qui ne peuvent pas encore ou ne peuvent plus couper eux-mêmes et digérer les os, par de la farine d'os (ne pas la chauffer, elle perdrait toutes ses qualités), de la pâte d'os (os crus réduits en poudre), des coquilles d'œufs ou du nitrate de calcium (mieux assimilé par l'organisme que le carbonate de calcium).

Mieux vaut diviser la ration quotidienne en quatre repas.

Les légumes de différentes sortes, crus et coupés fins (presque écrasés), sont un excellent complément alimentaire. Faire des mélanges selon les saisons. Couper les légumes en petits morceaux permet au chien d'en exploiter les précieux composants (vitamines, minéraux et oligo-éléments) qui lui apportent également des fibres. Le mélange de légumes doit être majoritairement composé de différentes salades vertes : laitue, roquette, épinards, pissenlit, jeunes orties, cresson, mâche, etc., le reste consistant, par exemple, en chou-rave, chou-fleur, céleri, poireau ou choux de Bruxelles. Le mélange doit toujours comporter un tiers de carottes car elles contiennent des fibres qui ont un effet favorable sur la flore intestinale et assurent l'apport essentiel en bêta-carotène.

Attention ! Les pommes de terre crues, haricots verts crus, piments ou aubergines crus peuvent contenir des substances toxiques.

Les fruits doivent être proposés au chien en petites quantités entre les repas.

Les matières grasses et les huiles fournissent de l'énergie et sont vitales pour le chien. Les huiles végétales contiennent une forte proportion d'acides gras non saturés, bénéfiques pour la peau et le poil. Les matières grasses facilitent l'assimilation des vitamines liposolubles et permettent une meilleure absorption des aliments. Pour couvrir les besoins en matières grasses, 10 à 15 % de l'alimentation carnée suffisent, avec un apport supplémentaire d'acides gras essentiels sous forme de, par exemple, huile de chardon à teneur élevée en acide linoléique (72 %).

Les produits laitiers sont très appréciés de nombreux chiens qui les tolèrent bien, même si la forte teneur en lactose pose des problèmes à certains (diarrhée). Un peu de lait dans l'eau du chien l'incitera à boire plus s'il a tendance à ne pas s'abreuver assez et si sa santé l'exige. Le lait aigre ou lait caillé, le yaourt et le kéfir sont également bien tolérés car une partie du lactose y a été transformée en acide lactique. Les petits dés de fromage sont des friandises appréciées en guise de récompense et également bien tolérés, de même que le fromage blanc avec un peu de miel et un jaune d'œuf cru.

Les glucides sont présents dans les flocons d'avoine ou de blé, le riz, le pain, les biscottes, les biscuits ou les aliments pour chiens en flocons. Les besoins du chien sont faibles car il ne peut naturellement pas transformer la cellulose, son tractus intestinal est trop court et sa flore intestinale inadaptée. Les producteurs d'aliments préparés « éliminent » les céréales et les rendent assimilables pour le chien par chauffage, ce qui les transforme en fécules. En ce qui me concerne, je couvre le faible besoin en glucides de mes chiens en dehors des repas carnés avec une tranche de pain dur, un petit-déjeuner de fromage blanc avec des flocons d'avoine et de la noix de coco en poudre, ou encore des biscuits pour chiens que je cuis moi-même.

Les compléments alimentaires : Selon l'âge et la santé du chien, un mélange de minéraux du commerce complète l'alimentation carnée, osseuse et végétale pour son bon développement physique. Demander conseil au vétérinaire. L'huile de lin ou les acides gras oméga 3 sous forme d'huile de saumon sont ajoutés notamment aux acides gras essentiels décrits page 64, de même que les algues marines du genre *Spirulina*, sous forme de poudre ou de comprimés.

LE SAVIEZ-VOUS ?

L'énorme estomac des chiens

Par rapport à la taille du corps, l'estomac d'un chien est presque huit fois plus gros que celui d'un cheval ! Le chien est donc, comme le loup, en mesure de dévorer de grandes quantités de nourriture. Le loup en a besoin car il ne prend pas tous les jours de proie et les louveteaux ou les membres âgés de la meute restés sur place le forcent, à coups de museau, à régurgiter une partie de son repas lorsqu'il revient de la chasse.

Le BARF

Cet acronyme signifie « Biologically Appropriate Raw Food » (alimentation naturelle à base de viande crue). Le concept a été développé par le vétérinaire australien Ian Billinghurst, qui a publié en 1993 son expérience de cette méthode d'alimentation des chiens, et se résume à un régime naturel dans le respect des besoins de l'espèce. Pour passer au BARF et nourrir un chien sainement selon cette méthode, pas besoin de tableaux ni de calculs scientifiques, la seule condition est de composer les menus en fonction de ses besoins avec les ingrédients nécessaires – qui diffèrent en fonction de l'âge et du poids de l'animal. Veillez à utiliser des produits naturels frais et crus et composez vos mélanges en vous inspirant des recettes qui suivent. Vous pouvez aussi vous informer sur Internet (❯ Adresses utiles, page 141).

Les quadrupèdes n'ont pas les mêmes goûts que nous. Les chiens préfèrent le plus souvent boire l'eau d'un étang que l'eau chlorée du robinet.

Pour une « belle bête »

La condition première du développement physique sain d'un chiot est une alimentation équilibrée. Les maîtres responsables en sont conscients.

LE LAIT MATERNEL doit être la seule nourriture du chiot jusqu'à la 4e semaine. À partir de la 4e ou 5e semaine, la mère louve régurgite pour ses louveteaux de la viande prédigérée en plus du lait, ce que nos chiennes ne font plus que rarement : les chiots nourris correctement reçoivent de leur éleveur, en plus du lait maternel, du lait spécial pour chiots, puis de la bouillie. Ils peuvent aussi absorber de minuscules portions de bœuf maigre coupé très fin.

Les régimes pour chiots

C'est au plus tard lorsqu'ils sont confiés à leur nouveau maître, au cours de la 8e semaine, que les chiots sont sevrés et commencent à manger d'eux-mêmes des aliments solides. Pour l'acheteur, il convient de choisir un mode d'alimentation avant même d'aller chercher le chiot.

Pour cela, quelques réflexions préalables s'imposent : informez-vous sur la qualité des aliments préparés que vous destinez à votre chiot (❯ page 61) et si vous préparez vous-même ses repas, vous aurez besoin de connaissances suffisantes sur ses besoins, la composition et la préparation des plats.

Préparer soi-même les repas prend du temps, mais peut aussi faire plaisir. Bien sûr, il est plus rapide d'ouvrir une boîte ou un paquet d'aliments préparés. Si vous souhaitez préparer vous-même le repas de vote chien, la première question qui se pose est celle de savoir si vous pouvez vous approvisionner en viande fraîche dans le voisinage et dans quelles conditions ? La viande provient-elle d'abattoirs inspectés et soumis au contrôle des denrées alimentaires ? Est-elle vraiment fraîche, ou correctement stockée s'il s'agit de viande congelée ? L'autre réflexion concerne le prix de l'alimentation de votre chien : comparez en calculant le coût d'une ration quotidienne.

Mon expérience m'a appris que la viande fraîche revient le moins cher à condition de disposer de possibilités d'achat bon marché. Mais c'est à chaque maître de décider lui-même du régime alimentaire de son chiot.

Un bon éleveur vous fournira un plan d'alimentation détaillé et la nourriture à laquelle le chiot est habitué pour les premiers jours. Une longue discussion vous aidera ensuite à prendre les bonnes décisions au cours des semaines qui suivront.

Enfin, c'est le chien lui-même qui vous montrera s'il se développe ou non harmonieusement avec le régime adopté et ce qu'il ne tolère éventuellement pas.

Autour de l'alimentation

1 **La gamelle :** Le support de gamelles à eau et à nourriture réglable en hauteur convient aux chiens trop empressés, ils peuvent ainsi manger plus calmement et avalent moins d'air.

2 **Les os :** Les chiens aiment ronger les os crus et cela prévient la formation de tartre.

3 **La boisson :** L'eau reste plus longtemps fraîche dans une gamelle en céramique. Le chien doit toujours avoir de l'eau potable à sa disposition.

Les quantités et fréquences des repas

Jusqu'à l'âge de six mois, la ration quotidienne du chiot doit être répartie en quatre petits repas. De six mois à un an, il tolère deux à trois portions plus importantes. L'estomac des chiots ne peut cependant pas encore transformer de trop grandes quantités de nourriture. De plus, un estomac trop plein risquerait de distendre la musculature de son dos, pas encore complètement formée, ce qui pourrait causer notamment un dos ensellé.

Le premier repas du matin dépend de votre emploi du temps mais ne devrait pas être servi après 8 heures. Comme les céréales ne doivent jamais être données au chien en même temps que la viande et qu'il n'en a pas besoin de beaucoup, je fais de ce premier repas un petit-déjeuner au fromage blanc pour mes chiots : fromage blanc maigre (20 % de matière grasse) en quantité adaptée à la taille du chiot (75 à 150 g env.), 1 cuill. à soupe bombée de flocons d'avoine, 1 cuill. à café bombée de noix de coco en poudre, 1 cuill. à café de germes de blé, 1 cuill. à café de miel, 1 cuill. à café de pollen de fleurs, 1 cuill. à café d'huile de chardon ou de tournesol, ½ cuill. à café de coquilles d'œuf finement écrasées et un jaune d'œuf frais un jour sur deux. Les bébés apprécient aussi un peu de pomme finement râpée avec la peau et si la bouillie est trop sèche, on peut la diluer avec un peu de yaourt nature ou de lait. Ce petit-déjeuner naturel à grande valeur nutritive réussit aussi très bien aux chiots nourris d'aliments préparés le reste de la journée, c'est alors un complément alimentaire précieux.

Les trois repas suivants des chiots se composent chez moi d'une bouillie à la viande préparée selon la recette suivante : 75 % (de la quantité totale › Les quantités, page 70) de muscle ou de tête de bœuf cru haché, 20 % de légumes (› page 64), blanchis les pre-

miers temps, puis crus après une longue acclimatation. Les légumes doivent être réduits en purée à la machine. Ajouter selon la saison 1 cuill. à soupe de feuilles fraîches de jeune ortie, de pissenlit ou d'ail sauvage finement hachées, 1 cuill. à café d'huile de chardon pressée à froid et en hiver 1 cuill. à café d'huile de foie de morue. Si vous ne donnez pas de petit-déjeuner au fromage blanc à votre chiot, ajouter 3 fois par semaine un jaune d'œuf frais (le blanc d'œuf doit uniquement être proposé cuit aux chiens) et un mélange de minéraux adapté pour un apport suffisant en calcium et autres minéraux et vitamines essentiels (❯ Les compléments alimentaires, page 65), à demander au vétérinaire.

Conseil : Si vous nourrissez votre chiot avec des aliments préparés, mieux vaut continuer de lui donner ceux que l'éleveur vous a recommandés et auxquels le chiot est déjà habitué.

Les modes d'alimentation

Faut-il laisser en permanence de la nourriture à la disposition du chien afin qu'il puisse manger quand il le veut ? Où vaut-il mieux le nourrir à des horaires fixes ?
La question fait régulièrement l'objet de discussions passionnées. Je vois pour ma part plusieurs raisons contre l'« offre permanente de nourriture » :

ASTUCE

Le menu unique

Changer sans cesse le menu du chien le rendra délicat et difficile. Si des raisons de santé imposent un changement, mélanger de petites quantités du nouvel aliment à l'ancien et les augmenter progressivement jusqu'à ce qu'il ait remplacé l'ancien produit.

CHECK-LIST

Les règles alimentaires de base

Pour les repas de votre chiot, suivre les règles suivantes :

- Toujours nourrir le chiot au même endroit et au même moment.
- Il doit se sentir bien et en sécurité à l'endroit où il prend ses repas.
- Le laisser manger sans que personne ne le dérange, y compris les enfants.
- Adapter les rations quotidiennes de manière à ce qu'il ne mange pas trop à chaque repas.
- Enlever les restes de nourriture dès qu'il se détourne de la gamelle.

- La plupart de nos compagnons à quatre pattes souffrent de suralimentation. Les chiens trop nourris et trop gras sont souvent malades physiquement et psychologiquement.
- Les organes digestifs ne peuvent pas se vider et se reposer parfaitement entre les repas.
- Les chiens sont difficiles à motiver et à influencer positivement pendant leur éducation ou leur formation car ils sont repus en permanence.
- L'alimentation en libre-service n'est possible qu'avec des aliments secs car la viande fraîche attire les mouches ou fermente dès qu'il fait chaud.
- Lorsque plusieurs chiens sont élevés ensemble, les plus gourmands ne tardent pas à trop manger et engraissent.

Le «rationnement» peut être pratiqué avec tous les types d'aliments. Le côlon du chien se règle sur certaines heures et les indispensables promenades sont plus faciles à planifier. Sans compter que des repas à heures fixes évitent au chien de mendier. Pour le nourrir, poser sa gamelle devant lui et l'observer pendant qu'il mange : il doit absorber la nourriture rapidement et avec appétit, si ce n'est pas le cas ou s'il s'éloigne de la gamelle, enlevez-la lui. Cette méthode permet d'éduquer les mauvais mangeurs et de contrôler parfaitement les quantités absorbées. Le chien ne reçoit sa ration habituelle qu'à l'heure du repas suivant. Ne changer en aucun cas la composition des repas, par exemple en y mélangeant des friandises qui servent sinon de récompense : le chien malin commencera sinon par refuser tous les jours son repas pour tenter d'obtenir quelques bouchées supplémentaires.

Conseil : le refus de s'alimenter peut aussi être un signe de maladie, mais il est alors la plupart du temps associé à d'autres symptômes comme l'apathie ou la fièvre (❯ page 86).

Les quantités : Si le chiot laisse de la nourriture dans sa gamelle, diminuer la portion suivante de la quantité correspondante. S'il semble au contraire pouvoir avaler plus et si son poids le permet (❯ Le contrôle du poids, page 71), augmenter la portion suivante.

L'endroit des repas : Toujours nourrir le chiot au même endroit, choisi pour qu'il puisse vider sa gamelle sans être dérangé. Après chaque repas, laver la gamelle à l'eau chaude. Jeter les restes et ne pas les remettre au réfrigérateur. Le chiot doit toujours avoir de l'eau fraîche à sa disposition. La gamelle d'eau elle aussi doit être lavée tous les jours à l'eau chaude (❯ page 68).

La qualité : Ne donner au chien que des produits en parfait état. Les plats maison laissés trop longtemps dehors peuvent fermenter et causer des diarrhées à l'animal. Le contenu des boîtes entamées doit être conservé au réfrigérateur dans une boîte en plastique fermée. Les aliments directement sortis du frigo rendent cependant les chiots malades, tandis qu'ils apprécient tout particulièrement les mets légèrement réchauffés car les éléments gustatifs s'y développent plus. Pour cela, verser de l'eau chaude sur les aliments secs et les laisser gonfler un court instant.

Le contrôle du poids

Les premières semaines, vérifier une fois par semaine que le chiot prend du poids de manière continue. Si c'est le cas, c'est aussi le signe qu'il est nourri sainement.

Conseil : Une suralimentation entre le 3e et le 6e mois peut entraîner chez les grandes races de chiens une croissance trop rapide qui laissera des séquelles définitives. En effet, les jeunes os des chiots sont encore souples et malléables, l'excès de poids qui pèse sur eux peut être à l'origine de malformations ou favoriser le développement d'une dysplasie de la hanche (HD) congénitale.

Pour le peser, c'est très simple : montez sur un pèse-personne et notez votre poids, prenez ensuite le chiot dans vos bras et montez de nouveau avec lui sur la balance, la différence entre les deux résultats donne le poids du chiot. La balance ne vous sera cependant pas d'une grande aide pour vérifier si votre chiot est trop ou pas assez nourri. Pour cela, il vous faut d'abord connaître le poids normal correspondant à son âge. Vous trouverez quelques valeurs indicatives ci-dessous :

Races moyennes : Poids d'une race de taille moyenne dont le poids adulte est de 20 kg : à la fin du 2e mois = 4,4 kg; à la fin du 3e mois = 7,4 kg; à la fin du 4e mois = 10,4 kg; à la fin du 6e mois = 14,0 kg; à la fin du 12e mois = 19,0 kg.

> Un chiot en bonne santé doit **prendre du poids,** sinon c'est le signe que quelque chose ne va pas bien.

Un pèse-lettre est presque suffisant pour peser un si minuscule bébé. ▸

Grandes races : Poids d'une race de grande taille dont le poids adulte est de 35 kg environ : à la fin du 2e mois = 7,0 kg; à la fin du 3e mois = 12,2 kg; à la fin du 4e mois = 16,8 kg; à la fin du 6e mois = 22,8 kg; à la fin du 12e mois = 29,8 kg.

Surveiller la ligne : Les maîtres intéressés apprennent rapidement à estimer l'équilibre nutritif de leur chien adulte. Pour cela, placez-vous derrière lui et posez vos mains sur sa cage thoracique à gauche et à droite, une légère pression doit vous permettre de bien sentir les côtes sur toute leur longueur. Si vous devez appuyer fortement pour les sentir, le chien est trop gros. En ce qui concerne les chiots, on évoque souvent les « rondeurs de bébé » qui disparaissent avec l'âge, mais cela ne s'applique que jusqu'à la 12e ou 14e semaine. Ensuite, le chiot doit devenir plutôt musclé et nerveux et toujours avoir un peu faim.

Les crottes

Les crottes d'un chien en bonne santé sont de forme ovoïde et élastiques, ni dures et friables, ni visqueuses. La couleur dépend de l'alimentation. Si elle est équilibrée, les crottes sont brun à brun foncé. Si le chiot mange trop d'os, ses crottes pourront être gris clair. Elles sont jaunâtres en cas d'excès de lait, presque noires et poisseuses en cas d'alimentation exclusivement hépatique. Si le chiot a la diarrhée, mais sans saignements, ne pas le nourrir pendant une

MON ANIMAL DOMESTIQUE

Quelle conscience de l'environnement a mon chiot ?

Une fois que le chiot s'est habitué à son nouveau logis, il cherche à explorer son environnement immédiat. C'est l'occasion de tester son assurance, ou au contraire son manque d'assurance.

Début du test :

Prendre progressivement contact avec des étrangers, des enfants et d'autres chiens. Comment le chiot réagit-il aux bruits de circulation ? Observez son comportement. Quelles sont les situations qui suscitent des réactions de peur ou qui l'effraient ? Faire durer le test plusieurs jours et ne pas trop solliciter le chiot avec de trop nombreuses impressions nouvelles.

Résultat du test :

Le chien ne peut pas ici être accusé de voler. L'étourderie de son maître lui vaut de trouver la saucisse et de la subtiliser sans attendre.

journée. Si la diarrhée persiste ou si les crottes sont mêlées de sang, consulter immédiatement un vétérinaire.

Les quantités : La quantité de crottes que fait un chiot en dit long sur la qualité de son alimentation : plus il absorbe de mets « indigestes » (par exemple des aliments préparés bon marché), plus il fera de crottes. En revanche, si la quantité de crottes est égale à la quantité de nourriture absorbée, ne pas hésiter à consulter un vétérinaire.

Les problèmes particuliers

Les aliments avariés et moisis forment des toxines susceptibles de causer de graves intoxications au chien et qui se multiplient lorsque les aliments, secs ou autres, sont conservés dans un endroit chaud et humide. Le chien est, certes, un charognard, ses acides gastriques et biliaires détruisent un certain nombre de bactéries, mais pas leurs toxines, aussi mieux vaut jeter tout le paquet dès l'apparition de moisissures.

L'herbe : Le chien peut en manger pour plusieurs raisons. Les plus fréquentes sont des troubles digestifs, très souvent dus à un excès d'acide gastrique. Le chien vomit alors l'herbe absorbée avec une mousse de couleur jaunâtre. Il peut aussi manger des herbes jeunes et juteuses pour compléter son alimentation – mais ne les vomit alors pas. Mon berger allemand actuel se régale ainsi des feuilles séchées de notre vigne vierge.

Les crottes : La coprophagie ou le fait de manger des excréments peut indiquer une carence. Si le chien mange ses crottes ou celles d'autres chiens, il souffre peut-être d'un manque d'enzymes digestives. S'il mange les excréments de chevaux, bœufs ou moutons, il peut s'agir d'une carence en protéines ou en vitamine B. Dans ce cas, vérifier la composition de ses repas et si tout est en ordre, le recours à des mesures éducatives s'impose. Les chiennes mangent aussi les crottes de leurs chiots, mais c'est un comportement parfaitement normal.

5. Soins et santé

Les soins réguliers contribuent de manière essentielle à la prévention et à la santé du chiot. S'il tombe malgré tout malade, n'hésitez pas à consulter un vétérinaire sans tarder.

Le chiot bien soigné : beau et sain

Habituez votre chiot dès son plus jeune âge à des soins « rituels » qu'il perçoit positivement : un massage doux à la brosse, des compliments de son maître ou de sa maîtresse et une friandise pour s'être bien comporté – cela ne peut que plaire au bébé.

LES SOINS RÉGULIERS du chien n'ont pas pour seuls objectifs l'hygiène et la beauté, ils permettent aussi de repérer plus rapidement les premiers symptômes de maladie. Sans compter que le « corps-à-corps » avec l'animal est une composante sociale importante : vous gagnez ainsi sa confiance et il ne la perdra plus, même s'il tombe malade ou s'il souffre et que vous devez l'examiner alors que cela lui est désagréable.

Le pelage

Il existe des chiens aux types de poil les plus divers : poil long (collie), poil court et lisse (berger allemand), poil court (boxer), poil raide (fox-terrier) et des chiens dont le standard de la race exige qu'ils soient tondus (caniche). Tous, sauf ceux qui sont tondus, subissent une « mue » deux fois par an au cours de laquelle ils perdent les vieux poils morts et le duvet, parfois par plaques entières pour les races au duvet très épais (races nordiques). Cette perte brutale peut être quelque peu adoucie par des peignages soigneux et réguliers.

Pour l'habituer aux soins du poil et du corps : Étalez une couverture sur la table et posez le chiot dessus. Amenez-le, par des caresses et des mots apaisants, à se coucher dans une position détendue. Dès qu'il commence à savourer et à se délecter d'être gratté et chatouillé sur le ventre, montrez-lui la brosse et le peigne et laissez-le les flairer. Commencez par lui donner quelques coups de brosse très doux dans le sens du poil sans appuyer et récompensez-le avec une friandise et de nombreux compliments au bout de deux ou trois. Interrompez là le soin du poil mais le lendemain, essayez de le brosser un peu plus longtemps et commencez aussi à employer le peigne avec précaution. Ne perdez surtout pas votre calme du début à la fin.

Les adorables chiots King Charles sont dès la naissance des petits êtres soignés de la tête aux pieds.

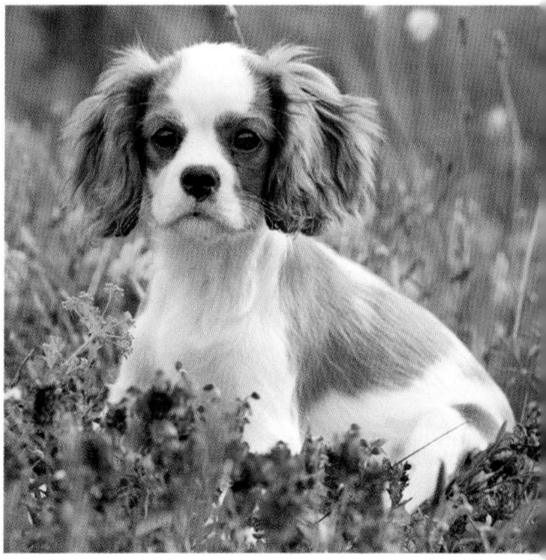

Les chiots auxquels un premier « soin » trop grossier et trop impatient fait mal ne se laisseront plus volontiers brosser et peigner par la suite. En revanche, dès que le chiot a compris que le brossage et le peignage lui font du bien et qu'il peut compter sur une friandise au cours de l'opération et à la fin, il se laissera soigner en toute confiance et avec plaisir.

Le bain : S'il est élevé dans un logement propre, brossé et peigné régulièrement, un chien ne doit normalement pas être baigné. Si cela devait néanmoins s'avérer nécessaire, utiliser un shampooing nourrissant pour chiens afin de ne pas détruire le manteau gras et acide de sa peau et veiller, surtout en hiver, à ce que son poil soit parfaitement sec avant de le laisser sortir. En revanche, dès que les températures estivales le permettent, inviter le chiot à barboter dans l'eau peu profonde (dans un bassin pour enfants) pour qu'il apprenne à aimer l'eau. Il n'y a rien de mieux pour le soin du poil que les baignades estivales régulières. Après le bain, lorsque le poil est sec, le peigner légèrement et brosser les sujets à poil court à contre poil pour leur masser la peau.

Les modifications pathologiques du poil : Une alimentation déficiente ou inadaptée peut être à l'origine d'un pelage terne, cassant, sec qui sent mauvais (le rance), associé à une peau sèche et à des pellicules. Parmi les remèdes possibles, un mélange de minéraux équilibrant (prescrit par le vétérinaire), de la levure de bière, un jaune d'œuf ou jusqu'à une cuill. à soupe d'huile de chardon par jour peuvent aider. Le mieux reste néanmoins de consulter un vétérinaire.

Le museau

La truffe – l'extrémité, de la consistance du cuir, du museau – doit toujours être humide et propre. La nettoyer à l'eau tiède après les « travaux de terrassement » du chiot et l'enduire de vaseline si elle est trop sèche pour lui conserver sa souplesse et éviter les coupures.

En cas d'écoulement nasal clair et aqueux accompagné de fièvre et d'un écoulement purulent, muqueux ou sanglant, consulter immédiatement un vétérinaire.

Le chiot doit aimer les soins prodigués par son maître.

Entraînez-vous au calme et à la patience.

L'agitation et la nervosité dégoûteront le bébé chien des soins.

Les babines

Les lèvres du chien sont normalement fermées et serrées. Les éleveurs sont cependant parvenus à obtenir des babines tombantes chez certaines races comme les dogues ou les mastiffs. Bien évidemment, ces chiens ne peuvent par conséquent faire autrement que de « baver » plus ou moins abondamment. Par ailleurs, restes de nourriture

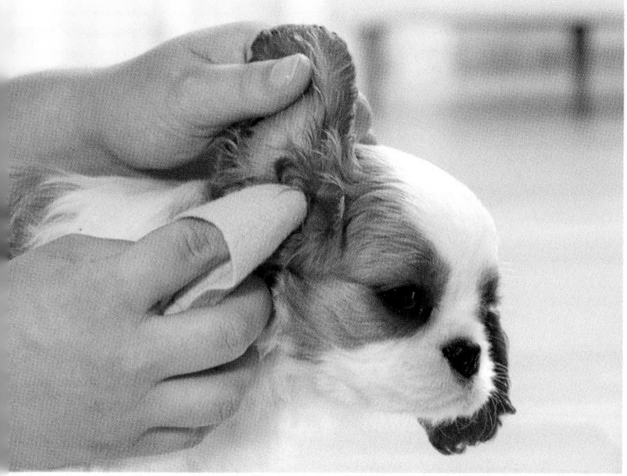

◀ 1 **Soin des oreilles :** Après y avoir versé quelques gouttes de liquide nettoyant (disponible en animalerie et à utiliser comme prescrit sur le mode d'emploi), l'oreille externe est soigneusement nettoyée avec un chiffon doux.

Contrôle dentaire : Vérifier régulièrement l'absence de corps étrangers entre les dents et de tartre. Surveiller également toute modification pathologique des gencives et de la gorge. 2 ▶

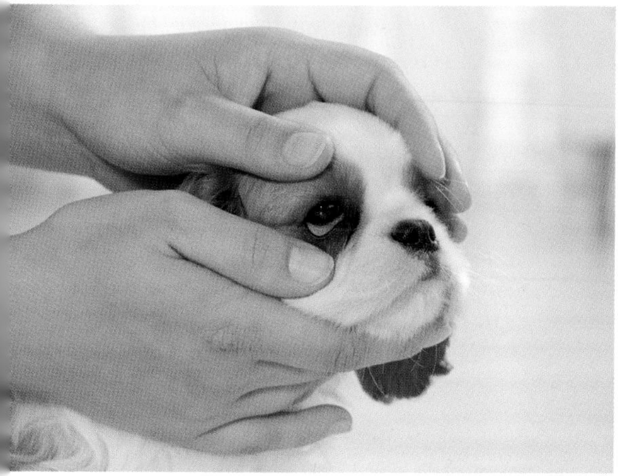

◀ 3 **Soin des yeux :** Retirer les croûtes aux coins des yeux à l'aide d'un chiffon doux et humide. Les écoulements purulents et les conjonctivites doivent faire l'objet d'un traitement vétérinaire (❯ page 78).

Soin des pattes : Les coussinets et espaces interdigitaux doivent être contrôlés pour vérifier qu'aucun corps étranger ne s'y est logé. Pour soigner les coussinets, les enduire de vaseline (❯ page 79). 4 ▶

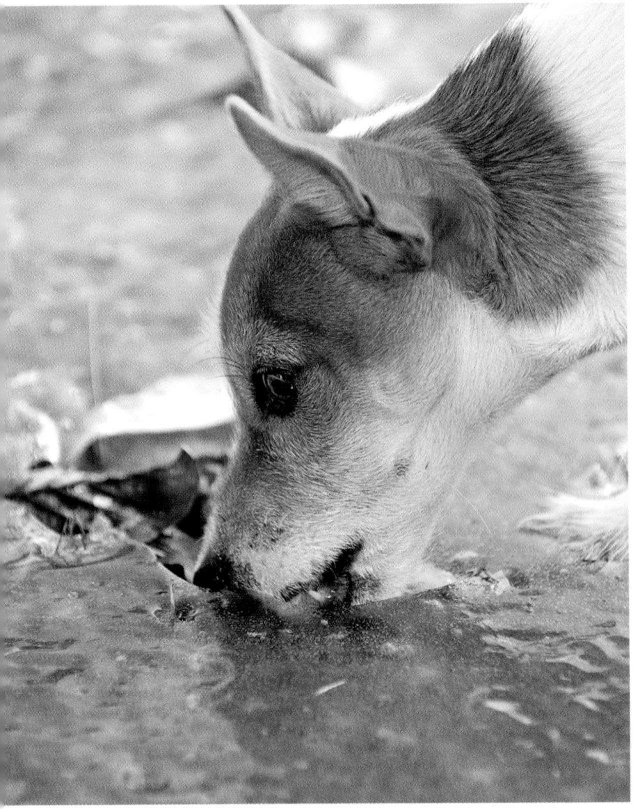

Le chiot ne doit pas manger la glace en hiver.

et impuretés s'accumulent dans les « poches » ainsi formées, collent en cas de soins insuffisants et ne peuvent alors plus être éliminés avec la seule langue du chien. Il en résulte souvent des gerçures ou un eczéma labial. Le nettoyage régulier à l'eau tiède et un peu de vaseline aux endroits durcis permettent de prévenir ces problèmes.

Les yeux

Ils doivent être clairs. Les paupières doivent être collées aux yeux et empêcher les impuretés d'y pénétrer. Retirer tous les matins avec un chiffon humide les croûtes au coin des yeux du chiot.
Les principaux signes anormaux sont : le trouble croissant et/ou le changement de couleur du corps vitré, les écoulements purulents, les conjonctivites et les yeux gonflés. Dans ce cas, une visite chez le vétérinaire s'impose.

Les dents

Contrôler régulièrement la dentition du chiot pour vérifier l'absence de tartre et d'impuretés entre les dents. S'il a été habitué tôt à se nettoyer les dents avec une brosse à dents pour chien et du dentifrice spécial, il tolérera ce traitement une fois adulte. Vérifier également qu'il possède toutes ses dents (28 dents de lait, 42 dents définitives).

Les oreilles

Les oreilles du chien peuvent être relevées, semi-dressées ou tombantes. Elles doivent être nettoyées régulièrement. Pour cela, le mieux est d'utiliser un liquide nettoyant spécial (en animalerie) à chauffer légèrement et à verser goutte à goutte dans l'oreille. Les oreilles tombantes nécessitent un soin particulier car leur forme les empêche de sécher toutes seules et des otites peuvent se développer en cas de soins insuffisants. Le chien montre qu'il a des problèmes d'oreilles d'abord en se grattant précautionneusement l'oreille, puis en secouant la tête et en la tenant penchée dans la direction de l'oreille malade. La mutilation (coupage) des oreilles est aujourd'hui interdite en France.

Les pattes et les griffes

Les pattes : Les coussinets sont plus ou moins l'équivalent de notre plante

du pied. Pour en prendre soin, les laver de temps en temps (entre les doigts aussi) et les graisser à la vaseline. En hiver, il convient aussi d'en retirer le sel de déneigement, très agressif, et de les protéger en les enduisant de suif de cerf ou d'un vaporisateur à cet effet (en animalerie). Les chiens aux poils épais entre les orteils souffrent par ailleurs des blocs de glace qui s'y forment. Là encore, le suif de cerf utilisé préventivement peut aider, ou l'élimination des poils trop longs.
Enfin, les tours en vélo sur des chaussées stabilisées peuvent littéralement « raboter » les pattes du chien et lui laisser les « pieds » en sang, des blessures susceptibles de s'enflammer ou de durcir.

Les griffes : Un chien qui a suffisamment de mouvement use normalement lui-même ses griffes. Néanmoins, de nombreuses races, notamment les plus grandes, appuient parfois tellement sur les articulations antérieures du pied à la suite de malnutrition que les griffes ne touchent plus suffisamment le sol. Dans ce cas, faites-vous montrer par le vétérinaire comment les couper.

Les parties génitales

Vérifier régulièrement la vulve de votre chienne pour être sûr qu'aucun écoulement anormal n'en sort. Les saignements menstruels, en revanche, sont parfaitement normaux – pour éviter les gouttes de sang sur le sol, on trouve des

1 **Soin du poil pour débuter :** Le brossage stimule les glandes cutanées qui produisent des matières grasses et donnent au poil un bel éclat. Lors de la première tentative de soin, se contenter d'habituer le chiot au contact avec la brosse.

2 **Soin du poil courant :** Le chiot sait désormais que la brosse lui fait du bien et peut-être aussi qu'une friandise l'attend après le soin. Il se couche sur le côté, détendu, et savoure le doux massage.

CHECK-LIST

Bilan de santé

Plus vous remarquerez tôt les éventuels signes de maladie chez votre chiot, meilleures seront ses chances de guérison.

- ○ Pendant ses périodes de réveil, le chiot est plein d'entrain et insouciant, curieux et toujours prêt à jouer.
- ○ Son corps est musclé, ni trop maigre, ni trop gros (❯ page 71).
- ○ Son poil est propre et luisant.
- ○ La peau est lisse, sans grosseurs sous-cutanées, humide et, bien sûr, sans le moindre parasite.
- ○ Les pattes sont souples et ne semblent lui causer aucune souffrance lorsqu'il marche.
- ○ Le chiot adopte une démarche harmonieuse à toutes les allures et ne se montre gêné par aucun mouvement.
- ○ Les coussinets ne sont pas sensibles au toucher.
- ○ Les oreilles sont propres et inodores.
- ○ Les yeux sont clairs et brillants.
- ○ Les dents sont blanches, saines et il n'en manque aucune (❯ page 78).
- ○ Les gencives et la langue sont humides et roses.

culottes de protection spéciales. Vérifier l'absence de tumeur ou de modification des testicules du chien et rincer son prépuce pour éviter d'éventuelles inflammations – après en avoir parlé à votre vétérinaire. De même, présentez au vétérinaire tout chiot qui ne présente qu'un testicule, ou aucun car les testicules non descendus qui restent dans la cavité abdominale peuvent être source de difficultés ultérieures.

Le postérieur, l'urine et les crottes

L'anus et la glande anale : Pensez à examiner souvent votre chien sous la queue. En règle générale, il se nettoie lui-même à cet endroit, mais au niveau de l'anus se trouve la glande anale qui produit une sécrétion à l'odeur forte lorsque le chien défèque, c'est sa « note parfumée » personnelle à laquelle ses congénères le reconnaissent. L'anus et la glande anale doivent toujours être propres. Les frotter éventuellement avec un chiffon humide et les enduire de temps en temps de vaseline. Lorsque les deux orifices de la glande anale restent collés trop longtemps, cela peut provoquer une obstruction et une inflammation nécessitant l'intervention du vétérinaire.
L'urine : Le chien ne doit pas uriner goutte à goutte mais produire un jet d'urine, jaune clair à jaune foncé.
Les crottes : Elles doivent être contrôlées tous les jours. Elles doivent former des boudins fermes, compacts et pas trop durs. En cas de diarrhée non sanglante, ne pas alimenter le chien pendant une journée et vérifier si sa nourriture est susceptible d'avoir causé la diarrhée (❯ page 72).

Prévention et guérison

Une alimentation saine, des soins consciencieux, suffisamment de mouvement et des activités intéressantes, tels sont les meilleurs garants d'une bonne santé stable du chiot. S'il tombe néanmoins malade, consulter aussitôt un vétérinaire.

C'EST AU QUOTIDIEN avec votre chiot et lors des soins que vous remarquerez le plus rapidement ce qui ne va pas et s'il couve éventuellement une maladie.

Symptômes des maladies

Les signes anormaux suivants sont visibles, même par un profane :
Modifications du comportement : Le chiot fait triste mine, n'a envie de rien, il est grincheux et de mauvaise humeur. Il change souvent de place, est peureux et extrêmement agité. Il erre sans but, hurle, gémit, crie ou pleure, est particulièrement craintif. Il semble un peu hébété et/ou se montre indifférent à son environnement. Il a le regard vide, sans expression, et une démarche lente et furtive. Il dort sans interruption. Il souffre de pertes de conscience provisoires, s'évanouit ou est victime d'étourdissements.
Modifications physiques : Les os sont visiblement mal positionnés, la forme du squelette se modifie. Le chien maigrit ou, au contraire, engraisse exagérément. La peau lui colle au corps. Les poils du chiot tombent ou perdent leur éclat.
Modifications cutanées : Les muqueuses visibles comme la conjonctive oculaire et la muqueuse gingivale (› Check-list, page 81) frappent par leur pâleur ou une autre coloration. La peau interne des cuisses et du ventre prend elle aussi couleur, elle est sèche, dure, chaude ou froide selon les cas. Les émanations cutanées sentent mauvais, la peau est sensible à la douleur ou présente des gonflements pâteux.
La température et le pouls : La température normale d'un chien se situe entre 37,5 et 39 °C, celle d'un chiot peut aller jusqu'à 39,5 °C.
Le pouls des gros chiens bat de 70 à 130 fois par minute, jusqu'à 180 fois pour les petites races et jusqu'à 220 fois pour les chiots.
Le pouls peut cependant aussi s'accélérer si le chien a peur, est inquiet, s'il

ASTUCE

Les vers

Les signes d'infection sont la diarrhée, les vomissements et les démangeaisons autour de l'anus. Si vous trouvez du sang dans ses crottes, il peut s'agir d'ascarides, les crottes noires indiquent la présence d'ankylostomes et peuvent signaler des hémorragies intestinales.

est joyeux, après une activité sportive intense ou tout autre effort. Il peut être mesuré sur la face interne des cuisses. Un ralentissement se produit parfois en cas d'intoxication, une accélération en cas de fièvre, de faiblesse cardiaque ou de perte de sang. Le chien au repos respire 10 à 30 fois par minute.

On remarque qu'un chiot est malade à des **modifications du comportement.** La visite chez le vétérinaire est alors incontournable.

Pour prendre sa température : Utiliser un thermomètre qui peut être introduit dans l'oreille, c'est la solution la plus rapide et qui pose beaucoup moins de problème que dans l'anus.

Si le chien reste couché sur son lit indifférent à tout, il est peut-être malade.

La visite chez le vétérinaire

Avant la consultation, notez les symptômes que vous avez remarqués chez votre chiot. Vous devez aussi être en mesure de renseigner le vétérinaire sur la nature des crottes et de l'urine, car sans ces indications, il ne lui sera peut-être pas possible de poser rapidement un diagnostic.

Prévention des maladies

Les vermifugations : Les chiots doivent être vermifugés tôt car ils peuvent être infectés de larves d'ascarides dans le ventre de leur mère par le sang de cette dernière et peuvent de nouveau être contaminés après la naissance par le lait maternel. C'est pourquoi la lutte contre les vers ronds ou nématodes (groupe dont font partie les ascarides) commence dès la 2e semaine et doit être répétée toutes les deux semaines jusqu'à la 12e semaine.
Les chiens adultes quant à eux ne sont plus aujourd'hui vermifugés sur de simples soupçons, mais uniquement lorsque des échantillons de crottes font état de la présence de vers quels qu'ils soient.
Ils doivent cependant être vermifugés avant toute vaccination car l'immunisation ne pourra pas se développer suffisamment sinon.
Les vaccinations : Pour les chiens aussi, des vaccins ont été développés pour de nombreuses maladies infectieuses parfois mortelles. Tous les chiots devraient recevoir les vaccinations de base, elles peuvent leur sauver la vie. Les maladies infectieuses les plus dangereuses sont :

- la maladie de Carré
- l'hépatite

VACCINATIONS CONTRE LES MALADIES INFECTIEUSES LES PLUS DANGEREUSES

ÂGE	VACCINATION
7e/8e semaine	Maladie de Carré, leptospirose, parvovirose, hépatite
11e/12e semaine	Maladie de Carré, leptospirose, parvovirose, hépatite, rage
15e/16e semaine	Éventuellement rappel de la rage
15e semaine	Maladie de Carré, leptospirose, parvovirose, hépatite, rage

Conseil : Les délais et la nécessité des rappels tels qu'ils étaient recommandés jusqu'à présent font aujourd'hui débat. Il existe désormais des vaccins qui assurent une protection bien plus longue que les recommandations et prescriptions officielles (par exemple contre la rage). Mieux vaut donc s'informer précisément et ne décider d'un calendrier de vaccinations pour son chiot qu'après avoir demandé conseil à son vétérinaire.

- la leptospirose
- la rage
- la parvovirose

Les chiots bénéficient d'une immunisation naturelle par le lait maternel, mais son effet est limité dans le temps et peut chuter brusquement entre la 6e et la 8e semaine. Le chiot est alors vacciné deux fois à un intervalle de quatre semaines dans le cadre de l'immunisation dite de base.

La protection n'est cependant complète qu'une à deux semaines après la vaccination. En attendant, le chiot doit être tenu à l'écart d'autres animaux susceptibles d'être malades.

Les principales maladies infectieuses

Sans vaccination, elles sont souvent mortelles pour le chien.

La maladie de Carré ou distemper canin. Les symptômes en sont : des poussées de fièvre variables, des vomissements, de la diarrhée, un écoulement nasal, d'abord aqueux, plus tard purulent, une inflammation de la muqueuse nasale, une pneumonie, une hypersensibilité à la lumière, une conjonctivite purulente, la cécité, la formation de pustules, des rougeurs cutanées sur la face interne des cuisses et l'abdomen, le poil terne et hérissé, toute la gamme des maladies nerveuses, des convul-

sions musculaires jusqu'à la paralysie. Les différentes formes évolutives peuvent apparaître successivement ou simultanément.
L'hépatite : Les symptômes en sont : fièvre, abattement, manque d'appétit, inflammation des amygdales, conjonctivite, difficultés à avaler, hémorragies des muqueuses, opacité provisoire de la cornée dans les cas les moins graves. Certaines formes évolutives sont marquées par des décès brusques qui font souvent naître à tort le soupçon d'une intoxication ou d'un empoisonnement.

Les vaccinations régulières peuvent sauver la vie du chien.

La leptospirose : Les symptômes en sont : fièvre, troubles généraux, faiblesse, hémorragies des muqueuses, coloration jaune des muqueuses due à une détérioration du foie et à la destruction de globules rouges, vomissements inapaisables, diarrhée, déshydratation. On connaît des formes évolutives légères, mais aussi mortelles.
La rage : La forme évolutive classique passe par trois phases : tout d'abord, le caractère du chien change, il devient craintif, se terre dans son coin, n'obéit plus, est nerveux et « attrape des mouches » imaginaires. Pendant la deuxième phase, l'animal devient agressif, il fugue (rage furieuse), les autres symptômes comprennent l'agitation, la combativité exacerbée, la bave, les appétits dénaturés (paille, textiles, bois, excréments), le chien mord les objets les plus divers et devient fou furieux. La troisième phase est marquée par l'épuisement, la paralysie et enfin la mort.
Il existe aussi une forme de rage « calme » qui s'accompagne d'indifférence, d'un regard fixe et sans expression, d'une paralysie de la mâchoire inférieure et d'une voix rauque.
La parvovirose : Les symptômes en sont : une diarrhée aqueuse et nauséabonde, parfois sanglante, des vomissements, un refus de s'alimenter, un abattement, une déshydratation massive, une inflammation du muscle cardiaque. Les décès sont fréquents chez les très jeunes chiens.

Les parasites externes

Les puces sont sans doute les parasites du chien les plus connus. Bien qu'à mon avis on ne puisse en vouloir à un chien d'attraper des puces, leurs attaques peuvent être très désagréables car une puce ne vient jamais seule. Le chien peut réagir aux agressions massives par des démangeaisons, des réactions allergiques à la salive de puce, la formation de croûtes et la perte de poils. Les puces adultes vivent dans le pelage du chien et sucent le sang de son épiderme – dont elles ont besoin pour pondre. Les œufs tombent du poil sur le lit du chien (panier, moquette ou fauteuil) et s'y développent. Les puces adultes ne représentent qu'un à cinq pour cent d'une population, de sorte qu'il ne suffit pas de traiter le chien, il faut aussi et surtout lutter dans tout son environnement contre les différents stades de l'évolution des insectes – œufs, larves, chrysalides. Des préparations « spot on » à verser goutte à goutter sur

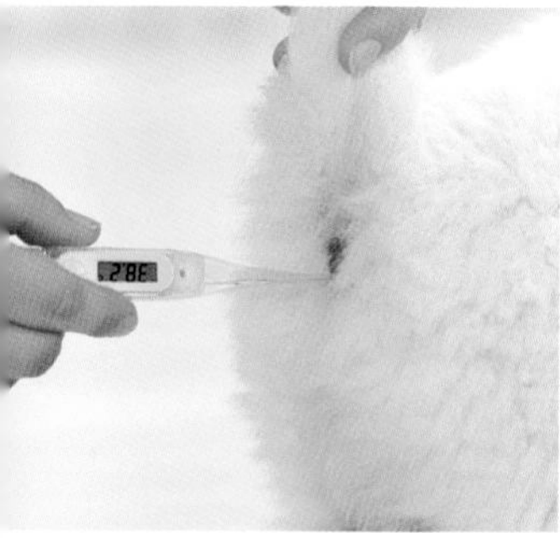

1 Prendre sa température : Introduire le thermomètre enduit de vaseline dans l'anus jusqu'à l'affichage de la température.

2 Mettre des gouttes dans les yeux : Tirer légèrement la paupière vers le bas avec le pouce de la main gauche en tenant bien la tête du chiot. Déposer les gouttes sur la paupière inférieure avec la main droite.

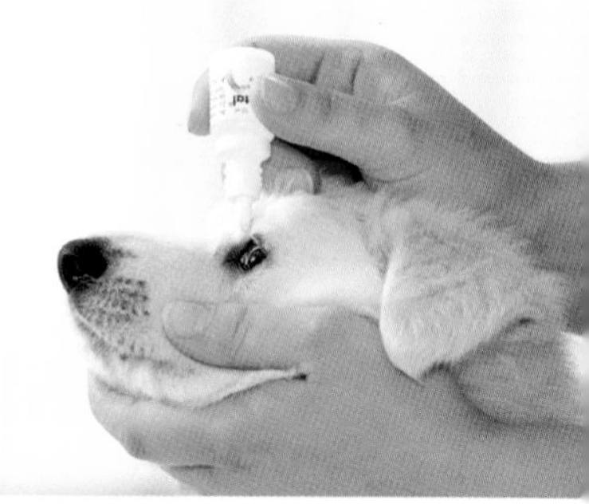

3 Le bander : Pour arrêter un saignement, il est parfois nécessaire de mettre un pansement. Pour cela, rester calme et patient.

le poil aident aujourd'hui à combattre les puces chez le chien, ainsi que des bains, poudres, sprays et colliers anti-puces. Les couvées de puces sont éliminées avec des régulateurs de croissance d'insectes (sprays, pulvérisations, comprimés). L'environnement du chien, notamment son lit, doit être nettoyé, aspiré, lavé et traité à l'aide de désinfectant anti-puces en vaporisateur.

Les tiques ou « tiques brunes du chien » sont également des insectes suceurs de sang qu'on trouve essentiellement dans les terrains forestiers au sous-bois abondant ou en lisière de champs et de prairies. Elles déploient leur activité principale en mai/juin et septembre/octobre. Comme les autres tiques, la tique brune du chien a été « importée » de régions tropicales et est porteuse de maladies graves telles que la borréliose, la babésiose, l'ehrlichiose et la FSME. Les mesures préventives comprennent des colliers anti-tiques et des préparations ou sprays « spot on ». Une astuce : ajouter de temps en temps une demi-gousse d'ail écrasée au repas du chiot s'il le tolère. Par ailleurs, après toute promenade en forêt ou dans la nature, le chien doit être brossé, frotté et examiné pour vérifier l'absence de tiques. Si vous en découvrez une, la saisir juste au-dessus de la peau avec une pince à tiques et la « dévisser ». Éviter cependant de tamponner l'endroit avec de l'huile, de l'essence ou de la colle : cela ferait vomir la tique et accroîtrait le risque de transmission d'agents pathogènes.

Les poux sont rares chez les chiens domestiques bien soignés et sont surtout présents chez les chiens des rues abandonnés. Ils causent agitation, déman-

LES MALADIES LES PLUS COURANTES

Premiers signes	Autres symptômes	Maladie éventuelle
Refuse de s'alimenter	Diarrhée, vomissements, fièvre, apathie, soif	Infection virale, inflammation utérine, corps étrangers dans l'intestin
Refuse de boire	Bave, toux, étouffements et étranglements, déglutition infondée	Présence de corps étrangers dans le gosier, paralysie du gosier
Boit beaucoup	Vomissements, température basse, vertige, apathie	Lésion rénale (avec urémie), diabète, infection utérine
Vomit	Glaires sanglantes, fièvre, absence de selles, tension abdominale	Gastrite, corps étrangers dans l'estomac, maladie hépatique ou rénale
Efforts vains pour uriner et crotter	Glaires sanglantes, saignement anal, urine sanglante	Obstruction, calculs urétraux ou vésicaux
Diarrhée	Sang dans les crottes, vomissements, déshydratation	Vers, infection gastro-intestinale, intoxication, maladie hépatique ou pancréatique
Tousse	Toux sèche avec étouffements muqueux, toux irritative avec mucosités sanglantes	Inflammation des amygdales, de la gorge ou du larynx (toux du chenil)
A mauvaise haleine	Bave, boit excessivement, haleine urineuse et putride	Tartre, parodontose, dent purulente, gastrite, maladie rénale
Tient la tête penchée ou la secoue	Oreilles nauséabondes, douleur lors des grattements	Présence d'un corps étranger dans l'oreille, excès de cérumen, acariens des oreilles, inflammation
Démangeaisons	Pustules, perte de poils, rougeurs cutanées, gonflements	Eczéma, attaque de parasites (puces, tiques), allergie, tumeur
Se lèche la région anale	Glissades sur l'arrière-train (« luge »)	Obstruction de la glande anale, vers
Boite	Paralysie et gonflements, marche sur trois pattes	Entorse, blessure ou maladie articulaire ou musculaire
Yeux larmoyants	Écoulement purulent, conjonctivite	Inflammation, infection, présence d'un corps étranger dans l'œil, maladie oculaire congénitale

geaisons, plaies, modifications cutanées humides et poisseuses, formation de croûtes et perte de poils. Contrairement aux puces, ils dépendent totalement du chien avec leur progéniture. On les trouve surtout sur la lèvre supérieure, au fond des oreilles et sur la gorge, ils collent leurs œufs (lentes) aux poils du chien. La meilleure prévention reste le soin régulier du poil et ils peuvent être sinon combattus à l'aide de poudres ou de bains spécifiques (en animalerie).

Les demodex sont des habitants naturels des follicules pileux et des glandes sébacées. Chez le chien, les symptômes de maladie apparaissent uniquement en cas d'accroissement massif des populations à la suite d'un défaut du système immunitaire; ils prennent alors la forme de rougeurs sans poils sur la lèvre supérieure, les paupières, le dos du nez, le front, les oreilles et les pattes antérieures ou de pellicules sur les membranes interdigitales, mais ne causent que des démangeaisons modérées. Les jeunes chiens et ceux au système immunitaire affaibli sont touchés en priorité, les parasites sont transmis par la mère lors de câlins trop rapprochés ou pendant la tétée. Lorsque des chiens plus âgés tombent malades, c'est qu'ils étaient déjà infectés dans leur jeune âge. On trouve des bains spécifiques, des solutions et/ou des injections (à faire par le vétérinaire) pour lutter contre l'agent pathogène et renforcer le système immunitaire du chien.

Les acariens des oreilles sont transmis par contact entre chiens ou entre chats et chiens. Ils s'attaquent au conduit auditif externe et à l'intérieur du lobe. Le chien souffre alors de démangeaisons et de prurit violents, il secoue la tête, se frotte les oreilles sur le sol, on assiste à la formation accrue de cérumen et à une inflammation du conduit auditif accompagnée d'une sécrétion brun-noir, sablonneuse ou friable. Dans les cas les plus graves, des perforations de la membrane du tympan, des otites et la surdité peuvent survenir. La prévention passe par un contrôle régulier des oreilles (› page 78). Les traitements avec des préparations anti-acariens sont à réserver au vétérinaire.

Combattez les parasites
dès leur apparition.

Les parasites internes

Les ascarides sont le type de vers le plus fréquent et tous les chiots sont considé-

Cette collerette souple gonflable empêche le chien de lécher ses plaies ou son eczéma.

rés comme touchés (› page 82). Ils sont blancs et ont un corps à section circulaire qui les fait ressembler à des spaghettis. Chez les chiots qui tètent encore, la migration des larves dans tout le corps peut causer des lésions pulmonaires et une pneumonie, les bébés toussent, ont le nez qui coule et vomissent, leur ventre est ballonné et sensible à la pression, leurs crottes informes et visqueuses, ils maigrissent, n'ont pas d'appétit et sont anémiques. Les amas de vers peuvent aussi causer une occlusion intestinale. La prévention passe par des vermifugations systématiques de la chienne et de ses chiots (› pages 81 et 82), le contrôle régulier des crottes du chien adulte, leur élimination et une bonne hygiène sont également importants. La question de la vermifugation doit être discutée avec le vétérinaire.

Le ver solitaire ou ténia *(Dipylidium caninum)* est le plus fréquent chez les chiens. Il est transmis par des puces qui le contiennent à des stades infectieux. Il ne nuit que rarement à la santé du chien, ce dernier peut tout au plus souffrir de variations d'appétit ou de diarrhée. Il élimine des morceaux de ténia avec les crottes, on peut aussi les trouver desséchés sous forme de formations rappelant des grains de riz dans le pelage des pattes arrière, sur la queue ou dans le lit du chien. La lutte systématique contre les puces permet aussi de prévenir le risque de ténia, réserver de préférence le traitement au vétérinaire.

LE SAVIEZ-VOUS ?

Les visites chez le vétérinaire ne souffrent aucun délai

Les symptômes suivants exigent d'agir rapidement : vomissements ininterrompus ou sanglants, difficultés respiratoires (éventuelle torsion de l'estomac) ; présence de sang dans l'urine ou les crottes (maladie grave ou lésion interne) ; modification nette du comportement au moment d'uriner (défaillance rénale, infection ou intoxication) ; confusion, vertige ou collapsus (problèmes cardiaques ou cérébraux, hypertension ou intoxication).

Les parasites exotiques

La babésiose (ou piroplasmose) est une maladie due à un parasite sanguin transmis par les piqûres de tiques et introduit dans nos régions par le « tourisme canin » dans le bassin méditerranéen. Les symptômes sont les suivants : le chien est épuisé et affaibli, il n'a pas d'appétit, une forte fièvre, les muqueuses sont pâles par suite d'anémie, elles sont jaunes et l'urine brun-vert en raison de la destruction des globules rouges, l'animal maigrit et respire avec effort. La babésiose est souvent mortelle par défaillance rénale. À titre préventif, n'emmenez pas votre chien avec vous en vacances au bord de la Méditerranée, nos compagnons sont malheureusement très réceptifs à l'agent pathogène. Il existe aussi un vaccin contre la babésiose. Si le chien est malade, le vétérinaire prescrira des médicaments et éventuellement des transfusions sanguines car le parasite détruit les globules rouges.

La leishmaniose est une infection transmise par des moucherons suceurs de sang. La maladie ne se déclare souvent que des mois ou des années après la piqûre par l'insecte. Le parasite est originaire du basin méditerranéen (Portugal) et de certaines régions de Suisse. Les chiens infectés subissent des modifications cutanées et du pelage, perdent notamment leurs poils, ont des pellicules rappelant l'amiante, des inflammations cutanées de type ulcère, des griffes sèches et cassantes, des gonflements des glandes lymphatiques, des poussées de fièvre variables, perdent du poids, ont un appétit variable, saignent du nez, sont anémiés, souffrent d'inflammations oculaires, de troubles de la fonction rénale, de paralysie et ont le ventre douloureux et sensible au toucher en raison d'une hypertrophie du foie et de la rate. La leishmaniose est souvent mortelle. À titre préventif, mieux vaut ne pas emmener son chien dans les régions à risque. Le traitement vétérinaire est très long et pas toujours couronné de succès, certains médicaments ont de nombreux effets secondaires.

La maladie du ver du cœur (ou dirofilariose) est transmise par des moustiques. Le ver exotique mène une existence de parasite dans le cœur et les artères pulmonaires du chien. Il a été introduit dans nos régions par le « tourisme canin » dans les zones chaudes et humides du Sud de l'Europe et d'Amérique. Il existe des médicaments préventifs, un traitement médicamenteux

L'administration de médicaments

1 **Les médicaments liquides** sont injectés latéralement dans la gueule du chien à l'aide d'une seringue à usage unique (sans aiguille). Important : lever légèrement la tête du chiot pour éviter que le médicament ne coule.

2 **Les cachets** sont placés tout à l'arrière de la langue du chiot. Lui maintenir ensuite le museau fermé jusqu'à ce qu'il ait avalé et le laisser impérativement boire.

est également possible et dans certains cas rares, les amas de vers doivent être retirés des vaisseaux sanguins par voie chirurgicale.

Castration ou traitement hormonal ?

Les chiennes sont en chaleur deux fois par an (› page 51). Si vous ne souhaitez pas vous lancer dans l'élevage ou si vous voulez intégrer la chienne à un foyer comportant plusieurs chiens des deux sexes, mieux vaut réfléchir à la manière d'éviter une gestation. Par ailleurs, de nombreuses chiennes souffrent de pseudo-gestation en l'absence de partenaire sexuel, ce qui peut entraîner des inflammations utérines (pyromètres), des maladies ovariennes et la formation de tumeurs mammaires. Deux solutions pour résoudre ces problèmes : faire castrer la chienne ou lui administrer des hormones pour empêcher l'apparition des chaleurs.

La castration : En France, la castration est autorisée même sans raisons médicales. Il s'agit de retirer les ovaires et l'utérus de la chienne. On recommande de procéder à la castration après les premières chaleurs, c'est-à-dire au plus tôt après le 7e mois selon la race de la chienne. Prendre rendez-vous à temps avec son vétérinaire car, plus la castration a lieu tôt, plus l'animal est protégé. L'opération a cependant aussi des effets secondaires. Comme pour toute autre opération, l'anesthésie présente un certain risque dont il faut tenir compte. La cicatrisation peut aussi être retardée car la chienne lèche la plaie, mais avec un désinfectant à vaporiser et un T-shirt pour couvrir la plaie, l'affaire est vite réglée. En règle générale, les fils sont retirés au bout de dix jours et la chienne se remet de l'opération. L'incontinence qui survient parfois concerne avant tout les chiennes corpulentes de grandes races et elle peut rapidement être soignée avec les médicaments adéquats. Chez les races à poil long, une prolifération des poils laineux se produit parfois, le pelage devient alors plus souple et plus doux, il ressemble à celui des chiots. La castration n'est pas responsable de ce que les chiennes castrées engraissent, mais leur maître : une alimentation contrôlée avec suffisamment de mouve-

La bonne vaccination du chiot empêche qu'il ne s'infecte au contact d'animaux malades.

Mon chiot va-t-il bien ?

Lorsqu'un chiot ne se sent pas bien, on le voit aussitôt à son comportement. Observez de près votre bébé chien et testez s'il est bien dans sa peau. Veillez tout particulièrement aux comportements positifs décrits ci-dessous.

Début du test :

- ○ Le chiot se déplace librement et en parfaite indépendance dans le logement.
- ○ Il mange de bon appétit.
- ○ Il dort calmement et en toute confiance.
- ○ Il ne réagit pas avec nervosité et inquiétude.
- ○ Il joue avec plaisir et s'intéresse à son environnement.

Résultat du test :

ment et d'activité permet d'éviter ce problème avant même son apparition.

Toutes mes chiennes ont été et sont castrées et je ne peux rapporter aucune mauvaise expérience. Les chiennes non castrées subissent deux fois par an, pendant leurs chaleurs, un énorme stress sexuel auquel elles ne peuvent trouver d'exutoire dans l'accouplement. Beaucoup réagissent alors de manière déconcertante et leur caractère change. La castration permet de leur épargner ce supplice.

En ce qui concerne la castration des mâles, elle n'a aucune justification médicale, elle peut uniquement aider lorsque le chien témoigne d'un comportement sexuel exacerbé ou présente une disposition aux tumeurs testiculaires.

Le traitement hormonal : L'efficacité d'un traitement hormonal régulier de la chienne dépend de la précision de l'administration : l'apport d'hormones doit impérativement intervenir pendant la phase de repos sexuel complet, c'est-à-dire au moins trois mois après la fin des dernières chaleurs et au plus un mois avant le début des suivantes. Si le cycle de la chienne est irrégulier, il est impossible de déterminer le moment exact, seul un frottis vaginal réalisé par le vétérinaire permet de le faire avec certitude. Malgré tout, il arrive toujours que la chienne soit en chaleur alors qu'elle a reçu un traitement approprié. Dans ce cas, des kystes ovariens peuvent se former, des inflammations utérines et des tumeurs mammaires apparaître.

6. Éducation et activité

Une bonne éducation procure au chien sécurité, mais aussi liberté, car vous pouvez alors l'emmener presque partout sans difficultés. Quant à l'activité, elle stimule et sollicite son intelligence.

L'éducation précoce : dès le premier jour

Pour que tout aille bien dès le début dans l'équipe homme-chien, il est indispensable d'éduquer ce dernier avec amour et cohérence. Pour cela, prenez le temps et soyez patient.

IL Y A PLUS DE TRENTE ANS, lorsque je me suis rendu avec mon chiot collie « Tasso » dans une association canine, tous deux heureux et impatients d'apprendre, j'ai reçu le conseil de rentrer chez moi et d'attendre que le chien ait un an. Heureusement, Eberhard Trummler, le premier chercheur comportemental à avoir alors écrit des ouvrages accessibles sur le comportement des chiens, m'a aidé à trouver seul ma voie. De même, de nombreux maîtres ne savent pas encore exactement à quel moment commencer à éduquer leur compagnon.

Les premières semaines

Dès la naissance du chien, la vie elle-même se charge des premiers apprentissages. Le chiot apprend instinctivement à trouver la source de lait maternel et sa mère lui enseigne les premières bonnes manières avant leur séparation, par exemple l'attitude à adopter envers des congénères de rang supérieur. Elle fixe aussi les premières limites en cas de comportement trop grossier envers elle ou les frères et sœurs du bébé (› photo ci-contre). Par ailleurs, un bon éleveur veille à donner au chiot de multiples impressions de son environnement pendant la première phase d'imprégnation (› page 8). À partir du moment où le chiot est donné à son maître définitif, c'est ce dernier qui est responsable de son développement et doit poursuivre sans transition l'éducation de la mère chienne et celle acquise avec l'éleveur. En effet, si vous attendez pour éduquer votre chien qu'il « vous mène par le bout du nez », c'est trop tard.

De la 4e à la 16e semaine, le chiot traverse les phases d'imprégnation, de socialisation et de hiérarchisation. Tout ce qu'il apprend – et ce qu'il n'apprend

La mère « mord » la gueule de son petit pour rétablir les limites à ne pas dépasser. ›

Tout est une question de laisse

1 **La laisse de 3 mètres :** Elle est la plus appropriée pour aller faire un tour « au coin de la rue » et pour les petites promenades dans les zones très fréquentées.

2 **La laisse de 10 mètres :** Elle permet d'assurer le chiot en terrain découvert et de lui apprendre à obéir.

3 **La laisse double de 2 mètres :** Elle peut être raccourcie à 1 mètre, c'est la laisse idéale pour l'éducation du chiot.

pas – pendant ce court laps de temps forme son caractère. Et les occasions manquées ne peuvent plus être rattrapées ensuite.

Le cœur et la raison

L'éducation d'un chien dure toute la vie car elle doit s'orienter vers la cohabitation avec l'homme. Cependant, la première année du chiot qui grandit est celle qui exige le plus de travail et de responsabilité de la part de son maître. Il est essentiel d'y consacrer du temps et de l'attention : c'est votre devoir de montrer au chiot ce qui est permis et ce qui ne l'est pas dans toutes les situations.

Sa personnalité : Aussi adaptée et raisonnable que soit l'éducation de votre chiot, il est essentiel de ne jamais oublier que c'est un être vivant qui mérite d'être traité avec respect et dont vous devez tenir compte de la personnalité propre. Après tout, le chiot que vous adoptez est arraché à son environnement familial habituel, il souffre encore au début du choc de la séparation et se sent désorienté.

Si l'éducation du chiot est importante dès le début, elle ne doit pas avoir pour but d'en faire un « récepteur d'ordres », mais un partenaire qui prend plaisir à vivre en harmonie avec les membres humains de sa meute. Votre tâche est donc de stimuler l'intelligence sociale de votre chien et de la développer par l'éducation.

La réussite : Apportez à votre chiot un ancrage solide en lui parlant avec supériorité et cohérence un langage clair et concis (› chapitre 7). L'éducation doit éveiller sa curiosité, elle doit comprendre des défis passionnants et des réussites motivantes. Pour cela, rien ne vaut la pratique quotidienne.

L'école pour chiens : Il serait faux de croire que votre chien apprendra tout le nécessaire dans un cours hebdomadaire d'une école pour chiens. Il n'en est pas moins conseillé de participer à un tel cours. Ce n'est pas le chien cependant,

mais bien son maître, qui doit y acquérir les connaissances requises pour les appliquer et éduquer correctement son compagnon à quatre pattes. Or, de nombreux maîtres ne font rien avec leur chien en dehors de l'école. Pourtant, l'éducation doit être étalée sur l'emploi du temps complet et le chiot apprend le mieux tout ce qui en fera un chien bien élevé dans les situations de la vie courante.

Sous surveillance : Quel que soit l'endroit où vous vous trouvez avec votre chiot et ce que vous faites avec lui, toutes ses actions exigent de votre part une réaction systématique, positive ou négative – vous pouvez aussi décider d'ignorer les comportements inopportuns.

Le cerveau du chien ne fait pas de pause dans l'apprentissage. Il ne différencie pas non plus le temps libre du travail. Si vous ne pouvez surveiller le chiot un court instant, mettez-le dans sa caisse pendant ce temps (❯ page 43). Il est important qu'il ne puisse pas faire de dégâts (ronger les meubles, mordre les chaussures, uriner à l'intérieur, etc.) sans surveillance. Le séjour provisoire dans la caisse est également un exercice préparatoire pour apprendre à rester seul. Occuper longuement le chiot auparavant afin qu'il passe le temps dans la caisse à dormir – les chiots, comme les petits enfants, ont encore besoin de beaucoup de calme.

ASTUCE

Comment lui donner une friandise

Il n'y a qu'une bonne manière de tenir les friandises données au chiot en guise de récompense. La bonne : la presser avec le pouce contre l'intérieur de la main, les autres doigts refermés dessus en poing. Le chien n'accède à sa récompense qu'en poussant vigoureusement votre pouce sur le côté avec son museau.

Il est important de toujours utiliser **les mêmes signaux vocaux.** Des instructions différentes pour une demande identique troubleraient le chiot.

L'apprentissage

Le quadrupède enregistre des impressions de son environnement, les stocke dans sa mémoire et affiche l'information correspondant à une certaine stimulation sous forme de comportement.

Le conditionnement opérant : Exemple : le chiot vient à l'ordre (signal vocal) « Ici ! » et reçoit pour cela une récompense. Il fait des expériences agréables/couronnées de succès ou désagréables/sans succès et apprend, comme nous les hommes, par l'expérience. Si ce principe de base est appliqué habilement pour son éducation, il refera à l'avenir toujours volontiers ce qu'il ressent comme agréable et évitera de faire ce qui a constitué pour lui une expérience désagréable (par exemple un « Non ! » ou la peur face à une boîte pleine d'objets métalliques agitée par son maître). On appelle ce principe d'apprentissage le « conditionnement opérant ».

Le conditionnement classique : Une stimulation neutre suffit à déclencher un comportement. Exemple : vous préparez le collier et la laisse, le chien éprouve une joie irrépressible à l'idée de la promenade imminente. Il a appris, en observant attentivement et en recoupant différents gestes, toujours identiques, de son maître, que la promenade convoitée va avoir lieu.

Les stimulations : La confrontation précoce, au cours des seize premières semaines, avec de nouveaux bruits, de nouvelles odeurs, de nouvelles personnes, d'autres animaux et des appareils stimule le développement cérébral du chiot. Les exercices faciles et amusants qu'il perçoit comme gratifiants accroissent son désir inné d'apprendre. À aucun autre moment de son développement ultérieur, il n'aura autant de facilité et de plaisir à apprendre. C'est aussi à cet âge que le chiot cherche un supérieur qu'il reconnaîtra comme tel et à l'autorité « bienveillante » duquel il pourra se soumettre sans conditions.

Dans tout ce qu'il fait, le bébé chien enregistre très exactement nos réactions à chacun de ses comportements et, si nous échouons à ses yeux par

En récompense de s'être comporté comme il le devait, le chiot reçoit son jouet favori.

incohérence, par emportement ou par des ordres peu explicites, il ne pourra pas nous reconnaître comme « chef de meute » (› page 33).

La confiance : L'attachement et la confiance sont les bases de l'intégration réussie du chiot à l'équipe homme-chien. Des règles claires rendent l'homme prévisible, donnent au chiot un sentiment de sécurité et renforcent sa confiance. En effet, un chien ne fait confiance à son maître que lorsqu'il est sûr qu'il ne lui arrivera rien au voisinage de ce dernier et un chiot qui fait pleinement confiance à son maître sera, lui aussi, toujours prévisible dans ses réactions et son comportement.

L'attachement à l'homme naît de contacts corporels réguliers, lorsque le chien est nourri, soigné et que tous deux se livrent à des entreprises communes dans la nature. Plus vous procurerez des occupations intéressantes à votre chiot, plus son attachement pour vous sera fort. Il ne vous quittera alors plus des yeux, ou presque, et il sera facile d'éveiller son attention pour l'éduquer. En revanche, si le chien n'est que peu attaché à son maître, tout, ou presque, lui semble plus important que ce dernier, il n'est pas rare qu'il ne lui accorde aucune attention et les tentatives d'éducation ne donnent rien.

La motivation : L'homme et le chien doivent se trouver « en tête-à-tête » et pour cela, le chien doit se concentrer sur son maître et lui montrer ainsi sa bonne volonté. Par conséquent, le chiot doit pouvoir être motivé à tout moment. Un grand nombre de facteurs y contribuent : d'une part, les stimulations externes telles qu'une friandise, un jeu animé avec son maître ou le ton encourageant de ce dernier ; d'autre part, des stimulations internes comme par exemple la curiosité du chiot. On distingue ainsi la motivation propre, fondée sur des stimulations internes, et la motivation extérieure, déclenchée par des stimulations externes. La condition principale pour motiver son chien reste

LE SAVIEZ-VOUS ?

Le chien se soumet volontiers à l'homme

Les chiens sont des animaux capables de s'adapter et, pour cette raison, se soumettent aux hommes qui font preuve de cohérence et de fermeté. Ils sont également égoïstes et l'obéissance à un ordre dépend souvent chez eux du profit qu'ils en tirent. Dans ce cas, il importe peu au chien que l'homme qui lui donne l'ordre lui soit ou non supérieur : l'homme est pour lui une sorte de « super-chien » avec lequel il cohabite en « s'adaptant » aux règles d'un ordre social donné.

cependant la satisfaction de ses besoins fondamentaux, notamment de la nourriture en suffisance, assez d'eau à boire, un sommeil ininterrompu, un sentiment de sécurité (choisir un environnement familier pour les exercices) et des structures sociales claires dans l'équipe chien-homme.

L'attention

Un exemple pratique de la manière dont j'oriente la concentration du chiot sur moi : mes mots clés sont « Viens voir ! », je les utilise pour motiver le chiot à chercher le contact visuel avec moi car l'exercice qui suit promet une délicieuse friandise en récompense.

Première étape : Offrir sa friandise préférée au chiot affamé assis devant vous. Au même instant (ni avant, ni après !) et pendant qu'il s'empare avidement de la gourmandise, dire très rapidement plusieurs fois de suite « Viens voir ! ». Répéter l'opération au moins cinq fois.

Deuxième étape : Attendre que le chien s'intéresse à autre chose à proximité de vous. Dire alors de nouveau plusieurs fois sur le même ton « Viens voir ! ». Si le chiot réagit rapidement et vous regarde d'un air intéressé, lui donner sa friandise.

Conseil : Pour le conditionnement, choisir de préférence un endroit où rien ne risque de distraire le chien. La motivation déclenchée par l'offre de nourriture doit laisser place avec le temps à la motivation propre du chien. Pour sti-

1 **L'exercice « Ici ! » :** S'accroupir pour se mettre au niveau du chiot et le motiver à venir en ouvrant les bras et en lui parlant sur un ton encourageant et attirant.

2 **« Me voilà ! » :** Le chiot a couru dans vos bras avec joie ? Super ! Maintenant qu'il a fait ce que vous voulez et s'est, en plus, gentiment assis, il attend tout naturellement sa récompense.

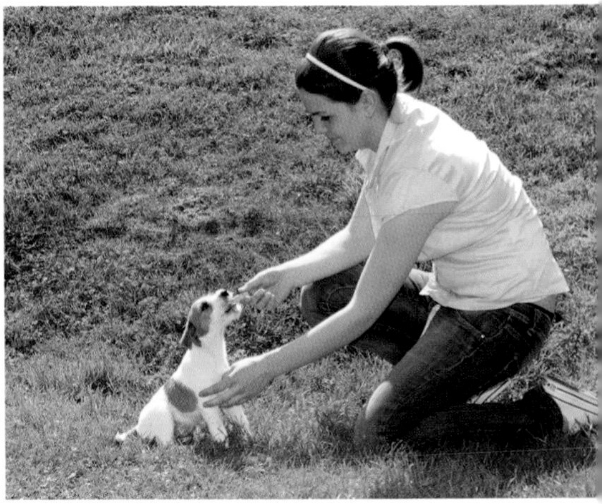

Attentif, le chiot attend le signal de sa maîtresse.

muler cette dernière, faire en sorte que l'apprentissage soit toujours couronné de succès pour le chiot. La réussite est alors assimilée à la récompense qu'elle remplace peu à peu. Les chiens uniquement stimulés par la nourriture, donc par des motivations externes, finissent par en attendre toujours plus et leur motivation diminue alors à vue d'œil.

L'obéissance

C'est la base d'une bonne éducation, on en voit la preuve en toutes circonstances. L'obéissance de base du chiot est introduite en même temps que les quatre ordres fondamentaux qu'il doit maîtriser parfaitement : « Ici ! », « Assis ! », « Couché ! » et « Non ! ». Ces quatre mots sont pour tous les chiens de famille la base même d'une existence sûre et équilibrée. Ce n'est qu'à partir du quatrième ou cinquième mois que le chiot est en mesure de se concentrer sur l'entraînement à ces exercices de base. Il doit alors apprendre les différents signaux vocaux et les associer, après les avoir répétés régulièrement, à certains actes pour les accomplir à chaque fois qu'il entend le signal. Pour cela, veiller à toujours utiliser les mêmes signaux vocaux pour les mêmes ordres, vous ne pourrez compter voir venir le chien si vous (ou les autres membres de la famille) l'appelez parfois en disant « Viens ! », parfois « Ici ! », ou encore « Suis-moi ! » : il ne peut alors associer aucun acte à un signal vocal donné. Par ailleurs, le chien apprend un grand nombre d'autres signaux (par exemple « faire un tour », les noms de ses amis chiens, etc.) en observant son maître au cours de son existence, ils le stimulent positivement et il sait en tirer profit, ces signaux comprennent aussi des bruits tels le bruissement du papier lorsque le maître ouvre une plaque de chocolat ou le bruit de sa voiture.

Les exercices de base

Pour apprendre les exercices de base, le chiot doit être tenu en laisse afin qu'il ne puisse pas s'échapper à la moindre distraction. Choisir pour cela la fine laisse de 3 mètres (› photo page 94). Quant aux exercices d'appel d'un chiot en liberté, ils doivent uniquement être pratiqués avec la laisse de 10 mètres sur un terrain sans aucun risque dû à la circulation (› photo page 94).

Quelle est la force de l'attachement que me porte mon chiot ?

Il peut être utile de tester l'attachement que vous porte votre chiot. Pour cela, demandez à une personne qui lui est familière de le tenir fermement et cachez-vous derrière un arbre ou au coin d'une maison pendant qu'il regarde.

Début du test :

○ Première étape : Lorsque vous appelez le chiot depuis votre cachette, votre partenaire le libère pour qu'il puisse se mettre à votre recherche.
○ Deuxième étape : Répétez l'opération, mais sans appeler le chiot.
○ Troisième étape : Les cachettes seront de plus en plus difficiles à trouver. Plus le chien cherchera à vous rejoindre rapidement, plus il manifeste qu'il vous est attaché.

Résultat du test :

L'exercice « Ici ! »

Première étape : Attendre que le chiot vienne joyeusement vers vous et cherche à prendre contact, s'accroupir rapidement, ouvrir les bras pour l'y recevoir et le motiver en répétant sur un ton amical « Ici ! ».
Deuxième étape : Une fois que le chiot vous a rejoint, le caresser affectueusement des deux mains sur tout le corps, de la tête vers le bas, et le complimenter abondamment.
Troisième étape : Pour finir, le récompenser avec une friandise particulièrement savoureuse.
Quatrième étape : Par la suite, essayer aussi de l'appeler par son nom et de l'inciter à venir avec le « Viens voir ! » qu'il connaît bien (❯ page 98) en vous tenant accroupi en terrain découvert (avec la laisse de 10 m). Dès qu'il se dirige joyeusement vers vous, crier deux ou trois fois « Ici ! » d'un ton encourageant et mettre fin à l'exercice comme décrit à la troisième étape. Si le chiot ne vient pas ou reste hésitant malgré tous vos efforts pour le motiver, éloignez-vous rapidement de lui : il a peur de vous perdre et cherche à vous rejoindre, s'il vous court alors après, tournez-vous vers lui, accroupissez-vous et procédez de nouveau comme décrit aux étapes 1 à 3.

L'exercice « Assis ! »

Pendant tout l'exercice, le chiot doit rester tenu à une laisse pas trop serrée.
Première étape : Le chiot se tient

devant ou à côté de vous. Passer la friandise de son museau au-dessus de sa tête : il essaie avec avidité d'attraper le délice convoité, mais ne le reçoit que lorsqu'il modifie sa position inconfortable en position assise.
Deuxième étape : Pendant qu'il s'assoit, prononcer le signal vocal « Assis ! » et lui donner la friandise dès que son arrière-train touche le sol.
Troisième étape : Il doit rester assis tant que vous le complimentez et le caressez de la tête au dos. Libérez-le au bout de quelques secondes avec un « Vas-y ! » ou « OK ! ».

L'exercice « Couché ! »

Pour cet exercice, le chiot doit maîtriser « Assis ! ».
Première étape : Le chiot s'assoit au signal vocal « Assis ! ».
Deuxième étape : Poser légèrement une main sur son arrière-train pour l'empêcher de se lever pendant l'exercice. Avec l'autre main, faire descendre une friandise devant son nez jusqu'au sol et la tirer vers l'avant, de telle sorte qu'il ne puisse l'atteindre sans se coucher.
Troisième étape : Dès que son ventre touche le sol, dire « Couché ! » et lui donner sa récompense. Le complimenter abondamment et le caresser tendrement sur la tête et le dos avec la main qui l'empêchait de se lever.

L'exercice « Non ! »

Le « Non ! » ferme doit inciter le chiot à interrompre aussitôt un acte déjà commencé, par exemple s'il mange des immondices pendant la promenade.
Première étape : S'il s'est emparé de quelque chose qui ne vous plaît pas, allez tranquillement vers lui, prenez-le par le collier et dites fermement « Non ! », mais sans crier. Poussez-le du collier pas trop fort pour le corriger.
Deuxième étape : Dès qu'il laisse tomber l'objet qu'il tient, complimentez-le abondamment et donnez-lui une friandise ou son jouet favori en échange.
Conseil : Restez maître de vous car si vous criez et vous précipitez sur le chiot, vous ne ferez que le faire fuir avec son butin pour aller le mettre en sûreté et il en fera rapidement un amusant jeu « de chat ».

Les chiots apprennent facilement l'ordre « Assis ! » car dès leur plus jeune âge, ils mendient ainsi de la nourriture à leur mère.

Cours de soutien

Pour les bébés chiens les plus éveillés, l'apprentissage doit se faire en jouant. Vous pouvez y contribuer en occupant abondamment votre chiot et en lui proposant des jeux intéressants. Le résultat : un chien de famille malin et équilibré.

LE JEU est un besoin naturel du chien. Les chiots ont recours à leurs frères et sœurs et à leur mère comme partenaires de jeu. Il s'agit alors essentiellement de jeux de chasse, de combat et de défense hors de tout contexte sérieux qui permettent aux bébés de mesurer leurs forces : les chamailleries parfois violentes contribuent à fortifier, notamment leur musculature, tandis qu'ils prennent lentement conscience de leur corps et de son fonctionnement. Les mécanismes innés du comportement social sont eux aussi testés par le jeu, entraînés et renforcés.

Les règles du jeu

Lorsque vous ramenez le chiot à la maison, le meilleur moyen de l'aider à surmonter la perte de sa mère, de ses frères et sœurs et de son environnement familier est de jouer gaiement avec lui. Les éleveurs avisés essaient dès le départ d'encourager la motivation et la disposition à apprendre des chiots par des jeux ciblés et adaptés. Par ces activités en commun, l'homme et le chien apprennent aussi à mieux se connaître, la confiance du chien envers son partenaire de jeu humain, comme la réciproque, est renforcée, l'assurance du chien croît, tandis que son maître apprend le langage corporel de son compagnon et découvre ses talents cachés. C'est en jouant que vous connaîtrez le tempérament et l'endurance de votre chien, s'il est dur ou tendre, un fonceur absolu ou un grand sensible. En effet, mieux vaut un caractère prudent et courageux qu'intrépide et affolé pour faire un bon chien de famille. Une éducation ludique vous permettra d'orienter son comportement dans la direction voulue.

L'importance du jeu : Seuls les chiots avec lesquels leur maître joue beaucoup développeront ce plaisir à jouer supérieur à la moyenne qui dure souvent toute la vie. Les chiens au comportement joueur aussi marqué sont les plus agréables à éduquer et, plus tard, à former sans violence par le jeu. En revanche, les chiens dont le plaisir à jouer décline rapidement ont visiblement manqué d'occasions de jouer lorsqu'ils étaient chiots et toutes les tentatives de les motiver plus tard ne connaissent que de modestes succès.

Éviter les distractions : Au début, le chiot ne doit pas être distrait du jeu. Pour cela, commencer par jouer dans son environnement familial direct où il se sent parfaitement en sécurité. Ce n'est que lorsque son envie de jouer croît que de petites distractions peuvent être introduites progressivement, par exemple en transférant le jeu de la

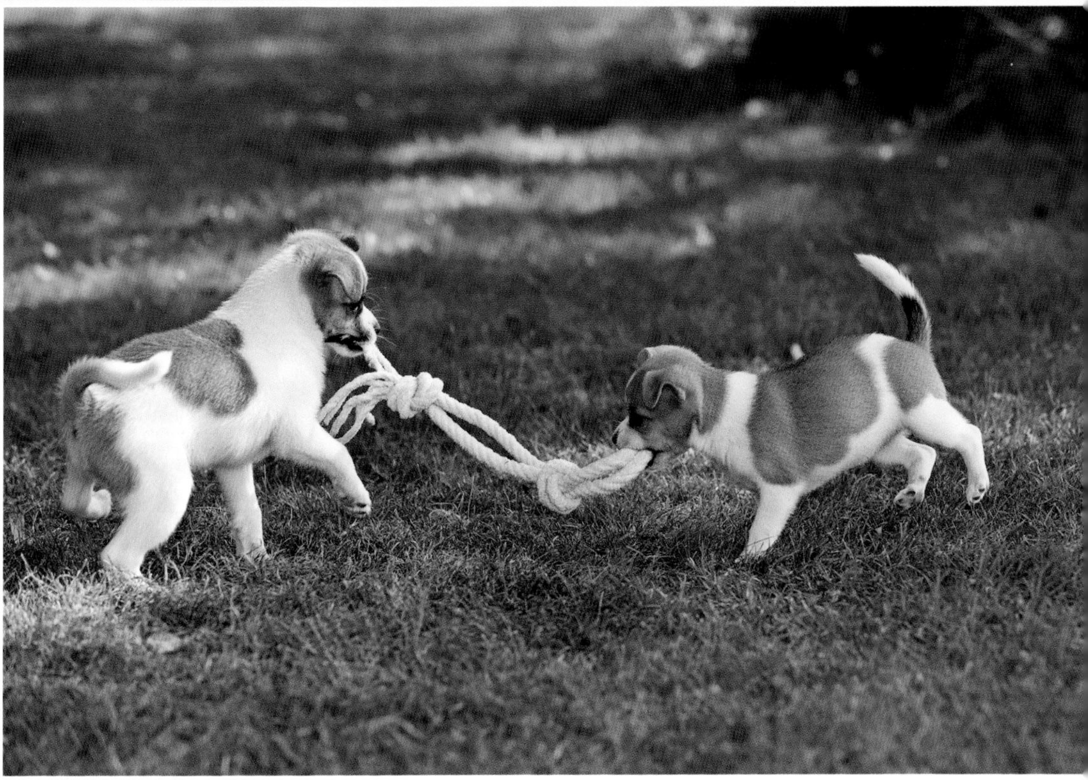

Un morceau de corde permet d'entraîner ses forces et sa capacité à s'imposer.

maison au jardin, puis dans une prairie hors des limites de ce dernier. Attendre que votre compagnon ait pris l'habitude des distractions pour rejoindre un terrain de jeux pour chiens.

Créer une bonne ambiance : Pour le chiot, il est extrêmement important de mettre en place autour du jeu une atmosphère de confiance, amicale et qui l'engage à jouer. En effet, votre état d'esprit du moment se répercute sur le chien (❯ chapitre 7). Si vous n'êtes pas de bonne humeur, mieux vaut l'emmener en promenade jusqu'à ce que vous soyez mieux disposé.

Fixer des limites sans attendre : Les premières semaines après la séparation d'avec sa mère sont très agitées pour le chiot. Sa curiosité le pousse d'une découverte à l'autre et les excès de zèle sont fréquents. Votre tâche consiste alors à l'accompagner dans ses explorations pour l'observer et intervenir lorsqu'il exagère. Les morsures par jeu, par exemple, sont un comportement très fortement ancré chez le chiot pendant les premiers corps à corps avec l'homme. Il importe ici de fixer à temps des limites au bébé.

Le chien doit acquérir dès son plus jeune âge l'inhibition absolue de morsure. Pour cela, interrompre le jeu en poussant un « Aïe ! » sonore dès qu'il commence à mordre, mais ne retirez votre main que lorsqu'il cède au « Aïe ! » et détournez son attention sur un jouet ou en lui lançant une balle. S'il vous mord plus tard la main par hasard dans la fièvre du jeu, il devra aussitôt vous libérer et faire preuve d'une inhibition de morsure intacte. De même, si le chiot fait mine de vous sauter dessus en pinçant votre jambe de pantalon, rappelez-le à l'ordre sans attendre d'un « Non ! » ferme ou en lui attrapant le museau d'une main (› photo page 119) et détournez son attention à l'aide d'un jouet.

Le jeu intense en commun renforce **l'attachement** entre le maître et son chien.

Montrer son autorité : Lors des séances de jeux avec son maître, le chien doit apprendre le plus rapidement possible que c'est l'homme qui prend les initiatives et qui décide quand, quoi, où, comment et surtout combien de temps et avec quoi jouer.

Ce jeu d'intelligence intéresse aussi beaucoup la chienne de quatre mois.

Le jeu avec d'autres chiens

Après la séparation de ses frères et sœurs, le chiot doit pouvoir participer au moins jusqu'à sa 14e semaine à des séances de jeu bien menées (association canine ou école pour chiens) qui lui permettent de s'entraîner avec d'autres aux divers comportements sociaux et à la communication.
Après leur maturité sexuelle, la plupart des chiens ne jouent plus en toute confiance qu'avec peu de congénères : ils ont tous fait au moins une fois la mauvaise expérience du rejet par un autre. En effet, les chiens ne diffèrent pas de nous sur ce point, tous les autres ne leur sont pas d'emblée sympathiques. Par conséquent, il n'est pas asocial pour un mâle d'entrer en conflit avec un autre. L'important n'est pas qu'il se batte, mais la manière dont il se bat et s'il respecte ou non les règles sociales de manière à régler l'affaire en limitant les dégâts – tant que l'homme ne s'en mêle pas.

L'éducation par le jeu

Je voudrais revenir ici sur l'éducation du chiot. Pour un chien éduqué et formé sans violence, par la motivation et l'encouragement positif, tout ce qu'il entreprend avec l'homme dans ce cadre est un jeu, ou presque. Les compliments et la satisfaction de ses instincts l'incitent sans cesse de nouveau à exécuter avec plaisir les tâches que nous lui fixons. Je souhaiterais personnellement que l'éducation du chien n'ait plus pour seul objectif – comme autrefois – sa soumission sans conditions. Au contraire, la connaissance de ses comportements spécifiques doit permettre de lui donner

LES JOUETS ADAPTÉS AUX CHIOTS

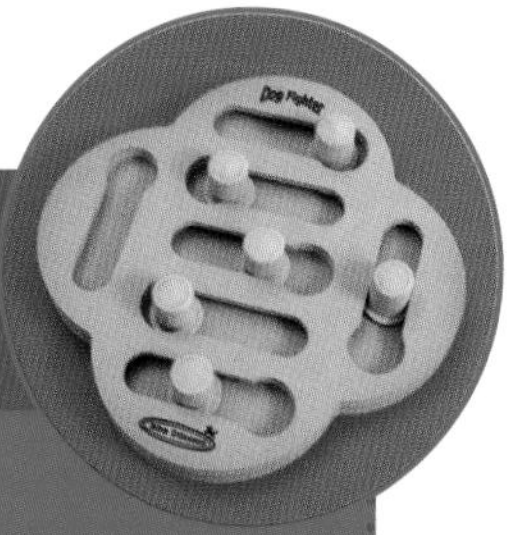

CE QU'AIMENT LES BÉBÉS CHIENS

Balle dure	À faire rouler et lancer, solide et facile à nettoyer.
Anneau dur	L'anneau peut rouler et être lancé, les chiots dès leur plus jeune âge peuvent parfaitement l'attraper dans leur gueule.
Dummy proie	Sachet à jeter empli de nourriture pour récompenser le chiot de sa « réussite » à la chasse.
Dummy flottant	Un jouet épatant pour les chiens qui aiment se baigner en été.
Corde à nœuds	De vieilles serviettes nouées font aussi l'affaire pour les jeux à tirer avec d'autres chiens ou des hommes.
Animal couineur	Motive les chiens peu enclins à jouer, mais énerve leur maître.
Boudin en jute	Idéal à traîner, lancer ou pour les jeux à mordre.
Cartons de différentes tailles	Constituent de fantastiques cachettes ou servent à chercher des objets, ou encore pour s'amuser à les déchirer et s'en donner à cœur joie.

la chance d'apprendre en jouant et de remplir des missions avec beaucoup de plaisir et de motivation.

L'aventure de la promenade

Pour un chien, il n'y a rien de plus intéressant que de partir à l'aventure avec son maître, et rien de plus ennuyeux que de voir ses sorties limitées au jardin pour aller faire ses besoins – jardin dont il connaît le moindre arbre, le moindre arbrisseau et la moindre odeur…
Prévoir par conséquent de varier les promenades, vous pouvez utiliser pour cela la laisse de 10 m au parc ou dans la nature. La recherche d'un objet « perdu » est notamment très appréciée des chiens : son jouet favori caché dans l'herbe ou les buissons sur le trajet. Ou alors vous laissez tomber discrètement un gant et envoyez le chien vous le chercher. Commencer avec des distances d'un à deux mètres pour les chiots et les augmenter progressivement. Cachez-vous et laissez le chiot flairer votre trace. Ce que le chien désire le plus cependant, c'est explorer les environs avec vous, attraper les feuilles qui volent, capter de nouvelles odeurs, courir le long du ruisseau, monter sur des troncs d'arbres tombés ou y marcher en équilibre et chercher des trous de souris. Le chiot veut faire ses expériences sous votre protection et en votre présence, mais pas pour autant être suivi et interrompu

1 **Jeu de balle :** Attraper et porter une balle fait partie des jeux de chasse classiques que les chiots connaissent sans avoir besoin de l'apprendre.

2 **Ascension :** L'ascension de l'accès en pente pour atteindre le point le plus haut d'un agrès demande courage et habileté. Des friandises posées sur le trajet peuvent aider.

3 **Tunnel :** Tous les chiots apprennent rapidement à ne plus avoir peur du court tunnel, on peut alors le rallonger.

sans cesse dans son entreprise par excès d'attention – n'intervenez que lorsqu'il est vraiment en danger.

Si vous vous tenez à proximité du chiot sans dire un mot, il s'orientera toujours selon vous. En revanche, si vous l'appelez sans cesse, il n'aura aucune raison de se montrer attentif envers vous puisqu'il entendra votre voix en permanence.

Conseil : Même si le chiot ne peut pas encore parcourir de grandes distances, les excursions doivent l'intéresser et le motiver. Si vous rencontrez d'autres chiens, assurez-vous qu'ils sont inoffensifs avant de laisser le chiot prendre contact.

Les jeux d'intérieur

À l'intérieur, on peut jouer avec le chiot sans être dérangé et donner progressivement le plaisir du jeu à un chiot un peu paresseux. Par mauvais temps en particulier, saisissez toutes les occasions d'occuper votre petit compagnon.

La recherche : Commencer par cacher des friandises en utilisant le stimulus vocal « Cherche ! » pour lancer la recherche. Une fois que le chiot a trouvé la friandise, passer à l'étape suivante : cacher son jouet favori et le désigner en même temps que le « Cherche ! », par exemple « Cherche l'ours ! » ou « Cherche la balle ! ». Au fur et à mesure que le chiot vieillit, vous pourrez placer en cercle plusieurs jouets désignés par leur nom et demander au chien de ne prendre que celui que vous lui demandez.

Le parcours de santé : Pour la forme physique du chien et en guise de petites épreuves de courage, vous pouvez construire avec des objets d'utilité courante un petit parcours que le chiot aura plaisir à suivre et qui lui donnera de l'expérience. Disposez par exemple des bouteilles en plastique pleines en slalom et attirez le chiot la première fois avec une friandise et le signal « Slalom ! ». De même, une planche à repasser sur des piles de livres de différentes hauteurs donne des « rampes » très utiles pour tester le courage du chiot. Enfin, des cartons bien stables font des tunnels et des cachettes fantastiques.

La bagarre : Une bagarre pour jouer avec son maître renforce le sentiment d'union et le chiot apprend ainsi à prendre confiance dans les contacts corporels. Pour les jeux les plus turbulents, éviter les sols lisses car les ligaments et les tendons du chiot ne sont pas encore très stables et pourraient se distendre. Jouer uniquement avec lui sur de la moquette ou un tapis.

Les jeux d'intelligence et de réflexion

On trouve aujourd'hui d'excellents jeux d'intelligence et de réflexion pour chiens. Parmi les plus conseillés figurent notamment ceux en bois scandinave naturel et non traité développés par la Suédoise Nina Ottoson. Ils stimulent l'intelligence et le plaisir d'apprendre du chiot qu'ils entraînent à la concentration. Si vous achetez des imitations, veillez à la qualité des matériaux utilisés et à ce qu'ils ne présentent aucun risque.

Si les chiots ne peuvent pas encore se concentrer longtemps pour résoudre un « problème » comme les chiens plus âgés, ils sont souvent dotés d'une inventivité étonnante. Déplacer des cubes en bois pour trouver une friandise cachée par-dessous ne pose aucun problème à ces jeunes génies canins.

Le labyrinthe : Il peut être assemblé à partir d'éléments préfabriqués. Certaines associations canines ou écoles pour chiens en proposent pour entraîner les chiens mais les bricoleurs les plus doués peuvent aussi en construire un eux-mêmes. Il permet de tester son compagnon et d'en apprendre plus sur son bon sens, sa réflexion ou son attachement envers son maître. La seule condition est que le chiot obéisse sans laisse. Le faire asseoir devant le labyrinthe, se poster à l'extrémité et l'appeler d'une voix joyeuse. Le chiot qui ignore son maître reste assis et attend, mais dans le cas contraire, il cherche la sortie car il veut rejoindre son maître ou sa maîtresse : le bébé chien est alors motivé et incité à parcourir le labyrinthe par la seule demande encourageante de son maître.

La cloison : Cette construction simple est elle aussi intéressante : se placer derrière une cloison en bois ou un paravent, le chiot est assis devant. Important : il doit pouvoir se rendre derrière la cloison pour retrouver son maître. Appeler le chien. Comment réagit-il ? Essaie-t-il de vous rejoindre ? Comment résout-il le problème qui se pose à lui ? Combien de temps lui faut-il pour découvrir qu'il peut contourner la cloison à gauche ou à droite pour pouvoir enfin vous rejoindre ?

Conseil : Les premiers exercices ne doivent pas être trop difficiles. Le chiot doit en effet remporter un succès à chaque jeu. Il convient de l'aider à y parvenir sans qu'il le remarque, ce qui exige beaucoup de tact et de doigté, car il doit être lui-même l'artisan de sa réussite.

Un chiot comme partenaire de jeu

Mon fils Tom a trois ans. Nous venons d'acheter un chiot comme partenaire de jeu pour lui. À quoi faut-il faire particulièrement attention lorsqu'ils jouent tous les deux ensemble ?

ENFANT ET ENFANT CHIEN – un mélange explosif. Vous ne devez en aucun cas les laisser jouer tous les deux sans surveillance. Ce sont deux êtres vivants dont le développement intellectuel est à peu près au même niveau. L'enfant comme le chien a encore des réactions totalement imprévisibles et ils doivent être lentement habitués l'un à l'autre. Par ailleurs, la motricité des petits enfants n'est pas encore parfaitement développée, de sorte qu'ils peuvent tenir le chiot trop fermement ou le laisser tomber en voulant le soulever – autant d'expériences douloureuses susceptibles d'inspirer au chien plus tard des réactions négatives envers les enfants.

Faire connaître et comprendre

Les parents doivent dès le début expliquer à leur enfant comment traiter correctement le chien et lui enseigner le respect de cet être vivant. L'enfant doit avant tout apprendre que l'adorable chiot n'est pas un jouet et qu'il faut le traiter avec ménagement. Le bébé chien ne doit notamment pas être dérangé dans son sommeil, l'endroit où il dort est une zone interdite aux enfants afin qu'il puisse s'y retirer toutes les fois où il veut avoir la paix. De même, le chiot ne doit bien évidemment pas être dérangé pendant qu'il mange. Pour faire comprendre tout cela à un enfant encore jeune, les jeux de rôles sont souvent très efficaces : donner à l'enfant le rôle du chiot qui, par exemple, est serré et pincé par vous (dans le rôle de l'enfant). Il comprendra rapidement que cela fait mal. Lui apprendre aussi à reconnaître les avertissements et les signes d'ennui donnés par le chiot et les raisons pour lesquelles il n'a peut-être pas toujours envie de jouer.

Interdire les jeux violents

Interdire à l'enfant les jeux de chasse ou les jeux à mordre et à tirer trop violents avec le chiot. En effet, l'animal risque de se surexciter et de faire alors sentir douloureusement ses dents de lait pointues à l'enfant. Les enfants ne sont généralement pas en mesure de fixer sérieusement des limites au jeune chien dans les jeux violents, toutes les tentatives timides de se défendre sont alors comprises par l'animal comme d'autres variantes du jeu et il redouble d'activité. Dans ce cas, un adulte doit intervenir et faire sortir au besoin le chien de la pièce jusqu'à ce qu'il se soit calmé. Multiplier les occasions de faire le fou avec d'autres chiens et proposer au chiot des occupations conformes à ses besoins lui permettent de libérer son trop-plein d'énergie et le rendent plus équilibré.

Les jeux en solitaire

Ce terme désigne pour les spécialistes toute occupation ludique du chien avec lui-même, par exemple lorsque les jeunes chiens prennent plaisir à découvrir leurs membres et leurs possibilités de mouvement. Ils sautent alors comme des cabris, se laissent tomber à terre ou se roulent sur le sol avec délice. Mon bouledogue français « Only », âgé de douze semaines, découvre en ce moment l'étang du jardin et ses pierres, pour certaines dans l'eau, sur lesquelles il grimpe avec précaution, puis regarde de tous côtés une fois qu'il y est parvenu non sans mal, fier comme s'il avait vaincu un sommet. On trouve aussi des jouets pour les « maîtres célibataires » à remplir de friandises qui en tombent lorsque le chien fait rouler l'objet. Certains pensent que c'est une sollicitation suffisante pour leur chiot, mais c'est une grave erreur !

Les objets à mâcher : La principale activité en solitaire des jeunes chiens, mais aussi des chiens plus âgés, consiste à grignoter et mâchouiller un objet des heures durant. Veiller à lui en proposer suffisamment, sans risques et non toxiques, sous forme de branches, morceaux de bois sans éclats, cuir ou oreille de bœuf, etc., pour ne pas qu'il se rabatte sinon sur les pieds de chaises ou les chaussures.

Les animaux en peluche : Beaucoup de chiens ont une peluche préférée qu'ils ne mordent pas. Ils gardent ce jouet généralement très longtemps et posent même la tête dessus pour dormir. Acheter uniquement des peluches convenant aux chiens.

Conseil : Les jouets utilisés pour motiver le chien pendant son éducation doivent être rangés entre chaque exercice.

Le chiot de droite exprime une invitation à jouer classique, son partenaire répond aussitôt et dresse la queue pour indiquer qu'il va bondir.

7. La communication

L'intensité et la clarté des « conversations » avec votre compagnon à quatre pattes dépendent de la connaissance que vous avez de ses modes d'expression et de leur interprétation.

Le chien multilingue

Si nous disposons d'un langage vocal et d'un langage corporel, le chien, de son côté, communique aussi par les odeurs et par des signaux dits « tactiles ».

L'EXPRESSION chez le chien désigne tous les comportements liés à la communication avec l'homme. En effet, parler ensemble (communiquer) est, chez l'homme comme chez le chien, la condition d'une cohabitation harmonieuse.

Les différentes formes de communication

L'homme possède un langage « narratif » grâce auquel il peut notamment raconter ce qu'il a fait hier ou ce qu'il prévoit de faire demain. Le chien quant à lui utilise un langage « indicatif » et peut uniquement dire ce qu'il ressent ou veut exprimer à un moment donné. Pour cela, il utilise des modes d'expression qui lui sont propres et qui sont très divers. Il « parle » ainsi avec :

- les mouvements de son corps = signaux optiques ;
- les odeurs qu'il émet = signaux olfactifs ;
- le contact = signaux tactiles ;
- les sons = signaux acoustiques.

Les chiens utilisent aussi ces multiples possibilités d'expression pour parler avec nous, les hommes – nous savons tous le sens d'une queue qui s'agite, d'un grognement ou d'un aboiement. Nous, les hommes, communiquons avec des mots dont chacun a un sens précis. Nous avons aussi un langage corporel, mais ne sommes malheureusement pas en mesure de l'employer délibérément dans la plupart des cas. Il ne joue qu'un rôle secondaire dans notre existence, alors même que ce serait le langage le plus compréhensible pour la communication avec nos fidèles compagnons car les chiens sont des observateurs très fins.
Malheureusement, seuls très peu de maîtres ont recours au langage corporel pour parler à leur chien. Or, savoir

On peut aussi s'occuper avec soi-même pour s'amuser.

interpréter le langage corporel des autres permet de reconnaître, par exemple si son interlocuteur est sûr de lui ou pas, ou encore s'il dit la vérité ou ment. Il existe des séminaires pour apprendre à utiliser le langage corporel de manière ciblée et souvent, cela permet de se présenter plus positivement, notamment lors d'un entretien d'embauche, et donc de décrocher l'emploi.

Le langage corporel du chien

Même sans rien savoir des modes d'expression du chien, on reconnaît immédiatement qu'il ne se sent pas en sécurité ou a peur lorsqu'il s'accroupit, le dos rond, la tête baissée et la queue entre les pattes. De même, il est évident qu'un chien qui vient vers vous les pattes raidies, les poils de l'échine hérissés et en montrant les dents n'a pas de bonnes intentions, tandis qu'il montre une approche amicale en donnant la patte ou vous léchant la main.

Ce serait cependant une erreur de croire que le seul balancement de la queue doit être imputé à l'amitié du chien sans prêter attention aux autres signaux corporels. En effet, seul l'ensemble de tous les signaux, l'attitude, la position des oreilles, la mimique et la queue permettent de déduire l'humeur du chien. Nos chiens disposent d'un vocabulaire très étendu pour s'exprimer et ils peuvent aussi combiner les différents signaux, de

LE SAVIEZ-VOUS ?

Les chiens n'ont pas besoin d'un sixième sens

Nos compagnons donnent parfois l'impression d'avoir un sixième sens. Ils réagissent aux changements d'humeur de leur maître, se souviennent des maladies et peuvent nous avertir d'une catastrophe qui approche, notamment d'un tremblement de terre, ils sont aussi capables d'annoncer une crise d'épilepsie ou une hypoglycémie éventuellement mortelle de leur maître avant même que ce dernier ne le remarque. L'explication est simple : les chiens le sentent.

Le chien quant à lui ne sait pas dissimuler. Son langage corporel affiche toujours uniquement ce qu'il ressent véritablement à un moment donné. C'est un langage des sentiments. Il n'a pas besoin de mots pour s'exprimer, il utilise toute la palette de son langage corporel et sonore pour communiquer avec ses congénères comme avec les hommes, sans oublier les signaux tactiles et olfactifs. Pour l'homme, il est donc important de connaître les moyens d'expression du chien pour être sûr de le comprendre.

sorte qu'un même geste peut être utilisé à différentes fins et exprime toujours quelque chose d'autre selon les autres gestes auxquels il est associé.

Le chien se sent en sécurité : Le comportement neutre d'un chien qui n'a rien à redouter dans son environnement familier se manifeste par la position de la tête normalement dressée, l'absence de tension des membres, qui sont légèrement fléchis lorsque l'animal est debout, et la position normale de la queue selon la race. Les oreilles relevées sont dirigées vers l'avant et légèrement redressées, tandis que la racine des oreilles tombantes est tirée vers l'avant.

Le chien n'est pas sûr de lui : On reconnaît le chien incertain ou inquiet à sa mimique. La peau du visage est tendue, les commissures des lèvres tirées vers l'arrière, comme si le chien ricanait. Le regard est agité et n'est dirigé vers aucun objet en particulier. Les oreilles, ou leur base pour les oreilles tombantes, sont déplacées vers l'arrière. La tête est baissée, le corps se replie sans cesse et la queue est coincée entre les pattes. Les chiens qui ont hérité d'un caractère faible et n'ont pas été, ou pas assez, socialisés pendant la phase d'imprégnation affichent ce comportement toute leur vie.

Le chien en impose : Les mâles les plus sûrs d'eux ont parfois tendance à vouloir s'imposer face à leurs rivaux. Chacun des deux veut alors afficher sa supériorité, ils se tournent autour les pattes raides, la queue portée plus ou moins haut et légèrement balancée d'un côté à l'autre dans l'expectative, essaient de se flairer par-devant ou par-derrière, la tête et le museau tenus à l'horizontale, mais en évitant strictement tout contact visuel. Les oreilles sont légèrement inclinées vers l'avant, l'un des deux peut afficher un comportement de menace défensive ou offensive, ou encore se soumettre, une attaque sans sommation est également possible.

L'autorité maternelle

1 Apaiser : Ces deux chiots tervuerens font preuve de soumission envers leur mère. Le corps de celui de gauche est replié sur lui-même, tandis que celui de droite fait un signe d'apaisement avec la patte.

2 Humbles : Ce chiot affiche également une soumission passive, couché et en tendant des pattes apaisantes vers le visage de sa mère qui remarque bien sûr ce comportement avec bienveillance.

Parmi les autres moyens d'expression d'un chien sûr de lui, le grattage après avoir uriné ou déféqué est réalisé avec les deux pattes postérieures ou avec les quatre pattes.

Le marquage des mâles (et souvent aussi des femelles) est un comportement hérité du loup pour faire valoir ses droits sur un territoire. En ville, les autres mâles n'en tiennent quasiment aucun compte, mais les multiples marquages provoquent une surexcitation olfactive et les chiens continuent de lever sans cesse la patte même lorsque leur vessie est vide depuis longtemps.

Le fait de se chevaucher, ou au moins de poser les pattes sur le dos de l'autre chien pour faire mine de le chevaucher, ne doit pas toujours être considéré comme un comportement sexuel, mais aussi comme une manière de s'imposer.

Certains mâles provoquent aussi leur concurrent en se postant perpendiculairement devant lui, ce qu'on appelle la position en T. Tous les comportements du chien dominant visent à afficher sa domination et sa force, mais comportent aussi une menace cachée.

Le chien menace d'attaquer : On parle aussi de menace offensive ou de comportement de menace agressif. Ce comportement est toujours dirigé vers l'adversaire. La tête est légèrement baissée, les dents découvertes, les lèvres paraissent « raccourcies », le chien fixe son adversaire. Les oreilles tirées en arrière, l'« assaillant » fait entendre un grondement ou un aboiement. Les membres tendus font paraître son corps plus grand, d'autant plus que les poils du dos sont hérissés. La queue est plus ou moins tendue au-dessus du dos selon la race. Chez le loup, l'explication s'arrête généralement là, tandis que chez nos chiens domestiques, l'attaque peut suivre immédiatement la menace, voire se passer de menace – ils ne savent parfois plus se battre sans faire du tort à l'autre.

Le chien se défend par la menace : La menace défensive prend la forme suivante : les commissures des lèvres tirées loin en arrière et les oreilles couchées, le chien – dans la plupart des cas peu sûr de lui – « mord » spontanément le vide, il se tient les pattes légèrement pliées, mais les poils peuvent malgré tout être hérissés. La queue est toujours étroitement serrée contre l'abdomen. S'il en a la possibilité, ce chien ne va pas tarder à se retirer. S'il ne peut s'écarter ou fuir, il se prépare à se défendre.

La plupart des morsures accidentelles sont dues à des chiens ainsi apeurés. La menace défensive peut aussi se prolonger par la soumission passive.

Le chien s'humilie : C'est ce qu'on appelle la soumission passive : le chien évite obstinément tout contact visuel et ne témoigne d'aucune agressivité. Les oreilles sont couchées en arrière, le visage rappelle celui d'un chiot, l'animal semble ricaner et il effectue des mouvements de léchage ciblés ou non. Il peut alors hurler, gémir, crier ou uriner. Son dos prend la position typique du chien soumis, un signal extrêmement fort qui déclenche l'inhibition de morsure ou de meurtre dans le combat comme dans le jeu.

La même inhibition peut être déclenchée avec un contact physique moins intense lorsque le chien qui se soumet, debout ou assis, tend la patte avant vers son partenaire en signe d'apaisement et l'agite de haut en bas. La queue est alors coincée entre les pattes.

Les signaux corporels
d'un seul coup d'œil

Confiant et «repentant» ▶
Le teckel de gauche tend son ventre avec confiance vers son maître : il réclame d'être gratté et chatouillé. Le teckel de droite a visiblement été mis en garde et affiche son regret.

◀ **Incertain et curieux**
Les oreilles couchées du chiot de gauche indiquent qu'il n'est pas sûr de lui. Ci-contre, il a redressé ses oreilles et son visage exprime une attente curieuse. Les poils qui couvrent le visage rendent l'interprétation plus difficile.

Calme et détendu ▶
Le fait de se lécher les babines, à gauche, est un signe de calme et de satisfaction. À droite, le chiot est couché sur son lit, parfaitement détendu, et jette un regard plein d'espoir à son maître ou sa maîtresse.

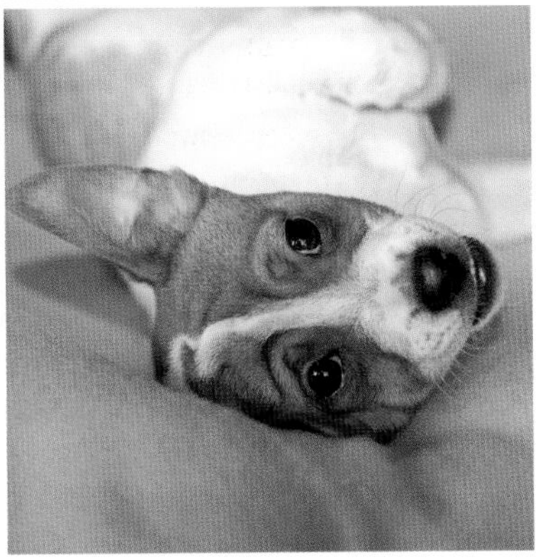

L'attitude ramassée du chiot indique la soumission active.

Le chien se soumet de son plein gré : C'est ce qu'on appelle la soumission active. Le regard du chien est dirigé avec confiance sur son partenaire, mais ne le fixe pas pour autant, ses membres sont fléchis de sorte que le corps paraît ramassé sur lui-même, la queue est basse (mais pas coincée entre les pattes) et agitée rapidement d'un côté à l'autre. La soumission active, par laquelle le chien se soumet sans contrainte à son maître ou à un congénère, devrait en principe être son comportement le plus fréquent. Malheureusement, de nombreux maîtres forcent leur compagnon au quotidien – par une attitude emportée ou en lui inculquant l'« obéissance d'un cadavre » – à une soumission passive permanente et font de leurs chiots, avec le temps, des « larves » sans aucune assurance, qui courbent l'échine et s'aplatissent par terre, quand ils ne hurlent ou n'urinent pas. La soumission active se prolonge souvent par un comportement joueur. Mon chien me donne ainsi la patte de son plein gré sans y avoir été dressé, me lèche la main ou se couche sur le dos à mes pieds afin que je lui gratte le ventre, il essaie aussi parfois de me lécher la bouche – une habitude de son enfance lorsqu'il amenait sa mère à régurgiter pour lui de la nourriture prédigérée en lui léchant les commissures des lèvres.

Le chien veut jouer : Son invite est très claire : l'avant du corps touche presque le sol, tandis que l'arrière-train reste soulevé, les pattes avant sont écartées et le chien agite la queue, il peut aussi tenir la tête penchée ou lui imprimer des mouvements brusques de va-et-vient.

Le langage parlé

Les chiens ne font pas qu'aboyer. Ils peuvent faire entendre un plaisir silencieux jusqu'à la 4e semaine lorsqu'ils tètent leur mère.

Le hurlement exprime le mal-être, poussé par les chiots comme par les chiens adultes en cas de soumission passive (❯ page 114). En cas de soumission active, le hurlement sert au chien à mendier l'attention de son maître (❯ ci-contre). Dans les deux cas, il peut faire place aux aboiements, alors associés à des gémissements, et augmenter d'intensité en cas de peur extrême ou de douleur dans le cadre de la soumission passive. L'aboiement apparaît chez les chiots à partir de la 4e semaine. Il per-

met au chien d'exprimer beaucoup de choses et les différences de ton, associées aux informations supplémentaires fournies par la mimique et le langage corporel selon les situations, nous le rendent compréhensible avec le temps.
Le grognement est à la fois l'expression de la supériorité et une menace. À partir de la huitième semaine, il arrive que les chiots grognent envers l'homme pour le tester et voir s'ils peuvent l'impressionner. Le grognement fait aussi partie du jeu avec l'homme.
Les chiens laissés trop longtemps seuls crient, un cri sans cesse interrompu par des aboiements.

Le langage des odeurs

La communication dite olfactive prend la forme d'urine, de crottes ou de la sécrétion de la glande anale. Elle permet aux chiens de se « parler » sans se rencontrer. Avec les marquages odorants qu'ils déposent sous forme d'urine et de crottes au coin des maisons, au pied des arbres ou des clôtures, ils transmettent des informations les concernant à leurs congénères. En les reniflant, le chien prend connaissance de toutes sortes de précisions sur son prédécesseur et réagit en conséquence. Un animal pas très sûr de lui sera intimidé par l'odeur d'un autre plus dominant et se gardera bien de déféquer ou d'uriner au même endroit, mais s'ils sont aussi dominants l'un que l'autre, le marquage odorant les provoque et chacun veut le recouvrir de son propre marquage pour en imposer à l'autre. Lorsque deux chiens se rencontrent, l'odorat est le sens le plus mis à contribution. Ils se reniflent mutuellement les commissures des lèvres, les parties génitales et l'anus et sont en mesure de reconnaître l'odeur de l'autre dès lors que ses marquages lui sont déjà « passés sous le nez » auparavant.

Les chiots sont curieux de nature et reniflent tout autour d'eux. Le parfum des fleurs semble cependant inquiéter ce bébé.

L'art de la conversation

Le chien est un observateur exceptionnel et il est désireux de nous plaire. Votre compagnon attend de vous des affirmations claires, des compliments qui le motivent et des signaux corporels. Ainsi, vous pourrez vous entendre à merveille.

TOUJOURS PLUS DE GENS ont toujours moins de temps pour des conversations directes – la plupart se déroulent par téléphone mobile ou ordinateur interposé. Avec ce mode de communication, il n'est plus possible, ni nécessaire, d'avoir recours à son langage corporel propre et d'interpréter celui de son interlocuteur, comme c'est le cas lors des conversations personnelles directes avec contact visuel. Les liens directs sont ainsi de plus en plus distendus. Il en va malheureusement de même pour la communication avec nos chiens.

S'exprimer clairement

Pour bien vous entendre avec le chien, votre présence directe et personnelle est fondamentale, au même titre que le langage corporel. Pour cela, essayez d'employer un langage corporel clair, en plus du langage parlé, lorsque vous vous adressez à votre chiot. De même, observez-le pour apprendre à interpréter correctement les signaux corporels qu'il émet, pour ainsi dire le « vocabulaire » de sa langue.

Les chiens observent très précisément le langage corporel de leur maître. Par conséquent, les mots que vous choisissez d'utiliser pour les différents ordres à votre compagnon ne sont pour lui qu'un détail qui l'aide à vous comprendre. En effet, la réaction du chien à nos signaux vocaux dépend également des mouvements dont nous les accompagnons, de notre attitude et de notre mimique.

Beaucoup de maîtres ne communiquent que verbalement avec leur chien et uniquement sur le ton de l'ordre à grand renfort de « Ici ! », « Assis ! », « Couché ! », etc. De même, la plupart des cours dans les écoles pour chiens visent uniquement à ce que le chien apprenne à exécuter correctement ces ordres. Mais comment avoir une conversation animée avec votre compagnon sur de telles bases ?

D'autres maîtres troublent et déconcertent leur chien avec des phrases et des sermons interminables. L'animal n'y comprend rien et finit par réagir avec une totale indifférence. Il ne sait pas ce que son maître attend de lui, c'est tout juste s'il se rend compte qu'il a fait quelque chose qui déplaît à ce dernier. Dans ce cas, le chien exprime avec son corps la soumission passive (❯ page 114), mais ce comportement est alors souvent interprété à tort par le maître comme de la mauvaise conscience, ou même de la honte.

Pour de tels maîtres, il est essentiel d'en apprendre plus sur le langage corporel du chien sous peine de voir les malen-

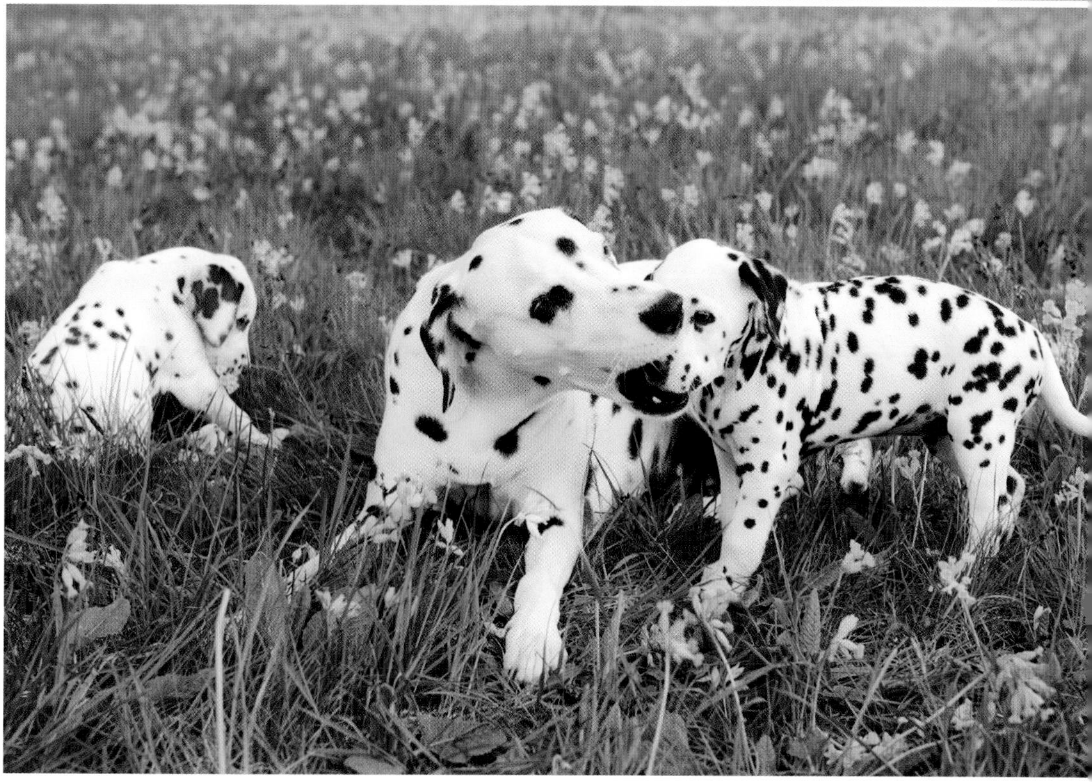

Pendant un jeu, le chiot est affectueusement remis à sa place par sa mère.

tendus les plus graves se multiplier, ce qui ne ferait que nuire à leur cohabitation harmonieuse avec l'animal. Un exemple : le chiot ne comprendra pas si vous essayez de lui faire comprendre verbalement son infériorité, en revanche il se sentira aussitôt remis à sa place si vous lui saisissez le museau car il a déjà fait l'expérience de la morsure sur le museau par sa mère ou d'autres chiens adultes et en connaît la signification (> photo ci-dessus). Ne pas attendre cependant pour vous y essayer que le chien adulte ait éventuellement déjà endossé le rôle de chef de famille à la suite de manquements dans son éducation, ou alors c'est lui qui vous disciplinera avec la plus grande sévérité, au besoin par une morsure.

L'importance des signaux vocaux : Bien entendu, la communication avec le chien ne peut se passer de nos signaux vocaux. Même un chiot moyennement doué est capable d'apprendre 20 à 30 ordres et certains spécialistes comme les bons chiens de garde ou les chiens guides d'aveugles maîtrisent souvent plus de 100 signaux vocaux. En effet, le chien est de lui-même parfaitement disposé à comprendre notre langage sonore et à répondre à nos demandes.

Le langage corporel humain : Les chiens sont très supérieurs à l'homme pour l'interprétation de notre langage corporel, bon nombre de maîtres ont du mal à s'en accommoder. Il est toujours étonnant de voir la vitesse à laquelle les chiens comprennent

Les signaux au chiot

1 **Motiver :** Si elle est accroupie et ouvre les bras d'un air engageant, le chiot viendra avec plaisir et sans crainte vers sa maîtresse.

2 **Menacer :** Se pencher au-dessus du chiot lui fait peur avec un langage corporel à l'aspect menaçant.

3 **Ignorer :** Si vous n'aimez pas que le chiot vous saute amicalement dessus, détournez-vous brusquement de lui et ignorez-le simplement.

intuitivement nos gestes pourtant le plus souvent inconscients. En effet, nous ne maîtrisons pas de nombreux éléments lorsque nous parlons – notre mimique, nos gestes, notre ton, la hauteur de notre voix ou d'autres spécificités élocutoires. Mais le chien dès son plus jeune âge perçoit l'humeur de son maître, il semblerait qu'il ait développé au cours de millénaires de cohabitation une forme spéciale d'intelligence pour mieux nous comprendre, nous les hommes.

Être disposé à parler

Au début, on ne saurait exiger plus d'un chiot que de venir rapidement sur ordre et de réagir au compliment ou à la critique comme le souhaite son maître. La condition pour la communication entre l'homme et le chien reste cependant la « disposition à parler ».

Les chiots sont par nature toujours prêts à « discuter ». Cette bonne disposition doit cependant être acceptée et confirmée par le maître. Si vous réagissez négativement à une demande de communication de votre chien, vous étouffez dans l'œuf son offre de discussion dès le départ.

Une mauvaise compréhension peut aussi gêner la conversation, c'est le cas notamment des discours embrouillés tenus au chien et/ou d'aides qui le déstabilisent, ou encore d'une mauvaise programmation dans l'apprentissage des exercices.

Un bon exemple : Vous souhaitez que le chiot vienne rapidement et de manière fiable à votre appel. Pour cela, une méthode simple.

Première étape : il a besoin d'un ordre clair et net : « Ici ! » de votre part. La première fois, accroupissez-vous pour ne pas le déstabiliser de toute votre hauteur.

Deuxième étape : l'ordre est accompagné d'un signal visuel toujours identique : écartez les bras, la paume des mains vers le haut et dirigée vers votre corps. Faites-lui signe du doigt. Votre

langage corporel indique clairement au chiot qu'il est le bienvenu. Comme de surcroît il sait par expérience qu'il reçoit parfois une récompense et des caresses en abondance lorsqu'il vient, il ne risque pas de passer à côté.

L'art de la critique

La critique n'a rien à voir avec la punition. La seconde n'a pas sa place dans l'éducation par l'encouragement positif. En effet, un chien puni après-coup pour un acte inopportun n'apprend strictement rien, la punition ne fait que le stresser, sans compter que sa disposition à communiquer en est interrompue. C'est pourquoi la critique doit être émise au moment où le chien fait une bêtise. Pour cela, essayez de prendre l'habitude de le gronder avec un «Non!» profond, et si vous arrivez à le faire sur un ton vraiment méchant, vous pouvez vous épargner le signal vocal «Non!» – il doit être uniquement ressenti comme négatif par le chien. Le signal négatif seul ne suffit cependant pas. Il permet seulement de faire comprendre au chien qu'il a fait quelque chose de mal, mais cette expérience négative doit toujours être suivie d'une alternative positive. Pour cela, aidez le chien à faire les choses correctement et donnez un sens encore plus positif à son action dès lors qu'il l'a effectuée avec votre aide. Par la suite, il deviendra toujours plus attentif (plus ouvert à la discussion) car il trouvera de

ASTUCE

Si le chien ne réagit pas normalement

Les comportements anormaux sont le plus souvent des névroses dues à l'homme, notamment par manque de socialisation et/ou de graves erreurs d'éducation, qui apparaissent chez le chiot. Des maladies telles que mal de dos, de hanches ou de tête du fait d'une tumeur au cerveau peuvent aussi en être la cause.

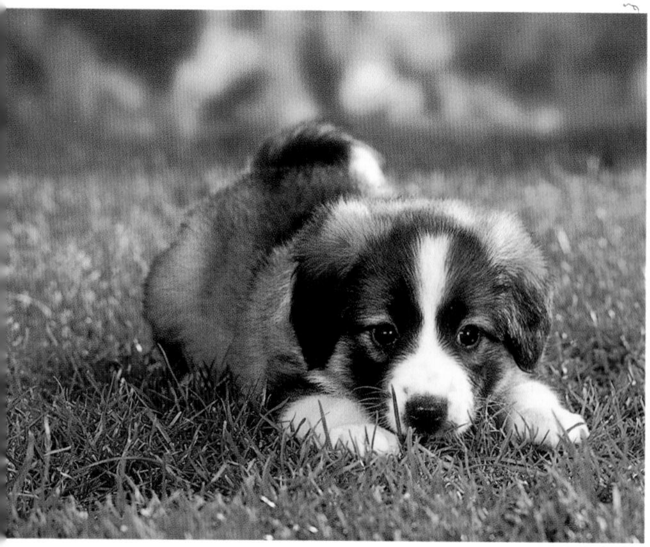

▲

Cette attitude est censée motiver un compagnon de jeu à se joindre à soi.

l'intérêt à exécuter les missions qui lui sont confiées de manière à vous satisfaire. Avec un chien dans une telle disposition et si ouvert à la discussion, la critique peut finalement être employée avec toujours moins de force.

Conseil : mes chiots sont tenus en laisse pendant toutes les phases de leur éducation et entraînements ciblés. La longueur de la laisse dépend de l'endroit ou de l'exercice (› pages 94-95). Le chien doit gagner sa liberté pendant une leçon en faisant la preuve de son esprit critique et de sa fiabilité.

Le tabou de la punition : Les maîtres de chiens sont nombreux à évoquer les punitions dites naturelles. En effet, les mères chiennes secoueraient aussi leurs petits par la peau du cou. Or, cet acte équivaut à un meurtre dans la nature et peut inspirer une peur mortelle à un chiot lorsqu'il est utilisé en guise de punition – aucune chienne ne ferait cela à son petit.

Quant au conseil de pincer ou de tordre l'oreille du chien, je le récuse également car il peut en résulter des blessures et parce que ma méthode d'éducation canine ne prévoit pas de faire mal à mon partenaire. J'arrête ici la liste des punitions soi-disant naturelles car je suis d'avis que la punition comme moyen coercitif, telle que de nombreux centres d'entraînement y ont encore recours aujourd'hui, n'a plus sa place dans l'éducation canine moderne. Le chien n'apprend pas par la punition car elle ne lui est infligée que lorsqu'il a déjà fait la bêtise. Mieux vaut anticiper pendant sa formation de manière à l'empêcher de faire la bêtise.

À voix basse et amicale

Ne criez jamais les signaux vocaux pour rappeler le chien à l'ordre : plus vous parlerez fort, moins l'animal sera attentif car la force de votre voix ne constituera pas à ses yeux une motivation pour faire attention. Les ordres vocaux doivent être clairs et nets, mais prononcés à voix basse et sur un ton amical. La seule violence de la voix ne rend pas le chien plus obéissant et vous capterez plus l'attention de votre chiot en lui parlant à voix basse. Il est d'autant plus inutile de crier que le chien a une ouïe beaucoup plus fine que la nôtre. Votre compagnon ne s'attend à rien de plus de votre part que des paroles claires et nettes sur un ton normal, accompagnées des gestes assortis.

La critique de mon berger allemand de sept ans « Itchy » à notre bouledogue français de treize semaines « Only » passe généralement par le contact visuel, au pire par un froncement du nez et un léger grognement de l'aîné. Les premières semaines, la critique était nettement plus intense et plus directe, mais jamais violente, sans aboiements ni blessures.

Le compliment approprié

Le compliment tient lieu de soutien et de réconfort lorsque le chiot s'est comporté selon le désir de son maître, la critique ne servant qu'à lui faire comprendre qu'il a fait quelque chose de mal (❯ page 121).
Il est souvent étonnant de voir ce que certains maîtres entendent par compliment. Certains tapotent vigoureusement leur chien sur la tête ou le « frappent » avec reconnaissance sur les côtes, d'autres émettent un « gentil » dénué de toute passion sans desserrer les dents, tandis que d'autres encore lui octroient sans raison des friandises en masse à chaque contact. Pourtant, aucun chien n'est en mesure d'interpréter de tels « compliments », encore moins de les associer à un comportement positif de sa part.
Le compliment joue un rôle central dans la communication entre l'homme et le chien. En premier lieu lorsqu'il prend la forme de caresses calmes et chaleureuses accompagnées de mots louangeurs. N'épargnez en aucun cas les compliments, mais utilisez-les toujours à bon escient ou l'effet sera manqué.
Le compliment est la clé du succès. Le chiot le comprendra le mieux si vous le récompensez gentiment à chaque fois qu'il franchit une étape au lieu d'attendre qu'il ait fini tout l'exercice. Le compliment approprié doit confirmer le chien dans sa manière d'agir à un moment donné et le motiver à continuer. Il doit ressentir le compliment comme positif et l'associer au comportement que vous, son maître, jugez souhaitable. Le compliment est une forme de communication intensive. C'est pourquoi la voix joyeuse et les gestes positifs qui l'expriment doivent parfaitement concorder et être sincères : le chien remarquera tout de suite que vous ne le complimentez que « pour la forme » ou que vous exagérez.

Entre quatre yeux

Le contact visuel n'importe pas uniquement pour la communication

Le chiot passe d'une attitude ramassée à une invitation à jouer – pourvu que quelqu'un y réponde.

Ce chiot berger allemand semble attendre avec patience son maître, dans l'espoir d'un jeu animé avec lui.

entre hommes, mais aussi avec le chien. En effet, le chien attentif et disposé à communiquer cherche le regard détendu de son maître. Il fait preuve de soumission active (❯ page 116).
Le regard fixe en revanche est considéré comme une menace ou un défi – un chien dominant pourrait y répondre par l'attaque.
Si par exemple le chiot se prend trop au jeu avec vous et que vous ne parvenez plus à le discipliner, ou dans toutes les occasions qui exigent de fixer des limites, le bon vieux « savon » a fait ses preuves : prenez la tête du chien entre vos deux mains et essayez d'entrer en contact visuel avec lui sans le fixer avec colère, parlez-lui calmement en insistant sur le mot « Arrête ! », sans secouer la tête du chien ni crier. Vous serez surpris de voir comme le chien se laisse gagner par votre calme et votre détermination. Après l'avoir ainsi « renvoyé », ignorez-le jusqu'à ce qu'il vous renouvelle son offre de communication à laquelle vous devez alors répondre en lui proposant une nouvelle activité.

Apaiser

Les chiens utilisent des signaux inhibiteurs d'agression pour calmer leur vis-à-vis. Le système fonctionne parfaitement entre chiens mais reste le plus souvent méconnu de leurs maîtres.
Le bâillement : Il permet au chien de modérer l'agression d'un adversaire menaçant. C'est un comportement qui s'oppose à une menace ou une attaque.
Le grattement : Il est souvent utilisé avec succès lorsque deux chiens se rencontrent pour calmer un adversaire trop agressif. Le chien qui se gratte doit être le plus sûr de lui car un chien plus faible n'a pas les nerfs assez solides pour s'asseoir en présence d'un rival qui le menace et se gratter sans besoin.
Le reniflement : On voit souvent ce comportement sur les terrains d'entraînement pour chiens, associé à un maître énervé ou emporté.
Un chien qui renifle montre qu'il a fait

de mauvaises expériences en répondant à l'appel de son maître. Il ne s'en approche alors qu'avec hésitation car il perçoit son mécontentement à ses seuls gestes. De même, un chien qui a appris la docilité en laisse par la violence (fortes secousses sur la laisse avec collier étrangleur ou à clous) marche en reniflant devant ou à côté de son maître dans l'espoir de le calmer. Il cherche ainsi à empêcher l'homme de lui infliger des souffrances supplémentaires.

Le léchage : Le chiot garde un vif souvenir de ce comportement qu'il utilisait pour mendier de la nourriture auprès de sa mère (❯ Lécher les commissures des lèvres, page 116). Il se lèche le museau à de multiples reprises lorsqu'il se sent en infériorité ou se contente de sortir plusieurs fois le bout de la langue s'il se sent menacé.

La patte : Lorsqu'un chien donne la patte, nous sommes nombreux à croire qu'il nous salue. En fait, il s'agit d'un geste d'apaisement classique que les autres chiens comprennent comme tel. Avec ce signal très prudent, le chien inférieur va parfois jusqu'à toucher de sa patte tendue l'adversaire qui le menace et évite ainsi toute morsure. En revanche, si le chien inférieur posait la patte sur l'épaule de l'autre ou le heurtait au visage, cela pourrait signifier une provocation.

MON ANIMAL DOMESTIQUE

À quel moment le chiot émet-il des signaux d'apaisement ?

Pour intensifier encore plus la communication avec votre chien, il importe d'apprendre à reconnaître et à comprendre toujours plus vite les signaux d'apaisement qu'il vous envoie à vous ou à ses congénères.

Début du test :

- ○ Observez au quotidien le langage corporel de votre jeune chien envers vous.
- ○ Notez ses signaux d'apaisement (❯ page 124) et les circonstances dans lesquelles il les fait. Si vous pensez avoir compris un signal, réfléchissez à l'erreur que vous pourriez avoir commise pour qu'il cherche à vous calmer.

Résultat du test :

Questions-réponses : La communication

Tous les dimanches matins, mon chien s'assoit joyeusement devant la porte car il sait que ce jour-là, nous l'emmenons au terrain de jeux pour chiots. Mais comment sait-il que c'est dimanche ?
C'est tout simple : votre compagnon le remarque au déroulement de la journée. C'est un jour différent des autres : vous dormez peut-être plus longtemps le matin, vous prenez tranquillement votre petit-déjeuner tous ensemble et vous avez peut-être mis des vêtements spéciaux que vous portez pour l'entraînement de votre chien. En tout cas, l'excursion dominicale semble lui faire très plaisir, sinon il ne s'en réjouirait pas autant.

Les chiens éprouvent-ils de la honte ?
Non, même si on a parfois l'impression que son chien a honte lorsque nous le critiquons parce qu'il a fait une bêtise. Il réagit alors plus ou moins à notre mécontentement selon sa force de caractère et montre tous les signes de la soumission. La honte suppose une conscience éthique, mais les chiens n'ont aucune conscience de ce qui est juste ou injuste, et ne connaissent pas, par conséquent, la mauvaise conscience. Ils n'agissent pas selon les principes du bien et du mal, mais suivent simplement leurs instincts (› page 13).

Pourquoi notre berger allemand de quatre mois, Mix, a-t-il peur de la circulation alors qu'il n'en a fait aucune mauvaise expérience car il a grandi dans une ferme isolée ?
Le chiot n'a vraisemblablement pas eu la possibilité de s'y habituer, dans son lieu de naissance éloigné de toute circulation. Familiarisez-le petit à petit avec ce bruit à un endroit ou à une heure peu fréquentés. Vous pouvez par exemple choisir de toujours faire vos exercices dans la même petite rue jusqu'à ce que le chien se soit habitué à la circulation dans ce lieu familier. Si le chiot se montre apeuré, ne surtout pas le plaindre, mais ne pas non plus se montrer impressionné et ne pas tenir compte de sa peur. Si vous êtes vous-même peureux et nerveux, laissez à quelqu'un d'autre le soin de cet entraînement, vous risqueriez sinon de transmettre votre disposition d'esprit au chien, il sentirait votre incertitude et cela ne ferait qu'aggraver son état.

Comment reconnaître et interpréter la mimique de mon chien ?
Le langage corporel du chien est très compréhensible, pour les hommes aussi. Sa mimique en revanche, soit les changements rapides d'expression du regard, des lèvres, des sourcils ou des rides du front, qui doit de surcroît être mise en relation avec les mouvements de la queue et du corps, est souvent difficile à juger et à inter-

préter correctement. Sans compter qu'elle est souvent impossible à déceler chez certaines races de chiens au visage très velu. Mon conseil par conséquent : étudiez vous-même l'expression du visage de votre compagnon dans différentes situations et prenez-en note. Vous serez surpris de tout ce que vous découvrirez d'intéressant à votre chien.

Mon fox-terrier à poil court de quatre mois dresse parfois les poils du dos lorsqu'il rencontre d'autres chiens. Est-ce une tendance agressive ?

Ce comportement est avant tout un signe de stress. Chez l'homme aussi, les cheveux peuvent littéralement se dresser sur la tête en cas de peur extrême. Si le chien n'est que légèrement énervé et reste sûr de lui, ses poils se dressent uniquement au niveau des épaules, il ne hérisse tous les poils du dos qu'en cas d'excitation extrême, de manque d'assurance intérieure et de peur. Dans tous les cas, l'élément déclencheur est l'hormone de stress adrénaline. Il arrive aussi que les chiots testent ce signal sans raison à partir de la 10e semaine. Proposez à votre bébé plus de contacts réguliers avec des chiens socialement forts.

Pourquoi notre chiot ne gratte-t-il pas la terre après avoir fait une crotte ?

Les chiens de vos voisins ont certainement déjà atteint leur maturité sexuelle et sont adultes. Les chiens ne grattent pas comme les chats pour enterrer leurs petites affaires. Au contraire, ils le font pour intensifier le marquage qu'ils laissent avec leurs crottes. En effet, les chiens ont des glandes sudoripares sur les pieds qui libèrent une note olfactive individuelle sur le sol lorsqu'ils le grattent, par ailleurs le sol ainsi gratté renforce le marquage olfactif. Lorsque votre bébé sera devenu un « vrai petit gars », il se comportera de la même manière que les chiens des voisins. Les chiennes marquent et grattent cependant moins que les chiens.

Comment m'y prendre pour présenter un chien étranger à mon chien ?

Même s'il s'agit encore de chiots, la première rencontre doit avoir lieu en terrain neutre, par exemple dans une grande prairie. Les deux chiens y disposent de suffisamment d'espace pour faire connaissance en jouant. En effet, les chiots développent des exigences territoriales chez eux et les défendent parfois. Lorsque les deux chiens sont amis, il n'y aura plus de problème entre eux, même chez l'un ou chez l'autre. Veillez cependant à ce que votre chien ait le plus de droits chez lui, son jouet favori notamment doit rester hors de portée de l'autre chien.

8. En cas de problème

Des problèmes peuvent se poser dans la relation homme-chien, ou de simples malentendus. Les causes en sont très diverses, mais ils peuvent presque toujours être facilement résolus.

Petits problèmes et solutions

Vous trouverez dans les pages qui suivent un choix de comportements du chien qui nous dérangent, nous les hommes. Pourtant, il n'est pas si difficile que cela de trouver un terrain d'entente avec son compagnon à quatre pattes.

MÊME LE MEILLEUR DES CHIENS peut parfois montrer un comportement indésirable. Et si vous vous contentez d'ignorer certaines particularités de votre chouchou et d'en rire, elles peuvent s'exacerber à l'excès. Avant de commencer à essayer de le rééduquer, cherchez à découvrir la cause de son comportement et à la supprimer. Si vous tentez par exemple de faire perdre à votre chien son fort instinct de chasse ou le plaisir des bagarres avec d'autres mâles, vous n'obtiendrez normalement aucun succès durable car ces habitudes font partie de son comportement normal, la seule mesure qui aide reste de garder le chien en laisse. En revanche, en cas de particularités dangereuses, comme par exemple le fait de mordre par peur ou d'attaquer l'homme, l'aide d'un thérapeute comportemental pour chiens expérimenté est incontournable.

Il court après les voitures et les vélos

Pourchasser les objets qui se déplacent rapidement est un comportement naturel du chien, un comportement inné (❯ Les fameux instincts, page 13). Le chien est un « chasseur à courre » et sa vision est donc avant tout une vision du mouvement : il perçoit le moindre déplacement. Les jeunes chiens en particulier chassent passionnément les feuilles qui volent, les papillons ou les bouts de papier. Avec l'âge, les vélos, ou même les voitures, deviennent des objets plus intéressants à pourchasser, surtout pour les chiens qui bénéficient de plus de liberté qu'ils ne connaissent l'obéissance et sont insuffisamment occupés.

Les solutions possibles : Empêcher toute tentative de poursuite spontanée (même des feuilles) du chien tenu en laisse dès son plus jeune âge, surtout

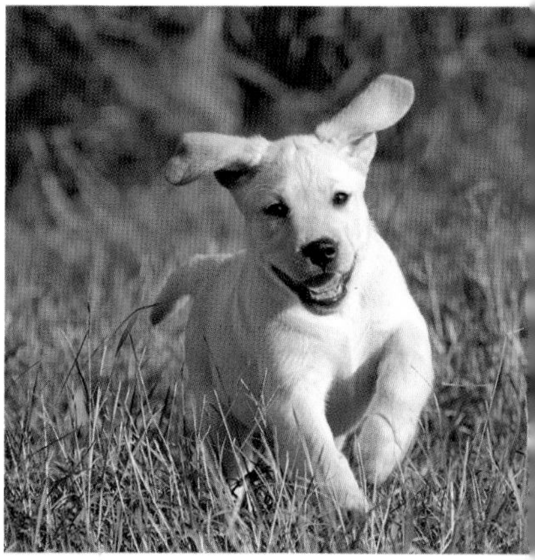

Plein de vie et d'exubérance, ce chiot court et saute dans l'herbe, pourvu qu'il ne « vise » aucune proie.

Comportement de chiot

1 Exubérance : Emporté par son jeu, le chiot cherche à attraper la main de sa maîtresse avec ses petites dents pointues. Ce comportement doit être réprimé dès le début.

2 Solitude : Le chiot montre sa peur d'être abandonné par des hurlements interrompus d'aboiements.

3 Soumission : Un gros chien étranger incite le chiot à la soumission passive, ce qui peut lui sauver la vie dans certains cas.

dans les endroits fréquentés. Si votre compagnon est vraiment un passionné de la chasse, l'entraîner très tôt à rapporter des objets lancés dans ce but ou à porter des objets. S'il chasse déjà les voitures ou les vélos, il ne doit plus être détaché mais dès qu'il commence à courir après le moindre objet, faire brusquement demi-tour et ne pas lésiner sur les compliments s'il se détourne alors de sa chasse. Ces mesures doivent être accompagnées d'un entraînement intensif à l'obéissance.

Il mordille

Les chiots, mais pas seulement, prennent plaisir à mordiller tout ce qui leur tombe sous la dent et n'épargnent ni les meubles, ni les tapis précieux. Les chaussures sont l'objet d'un intérêt particulier en raison de leur odeur de cuir, ou de celle du maître bien-aimé. Certains chiens ne rongent que lorsque leurs dents définitives poussent, d'autres toute leur vie.

Les chiens mordillent souvent parce qu'ils s'ennuient, ont peur, sont trop seuls et/ou pour dépenser un trop-plein d'énergie.

Les solutions possibles : Rangez hors de la portée du chien tous les objets auxquels vous tenez mais qui pourraient lui donner envie. Faites en sorte qu'il ait toujours quelque chose de nouveau à ronger, comme par exemple une oreille de bœuf, un morceau de cuir de bœuf, un sac en papier, un carton de lait vide, un morceau de corde ou un vieux balai inutilisable. S'il s'en prend aussi aux pieds de chaises ou autres meubles, les enduire d'une sauce au poivre bien relevée : les chiens détestent ce goût. Observez alors l'animal avec attention pour être sûr qu'il ne jette pas son dévolu sur un autre objet.

Il saute

Sauter sur les gens est un rituel de salut inné chez les chiens ; cette exubérance est donc un comportement naturel,

bien qu'indésirable, et le chien ne doit pas être puni pour cela.

Ignorez par conséquent les conseils traditionnels, mais vraiment dépassés, comme de laisser le chien se cogner douloureusement le genou lorsqu'il saute ou de lui marcher sur les pattes postérieures.

Les solutions possibles : À l'avenir, exiger du chien qu'il s'assoie pour dire bonjour et attendre qu'il l'ait fait pour le caresser, le récompenser de temps en temps d'une friandise. Repousser les tentatives de saut avec un « Non ! » tranchant et en vous détournant brusquement. Ne saluer le chien que lorsqu'il s'assoit à votre signal et demandez à vos amis de ne pas lui dire bonjour et de ne pas le regarder tant qu'il n'est pas assis.

Il creuse

Lorsqu'un chien plein d'énergie qui manque d'activité passe longtemps au jardin sans surveillance, il n'est pas rare qu'il trompe son ennui en creusant des trous souvent remarquables. C'est une activité qui lui fait plaisir, ou alors il a observé son maître « cacher » des oignons de tulipes et il veut l'imiter.

Les solutions possibles : Lui interdire dès son plus jeune âge toute activité dans ce sens et ne pas lui permettre non plus de creuser pendant les promenades – ou alors il ne comprendrait pas pourquoi il n'en a pas le droit à la maison. Lui proposer plus d'occupations

ASTUCE

La peur des autres chiens

Organisez une rencontre pendant la promenade entre un autre maître accompagné de son brave toutou et votre « trouillard ». Testez la distance à partir de laquelle votre chien cesse d'avoir peur de l'autre et réduisez-la petit à petit. Récompensez votre compagnon à chaque fois qu'il reste détendu.

Les comportements inopportuns du chiot doivent être corrigés **dès son plus jeune âge** pour assurer une future cohabitation harmonieuse.

pour éviter qu'il ne s'ennuie et ne pas le laisser sans surveillance au jardin. Un «Non!» ferme peut l'empêcher de creuser, mais uniquement lorsque vous êtes là. Enfin s'il creuse toujours au même endroit, combler le trou avec un peu de ses crottes légèrement recouvertes de terre.

Il a peur d'être abandonné

Les chiens qui ont peur de la séparation le manifestent par des aboiements, des hurlements ou des pleurs qui peuvent durer des heures, certains aussi détruisent le mobilier. Cette peur peut avoir plusieurs causes. Les chiens qui en sont victimes ont souvent déjà perdu une personne de référence, mais on la rencontre aussi chez des chiens qui n'ont jamais été laissés seuls car leur maître passe normalement toute la journée chez lui.

Les solutions possibles : Un entraînement progressif peut donner au chien un sentiment de sécurité pour qu'il soit assuré de votre retour. Tout d'abord, il est important de l'occuper pour le fatiguer, le conduire ensuite vers son lit et s'il se couche, quitter la pièce sans dire un mot et fermer la porte. Revenir au bout de quelques secondes, pas plus de cinq, mais ne pas parler au chien : il s'agit de l'habituer à vos allées et venues régulières. N'hésitez pas non plus à sortir de temps en temps de la maison après avoir mis votre manteau – mais sans faire durer votre absence trop longtemps.

Renoncez à toute cérémonie d'adieu ou salutation : le chien doit percevoir le départ et le retour de son maître comme quelque chose de parfaitement naturel. Une fois qu'il s'y est habitué, prolongez votre absence très progressivement de quelques minutes à chaque fois.

Lorsque les chiots grandissent avec les chats, il n'est pas rare de voir de vraies amitiés se développer.

Il a peur de l'orage et des feux d'artifice

Les chiens perçoivent la tension électrique dans l'atmosphère qui cause éclairs et tonnerre bien avant qu'un orage n'éclate. Ils y reconnaissent la puissance de la nature dont ils cherchent alors à se protéger.

Les chiens peureux et peu sûrs d'eux souffrent plus des orages, mais les chiens aux nerfs les plus solides ne sont souvent pas très à l'aise eux non plus, ils paniquent simplement moins facilement. Quant aux feux d'artifice, ils font à un chien nerveux la même impression qu'un orage. Ces animaux ont généralement peur aussi des coups de feu et sont particulièrement sensibles au bruit.

Les solutions possibles : Restez à la maison, fermez les fenêtres et les stores pour que le chien ne voie pas les éclairs ou les fusées et pour atténuer le bruit du tonnerre ou des feux d'artifices. Mettez de la musique et n'hésitez pas à monter le son. Ne plaignez ni ne maternez en aucun cas le chien apeuré, cela ne ferait que le confirmer dans son angoisse. Adoptez un comportement indifférent et essayez éventuellement de distraire votre compagnon par un jeu. Enfin, il existe aussi des calmants légers pour chiens (en accord avec le vétérinaire).

Vous pouvez aussi essayer d'habituer le chien au bruit de l'orage. Pour cela, enregistrer le tonnerre et lui passer l'enregistrement pendant qu'il mange, d'abord suffisamment bas pour qu'il ne montre aucun comportement de peur, puis augmenter le son chaque jour un peu plus et au prochain orage, proposez au chien le même repas que pendant l'entraînement avec l'enregistrement.

LE SAVIEZ-VOUS ?

Certains problèmes exigent l'aide d'un spécialiste

En cas de problèmes comportementaux graves, notamment l'agression envers l'homme, il importe de demander conseil à un spécialiste. Un bon thérapeute ne se consacrera pas uniquement au chien mais examinera aussi le comportement du maître. Pour conseiller ce dernier, il commencera par déterminer les causes du problème entre le chien et l'homme avant de fixer le déroulement du traitement. La recherche des causes constitue toujours l'essentiel de la thérapie.

Il « se parfume » et mange ses crottes

Se rouler dans des substances peu ragoûtantes est pour le chien un héritage de son ancêtre le loup.

Les loups dissimulaient leur odeur de prédateur en se roulant dans les déjections d'herbivores avant d'aller à la chasse. Nos compagnons le font de préférence d'autant plus souvent qu'ils sont lavés – ils ont une tout autre idée que nous de ce qui sent bon. Quant au fait de manger ses crottes, il peut avoir les

MON ANIMAL DOMESTIQUE

Quelles peuvent être les raisons d'un problème ?

Le chien n'est pas responsable de la plupart des problèmes et malentendus qui se posent au quotidien. Mais peut-être lui avez-vous donné des signaux erronés ou ne le comprenez-vous pas bien. Cherchez la cause des problèmes.

Début du test :

Votre chiot vous reconnaît-il comme de rang supérieur (❯ page 33) ? A-t-il une confiance absolue en vous ? Se sent-il en sécurité en votre présence ? Est-il malade ? L'avez-vous suffisamment motivé ? Était-il concentré sur vous et attentif ? Par quoi a-t-il été distrait ? Lui avez-vous donné des ordres clairs ? L'exercice était-il trop difficile pour lui, si vous avez par exemple sauté des étapes d'apprentissage ?

Résultat du test :

causes les plus diverses. Une alimentation déséquilibrée en est le plus souvent à l'origine, par manque de substances alcalines dont le chien a absolument besoin en tant que charognard. L'apport de certains minéraux peut également être insuffisant. Enfin, il se peut aussi que le chien se sente négligé.

Les solutions possibles : Si le chien a une préférence pour les immondices, seule votre vigilance et son obéissance peuvent aider. Il doit en effet cesser dès qu'il entend votre « Non ! » ferme ou votre « Pfff ! ».

Pour prévenir la coprophagie, commencer par retirer toutes les crottes du jardin. Tenir le chien en laisse pendant la promenade afin de pouvoir l'empêcher à temps de manger des crottes. Le faire examiner par un vétérinaire pour savoir s'il manque de certains nutriments et en cas de carence, réfléchir à un changement de régime, penser notamment à le nourrir à l'avenir de manière plus naturelle (de viande fraîche). Vous trouverez des recommandations précises à ce sujet au chapitre 4. Les chiens nourris de produits frais ne mangent pas leurs crottes, je peux vous le garantir.

« Je vais très bien ! » C'est ce qu'exprime ce petit Husky. ▶

Faire garder son chiot

Si vous ne pouvez pas emmener votre chiot avec vous, par exemple à l'hôpital, ou si vous ne voulez pas l'emmener en voyage et que quelqu'un s'occupe de lui pendant ce temps, notez ici tout ce que votre remplaçant doit savoir pour être sûr que votre compagnon sera soigné au mieux en votre absence.

Mon chiot s'appelle :

Quelques-unes de ses caractéristiques physiques :

Ce qu'il aime manger :

Tous les jours dans cette quantité :

Une fois par semaine dans cette quantité :

Des friandises de temps en temps :

Comme boisson :

Les heures des repas :

Les aliments sont rangés à cet endroit :

Ménage :

À nettoyer tous les jours :

À laver toutes les semaines :

Les petites attentions qu'il aime :

Comment l'occuper idéalement :

Ce qu'il n'aime pas du tout :

Ce qu'il n'a pas le droit de faire :

Autres points importants :

Son vétérinaire :

L'adresse et le numéro de téléphone où l'on peut me joindre :

INDEX

Les numéros de pages **en gras** renvoient à des illustrations.

ASSOCIATIONS

Fédération cynologique internationale (FCI)
place Albert Ier, 13
B-6530 Thuin
www.fci.be

Société centrale canine (SCC)
55, avenue Jean-Jaurès
93535 Aubervilliers Cedex
Téléphone :
+ 33 (0)1 49 37 54 00
Fax : + 33 (0)1 49 37 01 20
E-mail : contact@scc.asso.fr
www.scc.asso.fr

Pour les sociétés canines régionales et les associations de races, voir le site de la SCC.

Société protectrice des animaux (SPA)
39, boulevard Berthier
75847 Paris Cedex 17
Tél. : 01 43 80 40 66
Fax : 01 47 63 74 76
www.spa.asso.fr

Confédération nationale de protection des animaux de France
25, quai Jean-Moulin
69002 Lyon
Tél. : 04 78 38 71 71
www.spa-france.asso.fr

Fondation 30 millions d'amis
75402 Paris Cedex 08
Tél. : 01 56 59 04 44
Fax : + 33 (1) 58 56 33 55
www.30millionsdamis.fr

Protection suisse des animaux
Dornacherstr. 101
4008 Bâle
Tél. : 061 365 99 99
Fax : 061 365 99 90
www.protection-animaux.com

Pour un répertoire des associations dans le monde entier : www.worldanimal.net

Où demander conseil ?

Dans les magasins spécialisés et auprès de son vétérinaire.

Assurance responsabilité civile

Presque toutes les polices d'assurance responsabilité civile prennent en charge les dégâts causés par le chien pour un coût modique.

Assurance-maladie

Il existe de nombreuses possibilités d'assurer son chien. Se renseigner auprès du Centre de documentation et d'information de l'assurance (CDIA) : www.ffsa.fr

Enregistrement de chiens

Les inscriptions au fichier canin international se font auprès de la FCI, celles au fichier national canin (France) auprès de la SCC.

Les chiens sur Internet

www.fci.be
www.scc.asso.fr

www.chien.com
www.chiensderace.com
www.frenchtoutou.com
www.annoncesetanimaux.com

Et d'innombrables autres sites… les chiens sont très bien représentés sur Internet.

REMERCIEMENTS

Je remercie particulièrement mon épouse Hansi qui, outre la compréhension dont elle a fait preuve pendant quarante-cinq ans pour mes nombreuses activités canines, n'a jamais perdu patience, même lorsque la rédaction de mes livres me rendait invivable.
L'auteur et l'éditeur remercient la société Padvital GmbH de Karlsruhe, www.padvital.de, pour les jeux d'intelligence pour chiens développés par la Suédoise Nina Ottosson qui figurent sur les photos de ce livre.

Important

Les conseils et règles indiqués dans ce guide sont adaptés à des animaux jeunes normalement développés et de bonne lignée, soit des animaux sains et sans la moindre faiblesse de caractère.
Avant d'adopter un chien adulte, il faut être conscient qu'il a déjà subi une imprégnation déterminante par l'homme. Il importe par conséquent de l'observer avec une attention particulière, et notamment son comportement avec l'homme ; voir également ses anciens propriétaires.
Si le chien vient d'un refuge pour animaux, ses responsables peuvent éventuellement fournir des informations sur l'origine de l'animal et ses particularités.
Certains chiens présentent un comportement caractéristique dû aux mauvaises expériences qu'ils ont faites auparavant avec l'homme, ils peuvent aussi avoir tendance à mordre.
Ces chiens ne doivent être adoptés que par des éleveurs expérimentés.
Les chiens bien éduqués et soigneusement observés eux aussi peuvent causer des dommages à des tiers, voire même des accidents.
Dans tous les cas, il est vivement recommandé de souscrire une police d'assurance suffisante.

Crédits photographiques

Arco-Digital: 18-2, 19-3;
Debra Bardowicks: 48, 49-1, 49-2, 79-1, 79-2;
Thomas Brodmann: 94, 95-1, 95-2, 101, 104, 105, 106-1, 106-2, 106-3, 120, 121-1, 121-2, 130, 131-2; **Corbis:** 34, 108;
Oliver Giel: 7, 16-2, 17-2, 36, 39-1, 39-2, 51, 54, 68, 69-1, 69-2, 73, 75, 77-1, 77-2, 77-3, 77-4, 85-1, 85-2, 85-3, 87, 89-1, 89-2, 93, 96, 119;
Juniors: 20-3, 22-3, 23-1;
Angela Kraft: 2-2, 15, 23-2, 31, 32, 102, 124;
Regina Kuhn: 44, 47, 59-1, 59-2, 59-3, 67;
PantherMedia: 20-4, 27-3;
Sigrid Starick: 17-3, 19-2, 24-3, 26-2, 26-3;
Christine Steimer: 4, 11, 16-1, 18-1, 19-1, 20-1, 21-1, 21-3, 22-1, 23-3, 25-1, 25-3, 27-2, 29, 38, 41-1, 41-2, 41-3, 41-4, 41-5, 41-6, 52, 56, 64, 71, 81, 82, 86, 98-1, 98-2, 127-1, 127-2, 127-3, 129, 132;
Tierfotoagentur: 17-4, 21-2, 24-1, 24-2, 25-2, 25-4, 26-1, 27-1;
Monika Wegler: 2-1, 3, 5-1, 5-2, 6, 8-1, 8-2, 9, 10, 12, 14, 17-1, 18-3, 20-2, 22-2, 30, 35, 37, 40, 43, 45, 50, 53, 60, 61, 63, 65, 66, 74, 78, 83, 88, 90, 92, 97, 99, 103, 109, 110, 111, 112, 113-1, 113-2, 115-1, 115-2, 115-3, 115-4, 115-5, 115-6, 116, 117, 118, 122, 123, 128, 131-1, 133, 135, 145.

Édition originale

Rédaction : Nadja Harzdorf, Alexandra Stronski, Adriane Andreas
Maquette intérieure : independent Medien-Design
Repro : Longo AG, Bozen

Édition française
Traduction : Claire Debard
Réalisation : Philippe Brunet / PHB

ISBN : 978-2-501-06538-2
Codification : 40-7081-9
Dépôt légal : avril 2010
Édition 01

Imprimé en Espagne par Estella Gráficas